PENGUIN TWENTIETH-CENTURY CLASSICS

COLLECTED SHORT STORIES

VOLUME 4

William Somerset Maugham was born in 1874 and lived in Paris until he was ten years old. He was educated at The King's School, Canterbury, and at Heidelberg University. He later walked the wards of St. Thomas's Hospital with a view to practicing medicine, but when he had qualified, the success of his first novel, *Liza of Lambeth* (1897), won him over to letters. Some of his hospital experience is reflected in the story, as well as in his later masterpiece, *Of Human Bondage* (1915). With *The Moon and Sixpence* (1919) and *Cakes and Ale* (1930), his reputation as a novelist was further enhanced.

A celebrity by the age of thirty-three, when he became one of the most successful playwrights on the London stage, Maugham's Edwardian comedy *Lady Frederick*, his first hit (1907), was followed by a string of successes just before and then after the First World War. At one point Maugham had four plays running at the same time in London's West End. His theatre career ended with *Sheppey* (1933).

His fame as a short-story writer began in 1921 with *The Trembling of a Leaf*, subtitled *Little Stories of the South Sea Islands*, which contained "Rain." After initial magazine publication of each story he wrote, there were ten more collections. Somerset Maugham's general nonfiction books also reflect his love of travel; they include *On a Chinese Screen* (1922) and *Don Fernando* (1935), essays, criticism, and the self-revealing *The Summing Up* (1938) and *A Writer's Notebook* (1949).

He traveled widely in the Far East and throughout Europe. His permanent home since before the Second World War was on the French Riviera, which he vacated temporarily in 1940. He became Companion of Honor in 1954 and he died in 1965.

W. Somerset Maugham

COLLECTED SHORT STORIES

VOLUME 4

PENGUIN BOOKS

PENGUIN BOOKS
Published by the Penguin Group
Penguin Books USA Inc., 375 Hudson Street, New York, New York 10014, U.S.A.
Penguin Books Ltd, 27 Wrights Lane, London W8 5TZ, England
Penguin Books Australia Ltd, Ringwood, Victoria, Australia
Penguin Books Canada Ltd, 10 Alcorn Avenue, Toronto, Ontario, Canada M4V 3B2
Penguin Books (NZ) Ltd, 182–190 Wairau Road, Auckland 10, New Zealand

Penguin Books Ltd, Registered Offices: Harmondsworth, Middlesex, England

The Complete Short Stories first published in three volumes in Great Britain by
William Heinemann Ltd 1951
Published in four volumes in Penguin Books in Great Britain 1963

23   25   27   29   30   28   26   24   22

This volume published in Penguin Books in the United States of America by
arrangement with Doubleday & Company, Inc. 1978

ISBN 0 14 01.8592 5

Printed in the United States of America
Set in Monotype Times

CONTENTS

PREFACE

IN this final volume I have placed the rest of my stories the scene of which is set in Malaya. They were written long before the Second World War and I should tell the reader that the sort of life with which they deal no longer exists. When I first visited those countries the lives the white men and their wives led there differed but little from what they had been twenty-five years before. They got home leave once in five years. They had besides a few weeks leave every year. If they lived where the climate was exhausting they sought the fresh air of some hill-station not too far away; if, like some of the government servants, they lived where they might not see another white man for weeks on end, they went to Singapore so that they might consort for a time with their kind. *The Times* when it arrived at a station up-country, in Borneo for instance, was six weeks old, and they were lucky if they received the Singapore paper in a fortnight.

Aviation has changed all that. Even before the war people who could afford it were able to spend even their short leave at home. Papers, illustrated weeklies, magazines reached them fresh from the press. In the old days Sarawak, say, or Selangor were where they expected to spend their lives till it was time for them to retire on a pension; England was very far away and when at long intervals they went back was increasingly strange to them; their real home, their intimate friends, were in the land in which the better part of their lives was spent. But with the rapidity of communication it remained an alien land, a temporary rather than a permanent habitation, which circumstances obliged them for a spell to occupy; it was a longish halt in a life that had its roots in the Sussex downs or on the moors of Yorkshire. Their ties with the homeland, which before had insensibly loosened and sometimes broke asunder, remained fast. England, so to speak, was round the corner. They no longer felt cut off. It changed their whole outlook.

The countries of which I wrote were then at peace. It may be that some of those peoples, Malays, Dyaks, Chinese, were restive under the British rule, but there was no outward sign of it. The British gave them justice, provided them with hospitals and schools, and encouraged their industries. There was no more crime than anywhere else. An unarmed man could wander through the length of the Federated Malay States in perfect safety. The only real trouble was the low price of rubber.

There is one more point I want to make. Most of these stories are on the tragic side. But the reader must not suppose that the incidents I have narrated were of common occurrence. The vast majority of these people, government servants, planters, and traders, who spent their working lives in Malaya were ordinary people ordinarily satisfied with their station in life. They did the jobs they were paid to do more or less competently. They were as happy with their wives as are most married couples. They led humdrum lives and did very much the same things every day. Sometimes by way of a change they got a little shooting; but as a rule, after they had done their day's work, they played tennis if there were people to play with, went to the club at sundown if there was a club in the vicinity, drank in moderation, and played bridge. They had their little tiffs, their little jealousies, their little flirtations, their little celebrations. They were good, decent, normal people.

I respect, and even admire, such people, but they are not the sort of people I can write stories about. I write stories about people who have some singularity of character which suggests to me that they may be capable of behaving in such a way as to give me an idea that I can make use of, or about people who by some accident or another, accident of temperament, accident of environment, have been involved in unusual contingencies. But, I repeat, they are the exception.

THE BOOK-BAG

SOME people read for instruction, which is praiseworthy, and some for pleasure, which is innocent, but not a few read from habit, and I suppose that this is neither innocent nor praiseworthy. Of that lamentable company am I. Conversation after a time bores me, games tire me, and my own thoughts, which we are told are the unfailing resource of a sensible man, have a tendency to run dry. Then I fly to my book as the opium-smoker to his pipe. I would sooner read the catalogue of the Army and Navy Stores or Bradshaw's *Guide* than nothing at all, and indeed I have spent many delightful hours over both these works. At one time I never went out without a second-hand bookseller's list in my pocket. I know no reading more fruity. Of course to read in this way is as reprehensible as doping, and I never cease to wonder at the impertinence of great readers who, because they are such, look down on the illiterate. From the standpoint of what eternity is it better to have read a thousand books than to have ploughed a million furrows? Let us admit that reading with us is just a drug that we cannot do without – who of this band does not know the restlessness that attacks him when he has been severed from reading too long, the apprehension and irritability, and the sigh of relief which the sight of a printed page extracts from him? – and so let us be no more vainglorious than the poor slaves of the hypodermic needle or the pint-pot.

And like the dope-fiend who cannot move from place to place without taking with him a plentiful supply of his deadly balm I never venture far without a sufficiency of reading matter. Books are so necessary to me that when in a railway train I have become aware that fellow-travellers have come away without a single one I have been seized with a veritable dismay. But when I am starting on a long journey the problem is formidable. I have learnt my lesson. Once, imprisoned by illness for three months in a hill-town in Java, I came to the end of all the books I had brought with me, and knowing no Dutch was obliged to buy the schoolbooks from which intelligent Javanese, I suppose, acquired knowledge of French and German. So I read again after five-and-twenty years the frigid plays of Goethe, the fables of La Fontaine, and the tragedies of the tender and exact Racine. I have the greatest admiration for Racine, but I admit that to read his plays one after the other

9

requires a certain effort in a person who is suffering from colitis. Since then I have made a point of travelling with the largest sack made for carrying soiled linen and filling it to the brim with books to suit every possible occasion and every mood. It weighs a ton and strong porters reel under its weight. Custom-house officials look at it askance, but recoil from it with consternation when I give them my word that it contains nothing but books. Its inconvenience is that the particular work I suddenly hanker to read is always at the bottom and it is impossible for me to get it without emptying the book-bag's entire contents upon the floor. Except for this, however, I should perhaps never have heard the singular history of Olive Hardy.

I was wandering about Malaya, staying here and there, a week or two if there was a rest-house or a hotel, and a day or so if I was obliged to inflict myself on a planter or a District Officer whose hospitality I had no wish to abuse; and at the moment I happened to be at Penang. It is a pleasant little town, with a hotel that has always seemed to me very agreeable, but the stranger finds little to do there and time hung a trifle heavily on my hands. One morning I received a letter from a man I knew only by name. This was Mark Featherstone. He was Acting Resident, in the absence on leave of the Resident, at a place called Tenggarah. There was a sultan there and it appeared that a water festival of some sort was to take place which Featherstone thought would interest me. He said that he would be glad if I would come and stay with him for a few days. I wired to tell him that I should be delighted and next day took the train to Tenggarah. Featherstone met me at the station. He was a man of about thirty-five, I should think, tall and handsome, with fine eyes and a strong, stern face. He had a wiry black moustache and bushy eyebrows. He looked more like a soldier than a government official. He was very smart in white ducks, with a white topee, and he wore his clothes with elegance. He was a little shy, which seemed odd in a strapping fellow of resolute mien, but I surmised that this was only because he was unused to the society of that strange fish, a writer, and I hoped in a little to put him at his ease.

'My boys'll look after your barang,' he said. 'We'll go down to the club. Give them your keys and they'll unpack before we get back.'

I told him that I had a good deal of luggage and thought it better to leave everything at the station but what I particularly wanted. He would not hear of it.

'It doesn't matter a bit. It'll be safer at my house. It's always better to have one's barang with one.'

'All right.'

I gave my keys and the ticket for my trunk and my book-bag to a Chinese boy who stood at my host's elbow. Outside the station a car was waiting for us and we stepped in.

'Do you play bridge?' asked Featherstone.

'I do.'

'I thought most writers didn't.'

'They don't,' I said. 'It's generally considered among authors a sign of deficient intelligence to play cards.'

The club was a bungalow, pleasing but unpretentious; it had a large reading-room, a billiard-room with one table, and a small card-room. When we arrived it was empty but for one or two persons reading the English weeklies, and we walked through to the tennis courts, where a couple of sets were being played. A number of people were sitting on the veranda, looking on, smoking, and sipping long drinks. I was introduced to one or two of them. But the light was failing and soon the players could hardly see the ball. Featherstone asked one of the men I had been introduced to if he would like a rubber. He said he would. Featherstone looked about for a fourth. He caught sight of a man sitting a little by himself, paused for a second, and went up to him. The two exchanged a few words and then came towards us. We strolled in to the card-room. We had a very nice game. I did not pay much attention to the two men who made up the four. They stood me drinks and I, a temporary member of the club, returned the compliment. The drinks were very small, quarter whiskies, and in the two hours we played each of us was able to show his open-handedness without an excessive consumption of alcohol. When the advancing hour suggested that the next rubber must be the last we changed from whisky to gin pahits. The rubber came to an end. Featherstone called for the book and the winnings and losings of each one of us were set down. One of the men got up.

'Well, I must be going,' he said.

'Going back to the estate?' asked Featherstone.

'Yes,' he nodded. He turned to me. 'Shall you be here tomorrow?'

'I hope so.'

He went out of the room.

'I'll collect my mem and get along home to dinner,' said the other.

'We might be going too,' said Featherstone.

'I'm ready whenever you are,' I replied.

We got into the car and drove to his house. It was a longish drive. In the darkness I could see nothing much, but presently I realized that we were going up a rather steep hill. We reached the Residency.

It had been an evening like any other, pleasant, but not at all exciting, and I had spent I don't know how many just like it. I did not expect it to leave any sort of impression on me.

Featherstone led me into his sitting-room. It looked comfortable, but it was a trifle ordinary. It had large basket arm-chairs covered with cretonne and on the walls were a great many framed photographs; the tables were littered with papers, magazines, and official reports, with pipes, yellow tins of straight-cut cigarettes, and pink tins of tobacco. In a row of shelves were untidily stacked a good many books, their bindings stained with damp and the ravages of white ants. Featherstone showed me my room and left me with the words:

'Shall you be ready for a gin pahit in ten minutes?'

'Easily,' I said.

I had a bath and changed and went downstairs. Featherstone, ready before me, mixed our drink as he heard me clatter down the wooden staircase. We dined. We talked. The festival which I had been invited to see was the next day but one, but Featherstone told me he had arranged for me before that to be received by the Sultan.

'He's a jolly old boy,' he said. 'And the palace is a sight for sore eyes.'

After dinner we talked a little more, Featherstone put on the gramophone, and we looked at the latest illustrated papers that had arrived from England. Then we went to bed. Featherstone came to my room to see that I had everything I wanted.

'I suppose you haven't any books with you,' he said. 'I haven't got a thing to read.'

'Books?' I cried.

I pointed to my book-bag. It stood upright, bulging oddly, so that it looked like a humpbacked gnome somewhat the worse for liquor.

'Have you got books in there? I thought that was your dirty linen or a camp-bed or something. Is there anything you can lend me?'

'Look for yourself.'

Featherstone's boys had unlocked the bag, but quailing before the sight that then discovered itself had done no more. I knew from long experience how to unpack it. I threw it over on its side, seized its leather bottom and, walking backwards, dragged the sack away from its contents. A river of books poured on to the floor. A look of stupefaction came upon Featherstone's face.

'You don't mean to say you travel with as many books as that? By George, what a snip!'

He bent down and turning them over rapidly looked at the titles. There were books of all kinds. Volumes of verse, novels, philosophical works, critical studies (they say books about books are profitless, but they certainly make very pleasant reading), biographies, history; there were books to read when you were ill and books to read when your brain, all alert, craved for something to grapple with; there were books that you had always wanted to read, but in the hurry of life at home had never found time to; there were books to read at sea when you were meandering through narrow waters on a tramp steamer, and there were books for bad weather when your whole cabin creaked and you had to wedge yourself in your bunk in order not to fall out; there were books chosen solely for their length, which you took with you when on some expedition you had to travel light, and there were the books you could read when you could read nothing else. Finally Featherstone picked out a life of Byron that had recently appeared.

'Hullo, what's this?' he said. 'I read a review of it some time ago.'

'I believe it's very good,' I replied. 'I haven't read it yet.'

'May I take it? It'll do me for tonight at all events.'

'Of course. Take anything you like.'

'No, that's enough. Well, good night. Breakfast at eight-thirty.'

When I came down next morning the head boy told me that Featherstone, who had been at work since six, would be in shortly. While I waited for him I glanced at his shelves.

'I see you've got a grand library of books on bridge,' I remarked as we sat down to breakfast.

'Yes, I get every one that comes out. I'm very keen on it.'

'That fellow we were playing with yesterday plays a good game.'

'Which? Hardy?'

'I don't know. Not the one who said he was going to collect his wife. The other.'

'Yes, that was Hardy. That was why I asked him to play. He doesn't come to the club very often.'

'I hope he will tonight.'

'I wouldn't bank on it. He has an estate about thirty miles away. It's a longish ride to come just for a rubber of bridge.'

'Is he married?'

'No. Well, yes. But his wife is in England.'

'It must be awfully lonely for those men who live by themselves on those estates,' I said.

'Oh, he's not so badly off as some. I don't think he much cares about seeing people. I think he'd be just as lonely in London.'

There was something in the way Featherstone spoke that struck me as a little strange. His voice had what I can only describe as a shuttered tone. He seemed suddenly to have moved away from me. It was as though one were passing along a street at night and paused for a second to look in at a lighted window that showed a comfortable room and suddenly an invisible hand pulled down a blind. His eyes, which habitually met those of the person he was talking to with frankness, now avoided mine, and I had a notion that it was not only my fancy that read in his face an expression of pain. It was drawn for a moment as it might be by a twinge of neuralgia. I could not think of anything to say and Featherstone did not speak. I was conscious that his thoughts, withdrawn from me and what we were about, were turned upon a subject unknown to me. Presently he gave a little sigh, very slight, but unmistakable, and seemed with a deliberate effort to pull himself together.

'I'm going down to the office immediately after breakfast,' he said. 'What are you going to do with yourself?'

'Oh, don't bother about me. I shall slack around. I'll stroll down and look at the town.'

'There's not much to see.'

'All the better. I'm fed up with sights.'

I found that Featherstone's veranda gave me sufficient entertainment for the morning. It had one of the most enchanting views I had seen in the F.M.S. The Residency was built on the top of a hill and the garden was large and well cared for. Great trees gave it almost the look of an English park. It had vast lawns and there Tamils, black and emaciated, were scything with deliberate and beautiful gestures. Beyond and below, the jungle grew thickly to the bank of a broad, winding, and swiftly flowing river, and on the other side of this, as far as the eye could reach, stretched the wooded hills of Tenggarah. The contrast between the trim lawns, so strangely English, and the savage growth of the jungle beyond pleasantly titillated the fancy. I sat and read and smoked. It is my business to be curious about people and I asked myself how the peace of this scene, charged nevertheless with a tremulous and dark significance, affected Featherstone who lived with it. He knew it under every aspect: at dawn when the mist rising from the river shrouded it with a ghostly pall; in the splendour of noon; and at last when the shadowy gloaming crept softly out of the jungle, like an army making its way with caution in unknown country, and presently enveloped the green lawns and the great flowering trees and the flaunting cassias in the silent night. I wondered whether, unbeknownst to him, the tender and yet strangely sinister aspect of the scene, acting on his nerves and his loneliness, imbued him with some mystical quality so that the life he led, the life of the capable administrator, the sportsman, and the good fellow, on occasion seemed to him not quite real. I smiled at my own fancies, for certainly the conversation we had had the night before had not indicated in him any stirrings of the soul. I had thought him quite nice. He had been at Oxford and was a member of a good London club. He seemed to attach a good deal of importance to social things. He was a gentleman and slightly conscious of the fact that he belonged to a better class than most of the Englishmen his life brought him in contact with. I gathered from the various silver pots that adorned his dining-room that he excelled in games. He played tennis and billiards. When he went on leave he hunted and, anxious to keep his weight down, he dieted carefully. He talked a good deal of what he would do when he retired. He hankered after the life of a country gentleman. A little house in Leicestershire, a couple of hunters, and neighbours to play bridge with. He would have his pension and he had a little money of his own. But meanwhile he worked hard and did his work, if not brilliantly, certainly with competence. I have no doubt that he was looked upon by his superiors as a reliable officer. He was cut upon a pattern that I knew too well to find very interesting. He was like a novel that is careful, honest, and efficient, yet a little ordinary, so that you seem to have read it all before, and you turn the pages listlessly, knowing that it will never afford you a surprise or move you to excitement.

But human beings are incalculable and he is a fool who tells himself that he knows what a man is capable of.

In the afternoon Featherstone took me to see the Sultan. We were received by one of his sons, a shy, smiling youth who acted as his A.D.C. He was dressed in a neat blue suit, but round his waist he wore a sarong, white flowers on a yellow ground, on his head a red fez, and on his feet knobby American shoes. The palace, built in the Moorish style, was like a very big doll's house and it was painted bright yellow, which is the royal colour. We were led into a spacious room, furnished with the sort of furniture you would find in an English lodging-house at the seaside, but the chairs were covered with yellow silk. On the floor was a Brussels carpet and on the walls photographs in very grand gilt frames of the Sultan at various state functions. In a cabinet was a large collection of all kinds of fruit done entirely in crochet work. The Sultan came in with several attendants. He was a man of fifty, perhaps, short and stout, dressed in trousers and tunic of a large white-and-yellow check; round his middle he wore a very beautiful yellow sarong and on his head a white fez. He had large handsome friendly eyes. He gave us coffee to drink, sweet cakes to eat, and cheroots to smoke. Conversation was not difficult, for he was affable, and he told me that he had never been to a theatre or played cards, for he was very religious, and he had four wives and twenty-four children. The only bar to the happiness of his life seemed to be that common decency obliged him to divide his time equally between his four wives. He said that an hour with one was a month and with another five minutes. I remarked that Professor Einstein – or was it Bergson? – had made similar observations upon time and indeed on this question had given the world much to ponder over. Presently we took our leave and the Sultan presented me with some beautiful white Malaccas.

In the evening we went to the club. One of the men we had played with the day before got up from his chair as we entered.

'Ready for a rubber?' he said.

'Where's our fourth?' I asked.

'Oh, there are several fellows here who'll be glad to play.'

'What about that man we played with yesterday?' I had forgotten his name.

'Hardy? He's not here.'

'It's not worth while waiting for him,' said Featherstone.

'He very seldom comes to the club. I was surprised to see him last night.'

I did not know why I had the impression that behind the very ordinary words of these two men there was an odd sense of embarrassment. Hardy had made no impression on me and I did not even remember what he looked like. He was just a fourth at the bridge table. I had a feeling that they had something against him. It was no business of mine and I was quite content to play with a man who at that moment joined us. We certainly had a more cheerful game than before. A good deal of chaff passed from one side of the table to the other. We played less serious bridge. We laughed. I wondered if it was only that they were less shy of the stranger who had happened in upon them or if the presence of Hardy had caused in the other two a certain constraint. At half past eight we broke up and Featherstone and I went back to dine at his house.

After dinner we lounged in arm-chairs and smoked cheroots. For some reason our conversation did not flow easily. I tried topic after topic, but could not get Featherstone to interest himself in any of them. I began to think that in the last twenty-four hours he had said all he had to say. I fell somewhat discouraged into silence. It prolonged itself, and again, I did not know why, I had a faint sensation that it was charged with a significance that escaped me. I felt slightly uncomfortable. I had that queer feeling that one sometimes has when sitting in an empty room that one is not by oneself. Presently I was conscious that Featherstone was steadily looking at me. I was sitting by a lamp, but he was in shadow so that the play of his features was hidden from me. But he had very large brilliant eyes and in the half darkness they seemed to shine dimly. They were like new boot-buttons that caught a reflected light. I wondered why he looked at me like that. I gave him a glance and catching his eyes insistently fixed upon me faintly smiled.

'Interesting book that one you lent me last night,' he said suddenly, and I could not help thinking his voice did not sound quite natural. The words issued from his lips as though they were pushed from behind.

'Oh, the *Life of Byron?*' I said breezily. 'Have you read it already?'

'A good deal of it. I read till three.'

'I've heard it's very well done. I'm not sure that Byron interests me so much as all that. There was so much in him that was so frightfully second-rate. It makes one rather uncomfortable.'

'What do you think is the real truth of that story about him and his sister?'

'Augusta Leigh? I don't know very much about it. I've never read *Astarte.*'

'Do you think they were really in love with one another?'

'I suppose so. Isn't it generally believed that she was the only woman he ever genuinely loved?'

'Can you understand it?'

'I can't really. It doesn't particularly shock me. It just seems to me very unnatural. Perhaps "unnatural" isn't the right word. It's incomprehensible to me. I can't throw myself into the state of feeling in which such a thing seems possible. You know, that's how a writer gets to know the people he writes about, by standing himself in their shoes and feeling with their hearts.'

I know I did not make myself very clear, but I was trying to describe a sensation, an action of the subconscious, which from experience was perfectly familiar to me, but which no words I knew could precisely indicate. I went on:

'Of course she was only his half-sister, but just as habit kills love I should have thought habit would prevent its arising. When two persons have known one another all their lives and lived together in close contact I can't imagine how or why that sudden spark should flash that results in love. The probabilities are that they would be joined by mutual affection and I don't know anything that is more contrary to love than affection.'

I could just see in the dimness the outline of a smile flicker for a moment on my host's heavy, and it seemed to me then, somewhat saturnine face.

'You only believe in love at first sight?'

'Well, I suppose I do, but with the proviso that people may have met twenty times before seeing one another. "Seeing" has an active side and a passive one. Most people we run across mean so little to us that we never bestir ourselves to look at them. We just suffer the impression they make on us.'

'Oh, but one's often heard of couples who've known one another for years and it's never occurred to one they cared two straws for each other and suddenly they go and get married. How do you explain that?'

'Well, if you're going to bully me into being logical and consistent, I should suggest that their love is of a different kind. After all, passion isn't the only reason for marriage. It may not even be the best one. Two people may marry because they're lonely or because they're good friends or for convenience sake. Though I said that affection was the greatest enemy of love, I would never deny that it's a very good substitute. I'm not sure that a marriage founded on it isn't the happiest.'

'What did you think of Tim Hardy?'

I was a little surprised at the sudden question, which seemed to have nothing to do with the subject of our conversation.

'I didn't think of him very much. He seemed quite nice. Why?'

'Did he seem to you just like everybody else?'

'Yes. Is there anything peculiar about him? If you'd told me that, I'd have paid more attention to him.'

'He's very quiet, isn't he? I suppose no one who knew nothing about him would give him a second thought.'

I tried to remember what he looked like. The only thing that had struck me when we were playing cards was that he had fine hands. It passed idly through my mind that they were not the sort of hands I should have expected a planter to have. But why a planter should have different hands from anybody else I did not trouble to ask myself. His were somewhat large, but very well formed with peculiarly long fingers, and the nails were of an admirable shape. They were virile and yet oddly sensitive hands. I noticed this and thought no more about it. But if you are a writer instinct and the habit of years enable you to store up impressions that you are not aware of. Sometimes of course they do not correspond with the facts and a woman for example may remain in your subconsciousness as a dark, massive, and ox-eyed creature when she is indeed rather small and of a non-descript colouring. But that is of no consequence. The impression may very well be more exact than the sober truth. And now, seeking to call up from the depths of me a picture of this man I had a feeling of some ambiguity. He was clean-shaven and his face, oval but not thin, seemed strangely pale under the tan of long exposure to the tropical sun. His features were vague. I did not know whether I remembered it or only imagined now that his rounded chin gave one the impression of a certain weakness. He had thick brown hair, just turning grey, and a long wisp fell down constantly over his forehead. He pushed it back with a gesture that had become habitual. His brown eyes were rather large and gentle, but perhaps a little sad; they had a melting softness which, I could imagine, might be very appealing.

After a pause Featherstone continued:

'It's rather strange that I should run across Tim Hardy here after all these years. But that's the way of the F.M.S. People move about and you find yourself in the same place as a man you'd known years before in another part of the country. I first knew Tim when he had an estate near Sibuku. Have you ever been there?'

'No. Where is it?'

'Oh, it's up north. Towards Siam. It wouldn't be worth your while to go. It's just like every other place in the F.M.S. But it was rather nice. It had a very jolly little club and there were some quite decent people. There was the schoolmaster and the head of the police, the doctor, the padre, and the government engineer. The usual lot, you know. A few planters. Three or four women. I was A.D.O. It was one of my first jobs. Tim Hardy had an estate about twenty-five miles away. He lived there with his sister. They had a bit of money of their own and he'd bought the place. Rubber was pretty good then and he wasn't doing at all badly. We rather cottoned on to one another. Of course it's a toss-up with planters. Some of them are very good fellows, but they're not exactly . . .' he sought for a word or a phrase that did not sound snobbish. 'Well, they're not the sort of people you'd be likely to meet at home. Tim and Olive were of one's own class, if you understand what I mean.'

'Olive was the sister?'

'Yes. They'd had a rather unfortunate past. Their parents had separated when they were quite small, seven or eight, and the mother had taken Olive and the father had kept Tim. Tim went to Clifton, they were West Country people, and only came home for the holidays. His father was a retired naval man who lived at Fowey. But Olive went with her mother to Italy. She was educated in Florence; she spoke Italian perfectly and French too. For all those years Tim and Olive never saw one another once, but they used to write to one another regularly. They'd been very much attached when they were children. As far as I could understand, life when their people were living together had been rather stormy with all sorts of scenes and upsets, you know the sort of thing that happens when two people who are married don't get on together, and that had thrown them on their own resources. They were left a good deal to themselves. Then Mrs Hardy died and Olive came home to England and went back to her father. She was eighteen then and Tim was seventeen. A year later the war broke out. Tim joined up and his father, who was over fifty, got some job at Portsmouth. I take it he had been a hard liver and a heavy drinker. He broke down before the end of the war and died after a lingering illness. They don't seem to have had any relations. They were the last of a rather old family; they had a fine old house in Dorsetshire that had belonged to them for a good many genera-tions, but they had never been able to afford to live in it and it was always let. I remember seeing photographs of it. It was very much a gentleman's house, of grey stone and rather stately, with a coat of arms carved over the front door, and mullioned windows. Their great ambition was to make enough money to be able to live in it. They used to talk about it a lot. They never spoke as though either of them would marry, but always as though it were a settled thing that they would remain together. It was rather funny considering how young they were.'

'How old were they then?' I asked.

'Well, I suppose he was twenty-five or twenty-six and she was a year older. They were awfully kind to me when I first went up to Sibuku. They took a fancy to me at once. You see, we had more in common than most of the people there. I think they were glad of my company. They weren't particularly popular.'

'Why not?' I asked.

'They were rather reserved and you couldn't help seeing that they liked their own society better than other people's. I don't know if you've noticed it, but that always seems to put people's backs up. They resent it somehow if they have a feeling that you can get along very well without them.'

'It's tiresome, isn't it?' I said.

'It was rather a grievance to the other planters that Tim was his own master and had private means. They had to put up with an old Ford to get about in, but Tim had a real car. Tim and Olive were very nice when they came to the club and they played in the tennis tournaments and all that sort of thing, but you had an impression that they were always glad to get away again. They'd dine out with people and make themselves very pleasant, but it was pretty obvious that they'd just as soon have stayed at home. If you had any sense you couldn't blame them. I don't know if you've been much to planters' houses. They're a bit dreary. A lot of gimcrack furniture and silver ornaments and tiger skins. And the food's uneatable. But the Hardys had made their bungalow rather nice. There was nothing very grand in it; it was just easy and homelike and comfortable. Their living-room was like a drawing-room in an English country house. You felt that their things meant something to them and that they had had them a long time. It was a very jolly house to stay at. The bungalow was in the middle of the estate, but it was on the brow of a little hill and you looked right over the rubber trees to the sea in the distance. Olive took a lot of trouble with her garden and it was really topping. I never saw such a show of cannas. I used to go there for weekends. It was only about half an hour's drive to the sea and we'd take our lunch with us and bathe and sail. Tim kept a small boat there. Those days were grand. I never knew one could enjoy oneself so much. It's a beautiful bit of coast and it was really extraordinarily romantic. Then in the evenings we'd play patience and chess or turn on the gramophone. The cooking was damned good too. It was a change from what one generally got. Olive had taught their cook to make all sorts of Italian dishes and we used to have great wallops of macaroni and risotto and gnocchi and things like that. I couldn't help envying them their life, it was so jolly and peaceful, and when they talked of what they'd do when they went back to England for good I used to tell them they'd always regret what they'd left.

' "We've been very happy here," said Olive.

'She had a way of looking at Tim, with a slow, sidelong glance from under her long eyelashes, that was rather engaging.

'In their own house they were quite different from what they were when they went out. They were so easy and cordial. Everybody admitted that and I'm bound to say that people enjoyed going there. They often asked people over. They had the gift of making you feel at home. It was a very happy house, if you know what I mean. Of course no one could help seeing how attached they were to one another. And whatever people said about their being stand-offish and self-centred, they were bound to be rather touched by the affection they had for one another. People said they couldn't have been more united if they were married, and when you saw how some couples got on you couldn't help thinking they made most marriages look rather like a wash-out. They seemed to think the same things at the same time. They had little private jokes that made them laugh like children. They were so charming with one another, so gay and happy, that really to stay with them was, well, a spiritual refreshment. I don't know what else you could call it. When you left them, after a couple of days at the bungalow, you felt you'd absorbed some of their peace and their sober gaiety. It was as though your soul had been sluiced with cool clear water. You felt strangely purified.'

It was singular to hear Featherstone talking in this exalted strain. He looked so spruce in his smart white coat, technically known as a bum-freezer, his moustache was so trim, his thick curly hair so carefully brushed, that his high-flown language made me a trifle uncomfortable. But I realized that he was trying to express in his clumsy way a very sincerely felt emotion.

'What was Olive Hardy like?' I asked.

'I'll show you. I've got quite a lot of snapshots.'

He got up from his chair and going to a shelf brought me a large album. It was the usual thing, indifferent photographs of people in groups and unflattering likenesses of single figures. They were in bathing dress or in shorts or tennis things, generally with their faces screwed up because the sun blinded them, or puckered by the distortion of laughter. I recognized Hardy, not much changed after ten years, with his wisp of hair hanging across his forehead. I remembered him better now that I saw the snapshots. In them he looked nice and fresh and young. He had an alertness of expression that was attractive and that I certainly had not noticed when I saw him. In his eyes was a sort of eagerness for life that danced and sparkled through the fading print. I glanced at the photographs of his sister. Her bathing dress showed that she had a good figure, well-developed, but slender; and her legs were long and slim.

'They look rather alike,' I said.

'Yes, although she was a year older they might have been twins, they were so much alike. They both had the same oval face and that pale skin without any colour in the cheeks, and they both had those soft brown eyes, very liquid and appealing, so that you felt whatever they did you could never be angry with them. And they both had a sort of careless elegance that made them look charming whatever they wore and however untidy they were. He's lost that now, I suppose, but he certainly had it when I first knew him. They always rather reminded me of the brother and sister in *Twelfth Night*. You know whom I mean.'

'Viola and Sebastian.'

'They never seemed to belong quite to the present. There was something Elizabethan about them. I don't think it was only because I was very young then that I couldn't help feeling they were strangely romantic somehow. I could see them living in Illyria.'

I gave one of the snapshots another glance.

'The girl looks as though she had a good deal more character than her brother,' I remarked.

'She had. I don't know if you'd have called Olive beautiful, but she was awfully attractive. There was something poetic in her, a sort of lyrical quality, as it were, that coloured her movements, her acts, and everything about her. It seemed to exalt her above common cares. There was something so candid in her expression, so courageous and independent in her bearing, that – oh, I don't know, it made mere beauty just flat and dull.'

'You speak as if you'd been in love with her,' I interrupted.

'Of course I was. I should have thought you'd guessed that at once. I was frightfully in love with her.'

'Was it love at first sight?' I smiled.

'Yes, I think it was, but I didn't know it for a month or so. When it suddenly struck me that what I felt for her – I don't know how to explain it, it was a sort of shattering turmoil that affected every bit of me – that that was love, I knew I'd felt it all along. It was not only her looks, though they were awfully alluring, the smoothness of her pale skin and the way her hair fell over her forehead and the grave sweetness of her brown eyes, it was more than that; you had a sensation of well-being when you were with her, as though you could relax and be quite natural and needn't pretend to be anything you weren't. You felt she was incapable of meanness. It was impossible to think of her as envious of other people or catty. She seemed to have a natural generosity of soul. One could be silent with her for an hour at a time and yet feel that one had had a good time.'

'A rare gift,' I said.

'She was a wonderful companion. If you made a suggestion to do something she was always glad to fall in with it. She was the least exacting girl I ever knew. You could throw her over at the last minute and however disappointed she was it made no difference. Next time you saw her she was just as cordial and serene as ever.'

'Why didn't you marry her?'

Featherstone's cheroot had gone out. He threw the stub away and deliberately lit another. He did not answer for a while. It may seem strange to persons who live in a highly civilized state that he should confide these intimate things to a stranger; it did not seem strange to me. I was used to it. People who live so desperately alone, in the remote places of the earth, find it a relief to tell someone whom in all probability they will never meet again the story that has burdened perhaps for years their waking thoughts and their dreams at night. And I have an inkling that the fact of your being a writer attracts their confidence. They feel that what they tell you will excite your interest in an impersonal way that makes it easier for them to discharge their souls. Besides, as we all know from our own experience, it is never unpleasant to talk about oneself.

'Why didn't you marry her?' I had asked him.

'I wanted to badly enough,' Featherstone answered at length. 'But I hesitated to ask her. Although she was always so nice to me and so easy to get on with, and we were such good friends, I always felt that there was something a little mysterious in her. Although she was so simple, so frank and natural, you never quite got over the feeling of an inner kernel of aloofness, as if deep in her heart she guarded, not a secret, but a sort of privacy of the soul that not a living person would ever be allowed to know. I don't know if I make myself clear.'

'I think so.'

'I put it down to her upbringing. They never talked of their mother, but somehow I got the impression that she was one of those neurotic, emotional women who wreck their own happiness and are a pest to everyone connected with them. I had a suspicion that she'd led rather a hectic life in Florence and it struck me that Olive owed her beautiful serenity to a disciplined effort of her own will, and that her aloofness was a sort of citadel she'd built to protect herself from the knowledge of all sorts of shameful things. But of course that aloofness was awfully captivating. It was strangely exciting to think that if she loved you, and you were married to her, you would at last pierce right into the hidden heart of that mystery; and you felt that if you could share that with her it would be as it were a consummation of all you'd ever desired in your life. Heaven wouldn't be in it. You know, I felt about it just like Bluebeard's wife about the forbidden chamber in the castle. Every room was open to me, but I should never rest till I had gone into that last one that was locked against me.'

My eye was caught by a chik-chak, a little brown house lizard with a large head, high up on the wall. It is a friendly little beast and it is good to see it in a house. It watched a fly. It was quite still. On a sudden it made a dart and then as the fly flew away fell back with a sort of jerk into a strange immobility.

'And there was another thing that made me hesitate. I couldn't bear the thought that if I proposed to her and she refused me she wouldn't let me come to the bungalow in the same old way. I should have hated that, I enjoyed going there so awfully. It made me so happy to be with her. But you know, sometimes one can't help oneself. I did ask her at last, but it was almost by accident. One evening, after dinner, when we were sitting on the veranda by ourselves, I took her hand. She withdrew it at once.

' " Why did you do that?" I asked her.

' " I don't very much like being touched," she said. She turned her head a little and smiled. "Are you hurt? You mustn't mind, it's just a funny feeling I have. I can't help it."

' "I wonder if it's ever occurred to you that I'm frightfully fond of you," I said.

'I expect I was terribly awkward about it, but I'd never proposed to anyone before.' Featherstone gave a little sound that was not quite a chuckle and not quite a sigh. 'For the matter of that, I've never proposed to anyone since. She didn't say anything for a minute. Then she said:

' "I'm very glad, but I don't think I want you to be anything more than that."

' "Why not?" I asked.

' "I could never leave Tim."

' "But supposing he marries?"

' "He never will."

'I'd gone so far then that I thought I'd better go on. But my throat was so dry that I could hardly speak. I was shaking with nervousness.

' "I'm frightfully in love with you, Olive. I want to marry you more than anything in the world."

'She put her hand very gently on my arm. It was like a flower falling to the ground.

' "No, dear, I can't," she said.

'I was silent. It was difficult for me to say what I wanted to. I'm naturally rather shy. She was a girl. I couldn't very well tell her that it wasn't quite the same thing living with a husband and living with a brother. She was normal and healthy; she must want to have babies; it wasn't reasonable to starve her natural instincts. It was such waste of her youth. But it was she who spoke first.

' "Don't let's talk about this any more," she said. "D'you mind? It did strike me once or twice that perhaps you cared for me. Tim noticed it. I was sorry because I was afraid it would break up our friendship. I don't want it to do that, Mark. We do get on so well together, the three of us, and we have such jolly times. I don't know what we should do without you now."

' "I thought of that too," I said.

' "D'you think it need?" she asked me.

' "My dear, I don't want it to," I said. "You must know how much I love coming here. I've never been so happy anywhere before!"

' "You're not angry with me?"

' "Why should I be? It's not your fault. It only means that you're not in love with me. If you were you wouldn't care a hang about Tim."

' "You are rather sweet," she said.

'She put her arm round my neck and kissed me lightly on the cheek. I had a notion that in her mind it settled our relation. She adopted me as a second brother.

'A few weeks later Tim went back to England. The tenant of their house in Dorset was leaving and though there was another in the offing, he thought he ought to be on the spot to conduct negotiations. And he wanted some new machinery for the estate. He thought he'd get it at the same time. He didn't expect to be gone more than three months and Olive made up her mind not to go. She knew hardly anyone in England, and it was practically a foreign country to her, she didn't mind being left alone, and she wanted to look after the estate. Of course they could have put a manager in charge, but that wasn't the same thing. Rubber was falling and in case of accidents it was just as well that one or other of them should be there. I promised Tim I'd look after her and if she wanted me she could always call me up. My proposal hadn't changed anything. We carried on as though nothing had happened. I don't know whether she'd told Tim. He made no sign that he knew. Of course I loved her as much as ever, but I kept it to myself. I have a good deal of self-control, you know. I had a sort of feeling I hadn't a chance. I hoped eventually my love would change into something else and we could just be wonderful friends. It's funny, it never has, you know. I suppose I was hit too badly ever to get quite over it.

'She went down to Penang to see Tim off and when she came back I met her at the station and drove her home. I couldn't very well stay at the bungalow while Tim was away, but I went over every Sunday and had tiffin and we'd go down to the sea and have a bathe. People tried to be kind to her and asked her to stay with them, but she wouldn't. She seldom left the estate. She had plenty to do. She read a lot. She was never bored. She seemed quite happy in her own company, and when she had visitors it was only from a sense of duty. She didn't want them to think her ungracious. But it was an effort and she told me she heaved a sigh of relief when she saw the last of them and could again enjoy without disturbance the peaceful loneliness of the bungalow. She was a very curious girl. It was strange that at her age she

should be so indifferent to parties and the other small gaieties the
station afforded. Spiritually, if you know what I mean, she was
entirely self-supporting. I don't know how people found out that I
was in love with her; I thought I'd never given myself away in anything, but I had hints here and there that they knew. I gathered
they thought Olive hadn't gone home with her brother on my account. One woman, a Mrs Sergison, the policeman's wife, actually
asked me when they were going to be able to congratulate me. Of
course I pretended I didn't know what she was talking about, but
it didn't go down very well. I couldn't help being amused. I meant
so little to Olive in that way that I really believe she'd entirely
forgotten that I'd asked her to marry me. I can't say she was unkind to me, I don't think she could have been unkind to anyone;
but she treated me with just the casualness with which a sister
might treat a younger brother. She was two or three years older
than I. She was always terribly glad to see me, but it never occurred to her to put herself out for me; she was almost amazingly
intimate with me, but unconsciously, you know, as you might be
with a person you'd known so well all your life that you never
thought of putting on frills with him. I might not have been a man
at all, but an old coat that she wore all the time because it was
easy and comfortable and she didn't mind what she did in it. I
should have been crazy not to see that she was a thousand miles
away from loving me.

'Then one day, three or four weeks before Tim was due back,
when I went to the bungalow I saw she'd been crying. I was
startled. She was always so composed. I'd never seen her upset
over anything.

' "Hullo, what's the matter?" I said.

' "Nothing."

' "Come off it, darling," I said. "What have you been crying
about?"

'She tried to smile.

' "I wish you hadn't got such sharp eyes," she said. "I think
I'm being silly. I've just had a cable from Tim to say he's postponed his sailing."

' "Oh, my dear, I am sorry," I said. "You must be awfully
disappointed."

' "I've been counting the days. I want him back so
badly."

' "Does he say why he's postponing?" I asked.

' "No, he says he's writing. I'll show you the cable."

'I saw that she was very nervous. Her slow quiet eyes were filled with apprehension and there was a little frown of anxiety between her brows. She went into her bedroom and in a moment came back with the cable. I felt that she was watching me anxiously as I read. So far as I remember it ran: *Darling, I cannot sail on the seventh after all. Please forgive me. Am writing fully. Fondest love. Tim.*

' "Well, perhaps the machinery he wanted isn't ready and he can't bring himself to sail without it," I said.

' "What could it matter if it came by a later ship? Anyhow, it'll be hung up at Penang."

' "It may be something about the house."

' "If it is why doesn't he say so? He must know how frightfully anxious I am."

' "It wouldn't occur to him," I said. "After all, when you're away you don't realize that the people you've left behind don't know something that you take as a matter of course."

'She smiled again, but now more happily.

' "I dare say you're right. In point of fact Tim is a little like that. He's always been rather slack and casual. I dare say I've been making a mountain out of a molehill. I must just wait patiently for his letter."

'Olive was a girl with a lot of self-control and I saw her by an effort of will pull herself together. The little line between her eyebrows vanished and she was once more her serene, smiling, and kindly self. She was always gentle: that day she had a mildness so heavenly that it was shattering. But for the rest of the time I could see that she kept her restlessness in check only by the deliberate exercise of her common sense. It was as though she had a foreboding of ill. I was with her the day before the mail was due. Her anxiety was all the more pitiful to see because she took such pains to hide it. I was always busy on mail day, but I promised to go up to the estate later on and hear the news. I was just thinking of starting when Hardy's seis came along in the car with a message from the amah asking me to go at once to her mistress. The amah was a decent, elderly woman to whom I had given a dollar or two and said that if anything went wrong on the estate she was to let me know at once. I jumped into my car. When I arrived I found the amah waiting for me on the steps.

' "A letter came this morning," she said.

'I interrupted her. I ran up the steps. The sitting-room was empty.

' "Olive," I called.

'I went into the passage and suddenly I heard a sound that froze my heart. The amah had followed me and now she opened the door of Olive's room. The sound I had heard was the sound of Olive crying. I went in. She was lying on her bed, on her face, and her sobs shook her from head to foot. I put my hand on her shoulder.

' "Olive, what is it?" I asked.

' "Who's that?" she cried. She sprang to her feet suddenly, as though she were scared out of her wits. And then: "Oh, it's you," she said. She stood in front of me, with her head thrown back and her eyes closed, and the tears streamed from them. It was dreadful. "Tim's married," she gasped, and her face screwed up in a sort of grimace of pain

'I must admit that for one moment I had a thrill of exultation, it was like a little electric shock tingling through my heart; it struck me that now I had a chance, she might be willing to marry me; I know it was terribly selfish of me; you see, the news had taken me by surprise; but it was only for a moment, after that I was melted by her awful distress and the only thing I felt was deep sorrow because she was unhappy. I put my arm round her waist.

' "Oh, my dear, I'm so sorry," I said. "Don't stay here. Come into the sitting-room and sit down and we'll talk about it. Let me give you something to drink."

'She let me lead her into the next room and we sat down on the sofa. I told the amah to fetch the whisky and syphon and I mixed her a good strong stengah and made her drink a little. I took her in my arms and rested her head on my shoulder. She let me do what I liked with her. The great tears streamed down her poor face.

' "How could he?" she moaned. "How could he?"

' "My darling," I said, "it was bound to happen sooner or later. He's a young man. How could you expect him never to marry? It's only natural."

' "No, no, no," she gasped.

'Tight-clenched in her hand I saw that she had a letter and I guessed that it was Tim's.

' "What does he say?" I asked.

'She gave a frightened movement and clutched the letter to her heart as though she thought I would take it from her.

' "He says he couldn't help himself. He says he had to. What does it mean?"

' "Well, you know, in his way he's just as attractive as you are He has so much charm. I suppose he just fell madly in love with some girl and she with him."

' "He's so weak," she moaned.

' "Are they coming out?" I asked.

' "They sailed yesterday. He says it won't make any difference. He's insane. How *can* I stay here?"

'She began to cry hysterically. It was torture to see that girl, usually so calm, utterly shattered by her emotion. I had always felt that her lovely serenity masked a capacity for deep feeling. But the abandon of her distress simply broke me up. I held her in my arms and kissed her, her eyes and her wet cheek and her hair. I don't think she knew what I was doing. I was hardly conscious of it myself. I was so deeply moved.

' "What shall I do?" she wailed.

' "Why won't you marry me?" I said.

'She tried to withdraw herself from me, but I wouldn't let her go.

' "After all, it would be a way out," I said.

' "How can I marry you?" she moaned. "I'm years older than you are."

' "Oh, what nonsense, two or three. What do I care?"

' "No, no."

' "Why not?" I said.

' "I don't love you," she said.

' "What does that matter? I love you."

'I don't know what I said. I told her that I'd try to make her happy. I said I'd never ask anything from her but what she was prepared to give me. I talked and talked. I tried to make her see reason. I felt that she didn't want to stay there, in the same place as Tim, and I told her that I'd be moved soon to some other district. I thought that might tempt her. She couldn't deny that we'd always got on awfully well together. After a time she did seem to grow a little quieter. I had a feeling that she was listening to me. I had even a sort of feeling that she knew that she was lying in my arms and that it comforted her. I made her drink a drop more whisky. I gave her a cigarette. At last I thought I might be just mildly facetious.

' "You know, I'm not a bad sort really," I said. "You might do worse."

' "You don't know me," she said. "You know nothing whatever about me."

' "I'm capable of learning," I said.

'She smiled a little.

' "You're awfully kind, Mark," she said.

' "Say yes, Olive," I begged.

'She gave a deep sigh. For a long time she stared at the ground. But she did not move and I felt the softness of her body in my arms. I waited. I was frightfully nervous and the minutes seemed endless.

' "All right," she said at last, as though she were not conscious that any time had passed between my prayer and her answer.

'I was so moved that I had nothing to say. But when I wanted to kiss her lips, she turned her face away, and wouldn't let me. I wanted us to be married at once, but she was quite firm that she wouldn't. She insisted on waiting till Tim came back. You know how sometimes you see so clearly into people's thoughts that you're more certain of them than if they'd spoken them; I saw that she couldn't quite believe that what Tim had written was true and that she had a sort of miserable hope that it was all a mistake and he wasn't married after all. It gave me a pang, but I loved her so much, I just bore it. I was willing to bear anything. I adored her. She wouldn't even let me tell anyone that we were engaged. She made me promise not to say a word till Tim's return. She said she couldn't bear the thought of the congratulations and all that. She wouldn't even let me make any announcement of Tim's marriage. She was obstinate about it. I had a notion that she felt if the fact were spread about it gave it a certainty that she didn't want it to have.

'But the matter was taken out of her hands. News travels mysteriously in the East. I don't know what Olive had said in the amah's hearing when first she received the news of Tim's marriage; anyhow, the Hardy's seis told the Sergisons and Mrs Sergison attacked me the next time I went into the club.

' "I hear Tim Hardy's married," she said.

' "Oh?" I answered, unwilling to commit myself.

'She smiled at my blank face, and told me that her amah having told her the rumour she had rung up Olive and asked her if it was true. Olive's answer had been rather odd. She had not exactly confirmed it, but said that she had received a letter from Tim telling her he was married.

' "She's a strange girl," said Mrs Sergison. "When I asked her for details she said she had none to give and when I said: 'Aren't you thrilled?' she didn't answer."

' "Olive's devoted to Tim, Mrs Sergison," I said. "His marriage has naturally been a shock to her. She knows nothing about Tim's wife. She's nervous about her."

' "And when are you two going to be married?" she asked me abruptly.

' "What an embarrassing question!" I said, trying to laugh it off.

'She looked at me shrewdly.

' "Will you give me your word of honour that you're not engaged to her?"

'I didn't like to tell her a deliberate lie, nor to ask her to mind her own business, and I'd promised Olive faithfully that I would say nothing till Tim got back. I hedged.

' "Mrs Sergison," I said, "when there's anything to tell I promise that you'll be the first person to hear it. All I can say to you now is that I do want to marry Olive more than anything in the world."

' "I'm very glad that Tim's married," she answered. "And I hope she'll marry you very soon. It was a morbid and unhealthy life that they led up there, those two, they kept far too much to themselves and they were far too much absorbed in one another."

'I saw Olive practically every day. I felt that she didn't want me to make love to her, and I contented myself with kissing her when I came and when I went. She was very nice to me, kindly and thoughtful; I knew she was glad to see me and sorry when it was time for me to go. Ordinarily, she was apt to fall into silence but during this time she talked more than I had ever heard her talk before. But never of the future and never of Tim and his wife. She told me a lot about her life in Florence with her mother. She had led a strange lonely life, mostly with servants and governesses, while her mother, I suspected, engaged in one affair after another with vague Italian counts and Russian princes. I guessed that by the time she was fourteen there wasn't much she didn't know. It was natural for her to be quite unconventional: in the only world she knew till she was eighteen conventions weren't mentioned because they didn't exist. Gradually, Olive seemed to regain her serenity and I should have thought that she was beginning to accustom herself to the thought of Tim's marriage if it hadn't been that I couldn't but notice how pale and tired she looked. I made up my mind that the moment he arrived I'd press her to marry me at once. I could get short leave whenever I asked for it, and by the time that was up I thought I could manage a transfer to some other post. What she wanted was change of air and fresh scenes.

'We knew, of course, within a day when Tim's ship would reach Penang, but it was a question whether she'd get in soon enough for him to catch the train and I wrote to the P. & O. agent asking him to telegraph as soon as he had definite news. When I got the wire and took it up to Olive I found that she'd just received one from Tim. The ship had docked early and he was arriving next day. The train was supposed to get in at eight o'clock in the morning, but it was liable to be anything from one to six hours late, and I bore with me an invitation from Mrs Sergison asking Olive to come back with me to stay the night with her so that she would be on the spot and need not go to the station till the news came through that the train was coming.

'I was immensely relieved. I thought that when the blow at last fell Olive wouldn't feel it so much. She had worked herself up into such a state that I couldn't help thinking that she must have a reaction now. She might take a fancy to her sister-in-law. There was no reason why they shouldn't all three get on very well together. To my surprise Olive said she wasn't coming down to the station to meet them.

'"They'll be awfully disappointed," I said.

'"I'd rather wait here," she answered. She smiled a little. "Don't argue with me, Mark, I've quite made up my mind."

'"I've ordered breakfast in my house," I said.

'"That's all right. You meet them and take them to your house and give them breakfast, and then they can come along here afterwards. Of course I'll send the car down."

'"I don't suppose they'll want to breakfast if you're not there," I said.

'"Oh, I'm sure they will. If the train gets in on time they wouldn't have thought of breakfasting before it arrived and they'll be hungry. They won't want to take this long drive without anything to eat."

'I was puzzled. She had been looking forward so intensely to Tim's coming, it seemed strange that she should want to wait all by herself while the rest of us were having a jolly breakfast. I supposed she was nervous and wanted to delay as long as possible meeting the strange woman who had come to take her place. It seemed unreasonable, I couldn't see that an hour sooner or an hour later could make any difference, but I knew women were funny, and anyhow I felt Olive wasn't in the mood for me to press it.

' "Telephone when you're starting so that I shall know when to expect you," she said.

' "All right," I said, "but you know I shan't be able to come with them. It's my day for going to Lahad."

'This was a town that I had to go to once a week to take cases. It was a good way off and one had to ferry across a river, which took some time, so that I never got back till late. There were a few Europeans there and a club. I generally had to go on there for a bit to be sociable and see that things were getting along all right.

' "Besides," I added, "with Tim bringing his wife home for the first time I don't suppose he'll want me about. But if you'd like to ask me to dinner I'll be glad to come to that."

'Olive smiled.

' "I don't think it'll be my place to issue any more invitations, will it?" she said. "You must ask the bride."

'She said this so lightly that my heart leaped. I had a feeling that at last she had made up her mind to accept the altered circumstances and, what was more, was accepting them with cheerfulness. She asked me to stay to dinner. Generally I left about eight and dined at home. She was very sweet, almost tender, and I was happier than I'd been for weeks. I had never been more desperately in love with her. I had a couple of gin pahits and I think I was in rather good form at dinner. I know I made her laugh. I felt that at last she was casting away the load of misery that had oppressed her. That was why I didn't let myself be very much disturbed by what happened at the end.

' "Don't you think it's about time you were leaving a presumably maiden lady?" she said.

'She spoke in a manner that was so quietly gay that I answered without hesitation:

' "Oh, my dear, if you think you've got a shred of reputation left you deceive yourself. You're surely not under the impression that the ladies of Sibuku don't know that I've been coming to see you every day for a month. The general feeling is that if we're not married it's high time we were. Don't you think it would be just as well if I broke it to them that we're engaged?"

' "Oh, Mark, you mustn't take our engagement very seriously," she said.

'I laughed.

' "How else do you expect me to take it? It is serious."

'She shook her head a little.

35

' "No. I was upset and hysterical that day. You were being very sweet to me. I said yes because I was too miserable to say no. But now I've had time to collect myself. Don't think me unkind. I made a mistake. I've been very much to blame. You must forgive me."

' "Oh, darling, you're talking nonsense. You've got nothing against me."

'She looked at me steadily. She was quite calm. She had even a little smile at the back of her eyes.

' "I can't marry you. I can't marry anyone. It was absurd of me ever to think I could."

'I didn't answer at once. She was in a queer state and I thought it better not to insist.

' "I suppose I can't drag you to the altar by main force," I said.

'I held out my hand and she gave me hers. I put my arm round her, and she made no attempt to withdraw. She suffered me to kiss her as usual on her cheek.

'Next morning I met the train. For once in a way it was punctual. Tim waved to me as his carriage passed the place where I was standing, and by the time I had walked up he had already jumped out and was handing down his wife. He grasped my hand warmly.

' "Where's Olive?" he said, with a glance along the platform. "This is Sally."

'I shook hands with her and at the same time explained why Olive was not there.

' "It was frightfully early, wasn't it?" said Mrs Hardy.

'I told them that the plan was for them to come and have a bit of breakfast at my house and then drive home.

' "I'd love a bath," said Mrs Hardy.

' "You shall have one," I said.

'She was really an extremely pretty little thing, very fair, with enormous blue eyes and a lovely little straight nose. Her skin, all milk and roses, was exquisite. A little of the chorus girl typ , of course, and you may happen to think that rather namby-pamby, but in that style she was enchanting. We drove to my house, they both had a bath and Tim a shave; I just had two minutes alone with him. He asked me how Olive had taken his marriage. I told him she'd been upset.

' "I was afraid so," he said, frowning a little. He gave a short sigh. "I couldn't do anything else."

'I didn't understand what he meant. At that moment Mrs Hardy joined us and slipped her arm through her husband's. He took her hand in his and gently pressed it. He gave her a look that had in it something pleased and humorously affectionate, as though he didn't take her quite seriously, but enjoyed his sense of proprietorship and was proud of her beauty. She really was lovely. She was not at all shy, she asked me to call her Sally before we'd known one another ten minutes, and she was quick in the uptake. Of course, just then she was excited at arriving. She'd never been East and everything thrilled her. It was quite obvious that she was head over heels in love with Tim. Her eyes never left him and she hung on his words. We had a jolly breakfast and then we parted. They got into their car to go home and I into mine to go to Lahad. I promised to go straight to the estate from there and in point of fact it was out of my way to pass by my house. I took a change with me. I didn't see why Olive shouldn't like Sally very much, she was frank and gay, and ingenuous; she was extremely young, she couldn't have been more than nineteen, and her wonderful prettiness couldn't fail to appeal to Olive. I was just as glad to have had a reasonable excuse to leave the three of them by themselves for the day, but as I started out from Lahad I had a notion that by the time I arrived they would all be pleased to see me. I drove up to the bungalow and blew my horn two or three times, expecting someone to appear. Not a soul. The place was in total darkness. I was surprised. It was absolutely silent. I couldn't make it out. They must be in. Very odd, I thought. I waited a moment, then got out of the car and walked up the steps. At the top of them I stumbled over something. I swore and bent down to see what it was; it had felt like a body. There was a cry and I saw it was the amah. She shrank back cowering as I touched her and broke into loud wails.

' "What the hell's the matter?" I cried, and then I felt a hand on my arm and heard a voice: Tuan, Tuan. I turned and in the darkness recognized Tim's head boy. He began to speak in little frightened gasps. I listened to him with horror. What he told me was unspeakable. I pushed him aside and rushed into the house. The sitting-room was dark. I turned on the light. The first thing I saw was Sally huddled up in an arm-chair. She was startled by my sudden appearance and cried out. I could hardly speak. I asked her if it was true. When she told me it was I felt the room suddenly going round and round me. I had to sit down. As the car that bore Tim and Sally drove up the road that led to the house and Tim sounded the claxon to announce their arrival and the boys and the amah ran out to greet them there was the sound

of a shot. They ran to Olive's room and found her lying in front
of the looking-glass in a pool of blood. She had shot herself with
Tim's revolver.

' "Is she dead?" I said.

' "No, they sent for the doctor, and he took her to the hospital."

'I hardly knew what I was doing. I didn't even trouble to tell
Sally where I was going. I got up and staggered to the door. I
got into the car and told my seis to drive like hell to the hospital.
I rushed in. I asked where she was. They tried to bar my
way, but I pushed them aside. I knew where the private rooms
were. Someone clung to my arm, but I shook him off. I vaguely
understood that the doctor had given instructions that no one was
to go into the room. I didn't care about that. There was an orderly
at the door; he put out his arm to prevent me from passing. I
swore at him and told him to get out of my way. I suppose I made
a row, I was beside myself; the door was opened and the doctor
came out.

' "Who's making all this noise?" he said. "Oh, it's you. What
do you want?"

' "Is she dead?" I asked.

' "No. But she's unconscious. She never regained consciousness. It's only a matter of an hour or two."

' "I want to see her."

' "You can't."

' "I'm engaged to her."

' "You?" he cried, and even at that moment I was aware that
he looked at me strangely. "That's all the more reason."

' I didn't know what he meant. I was stupid with horror.

' "Surely you can do something to save her," I cried.

'He shook his head.

' "If you saw her you wouldn't wish it," he said.

'I stared at him aghast. In the silence I heard a man's convulsive sobbing.

' "Who's that?" I asked.

' "Her brother."

'Then I felt a hand on my arm. I looked round and saw it was
Mrs Sergison.

' "My poor boy," she said, "I'm so sorry for you."

' "What on earth made her do it?" I groaned.

' "Come away, my dear," said Mrs Sergison. "You can do no
good here."

' "No, I must stay," I said.

' "Well, go and sit in my room," said the doctor.

'I was so broken that I let Mrs Sergison take me by the arm and lead me into the doctor's private room. She made me sit down. I couldn't bring myself to realize that it was true. I thought it was a horrible nightmare from which I must awake. I don't know how long we sat there. Three hours. Four hours. At last the doctor came in.

' "It's all over," he said.

'Then I couldn't help myself, I began to cry. I didn't care what they thought of me. I was so frightfully unhappy.

'We buried her next day.

'Mrs Sergison came back to my house and sat with me for a while. She wanted me to go to the club with her. I hadn't the heart. She was very kind, but I was glad when she left me by myself. I tried to read, but the words meant nothing to me. I felt dead inside. My boy came in and turned on the lights. My head was aching like mad. Then he came back and said that a lady wished to see me. I asked who it was. He wasn't quite sure, but he thought it must be the new wife of the tuan at Putatan. I couldn't imagine what she wanted. I got up and went to the door. He was right. It was Sally. I asked her to come in. I noticed that she was deathly white. I felt sorry for her. It was a frightful experience for a girl of that age and for a bride a miserable home-coming. She sat down. She was very nervous. I tried to put her at her ease by saying conventional things. She made me very uncomfortable because she stared at me with those enormous blue eyes of hers, and they were simply ghastly with horror. She interrupted me suddenly.

' "You're the only person here I know," she said. "I had to come to you. I want you to get me away from here."

'I was dumbfounded.

' "What *do* you mean?" I said.

' "I don't want you to ask me any questions. I just want you to get me away. At once. I want to go back to England!"

' "But you can't leave Tim like that just now," I said. "My dear, you must pull yourself together. I know it's been awful for you. But think of Tim. If you have any love for him the least you can do is to try and make him a little less unhappy."

' "Oh, you don't know," she cried. "I can't tell you. It's too horrible. I beseech you to help me. If there's a train tonight let me get on it. If I can only get to Penang I can get a ship. I can't stay in this place another night. I shall go mad."

'I was absolutely bewildered.

' "Does Tim know?" I asked her.

' "I haven't seen Tim since last night. I'll never see him again. I'd rather die."

'I wanted to gain a little time.

' "But how can you go without your things? Have you got any luggage?"

' "What does that matter?" she cried impatiently. "I've got what I want for the journey."

' "Have you any money?"

' "Enough. Is there a train tonight?"

' "Yes," I said. "It's due just after midnight."

' "Thank God. Will you arrange everything? Can I stay here till then?"

' "You're putting me in a frightful position," I said. "I don't know what to do for the best. You know, it's an awfully serious step you're taking."

' "If you knew everything you'd know it was the only possible thing to do."

' "It'll create an awful scandal here. I don't know what people'll say. Have you thought of the effect on Tim?" I was worried and unhappy. "God knows I don't want to interfere in what isn't my business. But if you want me to help you I ought to know enough to feel justified in doing so. You must tell me what's happened."

' "I can't. I can only tell you that I know everything."

'She hid her face with her hands and shuddered. Then she gave herself a shake as though she were recoiling from some frightful sight.

' "He had no right to marry me. It was monstrous."

'And as she spoke her voice rose shrill and piercing. I was afraid she was going to have an attack of hysterics. Her pretty doll-like face was terrified and her eyes stared as though she could never close them again.

' "Don't you love him any more?" I asked.

' "After that?"

' "What will you do if I refuse to help you?" I said.

' "I suppose there's a clergyman here or a doctor. You can't refuse to take me to one of them."

' "How did you get here?"

' "The head boy drove me. He got a car from somewhere."

' "Does Tim know you've gone?"

' "I left a letter for him."

' "He'll know you're here."

' "He won't try to stop me. I promise you that. He daren't. For God's sake don't you try either. I tell you I shall go mad if I stay here another night."

'I sighed. After all she was of an age to decide for herself.'

I, the writer of this, hadn't spoken for a long time.

'Did you know what she meant?' I asked Featherstone.

He gave me a long, haggard look.

'There was only one thing she could mean. It was unspeakable. Yes, I knew all right. It explained everything. Poor Olive. Poor sweet. I suppose it was unreasonable of me, at that moment I only felt a horror of that little pretty fair-haired thing with her terrified eyes. I hated her. I didn't say anything for a while. Then I told her I'd do as she wished. She didn't even say thank you. I think she knew what I felt about her. When it was dinner-time I made her eat something and then she asked me if there was a room she could go and lie down in till it was time to go to the station. I showed her into my spare room and left her. I sat in the sitting-room and waited. My God, I don't think the time has ever passed so slowly for me. I thought twelve would never strike. I rang up the station and was told the train wouldn't be in till nearly two. At midnight she came back to the sitting-room and we sat there for an hour and a half. We had nothing to say to one another and we didn't speak. Then I took her to the station and put her on the train.'

'Was there an awful scandal?'

Featherstone frowned.

'I don't know. I applied for short leave. After that I was moved to another post. I heard that Tim had sold his estate and bought another. But I didn't know where. It was a shock to me at first when I found him here.'

Featherstone, getting up, went over to a table and mixed himself a whisky and soda. In the silence that fell now I heard the monotonous chorus of the croaking frogs. And suddenly the bird that is known as the fever-bird, perched in a tree close to the house, began to call. First, three notes in a descending, chromatic scale, then five, then four. The varying notes of the scale succeeded one another with maddening persistence. One was compelled to listen and to count them, and because one did not know how many there would be it tortured one's nerves.

'Blast that bird,' said Featherstone. 'That means no sleep for me tonight.'

FRENCH JOE

It was Captain Bartlett who told me of him. I do not think that many people have been to Thursday Island. It is in the Torres Straits and is so called because it was discovered on a Thursday by Captain Cook. I went there since they told me in Sydney that it was the last place God ever made. They said there was nothing to see and warned me that I should probably get my throat cut. I had come up from Sydney in a Japanese tramp and they put me ashore in a small boat. It was the middle of the night and there was not a soul on the jetty. One of the sailors who landed my kit told me that if I turned to the left I should presently come to a two-storey building and this was the hotel. The boat pushed off and I was left alone. I do not much like being separated from my luggage, but I like still less to pass the night on a jetty and sleep on hard stones; so I shouldered a bag and set out. It was pitch dark. I seemed to walk much more than a few hundred yards which they had spoken of and was afraid I had missed my way, but at last saw dimly a building which seemed to be important enough to suggest that it might be the hotel. No light showed, but my eyes by now were pretty well accustomed to the darkness and I found a door. I struck a match, but could see no bell. I knocked; there was no reply; I knocked again, with my stick, as loudly as I could, then a window above me was opened and a woman's voice asked me what I wanted.

'I've just got off the *Shika Maru*,' I said. 'Can I have a room?'
'I'll come down.'

I waited a little longer, and the door was opened by a woman in a red flannel dressing-gown. Her hair was hanging over her shoulders in long black wisps. In her hand she held a paraffin lamp. She greeted me warmly, a little stoutish woman, with keen eyes and a nose suspiciously red, and bade me come in. She took me upstairs and showed me a room.

'Now you sit down,' she said, 'and I'll make up the bed before you can say Jack Robinson. What will you 'ave? A drop of whisky would do you good, I should think. You won't want to be washing at this time of night, I'll bring you a towel in the morning.'

And while she made the bed she asked me who I was and what I had come to Thursday Island for. She could see I wasn't a sea-faring man – all the pilots came to this hotel and had done for twenty years – and she didn't know what business could have brought me. I wasn't that fellow as was coming to inspect the Customs was I? She'd 'eard they were sending someone from Sydney. I asked her if there were any pilots staying there then. Yes, there was one, Captain Bartlett, did I know him? A queer fish he was and no mistake. Hadn't got a hair on his head, but the way he could put his liquor away, well, it was a caution. There, the bed was ready and she expected I'd sleep like a top and one thing she could say was, the sheets were clean. She lit the end of a candle and bade me good night.

Captain Bartlett certainly was a queer fish, but he is of no moment to my present purpose; I made his acquaintance at dinner next day – before I left Thursday Island I had eaten turtle soup so often that I have ceased to look upon it as a luxury – and it was because in the course of conversation I mentioned that I spoke French that he asked me to go and see French Joe.

'It'll be a treat to the old fellow to talk his own lingo for a bit. He's ninety-three, you know.'

For the last two years, not because he was ill but because he was old and destitute, he had lived in the hospital and it was here that I visited him. He was lying in bed, in flannel pyjamas much too large for him, a little shrivelled old man with vivacious eyes, a short white beard, and bushy black eyebrows. He was glad to speak French with me, which he spoke with the marked accent of his native isle, for he was a Corsican, but he had dwelt so many years among English-speaking people that he no longer spoke his mother tongue with accuracy. He used English words as though they were French, making verbs of them with French termina-tions. He talked very quickly, with broad gestures, and his voice for the most part was clear and strong; but now and then it seemed suddenly to fade away so that it sounded as though he spoke from the grave. The hushed and hollow sound gave me an eerie feeling. Indeed I could not look upon him still as of this world. His real name was Joseph de Paoli. He was a nobleman and a gentleman. He was of the same family as the general we have all read of in Boswell's Johnson, but he showed no interest in his famous ancestor.

'We have had so many generals in our family,' he said. 'You know, of course, that Napoleon Bonaparte was a connexion of mine. No, I have never read Boswell. I have not read books. I have lived.'

He had entered the French army in 1851. Seventy-five years ago. It is terrifying. As a lieutenant of artillery ('like my cousin Bonaparte,' he said) he had fought the Russians in the Crimea and as a captain the Prussians in 1870. He showed me a scar on his bald pate from an Uhlan's lance and then with a dramatic gesture told how he had thrust his sword in the Uhlan's body with such violence that he could not withdraw it. The Uhlan fell dead and the sword remained in the body. But the Empire perished and he joined the communists. For six weeks he fought against the government troops under Monsieur Thiers. To me Thiers is but a shadowy figure, and it was startling and even a trifle comic to hear French Joe speak with passionate hatred of a man who has been dead for half a century. His voice rose into a shrill scream as he repeated the insults, Oriental in their imagery, which in the council he had flung at the head of this mediocre statesman. French Joe was tried and sentenced to five years in New Caledonia.

'They should have shot me,' he said, 'but, dirty cowards, they dared not.'

Then came the long journey in a sailing vessel, and the antipodes, and his wrath flamed out again when he spoke of the indignity thrust upon him, a political prisoner, when they herded him with vulgar criminals. The ship put in at Melbourne, and one of the officers, a fellow-Corsican, enabled him to slip over the side. He swam ashore and, taking his friend's advice, went straight to the police-station. No one there could understand a word he said, but an interpreter was sent for, his dripping papers were examined, and he was told that so long as he did not set foot on a French ship he was safe.

'Freedom,' he cried to me. 'Freedom.'

Then came a long series of adventures. He cooked, taught French, swept streets, worked in the gold mines, tramped, starved, and at last found his way to New Guinea. Here he underwent the most astonishing of his experiences, for drifting into the savage interior, and they are cannibals there still, after a hundred desperate adventures and hair-breadth escapes he made himself king of some wild tribe.

'Look at me, my friend,' he said, 'I who lie here on a hospital bed, the object of charity, have been monarch of all I surveyed. Yes, it is something to say that I have been a king.'

But eventually he came into collision with the British, and his sovereignty passed from him. He fled the country and started life once more. It is clear that he was a fellow of resource for eventually he came to own a fleet of pearling luggers on Thursday Island. It looked as though at last he had reached a haven of peace and, an elderly man now, he looked forward to a prosperous and even respectable old age. A hurricane destroyed his boats and ruin fell upon him. He never recovered. He was too old to make a fresh start, and since then had earned as best he could a precarious livelihood till at last, beaten, he had accepted the hospital's kindly shelter.

'But why did you not go back to France or Corsica? An amnesty was granted to the communists a quarter of a century ago.'

'What are France and Corsica to me after fifty years? A cousin of mine seized my land. We Corsicans never forget and never forgive. If I had gone back I should have had to kill him. He had his children.'

'Funny old French Joe,' smiled the hospital nurse who stood at the end of the bed.

'At all events you have had a fine life,' I said.

'Never. Never. I have had a frightful life. Misfortune has followed me wherever I turned my steps and look at me now: I am rotten, fit for nothing but the grave. I thank God that I had no children to inherit the curse that is upon me.'

'Why, Joe, I thought you didn't believe in God,' said the nurse.

'It is true. I am a sceptic. I have never seen a sign that there is in the scheme of things an intelligent purpose. If the universe is the contrivance of some being, that being can only be a criminal imbecile.' He shrugged his shoulders. 'Anyhow, I have not got much longer in this filthy world and then I shall go and see for myself what is the real truth of the whole business.'

The nurse told me it was time to leave the old man and I took his hand to bid him farewell. I asked him if there was anything I could do for him.

'I want nothing,' he said. 'I only want to die.' His black shining eyes twinkled. 'But meanwhile I should be grateful for a packet of cigarettes.'

GERMAN HARRY

I WAS in Thursday Island and I wanted very much to go to New Guinea. Now the only way in which I could do this was by getting a pearling lugger to take me across the Arafura Sea. The pearl fishery at that time was in a bad way and a flock of neat little craft lay anchored in the harbour. I found a skipper with nothing much to do (the journey to Merauke and back could hardly take him less than a month) and with him I made the necessary arrangements. He engaged four Torres Straits islanders as crew (the boat was but nineteen tons) and we ransacked the local store for canned goods. A day or two before I sailed a man who owned a number of pearlers came to me and asked whether on my way I would stop at the island of Trebucket and leave a sack of flour, another of rice, and some magazines for the hermit who lived there.

I pricked up my ears. It appeared that the hermit had lived by himself on this remote and tiny island for thirty years, and when opportunity occurred provisions were sent to him by kindly souls. He said that he was a Dane, but in the Torres Straits he was known as German Harry. His history went back a long way. Thirty years before, he had been an able seaman on a sailing vessel that was wrecked in those treacherous waters. Two boats managed to get away and eventually hit upon the desert island of Trebucket. This is well out of the line of traffic and it was three years before any ship sighted the castaways. Sixteen men had landed on the island, but when at last a schooner, driven from her course by stress of weather, put in for shelter, no more than five were left. When the storm abated the skipper took four of these on board and eventually landed them at Sydney. German Harry refused to go with them. He said that during those three years he had seen such terrible things that he had a horror of his fellow-men and wished never to live with them again. He would say no more. He was absolutely fixed in his determination to stay, entirely by himself, in that lonely place. Though now and then opportunity had been given him to leave he had never taken it.

A strange man and a strange story. I learned more about him as we sailed across the desolate sea. The Torres Straits are peppered with islands and at night we anchored on the lee of one or other of them. Of late new pearling grounds have been discovered near Trebucket, and in the autumn pearlers, visiting it now and then, have given German Harry various necessities so that he has been able to make himself sufficiently comfortable. They bring him papers, bags of flour and rice, and canned meats. He has a whale boat and used to go fishing in it, but now he is no longer strong enough to manage its unwieldy bulk. There is abundant pearl shell on the reef that surrounds his island and this he used to collect and sell to the pearlers for tobacco, and sometimes he found a good pearl for which he got a considerable sum. It is believed that he has, hidden away somewhere, a collection of magnificent pearls. During the war no pearlers came out and for years he never saw a living soul. For all he knew, a terrible epidemic had killed off the entire human race and he was the only man alive. He was asked later what he thought.

'I thought something had happened,' he said.

He ran out of matches and was afraid that his fire would go out, so he only slept in snatches, putting wood on his fire from time to time all day and night. He came to the end of his provisions and lived on chickens, fish, and coconuts. Sometimes he got a turtle.

During the last four months of the year there may be two or three pearlers about and not infrequently after the day's work they will row in and spend an evening with him. They try to make him drunk and then they ask him what happened during those three years after the two boat-loads came to the island. How was it that sixteen landed and at the end of that time only five were left? He never says a word. Drunk or sober he is equally silent on that subject and if they insist grows angry and leaves them.

I forget if it was four or five days before we sighted the hermit's little kingdom. We had been driven by bad weather to take shelter and had spent a couple of days at an island on the way. Trebucket is a low island, perhaps a mile round, covered with coconuts, just raised above the level of the sea and surrounded by a reef so that it can be approached only on one side. There is no opening in the reef and the lugger had to anchor a mile from the shore. We got into a dinghy with the provisions. It was a stiff pull and even within the reef the sea was choppy. I saw the little hut, sheltered by trees, in which German Harry lived, and as we approached he sauntered down slowly to the water's edge. We shouted a greeting, but he did not answer. He was a man of over seventy, very bald, hatchet-faced, with a grey beard, and he walked with a roll so that you could never have taken him for

47

anything but a sea-faring man. His sunburn made his blue eyes look very pale and they were surrounded by wrinkles as though for long years he had spent interminable hours scanning the vacant sea. He wore dungarees and a singlet, patched, but neat and clean. The house to which he presently led us consisted of a single room with a roof of corrugated iron. There was a bed in it, some rough stools which he himself had made, a table, and his various household utensils. Under a tree in front of it was a table and a bench. Behind was an enclosed run for his chickens.

I cannot say that he was pleased to see us. He accepted our gifts as a right, without thanks, and grumbled a little because something or other he needed had not been brought. He was silent and morose. He was not interested in the news we had to give him, for the outside world was no concern of his: the only thing he cared about was his island. He looked upon it with a jealous, proprietary right; he called it 'my health resort' and he feared that the coconuts that covered it would tempt some enterprising trader. He looked at me with suspicion. He was sombrely curious to know what I was doing in these seas. He used words with difficulty, talking to himself rather than to us, and it was a little uncanny to hear him mumble away as though we were not there. But he was moved when my skipper told him that an old man of his own age whom he had known for a long time was dead.

'Old Charlie dead – that's too bad. Old Charlie dead.'

He repeated it over and over again. I asked him if he read.

'Not much,' he answered indifferently.

He seemed to be occupied with nothing but his food, his dogs, and his chickens. If what they tell us in books were true his long communion with nature and the sea should have taught him many subtle secrets. It hadn't. He was a savage. He was nothing but a narrow, ignorant, and cantankerous sea-faring man. As I looked at the wrinkled, mean old face I wondered what was the story of those three dreadful years that had made him welcome this long imprisonment. I sought to see behind those pale blue eyes of his what secrets they were that he would carry to his grave. And then I foresaw the end. One day a pearl fisher would land on the island and German Harry would not be waiting for him, silent and suspicious, at the water's edge. He would go up to the hut and there, lying on the bed, unrecognizable, he would see all that remained of what had once been a man. Perhaps then he would hunt high and low for the great mass of pearls that has haunted the fancy of so many adventurers. But I do not believe he would find it: German Harry would have seen to it that none should discover the treasure, and the pearls would rot in their hiding place. Then the pearl fisher would go back into his dinghy and the island once more be deserted of man.

THE FOUR DUTCHMEN

THE Van Dorth Hotel at Singapore was far from grand. The bedrooms were dingy and the mosquito nets patched and darned; the bath-houses, all in a row and detached from the bedrooms, were dank and smelly. But it had character. The people who stayed there, masters of tramps whose round ended at Singapore, mining engineers out of a job, and planters taking a holiday, to my mind bore a more romantic air than the smart folk, globe-trotters, government officials and their wives, wealthy merchants, who gave luncheon-parties at the Europe and played golf and danced and were fashionable. The Van Dorth had a billiard-room, with a table with a threadbare cloth, where ships' engineers and clerks in insurance offices played snooker. The dining-room was large and bare and silent. Dutch families on the way to Sumatra ate solidly through their dinner without exchanging a word with one another, and single gentlemen on a business trip from Batavia devoured a copious meal while they intently read their paper. On two days a week there was rijstafel and then a few residents of Singapore who had a fancy for this dish came for tiffin. The Van Dorth Hotel should have been a depressing place, but somehow it wasn't; its quaintness saved it. It had a faint aroma of something strange and half-forgotten. There was a scrap of garden facing the street where you could sit in the shade of trees and drink cold beer. In that crowded and busy city, though motors whizzed past and rickshaws passed continuously, the coolies' feet pattering on the road and their bells ringing, it had the remote peacefulness of a corner of Holland. It was the third time I had stayed at the Van Dorth. I had been told about it first by the skipper of a Dutch tramp, the S.S. *Utrecht*, on which I had travelled from Merauke in New Guinea to Macassar. The journey took the best part of a month, since the ship stopped at a number of islands in the Malay Archipelago, the Aru and the Kei Islands, Banda-Neira, Amboina, and others of which I have even forgotten the names, sometimes for an hour or two, sometimes for a day, to take on or discharge cargo. It was a charming, monotonous, and diverting trip. When we dropped anchor the agent came out in his launch, and generally the Dutch Resident, and we gathered on deck under the awning and the captain ordered beer. The news of the island was exchanged for the news of the world. We brought papers and mail. If we were staying long enough the Resident asked us to dinner and, leaving the ship in charge of the second officer, we all (the captain, the chief officer, the engineer, the supercargo, and I) piled into the launch and went ashore. We spent a merry evening. These little islands, one so like another, allured my fancy just because I knew that I should never see them again. It made them strangely unreal, and as we sailed away and they vanished into the sea and sky it was only by an effort of the imagination that I could persuade myself that they did not with my last glimpse of them cease to exist.

But there was nothing illusive, mysterious, or fantastic about the captain, the chief officer, the chief engineer, and the supercargo. Their solidity was amazing. They were the four fattest men I ever saw. At first I had great difficulty in telling them apart, for though one, the supercargo, was dark and the others were fair, they looked astonishingly alike. They were all big, with large round bare red faces, with large fat arms and large fat legs and large fat bellies. When they went ashore they buttoned up their stengah-shifters and then their great double chins bulged over the collars and they looked as though they would choke. But generally they wore them unbuttoned. They sweated freely and wiped their shiny faces with bandanas and vigorously fanned themselves with palm-leaf fans.

It was a treat to see them at tiffin. Their appetites were enormous. They had rijstafel every day, and each seemed to vie with the other how high he could pile his plate. They loved it hot and strong.

'In dis country you can't eat a ting onless it's tasty,' said the skipper.

'De only way to keep yourself up in dis country is to eat hearty,' said the chief.

They were the greatest friends, all four of them; they were like schoolboys together, playing absurd little pranks with one another. They knew each other's jokes by heart and no sooner did one of them start the familiar lines than he would splutter with laughter so violently, the heavy shaking laughter of the fat man, that he could not go on, and then the others began to laugh too. They rolled about in their chairs, and grew redder and redder, hotter and hotter, till the skipper shouted for beer, and each, gasping but happy, drank his bottle in one enchanted draught. They had been on this run together for five years and when, a little time before, the chief officer had been offered a ship of his own he refused it. He would not leave his companions. They had made up their minds that when the first of them retired they would all retire.

'All friends and a good ship. Good grub and good beer. Vot can a sensible man vant more?'

At first they were a little stand-offish with me. Although the ship had accommodation for half a dozen passengers, they did not often get any, and never one whom they did not know. I was a stranger and a foreigner. They liked their bit of fun and did not want anyone to interfere with it. But they were all of them very fond of bridge, and on occasion the chief and the engineer had duties that prevented one or the other playing. They were willing to put up with me when they discovered that I was ready to make a fourth whenever I was wanted. Their bridge was as incredibly fantastic as they were. They played for infinitesimal stakes, five cents a hundred: they did not want to win one another's money, they said, it was the game they liked. But what a game! Each was wildly determined to play the hand and hardly one was dealt without at least a small slam being declared. The rule was that if you could get a peep at somebody else's cards you did, and if you could get away with a revoke you told your partner when there was no danger it could be claimed and you both roared with laughter till the tears rolled down your fat cheeks. But if your partner had insisted on taking the bid away from you and had called a grand slam on five spades to the queen, whereas you were positive on your seven little diamonds you could have made it easily, you could always score him off by redoubling without a trick in your hand. He went down two or three thousand and the glasses on the table danced with the laughter that shook your opponents.

I could never remember their difficult Dutch names, but knowing them anonymously as it were, only by the duties they performed, as one knows the characters Pantaloon, Harlequin, and Punchinello, of the old Italian comedy, added grotesquely to their drollery. The mere sight of them, all four together, set you laughing, and I think they got a good deal of amusement from the astonishment they caused in strangers. They boasted that they were the four most famous Dutchmen in the East Indies. To me not the least comic part of them was their serious side. Sometimes late at night, when they had given up all pretence of still wearing their uniforms, and one or the other of them lay by my side on a long chair in a pyjama jacket and a sarong, he would grow sentimental. The chief engineer, due to retire soon, was meditating marriage with a widow whom he had met when last he was home and spending the rest of his life in a little town with old red-brick houses on the shores of the Zuyder Zee. But the captain was very susceptible to the charms of the native girls and his thick English became almost unintelligible from emotion when he described to me the effect they had on him. One of these days he would buy himself a house on the hills in Java and marry a pretty little Javanese. They were so small and so gentle and they made no noise, and he would dress her in silk sarongs and give her gold chains to wear round her neck and gold bangles to put on her arms. But the chief mocked him.

'Silly all dat is. Silly. She goes mit all your friends and de house boys and everybody. By de time you retire, my dear, vot you'll vant vill be a nurse, not a vife.'

'Me?' cried the skipper. 'I shall want a vife ven I'm eighty!'

He had picked up a little thing last time the ship was at Macassar and as we approached that port he began to be all of a flutter. The chief officer shrugged fat and indulgent shoulders. The captain was always losing his head over one brazen hussy after another, but his passion never survived the interval between one stop at a port and the next, and then the chief was called in to smooth out the difficulties that ensued. And so it would be this time.

'De old man suffers from fatty degeneration of de heart. But so long as I'm dere to look after him not much harm comes of it. He vastes his money and dat's a pity, but as long as he's got it to vaste, why shouldn't he?'

The chief officer had a philosophic soul.

At Macassar then I disembarked, and bade farewell to my four fat friends.

'Make another journey with us,' they said. 'Come back next year or the year after. You'll find us all here just the same as ever.'

A good many months had passed since then and I had wandered through more than one strange land. I had been to Bali and Java and Sumatra; I had been to Cambodia and Annam; and now, feeling as though I were home again, I sat in the garden of the Van Dorth Hotel. It was cool in the very early morning and having had breakfast I was looking at back numbers of the *Straits Times* to find out what had been happening in the world since last I had been within reach of papers. Nothing very much. Suddenly my eyes caught a headline: *The* Utrecht *Tragedy. Supercargo and Chief Engineer. Not Guilty.* I read the paragraph carelessly and then I sat up. The *Utrecht* was the ship of my four fat Dutchmen and apparently the supercargo and the chief engineer had been on trial for murder. It couldn't be my two fat friends. The names were given, but the names meant nothing to me. The trial had taken place in Batavia. No details were given in this paragraph; it was only a brief announcement that after the judges had considered the speeches of the prosecution and of the defence their verdict was as stated. I was astounded. It was incredible that the men I knew could have committed a murder. I could not find out who had been murdered. I looked through back numbers of the paper. Nothing.

I got up and went to the manager of the hotel, a genial Dutchman, who spoke admirable English, and showed him the paragraph.

'That's the ship I sailed on. I was in her for nearly a month. Surely these fellows aren't the men I knew. The men I knew were enormously fat.'

'Yes, that's right,' he answered. 'They were celebrated all through the Dutch East Indies, the four fattest men in the service. It's been a terrible thing. It made a great sensation. And they were friends. I knew them all. The best fellows in the world.'

'But what happened?'

He told me the story and answered my horrified questions. But there were things I wanted to know that he couldn't tell me. It was all confused. It was unbelievable. What actually had happened was only conjecture. Then someone claimed the manager's attention and I went back to the garden. It was getting hot now and I went up to my room. I was strangely shattered.

It appeared that on one of the trips the captain took with him a Malay girl that he had been carrying on with and I wondered if it was the one he had been so eager to see when I was on board. The other three had been against her coming – what did they want with a woman in the ship? it would spoil everything – but the captain insisted and she came. I think they were all jealous of her. On that journey they didn't have the fun they generally had. When they wanted to play bridge the skipper was dallying with the girl in his cabin; when they touched at a port and went ashore the time seemed long to him till he could get back to her. He was crazy about her. It was the end of all their larks. The chief officer was more bitter against her than anybody: he was the captain's particular chum, they had been shipmates ever since they first came out from Holland; more than once high words passed between them on the subject of the captain's infatuation. Presently those old friends spoke to one another only when their duties demanded it. It was the end of the good fellowship that had so long obtained between the four fat men. Things went from bad to worse. There was a feeling among the junior officers that something untoward was pending. Uneasiness. Tension. Then one night the ship was aroused by the sound of a shot and the screams of the Malay girl. The supercargo and the chief engineer tumbled out of their bunks and they found the captain, a revolver in his hand, at the door of the chief officer's cabin. He pushed past them and went on deck. They entered and found the chief officer dead and the girl cowering behind the door. The captain had found them in bed together and had killed the chief. How he had discovered what was going on didn't seem to be known, nor what was the meaning of the intrigue. Had the chief induced the girl to come to his cabin in order to get back on the captain, or had she, knowing his ill-will and anxious to placate him, lured him to become her lover? It was a mystery that would never be solved. A dozen possible explanations flashed across my mind. While the engineer and the supercargo were in the cabin, horror-struck at the sight before them, another shot was heard. They knew at once what had happened. They rushed up the companion. The captain had gone to his cabin and blown his brains out. Then the story grew dark and enigmatic. Next morning the Malay girl was nowhere to be found and when the second officer, who had taken command of the ship, reported this to the super-cargo, the supercargo said: 'She's probably jumped overboard. It's the best thing she could have done. Good riddance to bad rubbish.' But one of the sailors on the watch, just before dawn, had seen the supercargo and the chief engineer carry something up on deck, a bulky package, about the size of a native woman, look about them to see that they were unobserved, and drop it overboard; and it was said all over the ship that these two to avenge their friends had sought the girl out in her cabin and strangled her and flung her body into the sea. When the ship arrived at Macassar they were arrested and taken to Batavia to be tried for murder. The evidence was flimsy and they were acquitted. But all through the East Indies they knew that the supercargo and the chief engineer had executed justice on the trollop who had caused the death of the two men they loved.

And thus ended the comic and celebrated friendship of the four fat Dutchmen.

THE BACK OF BEYOND

GEORGE MOON was sitting in his office. His work was finished, and he lingered there because he hadn't the heart to go down to the club. It was getting on towards tiffin time, and there would be a good many fellows hanging about the bar. Two or three of them would offer him a drink. He could not face their heartiness. Some he had known for thirty years. They had bored him, and on the whole he disliked them, but now that he was seeing them for the last time it gave him a pang. Tonight they were giving him a farewell dinner. Everyone would be there and they were presenting him with a silver tea-service that he did not in the least want. They would make speeches in which they would refer eulogistically to his work in the colony, express their regret at his departure, and wish him long life to enjoy his well-earned leisure. He would reply suitably. He had prepared a speech in which he surveyed the changes that had taken place in the F.M.S. since first, a raw cadet, he had landed at Singapore. He would thank them for their loyal cooperation with him during the term which it had been his privilege to serve as Resident at Timbang Belud, and draw a glowing picture of the future that awaited the country as a whole and Timbang Belud in particular. He would remind them that he had known it as a poverty-stricken village with a few Chinese shops and left it now a prosperous town with paved streets down which ran trams, with stone houses, a rich Chinese settlement, and a clubhouse second in splendour only to that of Singapore. They would sing 'For he's a jolly good fellow' and 'Auld Lang Syne'. Then they would dance and a good many of the younger men would get drunk. The Malays had already given him a farewell party and the Chinese an interminable feast. Tomorrow a vast concourse would see him off at the station and that would be the end of him. He wondered what they would say of him. The Malays and the Chinese would say that he had been stern, but acknowledge that he had been just. The planters had not liked him. They thought him hard because he would not let them ride roughshod over their labour. His subordinates had feared him. He drove them. He had no patience with slackness or inefficiency. He had never spared himself and saw no reason why he should spare others. They thought him inhuman. It was true that there was nothing come-hither in him. He could not throw off his

56

official position when he went to the club and laugh at bawdy stories, chaff and be chaffed. He was conscious that his arrival cast a gloom, and to play bridge with him (he liked to play every day from six to eight) was looked upon as a privilege rather than an entertainment. When at some other table a young man's four as the evening wore on grew hilarious, he caught glances thrown in his direction and sometimes an older member would stroll up to the noisy ones and in an undertone advise them to be quiet. George Moon sighed a little. From an official standpoint his career had been a success, he had been the youngest Resident ever appointed in the F.M.S., and for exceptional services a C.M.G. had been conferred upon him; but from the human it had perhaps been otherwise. He had earned respect, respect for his ability, industry, and trustworthiness, but he was too clear-sighted to think for a moment that he had inspired affection. No one would regret him. In a few months he would be forgotten.

He smiled grimly. He was not sentimental. He had enjoyed his authority, and it gave him an austere satisfaction to know that he had kept everyone up to the mark. It did not displease him to think that he had been feared rather than loved. He saw his life as a problem in higher mathematics, the working-out of which had required intense application of all his powers, but of which the result had not the least practical consequence. Its interest lay in its intricacy and its beauty in its solution. But like pure beauty it led nowhither. His future was blank. He was fifty-five, and full of energy, and to himself his mind seemed as alert as ever, his experience of men and affairs was wide: all that remained to him was to settle down in a country town in England or in a cheap part of the Riviera and play bridge with elderly ladies and golf with retired colonels. He had met, when on leave, old chiefs of his, and had observed with what difficulty they adapted themselves to the change in their circumstances. They had looked forward to the freedom that would be theirs when they retired and had pictured the charming uses to which they would put their leisure. Mirage. It was not very pleasant to be obscure after having dwelt in a spacious Residency, to make do with a couple of maids when you had been accustomed to the service of half a dozen Chinese boys and, above all, it was not pleasant to realize that you did not matter a row of beans to anyone when you had grown used to the delicate flattery of knowing that a word of praise could delight and a frown humiliate all sorts and conditions of men.

George Moon stretched out his hand and helped himself to a

cigarette from the box on his desk. As he did so he noticed all the little lines on the back of his hand and the thinness of his shrivelled fingers. He frowned with distaste. It was the hand of an old man. There was in his office a Chinese mirror-picture that he had bought long ago and that hè was leaving behind. He got up and looked at himself in it. He saw a thin yellow face, wrinkled and tight-lipped, thin grey hair, and grey tired eyes. He was tallish, very spare, with narrow shoulders, and he held himself erect. He had always played polo and even now could beat most of the younger men at tennis. When you talked to him he kept his eyes fixed on your face, listening attentively, but his expression did not change, and you had no notion what effect your words had on him. Perhaps he did not realize how disconcerting this was. He seldom smiled.

An orderly came in with a name written on a chit. George Moon looked at it and told him to show the visitor in. He sat down once more in his chair and looked with his cold eyes at the door through which in a moment the visitor would come. It was Tom Saffary, and he wondered what he wanted. Presumably something to do with the festivity that night. It had amused him to hear that Tom Saffary was the head of the committee that had organized it, for their relations during the last year had been far from cordial. Saffary was a planter and one of his Tamil overseers had lodged a complaint against him for assault. The Tamil had been grossly insolent to him and Saffary had given him a thrashing. George Moon realized that the provocation was great, but he had always set his face against the planters taking the law in their own hands, and when the case was tried he sentenced Saffary to a fine. But when the court rose, to show that there was no ill-feeling he asked Saffary to luncheon: Saffary, resentful of what he thought an unmerited affront, curtly refused and since then had declined to have any social relations with the Resident. He answered when George Moon, casually, but resolved not to be affronted, spoke to him; but would play neither bridge nor tennis with him. He was manager of the largest rubber estate in the district, and George Moon asked himself sardonically whether he had arranged the dinner and collected subscriptions for the presentation because he thought his dignity required it or whether, now that his Resident was leaving, it appealed to his sentimentality to make a noble gesture. It tickled George Moon's frigid sense of humour to think that it would fall to Tom Saffary to make the principal speech of the evening, in which he would enlarge upon the departing Resident's admirable qualities and voice the community's regret at their irreparable loss.

Tom Saffary was ushered in. The Resident rose from his chair, shook hands with him and thinly smiled.

'How do you do? Sit down. Won't you have a cigarette?'

'How do you do?'

Saffary took the chair to which the Resident motioned him, and the Resident waited for him to state his business. He had a notion that his visitor was embarrassed. He was a big, burly, stout fellow, with a red face and a double chin, curly black hair, and blue eyes. He was a fine figure of a man, strong as a horse, but it was plain he did himself too well. He drank a good deal and ate too heartily. But he was a good business man and a hard worker. He ran his estate efficiently. He was popular in the community. He was generally known as a good chap. He was free with his money and ready to lend a helping hand to anyone in distress. It occurred to the Resident that Saffary had come in order before the dinner to compose the difference between them. The emotion that might have occasioned such a desire excited in the Resident's sensibility a very faint, good-humoured contempt. He had no enemies because individuals did not mean enough to him for him to hate any of them, but if he had, he thought, he would have hated them to the end.

'I dare say you're a bit surprised to see me here this morning, and I expect, as it's your last day and all that, you're pretty busy.'

George Moon did not answer, and the other went on.

'I've come on rather an awkward business. The fact is that my wife and I won't be able to come to the dinner tonight, and after that unpleasantness we had together last year I thought it only right to come and tell you that it has nothing to do with that. I think you treated me very harshly; it's not the money I minded, it was the indignity, but bygones are bygones. Now that you're leaving I don't want you to think that I bear any more ill-feeling towards you.'

'I realized that when I heard that you were chiefly responsible for the send-off you're giving me,' answered the Resident civilly. 'I'm sorry that you won't be able to come tonight.'

'I'm sorry, too. It's on account of Knobby Clarke's death.' Saffary hesitated for a moment. 'My wife and I were very much upset by it.'

'It was very sad. He was a great friend of yours, wasn't he?'

'He was the greatest friend I had in the colony.'

Tears shone in Tom Saffary's eyes. Fat men are very emotional, thought George Moon.

'I quite understand that in that case you should have no heart for what looks like being a rather uproarious party,' he said kindly. 'Have you heard anything of the circumstances?'

'No, nothing but what appeared in the paper.'

'He seemed all right when he left here.'

'As far as I know he'd never had a day's illness in his life.'

'Heart, I suppose. How old was he?'

'Same age as me. Thirty-eight.'

'That's young to die.'

Knobby Clarke was a planter and the estate he managed was next door to Saffary's. George Moon had liked him. He was a rather ugly man, sandy, with high cheek-bones and hollow temples, large pale eyes in deep sockets and a big mouth. But he had an attractive smile and an easy manner. He was amusing and could tell a good story. He had a careless good-humour that people found pleasing. He played games well. He was no fool. George Moon would have said he was somewhat colourless. In the course of his career he had known a good many men like him. They came and went. A fortnight before, he had left for England on leave and the Resident knew that the Saffarys had given a large dinner-party on his last night. He was married and his wife of course went with him.

'I'm sorry for her,' said George Moon. 'It must have been a terrible blow. He was buried at sea, wasn't he?'

'Yes. That's what it said in the paper.'

The news had reached Timbang the night before. The Singapore papers arrived at six, just as people were getting to the club, and a good many men waited to play bridge or billiards till they had had a glance at them. Suddenly one fellow had called out:

'I say, do you see this? Knobby's dead.'

'Knobby who? Not Knobby Clarke?'

There was a three-line paragraph in a column of general intelligence:

Messrs Star, Mosley and Co. have received a cable informing them that Mr Harold Clarke of Timbang Batu died suddenly on his way home and was buried at sea.

A man came up and took the paper from the speaker's hand, and incredulously read the note for himself. Another peered over his shoulder. Such as happened to be reading the paper turned to the page in question and read the three different lines.

'By George,' cried one.

'I say, what tough luck,' said another.

'He was as fit as a fiddle when he left here.'

A shiver of dismay pierced those hearty, jovial, careless men, and each one for a moment remembered that he too was mortal. Other members came in and as they entered, braced by the thought of the six o'clock drink, and eager to meet their friends, they were met by the grim tidings.

'I say, have you heard? Poor Knobby Clarke's dead.'

'No? I say, how awful!'

'Rotten luck, isn't it?'

'Rotten.'

'Damned good sort.'

'One of the best.'

'It gave me quite a turn when I saw it in the paper just by chance.'

'I don't wonder.'

One man with the paper in his hand went into the billiard-room to break the news. They were playing off the handicap for the Prince of Wales's Cup. That august personage had presented it to the club on the occasion of his visit to Timbang Belud. Tom Saffary was playing against a man called Douglas, and the Resident, who had been beaten in the previous round, was seated with about a dozen others watching the game. The marker was monotonously calling out the score. The newcomer waited for Saffary to finish his break and then called out to him.

'I say, Tom, Knobby's dead.'

'Knobby? It's not true.'

The other handed him the paper. Three or four gathered round to read with him.

'Good God!'

There was a moment's awed silence. The paper was passed from hand to hand. It was odd that none seemed willing to believe till he saw it for himself in black and white.

'Oh, I am sorry.'

'I say, it's awful for his wife,' said Tom Saffary. 'She was going to have a baby. My poor missus'll be upset.'

'Why, it's only a fortnight since he left here.'

'He was all right then.'

'In the pink.'

Saffary, his fat red face sagging a little, went over to a table and, seizing his glass, drank deeply.

'Look here, Tom,' said his opponent, 'would you like to call the game off?'

'Can't very well do that.' Saffary's eye sought the score board and he saw that he was ahead. 'No, let's finish. Then I'll go home and break it to Violet.'

Douglas had his shot and made fourteen. Tom Saffary missed an easy in-off, but left nothing. Douglas played again, but did not score and again Saffary missed a shot that ordinarily he could have been sure of. He frowned a little. He knew his friends had betted on him pretty heavily and he did not like the idea of failing them. Douglas made twenty-two. Saffary emptied his glass and by an effort of will that was quite patent to the sympathetic on-lookers settled down to concentrate on the game. He made a break of eighteen and when he just failed to do a long Jenny they gave him a round of applause. He was sure of himself now and began to score quickly. Douglas was playing well too, and the match grew exciting to watch. The few minutes during which Saffary's attention wandered had allowed his opponent to catch up with him, and now it was anybody's game.

'Spot two hundred and thirty-five,' called the Malay, in his queer clipped English. 'Plain two hundred and twenty-eight. Spot to play.'

Douglas made eight, and then Saffary, who was plain, drew up to two hundred and forty. He left his opponent a double balk. Douglas hit neither ball, and so gave Saffary another point.

'Spot two hundred and forty-three,' called the marker. 'Plain two hundred and forty-one. Plain to play.'

Saffary played three beautiful shots off the red and finished the game.

'A popular victory,' the bystanders cried.

'Congratulations, old man,' said Douglas.

'Boy,' called Saffary, 'ask these gentlemen what they'll have. Poor old Knobby.'

He sighed heavily. The drinks were brought and Saffary signed the chit. Then he said he'd be getting along. Two others had already begun to play.

'Sporting of him to go on like that,' said someone when the door was closed on Saffary.

'Yes, it shows grit.'

'For a while I thought his game had gone all to pieces.'

'He pulled himself together in grand style. He knew there were a lot of bets on him. He didn't want to let his backers down.'

'Of course it's a shock, a thing like that.'

'They were great pals. I wonder what he died of.'

'Good shot, sir.'

George Moon, remembering this scene, thought it strange that Tom Saffary, who on hearing of his friend's death had shown such self-control, should now apparently take it so hard. It might be that just as in the war a man when hit often did not know it till some time afterwards, Saffary had not realized how great a blow to him Harold Clarke's death was till he had had time to think it over. It seemed to him, however, more probable that Saffary, left to himself, would have carried on as usual, seeking sympathy for his loss in the company of his fellows, but that his wife's conventional sense of propriety had insisted that it would be bad form to go to a party when the grief they were suffering from made it only decent for them to eschew for a little festive gatherings. Violet Saffary was a nice little woman, three or four years younger than her husband; not very pretty, but pleasant to look at and always becomingly dressed; amiable, ladylike, and unassuming. In the days when he had been on friendly terms with the Saffarys the Resident had from time time dined with them. He had found her agreeable, but not very amusing. They had never talked but of commonplace things. Of late he had seen little of her. When they chanced to meet she always gave him a friendly smile, and on occasion he said one or two civil words to her. But it was only by an effort of memory that he distinguished her from half a dozen of the other ladies in the community whom his official position brought him in contact with.

Saffary had presumably said what he had come to say and the Resident wondered why he did not get up and go. He sat heaped up in his chair oddly, so that it gave you the feeling that his skeleton had ceased to support him and his considerable mass of flesh was falling in on him. He looked dully at the desk that separated him from the Resident. He sighed deeply.

'You must try not to take it too hard, Saffary,' said George Moon. 'You know how uncertain life is in the East. One has to resign oneself to losing people one's fond of.'

Saffary's eyes slowly moved from the desk, and he fixed them on George Moon's. They stared unwinking. George Moon liked people to look him in the eyes. Perhaps he felt that when he thus held their vision he held them in his power. Presently two tears formed themselves in Saffary's blue eyes and slowly ran down his cheeks. He had a strangely puzzled look. Something had frightened him. Was it death? No. Something that he thought worse. He looked cowed. His mien was cringing so that he made you think of a dog unjustly beaten.

'It's not that,' he faltered. 'I could have borne that.'

George Moon did not answer. He held that big, powerful man with his cold level gaze and waited. He was pleasantly conscious of his absolute indifference. Saffary gave a harassed glance at the papers on the desk.

'I'm afraid I'm taking up too much of your time.'

'No, I have nothing to do at the moment.'

Saffary looked out of the window. A little shudder passed between his shoulders. He seemed to hesitate.

'I wonder if I might ask your advice,' he said at last.

'Of course,' said the Resident, with the shadow of a smile, 'that's one of the things I'm here for.'

'It's a purely private matter.'

'You may be quite sure that I shan't betray any confidence you place in me.'

'No, I know you wouldn't do that, but it's rather an awkward thing to speak about, and I shouldn't feel very comfortable meeting you afterwards. But you're going away tomorrow, and that makes it easier, if you understand what I mean.'

'Quite.'

Saffary began to speak, in a low voice, sulkily, as though he were ashamed, and he spoke with the awkwardness of a man unused to words. He went back and said the same thing over again. He got mixed up. He started a long, elaborate sentence and then broke off abruptly because he did not know how to finish it. George Moon listened in silence, his face a mask, smoking, and he only took his eyes off Saffary's face to reach for another cigarette from the box in front of him and light it from the stub of that which he was just finishing. And while he listened he saw, as it were a background, the monotonous round of the planter's life. It was like an accompaniment of muted strings that threw into sharper relief the calculated dissonances of an unexpected melody.

With rubber at so low a price every economy had to be exercised and Tom Saffary, notwithstanding the size of the estate, had to do work which in better times he had had an assistant for. He rose before dawn and went down to the lines where the coolies were assembled. When there was just enough light to see he read out the names, ticking them off according to the answers, and assigned the various squads to their work. Some tapped, some weeded, and others tended the ditches. Saffary went back to his solid breakfast, lit his pipe, and sallied forth again to inspect the coolies quarters. Children were playing and babies sprawling here and there. On the sidewalks Tamil women cooked their rice. Their black skins shone with oil. They were draped about in dull red cotton and wore gold ornaments in their hair. There were handsome creatures among them, upright of carriage, with delicate features and small, exquisite hands; but Saffary looked upon them only with distaste. He set out on his rounds. On his well-grown estate the trees planted in rows gave one a charming feeling of the prim forest of a German fairy-tale. The ground was thick with dead leaves. He was accompanied by a Tamil overseer, his long black hair done in a chignon, barefooted, in sarong and baju, with a showy ring on his finger. Saffary walked hard, jumping the ditches when he came to them, and soon he dripped with sweat. He examined the trees to see that they were properly tapped, and when he came across a coolie at work looked at the shavings and if they were too thick swore at him and docked him half a day's pay. When a tree was not to be tapped any more he told the overseer to take away the cup and the wire that held it to the trunk. The weeders worked in gangs.

At noon Saffary returned to the bungalow and had a drink of beer which, because there was no ice, was luke-warm. He stripped off the khaki shorts, the flannel shirt, the heavy boots and stockings in which he had been walking, and shaved and bathed. He lunched in a sarong and baju. He lay off for half an hour, and then went down to his office and worked till five; he had tea and went to the club. About eight he started back for the bungalow, dined, and half an hour after went to bed.

But last night he went home immediately he had finished his match. Violet had not accompanied him that day. When the Clarkes were there they had met at the club every afternoon, but now they had gone home she came less often. She said there was no one there who much amused her and she had heard everything everyone had to say till she was fed to the teeth. She did not play bridge and it was dull for her to wait about while he played. She told Tom he need not mind leaving her alone. She had plenty of things to do in the house.

As soon as she saw him back so early she guessed that he had come to tell her that he had won his match. He was like a child in his self-satisfaction over one of these small triumphs. He was a kindly, simple creature and she knew that his pleasure at winning was not only on his own account, but because he thought it must give her pleasure too. It was rather sweet of him to hurry home in order to tell her all about it without delay.

'Well, how did your match go?' she said as soon as he came lumbering into the sitting-room.

'I won.'

'Easily?'

'Well, not as easily as I should have. I was a bit ahead, and then I stuck, I couldn't do a thing, and you know what Douglas is, not at all showy, but steady, and he pulled up with me. Then I said to myself, well, if I don't buck up I shall get a licking, I had a bit of luck here and there, and then, to cut a long story short, I beat him by seven.'

'Isn't that splendid? You ought to win the cup now, oughtn't you?'

'Well, I've got three matches more. If I can get into the semi-finals I ought to have a chance.'

Violet smiled. She was anxious to show him that she was as much interested as he expected her to be.

'What made you go to pieces when you did?'

His faced sagged.

'That's why I came back at once. I'd have scratched only I thought it wasn't fair on the fellows who'd backed me. I don't know how to tell you, Violet.'

She gave him a questioning look.

'Why, what's the matter? Not bad news?'

'Rotten. Knobby's dead.'

For a full minute she stared at him, and her face, her neat friendly little face, grew haggard with horror. At first it seemed as though she could not understand.

'What *do* you mean?' she cried.

'It was in the paper. He died on board. They buried him at sea.'

Suddenly she gave a piercing cry and fell headlong to the floor. She had fainted dead away.

'Violet,' he cried, and threw himself down on his knees and took her head in his arms. 'Boy, boy.'

A boy, startled by the terror in his master's voice, rushed in, and Saffary shouted to him to bring brandy. He forced a little between Violet's lips. She opened her eyes, and as she remembered they grew dark with anguish. Her face was screwed up like a little child's when it is just going to burst into tears. He lifted her up in his arms and laid her on the sofa. She turned her head away.

'Oh, Tom, it isn't true. It can't be true.'

'I'm afraid it is.'

'No, no, no.'

She burst into tears. She wept convulsively. It was dreadful to hear her. Saffary did not know what to do. He knelt beside her and tried to soothe her. He sought to take her in his arms, but with a sudden gesture she repelled him.

'Don't touch me,' she cried, and she said it so sharply that he was startled.

He rose to his feet.

'Try not to take it too hard, sweetie,' he said. 'I know it's been an awful shock. He was one of the best.'

She buried her face in the cushions and wept despairingly. It tortured him to see her body shaken by those uncontrollable sobs. She was beside herself. He put his hand gently on her shoulder.

'Darling, don't give way like that. It's so bad for you.'

She shook herself free from his hand.

'For God's sake leave me alone,' she cried. 'Oh, Hal, Hal.' He had never heard her call the dead man that before. Of course his name was Harold, but everyone called him Knobby. 'What shall I do?' she wailed. 'I can't bear it. I can't bear it.'

Saffary began to grow a trifle impatient. So much grief did seem to him exaggerated. Violet was not normally so emotional. He supposed it was the damned climate. It made women nervous and high-strung. Violet hadn't been home for four years. She was not hiding her face now. She lay, almost falling off the sofa, her mouth open in the extremity of her pain, and the tears streamed from her staring eyes. She was distraught.

'Have a little more brandy,' he said. 'Try to pull yourself together, darling. You can't do Knobby any good by getting in such a state.'

With a sudden gesture she sprang to her feet and pushed him aside. She gave him a look of hatred.

'Go away, Tom. I don't want your sympathy. I want to be left alone.'

She walked swiftly over to an arm-chair and threw herself down in it. She flung back her head and her poor white face was wrenched into a grimace of agony.

'Oh, it's not fair,' she moaned. 'What's to become of me now? Oh, God, I wish I were dead.'

'Violet.'

His voice quavered with pain. He was very nearly crying too. She stamped her foot impatiently.

'Go away, I tell you. Go away.'

He started. He stared at her and suddenly gasped. A shudder passed through his great bulk. He took a step towards her and stopped, but his eyes never left her white, tortured face; he stared as though he saw in it something that appalled him. Then he dropped his head and without a word walked out of the room. He went into a little sitting-room they had at the back, but seldom used, and sank heavily into a chair. He thought. Presently the gong sounded for dinner. He had not had his bath. He gave his hands a glance. He could not be bothered to wash them. He walked slowly into the dining-room. He told the boy to go and tell Violet that dinner was ready. The boy came back and said she did not want any.

'All right. Let me have mine then,' said Saffary.

He sent Violet in a plate of soup and a piece of toast, and when the fish was served he put some on a plate for her and gave it to the boy. But the boy came back with it at once.

'Mem, she say no wantchee,' he said.

Saffary ate his dinner alone. He ate from habit, solidly, through the familiar courses. He drank a bottle of beer. When he had finished the boy brought him a cup of coffee and he lit a cheroot. Saffary sat still till he had finished it. He thought. At last he got up and went back into the large veranda which was where they always sat. Violet was still huddled in the chair in which he had left her. Her eyes were closed, but she opened them when she heard him come. He took a light chair and sat down in front of her.

'What *was* Knobby to you, Violet?' he said.

She gave a slight start. She turned away her eyes, but did not speak.

'I can't quite make out why you should have been so frightful*/* upset by the news of his death.'

'It was an awful shock.'

'Of course. But it seems very strange that anyone should go simply to pieces over the death of a friend.'

'I don't understand what you mean,' she said.

She could hardly speak the words and he saw that her lips were trembling.

'I've never heard you call him Hal. Even his wife called him Knobby.'

She did not say anything. Her eyes, heavy with grief, were fixed on vacancy.

'Look at me, Violet.'

She turned her head slightly and listlessly gazed at him.

'Was he your lover?'

She closed her eyes and tears flowed from them. Her mouth was strangely twisted.

'Haven't you got anything to say at all?'

She shook her head.

'You must answer me, Violet.'

'I'm not fit to talk to you now,' she moaned. 'How can you be so heartless?'

'I'm afraid I don't feel very sympathetic at the moment. We must get this straight now. Would you like a drink of water?'

'I don't want anything.'

'Then answer my question.'

'You have no right to ask it. It's insulting.'

'Do you ask me to believe that a woman like you who hears of the death of someone she knew is going to faint dead away and then, when she comes to, is going to cry like that? Why, one wouldn't be so upset over the death of one's only child. When we heard of your mother's death you cried of course, anyone would, and I know you were utterly miserable, but you came to me for comfort and you said you didn't know what you'd have done without me.'

'This was so frightfully sudden.'

'Your mother's death was sudden, too.'

'Naturally I was very fond of Knobby.'

'How fond? So fond that when you heard he was dead you didn't know and you didn't care what you said? Why did you say it wasn't fair? Why did you say, "What's going to become of me now?" ?'

She sighed deeply. She turned her head this way and that like a sheep trying to avoid the hands of the butcher.

'You mustn't take me for an utter fool, Violet. I tell you it's impossible that you should be so shattered by the blow if there hadn't been something between you.'

'Well, if you think that, why do you torture me with questions?'

'My dear, it's no good shilly-shallying. We can't go on like this. What d'you think I'm feeling?'

She looked at him when he said this. She hadn't thought of him at all. She had been too much absorbed in her own misery to be concerned with his.

'I'm so tired,' she sighed.

He leaned forward and roughly seized her wrist.

'Speak,' he cried.

'You're hurting me.'

'And what about me? D'you think you're not hurting me? How can you have the heart to let me suffer like this?'

He let go of her arm and sprang to his feet. He walked to the end of the room and back again. It looked as though the movement had suddenly roused him to fury. He caught her by the shoulders and dragged her to her feet. He shook her.

'If you don't tell me the truth I'll kill you,' he cried.

'I wish you would,' she said.

'He was your lover?'

'Yes.'

'You swine.'

With one hand still on her shoulder so that she could not move he swung back his other arm and with a flat palm struck her repeatedly, with all his strength, on the side of her face. She quivered under the blows, but did not flinch or cry out. He struck her again and again. All at once he felt her strangely inert, he let go of her and she sank unconscious to the floor. Fear seized him. He bent down and touched her, calling her name. She did not move. He lifted her up and put her back into the chair from which a little while before he had pulled her. The brandy that had been brought when first she fainted was still in the room and he fetched it and tried to force it down her throat. She choked and it spilt over her chin and neck. One side of her pale face was livid from the blows of his heavy hand. She sighed a little and opened her eyes. He held the glass again to her lips, supporting her head, and she sipped a little of the neat spirit. He looked at her with penitent, anxious eyes.

'I'm sorry, Violet. I didn't mean to do that. I'm dreadfully ashamed of myself. I never thought I could sink so low as to hit a woman.'

Though she was feeling very weak and her face was hurting, the flicker of a smile crossed her lips. Poor Tom. He did say things like that. He felt like that. And how scandalized he would be if you asked him why a man shouldn't hit a woman. But Saffary, seeing the wan smile, put it down to her indomitable courage. By God, she's a plucky little woman, he thought. Game isn't the word.

'Give me a cigarette,' she said.

He took one out of his case and put it in her mouth. He made two or three ineffectual attempts to strike his lighter. It would not work.

'Hadn't you better get a match?' she said.

For the moment she had forgotten her heart-rending grief and was faintly amused at the situation. He took a box from the table and held the lighted match to her cigarette. She inhaled the first puff with a sense of infinite relief.

'I can't tell you how ashamed I am, Violet,' he said. 'I'm disgusted with myself. I don't know what came over me.'

'Oh, that's all right. It was very natural. Why don't you have a drink? It'll do you good.'

Without a word, his shoulders all hunched up as though the burden that oppressed him were material, he helped himself to a brandy and soda. Then, still silent, he sat down. She watched the blue smoke curl into the air.

'What are you going to do?' she said at last.

He gave a weary gesture of despair.

'We'll talk about that tomorrow. You're not in a fit state tonight. As soon as you've finished your cigarette you'd better go to bed.'

'You know so much, you'd better know everything.'

'Not now, Violet.'

'Yes, now.'

She began to speak. He heard her words, but could hardly make sense of them. He felt like a man who has built himself a house with loving care and thought to live in it all his life, and then, he does not understand why, sees the housebreakers come and with their picks and heavy hammers destroy it room by room, till what was a fair dwelling-place is only a heap of rubble. What made it so awful was that it was Knobby Clarke who had done this thing. They had come out to the F.M.S. on the same ship and had worked at first on the same estate. They call the young planter a creeper and you can tell him in the streets of Singapore by his double felt hat and his khaki coat turned up at the wrists. Callow youths who saunter about staring and are inveigled by wily Chinese into buying worthless truck from Birmingham which they send home as Eastern curios, sit in the lounges of cheap hotels drinking innumerable stengahs, and after an evening at the pictures get into rickshaws and finish the night in the Chinese quarter. Tom and Knobby were inseparable. Tom, a big, powerful fellow, simple, very honest, hard-working; and Knobby, ungainly, but curiously attractive, with his deep-set eyes, hollow cheeks, and large humorous mouth. It was Knobby who made the jokes and Tom who laughed at them. Tom married first. He met Violet when he went on leave. The daughter of a doctor killed in the war, she was governess in the house of some people who lived in the same place as his father. He fell in love with her because she was alone in the world, and his tender heart was touched by the thought of the drab life that lay before her. But Knobby married, because Tom had and he felt lost without him, a girl who had come East to spend the winter with relations. Enid Clarke had been very pretty then in her blonde way, and full-face she was pretty still, though her skin, once so clear and fresh, was already faded; but she had a very weak, small, insignificant chin and in profile reminded you of a sheep. She had pretty flaxen hair, straight, because in the heat it would not keep its wave, and china-blue eyes. Though but twenty-six, she had already a tired look. A year after marriage she had a baby, but it died when only two years old. It was after this that Tom Saffary managed to get Knobby the post of manager of the estate next his own. The two men pleasantly resumed their old familiarity, and their wives, who till then had not known one another very well, soon made friends. They copied one another's frocks and lent one another servants and crockery when they gave a party. The four of them met every day. They went everywhere together. Tom Saffary thought it grand.

The strange thing was that Violet and Knobby Clarke lived on these terms of close intimacy for three years before they fell in love with one another. Neither saw love approaching. Neither suspected that in the pleasure each took in the other's company there was anything more than the casual friendship of two persons thrown together by the circumstances of life. To be together gave them no particular happiness, but merely a quiet sense of comfort. If by chance a day passed without their meeting they felt unaccountably bored. That seemed very natural. They played games together. They danced together. They chaffed one another. The revelation came to them by what looked like pure accident. They had all been to a dance at the club and were driving home in Saffary's car. The Clarke's estate was on the way and he was dropping them at their bungalow. Violet and Knobby sat in the back. He had had a good deal to drink, but was not drunk; their hands touched by chance, and he took hers and held it. They did not speak. They were all tired. But suddenly the exhilaration of the champagne left him and he was cold sober. They knew in a flash that they were madly in love with one another and at the same moment they realized they had never been in love before. When they reached the Clarkes's Tom said:

'You'd better hop in beside me, Violet.'

'I'm too exhausted to move,' she said.

Her legs seemed so weak that she thought she would never be able to stand.

When they met next day neither referred to what had happened, but each knew that something inevitable had passed. They behaved to one another as they had always done, they continued to behave so for weeks, but they felt that everything was different. At last flesh and blood could stand it no longer and they became lovers. But the physical tie seemed to them the least important element in their relation, and indeed their way of living made it impossible for them, except very seldom, to enjoy any intimate connexion. It was enough that they saw one another, though in the company of others, every day; a glance, a touch of the hand, assured them of their love, and that was all that mattered. The sexual act was no more than an affirmation of the union of their souls.

They very seldom talked of Tom or Enid. If sometimes they laughed together at their foibles it was not unkindly. It might have seemed odd to them to realize how completely these two people whom they saw so constantly had ceased to matter to them if they had given them enough thought to consider the matter. Their relations with them fell into the routine of life that nobody notices, like shaving oneself, dressing, and eating three meals a day. They felt tenderly towards them. They even took pains to please them, as you would with a bed-ridden invalid, because their own happiness was so great that in charity they must do what they could for others less fortunate. They had no scruples. They were too much absorbed in one another to be touched even for a moment by remorse. Beauty now excitingly kindled the pleasant humdrum life they had led so long.

But then an event took place that filled them with consternation. The company for which Tom worked entered into negotiations to buy extensive rubber plantations in British North Borneo and invited Tom to manage them. It was a better job than his present one, with a higher salary, and since he would have assistants under him he would not have to work so hard. Saffary welcomed the offer. Both Clarke and Saffary were due for leave and the two couples had arranged to travel home together. They had already booked their passages. This changed everything. Tom would not be able to get away for at least a year. By the time the Clarkes came back the Saffarys would be settled in Borneo. It did not take Violet and Knobby long to decide that there was only one thing to do. They had been willing enough to go on as they were, notwithstanding the hindrances to the enjoyment of their love, when they were certain of seeing one another continually; they felt that they had endless time before them and the future was coloured with a happiness that seemed to have no limit; but neither could suffer for an instant the thought of separation. They made up their minds to run away together, and then it seemed to them on a sudden that every day that passed before they could be together always and all the time was a day lost. Their love took another guise. It flamed into a devouring passion that left them no emotion to waste on others. They cared little for the pain they must cause Tom and Enid. It was unfortunate, but inevitable. They made their plans deliberately. Knobby on the pretence of business would go to Singapore and Violet, telling Tom that she was going to spend a week with friends on an estate down the line, would join him there. They would go over to Java and thence take ship to Sydney. In Sydney Knobby would look for a job. When Violet told Tom that the Mackenzies had asked her to spend a few days with them, he was pleased.

'That's grand. I think you want a change, darling,' he said. 'I've fancied you've been looking a bit peaked lately.'

He stroked her cheek affectionately. The gesture stabbed her heart.

'You've always been awfully good to me, Tom,' she said, her eyes suddenly filled with tears.

'Well, that's the least I could be. You're the best little woman in the world.'

'Have you been happy with me these eight years?'

'Frightfully.'

'Well, that's something, isn't it? No one can ever take that away from you.'

She told herself that he was the kind of man who would soon console himself. He liked women for themselves and it would not be long after he had regained his freedom before he found someone that he would wish to marry. And he would be just as happy with his new wife as he had been with her. Perhaps he would marry Enid. Enid was one of those dependent little things that somewhat exasperated her and she did not think her capable of deep feeling. Her vanity would be hurt; her heart would not be broken. But now that the die was cast, everything settled and the day fixed, she had a qualm. Remorse beset her. She wished that it had been possible not to cause those two people such fearful distress. She faltered.

'We've had a very good time here, Tom,' she said. 'I wonder if it's wise to leave it all. We're giving up a certainty for we don't know what.'

'My dear child, it's a chance in a million and much better money.'

'Money isn't everything. There's happiness.'

'I know that, but there's no reason why we shouldn't be just as happy in B.N.B. And besides, there was no alternative. I'm not my own master. The directors want me to go and I must, and that's all there is to it.'

She sighed. There was no alternative for her either. She shrugged her shoulders. It was hateful to cause others pain; sometimes you couldn't help yourself. Tom meant no more to her than the casual man on the voyage out who was civil to you: it was absurd that she should be asked to sacrifice her life for him.

The Clarkes were due to sail for England in a fortnight and this determined the date of their elopement. The days passed. Violet was restless and excited. She looked forward with a joy that was almost painful to the peace that she anticipated when they were once on board the ship and could begin the life which she was sure would give her at last perfect happiness.

She began to pack. The friends she was supposed to be going to stay with entertained a good deal and this gave her an excuse to take quite a lot of luggage. She was starting next day. It was eleven o'clock in the morning and Tom was making his round of the estate. One of the boys came to her room and told her that Mrs Clarke was there and at the same moment she heard Enid calling her. Quickly closing the lid of her trunk, she went out on to the veranda. To her astonishment Enid came up to her, flung her arms round her neck and kissed her eagerly. She looked at Enid and saw that her cheeks, usually pale, were flushed and that her eyes were shining. Enid burst into tears.

'What on earth's the matter, darling?' she cried.

For one moment she was afraid that Enid knew everything. But Enid was flushed with delight and not with jealousy or anger.

'I've just seen Dr Harrow,' she said. 'I didn't want to say anything about it. I've had two or three false alarms, but this time he says it's all right.'

A sudden coldness pierced Violet's heart.

'What do you mean? You're not going to . . .'

She looked at Enid and Enid nodded.

'Yes, he says there's no doubt about it at all. He thinks I'm at least three months gone. Oh, my dear, I'm so wildly happy.'

She flung herself again into Violet's arms and clung to her, weeping.

'Oh, darling, don't.'

Violet felt herself grow pale as death and knew that if she didn't keep a tight hold of herself she would faint.

'Does Knobby know?'

'No, I didn't say a word. He was so disappointed before. He was so frightfully cut up when baby died. He's wanted me to have another so badly.'

Violet forced herself to say the things that were expected of her, but Enid was not listening. She wanted to tell the whole story of her hopes and fears, of her symptoms, and then of her interview with the doctor. She went on and on.

'When are you going to tell Knobby?' Violet asked at last. 'Now, when he gets in?'

'Oh, no, he's tired and hungry when he gets back from his round. I shall wait till tonight after dinner.'

Violet repressed a movement of exasperation; Enid was going to make a scene of it and was choosing her moment; but after all, it was only natural. It was lucky, for it would give her the chance to see Knobby first. As soon as she was rid of her she rang him up. She knew that he always looked in at his office on his way home, and she left a message asking him to call her. She was only afraid that he would not do so till Tom was back, but she had to take a chance of that. The bell rang and Tom had not come in.

'Hal?'

'Yes.'

'Will you be at the hut at three?'

'Yes. Has anything happened?'

'I'll tell you when I see you. Don't worry.'

76

She rang off. The hut was a little shelter on Knobby's estate which she could get to without difficulty and where they occasionally met. The coolies passed it while they worked and it had no privacy; but it was a convenient place for them without exciting comment to exchange a few minutes' conversation. At three Enid would be resting and Tom at work in his office.

When Violet walked up Knobby was already there. He gave a gasp.

'Violet, how white you are.'

She gave him her hand. They did not know what eyes might be watching them and their behaviour here was always such as anyone could observe.

'Enid came to see me this morning. She's going to tell you tonight. I thought you ought to be warned. She's going to have a baby.'

'Violet!'

He looked at her aghast. She began to cry. They had never talked of the relations they had, he with his wife and she with her husband. They ignored the subject because it was to each horribly painful. Violet knew what her own life was; she satisfied her husband's appetite, but, with a woman's strange nonchalance, because to do so gave her no pleasure, attached no importance to it; but somehow she had persuaded herself that with Hal it was different. He felt now instinctively how bitterly what she had learned wounded her. He tried to excuse himself.

'Darling, I couldn't help myself.'

She cried silently and he watched her with miserable eyes.

'I know it seems beastly,' he said, 'but what could I do? It wasn't as if I had any reason to . . .'

She interrupted him.

'I don't blame you. It was inevitable. It's only because I'm stupid that it gives me such a frightful pain in my heart.'

'Darling!'

'We ought to have gone away together two years ago. It was madness to think we could go on like this.'

'Are you sure Enid's right? She thought she was in the family way three or four years ago.'

'Oh, yes, she's right. She's frightfully happy. She says you wanted a child so badly.'

'It's come as such an awful surprise. I don't seem able to realize it yet.'

She looked at him. He was staring at the leaf-strewn earth with harassed eyes. She smiled a little.

'Poor Hal.' She sighed deeply. 'There's nothing to be done about it. It's the end of us.'

'What do you mean?' he cried.

'Oh, my dear, you can't very well leave her now, can you? It was all right before. She would have been unhappy, but she would have got over it. But now it's different. It's not a very nice time for a woman anyhow. For months she feels more or less ill. She wants affection. She wants to be taken care of. It would be frightful to leave her to bear it all alone. We couldn't be such beasts.'

'Do you mean to say you want me to go back to England with her?'

She nodded gravely.

'It's lucky you're going. It'll be easier when you get away and we don't see one another every day.'

'But I can't live without you now.'

'Oh, yes, you can. You must. I can. And it'll be worse for me, because I stay behind and I shall have nothing.'

'Oh, Violet, it's impossible.'

'My dear, it's no good arguing. The moment she told me I saw it meant that. That's why I wanted to see you first. I thought the shock might lead you to blurt out the whole truth. You know I love you more than anything in the world. She's never done me any harm. I couldn't take you away from her now. It's bad luck on both of us, but there it is, I simply wouldn't dare to do a filthy thing like that.'

'I wish I were dead,' he moaned.

'That wouldn't do her any good, or me either,' she smiled.

'What about the future? Have we got to sacrifice our whole lives?'

'I'm afraid so. It sounds rather grim, darling, but I suppose sooner or later we shall get over it. One gets over everything.'

She looked at her wrist-watch.

'I ought to be getting back. Tom will be in soon. We're all meeting at the club at five.'

'Tom and I are supposed to be playing tennis.' He gave her a pitiful look. 'Oh, Violet, I'm so frightfully unhappy.'

'I know. So am I. But we shan't do any good by talking about it.'

She gave him her hand, but he took her in his arms and kissed her, and when she released herself her cheeks were wet with his tears. But she was so desperate she could not cry.

Ten days later the Clarkes sailed.

While George Moon was listening to as much of this story as Tom Saffary was able to tell him, he reflected in his cool, detached way how odd it was that these commonplace people, leading lives so monotonous, should have been convulsed by such a tragedy. Who would have thought that Violet Saffary, so neat and demure, sitting in the club reading the illustrated papers or chatting with her friends over a lemon squash, should have been eating her heart out for love of that ordinary man? George Moon remembered seeing Knobby at the club the evening before he sailed. He seemed in great spirits. Fellows envied him because he was going home. Those who had recently come back told him by no means to miss the show at the Pavilion. Drink flowed freely. The Resident had not been asked to the farewell party the Saffarys gave for the Clarkes, but he knew very well what it had been like, the good cheer, the cordiality, the chaff, and then after dinner the gramophone turned on and everyone dancing. He wondered what Violet and Clarke had felt as they danced together. It gave him an odd sensation of dismay to think of the despair that must have filled their hearts while they pretended to be so gay.

And with another part of his mind George Moon thought of his own past. Very few knew that story. After all, it had happened twenty-five years ago.

'What are you going to do now, Saffary?' he asked.

'Well, that's what I wanted you to advise me about. Now that Knobby's dead I don't know what's going to happen to Violet if I divorce her. I was wondering if I oughtn't to let her divorce me.'

'Oh, you want to divorce?'

'Well, I must.'

George Moon lit another cigarette and watched for a moment the smoke that curled away into the air.

'Did you ever know that I'd been married?'

'Yes, I think I'd heard. You're a widower, aren't you?'

'No, I divorced my wife. I have a son of twenty-seven. He's farming in New Zealand. I saw my wife the last time I was home on leave. We met at a play. At first we didn't recognize one another. She spoke to me. I asked her to lunch at the Berkeley.'

George Moon chuckled to himself. He was alone. It was a musical comedy. He found himself sitting next to a large fat dark woman whom he vaguely thought he had seen before, but the play was just starting and he did not give her a second look. When the curtain fell after the first act she looked at him with bright eyes and spoke.

'How are you, George?'

It was his wife. She had a bold, friendly manner and was very much at her ease.

'It's a long time since we met,' she said.

'It is.'

'How has life been treating you?'

'Oh, all right.'

'I suppose you're a Resident now. You're still in the Service, aren't you?'

'Yes. I'm retiring soon, worse luck.'

'Why? You look very fit.'

'I'm reaching the age limit. I'm supposed to be an old buffer and no good any more.'

'You're lucky to have kept so thin. I'm terrible, aren't I?'

'You don't look as though you were wasting away.'

'I know. I'm stout and I'm growing stouter all the time. I can't help it and I love food. I can't resist cream and bread and potatoes.'

George Moon laughed, but not at what she said; at his own thoughts. In years gone by it had sometimes occurred to him that he might meet her, but he had never thought that the meeting would take this turn. When the play was ended and with a smile she bade him good night, he said:

'I suppose you wouldn't lunch with me one day?'

'Any day you like.'

They arranged a date and duly met. He knew that she had married the man on whose account he had divorced her, and he judged by her clothes that she was in comfortable circumstances. They drank a cocktail. She ate the *hors-d'œuvre* with gusto. She was fifty if she was a day, but she carried her years with spirit. There was something jolly and careless about her, she was quick on the uptake, chatty, and she had the hearty, infectious laugh of the fat woman who has let herself go. If he had not known that her family had for a century been in the Indian Civil Service he would have thought that she had been a chorus girl. She was not flashy, but she had a sort of flamboyance of nature that suggested the stage. She was not in the least embarrassed.

'You never married again, did you?' she asked him.

'No.'

'Pity. Because it wasn't a success the first time there's no reason why it shouldn't have been the second.'

'There's no need for me to ask if you've been happy.'

'I've got nothing to complain of. I think I've got a happy nature. Jim's always been very good to me; he's retired now, you know, and we live in the country, and I adore Betty.'

'Who's Betty?'

'Oh, she's my daughter. She got married two years ago. I'm expecting to be a grandmother almost any day.'

'That ages us a bit.'

She gave a laugh.

'Betty's twenty-two. It was nice of you to ask me to lunch, George. After all, it would be silly to have any feelings about something that happened so long ago as all that.'

'Idiotic.'

'We weren't fitted to one another and it's lucky we found it out before it was too late. Of course I was foolish, but then I was very young. Have you been happy too?'

'I think I can say I've been a success.'

'Oh, well, that's probably all the happiness you were capable of.'

He smiled in appreciation of her shrewdness. And then, putting the whole matter aside easily, she began to talk of other things. Though the courts had given him custody of their son, he, unable to look after him, had allowed his mother to have him. The boy had emigrated at eighteen and was now married. He was a stranger to George Moon, and he was aware that if he met him in the street he would not recognize him. He was too sincere to pretend that he took much interest in him. They talked of him, however, for a while, and then they talked of actors and plays.

'Well,' she said at last, 'I must be running away. I've had a lovely lunch. It's been fun meeting you, George. Thanks so much.'

He put her into a taxi and taking off his hat walked down Piccadilly by himself. He thought her quite a pleasant, amusing woman: he laughed to think that he had ever been madly in love with her. There was a smile on his lips when he spoke again to Tom Saffary.

'She was a damned good-looking girl when I married her. That was the trouble. Though, of course, if she hadn't been I'd never have married her. They were all after her like flies round a honeypot. We used to have awful rows. And at last I caught her out. Of course I divorced her.'

'Of course.'

'Yes, but I know I was a damned fool to do it.' He leaned forward. 'My dear Saffary, I know now that if I'd had any sense I'd have shut my eyes. She'd have settled down and made me an excellent wife.'

He wished he were able to explain to his visitor how grotesque it had seemed to him when he sat and talked with that jolly, comfortable, and good-humoured woman that he should have made so much fuss about what now seemed to him to matter so little.

'But one has one's honour to think of,' said Saffary.

'Honour be damned. One has one's happiness to think of. Is one's honour really concerned because one's wife hops into bed with another man? We're not crusaders, you and I, or Spanish grandees. I *liked* my wife. I don't say I haven't had other women. I have. But she had just that something that none of the others could give me. What a fool I was to throw away what I wanted more than anything in the world because I couldn't enjoy exclusive possession of it!'

'You're the last man I should ever have expected to hear speak like that.'

George Moon smiled thinly at the embarrassment that was so clearly expressed on Saffary's fat troubled face.

'I'm probably the first man you've heard speak the naked truth,' he retorted.

'Do you mean to say that if it were all to do over again you would act differently?'

'If I were twenty-seven again I suppose I should be as big a fool as I was then. But if I had the sense I have now I'll tell you what I'd do if I found my wife had been unfaithful to me. I'd do just what you did last night: I'd give her a damned good hiding and let it go at that.'

'Are you asking me to forgive Violet?'

The Resident shook his head slowly and smiled.

'No. You've forgiven her already. I'm merely advising you not to cut off your nose to spite your face.'

Saffary gave him a worried look. It disconcerted him to know that this cold precise man should see in his heart emotions which seemed so unnatural to himself that he thrust them out of his consciousness.

'You don't know the circumstances,' he said. 'Knobby and I were almost like brothers. I got him this job. He owed everything to me. And except for me Violet might have gone on being a governess for the rest of her life. It seemed such a waste; I couldn't help feeling sorry for her. If you know what I mean, it was pity that first made me take any notice of her. Don't you think it's a bit thick that when you've been thoroughly decent with people they should go out of their way to do the dirty on you? It's such awful ingratitude.'

'Oh, my dear boy, one mustn't expect gratitude. It's a thing that no one has a right to. After all, you do good because it gives you pleasure. It's the purest form of happiness there is. To expect thanks for it is really asking too much. If you get it, well, it's like a bonus on shares on which you've already received a dividend; it's grand, but you mustn't look upon it as your due.'

Saffary frowned. He was perplexed. He could not quite make it out that George Moon should think so oddly about things that it had always seemed to him there were no two ways of thinking about. After all there were limits. I mean, if you had any sense of decency you had to behave like a tuan. There was your own self-respect to think of. It was funny that George Moon should give reasons that looked so damned plausible for doing something that, well, damn it, you had to admit you'd be only too glad to do if you could see your way to it. Of course George Moon was queer. No one ever quite understood him.

'Knobby Clarke is dead, Saffary. You can't be jealous of him any more. No one knows a thing except you and me and your wife, and tomorrow I'm going away for ever. Why don't you let bygones be bygones?'

'Violet would only despise me.'

George Moon smiled and, unexpectedly on that prim, fastidious face, his smile had a singular sweetness.

'I know her very little. I always thought her a very nice woman. Is she as detestable as that?'

Saffary gave a start and reddened to his ears.

'No, she's an angel of goodness. It's me who's detestable for saying that of her.' His voice broke and he gave a little sob. 'God knows I only want to do the right thing.'

'The right thing is the kind thing.'

Saffary covered his face with his hands. He could not curb the emotion that shook him.

'I seem to be giving, giving all the time, and no one does a God-damned thing for me. It doesn't matter if my heart is broken, I must just go on.' He drew the back of his hand across his eyes and sighed deeply. 'I'll forgive her.'

George Moon looked at him reflectively for a little.

'I wouldn't make too much of a song and dance about it, if I were you,' he said. 'You'll have to walk warily. She'll have a lot to forgive too.'

'Because I hit her, you mean? I know, that was awful of me.'

'Not a bit. It did her a power of good. I didn't mean that. You're behaving generously, old boy, and, you know, one needs a devil of a lot of tact to get people to forgive one one's generosity. Fortunately women are frivolous and they very quickly forget the benefits conferred upon them. Otherwise, of course, there'd be no living with them.'

Saffary looked at him open-mouthed.

'Upon my word you're a rum 'un, Moon,' he said. 'Sometimes you seem as hard as nails and then you talk so that one thinks you're almost human, and then, just as one thinks one's misjudged you and you have a heart after all, you come out with something that just shocks one. I suppose that's what they call a cynic.'

'I haven't deeply considered the matter,' smiled George Moon, 'but if to look truth in the face and not resent it when it's unpalatable, and take human nature as you find it, smiling when it's absurd and grieved without exaggeration when it's pitiful, is to be cynical, then I suppose I'm a cynic. Mostly human nature is both absurd and pitiful, but if life has taught you tolerance you find in it more to smile at than to weep.'

When Tom Saffary left the room the Resident lit himself with deliberation the last cigarette he meant to smoke before tiffin. It was a new role for him to reconcile an angry husband with an erring wife and it caused him a discreet amusement. He continued to reflect upon human nature. A wintry smile hovered upon his thin and pallid lips. He recalled with what interest in the dry creeks of certain places along the coast he had often stood and watched the Jumping Johnnies. There were hundreds of them sometimes, from little things of a couple of inches long to great fat fellows as long as your foot. They were the colour of the mud they lived in. They sat and looked at you with large round eyes and then with a sudden dash buried themselves in their holes. It was extraordinary to see them scudding on their flappers over the surface of the mud. It teemed with them. They gave you a fearful feeling that the mud itself was mysteriously become alive and an atavistic terror froze your heart when you remembered that such creatures, but gigantic and terrible, were once the only inhabitants of the earth. There was something uncanny about them, but something amusing too. They reminded you very much of human beings. It was quite entertaining to stand there for half an hour and observe their gambols.

George Moon took his topee off the peg and not displeased with life stepped out into the sunshine.

P. & O.

MRS HAMLYN lay on her long chair and lazily watched the passengers come along the gangway. The ship had reached Singapore in the night, and since dawn had been taking on cargo; the winches had been grinding away all day, but by now her ears were accustomed to their insistent clamour. She had lunched at the Europe, and for lack of anything better to do had driven in a rickshaw through the gay, multitudinous streets of the city. Singapore is the meeting-place of many races. The Malays, though natives of the soil, dwell uneasily in towns, and are few; and it is the Chinese, supple, alert, and industrious, who throng the streets; the dark-skinned Tamils walk on their silent, naked feet, as though they were but brief sojourners in a strange land, but the Bengalis, sleek and prosperous, are easy in their surroundings, and self-assured; the sly and obsequious Japanese seem busy with pressing and secret affairs; and the English in their topees and white ducks, speeding past in motor-cars or at leisure in their rickshaws, wear a nonchalant and careless air. The rulers of these teeming peoples take their authority with a smiling unconcern. And now, tired and hot, Mrs Hamlyn waited for the ship to set out again on her long journey across the Indian Ocean.

She waved a rather large hand, for she was a big woman, to the doctor and Mrs Linsell as they came on board. She had been on the ship since she left Yokohama, and had watched with acid amusement the intimacy which had sprung up between the two. Linsell was a naval officer who had been attached to the British Embassy at Tokio, and she had wondered at the indifference with which he took the attentions that the doctor paid his wife. Two men came along the gangway, new passengers, and she amused herself by trying to discover from their demeanour whether they were single or married. Close by, a group of men were sitting together on rattan chairs, planters she judged by their khaki suits and wide-brimmed double felt hats, and they kept the deck-steward busy with their orders. They were talking loudly and laughing, for they had all drunk enough to make them somewhat foolishly hilarious, and they were evidently giving one of their number a send-off; but Mrs Hamlyn could not tell which it was that was to be a fellow-passenger. The time was growing short. More passengers arrived, and then Mr Jephson with dignity strolled up the gangway. He was a consul and was going home on leave. He had joined the ship at Shanghai and had immediately set about making himself agreeable to Mrs Hamlyn. But just then she was disinclined for anything in the nature of a flirtation. She frowned as she thought of the reason which was taking her back to England. She would be spending Christmas at sea, far from anyone who cared two straws about her, and for a moment she felt a little twist of her heartstrings; it vexed her that a subject which she was so resolute to put away from her should so constantly intrude on her unwilling mind.

But a warning bell clanged loudly, and there was a general movement among the men who sat beside her.

'Well, if we don't want to be taken on we'd better be toddling,' said one of them.

They rose and walked towards the gangway. Now that they were all shaking hands she saw who it was that they had come to see the last of. There was nothing very interesting about the man on whom Mrs Hamlyn's eyes rested, but because she had nothing better to do she gave him more than a casual glance. He was a big fellow, well over six feet high, broad and stout; he was dressed in a bedraggled suit of khaki drill and his hat was battered and shabby. His friends left him, but they bandied chaff from the quay, and Mrs Hamlyn noticed that he had a strong Irish brogue; his voice was full, loud, and hearty.

Mrs Linsell had gone below and the doctor came and sat down beside Mrs Hamlyn. They told one another their small adventures of the day. The bell sounded again and presently the ship slid away from the wharf. The Irishman waved a last farewell to his friends, and then sauntered towards the chair on which he had left papers and magazines. He nodded to the doctor.

'Is that someone you know?' asked Mrs Hamlyn.

'I was introduced to him at the club before tiffin. His name is Gallagher. He's a planter.'

After the hubbub of the port and the noisy bustle of departure, the silence of the ship was marked and grateful. They steamed slowly past green-clad, rocky cliffs (the P. & O. anchorage was in a charming and secluded cove), and came out into the main harbour. Ships of all nations lay at anchor, a great multitude, passenger boats, tugs, lighters, tramps; and beyond, behind the breakwater, you saw the crowded masts, a bare straight forest, of the native junks. In the soft light of the evening the busy scene was strangely touched with mystery, and you felt that all those vessels, their activity for the moment suspended, waited for some event of a peculiar significance.

Mrs Hamlyn was a bad sleeper and when the dawn broke she was in the habit of going on deck. It rested her troubled heart to watch the last faint stars fade before the encroaching day, and at that early hour the glassy sea had often an immobility which seemed to make all earthly sorrows of little consequence. The light was wan, and there was a pleasant shiver in the air. But next morning, when she went to the end of the promenade deck, she found that someone was up before her. It was Mr Gallagher. He was watching the low coast of Sumatra which the sunrise like a magician seemed to call forth from the dark sea. She was startled and a little vexed, but before she could turn away he had seen her and nodded.

'Up early,' he said. 'Have a cigarette?'

He was in pyjamas and slippers. He took his case from his coat pocket and handed it to her. She hesitated. She had on nothing but a dressing-gown and a little lace cap which she had put over her tousled hair, and she knew that she must look a sight; but she had her reasons for scourging her soul.

'I suppose a woman of forty has no right to mind how she looks,' she smiled, as though he must know what vain thoughts occupied her. She took the cigarette. 'But you're up early too.'

'I'm a planter. I've had to get up at five in the morning for so many years that I don't know how I'm going to get out of the habit.'

'You'll not find it will make you very popular at home.'

She saw his face better now that it was not shadowed by a hat. It was agreeable without being handsome. He was of course much too fat, and his features, which must have been good enough when he was a young man, were thickened. His skin was red and bloated. But his dark eyes were merry; and though he could not have been less than five and forty his hair was black and thick. He gave you an impression of great strength. He was a heavy, ungraceful, commonplace man, and Mrs Hamlyn, except for the promiscuity of ship-board, would never have thought it worth while to talk to him.

'Are you going home on leave?' she hazarded.

'No, I'm going home for good.'

His black eyes twinkled. He was of a communicative turn, and before it was time for Mrs Hamlyn to go below in order to have her bath he had told her a good deal about himself. He had been in the Federated Malay States for twenty-five years, and for the last ten had managed an estate in Selatan. It was a hundred miles from anything that could be described as civilization and the life had been lonely; but he had made money; during the rubber boom he had done very well, and with an astuteness which was unexpected in a man who looked so happy-go-lucky he had invested his savings in government stock. Now that the slump had come he was prepared to retire.

'What part of Ireland do you come from?' asked Mrs Hamlyn.

'Galway.'

Mrs Hamlyn had once motored through Ireland and she had a vague recollection of a sad and moody town with great stone warehouses, deserted and crumbling, which faced the melancholy sea. She had a sensation of greenness and of soft rain, of silence and of resignation. Was it here that Mr Gallagher meant to spend the rest of his life? He spoke of it with boyish eagerness. The thought of his vitality in that grey world of shadows was so incongruous that Mrs Hamlyn was intrigued.

'Does your family live there?' she asked.

'I've got no family. My mother and father are dead. So far as I know I haven't a relation in the world.'

He had made all his plans, he had been making them for twenty-five years, and he was pleased to have someone to talk to of all these things that he had been obliged for so long only to talk to himself about. He meant to buy a house and he would keep a motor-car. He was going to breed horses. He didn't much care about shooting; he had shot a lot of big game during his first years in the F.M.S.; but now he had lost his zest. He didn't see why the beasts of the jungle should be killed; he had lived in the jungle so long. But he could hunt.

'Do you think I'm too heavy?' he asked.

Mrs Hamlyn, smiling, looked him up and down with appraising eyes.

'You must weigh a ton,' she said.

He laughed. The Irish horses were the best in the world, and he'd always kept pretty fit. You had a devil of a lot of walking exercise on a rubber estate and he'd played a good deal of tennis. He'd soon get thin in Ireland. Then he'd marry. Mrs Hamlyn looked silently at the sea coloured now with the tenderness of the sunrise. She sighed.

'Was it easy to drag up all your roots? Is there no one you regret leaving behind? I should have thought after so many years, however much you'd looked forward to going home, when the time came at last to go it must have given you a pang.'

'I was glad to get out. I was fed up. I never want to see the country again or anyone in it.'

One or two early passengers now began to walk round the deck and Mrs Hamlyn, remembering that she was scantily clad, went below.

During the next day or two she saw little of Mr Gallagher, who passed his time in the smoking-room. Owing to a strike the ship was not touching at Colombo and the passengers settled down to a pleasant voyage across the Indian Ocean. They played deck games, they gossiped about one another, they flirted. The approach of Christmas gave them an occupation, for someone had suggested that there should be a fancy-dress dance on Christmas Day, and the ladies set about making their dresses. A meeting was held of the first-class passengers to decide whether the second-class passengers should be invited, and notwithstanding the heat the discussion was animated. The ladies said that the second-class passengers would only feel ill-at-ease. On Christmas Day it was to be expected that they would drink more than was good for them and unpleasantness might ensue. Everyone who spoke insisted that there was in his (or her) mind no idea of class distinction, no one would be so snobbish as to think there was any difference between first and second-class passengers as far as that went, but it would really be kinder to the second-class passengers not to put them in a false position. They would enjoy themselves much more if they had a party of their own in the second-class cabin. On the other hand, no one wanted to hurt their feelings, and of course one had to be more democratic nowadays (this was in reply to the wife of a missionary in China who said she had travelled on the P. & O. for thirty-five years and she had never heard of the second-class passengers being invited to a dance in the first-class saloon) and even though they wouldn't enjoy it, they might like to come. Mr Gallagher, dragged unwillingly from the card-table, because it had been foreseen that the voting would be close, was asked his opinion by the consul. He was taking home in the second-class a man who had been employed on his estate. He raised his massive bulk from the couch on which he sat.

'As far as I'm concerned I've only got this to say: I've got the man who was looking after our engines with me. He's a rattling good fellow, and he's just as fit to come to your party as I am. But he won't come because I'm going to make him so drunk on

Christmas Day that by six o'clock he'll be fit for nothing but to be put to bed.'

Mr Jephson, the consul, gave a distorted smile. On account of his official position, he had been chosen to preside at the meeting and he wished the matter to be taken seriously. He was a man who often said that if a thing was worth doing it was worth doing well.

'I gather from your observations,' he said, not without acidity, 'that the question before the meeting does not seem to you of great importance.'

'I don't think it matters a tinker's curse,' said Gallagher, with twinkling eyes.

Mrs Hamlyn laughed. The scheme was at last devised to invite the second-class passengers, but to go to the captain privily and point out to him the advisability of withholding his consent to their coming into the first-class saloon. It was on the evening of the day on which this happened that Mrs Hamlyn, having dressed for dinner, came on deck at the same time as Mr Gallagher.

'Just in time for a cocktail, Mrs Hamlyn,' he said jovially.

'I'd like one. To tell you the truth I need cheering up.'

'Why?' he smiled.

Mrs Hamlyn thought his smile attractive, but she did not want to answer his question.

'I told you the other morning,' she answered cheerfully. 'I'm forty.'

'I never met a woman who insisted on the fact so much.'

They went into the lounge and the Irishman ordered a dry Martini for her and a gin pahit for himself. He had lived too long in the East to drink anything else.

'You've got hiccups,' said Mrs Hamlyn.

'Yes, I've had them all the afternoon,' he answered carelessly. 'It's rather funny, they came on just as we got out of sight of land.'

'I daresay they'll pass off after dinner.'

They drank, the second bell rang, and they went into the dining-saloon.

'You don't play bridge?' he said, as they parted.

'No.'

Mrs Hamlyn did not notice that she saw nothing of Gallagher for two or three days. She was occupied with her own thoughts. They crowded upon her when she was sewing; they came between her and the novel with which she sought to cheat their insistence.

She had hoped that as the ship took her further away from the scene of her unhappiness, the torment of her mind would be eased; but contrariwise, each day that brought her nearer England increased her distress. She looked forward with dismay to the bleak emptiness of the life that awaited her; and then, turning her exhausted wits from a prospect that made her flinch, she considered, as she had done she knew not how many times before, the situation from which she had fled.

She had been married for twenty years. It was a long time and of course she could not expect her husband to be still madly in love with her; she was not madly in love with him; but they were good friends and they understood one another. Their marriage, as marriages go, might very well have been looked upon as a success. Suddenly she discovered that he had fallen in love. She would not have objected to a flirtation, he had had those before, and she had chaffed him about them; he had not minded that, it somewhat flattered him, and they had laughed together at an inclination which was neither deep nor serious. But this was different. He was in love as passionately as a boy of eighteen. He was fifty-two. It was ridiculous. It was indecent. And he loved without sense or prudence; by the time the hideous fact was forced upon her all the foreigners in Yokohama knew it. After the first shock of astonished anger, for he was the last man from whom such a folly might have been expected, she tried to persuade herself that she could have understood, and so have forgiven, if he had fallen in love with a girl. Middle-aged men often make fools of themselves with flappers, and after twenty years in the Far East she knew that the fifties were the dangerous age for men. But he had no excuse. He was in love with a woman eight years older than herself. It was grotesque, and it made her, his wife, perfectly absurd. Dorothy Lacom was hard on fifty. He had known her for eighteen years, for Lacom, like her own husband, was a silk merchant in Yokohama. Year in, year out, they had seen one another three or four times a week, and once, when they happened to be in England together, had shared a house at the seaside. But nothing! Not till a year ago had there been anything between them but a chaffing friendship. It was incredible. Of course Dorothy was a handsome woman; she had a good figure, over-developed, perhaps, but still comely; with bold black eyes and a red mouth and lovely hair; but all that she had had years before. She was forty-eight. Forty-eight!

Mrs Hamlyn tackled her husband at once. At first he swore

that there was not a word of truth in what she accused him of, but she had her proofs; he grew sulky; and at last he admitted what he could no longer deny. Then he said an astonishing thing.

'Why should you care?' he asked.

It maddened her. She answered him with angry scorn. She was voluble, finding in the bitterness of her heart wounding things to say. He listened to her quietly.

'I've not been such a bad husband to you for the twenty years we've been married. For a long time now we've only been friends. I have a great affection for you, and this hasn't altered it in the very smallest degree. I'm giving Dorothy nothing that I take away from you.'

'But what have you to complain of in me?'

'Nothing. No man could want a better wife.'

'How can you say that when you have the heart to treat me so cruelly?'

'I don't want to be cruel to you. I can't help myself.'

'But what on earth made you fall in love with her?'

'How can I tell? You don't think I wanted to, do you?'

'Couldn't you have resisted?'

'I tried. I think we both tried.'

'You talk as though you were twenty. Why, you're both middle-aged people. She's eight years older than I am. It makes me look such a perfect fool.'

He did not answer. She did not know what emotions seethed in her heart. Was it jealousy that seemed to clutch at her throat, anger, or was it merely wounded pride?

'I'm not going to let it go on. If only you and she were concerned I would divorce you, but there's her husband, and then there are the children. Good heavens, does it occur to you that if they were girls instead of boys she might be a grandmother by now?'

'Easily.'

'What a mercy that we have no children!'

He put out an affectionate hand as though to caress her, but she drew back with horror.

'You've made me the laughing-stock of all my friends. For all our sakes I'm willing to hold my tongue, but only on the condition that everything stops now, at once, and for ever.'

He looked down and played reflectively with a Japanese knick-knack that was on the table.

'I'll tell Dorothy what you say,' he replied at last.

She gave him a little bow, silently, and walked past him out of the room. She was too angry to observe that she was somewhat melodramatic.

She waited for him to tell her the result of his interview with Dorothy Lacom, but he made no further reference to the scene. He was quiet, polite, and silent; and at last she was obliged to ask him.

'Have you forgotten what I said to you the other day?' she inquired, frigidly.

'No. I talked to Dorothy. She wished me to tell you that she is desperately sorry that she has caused you so much pain. She would like to come and see you, but she is afraid you wouldn't like it.'

'What decision have you come to?'

He hesitated. He was very grave, but his voice trembled a little.

'I'm afraid there's no use in our making a promise we shouldn't be able to keep.'

'That settles it then,' she answered.

'I think I should tell you that if you brought an action for divorce we should have to contest it. You would find it impossible to get the necessary evidence and you would lose your case.'

'I wasn't thinking of doing that. I shall go back to England and consult a lawyer. Nowadays these things can be managed fairly easily, and I shall throw myself on your generosity. I dare say you will enable me to get my freedom without bringing Dorothy Lacom into the matter.'

He sighed.

'It's an awful muddle, isn't it? I don't want you to divorce me, but of course I'll do anything I can to meet your wishes.'

'What on earth do you expect me to do?' she cried, her anger rising again. 'Do you expect me to sit still and be made a damned fool of?'

'I'm awfully sorry to put you in a humiliating position.' He looked at her with harassed eyes. 'I'm quite sure we didn't want to fall in love with one another. We're both of us very conscious of our age. Dorothy, as you say is old enough to be a grandmother and I'm a baldish, stoutish gentleman of fifty-two. When you fall in love at twenty you think your love will last for ever, but at fifty you know so much, about life and about love, and you know that it will last so short a time.' His voice was low and rueful. It was as though before his mind's eye he saw the sadness of autumn and the leaves falling from the trees. He looked at her gravely. 'And at that age you feel that you can't afford to throw away the chance of happiness which a freakish destiny has given you. In five years it will certainly be over, and perhaps in six months. Life is rather drab and grey, and happiness is so rare. We shall be dead so long.'

It gave Mrs Hamlyn a bitter sensation of pain to hear her husband, a matter-of-fact and practical man, speak in a strain which was quite new to her. He had gained on a sudden a wistful and tragic personality of which she knew nothing. The twenty years during which they had lived together had no power over him and she was helpless in face of his determination. She could do nothing but go, and now, resentfully determined to get the divorce with which she had threatened him, she was on her way to England.

The smooth sea, upon which the sun beat down so that it shone like a sheet of glass, was as empty and hostile as life in which there was no place for her. For three days no other craft had broken in upon the solitariness of that expanse. Now and again its even surface was scattered for the twinkling of an eye by the scurry of flying fish. The heat was so great that even the most energetic of passengers had given up deck games, and now (it was after luncheon) such as were not resting in their cabins lay about on chairs. Linsell strolled towards her and sat down.

'Where's Mrs Linsell?' asked Mrs Hamlyn.

'Oh, I don't know. She's about somewhere.'

His indifference exasperated her. Was it possible that he did not see that his wife and the surgeon were falling in love with one another? Yet, not so very long ago, he must have cared. Their marriage had been romantic. They had become engaged when Mrs Linsell was still at school and he little more than a boy. They must have been a charming, handsome pair, and their youth and their mutual love must have been touching. And now, after so short a time, they were tired of one another. It was heartbreaking. What had her husband said?

' I suppose you're going to live in London when you get home?' asked Linsell lazily, for something to say.

'I suppose so,' said Mrs Hamlyn.

It was hard to reconcile herself to the fact that she had nowhere to go, and where she lived mattered not in the least to anyone alive. Some association of ideas made her think of Gallagher. She envied the eagerness with which he was returning to his native land, and she was touched, and at the same time amused, when she remembered the exuberant imagination he showed in describing the house he meant to live in and the wife he meant to marry. Her friends in Yokohama, apprised in confidence of her determination to divorce her husband, had assured her that she would marry again. She did not much want to enter a second time upon a state which had once so disappointed her, and besides, most men would think twice before they suggested marriage to a woman of forty. Mr Gallagher wanted a buxom young person.

'Where is Mr Gallagher?' she asked the submissive Linsell. 'I haven't seen him for the last day or two.'

'Didn't you know? He's ill.'

'Poor thing. What's the matter with him?'

'He's got hiccups.'

Mrs Hamlyn laughed.

'Hiccups don't make one ill, do they?'

'The surgeon is rather worried. He's tried all sorts of things, but he can't stop them.'

'How very odd.'

She thought no more about it, but next morning, chancing upon the surgeon, she asked him how Mr Gallagher was. She was surprised to see his boyish, cheerful face darken and grow perplexed.

'I'm afraid he's very bad, poor chap.'

'With hiccups?' she cried in amazement.

It was a disorder that really it was impossible to take seriously.

'You see, he can't keep any food down. He can't sleep. He's fearfully exhausted. I've tried everything I can think of.' He hesitated. 'Unless I can stop them soon – I don't quite know what'll happen.'

Mrs Hamlyn was startled.

'But he's so strong. He seemed so full of vitality.'

'I wish you could see him now.'

'Would he like me to go and see him?'

'Come along.'

Gallagher had been moved from his cabin into the ship's hospital, and as they approached it they heard a loud hiccup. The sound, perhaps owing to its connexion with insobriety, had in it something ludicrous. But Gallagher's appearance gave Mrs Hamlyn a shock. He had lost flesh and the skin hung about his neck in loose folds; under the sunburn his face was pale. His eyes, before full of fun and laughter, were haggard and tormented. His great body was shaken incessantly by the hiccups and now there was nothing ludicrous in the sound; to Mrs Hamlyn, for no reason that she knew, it seemed strangely terrifying. He smiled when she came in.

'I'm sorry to see you like this,' she said.

'I shan't die of it, you know,' he gasped. 'I shall reach the green shores of Erin all right.'

There was a man sitting beside him and he rose as they entered.

'This is Mr Pryce,' said the surgeon. 'He was in charge of the machinery on Mr Gallagher's estate.'

Mrs Hamlyn nodded. This was the second-class passenger to whom Gallagher had referred when they had discussed the party which was to be given on Christmas Day. He was a very small man, but sturdy, with a pleasantly impudent countenance and an air of self-assurance.

'Are you glad to be going home?' asked Mrs Hamlyn.

'You bet I am, lady,' he answered.

The intonation of the few words told Mrs Hamlyn that he was a cockney and, recognizing the cheerful, sensible, good-humoured, and careless type, her heart warmed to him.

'You're not Irish?' she smiled.

'Not me, miss. London's my 'ome and I shan't be sorry to see it again, I can tell you.'

Mrs Hamlyn never thought it offensive to be called miss.

'Well, sir, I'll be getting along,' he said to Gallagher, with the beginning of a gesture as though he were going to touch a cap which he hadn't got on.

Mrs Hamlyn asked the sick man whether she could do anything for him and in a minute or two left him with the doctor. The little cockney was waiting outside the door.

'Can I speak to you a minute or two, miss?' he asked.

'Of course.'

The hospital cabin was aft and they stood, leaning against the rail, and looked down on the well-deck where lascars and stewards off duty were lounging about on the covered hatches.

'I don't know exactly 'ow to begin,' said Pryce, uncertainly, a serious look strangely changing his lively, puckered face. 'I've been with Mr Gallagher for four years now and a better gentleman you wouldn't find in a week of Sundays.'

He hesitated again.

'I don't like it and that's the truth.'

'What don't you like?'

'Well, if you ask me 'e's for it, and the doctor don't know it. I told 'im, but 'e won't listen to a word I say.'

'You mustn't be too depressed, Mr Pryce. Of course the doctor's young, but I think he's quite clever, and people don't die of hiccups, you know. I'm sure Mr Gallagher will be all right in a day or two.'

'You know when it came on? Just as we was out of sight of land. She said 'e'd never see 'is 'ome.'

Mrs Hamlyn turned and faced him. She stood a good three inches taller than he.

'What do you mean?'

'My belief is, it's a spell been put on 'im, if you understand what I mean. Medicine's going to do 'im no good. You don't know them Malay women like what I do.'

For a moment Mrs Hamlyn was startled, and because she was startled she shrugged her shoulders and laughed.

'Oh, Mr Pryce, that's nonsense.'

'That's what the doctor said when I told 'im. But you mark my words, 'e'll die before we see land again.'

The man was so serious that Mrs Hamlyn, vaguely uneasy, was against her will impressed.

'Why should anyone cast a spell on Mr Gallagher?' she asked.

'Well, it's a bit awkward speakin' of it to a lady.'

'Please tell me.'

Pryce was so embarrassed that at another time Mrs Hamlyn would have had difficulty in concealing her amusement.

'Mr Gallagher's lived a long time up-country, if you understand what I mean, and of course it's lonely, and you know what men are, miss.'

'I've been married for twenty years,' she replied, smiling.

'I beg your pardon, ma'am. The fact is he had a Malay girl living with him. I don't know 'ow long, ten or twelve years, I think. Well, when 'e made up 'is mind to come 'ome for good she didn't say nothing. She just sat there. He thought she'd carry on no end, but she didn't. Of course 'e provided for 'er all right, 'e gave 'er a little 'ouse for herself, an' 'e fixed it up so as so much should be paid 'er every month. 'E wasn't mean, I will say that for 'im, an' she knew all along as 'e'd be going some time. She didn't cry or anything. When 'e packed up all 'is things and sent them off, she just sat there an' watched 'em go. And when 'e sold 'is furniture to the Chinks she never said a word. He'd give 'er all she wanted. And when it was time for 'im to go so as to

catch the boat she just kep' on sitting on the steps of the bungalow, you know, and she just looked an' said nothing. He wanted
to say good-bye to 'er, same as anyone would, an', would you
believe it? she never even moved. "Aren't you going to say good-
bye to me?" he says. A rare funny look come over 'er face. And
do you know what she says? "You go," she says; they 'ave a
funny way of talking, them natives, not like we 'ave, "you go,"
she says, "but I tell you that you will never come to your own
country. When the land sinks into the sea, death will come upon
you, an' before them as goes with you sees the land again, death
will have took you." It gave me quite a turn.'

'What did Mr Gallagher say?' asked Mrs Hamlyn.

'Oh, well, you know what 'e is. He just laughed. "Always
merry and bright," 'e says and 'e jumps into the motor, an' off we
go.'

Mrs Hamlyn saw the bright and sunny road that ran through
the rubber estates, with their trim green trees, carefully spaced,
and their silence, and then wound its way up hill and down
through the tangled jungle. The car raced on, driven by a reckless
Malay, with its white passengers, past Malay houses that stood
away from the road among the coconut trees, sequestered and
taciturn, and through busy villages where the market-place was
crowded with dark-skinned little people in gay sarongs. Then
towards evening it reached the trim, modern town, with its clubs
and its golf links, its well-ordered rest-house, its white people,
and its railway-station, from which the two men could take the
train to Singapore. And the woman sat on the steps of the bungalow, empty till the new manager moved in, and watched the road
down which the car had panted, watched the car as it sped on,
and watched till at last it was lost in the shadow of the night.

'What was she like?' Mrs Hamlyn asked.

'Oh, well, to my way of thinking them Malay women are all
very much alike, you know,' Pryce answered. 'Of course she
wasn't so young any more, and you know what they are, them
natives, they run to fat something terrible.'

'Fat?'

The thought, absurdly enough, filled Mrs Hamlyn with dismay.

'Mr Gallagher was always one to do himself well, if you understand what I mean.'

The idea of corpulence at once brought Mrs Hamlyn back to
common sense. She was impatient with herself because for an
instant she had seemed to accept the little cockney's suggestion.

'It's perfectly absurd, Mr Pryce. Fat women can't throw spells on people at a distance of a thousand miles. In fact life is very difficult for a fat woman anyway.'

'You can laugh, miss, but unless something's done, you mark my words, the governor's for it. And medicine ain't goin' to save him, not white man's medicine.'

'Pull yourself together, Mr Pryce. This fat lady had no particular grievance against Mr Gallagher. As these things are done in the East he seems to have treated her very well. Why should she wish him any harm?'

'We don't know 'ow they look at things. Why, a man can live there for twenty years with one them natives, and d'you think 'e knows what's goin' on in that black heart of hers? Not 'im!'

She could not smile at his melodramatic language, for his intensity was impressive. And she knew, if anyone did, that the hearts of men, whether their skins are yellow or white or brown, are incalculable.

'But even if she felt angry with him, even if she hated him and wanted to kill him, what could she do?' It was strange that Mrs Hamlyn with her questions was trying now, unconsciously, to reassure herself. 'There's no poison that could start working after six or seven days.'

'I never said it was poison.'

'I'm sorry, Mr Pryce,' she smiled, 'but I'm not going to believe in a magic spell, you know.'

'You've lived in the East?'

'Off and on for twenty years.'

'Well, if you can say what they can do and what they can't, it's more than I can.' He clenched his fist and beat it on the rail with sudden, angry violence. 'I'm fed up with the bloody country. It's got on my nerves, that's what it is. We're no match for them, us white men, and that's a fact. If you'll excuse me I think I'll go an' 'ave a tiddley. I've got the jumps.'

He nodded abruptly and left her. Mrs Hamlyn watched him, a sturdy, shuffling little man in shabby khaki, slither down the companion into the waist of the ship, walk across it with bent head, and disappear into the second-class saloon. She did not know why he left with her a vague uneasiness. She could not get out of her mind that picture of a stout woman, no longer young, in a sarong, a coloured jacket, and gold ornaments, who sat on the steps of a bungalow looking at an empty road. Her heavy face was painted, but in her large, tearless eyes there was no expression. The men who drove in the car were like schoolboys going home for the holidays. Gallagher gave a sigh of relief. In the early morning, under the bright sky, his spirits bubbled. The future was like a sunny road that wandered through a wide-flung, wooded plain.

Later in the day Mrs Hamlyn asked the doctor how his patient did. The doctor shook his head.

'I'm done. I'm at the end of my tether.' He frowned unhappily. 'It's rotten luck, striking a case like this. It would be bad enough at home, but on board ship . . .'

He was an Edinburgh man, but recently qualified, and he was taking his voyage as a holiday before settling down to practice. He felt himself aggrieved. He wanted to have a good time and, faced with this mysterious illness, he was worried to death. Of course he was inexperienced, but he was doing everything that could be done and it exasperated him to suspect that the passengers thought him an ignorant fool.

'Have you heard what Mr Pryce thinks?' asked Mrs Hamlyn.

'I never heard such rot. I told the captain and he's right up in the air. He doesn't want it talked about. He thinks it'll upset the passengers.'

'I'll be as silent as the grave.'

The surgeon looked at her sharply.

'Of course you don't believe that there can be any truth in nonsense of that sort?' he asked.

'Of course not.' She looked out at the sea, which shone, blue and oily and still, all round them. 'I've lived in the East a long time,' she added. 'Strange things happen there.'

'This is getting on my nerves,' said the doctor.

Near them two little Japanese gentlemen were playing deck quoits. They were trim and neat in their tennis shirts, white trousers, and buckram shoes. They looked very European, they even called the score to one another in English, and yet somehow to look at them filled Mrs Hamlyn at that moment with a vague disquiet. Because they seemed to wear so easily a disguise there was about them something sinister. Her nerves too were on edge.

And presently, no one quite knew how, the notion spread through the ship that Gallagher was bewitched. While the ladies sat about on their deck-chairs, stitching away at the costumes they were making for the fancy-dress party on Christmas Day, they gossiped about it in undertones, and the men in the smoking-room talked of it over their cocktails. A good many of the passengers had lived long in the East and from the recesses of their memory they produced strange and inexplicable stories. Of course it was absurd to think seriously that Gallagher was suffering from a malignant spell, such things were impossible, and yet this and that was a fact and no one had been able to explain it. The doctor had to confess that he could suggest no cause for Gallagher's condition, he was able to give a physiological explanation, but why these terrible spasms should have suddenly assailed him he did not say. Feeling vaguely to blame, he tried to defend himself.

'Why, it's the sort of case you might never come across in the whole of your practice,' he said. 'It's rotten luck.'

He was in wireless communication with passing ships, and suggestions for treatment came from here and there.

'I've tried everything they tell me,' he said irritably. 'The doctor of the Japanese boat advised adrenalin. How the devil does he expect me to have adrenalin in the middle of the Indian Ocean?'

There was something impressive in the thought of this ship speeding through a deserted sea, while to her from all parts came unseen messages. She seemed at that moment strangely alone and yet the centre of the world. In the lazaret the sick man, shaken by the cruel spasms, gasped for life. Then the passengers became conscious that the ship's course was altered, and they heard that the captain had made up his mind to put in at Aden. Gallagher was to be landed there and taken to the hospital, where he could have attention which on board was impossible. The chief engineer received orders to force his engines. The ship was an old one and she throbbed with the greater effort. The passengers had grown used to the sound and feel of her engines, and now the greater vibration shook their nerves with a new sensation. It would not pass into each one's unconsciousness, but beat on their sensibilities so that each felt a personal concern. And still the wide sea was empty of traffic, so that they seemed to traverse an empty world. And now the uneasiness which had descended upon the ship, but which no one had been willing to acknowledge, became a definite malaise. The passengers grew irritable, and people quarrelled over trifles which at another time would have seemed insignificant. Mr Jephson made his hackneyed jokes, but no one any longer repaid him with a smile. The Linsells had an altercation, and Mrs Linsell was heard late at night walking round the

deck with her husband and uttering in a low, tense voice a stream
of vehement reproaches. There was a violent scene in the smoking-
room one night over a game of bridge, and the reconciliation
which followed it was attended with general intoxication. People
talked little of Gallagher, but he was seldom absent from their
thoughts. They examined the route map. The doctor said now that
Gallagher could not live more than three or four days, and they
discussed acrimoniously what was the shortest time in which
Aden could be reached. What happened to him after he was
landed was no affair of theirs; they did not want him to die on
board.

Mrs Hamlyn saw Gallagher every day. With the suddenness
with which after tropical rain in the spring you seem to see the
herbage grow before your very eyes, she saw him go to pieces.
Already his skin hung loosely on his bones, and his double chin
was like the wrinkled wattle of a turkey-cock. His cheeks were
sunken. You saw now how large his frame was, and through the
sheet under which he lay his bony structure was like the skeleton
of a prehistoric giant. For the most part he lay with his eyes
closed, torpid with morphia, but shaken still with terrible spasms,
and when now and again he opened his eyes they were preter-
naturally large; they looked at you vaguely, perplexed and
troubled, from the depths of their bony sockets. But when,
emerging from his stupor, he recognized Mrs Hamlyn, he forced
a gallant smile to his lips.

'How are you, Mr Gallagher?' she said.

'Getting along, getting along. I shall be all right when we get
out of this confounded heat. Lord, how I look forward to a dip
in the Atlantic. I'd give anything for a good long swim. I want
to feel the cold grey sea of Galway beating against my chest.'

Then the hiccup shook him from the crown of his head to the
sole of his foot. Mr Pryce and the stewardess shared the care of
him. The little cockney's face wore no longer its look of impudent
gaiety, but instead was sullen.

'The captain sent for me yesterday,' he told Mrs Hamlyn when
they were alone. 'He gave me a rare talking to.'

'What about?'

'He said 'e wouldn't 'ave all this hoodoo stuff. He said it was
frightening the passengers and I'd better keep a watch on me
tongue or I'd 'ave 'im to reckon with. It's not my doing. I never
said a word except to you and the doctor.'

'It's all over the ship.'

'I know it is. D'you think it's only me that's saying it? All them Lascars and the Chinese, they all know what's the matter with him. You don't think you can teach them much, do you? They know it ain't a natural illness.'

Mrs Hamlyn was silent. She knew through the amahs of some of the passengers that there was no one on the ship, except the whites, who doubted that the woman whom Gallagher had left in distant Selantan was killing him with her magic. All were convinced that as they sighted the barren rocks of Arabia his soul would be parted from his body.

'The captain says if he hears of me trying any hanky-panky he'll confine me to my cabin for the rest of the voyage,' said Pryce, suddenly, a surly frown on his puckered face.

'What do you mean by hanky-panky?'

He looked at her for a moment fiercely as though she too were an object of the anger he felt against the captain.

'The doctor's tried every damned thing he knows, and he's wirelessed all over the place, and what good 'as 'e done? Tell me that. Can't 'e see the man's dying? There's only one way to save him now.'

'What do you mean?'

'It's magic what's killing 'im, and it's only magic what'll save him. Oh, don't say it can't be done. I've seen it with me own eyes.' His voice rose, irritable and shrill. 'I've seen a man dragged from the jaws of death, as you might say, when they got in a *pawang*, what we call a witch-doctor, an' 'e did 'is little tricks. I seen it with me own eyes, I tell you.'

Mrs Hamlyn did not speak. Pryce gave her a searching look.

'One of them Lascars on board, he's a witch-doctor, same as the *pawang* thet we 'ave in the F.M.S. An' 'e says he'll do it. Only he must 'ave a live animal. A cock would do.'

'What do you want a live animal for?' Mrs Hamlyn asked, frowning a little.

The cockney looked at her with quick suspicion.

'If you take my advice you won't know anything about it. But I tell you what, I'm going to leave no stone unturned to save my governor. An' if the captain 'ears of it and shuts me up in me cabin, well, let 'im.'

At that moment Mrs Linsell came up and Pryce with his quaint gesture of salute left them. Mrs Linsell wanted Mrs Hamlyn to fit the dress she had been making herself for the fancy-dress ball, and on the way down to the cabin she spoke to her anxiously of the possibility that Mr Gallagher might die on Christmas Day. They could not possibly have the dance if he did. She had told the doctor that she would never speak to him again if this happened, and the doctor had promised her faithfully that he would keep the man alive over Christmas Day somehow.

'It would be nice for him, too,' said Mrs Linsell.

'For whom?' asked Mrs Hamlyn.

'For poor Mr Gallagher. Naturally no one likes to die on Christmas Day. Do they?'

'I don't really know,' said Mrs Hamlyn.

That night, after she had been asleep a little while, she awoke weeping. It dismayed her that she should cry in her sleep. It was as though then the weakness of the flesh mastered her, and, her will broken, she were defenceless against a natural sorrow. She turned over in her mind, as so often before, the details of the disaster which had so profoundly affected her; she repeated the conversations with her husband, wishing she had said this and blaming herself because she had said the other. She wished with all her heart that she had remained in comfortable ignorance of her husband's infatuation, and asked herself whether she would not have been wiser to pocket her pride and shut her eyes to the unwelcome truth. She was a woman of the world, and she knew too well how much more she lost in separating herself from her husband than his love; she lost the settled establishment and the assured position, the ample means and the support of a recognized background. She had known of many separated wives, living equivocally on smallish incomes, and knew how quickly their friends found them tiresome. And she was lonely. She was as lonely as the ship that throbbed her hasting way through an unpeopled sea, and lonely as the friendless man who lay dying in the ship's lazaret. Mrs Hamlyn knew that her thoughts had got the better of her now and that she would not easily sleep again. It was very hot in her cabin. She looked at the time; it was between four and half past; she must pass two mortal hours before broke the reassuring day.

She slipped into a kimono and went on deck. The night was sombre and although the sky was unclouded no stars were visible. Panting and shaking, the old ship under full steam lumbered through the darkness. The silence was uncanny. Mrs Hamlyn with bare feet groped her way slowly along the deserted deck.

It was so black that she could see nothing. She came to the end

105

of the promenade deck and leaned against the rail. Suddenly she started and her attention was fixed, for on the lower deck she caught a fitful glow. She leaned forward cautiously. It was a little fire, and she saw only the glow because the naked backs of men, crouched round, hid the flame. At the edge of the circle she divined, rather than saw, a stocky figure in pyjamas. The rest were natives, but this was a European. It must be Pryce and she guessed immediately that some dark ceremony of exorcism was in progress. Straining her ears she heard a low voice muttering a string of secret words. She began to tremble. She was aware that they were too intent upon their business to think that anyone was watching them, but she dared not move. Suddenly, rending the sultry silence of the night like a piece of silk violently torn in two, came the crowing of a cock. Mrs Hamlyn almost shrieked. Mr Pryce was trying to save the life of his friend and master by a sacrifice to the strange gods of the East. The voice went on, low and insistent. Then in the dark circle there was a movement, something was happening, she knew not what; there was a cluck-cluck from the cock, angry and frightened, and then a strange, indescribable sound; the magician was cutting the cock's throat; then silence; there were vague doings that she could not follow, and in a little while it looked as though someone were stamping out the fire. The figures she had dimly seen were dissolved in the night and all once more was still. She heard again the regular throbbing of the engines.

Mrs Hamlyn stood still for a little while, strangely shaken, and then walked slowly along the deck. She found a chair and lay down in it. She was trembling still. She could only guess what had happened. She did not know how long she lay there, but at last she felt that the dawn was approaching. It was not yet day, and it was no longer night. Against the darkness of the sky she could now see the ship's rail. Then she saw a figure come towards her. It was a man in pyjamas.

'Who's that?' she cried nervously.

'Only the doctor,' came a friendly voice.

'Oh! What are you doing here at this time of night?'

'I've been with Gallagher.' He sat down beside her and lit a cigarette. 'I've given him a good strong hypodermic and he's quiet now.'

'Has he been very ill?'

'I thought he was going to pass out. I was watching him, and suddenly he started up on his bed and began to talk Malay. Of course I couldn't understand a thing. He kept on saying one word over and over again.'

'Perhaps it was a name, a woman's name.'

'He wanted to get out of bed. He's a damned powerful man even now. By George, I had a struggle with him. I was afraid he'd throw himself overboard. He seemed to think someone was calling him.'

'When was that?' asked Mrs Hamlyn slowly.

'Between four and half past. Why?'

'Nothing.'

She shuddered.

Later in the morning when the ship's life was set upon its daily round, Mrs Hamlyn passed Pryce on the deck, but he gave her a brief greeting and walked on with quickly averted gaze. He looked tired and overwrought. Mrs Hamlyn thought again of that fat woman, with golden ornaments in her thick, black hair, who sat on the steps of the deserted bungalow and looked at the road which ran through the trim lines of the rubber trees.

It was fearfully hot. She knew now why the night had been so dark. The sky was no longer blue, but a dead, level white; its surface was too even to give the effect of cloud; it was as though in the upper air the heat hung like a pall. There was no breeze, and the sea, as colourless as the sky, was smooth and shining like the dye in a dyer's vat. The passengers were listless; when they walked round the deck they panted, and beads of sweat broke out on their foreheads. They spoke in undertones. Something uncanny and disquieting brooded over the ship, and they could not bring themselves to laugh. A feeling of resentment arose in their hearts; they were alive and well, and it exasperated them that, so near, a man should be dying and by the fact (which was after all no concern of theirs) so mysteriously affect them. A planter in the smoking-room over a gin sling said brutally what most of them felt, though none had confessed.

'Well, if he's going to peg out,' he said, 'I wish he'd hurry up and get it over. It gives me the creeps.'

The day was interminable. Mrs Hamlyn was thankful when the dinner hour arrived. So much time, at all events, was passed. She sat at the doctor's table.

'When do we reach Aden?' she asked.

'Some time tomorrow. The captain says we shall sight land between five and six in the morning.'

She gave him a sharp look. He stared at her for a moment,

then dropped his eyes and reddened. He remembered that the woman, the fat woman sitting on the bungalow steps, had said that Gallagher would never see the land. Mrs Hamlyn wondered whether he, the sceptical, matter-of-fact young doctor, was wavering at last. He frowned a little and then, as though he sought to pull himself together, looked at her once more.

'I shan't be sorry to hand over my patient to the hospital people at Aden, I can tell you,' he said.

Next day was Christmas Eve. When Mrs Hamlyn awoke from a troubled sleep the dawn was breaking. She looked out of her port-hole and saw that the sky was clear and silvery; during the night the haze had melted, and the morning was brilliant. With a lighter heart she went on deck. She walked as far forward as she could go. A late star twinkled palely close to the horizon. There was a shimmer on the sea as though a loitering breeze passed playful fingers over its surface. The light was wonderfully soft, tenuous like a budding wood in spring, and crystalline so that it reminded you of the bubbling of water in a mountain brook. She turned to look at the sun rising rosy in the east, and saw coming towards her the doctor. He wore his uniform; he had not been to bed all night; he was dishevelled and he walked, with bowed shoulders, as though he were dog-tired. She knew at once that Gallagher was dead. When he came up to her she saw that he was crying. He looked so young then that her heart went out to him. She took his hand.

'You poor dear,' she said. 'You're tired out.'

'I did all I could,' he said. 'I wanted so awfully to save him.' His voice shook and she saw that he was almost hysterical.

'When did he die?' she asked.

He closed his eyes, trying to control himself, and his lips trembled.

'A few minutes ago.'

Mrs Hamlyn sighed. She found nothing to say. Her gaze wandered across the calm, dispassionate, and ageless sea. It stretched on all sides of them as infinite as human sorrow. But on a sudden her eyes were held, for there, ahead of them, on the horizon was something which looked like a precipitous and massy cloud. But its outline was too sharp to be a cloud's. She touched the doctor on the arm.

'What's that?'

He looked at it for a moment and under his sunburn she saw him grow white.

'Land.'

Once more Mrs Hamlyn thought of the fat Malay woman who sat silent on the steps of Gallagher's bungalow. Did she know?

They buried him when the sun was high in the heavens. They stood on the lower deck and on the hatches, the first- and second-class passengers, the white stewards and the European officers. The missionary read the burial service.

'*Man that is born of a woman hath but a short time to live, and is full of misery. He cometh up, and is cut down, like a flower; he fleeth as it were a shadow, and never continueth in one stay.*'

Pryce looked down at the deck with knit brows. His teeth were tight clenched. He did not grieve, for his heart was hot with anger. The doctor and the consul stood side by side. The consul bore to a nicety the expression of an official regret, but the doctor, clean-shaven now, in his neat fresh uniform and his gold braid, was pale and harassed. From him Mrs Hamlyn's eyes wandered to Mrs Linsell. She was pressed against her husband, weeping, and he was holding her hand tenderly. Mrs Hamlyn did not know why this sight singularly affected her. At that moment of grief, her nerves distraught, the little woman went by instinct to the protection and support of her husband. But then Mrs Hamlyn felt a little shudder pass through her and she fixed her eyes on the seams in the deck, for she did not want to see what was toward. There was a pause in the reading. There were various movements. One of the officers gave an order. The missionary's voice continued:

'*Forasmuch as it has pleased Almighty God of his great mercy to take unto himself the soul of our dear brother here departed: we therefore commend his body to the deep, to be turned into corruption, looking for the resurrection of the body when the sea shall give up its dead.*'

Mrs Hamlyn felt the hot tears flow down her cheeks. There was a dull splash. The missionary's voice went on.

When the service was finished the passengers scattered; the second-class passengers returned to their quarters and a bell rang to summon them to luncheon. But the first-class passengers sauntered aimlessly about the promenade deck. Most of the men made for the smoking-room and sought to cheer themselves with whiskies and sodas and with gin slings. But the consul put up a notice on the board outside the dining-saloon summoning the passengers to a meeting. Most of them had an idea for what purpose it was called, and at the appointed hour they assembled.

They were more cheerful than they had been for a week and they chattered with a gaiety which was only subdued by a mannerly reserve. The consul, an eyeglass in his eye, said that he had gathered them together to discuss the question of the fancy-dress dance on the following day. He knew they all had the deepest sympathy for Mr Gallagher and he would have proposed that they should combine to send an appropriate message to the deceased's relatives; but his papers had been examined by the purser and no trace could be found of any relative or friend with whom it was possible to communicate. The late Mr Gallagher appeared to be quite alone in the world. Meanwhile he (the consul) ventured to offer his sincere sympathy to the doctor, who, he was quite sure, had done everything that was possible in the circumstances.

'Hear, hear,' said the passengers.

They had all passed through a very trying time, proceeded the consul, and to some it might seem that it would be more respectful to the deceased's memory if the fancy-dress ball were postponed till New Year's Eve. This, however, he told them frankly was not his view, and he was convinced that Mr Gallagher himself would not have wished it. Of course it was a question for the majority to decide. The doctor got up and thanked the consul and the passengers for the kind things that had been said of him, it had of course been a very trying time, but he was authorized by the captain to say that the captain expressly wished all the festivities to be carried out on Christmas Day as though nothing had happened. He (the doctor) told them in confidence that the captain felt the passengers had got into a rather morbid state, and thought it would do them all good if they had a jolly good time on Christmas Day. Then the missionary's wife rose and said they mustn't think only of themselves; it had been arranged by the Entertainment Committee that there should be a Christmas Tree for the children, immediately after the first-class passengers' dinner, and the children had been looking forward to seeing everyone in fancy-dress; it would be too bad to disappoint them; she yielded to no one in her respect for the dead, and she sympathized with anyone who felt too sad to think of dancing just then, her own heart was very heavy, but she did feel it would be merely selfish to give way to a feeling which could do no good to anyone. Let them think of the little ones. This very much impressed the passengers. They wanted to forget the brooding terror which had hung over the boat for so many days, they were alive and they wanted to enjoy themselves; but they had an uneasy notion that it would be decent to exhibit a certain grief. It was quite another matter if they could do as they wished from altruistic motives. When the consul called for a show of hands everyone but Mrs Hamlyn, and one old lady who was rheumatic, held up an eager arm.

'The ayes have it,' said the consul. 'And I venture to congratulate the meeting on a very sensible decision.'

It was just going to break up when one of the planters got on his feet and said he wished to offer a suggestion. Under the circumstances didn't they all think it would be as well to invite the second-class passengers? They had all come to the funeral that morning. The missionary jumped up and seconded the motion. The events of the last few days had drawn them all together, he said, and in the presence of death all men were equal. The consul again addressed them. This matter had been discussed at a previous meeting, and the conclusion had been reached that it would be pleasanter for the second-class passengers to have their own party, but circumstances alter cases, and he was distinctly of opinion that their previous decision should be reversed.

'Hear, hear,' said the passengers.

A wave of democratic feeling swept over them and the motion was carried by acclamation. They separated light-heartedly, they felt charitable and kindly. Everyone stood everyone else drinks in the smoking-room.

And so, on the following evening, Mrs Hamlyn put on her fancy-dress. She had no heart for the gaiety before her, and for a moment had thought of feigning illness, but she knew no one would believe her, and was afraid to be thought affected. She was dressed as Carmen and she could not resist the vanity of making herself as attractive as possible. She darkened her eyelashes and rouged her cheeks. The costume suited her. When the bugle sounded and she went into the saloon she was received with flattering surprise. The consul (always a humorist) was dressed as a ballet-girl and was greeted with shouts of delighted laughter. The missionary and his wife, self-conscious but pleased with themselves, were very grand as Manchus. Mrs Linsell, as Columbine, showed all that was possible of her very pretty legs. Her husband was an Arab sheik and the doctor was a Malay sultan.

A subscription had been collected to provide champagne at dinner and the meal was hilarious. The company had provided crackers in which were paper hats of various shapes and these the

passengers put on. There were paper streamers too which they
threw at one another and little balloons which they beat from one
to the other across the room. They laughed and shouted. They
were very gay. No one could say that they were not having a good
time. As soon as dinner was finished they went into the saloon,
where the Christmas Tree, with candles lit, was ready, and the
children were brought in, shrieking with delight, and given presents. Then the dance began. The second-class passengers stood
about shyly round the part of the deck reserved for dancing and
occasionally danced with one another.

'I'm glad we had them,' said the consul, dancing with Mrs
Hamlyn. 'I'm all for democracy, and I think they're very sensible
to keep themselves to themselves.'

But she noticed that Pryce was not to be seen, and when an
opportunity presented asked one of the second-class passengers
where he was.

'Blind to the world,' was the answer. 'We put him to bed in
the afternoon and locked him up in his cabin.'

The consul claimed her for another dance. He was very facetious. Suddenly Mrs Hamlyn felt that she could not bear it any
more, the noise of the amateur band, the consul's jokes, the gaiety
of the dancers. She knew not why, but the merriment of those
people passing on their ship through the night and the solitary
sea affected her on a sudden with horror. When the consul released her she slipped away and, with a look to see that no one
had noticed her, ascended the companion to the boat deck. Here
everything was in darkness. She walked softly to a spot where she
knew she would be safe from all intrusion. But she heard a faint
laugh and she caught sight in a hidden corner of a Columbine and
a Malay sultan. Mrs Linsell and the doctor had resumed already
the flirtation which the death of Gallagher had interrupted.

Already all those people had put out of their minds with a kind
of ferocity the thought of that poor lonely man who had so
strangely died in their midst. They felt no compassion for him,
but resentment rather, because on his account they had been ill-
at-ease. They seized upon life avidly. They made their jokes, they
flirted, they gossiped. Mrs Hamlyn remembered what the consul
had said, that among Mr Gallagher's papers no letters could be
found, not the name of a single friend to whom the news of his
death might be sent, and she knew not why this seemed to her
unbearably tragic. There was something mysterious in a man who
could pass through the world in such solitariness. When she

remembered how he had come on deck in Singapore, so short a while since, in such rude health, full of vitality, and his arrogant plans for the future, she was seized with dismay. Those words of the burial service filled her with a solemn awe: *Man that is born of a woman hath but a short time to live, and is full of misery. He cometh up, and is cut down, like a flower* . . . Year in, year out, he had made his plans for the future, he wanted to live so much and he had so much to live for, and then just when he stretched out his hand – oh, it was pitiful; it made all the other distresses of the world of small account. Death with its mystery was the only thing that really mattered. Mrs Hamlyn leaned over the rail and looked at the starry sky. Why did people make themselves unhappy? Let them weep for the death of those they loved, death was terrible always, but for the rest, was it worth while to be wretched, to harbour malice, to be vain and uncharitable? She thought again of herself and her husband and the woman he so strangely loved. He too had said that we live to be happy so short a time and we are so long dead. She pondered long and intently, and suddenly, as summer lightning flashes across the darkness of the night, she made a discovery which filled her with tremulous surprise; for she found that in her heart was no longer anger with her husband nor jealousy of her rival. A notion dawned on some remote horizon of her consciousness and like the morning sun suffused her soul with a tender, blissful glow. Out of the tragedy of that unknown Irishman's death she gathered elatedly the courage for a desperate resolution. Her heart beat quickly, she was impatient to carry it into effect. A passion for self-sacrifice seized her.

The music had stopped, the ball was over; most of the passengers would have gone to bed and the rest would be in the smoking-room. She went down to her cabin and met no one on the way. She took her writing pad and wrote a letter to her husband:

My dear,
It is Christmas Day and I want to tell you that my heart is filled with kindly thoughts towards both of you. I have been foolish and unreasonable. I think we should allow those we care for to be happy in their own way, and we should care for them enough not to let it make us unhappy. I want you to know that I grudge you none of the joy that has so strangely come into your life. I am no longer jealous, nor hurt, nor vindictive. Do not think I shall be unhappy or lonely. If ever you feel that you need me, come to me, and I will welcome you with a cheerful spirit and without reproach or ill-will. I am most grateful for all the

years of happiness and of tenderness that you gave me, and in return I wish to offer you an affection which makes no claim on you and is, I hope, utterly disinterested. Think kindly of me and be happy, happy, happy.

She signed her name and put the letter into an envelope. Though it would not go till they reached Port Said she wanted to place it at once in the letter-box. When she had done this, beginning to undress, she looked at herself in the glass. Her eyes were shining and under her rouge her colour was bright. The future was no longer desolate, but bright with a fair hope. She slipped into bed and fell at once into a sound and dreamless sleep.

EPISODE

IT was quite a small party, because our hostess liked general conversation; we never sat down to dinner more than eight, and generally only six, and after dinner when we went up to the drawing-room the chairs were so arranged that it was impossible for two persons to go into a huddle in a corner and so break things up. I was glad on arriving to find that I knew everyone. There were two nice clever women besides our hostess and two men besides myself. One was my friend Ned Preston. Our hostess made it a point never to ask wives with their husbands, because she said each cramped the other's style and if they didn't like to come separately they needn't come at all. But since her food and her wine were good and the talk almost always entertaining they generally came. People sometimes accused her of asking husbands more often than wives, but she defended herself by saying that she couldn't possibly help it because more men were husbands than women were wives.

Ned Preston was a Scot, a good-humoured, merry soul, with a gift for telling a story, sometimes too lengthily, for he was uncommonly loquacious, but with dramatic intensity. He was a bachelor with a small income which sufficed for his modest needs, and in this he was lucky since he suffered from that form of chronic tuberculosis which may last for years without killing you, but which prevents you from working for your living. Now and then he would be ill enough to stay in bed for two or three weeks, but then he would get better and be as gay, cheerful, and talkative as ever. I doubt whether he had enough money to live in an expensive sanatorium and he certainly hadn't the temperament to suit himself to its life. He was worldly. When he was well he liked to go out, out to lunch, out to dinner, and he liked to sit up late into the night smoking his pipe and drinking a good deal of whisky. If he had been content to live the life of an invalid he might have been alive now, but he wasn't; and who can blame him? He died at the age of fifty-five of a haemorrhage which he had one night after coming home from some house where, he may well have flattered himself, he was the success of the party.

He had that febrile vitality that some consumptives have, and was always looking for an occupation to satisfy his desire for activity. I don't know how he heard that at Wormwood Scrubs

115

they were in want of prison visitors, but the idea took his fancy so he went to the Home Office and saw the official in charge of prisons to offer his services. The job is unpaid, and though a number of persons are willing to undertake it, either from compassion or curiosity, they are apt to grow tired of it, or find it takes up too much time, and the prisoners whose problems, interests and future they have been concerned with are left somewhat in the lurch. The Home Office people consequently are wary of taking on anyone who does not look as if he would persevere, and they make careful inquiries into the applicant's antecedents, character, and general suitability. Then he is given a trial, is discreetly watched, and if the impression is unfavourable is politely thanked and told that his services are no longer required. But Ned Preston satisfied the dour and shrewd official who interviewed him that he was in every way reliable, and from the beginning he got on well with the governor, the warders, and the prisoners. He was entirely lacking in class-consciousness, so prisoners, whatever their station in life, felt at ease with him. He neither preached nor moralized. He had never done a criminal, or even a mean, thing in his life, but he treated the crime of the prisoners he had to deal with as though it were an illness like his own tuberculosis which was a nuisance you had to put up with, but which it did no good to talk about.

Wormwood Scrubs is a first offenders' prison and it is a building, grim and cold, of forbidding appearance. Ned took me over it once and I had goose-flesh as the gates were unlocked for us and we went in. We passed through the halls in which the men were working.

'If you see any pals of yours take no notice of them,' Ned said to me. 'They don't like it.'

'Am I likely to see any pals of mine?' I asked drily.

'You never can tell. I shouldn't be surprised if you had had friends who'd passed bad cheques once too often or were caught in a compromising situation in one of the parks. You'd be surprised how often I run across chaps I've met out at dinner.'

One of Ned's duties was to see prisoners through the first difficult days of their confinement. They were often badly shaken by their trial and sentence; and when, after the preliminary proceedings they had to go through on entering the jail, the stripping, the bath, the medical examination and the questioning, the getting into prison clothes, they were led into a cell and locked up, they were apt to break down. Sometimes they cried hysterically; sometimes they could neither eat nor sleep. Ned's business then was to cheer them, and his breezy manner, his natural kindliness, often worked wonders. If they were anxious about their wives and children he would go to see them and if they were destitute provide them with money. He brought them news so that they might get over the awful feeling that they were shut away from the common interests of their fellow-men. He read the sporting papers to be able to tell them what horse had won an important race or whether the champion had won his fight. He would advise them about their future, and when the time approached for their release see what jobs they were fitted for and then persuade employers to give them a chance to make good.

Since everyone is interested in crime it was inevitable that sooner or later, with Ned there, the conversation should turn upon it. It was after dinner and we were sitting comfortably in the drawing-room with drinks in our hands.

'Had any interesting cases at the Scrubs lately, Ned?' I asked him.

'No, nothing much.'

He had a high, rasping voice and his laugh was a raucous cackle. He broke into it now.

'I went to see an old girl today who was a packet of fun. Her husband's a burglar. The police have known about him for years, but they've never been able to get him till just now. Before he did a job he and his wife concocted an alibi, and though he's been arrested three or four times and sent up for trial, the police have never been able to break it and he's always got off. Well, he was arrested again a little while ago, but he wasn't upset, the alibi he and his wife had made up was perfect and he expected to be acquitted as he'd been before. His wife went into the witness-box and to his utter amazement she didn't give the alibi and he was convicted. I went to see him. He wasn't so much worried at being in gaol as puzzled by his wife not having spoken up, and he asked me to go and see her and ask what the game was. Well I went, and d'you know what she said to me? She said: "Well, sir, it's like this; it was such a beautiful alibi I just couldn't bear to waste it." '

Of course we all laughed. The story-teller likes an appreciative audience, and Ned Preston was never disinclined to hold the floor. He narrated two or three more anecdotes. They tended to prove a point he was fond of making, that in what till we all got democratic in England were called the lower orders there was more passion, more romance, more disregard of consequences than could ever be found in the well-to-do and presumably educated classes, whom prudence has made timid and convention inhibited.

'Because the working man doesn't read much,' he said, 'because he has no great gift for expressing himself, you think he has no imagination. You're wrong. He's extravagantly imaginative. Because he's a great husky brute you think he has no nerves. You're wrong again. He's a bundle of nerves.'

Then he told us a story which I shall tell as best I can in my own words.

Fred Manson was a good-looking fellow, tall, well-made, with blue eyes, good features, and a friendly, agreeable smile, but what made him remarkable so that people turned round in the streets to stare at him was that he had a thick head of hair, with a great wave in it, of a deep rich red. It was really a great beauty. Perhaps it was this that gave him so sensual a look. His maleness was like a heady perfume. His eyebrows were thick, only a little lighter than his hair, and he was lucky enough not to have the ugly skin that so disfigures red-heads. His was a smooth olive. His eyes were bold, and when he smiled or laughed, which in the healthy vitality of his youth he did constantly, his expression was wonderfully alluring. He was twenty-two and he gave you the rather pleasant impression of just loving to be alive. It was inevitable that with such looks and above all with that troubling sexuality he should have success with women. He was charming, tender, and passionate, but immensely promiscuous. He was not exactly callous or brazen, he had a kindly nature, but somehow or other he made it quite clear to the objects of his passing fancy that all he wanted was a little bit of fun and it was impossible for him to remain faithful to anyone.

Fred was a postman. He worked in Brixton. It is a densely populated part of London, and has the curious reputation of harbouring more criminals than any other suburb because trams run to it from across the river all night long, so that when a man has done a job of housebreaking in the West End he can be sure of getting home without difficulty. Fred liked his job. Brixton is a district of innumerable streets lined with little houses inhabited, by the people who work in the neighbourhood and also by clerks, shop-assistants, skilled workers of one sort or another whose jobs take them every day across the river. He was strong and healthy and it was a pleasure to him to walk from street to street delivering the letters. Sometimes there would be a postal packet to hand in or a registered letter that had to be signed for, and then he would have the opportunity of seeing people. He was a sociable creature. It was never long before he was well known on whatever round he was assigned to. After a time his job was changed. His duty then was to go to the red pillar-boxes into which the letters were put, empty them, and take the contents to the main post-office of the district. His bag would be pretty heavy sometimes by the time he was through, but he was proud of his strength and the weight only made him laugh.

One day he was emptying a box in one of the better streets, a street of semi-detached houses, and had just closed his bag when a girl came running along.

'Postman,' she cried, 'take this letter, will you. I want it to go by this post most particularly.'

He gave her his good-natured smile.

'I never mind obliging a lady,' he said, putting down his bag and opening it.

'I wouldn't trouble you, only it's urgent,' she said as she handed him the letter she had in her hand.

'Who is it to – a feller?' he grinned.

'None of your business.'

'All right, be haughty. But I tell you this, he's no good. Don't you trust him.'

'You've got a nerve,' she said.

'So they tell me.'

He took off his cap and ran his hand through his mop of curling red hair. The sight of it made her gasp.

'Where d'you get your perm?' she asked with a giggle.

'I'll show you one of these days if you like.'

He was looking down at her with his amused eyes, and there was something about him that gave her a funny little feeling in the pit of her stomach.

'Well, I must be on my way,' he said. 'If I don't get on with the job pretty damn quick I don't know what'll happen to the country.'

'I'm not detaining you,' she said coolly.

'That's where you make a mistake,' he answered.

He gave her a look that made her heart beat nineteen to the dozen and she felt herself blushing all over. She turned away and ran back to the house. Fred noticed it was four doors away from the pillar-box. He had to pass it and as he did so he looked up. He saw the net curtains twitch and knew she was watching. He felt pleased with himself. During the next few days he looked at the house whenever he passed it, but never caught a glimpse of the girl. One afternoon he ran across her by chance just as he was entering the street in which she lived.

'Hullo,' he said, stopping.

'Hullo.'

She blushed scarlet.

'Haven't seen you about lately.'

'You haven't missed much.'

'That's what you think.'

She was prettier than he remembered, dark-haired, dark-eyed, rather tall, slight, with a good figure, a pale skin, and very white teeth.

'What about coming to the pictures with me one evening?'

'Taking a lot for granted, aren't you?'

'It pays,' he said with his impudent, charming grin.

She couldn't help laughing.

'Not with me, it doesn't.'

'Oh, come on. One's only young once.'

There was something so attractive in him that she couldn't bring herself to give him a saucy answer.

'I couldn't really. My people wouldn't like me going out with a fellow I don't know. You see, I'm the only one they have and they think a rare lot of me. Why, I don't even know your name.'

'Well, I can tell you, can't I? Fred. Fred Manson. Can't you say you're going to the pictures with a girl friend?'

She had never felt before what she was feeling then. She didn't know if it was pain or pleasure. She was strangely breathless.

'I suppose I could do that.'

They fixed the night, the time, and the place. Fred was waiting for her and they went in, but when the picture started and he put his arm round her waist, without a word, her eyes fixed on the screen, she quietly took it away. He took hold of her hand, but she withdrew it. He was surprised. That wasn't the way girls usually behaved. He didn't know what one went to the pictures for if it wasn't to have a bit of a cuddle. He walked home with her after the show. She told him her name. Grace Carter. Her father had a shop of his own in the Brixton Road, he was a draper and he had four assistants.

'He must be doing well,' said Fred.

'He doesn't complain.'

Gracie was a student at London University. When she got her degree she was going to be a school teacher.

'What d'you want to do that for when there's a good business waiting for you?'

'Pa doesn't want me to have anything to do with the shop – not after the education he's given me. He wants me to better myself, if you know what I mean.'

Her father had started life as an errand boy, then become a draper's assistant, and because he was hard-working, honest, and intelligent was now owner of a prosperous little business. Success had given him grand ideas for his only child. He didn't want her to have anything to do with trade. He hoped she'd marry a professional man perhaps, or at least someone in the City. Then he'd sell the business and retire, and Gracie would be quite the lady.

When they reached the corner of her street Gracie held out her hand.

'You'd better not come to the door,' she said.

'Aren't you going to kiss me good night?'

'I am not.'

'Why?'

'Because I don't want to.'

'You'll come to the pictures again, won't you?'

'I think I'd better not.'

'Oh, come on.'

There was such a warm urgency in his voice that she felt as though her knees would give way.

'Will you behave if I do?' He nodded. 'Promise?'

'Swop me bob.'

He scratched his head when he left her. Funny girl. He'd never met anyone quite like her. Superior, there was no doubt about that. There was something in her voice that got you. It was warm and soft. He tried to think what it was like. It was like as if the words kissed you. Sounded silly, that did, but that's just what it was like.

From then on they went to the pictures once or twice a week. After a while she allowed him to put his arm round her waist and to hold her hand, but she never let him go farther than that.

'Have you ever been kissed by a fellow?' he asked her once.

'No, I haven't,' she said simply. 'My ma's funny, she says you've got to keep a man's respect.'

'I'd give anything in the world just to kiss you, Gracie.'

'Don't be so silly.'

'Won't you let me just once?' She shook her head. 'Why not?'

'Because I like you too much,' she said hoarsely, and then walked quickly away from him.

It gave him quite a turn. He wanted her as he'd never wanted a woman before. What she'd said finished him. He'd been thinking of her a lot, and he'd looked forward to the evenings they spent together as he'd never looked forward to anything in his life. For the first time he was uncertain of himself. She was above him in every way, what with her father making money hand over fist and her education and everything, and him only a postman. They had made a date for the following Friday night and he was in a fever of anxiety lest she shouldn't come. He repeated to himself over and over again what she'd said: perhaps it meant that she'd made up her mind to drop him. When at last he saw her walking along the street he almost sobbed with relief. That evening he neither put his arm round her nor took her hand and when he walked her home he never said a word.

'You're very quiet tonight, Fred,' she said at last. 'What's the matter with you?'

He walked a few steps before he answered.

'I don't like to tell you.'

She stopped suddenly and looked up at him. There was terror on her face.

'Tell me whatever it is,' she said unsteadily.

'I'm gone, I can't help myself, I'm so stuck on you I can't see straight. I didn't know what it was to love like I love you.'

'Oh, is that all? You gave me such a fright. I thought you were going to say you were going to be married.'

'Me? Who d'you take me for? It's you I want to marry.'

'Well, what's to prevent you, silly?'

'Gracie! D'you mean it?'

He flung his arms round her and kissed her full on the mouth. She didn't resist. She returned his kiss and he felt in her a passion as eager as his own.

They arranged that Gracie should tell her parents that she was engaged to him and that on the Sunday he should come and be introduced to them. Since the shop stayed open late on Saturday and by the time Mr Carter got home he was tired out, it was not till after dinner on Sunday that Gracie broke her news. George Carter was a brisk, not very tall man, but sturdy, with a high colour, who with increasing prosperity had put on weight. He was more than rather bald and he had a bristle of grey moustache. Like many another employer who has risen from the working class he was a slave-driver and he got as much work out of his assistants for as little money as was possible. He had an eye for everything and he wouldn't put up with any nonsense, but he was reasonable and even kindly, so that they did not dislike him. Mrs Carter was a quiet, nice woman, with a pleasant face and the remains of good looks. They were both in the early fifties, for they had married late after 'walking out' for nearly ten years.

They were very much surprised when Gracie told them what she had to tell, but not displeased.

'You are a sly one,' said her father. 'Why, I never suspected for a minute you'd taken up with anyone. Well, I suppose it had to come sooner or later. What's his name?'

'Fred Manson.'

'A fellow you met at college?'

'No. You must have seen him about. He clears our pillar-box. He's a postman.'

'Oh, Gracie,' cried Mrs Carter, 'you can't mean it. You can't marry a common postman, not after all the education we've given you.'

For an instant Mr Carter was speechless. He got redder in the face than ever.

'Your ma's right, my girl,' he burst out now. 'You can't throw yourself away like that. Why, it's ridiculous.'

'I'm not throwing myself away. You wait till you see him.'

Mrs Carter began to cry.

'It's such a come-down. It's such a humiliation. I shall never be able to hold up my head again.'

'Oh, Ma, don't talk like that. He's a nice fellow and he's got a good job.'

'You don't understand,' she moaned.

'How d'you get to know him?' Mr Carter interrupted. 'What sort of a family's he got?'

'His pa drives one of the post-office vans,' Gracie answered defiantly.

'Working-class people.'

'Well, what of it? His pa's worked twenty-four years for the post-office and they think a lot of him.'

Mrs Carter was biting the corner of her handkerchief.

'Gracie, I want to tell you something. Before your pa and me got married I was in domestic service. He wouldn't ever let me tell you because he didn't want you to be ashamed of me. That's why we was engaged all those years. The lady I was with said she'd leave me something in her will if I stayed with her till she passed away.'

'It was that money that gave me my start,' Mr Carter broke in. 'Except for that I'd never have been where I am today. And I don't mind telling you your ma's the best wife a man ever had.'

'I never had a proper education,' Mrs Carter went on, 'but I always was ambitious. The proudest moment of my life was when your pa said we could afford a girl to help me and he said then: "The time'll come when you have a cook *and* a house-maid," and he's been as good as his word, and now you're going back to what I come from. I'd set my heart on your marrying a gentleman.'

She began crying again. Gracie loved her parents and couldn't bear to see them so distressed.

'I'm sorry, Ma, I knew it would be a disappointment to you, but I can't help it, I can't really. I love him so. I love him so terribly. I'm sure you'll like him when you see him. We're going for a walk on the Common this afternoon. Can't I bring him back to supper?'

Mrs Carter gave her husband a harassed look. He sighed.

'I don't like it and it's no good pretending I do, but I suppose we'd better have a look at him.'

Supper passed off better than might have been expected. Fred wasn't shy, and he talked to Gracie's parents as though he had known them all his life. If to be waited on by a maid, if to sup in a dining-room furnished in solid mahogany and afterwards to sit in a drawing-room that had a grand piano in it was new to him, he showed no embarrassment. After he had gone and they were alone in their bedroom Mr and Mrs Carter talked him over.

'He is handsome, you can't deny that,' she said.

'Handsome is as handsome does. D'you think he's after her money?'

'Well, he must know that you've got a tidy little bit tucked away somewhere, but he's in love with her all right.'

'Oh, what makes you think that?'

'Why, you've only got to see the way he looks at her.'

'Well, that's something at all events.'

In the end the Carters withdrew their opposition on the condition that the young things shouldn't marry until Gracie had taken her degree. That would give them a year, and at the back of their minds was the hope that by then she would have changed her mind. They saw a good deal of Fred after that. He spent every Sunday with them. Little by little they began quite to like him. He was so easy, so gay, so full of high spirits, and above all so obviously head over ears in love with Gracie, that Mrs Carter soon succumbed to his charm, and after a while even Mr Carter was prepared to admit that he didn't seem a bad fellow. Fred and Gracie were happy. She went to London every day to attend lectures and worked hard. They spent blissful evenings together. He gave her a very nice engagement ring and often took her out to dinner in the West End and to a play. On fine Sundays he drove her out into the country in a car that he said a friend had lent him. When she asked him if he could afford all the money he spent on her he laughed, and said a chap had given him a tip on an outsider and he'd made a packet. They talked interminably of the little flat they would have when they were married and the fun it would be to furnish it. They were more in love with one another than ever.

Then the blow fell. Fred was arrested for stealing money from the letters he collected. Many people, to save themselves the trouble of buying postal orders, put notes in their envelopes, and it wasn't difficult to tell that they were there. Fred went up for trial, pleaded guilty, and was sentenced to two years' hard labour. Gracie went to the trial. Up to the last moment she had hoped that he would be able to prove his innocence. It was a dreadful shock to her when he pleaded guilty. She was not allowed to see him. He went straight from the dock to the prison van. She went home and, locking herself up in her bedroom, threw herself on the bed and wept. When Mr Carter came back from the shop Gracie's mother went up to her room.

'Gracie, you're to come downstairs,' she said. 'Your father wants to speak to you.'

Gracie got up and went down. She did not trouble to dry her eyes.

'Seen the paper?' he said, holding out to her the *Evening News*. She didn't answer.

'Well, that's the end of that young man,' he went on harshly.

They too, Gracie's parents, had been shocked when Fred was arrested, but she was so distressed, she was so convinced that everything could be explained, that they hadn't had the heart to tell her that she must have nothing more to do with him. But now they felt it time to have things out with her.

'So that's where the money came from for those dinners and theatres. And the car. I thought it funny he should have a friend who'd lend him a car on Sundays when he'd be wanting it himself. He hired it, didn't he?'

'I suppose so,' she answered miserably. 'I just believed what he told me.'

'You've had a lucky escape, my girl, that's all I can say.'

'He only did it because he wanted to give me a good time. He didn't want me to think I couldn't have everything as nice when I was with him as what I've been used to at home.'

'You're not going to make excuses for him, I hope. He's a thief that's what he is.'

'I don't care,' she said sullenly.

'You don't care? What d'you mean by that?'

'Exactly what I say. I'm going to wait for him and the moment he comes out I'm going to marry him.'

Mrs Carter gave a gasp of horror.

'Gracie, you can't do a thing like that,' she cried. 'Think of the disgrace. And what about us? We've always held our heads high. He's a thief, and once a thief always a thief.'

'Don't go on calling him a thief,' Gracie shrieked, stamping her foot with rage. 'What he did he did just because he loved me. I don't care if he is a thief. I love him more than ever I loved him. You don't know what love is. You waited ten years to marry Pa just so as an old woman should leave you some money. D'you call that love?'

'You leave your ma out of this,' Mr Carter shouted. Then an idea occurred to him and he gave her a piercing glance. 'Have you *got* to marry the feller?'

Gracie blushed furiously.

'No. There's never been anything of that sort. And not through any fault of mine either. He loved me too much. He didn't want to do anything perhaps he'd regret afterwards.'

Often on summer evenings in the country when they'd been lying in a field in one another's arms, mouth to mouth, her desire had been as intense as his. She knew how much he wanted her and she was ready to give him what he asked. But when things got too desperate he'd suddenly jump up and say:

'Come on, let's walk.'

He'd drag her to her feet. She knew what was in his mind. He wanted to wait till they were married. His love had given him a delicacy of sentiment that he'd never known before. He couldn't

126

make it out himself, but he had a funny sort of feeling about her, he felt that if he had her before marriage it would spoil things. Because she guessed what was in his heart she loved him all the more.

'I don't know what's come over you,' moaned Mrs Carter. 'You was always such a good girl. You've never given us a day's uneasiness.'

'Stop it, Ma,' said Mr Carter violently. 'We've got to get this straight once and for all. You've got to give up this man, see? I've got me own position to think of and if you think I'm going to have a gaol-bird for a son-in-law you'd better think again. I've had enough of this nonsense. You've got to promise me that you'll have nothing more to do with the feller ever.'

'D'you think I'm going to give him up now? How often d'you want me to tell you I'm going to marry him the moment he gets out?'

'All right, then you can get out of my house and get out pretty damn quick. And stay out.'

'Pa!' cried Mrs Carter.

'Shut up.'

'I'll be glad to go,' said Gracie.

'Oh, will you? And how d'you think you're going to live?'

'I can work, can't I? I can get a job at Payne and Perkins. They'll be glad to have me.'

'Oh, Gracie, you couldn't go and work in a shop. You can't demean yourself like that,' said Mrs Carter.

'Will you shut up, Ma,' shouted Mr Carter, beside himself now with rage. 'Work, will you? You that's never done a stroke of work in your life except that tomfoolery at the college. Bright idea it was of your ma's to give you an education. Fat lot of good it'll be to you when you've got to stand on your feet for hours and got to be civil and pleasant to a lot of old trouts who just try and give you all the trouble they can just to show how superior they are. I bet you'll like it when you're bawled out by the manageress because you're not bright and snappy. All right, marry your gaol-bird. I suppose you know you'll have to keep him too. You don't think anyone's going to give him a job, do you, not with his record. Get out, get out, get out.'

He had worked himself up to such a pitch of fury that he sank panting into a chair. Mrs Carter, frightened, poured out a glass of water and gave him some to drink. Gracie slipped out of the room.

Next day, when her father had gone to work and her mother was out shopping, she left the house with such effects as she could get into a suit-case. Payne and Perkins was a large department store in the Brixton Road, and with her good appearance and pleasant manner she found no difficulty in getting taken on. She was put in the ladies' lingerie. For a few days she stayed at the Y.W.C.A. and then arranged to share a room with one of the girls who worked with her.

Ned Preston saw Fred in the evening of the day he went to gaol. He found him shattered, but only because of Gracie. He took his thieving very lightly.

'I had to do the right thing by her, didn't I? Her people, they didn't think I was good enough for her; I wanted to show them I was just as good as they were. When we went up to the West End I couldn't give her a sandwich and half of bitter in a pub, why, she's never been in a pub in her life, I *had* to take her to a restaurant. If people are such fools as to put money in letters, well, they're just asking for it.'

But he was frightened. He wasn't sure that Gracie would see it like that.

'I've got to know what she's going to do. If she chucks me now – well, it's the end of everything for me, see? I'll find some way of doing meself in, I swear to God I will.'

He told Ned the whole story of his love for Gracie.

'I could have had her over and over again if I'd wanted to. And I did want to and so did she. I knew that. But I respected her, see? She's not like other girls. She's one in a thousand, I tell you.'

He talked and talked. He stormed, he wept. From that confused torrent of words emerged one thing very clearly. A passionate, a frenzied love. Ned promised that he would see the girl.

'Tell her I love her, tell her that what I did I just did because I wanted her to have the best of everything, and tell her I just can't live without her.'

As soon as he could find time Ned Preston went to the Carters' house, but when he asked for Gracie the maid who opened the door told him that she didn't live there any more. Then he asked to see her mother.

'I'll go and see if she's in.'

He gave the maid his card, thinking the name of his club engraved in the corner would impress Mrs Carter enough to make her willing to see him. The maid left him at the door, but in a minute or two asked him to come in. He was shown into the stiff

and little-used sitting-room. Mrs Carter kept him waiting for some time and when she came in, holding his card in the tips of her fingers, he guessed it was because she had thought fit to change her dress. The black silk she wore was evidently a dress for occasions. He told her his connexion with Wormwood Scrubs and said that he had to do with a man named Frederick Manson. The moment he mentioned the name Mrs Carter assumed a hostile attitude.

'Don't speak to me of that man,' she cried. 'A thief, that's what he is. The trouble he's caused us. They ought to have given him five years, they ought.'

'I'm sorry he's caused you trouble,' said Ned mildly. 'Perhaps if you'd give me a few facts I might help to straighten things out.'

Ned Preston certainly had a way with him. Perhaps Mrs Carter was impressed because he was a gentleman. 'Class he is,' she probably said to herself. Anyhow it was not long before she was telling him the whole story. She grew upset as she told it and began to cry.

'And now she's gone and left us. Run away. I don't know how she could bring herself to do a thing like that. God knows, we love her. She's all we've got and we done everything in the world for her. Her pa never meant it when he told her to get out of the house. Only she was so obstinate. He got in a temper, he always was a quick-tempered man, he was just as upset as I was when we found she'd gone. And d'you know what's she's been and gone and done? Got herself a job at Payne and Perkins. Mr Carter can't abide them. Cutting prices all the time they are. Unfair competition, he calls it. And to think of our Gracie working with a lot of shop-girls – oh, it's so humiliating.'

Ned made a mental note of the store's name. He hadn't been at all sure of getting Gracie's address out of Mrs Carter.

'Have you seen her since she left you?' he asked.

'Of course I have. I knew they'd jump at her at Payne and Perkins, a superior girl like that, and I went there, and there she was, sure enough – in the ladies' lingerie. I waited outside till closing time and then I spoke to her. I asked her to come home. I said her pa was willing to let bygones be bygones. And d'you know what she said? She said she'd come home if we never said a word against Fred and if we was prepared to have her marry him as soon as ever he got out. Of course I had to tell her pa. I never saw him in such a state, I thought he was going to have a fit, he said he'd rather see her dead at his feet than married to that gaol-bird.'

Mrs Carter again burst into tears and as soon as he could Ned Preston left her. He went to the department store, up to the ladies' lingerie, and asked for Grace Carter. She was pointed out to him and he went up to her.

'Can I speak to you for a minute? I've come from Fred Manson.'

She went deathly white. For a moment it seemed that she could not utter a word.

'Follow me, please.'

She took him into a passage smelling of disinfectants which seemed to lead to the lavatories. They were alone. She stared at him anxiously.

'He sends you his love. He's worried about you. He's afraid you're awfully unhappy. What he wants to know really is if you're going to chuck him.'

'Me?' Her eyes filled with tears, but on her face was a look of ecstasy. 'Tell him that nothing matters to me as long as he loves me. Tell him I'd wait twenty years for him if I had to. Tell him I'm counting the days till he gets out so as we can get married.'

For fear of the manageress she couldn't stay away from her work for more than a minute or two. She gave Ned all the loving messages she could get into the time to give Fred Manson. Ned didn't get to the Scrubs till nearly six. The prisoners are allowed to put down their tools at five-thirty and Fred had just put his down. When Ned entered the cell he turned pale and sank on to the bed as though his anxiety was such that he didn't trust his legs. But when Ned told him his news he gave a gasp of relief. For a while he couldn't trust himself to speak.

'I knew you'd seen her the moment you came in. I smelt her.'

He sniffed as though the smell of her body were strong in his nostrils, and his face was as it were a mask of desire. His features on a sudden seemed strangely blurred.

'You know, it made me feel quite uncomfortable so that I had to look the other way,' said Ned Preston when he told us this, with a cackle of his shrill laughter. 'It was sex in its nakedness all right.'

Fred was an exemplary prisoner. He worked well, he gave no trouble. Ned suggested books for him to read and he took them out of the library, but that was about as far as he got.

'I can't get on well with them somehow,' he said. 'I start reading and then I begin thinking of Gracie. You know, when she kisses you ordinary-like – oh, it's so sweet, but when she kisses you really, my God, it's lovely.'

Fred was allowed to see Gracie once a month, but their meetings, with a glass screen between, under the eyes of a warder, were so painful that after several visits they agreed it would be better if she didn't come any more. A year passed. Owing to his good behaviour he could count on a remittance of his sentence and so would be free in another six months. Gracie had saved every penny she could out of her wages and now as the time approached for Fred's release she set about getting a home ready for him. She took two rooms in a house and furnished them on the hire purchase system. One room of course was to be their bedroom and the other the living-room and kitchen. There was an old-fashoned range in it and this she had taken out and replaced by a gas-stove. She wanted everything to be nice and new and clean and comfortable. She took pains to make the two little rooms bright and pretty. To do all this she had to go without all the barest necessities of existence and she grew thin and pale. Ned suspected that she was starving herself and when he went to see her took a box of chocolates or a cake so that she should have at least something to eat. He brought the prisoner news of what Gracie was doing and she made him promise to give him accurate accounts of every article she bought. He took fond, more than fond, passionate messages from one to the other. He was convinced that Fred would go straight in future and he got him a job as commissionaire from a firm that had a chain of restaurants in London. The wages were good and by calling taxis or fetching cars he would be able to make money on the side. He was to start work as soon as he came out of gaol. Gracie took the necessary steps so that they could get married at once. The eighteen months of Fred's imprisonment were drawing to an end. Gracie was in a fever of excitement.

It happened then that Ned Preston had one of his periodical bouts of illness and was unable to go to the prison for three weeks. It bothered him, for he didn't like to abandon his prisoners, so as soon as he could get out of bed he went to the Scrubs. The chief warder told him that Manson had been asking for him.

'I think you'd better go and see him. I don't know what's the matter with him. He's been acting rather funny since you've been away.'

It was just a fortnight before Fred was due to be released. Ned Preston went to his cell.

'Well, Fred, how are you?' he asked. 'Sorry I haven't been able to come and see you. I've been ill, and I haven't been able to see Gracie either. She must be all of a dither by now.'

'Well, I want you to go and see her.'

His manner was so surly that Ned was taken aback. It was unlike him to be anything but pleasant and civil.

'Of course I will.'

'I want you to tell her that I'm not going to marry her.'

Ned was so astounded that for a minute he could only stare blankly at Fred Manson.

'What on earth d'you mean?'

'Exactly what I say.'

'You can't let her down now. Her people have thrown her out. She's been working all this time to get a home ready for you. She's got the licence and everything.'

'I don't care. I'm not going to marry her.'

'But why, why, why?'

Ned was flabbergasted. Fred Manson was silent for a bit. His face was dark and sullen.

'I'll tell you. I've thought about her night and day for eighteen months and now I'm sick to death of her.'

When Ned Preston reached this point of his story our hostess and our fellow guests broke into loud laughter. He was plainly taken aback. There was some little talk after that and the party broke up. Ned and I, having to go in the same direction, walked along Piccadilly together. For a time we walked in silence.

'I noticed you didn't laugh with the others,' he said abruptly.

'I didn't think it funny.'

'What d'you make of it?'

'Well, I can see his point, you know. Imagination's an odd thing, it dries up; I suppose, thinking of her incessantly all th-t time he'd exhausted every emotion she could give him, and I think it was quite literally true, he'd just got sick to death of her. He'd squeezed the lemon dry and there was nothing to do but throw away the rind.'

'I didn't think it funny either. That's why I didn't tell them the rest of the story. I wouldn't accept it at first. I thought it was just hysteria or something. I went to see him two or three days running. I argued with him. I really did my damnedest. I thought if he'd only see her it would be all right, but he wouldn't even do that. He said he hated the sight of her. I couldn't move him. At last I had to go and tell her.'

We walked on a little longer in silence.

'I saw her in that beastly, stinking corridor. She saw at once there was something the matter and she went awfully white. She wasn't a girl to show much emotion. There was something gracious and rather noble about her face. Tranquil. Her lips quivered a bit when I told her and she didn't say anything for a minute. When she spoke it was quite calmly, as though – well, as though she'd just missed a bus and would have to wait for another. As though it was a nuisance, you know, but nothing to make a song and dance about. "There's nothing for me to do now but put my head in the gas-oven," she said.

'And she did.'

THE KITE

I KNOW this is an odd story. I don't understand it myself and if I set it down in black and white it is only with a faint hope that when I have written it I may get a clearer view of it, or rather with the hope that some reader, better acquainted with the complications of human nature than I am, may offer me an explanation that will make it comprehensible to me. Of course the first thing that occurs to me is that there is something Freudian about it. Now, I have read a good deal by Freud, and some books by his followers, and intending to write this story I have recently flipped through again the volume published by the Modern Library which contains his basic writings. It was something of a task, for he is a dull and verbose writer, and the acrimony with which he claims to have originated such and such a theory shows a vanity and a jealousy of others working in the same field which somewhat ill become the man of science. I believe, however, that he was a kindly and benign old party. As we know, there is often a great difference between the man and the writer. The writer may be bitter, harsh, and brutal, while the man may be so meek and mild that he wouldn't say boo to a goose. But that is neither here nor there. I found nothing in my re-reading of Freud's works that cast any light on the subject I had in mind. I can only relate the facts and leave it at that.

First of all I must make it plain that it is not my story and that I knew none of the persons with whom it is concerned. It was told me one evening by my friend Ned Preston, and he told it me because he didn't know how to deal with the circumstances and he thought, quite wrongly as it happened, that I might be able to give him some advice that would help him. In a previous story I have related what I thought the reader should know about Ned Preston, and so now I need only remind him that my friend was a prison visitor at Wormwood Scrubs. He took his duties very seriously and made the prisoners' troubles his own. We had been dining together at the Café Royal in that long, low room with its absurd and charming decoration which is all that remains of the old Café Royal that painters have loved to paint; and we were sitting over our coffee and liqueurs and, so far as Ned was concerned against his doctor's orders, smoking very long and very good Havanas.

'I've got a funny chap to deal with at the Scrubs just now,' he said, after a pause, 'and I'm blowed if I know how to deal with him.'

'What's he in for?' I asked.

'He left his wife and the court ordered him to pay so much a week in alimony and he's absolutely refused to pay it. I've argued with him till I was blue in the face. I've told him he's only cutting off his nose to spite his face. He says he'll stay in jail all his life rather than pay her a penny. I tell him he can't let her starve, and all he says is: "Why not?" He's perfectly well behaved, he's no trouble, he works well, he seems quite happy, he's just getting a lot of fun out of thinking what a devil of a time his wife is having.'

'What's he got against her?'

'She smashed his kite.'

'She did what?' I cried.

'Exactly that. She smashed his kite. He says he'll never forgive her for that till his dying day.'

'He must be crazy.'

'No, he isn't, he's a perfectly reasonable, quite intelligent, decent fellow.'

Herbert Sunbury was his name, and his mother, who was very refined, never allowed him to be called Herb or Bertie, but always Herbert, just as she never called her husband Sam but only Samuel. Mrs Sunbury's first name was Beatrice, and when she got engaged to Mr Sunbury and he ventured to call her Bea she put her foot down firmly.

'Beatrice I was christened,' she said, 'and Beatrice I always have been and always shall be, to you and to my nearest and dearest.'

She was a little woman, but strong, active, and wiry, with a sallow skin, sharp, regular features, and small, beady eyes. Her hair, suspiciously black for her age, was always very neat, and she wore it in the style of Queen Victoria's daughters, which she had adopted as soon as she was old enough to put it up and had never thought fit to change. The possibility that she did something to keep her hair its original colour was, if such was the case, her only concession to frivolity, for, far from using rouge or lipstick, she had never in her life so much as passed a powder-puff over her nose. She never wore anything but black dresses of good material, but made (by a little woman round the corner) regardless of fashion after a pattern that was both serviceable and decorous. Her only ornament was a thin gold chain from which hung a small gold cross.

Samuel Sunbury was a little man too. He was as thin and spare as his wife, but he had sandy hair, gone very thin now so that he had to wear it very long on one side and brushed it carefully over the large bald patch. He had pale blue eyes and his complexion was pasty. He was a clerk in a lawyer's office and had worked his way up from office boy to a respectable position. His employer called him Mr Sunbury and sometimes asked him to see an unimportant client. Every morning for twenty-four years Samuel Sunbury had taken the same train to the City, except of course on Sundays and during his fortnight's holiday at the seaside, and every evening he had taken the same train back to the suburb in which he lived. He was neat in his dress; he went to work in quiet grey trousers, a black coat, and a bowler hat, and when he came home he put on his slippers and a black coat which was too old and shiny to wear at the office; but on Sundays when he went to the chapel he and Mrs Sunbury attended he wore a morning coat with his bowler. Thus he showed his respect for the day of rest and at the same time registered a protest against the ungodly who went bicycling or lounged about the streets until the pubs opened. On principle the Sunburys were total abstainers, but on Sundays, when to make up for the frugal lunch, consisting of a scone and butter with a glass of milk, which Samuel had during the week, Beatrice gave him a good dinner of roast beef and Yorkshire pudding, for his health's sake she liked him to have a glass of beer. Since she wouldn't for the world have kept liquor in the house, he sneaked out with a jug after morning service and got a quart from the pub round the corner; but nothing would induce him to drink alone, so, just to be sociable-like, she had a glass too.

Herbert was the only child the Lord had vouchsafed to them, and this certainly through no precaution on their part. It just happened that way. They doted on him. He was a pretty baby and then a good-looking child. Mrs Sunbury brought him up carefully. She taught him to sit up at table and not put his elbows on it, and she taught him how to use his knife and fork like a little gentleman. She taught him to stretch out his little finger when he took his tea-cup to drink out of it and when he asked why, she said:

'Never you mind. That's how it's done. It shows you know what's what.'

In due course Herbert grew old enough to go to school. Mrs Sunbury was anxious because she had never let him play with the children in the street.

'Evil communications corrupt good manners,' she said. 'I always have kept myself to myself and I always shall keep myself to myself.'

Although they had lived in the same house ever since they were married she had taken care to keep her neighbours at a distance.

'You never know who people are in London,' she said. 'One thing leads to another, and before you know where you are you're mixed up with a lot of riff-raff and you can't get rid of them.'

She didn't like the idea of Herbert being thrown into contact with a lot of rough boys at the County Council school and she said to him:

'Now, Herbert, do what I do; keep yourself to yourself and don't have anything more to do with them than you can help.'

But Herbert got on very well at school. He was a good worker and far from stupid. His reports were excellent. It turned out that he had a good head for figures.

'If that's a fact,' said Samuel Sunbury, 'he'd better be an accountant. There's always a good job waiting for a good accountant.'

So it was settled there and then that this was what Herbert was to be. He grew tall.

'Why, Herbert,' said his mother, 'soon you'll be as tall as your dad.'

By the time he left school he was two inches taller, and by the time he stopped growing he was five feet ten.

'Just the right height,' said his mother. 'Not too tall and not too short.'

He was a nice-looking boy, with his mother's regular features and dark hair, but he had inherited his father's blue eyes, and though he was rather pale his skin was smooth and clear. Samuel Sunbury had got him into the office of the accountants who came twice a year to do the accounts of his own firm and by the time he was twenty-one he was able to bring back to his mother every week quite a nice little sum. She gave him back three half-crowns for his lunches and ten shillings for pocket money, and the rest she put in the Savings Bank for him against a rainy day.

When Mr and Mrs Sunbury went to bed on the night of Herbert's twenty-first birthday, and in passing I may say that Mrs Sunbury never went to bed, she retired, but Mr Sunbury, who was not quite so refined as his wife, always said: 'Me for Bedford,' – when then Mr and Mrs Sunbury went to bed, Mrs Sunbury said:

'Some people don't know how lucky they are; thank the Lord, I do. No one's ever had a better son than our Herbert. Hardly a day's illness in his life and he's never given me a moment's worry. It just shows if you bring up somebody right they'll be a credit to you. Fancy him being twenty-one, I can hardly believe it.'

'Yes, I suppose before we know where we are he'll be marrying and leaving us.'

'What should he want to do that for?' asked Mrs Sunbury with asperity. 'He's got a good home here, hasn't he? Don't you go putting silly ideas into his head, Samuel, or you and me'll have words and you know that's the last thing I want. Marry indeed! He's got more sense than that. He knows when he's well off. He's got sense, Herbert has.'

Mr Sunbury was silent. He had long ago learnt that it didn't get him anywhere with Beatrice to answer back.

'I don't hold with a man marrying till he knows his own mind,' she went on. 'And a man doesn't know his own mind till he's thirty or thirty-five.'

'He was pleased with his presents,' said Mr Sunbury to change the conversation.

'And so he ought to be,' said Mrs Sunbury still upset.

They had in fact been handsome. Mr Sunbury had given him a silver wrist-watch, with hands that you could see in the dark, and Mrs Sunbury had given him a kite. It wasn't by any means the first one she had given him. That was when he was seven years old, and it happened this way. There was a large common near where they lived and on Saturday afternoons when it was fine Mrs Sunbury took her husband and son for a walk there. She said it was good for Samuel to get a breath of fresh air after being cooped up in a stuffy office all the week. There were always a lot of people on the common, but Mrs Sunbury who liked to keep herself to herself kept out of their way as much as possible.

'Look at them kites, Mum,' said Herbert suddenly one day.

There was a fresh breeze blowing and a number of kites, small and large, were sailing through the air.

'*Those*, Herbert, not them,' said Mrs Sunbury.

'Would you like to go and see where they start, Herbert?' asked his father.

'Oh, yes, Dad.'

There was a slight elevation in the middle of the common and as they approached it they saw boys and girls and some men racing down it to give their kites a start and catch the wind. Sometimes they didn't and fell to the ground, but when they did they would rise, and as the owner unravelled his string go higher and higher. Herbert looked with ravishment.

'Mum, can I have a kite?' he cried.

He had already learnt that when he wanted anything it was better to ask his mother first.

'Whatever for?' she said.

'To fly it, Mum.'

'If you're so sharp you'll cut yourself,' she said.

Mr and Mrs Sunbury exchanged a smile over the little boy's head. Fancy him wanting a kite. Growing quite a little man he was.

'If you're a good boy and wash your teeth regular every morning without me telling you I shouldn't be surprised if Santa Claus didn't bring you a kite on Christmas Day.'

Christmas wasn't far off and Santa Claus brought Herbert his first kite. At the beginning he wasn't very clever at managing it, and Mr Sunbury had to run down the hill himself and start it for him. It was a very small kite, but when Herbert saw it swim through the air and felt the little tug it gave his hand he was thrilled; and then every Saturday afternoon, when his father got back from the City, he would pester his parents to hurry over to the common. He quickly learnt how to fly it, and Mr and Mrs Sunbury, their hearts swelling with pride, would watch him from the top of the knoll while he ran down and as the kite caught the breeze lengthened the cord in his hand.

It became a passion with Herbert, and as he grew older and bigger his mother bought him larger and larger kites. He grew very clever at gauging the winds and could do things with his kite you wouldn't have thought possible. There were other kite-flyers on the common, not only children, but men, and since nothing brings people together so naturally as a hobby they share it was not long before Mrs Sunbury, notwithstanding her exclusiveness, found that she, her Samuel, and her son were on speaking terms with all and sundry. They would compare their respective kites and boast of their accomplishments. Sometimes Herbert, a big boy of sixteen now, would challenge another kite-flyer. Then he would manoeuvre his kite to windward of the other fellow's, allow his cord to drift against his, and by a sudden jerk bring the enemy kite down. But long before this Mr Sunbury had succumbed to his son's enthusiasm and he would often ask to have a go himself. It must have been a funny sight to see him running down the hill in his striped trousers, black coat, and bowler hat. Mrs Sunbury would trot sedately behind him and when the kite was sailing free would take the cord from him and watch it as it soared. Saturday afternoon became the great day of the week for them, and when Mr Sunbury and Herbert left the house in the morning to catch their train to the City the first thing they did was to look up at the sky to see if it was flying weather. They liked best of all a gusty day, with uncertain winds, for that gave them the best chance to exercise their skill. All through the week, in the evenings, they talked about it. They were contemptuous of smaller kites than theirs and envious of bigger ones. They discussed the performances of other flyers as hotly, and as scornfully, as boxers or football-players discuss their rivals. Their ambition was to have a bigger kite than anyone else and a kite that would go higher. They had long given up a cord, for the kite they gave Herbert on his twenty-first birthday was seven feet high, and they used piano wire wound round a drum. But that did not satisfy Herbert. Somehow or other he had heard of a box-kite which had been invented by somebody, and the idea appealed to him at once. He thought he could devise something of the sort himself and since he could draw a little he set about making designs of it. He got a small model made and tried it out one afternoon, but it wasn't a success. He was a stubborn boy and he wasn't going to be beaten. Something was wrong, and it was up to him to put it right.

Then an unfortunate thing happened. Herbert began to go out after supper. Mrs Sunbury didn't like it much, but Mr Sunbury reasoned with her. After all, the boy was twenty-two, and it must be dull for him to stay home all the time. If he wanted to go for a walk or see a movie there was no great harm. Herbert had fallen in love. One Saturday evening, after they'd had a wonderful time on the common, while they were at supper, out of a clear sky he said suddenly:

'Mum, I've asked a young lady to come in to tea tomorrow. Is that all right?'

'You done what?' said Mrs Sunbury, for a moment forgetting her grammar.

'You heard, Mum.'

'And may I ask who she is and how you got to know her?'

'Her name's Bevan. Betty Bevan, and I met her first at the pictures one Saturday afternoon when it was raining. It was an accident-like. She was sitting next to me and she dropped her bag

140

and I picked it up and she said thank you and so naturally we got talking.'

'And d'you mean to tell me you fell for an old trick like that? Dropped her bag indeed!'

'You're making a mistake, Mum, she's a nice girl, she is really and well educated too.'

'And when did all this happen?'

'About three months ago.'

'Oh, you met her three months ago and you've asked her to come to tea tomorrow?'

'Well, I've seen her since of course. That first day, after the show, I asked her if she'd come to the pictures with me on the Tuesday evening, and she said she didn't know, perhaps she would and perhaps she wouldn't. But she came all right.'

'She would. I could have told you that.'

'And we've been going to the pictures about twice a week ever since.'

'So that's why you've taken to going out so often?'

'That's right. But, look, I don't want to force her on you, if you don't want her to come to tea I'll say you've got a headache and take her out.'

'Your mum will have her to tea all right,' said Mr Sunbury. 'Won't you, dear? It's only that your mum can't abide strangers. She never has liked them.'

'I keep myself to myself,' said Mrs Sunbury gloomily. 'What does she do?'

'She works in a typewriting office in the City and she lives at home, if you call it home; you see, her mum died and her dad married again, and they've got three kids and she doesn't get on with her step-ma. Nag, nag, nag all the time, she says.'

Mrs Sunbury arranged the tea very stylishly. She took the knick-knacks off a little table in the sitting room, which they never used, and put a tea-cloth on it. She got out the tea-service and the plated tea-kettle which they never used either, and she made scones, baked a cake, and cut thin bread-and-butter.

'I want her to see that we're not just nobody,' she told her Samuel.

Herbert went to fetch Miss Bevan, and Mr Sunbury intercepted them at the door in case Herbert should take her into the dining-room where normally they ate and sat. Herbert gave the tea-table a glance of surprise as he ushered the young woman into the sitting-room.

'This is Betty, Mum,' he said.

'Miss Bevan, I presume,' said Mrs Sunbury.

'That's right, but call me Betty, won't you?'

'Perhaps the acquaintance is a bit short for that,' said Mrs Sunbury with a gracious smile. 'Won't you sit down, Miss Bevan?'

Strangely enough, or perhaps not strangely at all, Betty Bevan looked very much as Mrs Sunbury must have looked at her age. She had the same sharp features and the same rather small beady eyes, but her lips were scarlet with paint, her cheeks lightly rouged, and her short black hair permanently waved. Mrs Sunbury took in all this at a glance, and she reckoned to a penny how much her smart rayon dress had cost, her extravagantly high-heeled shoes, and the saucy hat on her head. Her frock was very short and she showed a good deal of flesh-coloured stocking. Mrs Sunbury, disapproving of her make-up and of her apparel, took an instant dislike to her, but she had made up her mind to behave like a lady, and if she didn't know how to behave like a lady nobody did, so that at first things went well. She poured out tea and asked Herbert to give a cup to his lady friend.

'Ask Miss Bevan if she'll have some bread-and-butter or a scone, Samuel, my dear.'

'Have both,' said Samuel, handing round the two plates, in his coarse way. 'I like to see people eat hearty.'

Betty insecurely perched a piece of bread-and-butter and a scone on her saucer and Mrs Sunbury talked affably about the weather. She had the satisfaction of seeing that Betty was getting more and more ill-at-ease. Then she cut the cake and pressed a large piece on her guest. Betty took a bite at it and when she put it in her saucer it fell to the ground.

'Oh, I am sorry,' said the girl, as she picked it up.

'It doesn't matter at all, I'll cut you another piece,' said Mrs Sunbury.

'Oh, don't bother, I'm not particular. The floor's clean.'

'I hope so,' said Mrs Sunbury with an acid smile, 'but I wouldn't dream of letting you eat a piece of cake that's been on the floor. Bring it here, Herbert, and I'll give Miss Bevan some more.'

'I don't want any more, Mrs Sunbury, I don't really.'

'I'm sorry you don't like my cake. I made it specially for you.' She took a bit. 'It tastes all right to me.'

'It's not that, Mrs Sunbury, it's a beautiful cake, it's only that I'm not hungry.'

She refused to have more tea and Mrs Sunbury saw she was glad to get rid of the cup. 'I expect they have their meals in the kitchen,' she said to herself. Then Herbert lit a cigarette.

'Give us a fag, Herb,' said Betty. 'I'm simply dying for a smoke.'

Mrs Sunbury didn't approve of women smoking, but she only raised her eyebrows slightly.

'We prefer to call him Herbert, Miss Bevan,' she said.

Betty wasn't such a fool as not to see that Mrs Sunbury had been doing all she could to make her uncomfortable, and now she saw a chance to get back on her.

'I know,' she said. 'When he told me his name was Herbert I nearly burst out laughing. Fancy calling anyone Herbert. A scream, I call it.'

'I'm sorry you don't like the name my son was given at his baptism. I think it's a very nice name. But I suppose it all depends on what sort of class of people one is.'

Herbert stepped in to the rescue.

'At the office they call me Bertie, Mum.'

'Then all I can say is, they're a lot of very common men.'

Mrs Sunbury lapsed into a dignified silence and the conversation, such as it was, was maintained by Mr Sunbury and Herbert. It was not without satisfaction that Mrs Sunbury perceived that Betty was offended. She also perceived that the girl wanted to go, but didn't quite know how to manage it. She was determined not to help her. Finally Herbert took the matter into his own hands.

'Well, Betty, I think it's about time we were getting along,' he said. 'I'll walk back with you.'

'Must you go already?' said Mrs Sunbury, rising to her feet. 'It's been a pleasure, I'm sure.'

'Pretty little thing,' said Mr Sunbury tentatively after the young things had left.

'Pretty my foot. All that paint and powder. You take my word for it, she'd look very different with her face washed and without a perm. Common, that's what she is, common as dirt.'

An hour later Herbert came back. He was angry.

'Look here, Mum, what d'you mean by treating the poor girl like that? I was simply ashamed of you.'

'Don't talk to your mother like that, Herbert,' she flared up. 'You didn't ought to have brought a woman like that into my house. Common, she is, common as dirt.'

When Mrs Sunbury got angry not only did her grammar grow shaky, but she wasn't quite safe on her aitches. Herbert took no notice of what she said.

'She said she'd never been so insulted in her life. I had a rare job pacifying her.'

'Well, she's never coming here again, I tell you that straight.'

'That's what you think. I'm engaged to her, so put that in your pipe and smoke it.'

Mrs Sunbury gasped.

'You're not?'

'Yes, I am. I've been thinking about it for a long time, and then she was so upset tonight I felt sorry for her, so I popped the question and I had a rare job persuading her, I can tell you.'

'You fool,' screamed Mrs Sunbury. 'You fool.'

There was quite a scene then. Mrs Sunbury and her son went at it hammer and tongs, and when poor Samuel tried to intervene they both told him roughly to shut up. At last Herbert flung out of the room and out of the house and Mrs Sunbury burst into angry tears.

No reference was made next day to what had passed. Mrs Sunbury was frigidly polite to Herbert and he was sullen and silent. After supper he went out. On Saturday he told his father and mother that he was engaged that afternoon and wouldn't be able to come to the common with them.

'I dare say we shall be able to do without you,' said Mrs Sunbury grimly.

It was getting on to the time for their usual fortnight at the seaside. They always went to Herne Bay, because Mrs Sunbury said you had a nice class of people there, and for years they had taken the same lodgings. One evening, in as casual a way as he could, Herbert said:

'By the way, Mum, you'd better write and tell them I shan't be wanting my room this year. Betty and me are getting married and we're going to Southend for the honeymoon.'

For a moment there was dead silence in the room.

'Bit sudden-like, isn't it, Herbert?' said Mr Sunbury uneasily.

'Well, they're cutting down at Betty's office and she's out of a job, so we thought we'd better get married at once. We've taken two rooms in Dabney Street and we're furnishing out of my Savings Bank money.'

Mrs Sunbury didn't say a word. She went deathly pale and tears rolled down her thin cheeks.

'Oh, come on, Mum, don't take it so hard,' said Herbert. 'A fellow has to marry sometime. If Dad hadn't married you, I shouldn't be here now, should I?'

Mrs Sunbury brushed her tears away with an impatient hand.

'Your dad didn't marry me; I married 'im. I knew he was steady and respectable. I knew he'd make a good 'usband and father. I've never 'ad cause to regret it and no more 'as your dad. That's right, Samuel, isn't it?'

'Right as rain, Beatrice,' he said quickly.

'You know, you'll like Betty when you get to know her. She's a nice girl, she is really. I believe you'd find you had a lot in common. You must give her a chance, Mum.'

'She's never going to set foot in this house only over my dead body.'

'That's absurd, Mum. Why, everthing'll be just the same if you'll only be reasonable. I mean, we can go flying on Saturday afternoons same as we always did. Just this time I've been engaged it's been difficult. You see, she can't see what there is in kite-flying, but she'll come round to it, and after I'm married it'll be different, I mean I can come and fly with you and Dad; that stands to reason.'

'That's what you think. Well, let me tell you that if you marry that woman you're not going to fly my kite. I never gave it you, I bought it out of the housekeeping money, and it's mine see.'

'All right then, have it your own way. Betty says it's a kid's game anyway and I ought to be ashamed of myself, flying a kite at my age.'

He got up and once more stalked angrily out of the house. A fortnight later he was married. Mrs Sunbury refused to go to the wedding and wouldn't let Samuel go either. They went for their holiday and came back. They resumed their usual round. On Saturday afternoons they went to the common by themselves and flew their enormous kite. Mrs Sunbury never mentioned her son. She was determined not to forgive him. But Mr Sunbury used to meet him on the morning train they both took and they chatted a little when they managed to get into the same carriage. One morning Mr Sunbury looked up at the sky.

'Good flying weather today,' he said.

'D'you and Mum still fly?'

'What do you think? She's getting as clever as I am. You should see her with her skirts pinned up running down the hill.

I give you my word, I never knew she had it in her. Run? Why, she can run better than what I can.'

'Don't make me laugh, Dad!'

'I wonder you don't buy a kite of your own, Herbert. You've been always so keen on it.'

'I know I was. I did suggest it once, but you know what women are, Betty said: "Be your age," and oh, I don't know what all. I don't want a kid's kite, of course, and them big kites cost money. When we started to furnish Betty said it was cheaper in the long run to buy the best and so we went to one of them hire purchase places and what with paying them every month and the rent, well, I haven't got any more money than just what we can manage on. They say it doesn't cost any more to keep two than one, well, that's not my experience so far.'

'Isn't she working?'

'Well, no, she says after working for donkeys' years as you might say, now she's married she's going to take it easy, and of course someone's got to keep the place clean and do the cooking.'

So it went on for six months, and then one Saturday afternoon when the Sunburys were as usual on the common Mrs Sunbury said to her husband:

'Did you see what I saw, Samuel?'

'I saw Herbert, if that's what you mean. I didn't mention it because I thought it would only upset you.'

'Don't speak to him. Pretend you haven't see him.'

Herbert was standing among the idle lookers-on. He made no attempt to speak to his parents, but it did not escape Mrs Sunbury that he followed with all his eyes the flight of the big kite he had flown so often. It began to grow chilly and the Sunburys went home. Mrs Sunbury's face was brisk with malice.

'I wonder if he'll come next Saturday,' said Samuel.

'If I didn't think betting wrong I'd bet you sixpence he will, Samuel. I've been waiting for this all along.'

'You have?'

'I knew from the beginning he wouldn't be able to keep away from it.'

She was right. On the following Saturday and on every Saturday after that when the weather was fine Herbert turned up on the common. No intercourse passed. He just stood there for a while looking on and then strolled away. But after things had been going on like this for several weeks, the Sunburys had a surprise for him. They weren't flying the big kite which he was used to,

but a new one, a box-kite, a small one, on the model for which he
had made the designs himself. He saw it was creating a lot of interest among the other kite-flyers; they were standing round it
and Mrs Sunbury was talking volubly. The first time Samuel ran
down the hill with it the thing didn't rise, but flopped miserably
on the ground, and Herbert clenched his hands and ground his
teeth. He couldn't bear to see it fail. Mr Sunbury climbed up the
little hill again, and the second time the box-kite took the air.
There was a cheer among the bystanders. After a while Mr Sunbury pulled it down and walked back with it to the hill. Mrs
Sunbury went up to her son.

'Like to have a try, Herbert?'

He caught his breath.

'Yes, Mum, I should.'

'It's just a small one because they say you have to get the
knack of it. It's not like the old-fashioned sort. But we've got
specifications for a big one, and they say when you get to know
about it and the wind's right you can go up to two miles with it.'

Mr Sunbury joined them.

'Samuel, Herbert wants to try the kite.'

Mr Sunbury handed it to him, a pleased smile on his face, and
Herbert gave his mother his hat to hold. Then he raced down the
hill, the kite took the air beautifully, and as he watched it rise his
heart was filled with exultation. It was grand to see that little
black thing soaring so sweetly, but even as he watched it he
thought of the great big one they were having made. They'd never
be able to manage that. Two miles in the air, mum had said.
Whew!

'Why don't you come back and have a cup of tea, Herbert,'
said Mrs Sunbury, 'and we'll show you the designs for the new
one they want to build for us. Perhaps you could make some
suggestions.'

He hesitated. He'd told Betty he was just going for a walk to
stretch his legs, she didn't know he'd been coming to the common
every week, and she'd be waiting for him. But the temptation was
irresistible.

'I don't mind if I do,' he said.

After tea they looked at the specifications. The kite was huge,
with gadgets he had never seen before, and it would cost a lot of
money.

'You'll never be able to fly it by yourselves,' he said.

'We can try.'

'I suppose you wouldn't like me to help you just at first?' he asked uncertainly.

'Mightn't be a bad idea,' said Mrs Sunbury.

It was late when he got home, much later than he thought, and Betty was vexed.

'Wherever have you been, Herb? I thought you were dead. Supper's waiting and everything.'

'I met some fellows and got talking.'

She gave him a sharp look, but didn't answer. She sulked.

After supper he suggested they should go to a movie, but she refused.

'You go if you want to,' she said. 'I don't care to.'

On the following Saturday he went again to the common and again his mother let him fly the kite. They had ordered the new one and expected to get it in three weeks. Presently his mother said to him:

'Elizabeth is here.'

'Betty?'

'Spying on you.'

It gave him a nasty turn, but he put on a bold front.

'Let her spy. I don't care.'

But he was nervous and wouldn't go back to tea with his parents. He went straight home. Betty was waiting for him.

'So that's the fellows you got talking to. I've been suspicious for some time, you going for a walk on Saturday afternoons, and all of a sudden I tumbled to it. Flying a kite, you, a grown man. Contemptible I call it.'

'I don't care what you call it. I like it, and if you don't like it you can lump it.'

'I won't have it and I tell you that straight. I'm not going to have you make a fool of yourself.'

'I've flown a kite every Saturday afternoon ever since I was a kid, and I'm going to fly a kite as long as ever I want to.'

'It's that old bitch, she's just trying to get you away from me. I know her. If you were a man you'd never speak to her again, not after the way she's treated me.'

'I won't have you call her that. She's my mother and I've got the right to see her as often as ever I want to.'

The quarrel went on hour after hour. Betty screamed at him and Herbert shouted at her. They had had trifling disagreements before, because they were both obstinate, but this was the first serious row they had had. They didn't speak to one another on the Sunday, and during the rest of the week, though outwardly there was peace between them, their ill-feeling rankled. It happened that the next two Saturdays it poured with rain. Betty smiled to herself when she saw the downpour, but if Herbert was disappointed he gave no sign of it. The recollection of their quarrel grew dim. Living in two rooms as they did, sleeping in the same bed, it was inevitable that they should agree to forget their differences. Betty went out of her way to be nice to her Herb, and she thought that now she had given him a taste of her tongue and he knew she wasn't going to be put upon by anyone, he'd be reasonable. He was a good husband in his way, generous with his money and steady. Give her time and she'd manage him all right.

But after a fortnight of bad weather it cleared.

'Looks as if we're going to have good flying weather tomorrow,' said Mr Sunbury as they met on the platform to await their morning train. 'The new kite's come.'

'It has?'

'Your mum says of course we'd like you to come and help us with it, but no one's got the right to come between a man and his wife, and if you're afraid of Betty, her kicking up a rumpus, I mean, you'd better not come. There's a young fellow we've got to know on the common who's just mad about it, and he says he'll get it to fly if anybody can.'

Herbert was seized with a pang of jealousy.

'Don't you let any strangers touch our kite. I'll be there all right.'

'Well, you think it over, Herbert, and if you don't come we shall quite understand.'

'I'll come,' said Herbert.

So next day when he got back from the City he changed from his business clothes into slacks and an old coat. Betty came into the bedroom.

'What are you doing?'

'Changing,' he answered gaily. He was so excited, he couldn't keep the secret to himself. 'Their new kite's come and I'm going to fly it.'

'Oh no, you're not,' she said. 'I won't have it.'

'Don't be a fool, Betty. I'm going, I tell you, and if you don't like it you can do the other thing.'

'I'm not going to let you, so that's that.'

She shut the door and stood in front of it. Her eyes flashed and her jaw was set. She was a little thing and he was a tall strong man. He took hold of her two arms to push her out of the way, but she kicked him violently on the shin.

'D'you want me to give you a sock on the jaw?'

'If you go you don't come back,' she shouted.

He caught her up, though she struggled and kicked, threw her on to the bed and went out.

If the small box-kite had caused an excitement on the common it was nothing to what the new one caused. But it was difficult to manage, and though they ran and panted and other enthusiastic flyers helped them Herbert couldn't get it up.

'Never mind,' he said, 'we'll get the knack of it presently. The wind's not right today, that's all.'

He went back to tea with his father and mother and they talked it over just as they had talked in the old days. He delayed going because he didn't fancy the scene Betty would make him, but when Mrs Sunbury went into the kitchen to get supper ready he had to go home. Betty was reading the paper. She looked up.

'Your bag's packed,' she said.

'My what?'

'You heard what I said. I said if you went you needn't come back. I forgot about your things. Everything's packed. It's in the bedroom.'

He looked at her for a moment with surprise. She pretended to be reading again. He would have liked to give her a good hiding.

'All right, have it your own way,' he said.

He went into the bedroom. His clothes were packed in a suit-case, and there was a brown-paper parcel in which Betty had put whatever was left over. He took the bag in one hand, the parcel in the other, walked through the sitting-room without a word and out of the house. He walked to his mother's and rang the bell. She opened the door.

'I've come home, Mum,' he said.

'Have you, Herbert? Your room's ready for you. Put your things down and come in. We were just sitting down to supper.' They went into the dining-room. 'Samuel, Herbert's come home. Run out and get a quart of beer.'

Over supper and during the rest of the evening he told them the trouble he had had with Betty.

'Well, you're well out of it, Herbert,' said Mrs Sunbury when he had finished. 'I told you she was no wife for you. Common she is, common as dirt, and you who's always been brought up so nice.'

He found it good to sleep in his own bed, the bed he'd been used to all his life, and to come down to breakfast on the Sunday morning, unshaved and unwashed, and read the *News of the World*.

'We won't go to chapel this morning,' said Mrs Sunbury. 'It's been an upset to you, Herbert; we'll all take it easy today.'

During the week they talked a lot about the kite, but they also talked a lot about Betty. They discussed what she would do next.

'She'll try and get you back,' said Mrs Sunbury.

'A fat chance she's got of doing that,' said Herbert.

'You'll have to provide for her,' said his father.

'Why should he do that?' cried Mrs Sunbury. 'She trapped him into marrying her and now she's turned him out of the home he made for her.'

'I'll give her what's right as long as she leaves me alone.'

He was feeling more comfortable every day, in fact he was beginning to feel as if he'd never been away, he settled in like a dog in its own particular basket; it was nice having his mother to brush his clothes and mend his socks; she gave him the sort of things he'd always eaten and liked best; Betty was a scrappy sort of cook, it had been fun just at first, like picnicking, but it wasn't the sort of eating a man could get his teeth into, and he could never get over his mother's idea that fresh food was better than the stuff you bought in tins. He got sick of the sight of tinned salmon. Then it was nice to have space to move about in rather than be cooped up in two small rooms, one of which had to serve as a kitchen as well.

'I never made a bigger mistake in my life than when I left home, Mum,' he said to her once.

'I know that, Herbert, but you're back now and you've got no cause ever to leave it again.'

His salary was paid on Friday and in the evening when they had just finished supper the bell rang.

'That's her,' they said with one voice.

Herbert went pale. His mother gave him a glance.

'You leave it to me,' she said. 'I'll see her.'

She opened the door. Betty was standing on the threshold. She tried to push her way in, but Mrs Sunbury prevented her.

'I want to see Herb.'

'You can't. He's out.'

'No, he isn't. I watched him go in with his dad and he hasn't come out again.'

'Well, he doesn't want to see you, and if you start making a disturbance I'll call the police.'

'I want my week's money.'

'That's all you've ever wanted of him.' She took out her purse. 'There's thirty-five shillings for you.'

'Thirty-five shillings? The rent's twelve shillings a week.'

'That's all you're going to get. He's got to pay his board here, hasn't he?'

'And then there's the instalments on the furniture.'

'We'll see about that when the time comes. D'you want the money or don't you?'

Confused, unhappy, browbeaten, Betty stood irresolutely. Mrs Sunbury thrust the money in her hand and slammed the door in her face. She went back to the dining-room.

'I've settled her hash all right,' she said.

The bell rang again, it rang repeatedly, but they did not answer it, and presently it stopped. They guessed that Betty had gone away.

It was fine next day, with just the right velocity in the wind, and Herbert, after failing two or three times, found he had got the knack of flying the big box-kite. It soared into the air and up and up as he unreeled the wire.

'Why, it's a mile up if it's a yard,' he told his mother excitedly. He had never had such a thrill in his life.

Several weeks passed by. They concocted a letter for Herbert to write in which he told Betty that so long as she didn't molest him or members of his family she would receive a postal order for thirty-five shillings every Saturday morning and he would pay the instalments on the furniture as they came due. Mrs Sunbury had been much against this, but Mr Sunbury, for once at variance with her, and Herbert agreed that it was the right thing to do. Herbert by then had learnt the ways of the new kite and was able to do great things with it. He no longer bothered to have contests with the other kite-flyers. He was out of their class. Saturday afternoons were his moments of glory. He revelled in the admiration he aroused in the bystanders and enjoyed the envy he knew he excited in the less fortunate flyers. Then one evening when he was walking back from the station with his father Betty waylaid him.

'Hullo, Herb,' she said.

'Hullo.'

'I want to talk to my husband alone, Mr Sunbury.'

'There's nothing you've got to say to me that my dad can't hear,' said Herbert sullenly.

She hesitated. Mr Sunbury fidgeted. He didn't know whether to stay or go.

'All right, then,' she said. 'I want you to come back home, Herb. I didn't mean it that night when I packed your bag. I only did it to frighten you. I was in a temper. I'm sorry for what I did. It's all so silly, quarrelling about a kite.'

'Well, I'm not coming back, see. When you turned me out you did me the best turn you ever did me.'

Tears began to trickle down Betty's cheeks.

'But I love you, Herb. If you want to fly your silly old kite, you fly it, I don't care so long as you come back.'

'Thank you very much, but it's not good enough. I know when I'm well off and I've had enough of married life to last me a lifetime. Come on, Dad.'

They walked on quickly and Betty made no attempt to follow them. On the following Sunday they went to chapel and after dinner Herbert went to the coal-shed where he kept the kite to have a look at it. He just couldn't keep away from it. He doted on it. In a minute he rushed back, his face white, with a hatchet in his hand.

'She's smashed it up. She did it with this.'

The Sunburys gave a cry of consternation and hurried to the coal-shed. What Herbert had said was true. The kite, the new expensive kite, was in fragments. It had been savagely attacked with the hatchet, the woodwork was all in pieces, the reel was hacked to bits.

'She must have done it while we were at chapel. Watched us go out, that's what she did.'

'But how did she get in?' asked Mr Sunbury.

'I had two keys. When I came home I noticed one was missing, but I didn't think anything about it.'

'You can't be sure she did it, some of them fellows on the common have been very snooty, I wouldn't put it past them to have done this.'

'Well, we'll soon find out,' said Herbert. 'I'll go and ask her, and if she did it I'll kill her.'

His rage was so terrible that Mrs Sunbury was frightened.

'And get yourself hung for murder? No, Herbert, I won't let you go. Let your dad go, and when he comes back we'll decide what to do.'

'That's right, Herbert, let me go.'

They had a job to persuade him, but in the end Mr Sunbury went. And in half an hour he came back.

'She did it all right. She told me straight out. She's proud of it. I won't repeat her language, it fair startled me, but the long and short of it was she was jealous of the kite. She said Herbert loved the kite more than he loved her and so she smashed it up and if she had to do it again she'd do it again.'

'Lucky she didn't tell me that. I'd have wrung her neck even if I'd had to swing for it. Well, she never gets another penny out of me, that's all.'

'She'll sue you,' said his father.

'Let her.'

'The instalment on the furniture is due next week, Herbert,' said Mrs Sunbury quietly. 'In your place I wouldn't pay it.'

'Then they'll just take it away,' said Samuel, 'and all the money he's paid on it so far will be wasted.'

'Well, what of it?' she answered. 'He can afford it. He's rid of her for good and all and we've got him back and that's the chief thing.'

'I don't care twopence about the money,' said Herbert. 'I can see her face when they come to take the furniture away. It meant a lot to her, it did, and the piano, she set a rare store on that piano.'

So on the following Friday he did not send Betty her weekly money, and when she sent him on a letter from the furniture people to say that if he didn't pay the instalment due by such and such a date they would remove it, he wrote back and said he wasn't in a position to continue the payments and they could remove the furniture at their convenience. Betty took to waiting for him at the station, and when he wouldn't speak to her followed him down the street screaming curses at him. In the evenings she would come to the house and ring the bell till they thought they would go mad, and Mr and Mrs Sunbury had the greatest difficulty in preventing Herbert from going out and giving her a sound thrashing. Once she threw a stone and broke the sitting-room window. She wrote obscene and abusive postcards to him at his office. At last she went to the magistrate's court and complained that her husband had left her and wasn't providing for her support. Herbert received a summons. They both told their story and if the magistrate thought it a strange one he didn't say so. He tried to effect a reconciliation between them, but Herbert resolutely refused to go back to his wife. The magistrate ordered him to pay Betty twenty-five shillings a week. He said he wouldn't pay it.

'Then you'll go to prison,' said the magistrate. 'Next case.'

But Herbert meant what he said. On Betty's complaint he was brought once more before the magistrate, who asked him what reason he had for not obeying the order.

'I said I wouldn't pay her and I won't, not after she smashed my kite. And if you send me to prison I'll go to prison.'

The magistrate was stern with him this time.

'You're a very foolish young man,' he said. 'I'll give you a week to pay the arrears, and if I have any more nonsense from you you'll go to prison till you come to your senses.'

Herbert didn't pay, and that is how my friend Ned Preston came to know him and I heard the story.

'What d'you make of it?' asked Ned as he finished. 'You know, Betty isn't a bad girl. I've seen her several times, there's nothing wrong with her except her insane jealousy of Herbert's kite; and he isn't a fool by any means. In fact he's smarter than the average. What d'you suppose there is in kite-flying that makes the damned fool so mad about it?'

'I don't know,' I answered. I took my time to think. 'You see, I don't know a thing about flying a kite. Perhaps it gives him a sense of power as he watches it soaring towards the clouds and of mastery over the elements as he seems to bend the winds of heaven to his will. It may be that in some queer way he identifies himself with the kite flying so free and so high above him, and it's as it were an escape from the monotony of life. It may be that in some dim, confused way it represents an ideal of freedom and adventure. And you know, when a man once gets bitten with the virus of the ideal not all the King's doctors and not all the King's surgeons can rid him of it. But all this is very fanciful and I dare say it's just stuff and nonsense. I think you'd better put your problem before someone who knows a lot more about the psychology of the human animal than I do.'

A WOMAN OF FIFTY

My friend Wyman Holt is a professor of English Literature in one of the smaller universities of the Middle West, and hearing that I was speaking in a near-by city – near-by as distances go in the vastness of America – he wrote to ask me if I would come and give a talk to his class. He suggested that I should stay with him for a few days so that he could show me something of the surrounding country. I accepted the invitation, but told him that my engagements would prevent me from spending more than a couple of nights with him. He met me at the station, drove me to his house, and after we had had a drink we walked over to the campus. I was somewhat taken aback to find so many people in the hall in which I was to speak, for I had not expected more than twenty at the outside and I was not prepared to give a solemn lecture, but only an informal chat. I was more than a little intimidated to see a number of middle-aged and elderly persons, some of whom I suspected were members of the faculty, and I was afraid they would find what I had to say very superficial. However, there was nothing to do but to start and, after Wyman had introduced me to the audience in a manner that I very well knew I couldn't live up to, that is what I did. I said my say, I answered as best I could a number of questions, and then I retired with Wyman into a little room at the back of the stage from which I had spoken.

Several people came in. They said the usual kindly things to me that are said on these occasions, and I made the usual polite replies. I was thirsting for a drink. Then a woman came in and held out her hand to me.

'How very nice it is to see you again,' she said. 'It's years since we last met.'

To the best of my belief I'd never set eyes on her before. I forced a cordial smile to my tired, stiff lips, shook her proffered hand effusively and wondered who the devil she was. My professor must have seen from my face that I was trying to place her, for he said:

'Mrs Greene is married to a member of our faculty and she gives a course on the Renaissance and Italian literature.'

'Really,' I said. 'Interesting.'

I was no wiser than before.

'Has Wyman told you that you're dining with us tomorrow night?'

'I'm very glad,' I said.

'It's not a party. Only my husband, his brother, and my sister-in-law. I suppose Florence has changed a lot since then.'

'Florence?' I said to myself. 'Florence?'

That was evidently where I'd known her. She was a woman of about fifty with grey hair simply done and marcelled without exaggeration. She was a trifle too stout and she was dressed neatly enough, but without distinction, in a dress that I guessed had been bought ready-made at the local branch of a big store. She had rather large eyes of a pale blue and a poor complexion; she wore no rouge and had used a lipstick but sparingly. She seemed a nice creature. There was something maternal in her demeanour, something placid and fulfilled, which I found appealing. I supposed that I had run across her on one of my frequent visits to Florence and because it was perhaps the only time she had been there our meeting made more of an impression on her than on me. I must confess that my acquaintance with the wives of members of a faculty is very limited, but she was just the sort of person I should have expected the wife of a professor to be, and picturing her life, useful but uneventful, on scanty means, with its little social gatherings, its bickerings, its gossip, its busy dullness, I could easily imagine that her trip to Florence must linger with her as a thrilling and unforgettable experience.

On the way back to his house Wyman said to me:

'You'll like Jasper Greene. He's clever.'

'What's he a professor of?'

'He's not a professor; he's an instructor. A fine scholar. He's her second husband. She was married to an Italian before.'

'Oh?' That didn't chime in with my ideas at all. 'What was her name?'

'I haven't a notion. I don't believe it was a great success.' Wyman chuckled. 'That's only a deduction I draw from the fact that she hasn't a single thing in the house to suggest that she ever spent any time in Italy. I should have expected her to have at least a refectory table, an old chest or two, and an embroidered cope hanging on the wall.'

I laughed. I knew those rather dreary pieces that people buy when they're in Italy, the gilt wooden candlesticks, the Venetian glass mirrors, and the high-backed, comfortless chairs. They look well enough when you see them in the crowded shops of the dealers in antiques, but when you bring them to another country they're too often a sad disappointment. Even if they're genuine, which they seldom are, they look ill-at-ease and out of place.

'Laura has money,' Wyman went on. 'When they married she furnished the house from cellar to attic in Chicago. It's quite a show place; it's a little masterpiece of hideousness and vulgarity. I never go into the living-room without marvelling at the unerring taste with which she picked out exactly what you'd expect to find in the bridal suite of a second-class hotel in Atlantic City.'

To explain this irony I should state that Wyman's living-room was all chromium and glass, rough modern fabrics, with a boldly Cubist rug on the floor, and on the walls Picasso prints and drawings by Tchelicheff. However, he gave me a very good dinner. We spent the evening chatting pleasantly about things that mutually interested us and finished it with a couple of bottles of beer. I went to bed in a room of somewhat aggressive modernity. I read for a while and then putting out the light composed myself to sleep.

'Laura?' I said to myself. 'Laura what?'

I tried to think back. I thought of all the people I knew in Florence, hoping that by association I might recall when and where I had come in contact with Mrs Greene. Since I was going to dine with her I wanted to recall something that would prove that I had not forgotten her. People look upon it as a slight if you don't remember them. I suppose we all attach a sort of importance to ourselves, and it is humiliating to realize that we have left no impression at all upon the persons we have associated with. I dozed off, but before I fell into the blessedness of deep sleep, my subconscious, released from the effort of striving at recollection, I suppose, grew active and I was suddenly wide awake, for I remembered who Laura Greene was. It was no wonder that I had forgotten her, for it was twenty-five years since I had seen her, and then only haphazardly during a month I spent in Florence.

It was just after the First World War. She had been engaged to a man who was killed in it and she and her mother had managed to get over to France to see his grave. They were San Francisco people. After doing their sad errand they had come down to Italy and were spending the winter in Florence. At that time there was quite a large colony of English and Americans. I had some American friends, a Colonel Harding and his wife, colonel because he had occupied an important position in the Red Cross, who had a handsome villa in the Via Bolognese, and they asked me to stay with them. I spent most of my mornings sightseeing and met my friends at Doney's in the Via Tornabuoni round about noon to drink a cocktail. Doney's was the gathering-place of everybody one knew, Americans, English, and such of the Italians as frequented their society. There you heard all the gossip of the town. There was generally a lunch-party either at a restaurant or at one or other of the villas with their fine old gardens a mile or two from the centre of the city. I had been given a card to the Florence Club, and in the afternoon Charley Harding and I used to go there to play bridge or a dangerous game of poker with a pack of thirty-two cards. In the evening there would be a dinner-party with more bridge perhaps and often dancing. One met the same people all the time, but the group was large enough, the people sufficiently various, to prevent it from being tedious. Everyone was more or less interested in the arts, as was only right and proper in Florence, so that, idle as life seemed, it was not entirely frivolous.

Laura and her mother, Mrs Clayton, a widow, lived in one of the better boarding-houses. They appeared to be comfortably off. They had come to Florence with letters of introduction and soon made many friends. Laura's story appealed to the sympathies, and people were glad on that account to do what they could for the two women, but they were in themselves nice and quickly became liked for themselves. They were hospitable and gave frequent lunches at one or other of the restaurants where one ate macaroni and the inevitable scaloppini, and drank Chianti. Mrs Clayton was perhaps a little lost in this cosmopolitan society, where matters that were strange to her were seriously or gaily talked about, but Laura took to it as though it were her native element. She engaged an Italian woman to teach her the language and soon was reading the *Inferno* with her; she devoured books on the art of the Renaissance and on Florentine history, and I sometimes came across her, Baedeker in hand, at the Uffizzi or in some church studiously examining works of art.

She was twenty-four or twenty-five then and I was well over forty, so that though we often met we became cordially acquainted rather than intimate. She was by no means beautiful, but she was comely in rather an unusual way; she had an oval face with bright blue eyes and very dark hair which she wore very simply, parted in the middle, drawn over her ears and tied in a chignon low on the nape of her neck. She had a good skin and a naturally high colour; her features were good without being remarkable, and her teeth were even, small, and white; but her chief asset was her easy grace of movement, and I was not surprised when they told me that she danced 'divinely'. Her figure was very good, somewhat fuller than was the fashion of the moment; and I think what made her attractive was the odd mingling in her appearance of the Madonna in an altar-piece by one of the later Italian painters and a suggestion of sensuality. It certainly made her very alluring to the Italians who gathered at Doney's in the morning or were occasionally invited to lunch or dinner in the American or English villas. She was evidently accustomed to dealing with amorous young men, for though she was charming, gracious, and friendly with them she kept them at their distance. She quickly discovered that they were all looking for an American heiress who would restore the family fortunes, and with a demure amusement which I found admirable made them delicately understand that she was far from rich. They sighed a little and turned their attentions at Doney's, which was their happy hunting-ground, to more likely objects. They continued to dance with her, and to keep their hand in flirted with her, but their aspirations ceased to be matrimonial.

But there was one young man who persisted. I knew him slightly because he was one of the regular poker-players at the club. I played occasionally. It was impossible to win and the disgruntled foreigners used sometimes to say that the Italians ganged up on us, but it may be only that they knew the particular game they played better than we did. Laura's admirer, Tito di San Pietro, was a bold and even reckless player and would often lose sums he could ill afford. (That was not his real name, but I call him that since his own is famous in Florentine history.) He was a good-looking youth, neither short nor tall, with fine black eyes, thick black hair brushed back from his forehead and shining with oil, an olive skin, and features of classical regularity. He was poor and he had some vague occupation, which did not seem to interfere with his amusements, but he was always beautifully dressed. No one quite knew where he lived, in a furnished room perhaps or in the attic of some relation; and all that remained of his ancestors' great possessions was a Cinquecento villa about thirty miles from the city. I never saw it, but I was told that it was of amazing beauty, with a great neglected garden of cypresses and live oaks, overgrown borders of box, terraces, artificial grottoes, and crumbling statues. His widowed father, the count, lived there alone and subsisted on the wine he made from the vines of the small property he still owned and the oil from his olive trees. He seldom came to Florence, so I never met him, but Charley Harding knew him fairly well.

'He's a perfect specimen of the Tuscan nobleman of the old school,' he said. 'He was in the diplomatic service in his youth and he knows the world. He has beautiful manners and such an air, you almost feel he's doing you a favour when he says how d'you do to you. He's a brilliant talker. Of course he hasn't a penny, he squandered the little he inherited on gambling and women, but he bears his poverty with great dignity. He acts as though money were something beneath his notice.'

'What sort of age is he?' I asked.

'Fifty, I should say, but he's still the handsomest man I've ever seen in my life.'

'Oh?'

'You describe him, Bessie. When he first came here he made a pass at Bessie. I've never been quite sure how far it went.'

'Don't be a fool, Charley,' Mrs Harding laughed.

She gave him the sort of look a woman gives her husband when she has been married to him many years and is quite satisfied with him.

'He's very attractive to women and he knows it,' she said. 'When he talks to you he gives you the impression that you're the only woman in the world and of course it's flattering. But it's only a game and a woman would have to be a perfect fool to take him seriously. He *is* very handsome. Tall and spare and he holds himself well. He has great dark liquid eyes, like the boy's; his hair is snow-white, but very thick still, and the contrast with his bronzed, young face is really breath-taking. He has a ravaged, rather battered look, but at the same time a look of such distinction, it's really quite incredibly romantic.'

'He also has his great dark liquid eyes on the main chance,' said Charley Harding dryly. 'And he'll never let Tito marry a girl who has no more money than Laura.'

'She has about five thousand dollars a year of her own,' said Bessie. 'And she'll get that much more when her mother dies.'

'Her mother can live for another thirty years, and five thousand a year won't go far to keep a husband, a father, and two or three children, and restore a ruined villa with practically not a stick of furniture in it.'

'I think the boy's desperately in love with her.'

'How old is he?' I asked.

'Twenty-six.'

A few days after this Charley, on coming back to lunch, since for once we were lunching by ourselves, told me that he had run across Mrs Clayton in the Via Tornabuoni and she had said that she and Laura were driving out that afternoon with Tito to meet his father and see the villa.

'What d'you suppose that means?' asked Bessie.

'My guess is that Tito is taking Laura to be inspected by his old man, and if he approves he's going to ask her to marry him.'

'And will he approve?'

'Not on your life.'

But Charley was wrong. After the two women had been shown over the house they were taken for a walk round the garden. Without exactly knowing how it had happened Mrs Clayton found herself alone in an alley with the old count. She spoke no Italian, but he had been an attaché in London and his English was tolerable.

'Your daughter is charming, Mrs Clayton,' he said. 'I am not surprised that my Tito has fallen in love with her.'

Mrs Clayton was no fool and it may be that she too had guessed why the young man had asked them to go and see the ancestral villa.

'Young Italians are very impressionable. Laura is sensible enough not to take their attention too seriously.'

'I was hoping she was not quite indifferent to the boy.'

'I have no reason to believe that she likes him any more than any other of the young men who dance with her,' Mrs Clayton answered somewhat coldly. 'I think I should tell you at once that my daughter has a very moderate income and she will have no more till I die.'

'I will be frank with you. I have nothing in the world but this house and the few acres that surround it. My son could not afford to marry a penniless girl, but he is not a fortune-hunter and he loves your daughter.'

The count had not only the grand manner, but a great deal of charm and Mrs Clayton was not insensible to it. She softened a little.

'All that is neither here nor there. We don't arrange our children's marriages in America. If Tito wants to marry her, let him ask her, and if she's prepared to marry him she'll presumably say so.'

'Unless I am greatly mistaken that is just what he is doing now. I hope with all my heart that he will be successful.'

They strolled on and presently saw walking towards them the two young people hand in hand. It was not difficult to guess what had passed. Tito kissed Mrs Clayton's hand and his father on both cheeks.

'Mrs Clayton, Papa, Laura has consented to be my wife.'

The engagement made something of a stir in Florentine society and a number of parties were given for the young couple. It was quite evident that Tito was very much in love, but less so that Laura was. He was good-looking, adoring, high-spirited, and gay; it was likely enough that she loved him; but she was a girl who did not display emotion and she remained what she had always been, somewhat placid, amiable, serious but friendly, and easy to talk to. I wondered to what extent she had been influenced to accept Tito's offer by his great name, with its historical associations, and the sight of that beautiful house with its lovely view and the romantic garden.

'Anyhow there's no doubt about its being a love match on his side,' said Bessie Harding, when we were talking it over. 'Mrs Clayton tells me that neither Tito nor his father has shown any desire to know how much Laura has.'

'I'd bet a million dollars that they know to the last cent what she's got and they've calculated exactly how much it comes to in *lire*,' said Harding with a grunt.

'You're a beastly old man, darling,' she answered.

He gave another grunt.

Shortly after that I left Florence. The marriage took place from the Hardings' house and a vast crowd came to it, ate their food and drank their champagne. Tito and his wife took an apartment on the Lungarno and the old count returned to his lonely villa in the hills. I did not go to Florence again for three years and then only for a week. I was staying once more with the Hardings. I asked about my old friends and then remembered Laura and her mother.

'Mrs Clayton went back to San Francisco,' said Bessie, 'and Laura and Tito live at the villa with the count. They're very happy.'

'Any babies?'

'No.'

'Go on,' said Harding.

Bessie gave her husband a look.

'I cannot imagine why I've lived thirty years with a man I dislike so much,' she said. 'They gave up the apartment on the

Lungarno. Laura spent a good deal of money doing things to the villa, there wasn't a bathroom in it, she put in central heating, and she had to buy a lot of furniture to make it habitable, and then Tito lost a small fortune playing poker and poor Laura had to pay up.'

'Hadn't he got a job?'

'It didn't amount to anything and it came to an end.'

'What Bessie means by that is that he was fired,' Harding put in.

'Well, to cut a long story short, they thought it would be more economical to live at the villa and Laura had the idea that it would keep Tito out of mischief. She loves the garden and she's made it lovely. Tito simply worships her and the old count's taken quite a fancy to her. So really it's all turned out very well.'

'It may interest you to know that Tito was in last Thursday,' said Harding. 'He played like a madman and I don't know how much he lost.'

'Oh, Charley. He promised Laura he'd never play again.'

'As if a gambler ever kept a promise like that. It'll be like last time. He'll burst into tears and say he loves her and it's a debt of honour and unless he can get the money he'll blow his brains out. And Laura will pay as she paid before.'

'He's weak, poor dear, but that's his only fault. Unlike most Italian husbands he's absolutely faithful to her and he's kindness itself.' She looked at Harding with a sort of humorous grimness. 'I've yet to find a husband who was perfect.'

'You'd better start looking around pretty soon, dear, or it'll be too late,' he retorted with a grin.

I left the Hardings and returned to London. Charley Harding and I corresponded in a desultory sort of way, and about a year later I got a letter from him. He told me as usual what he had been doing in the interval, and mentioned that he had been to Montecatini for the baths and had gone with Bessie to vis't friends in Rome; he spoke of the various people I knew in Florence, So-and-so had just bought a Bellini and Mrs Such-and-such had gone to America to divorce her husband. Then he went on: 'I suppose you've heard about the San Pietros. It's shaken us all and we can talk of nothing else. Laura's terribly upset, poor thing, and she's going to have a baby. The police keep on questioning her and that doesn't make it any easier for her. Of course we brought her to stay here. Tito comes up for trial in another month.'

I hadn't the faintest notion what all this was about. So I wrote at once to Harding asking him what it meant. He answered with a long letter. What he had to tell me was terrible. I will relate the bare and brutal facts as shortly as I can. I learned them partly from Harding's letter and partly from what he and Bessie told me when two years later I was with them once more.

The count and Laura took to one another at once and Tito was pleased to see how quickly they had formed an affectionate friendship, for he was as devoted to his father as he was in love with his wife. He was glad that the count began to come more often to Florence than he had been used to. They had a spare room in the apartment and on occasion he spent two or three nights with them. He and Laura would go bargain-hunting in the antique shops and buy old pieces to put in the villa. He had tact and knowledge and little by little the house, with its spacious rooms and marble floors, lost its forlorn air and became a friendly place to live in. Laura had a passion for gardening and she and the count spent long hours together planning and then supervising the workmen who were restoring the gardens to their ancient, rather stately, beauty.

Laura made light of it when Tito's financial difficulties forced them to give up the apartment in Florence; she had had enough of Florentine society by then and was not displeased to live altogether in the grand house that had belonged to his ancestors. Tito liked city life and the prospect dismayed him, but he could not complain since it was his own folly that had made it necessary for them to cut down expenses. They still had the car and he amused himself by taking long drives while his father and Laura were busy, and if they knew that now and then he went into Florence to have a flutter at the club they shut their eyes to it. So a year passed. Then, he hardly knew why, he was seized with a vague misgiving. He couldn't put his finger on anything; he had an uneasy feeling that perhaps Laura didn't care for him so much as she had at first; sometimes it seemed to him that his father was inclined to be impatient with him; they appeared to have a great deal to say to one another, but he got the impression that he was being edged out of their conversation, as though he were a child who was expected to sit still and not interrupt while his elders talked of things over his head; he had a notion that often his presence was unwelcome to them and that they were more at their ease when he was not there. He knew his father, and his reputation, but the suspicion that arose in him was so horrible that he refused to entertain it. And yet sometimes he caught a look passing between them that disconcerted him, there was a tender possessiveness in his father's eyes, a sensual complacency in Laura's, which, if he had seen it in others, would have convinced him that they were lovers. But he couldn't, he wouldn't, believe that there was anything between them. The count couldn't help making love to a woman and it was likely enough that Laura felt his extraordinary fascination, but it was shameful to suppose for a moment that they, these two people he loved, had formed a criminal, almost an incestuous, connexion. He was sure that Laura had no idea that there was anything more in her feeling than the natural affection of a young, happily married woman for her father-in-law. Notwithstanding he thought it better that she should not remain in everyday contact with his father, and one day he suggested that they should go back to live in Florence. Laura and the count were astonished that he should propose such a thing and would not hear of it. Laura said that, having spent so much money on the villa, she couldn't afford to set up another establishment, and the count that it was absurd to leave it, now that Laura had made it so comfortable, to live in a wretched apartment in the city. An argument started and Tito got rather excited. He took some remark of Laura's to mean that if she lived at the villa it was to keep him out of temptation. This reference to his losses at the poker-table angered him.

'You always throw your money in my face,' he said passionately. 'If I'd wanted to marry money I'd have had the sense to marry someone who had a great deal more than you.'

Laura went very pale and glanced at the count.

'You have no right to speak to Laura like that,' he said. 'You are an ill-mannered oaf.'

'I shall speak to my wife exactly as I choose.'

'You are mistaken. So long as you are in my house you will treat her with the respect which is her right and your duty.'

'When I want lessons in behaviour from you, Father, I will let you know.'

'You are very impertinent, Tito. You will kindly leave the room.'

He looked very stern and dignified, and Tito, furious and yet slightly intimidated, leapt to his feet and stalked out slamming the door behind him. He took the car and drove in to Florence. He won quite a lot of money that day (lucky at cards, unlucky in love) and to celebrate his winnings got more than a little drunk. He did not go back to the villa till the following morning. Laura was as friendly and placid as ever, but his father was somewhat cool. No reference was made to the scene. But from then on things went from bad to worse. Tito was sullen and moody, the count critical, and on occasion sharp words passed between them. Laura did not interfere, but Tito gained the impression that after a dispute that had been more than acrimonious Laura interceded with his father, for the count thenceforward, refusing to be annoyed, began to treat him with the tolerant patience with which you would treat a wayward child. He convinced himself that they were acting in concert and his suspicions grew formidable. They even increased when Laura in her good-natured way, saying that it must be very dull for him to remain so much in the country, encouraged him to go more often to Florence to see his friends.

He jumped to the conclusion that she said this only to be rid of him. He began to watch them. He would enter suddenly a room in which he knew they were, expecting to catch them in a compromising position, or silently follow them to a secluded part of the garden. They were chatting unconcernedly of trivial things. Laura greeted him with a pleasant smile. He could put his finger on nothing to confirm his torturing suspicions. He started to drink. He grew nervous and irritable. He had no proof, no proof whatever, that there was anything between them, and yet in his bones he was certain that they were grossly, shockingly deceiving him. He brooded till he felt he was going mad. A dark aching fire within him consumed his being. On one of his visits to Florence he bought a pistol. He made up his mind that if he could have proof of what in his heart he was certain of, he would kill them both.

I don't know what brought on the final catastrophe. All that came out at the trial was that, driven beyond endurance, Tito had gone one night to his father's room to have it out with him. His father mocked and laughed at him. They had a furious quarrel and Tito took out his pistol and shot the count dead. Then he collapsed and fell, weeping hysterically, on his father's body; the repeated shots brought Laura and the servants rushing in. He jumped up and grabbed the pistol, to shoot himself he said afterwards, but he hesitated or they were too quick for him, and they snatched it out of his hand. The police were sent for. He spent most of his time in prison weeping; he would not eat and had to be forcibly fed; he told the examining magistrate that he had killed his father because he was his wife's lover. Laura, examined and examined again, swore that there had never been anything between the count and herself but a natural affection. The murder filled the Florentine public with horror. The Italians were convinced of her guilt, but her friends, English and American, felt that she was incapable of the crime of which she was accused. They went about saying that Tito was neurotic and insanely jealous and in his stupid way had mistaken her American freedom of behaviour for a criminal passion. On the face of it Tito's charge was absurd. Carlo di San Pietro was nearly thirty years older than she, an elderly man with white hair; who could suppose that there would have been anything between her and her father-in-law, when her husband was young, handsome, and in love with her?

It was in Harding's presence that she saw the examining magistrate and the lawyers who had been engaged to defend Tito. They had decided to plead insanity. Experts for the defence examined him and decided that he was insane, experts for the prosecution examined him and decided that he was sane. The fact that he had bought a pistol three months before he committed the dreadful crime went to prove that it was premeditated. It was discovered that he was deeply in debt and his creditors were pressing him; the only means he had of settling with them was by selling the villa, and his father's death put him in possession of it. There is no capital punishment in Italy, but murder with premeditation is punished by solitary confinement for life. On the approach of the trial the lawyers came to Laura and told her that the only way in which Tito could be saved from this was for her to admit in court that the count had been her lover. Laura went very pale. Harding protested violently. He said they had no right to ask her to perjure herself and ruin her reputation to save that shiftless, drunken gambler whom she had been so unfortunate as to marry. Laura remained silent for a while.

'Very well,' she said at last, 'if that's the only way to save him I'll do it.'

Harding tried to dissuade her, but she was decided.

'I should never have a moment's peace if I knew that Tito had to spend the rest of his life alone in a prison cell.'

And that is what happened. The trial opened. She was called and under oath stated that for more than a year her father-in-law had been her lover. Tito was declared insane and sent to an asylum. Laura wanted to leave Florence at once, but in Italy the preliminaries to a trial are endless and by then she was near her time. The Hardings insisted on her remaining with them till she was confined. She had a child, a boy, but it only lived twenty-four hours. Her plan was to go back to San Francisco and live with her mother till she could find a job, for Tito's extravagance, the money she had spent on the villa, and then the cost of the trial had seriously impoverished her.

It was Harding who told me most of this; but one day when he was at the club and I was having a cup of tea with Bessie and we were again talking over these tragic happenings she said to me:

'You know, Charley hasn't told you the whole story because he doesn't know it. I never told him. Men are funny in some ways; they're much more easily shocked than women.'

I raised my eyebrows, but said nothing.

'Just before Laura went away we had a talk. She was very low and I thought she was grieving over the loss of her baby. I wanted to say something to help her. "You mustn't take the baby's death too hardly," I said. "As things are, perhaps it's better it died." "Why?" she said. "Think what the poor little thing's future would have been with a murderer for his father." She looked at me for a moment in that strange quiet way of hers. And then what d'you think she said?'

'I haven't a notion,' said I.

'She said: "What makes you think his father was a murderer?"

I felt myself grow as red as a turkey-cock. I could hardly believe my ears. "Laura, what *do* you mean?" I said. "You were in court," she said. "You heard me say Carlo was my lover." '

Bessie Harding stared at me as she must have stared at Laura.

'What did you say then?' I asked.

'What was there for me to say? I said nothing. I wasn't so much horrified, I was bewildered. Laura looked at me and, believe it or not, I'm convinced there was a twinkle in her eyes. I felt a perfect fool.'

'Poor Bessie,' I smiled.

Poor Bessie, I repeated to myself now as I thought of this strange story. She and Charley were long since dead and by their death I had lost good friends. I went to sleep then, and next day Wyman Holt took me for a long drive.

We were to dine with the Greenes at seven and we reached their house on the dot. Now that I had remembered who Laura was I was filled with an immense curiosity to see her again. Wyman had exaggerated nothing. The living-room into which we went was the quintessence of commonplace. It was comfortable enough, but there was not a trace of personality in it. It might have been furnished *en bloc* by a mail-order house. It had the bleakness of a government office. I was introduced first to my host Jasper Greene and then to his brother Emery and to his brother's wife Fanny. Jasper Greene was a large, plump man with a moon face and a shock of black, coarse, unkempt hair. He wore large cellulose-rimmed spectacles. I was staggered by his youth. He could not have been much over thirty and was therefore nearly twenty years younger than Laura. His brother, Emery, a composer and teacher in a New York school of music, might have been seven or eight and twenty. His wife, a pretty little thing, was an actress for the moment out of a job. Jasper Green mixed us some very adequate cocktails but for a trifle too much vermouth, and we sat down to dinner. The conversation was gay and even boisterous. Jasper and his brother were loud-voiced and all three of them, Jasper, Emery, and Emery's wife, were loquacious talkers. They chaffed one another, they joked and laughed; they discussed art, literature, music, and the theatre. Wyman and I joined in when we had a chance, which was not often; Laura did not try to. She sat at the head of the table, serene, with an amused, indulgent smile on her lips as she listened to their scatter-brained nonsense; it was not stupid nonsense, mind you, it was intelligent and modern, but it was nonsense all the same. There was something maternal in her attitude, and I was reminded oddly of a sleek dachshund lying quietly in the sun while she looks lazily, and yet watchfully, at her litter of puppies romping round her. I wondered whether it crossed her mind that all this chatter about art didn't amount to much when compared with those incidents of blood and passion that she remembered. But did she remember? It had all happened a long time ago and perhaps it seemed no more than a bad dream. Perhaps these commonplace surroundings were part of her deliberate effort to forget, and to be among these young people was restful to her spirit. Perhaps Jasper's clever stupidity was a comfort. After that searing tragedy it might be that she wanted nothing but the security of the humdrum.

Possibly because Wyman was an authority on the Elizabethan drama the conversation at one moment touched on that. I had already discovered that Jasper Greene was prepared to lay down the law on subjects all and sundry, and now he delivered himself as follows:

'Our theatre has gone all to pot because the dramatists of our day are afraid to deal with the violent emotions which are the proper subject matter of tragedy,' he boomed. 'In the sixteenth century they had a wealth of melodramatic and bloody themes to suit their purpose and so they produced great plays. But where can our playwrights look for themes? Our Anglo-Saxon blood is too phlegmatic, too supine, to provide them with material they can make anything of, and so they are condemned to occupy themselves with the trivialities of social intercourse.'

I wondered what Laura thought of this, but I took care not to catch her eye. She could have told them a story of illicit love, jealousy, and parricide which would have been meat to one of Shakespeare's successors, but had he treated it, I suppose he would have felt bound to finish it with at least one more corpse strewn about the stage. The end of her story, as I knew it now, was unexpected certainly, but sadly prosaic and a trifle grotesque. Real life more often ends things with a whimper than with a bang. I wondered too why she had gone out of her way to renew our old acquaintance. Of course she had no reason to suppose that I knew as much as I did; perhaps with a true instinct she was confident that I would not give her away; perhaps she didn't care if I did. I stole a glance at her now and then while she was quietly listening to the excited babbling of the three young people, but her friendly, pleasant face told me nothing. If I hadn't known otherwise I would have sworn that no untoward circumstance had ever troubled the course of her uneventful life.

The evening came to an end and this is the end of my story, but for the fun of it I am going to relate a small incident that happened when Wyman and I got back to his house. We decided to have a bottle of beer before going to bed and went into the kitchen to fetch it. The clock in the hall struck eleven and at that moment the phone rang. Wyman went to answer it and when he came back was quietly chortling to himself.

'What's the joke?' I asked.

'It was one of my students. They're not supposed to call members of the faculty after ten-thirty, but he was all hot and bothered. He asked me how evil had come into the world.'

'And did you tell him?'

'I told him that St Thomas Aquinas had got hot and bothered

too about that very question and he'd better worry it out for himself. I said that when he found the solution he was to call me, no matter what time it was. Two o'clock in the morning if he liked.'

'I think you're pretty safe not to be disturbed for many a long night,' I said.

'I won't conceal from you that I have formed pretty much the same impression myself,' he grinned.

MAYHEW

THE lives of most men are determined by their environment. They accept the circumstances amid which fate has thrown them not only with resignation but even with good will. They are like street-cars running contentedly on their rails and they despise the sprightly flivver that dashes in and out of the traffic and speeds so jauntily across the open country. I respect them; they are good citizens, good husbands, and good fathers, and of course some-body has to pay the taxes; but I do not find them exciting. I am fascinated by the men, few enough in all conscience, who take life in their own hands and seem to mould it to their own liking. It may be that we have no such thing as free will, but at all events we have the illusion of it. At a cross-road it does seem to us that we might go either to the right or the left and, the choice once made, it is difficult to see that the whole course of the world's history obliged us to take the turning we did.

I never met a more interesting man than Mayhew. He was a lawyer in Detroit. He was an able and a successful one. By the time he was thirty-five he had a large and a lucrative practice, he had amassed a competence, and he stood on the threshold of a distinguished career. He had an acute brain, an attractive person-ality, and uprightness. There was no reason why he should not become, financially or politically, a power in the land. One even-ing he was sitting in his club with a group of friends and they were perhaps a little worse (or the better) for liquor. One of them had recently come from Italy and he told them of a house he had seen at Capri, a house on the hill, overlooking the Bay of Naples, with a large and shady garden. He described to them the beauty of the most beautiful island in the Mediterranean.

'It sounds fine,' said Mayhew. 'Is that house for sale?'

'Everything is for sale in Italy.'

'Let's send 'em a cable and make an offer for it.'

'What in heaven's name would you do with a house in Capri?'

'Live in it,' said Mayhew.

He sent for a cable form, wrote it out, and dispatched it. In a few hours the reply came back. The offer was accepted.

Mayhew was no hypocrite and he made no secret of the fact that he would never have done so wild a thing if he had been sober, but when he was he did not regret it. He was neither an impulsive nor an emotional man, but a very honest and sincere one. He would never have continued from bravado in a course that he had come to the conclusion was unwise. He made up his mind to do exactly as he had said. He did not care for wealth and he had enough money on which to live in Italy. He thought he could do more with life than spend it on composing the trivial quarrels of unimportant people. He had no definite plan. He merely wanted to get away from a life that had given him all it had to offer. I suppose his friends thought him crazy; some must have done all they could to dissuade him. He arranged his affairs, packed up his furniture, and started.

Capri is a gaunt rock of austere outline, bathed in a deep blue sea; but its vineyards, green and smiling, give it a soft and easy grace. It is friendly, remote, and debonair. I find it strange that Mayhew should have settled on this lovely island, for I never knew a man more insensible to beauty. I do not know what he sought there: happiness, freedom, or merely leisure; I know what he found. In this place which appeals so extravagantly to the senses he lived a life entirely of the spirit. For the island is rich with historic associations and over it broods always the enigmatic memory of Tiberius the Emperor. From his windows which overlooked the Bay of Naples, with the noble shape of Vesuvius changing colour with the changing light, Mayhew saw a hundred places that recalled the Romans and the Greeks. The past began to haunt him. All that he saw for the first time, for he had never been abroad before, excited his fancy; and in his soul stirred the creative imagination. He was a man of energy. Presently he made up his mind to write a history. For some time he looked about for a subject, and at last decided on the second century of the Roman Empire. It was little known and it seemed to him to offer problems analogous with those of our own day.

He began to collect books and soon he had an immense library. His legal training had taught him to read quickly. He settled down to work. At first he had been accustomed to foregather in the evening with the painters, writers, and suchlike who met in the little tavern near the Piazza, but presently he withdrew himself, for his absorption in his studies became more pressing. He had been accustomed to bathe in that bland sea and to take long walks among the pleasant vineyards, but little by little, grudging the time, he ceased to do so. He worked harder than he had ever worked in Detroit. He would start at noon and work all through the night till the whistle of the steamer that goes every morning from Capri to Naples told him that it was five o'clock and time to go to bed. His subject opened out before him, vaster and more significant, and he imagined a work that would put him for ever beside the great historians of the past. As the years went by he was to be found seldom in the ways of men. He could be tempted to come out of his house only by a game of chess or the chance of an argument. He loved to set his brain against another's. He was widely read now, not only in history, but in philosophy and science; and he was a skilful controversialist, quick, logical, and incisive. But he had good-humour and kindliness; though he took a very human pleasure in victory, he did not exult in it to your mortification.

When first he came to the island he was a big, brawny fellow, with thick black hair and a black beard, of a powerful physique; but gradually his skin became pale and waxy; he grew thin and frail. It was an odd contradiction in the most logical of men that, though a convinced and impetuous materialist, he despised the body; he looked upon it as a vile instrument which he could force to do the spirit's bidding. Neither illness nor lassitude prevented him from going on with his work. For fourteen years he toiled unremittingly. He made thousands and thousands of notes. He sorted and classified them. He had his subject at his finger ends, and at last was ready to begin. He sat down to write. He died.

The body that he, the materialist, had treated so contumeliously took its revenge on him.

That vast accumulation of knowledge is lost for ever. Vain was that ambition, surely not an ignoble one, to set his name beside those of Gibbon and Mommsen. His memory is treasured in the hearts of a few friends, fewer, alas! as the years pass on, and to the world he is unknown in death as he was in life.

And yet to me his life was a success. The pattern is good and complete. He did what he wanted, and he died when his goal was in sight and never knew the bitterness of an end achieved.

THE LOTUS EATER

MOST people, the vast majority in fact, lead the lives that circumstances have thrust upon them, and though some repine, looking upon themselves as round pegs in square holes, and think that if things had been different they might have made a much better showing, the greater part accept their lot, if not with serenity, at all events with resignation. They are like tram-cars travelling for ever on the selfsame rails. They go backwards and forwards, backwards and forwards, inevitably, till they can go no longer and then are sold as scrap-iron. It is not often that you find a man who has boldly taken the course of his life into his own hands. When you do, it is worth while having a good look at him.

That was why I was curious to meet Thomas Wilson. It was an interesting and a bold thing he had done. Of course the end was not yet and until the experiment was concluded it was impossible to call it successful. But from what I had heard it seemed he must be an odd sort of fellow and I thought I should like to know him. I had been told he was reserved, but I had a notion that with patience and tact I could persuade him to confide in me. I wanted to hear the facts from his own lips. People exaggerate, they love to romanticize, and I was quite prepared to discover that his story was not nearly so singular as I had been led to believe.

And this impression was confirmed when at last I made his acquaintance. It was on the Piazza in Capri, where I was spending the month of August at a friend's villa, and a little before sunset, when most of the inhabitants, native and foreign, gather together to chat with their friends in the cool of the evening. There is a terrace that overlooks the Bay of Naples, and when the sun sinks slowly into the sea the island of Ischia is silhouetted against a blaze of splendour. It is one of the most lovely sights in the world. I was standing there with my friend and host watching it, when suddenly he said:

'Look, there's Wilson.'

'Where?'

'The man sitting on the parapet, with his back to us. He's got a blue shirt on.'

I saw an undistinguished back and a small head of grey hair, short and rather thin.

'I wish he'd turn round,' I said.

'He will presently.'

'Ask him to come and have a drink with us at Morgano's.'

'All right.'

The instant of overwhelming beauty had passed and the sun, like the top of an orange, was dipping into a wine-red sea. We turned round and leaning our backs against the parapet looked at the people who were sauntering to and fro. They were all talking their heads off and the cheerful noise was exhilarating. Then the church bell, rather cracked, but with a fine resonant note, began to ring. The Piazza at Capri, with its clock tower over the footpath that leads up from the harbour, with the church up a flight of steps, is a perfect setting for an opera by Donizetti, and you felt that the voluble crowd might at any moment break out into a rattling chorus. It was charming and unreal.

I was so intent on the scene that I had not noticed Wilson get off the parapet and come towards us. As he passed us my friend stopped him.

'Hullo, Wilson, I haven't seen you bathing the last few days.'

'I've been bathing on the other side for a change.'

My friend then introduced me. Wilson shook hands with me politely, but with indifference; a great many strangers come to Capri for a few days, or a few weeks, and I had no doubt he was constantly meeting people who came and went; and then my friend asked him to come along and have a drink with us.

'I was just going back to supper,' he said.

'Can't it wait?' I asked.

'I suppose it can,' he smiled.

Though his teeth were not very good his smile was attractive. It was gentle and kindly. He was dressed in a blue cotton shirt and a pair of grey trousers, much creased and none too clean, of a thin canvas, and on his feet he wore a pair of very old espadrilles. The get-up was picturesque, and very suitable to the place and the weather, but it did not at all go with his face. It was a lined, long face, deeply sunburned, thin-lipped, with small grey eyes rather close together and tight, neat features. The grey hair was carefully brushed. It was not a plain face, indeed in his youth Wilson might have been good-looking, but a prim one. He wore the blue shirt, open at the neck, and the grey canvas trousers, not as though they belonged to him, but as though, shipwrecked in his pyjamas, he had been fitted out with odd garments by compassionate strangers. Notwithstanding this careless attire he looked like the manager of a branch office in an insurance company, who should by rights be wearing a black coat with pepper-and-salt trousers, a white collar, and an unobjectionable tie. I could very well see myself going to him to claim the insurance money when I had lost a watch, and being rather disconcerted while I answered the questions he put to me by his obvious impression, for all his politeness, that people who made such claims were either fools or knaves.

Moving off, we strolled across the Piazza and down the street till we came to Morgano's. We sat in the garden. Around us people were talking in Russian, German, Italian, and English. We ordered drinks. Donna Lucia, the host's wife, waddled up and in her low, sweet voice passed the time of day with us. Though middle-aged now and portly, she had still traces of the wonderful beauty that thirty years before had driven artists to paint so many bad portraits of her. Her eyes, large and liquid, were the eyes of Hera and her smile was affectionate and gracious. We three gossiped for a while, for there is always a scandal of one sort or another in Capri to make a topic of conversation, but nothing was said of particular interest and in a little while Wilson got up and left us. Soon afterwards we strolled up to my friend's villa to dine. On the way he asked me what I had thought of Wilson.

'Nothing,' I said. 'I don't believe there's a word of truth in your story.'

'Why not?'

'He isn't the sort of man to do that sort of thing.'

'How does anyone know what anyone is capable of?'

'I should put him down as an absolutely normal man of business who's retired on a comfortable income from gilt-edged securities. I think your story's just the ordinary Capri tittle-tattle.'

'Have it your own way,' said my friend.

We were in the habit of bathing at a beach called the Baths of Tiberius. We took a fly down the road to a certain point and then wandered through lemon groves and vineyards, noisy with cicadas and heavy with the hot smell of the sun, till we came to the top of the cliff down which a steep winding path led to the sea. A day or two later, just before we got down my friend said:

'Oh, there's Wilson back again.'

We scrunched over the beach, the only drawback to the bathing-place being that it was shingle and not sand, and as we came along Wilson saw us and waved. He was standing up, a pipe in his mouth, and he wore nothing but a pair of trunks. His body was dark brown, thin but not emaciated, and, considering his wrinkled face and grey hair, youthful. Hot from our walk, we undressed quickly and plunged at once into the water. Six feet from the shore it was thirty feet deep, but so clear that you could see the bottom. It was warm, yet invigorating.

When I got out Wilson was lying on his belly, with a towel under him reading a book. I lit a cigarette and went and sat down beside him.

'Had a nice swim?' he asked.

He put his pipe inside his book to mark the place and closing it put it down on the pebbles beside him. He was evidently willing to talk.

'Lovely,' I said. 'It's the best bathing in the world.'

'Of course people think those were the Baths of Tiberius.' He waved his hand towards a shapeless mass of masonry that stood half in the water and half out. 'But that's all rot. It was just one of his villas, you know.'

I did. But it is just as well to let people tell you things when they want to. It disposes them kindly towards you if you suffer them to impart information. Wilson gave a chuckle.

'Funny old fellow, Tiberius. Pity they're saying now there's not a word of truth in all those stories about him.'

He began to tell me all about Tiberius. Well, I had read my Suetonius too and I had read histories of the Early Roman Empire, so there was nothing very new to me in what he said. But I observed that he was not ill-read. I remarked on it.

'Oh, well, when I settled down here I was naturally interested, and I have plenty of time for reading. When you live in a place like this, with all its associations, it seems to make history so actual. You might almost be living in historical times yourself.'

I should remark here that this was in 1913. The world was an easy, comfortable place and no one could have imagined that anything might happen seriously to disturb the serenity of existence.

'How long have you been here?' I asked.

'Fifteen years.' He gave the blue and placid sea a glance, and a strangely tender smile hovered on his thin lips. 'I fell in love with the place at first sight. You've heard, I daresay, of the mythical German who came here on the Naples boat just for lunch and a look at the Blue Grotto and stayed forty years; well, I can't say I exactly did that, but it's come to the same thing in the end. Only it won't be forty years in my case. Twenty-five. Still, that's better than a poke in the eye with a sharp stick.'

I waited for him to go on. For what he had just said looked indeed as though there might be something after all in the singular story I had heard. But at that moment my friend came dripping out of the water very proud of himself because he had swum a mile, and the conversation turned to other things.

After that I met Wilson several times, either in the Piazza or on the beach. He was amiable and polite. He was always pleased to have a talk and I found out that he not only knew every inch of the island but also the adjacent mainland. He had read a great deal on all sorts of subjects, but his speciality was the history of Rome and on this he was very well informed. He seemed to have little imagination and to be of no more than average intelligence. He laughed a good deal, but with restraint, and his sense of humour was tickled by simple jokes. A commonplace man. I did not forget the odd remark he had made during the first short chat we had had by ourselves, but he never so much as approached the topic again. One day on our return from the beach, dismissing the cab at the Piazza, my friend and I told the driver to be ready to take us up to Anacapri at five. We were going to climb Monte Solaro, dine at a tavern we favoured, and walk down in the moonlight. For it was full moon and the views by night were lovely. Wilson was standing by while we gave the cabman instructions, for we had given him a lift to save him the hot dusty walk, and more from politeness than for any other reason I asked him if he would care to join us.

'It's my party,' I said.

'I'll come with pleasure,' he answered.

But when the time came to set out my friend was not feeling well, he thought he had stayed too long in the water, and would not face the long and tiring walk. So I went alone with Wilson. We climbed the mountain, admired the spacious view, and got back to the inn as night was falling, hot, hungry, and thirsty. We had ordered our dinner beforehand. The food was good, for Antonio was an excellent cook, and the wine came from his own vineyard. It was so light that you felt you could drink it like water and we finished the first bottle with our macaroni. By the time we had finished the second we felt that there was nothing much wrong with life. We sat in a little garden under a great vine laden with grapes. The air was exquisitely soft. The night was still and we were alone. The maid brought us *bel paese* cheese and a plate of figs. I ordered coffee and strega, which is the best liqueur they make in Italy. Wilson would not have a cigar, but lit his pipe.

'We've got plenty of time before we need start,' he said, 'the moon won't be over the hill for another hour.'

'Moon or no moon,' I said briskly, 'of course we've got plenty of time. That's one of the delights of Capri, that there's never any hurry.'

'Leisure,' he said. 'If people only knew! It's the most priceless thing a man can have and they're such fools they don't even know it's something to aim at. Work? They work for work's sake. They haven't got the brains to realize that the only object of work is to obtain leisure.'

Wine has the effect on some people of making them indulge in general reflections. These remarks were true, but no one could have claimed that they were original. I did not say anything, but struck a match to light my cigar.

'It was full moon the first time I came to Capri,' he went on reflectively. 'It might be the same moon as tonight.'

'It was, you know,' I smiled.

He grinned. The only light in the garden was what came from an oil lamp that hung over our heads. It had been scanty to eat by, but it was good now for confidences.

'I didn't mean that. I mean, it might be yesterday. Fifteen years it is, and when I look back it seems like a month. I'd never been to Italy before. I came for my summer holiday. I went to Naples by boat from Marseilles and I had a look round, Pompeii, you know, and Paestum and one or two places like that; then I came here for a week. I liked the look of the place right away, from the sea, I mean, as I watched it come closer and closer; and then when we got into the little boats from the steamer and landed at the quay, with all that crowd of jabbering people who wanted to take your luggage, and the hotel touts, and the tumbledown houses on the Marina and the walk up to the hotel, and dining on the terrace – well, it just got me. That's the truth. I didn't know if I was standing on my head or my heels. I'd never drunk Capri wine before, but I'd heard of it; I think I must have got a bit tight. I sat on that terrace after they'd all gone to bed and watched the moon over the sea, and there was Vesuvius with a great red plume of smoke rising up from it. Of course I know now that wine I drank was ink, Capri wine my eye, but I thought it all right then. But it wasn't the wine that made me drunk, it was the shape of the island and those jabbering people, the moon and the sea and the oleander in the hotel garden. I'd never seen an oleander before.'

It was a long speech and it had made him thirsty. He took up his glass, but it was empty. I asked him if he would have another strega.

'It's sickly stuff. Let's have a bottle of wine. That's sound, that is, pure juice of the grape and can't hurt anyone.'

I ordered more wine, and when it came filled the glasses. He took a long drink and after a sigh of pleasure went on.

'Next day I found my way to the bathing-place we go to. Not bad bathing, I thought. Then I wandered about the island. As luck would have it, there was a *festa* up at the Punta di Timberio and I ran straight into the middle of it. An image of the Virgin and priests, acolytes swinging censers, and a whole crowd of jolly, laughing, excited people, a lot of them all dressed up. I ran across an Englishman there and asked him what it was all about. "Oh, it's the feast of the Assumption," he said, "at least that's what the Catholic Church says it is, but that's just their hanky-panky. It's the festival of Venus. Pagan, you know. Aphrodite rising from the sea and all that." It gave me quite a funny feeling to hear him. It seemed to take one a long way back, if you know what I mean. After that I went down one night to have a look at the Faraglioni by moonlight. If the fates had wanted me to go on being a bank manager they oughtn't to have let me take that walk.'

'You were a bank manager, were you?' I asked.

I had been wrong about him, but not far wrong.

'Yes. I was manager of the Crawford Street branch of the York and City. It was convenient for me because I lived up Hendon way. I could get from door to door in thirty-seven minutes.'

He puffed at his pipe and relit it.

'That was my last night, that was. I'd got to be back at the bank on Monday morning. When I looked at those two great rocks sticking out of the water, with the moon above them, and all the little lights of the fishermen in their boats catching cuttlefish, all so peaceful and beautiful, I said to myself, well, after all, why should I go back? It wasn't as if I had anyone dependent on me. My wife had died of bronchial pneumonia four years before and the kid went to live with her grandmother, my wife's mother. She was an old fool, she didn't look after the kid properly and she got blood-poisoning, they amputated her leg, but they couldn't save her and she died, poor little thing.'

'How terrible,' I said.

'Yes, I was cut up at the time, though of course not so much as if the kid had been living with me, but I dare say it was a mercy. Not much chance for a girl with only one leg. I was sorry about my wife too. We got on very well together. Though I don't know if it would have continued. She was the sort of woman who was always bothering about what other people'd think. She didn't like travelling. Eastbourne was her idea of a holiday. D'you know, I'd never crossed the Channel till after her death.'

'But I suppose you've got other relations, haven't you?'

'None. I was an only child. My father had a brother, but he went to Australia before I was born. I don't think anyone could easily be more alone in the world than I am. There wasn't any reason I could see why I shouldn't do exactly what I wanted. I was thirty-four at that time.'

He had told me he had been on the island for fifteen years. That would make him forty-nine. Just about the age I should have given him.

'I'd been working since I was seventeen. All I had to look forward to was doing the same old thing day after day till I retired on my pension. I said to myself, is it worth it? What's wrong with chucking it all up and spending the rest of my life down here? It was the most beautiful place I'd ever seen. But I'd had a business training, I was cautious by nature. "No," I said, "I won't be carried away like this, I'll go tomorrow like I said I would and think it over. Perhaps when I get back to London I'll think quite differently." Damned fool, wasn't I? I lost a whole year that way.'

'You didn't change your mind, then?'

'You bet I didn't. All the time I was working I kept thinking of the bathing here and the vineyards and the walks over the hills and the moon and the sea, and the Piazza in the evening when everyone walks about for a bit of a chat after the day's work is over. There was only one thing that bothered me: I wasn't sure if I was justified in not working like everybody else did. Then I read a sort of history book, by a man called Marion Crawford it was, and there was a story about Sybaris and Crotona. There were two cities; and in Sybaris they just enjoyed life and had a good time, and in Crotona they were hardy and industrious and all that. And one day the men of Crotona came over and wiped Sybaris out, and then after a while a lot of other fellows came over from somewhere else and wiped Crotona out. Nothing remains of Sybaris, not a stone, and all that's left of Crotona is just one column. That settled the matter for me.'

'Oh?'

'It came to the same in the end, didn't it? And when you look back now, who were the mugs?'

I did not reply and he went on.

'The money was rather a bother. The bank didn't pension one off till after thirty years' service, but if you retired before that they gave you a gratuity. With that and what I'd got for the sale of my house and the little I'd managed to save, I just hadn't enough to buy an annuity to last the rest of my life. It would have been silly to sacrifice everything so as to lead a pleasant life and not have a sufficient income to make it pleasant. I wanted to have a little place of my own, a servant to look after me, enough to buy tobacco, decent food, books now and then, and something over for emergencies. I knew pretty well how much I needed. I found I had just enough to buy an annuity for twenty-five years.'

'You were thirty-five at the time?'

'Yes. It would carry me on till I was sixty. After all, no one can be certain of living longer than that, a lot of men die in their fifties, and by the time a man's sixty he's had the best of life.'

'On the other hand no one can be sure of dying at sixty,' I said.

'Well, I don't know. It depends on himself, doesn't it?'

'In your place I should have stayed on at the bank till I was entitled to my pension.'

'I should have been forty-seven then. I shouldn't have been too old to enjoy my life here, I'm older than that now and I enjoy it as much as I ever did, but I should have been too old to experience the particular pleasure of a young man. You know, you can have just as good a time at fifty as you can at thirty, but it's not the same sort of good time. I wanted to live the perfect life while I still had the energy and the spirit to make the most of it. Twenty-five years seemed a long time to me, and twenty-five years of happiness seemed worth paying something pretty substantial for. I'd made up my mind to wait a year and I waited a year. Then I sent in my resignation and as soon as they paid me my gratuity I bought the annuity and came on here.'

'An annuity for twenty-five years?'

'That's right.'

'Have you never regretted?'

'Never. I've had my money's worth already. And I've got ten years more. Don't you think after twenty-five years of perfect happiness one ought to be satisfied to call it a day?'

'Perhaps.'

He did not say in so many words what he would do then, but his intention was clear. It was pretty much the story my friend had told me, but it sounded different when I heard it from his own lips. I stole a glance at him. There was nothing about him that was not ordinary. No one, looking at that neat, prim face, could have thought him capable of an unconventional action. I did not blame him. It was his own life that he had arranged in this strange manner, and I did not see why he should not do what he liked with it. Still, I could not prevent the little shiver that ran down my spine.

'Getting chilly?' he smiled. 'We might as well start walking down. The moon'll be up by now.'

Before we parted Wilson asked me if I would like to go and see his house one day; and two or three days later, finding out where he lived, I strolled up to see him. It was a peasant's cottage, well away from the town, in a vineyard, with a view of the sea. By the side of the door grew a great oleander in full flower. There were only two small rooms, a tiny kitchen, and a lean-to in which firewood could be kept. The bedroom was furnished like a monk's cell, but the sitting-room, smelling agreeably of tobacco, was comfortable enough, with two large arm-chairs that he had brought from England, a large roll-top desk, a cottage piano, and crowded bookshelves. On the walls were framed engravings of pictures by G. F. Watts and Lord Leighton. Wilson told me that the house belonged to the owner of the vineyard who lived in another cottage higher up the hill, and his wife came in every day to do the rooms and the cooking. He had found the place on his first visit to Capri, and taking it on his return for good had been there ever since. Seeing the piano and music open on it, I asked him if he would play.

'I'm no good, you know, but I've always been fond of music and I get a lot of fun out of strumming.'

He sat down at the piano and played one of the movements from a Beethoven sonata. He did not play very well. I looked at his music, Schumann and Schubert, Beethoven, Bach, and Chopin. On the table on which he had his meals was a greasy pack of cards. I asked him if he played patience.

'A lot.'

From what I saw of him then and from what I heard from other people I made for myself what I think must have been a fairly accurate picture of the life he had led for the last fifteen years. It was certainly a very harmless one. He bathed; he walked a great deal, and he seemed never to lose his sense of the beauty of the island which he knew so intimately; he played the piano and he played patience; he read. When he was asked to a party he went and, though a trifle dull, was agreeable. He was not affronted if he was neglected. He liked people, but with an aloofness that prevented intimacy. He lived thriftily, but with sufficient comfort. He never owed a penny. I imagine he had never been a man whom sex had greatly troubled, and if in his younger days he had had now and then a passing affair with a visitor to the island whose head was turned by the atmosphere, his emotion, while it lasted, remained, I am pretty sure, well under his control. I think he was determined that nothing should interfere with his independence of spirit. His only passion was for the beauty of nature, and he sought felicity in the simple and natural things that life offers to everyone. You may say that it was a grossly selfish existence. It was. He was of no use to anybody, but on the other hand he did nobody any harm. His only object was his own happiness, and it looked as though he had attained it. Very few people know where to look for happiness; fewer still find it. I don't know whether he was a fool or a wise man. He was certainly a man who knew his own mind. The odd thing about him to me was that he was so immensely commonplace. I should never have given him a second thought but for what I knew, that on a certain day, ten years from then, unless a chance illness cut the thread before, he must deliberately take leave of the world he loved so well. I wondered whether it was the thought of this, never quite absent from his mind, that gave him the peculiar zest with which he enjoyed every moment of the day.

I should do him an injustice if I omitted to state that he was not at all in the habit of talking about himself. I think the friend I was staying with was the only person in whom he had confided. I believe he only told me the story because he suspected I already knew it, and on the evening on which he told it me he had drunk a good deal of wine.

My visit drew to a close and I left the island. The year after, war broke out. A number of things happened to me, so that the course of my life was greatly altered, and it was thirteen years before I went to Capri again. My friend had been back some time, but he was no longer so well off, and had moved into a house that had no room for me; so I was putting up at the hotel. He came to meet me at the boat and we dined together. During dinner I asked him where exactly his house was.

'You know it,' he answered. 'It's the little place Wilson had. I've built on a room and made it quite nice.'

With so many other things to occupy my mind I had not given

Wilson a thought for years; but now, with a little shock, I remembered. The ten years he had before him when I made his acquaintance must have elapsed long ago.

'Did he commit suicide as he said he would?'

'It's rather a grim story.'

Wilson's plan was all right. There was only one flaw in it and this, I suppose, he could not have foreseen. It had never occurred to him that after twenty-five years of complete happiness, in this quiet backwater, with nothing in the world to disturb his serenity, his character would gradually lose its strength. The will needs obstacles in order to exercise its power; when it is never thwarted, when no effort is needed to achieve one's desires, because one has placed one's desires only in the things that can be obtained by stretching out one's hand, the will grows impotent. If you walk on a level all the time the muscles you need to climb a mountain will atrophy. These observations are trite, but there they are. When Wilson's annuity expired he had no longer the resolution to make the end which was the price he had agreed to pay for that long period of happy tranquillity. I do not think, as far as I could gather, both from what my friend told me and afterwards from others, that he wanted courage. It was just that he couldn't make up his mind. He put it off from day to day.

He had lived on the island for so long and had always settled his accounts so punctually that it was easy for him to get credit; never having borrowed money before, he found a number of people who were willing to lend him small sums when now he asked for them. He had paid his rent regularly for so many years that his landlord, whose wife Assunta still acted as his servant, was content to let things slide for several months. Everyone believed him when he said that a relative had died and that he was temporarily embarrassed because owing to legal formalities he could not for some time get the money that was due to him. He managed to hang on after this fashion for something over a year. Then he could get no more credit from the local tradesmen, and there was no one to lend him any more money. His landlord gave him notice to leave the house unless he paid up the arrears of rent before a certain date.

The day before this he went into his tiny bedroom, closed the door and the window, drew the curtain, and lit a brazier of charcoal. Next morning when Assunta came to make his breakfast she found him insensible but still alive. The room was draughty, and though he had done this and that to keep out the fresh air he had not done it very thoroughly. It almost looked as though at the last moment, and desperate though his situation was, he had suffered from a certain infirmity of purpose. Wilson was taken to the hospital, and though very ill for some time he at last recovered. But as a result either of the charcoal poisoning or of the shock he was no longer in complete possession of his faculties. He was not insane, at all events not insane enough to be put in an asylum, but he was quite obviously no longer in his right mind.

'I went to see him,' said my friend. 'I tried to get him to talk, but he kept looking at me in a funny sort of way, as though he couldn't quite make out where he'd seen me before. He looked rather awful lying there in bed, with a week's growth of grey beard on his chin; but except for that funny look in his eyes he seemed quite normal.'

'What funny look in his eyes?'

'I don't know exactly how to describe it. Puzzled. It's an absurd comparison, but suppose you threw a stone up into the air and it didn't come down but just stayed there . . .'

'It would be rather bewildering,' I smiled.

'Well, that's the sort of look he had.'

It was difficult to know what to do with him. He had no money and no means of getting any. His effects were sold, but for too little to pay what he owed. He was English, and the Italian authorities did not wish to make themselves responsible for him. The British Consul in Naples had no funds to deal with the case. He could of course be sent back to England, but no one seemed to know what could be done with him when he got there. Then Assunta, the servant, said that he had been a good master and a good tenant, and as long as he had the money had paid his way; he could sleep in the woodshed in the cottage in which she and her husband lived, and he could share their meals. This was suggested to him. It was difficult to know whether he understood or not. When Assunta came to take him from the hospital he went with her without remark. He seemed to have no longer a will of his own. She had been keeping him now for two years.

'It's not very comfortable, you know,' said my friend. 'They've rigged him up a ramshackle bed and given him a couple of blankets, but there's no window, and it's icy cold in winter and like an oven in summer. And the food's pretty rough. You know how these peasants eat: macaroni on Sundays and meat once in a blue moon.'

'What does he do with himself all the time?'

'He wanders about the hills. I've tried to see him two or three times, but it's no good; when he sees you coming he runs like a hare. Assunta comes down to have a chat with me now and then and I give her a bit of money so that she can buy him tobacco, but God knows if he ever gets it.'

'Do they treat him all right?' I asked.

'I'm sure Assunta's kind enough. She treats him like a child. I'm afraid her husband's not very nice to him. He grudges the cost of his keep. I don't believe he's cruel or anything like that, but I think he's a bit sharp with him. He makes him fetch water and clean the cow-shed and that sort of thing.'

'It sounds pretty rotten,' I said.

'He brought it on himself. After all, he's only got what he deserved.'

'I think on the whole we all get what we deserve,' I said. 'But that doesn't prevent its being rather horrible.'

Two or three days later my friend and I were taking a walk. We were strolling along a narrow path through an olive grove.

'There's Wilson,' said my friend suddenly. 'Don't look, you'll only frighten him. Go straight on.'

I walked with my eyes on the path, but out of the corners of them I saw a man hiding behind an olive tree. He did not move as we approached, but I felt that he was watching us. As soon as we had passed I heard a scamper. Wilson, like a hunted animal, had made for safety. That was the last I ever saw of him.

He died last year. He had endured that life for six years. He was found one morning on the mountainside lying quite peacefully as though he had died in his sleep. From where he lay he had been able to see those two great rocks called the Faraglioni which stand out of the sea. It was full moon and he must have gone to see them by moonlight. Perhaps he died of the beauty of that sight.

SALVATORE

I wonder if I can do it.

I knew Salvatore first when he was a boy of fifteen with a pleasant, ugly face, a laughing mouth, and care-free eyes. He used to spend the morning lying about the beach with next to nothing on and his brown body was as thin as a rail. He was full of grace. He was in and out of the sea all the time, swimming with the clumsy, effortless stroke common to the fisher boys. Scrambling up the jagged rocks on his hard feet, for except on Sundays he never wore shoes, he would throw himself into the deep water with a cry of delight. His father was a fisherman who owned his own little vineyard and Salvatore acted as nursemaid to his two younger brothers. He shouted to them to come inshore when they ventured out too far and made them dress when it was time to climb the hot, vineclad hill for the frugal midday meal.

But boys in those Southern parts grow apace and in a little while he was madly in love with a pretty girl who lived on the Grande Marina. She had eyes like forest pools and held herself like a daughter of the Caesars. They were affianced, but they could not marry till Salvatore had done his military service, and when he left the island which he had never left in his life before, to become a sailor in the navy of King Victor Emmanuel, he wept like a child. It was hard for one who had never been less free than the birds to be at the beck and call of others; it was harder still to live in a battleship with strangers instead of in a little white cottage among the vines; and when he was ashore, to walk in noisy, friendless cities with streets so crowded that he was frightened to cross them, when he had been used to silent paths and the mountains and the sea. I suppose it had never struck him that Ischia, which he looked at every evening (it was like a fairy island in the sunset) to see what the weather would be like next day, or Vesuvius, pearly in the dawn, had anything to do with him at all; but when he ceased to have them before his eyes he realized in some dim fashion that they were as much part of him as his hands and his feet. He was dreadfully homesick. But it was hardest of all to be parted from the girl he loved with all his passionate young heart. He wrote to her (in his childlike handwriting) long, ill-spelt letters in which he told her how constantly he thought of her and how much he longed to be back. He was sent here and there, to Spezzia, to Venice, to Bari, and finally to China. Here he fell ill of some mysterious ailment that kept him in hospital for months. He bore it with the mute and uncomprehending patience of a dog. When he learnt that it was a form of rheumatism that made him unfit for further service his heart exulted, for he could go home; and he did not bother, in fact he scarcely listened, when the doctors told him that he would never again be quite well. What did he care when he was going back to the little island he loved so well and the girl who was waiting for him?

When he got into the rowing-boat that met the steamer from Naples and was rowed ashore he saw his father and mother standing on the jetty, and his two brothers, big boys now, and he waved to them. His eyes searched among the crowd that waited there, for the girl. He could not see her. There was a great deal of kissing when he jumped up the steps and they all, emotional creatures, cried a little as they exchanged their greetings. He asked where the girl was. His mother told him that she did not know; they had not seen her for two or three weeks; so in the evening when the moon was shining over the placid sea and the lights of Naples twinkled in the distance he walked down to the Grande Marina to her house. She was sitting on the doorstep with her mother. He was a little shy because he had not seen her for so long. He asked her if she had not received the letter that he had written to her to say that he was coming home. Yes, they had received a letter, and they had been told by another of the island boys that he was ill. Yes, that was why he was back; was it not a piece of luck? Oh, but they had heard that he would never be quite well again. The doctors talked a lot of nonsense, but he knew very well that now he was home again he would recover. They were silent for a little, and then the mother nudged the girl. She did not try to soften the blow. She told him straight out, with the blunt directness of her race, that she could not marry a man who would never be strong enough to work like a man. They had made up their minds, her mother and father and she, and her father would never give his consent.

When Salvatore went home he found that they all knew. The girl's father had been to tell them what they had decided, but they had lacked the courage to tell him themselves. He wept on his mother's bosom. He was terribly unhappy, but he did not blame the girl. A fisherman's life is hard and it needs strength and endurance. He knew very well that a girl could not afford to marry a man who might not be able to support her. His smile was very sad and his eyes had the look of a dog that has been beaten, but he did not complain, and he never said a hard word of the girl he had loved so well. Then, a few months later, when he had settled down to the common round, working in his father's vineyard and fishing, his mother told him that there was a young woman in the village who was willing to marry him. Her name was Assunta.

'She's as ugly as the devil,' he said.

She was older than he, twenty-four or twenty-five, and she had been engaged to a man who, while doing his military service, had been killed in Africa. She had a little money of her own and if Salvatore married her she could buy him a boat of his own and they could take a vineyard that by a happy chance happened at that moment to be without a tenant. His mother told him that Assunta had seen him at the *festa* and had fallen in love with him. Salvatore smiled his sweet smile and said he would think about it. On the following Sunday, dressed in the stiff black clothes in which he looked so much less well than in the ragged shirt and trousers of every day, he went up to High Mass at the parish church and placed himself so that he could have a good look at the young woman. When he came down again he told his mother that he was willing.

Well, they were married and they settled down in a tiny whitewashed house in the middle of a handsome vineyard. Salvatore was now a great big husky fellow, tall and broad, but still with that ingenuous smile and those trusting, kindly eyes that he had had as a boy. He had the most beautiful manners I have ever seen in my life. Assunta was a grim-visaged female, with decided features, and she looked old for her years. But she had a good heart and she was no fool. I used to be amused by the little smile of devotion that she gave her husband when he was being very masculine and masterful; she never ceased to be touched by his gentle sweetness. But she could not bear the girl who had thrown him over, and notwithstanding Salvatore's smiling expostulations she had nothing but harsh words for her. Presently children were born to them.

It was a hard enough life. All through the fishing season towards evening he set out in his boat with one of his brothers for the fishing grounds. It was a long pull of six or seven miles, and he spent the night catching the profitable cuttlefish. Then there was the long row back again in order to sell the catch in time for it to go on the early boat to Naples. At other times he was working in his vineyard from dawn till the heat drove him to rest and then again, when it was a trifle cooler, till dusk. Often his rheumatism prevented him from doing anything at all and then he would lie about the beach, smoking cigarettes, with a pleasant word for everyone notwithstanding the pain that racked his limbs. The foreigners who came down to bathe and saw him there said that these Italian fishermen were lazy devils.

Sometimes he used to bring his children down to give them a bath. They were both boys and at this time the elder was three and the younger less than two. They sprawled about at the water's edge stark naked and Salvatore standing on a rock would dip them in the water. The elder one bore it with stoicism, but the baby screamed lustily. Salvatore had enormous hands, like legs of mutton, coarse and hard from constant toil, but when he bathed his children, holding them so tenderly, drying them with delicate care, upon my word they were like flowers. He would seat the naked baby on the palm of his hand and hold him up, laughing a little at his smallness, and his laugh was like the laughter of an angel. His eyes then were as candid as his child's.

I started by saying that I wondered if I could do it and now I must tell you what it is that I have tried to do. I wanted to see whether I could hold your attention for a few pages while I drew for you the portrait of a man, just an ordinary fisherman who possessed nothing in the world except a quality which is the rarest, the most precious and the loveliest that anyone can have. Heaven only knows why he should so strangely and unexpectedly have possessed it. All I know is that it shone in him with a radiance that, if it had not been so unconscious and so humble, would have been to the common run of men hardly bearable. And in case you have not guessed what the quality was, I will tell you. Goodness, just goodness.

THE WASH-TUB

POSITANO stands on the side of a steep hill, a disarray of huddled white houses, their tiled roofs washed pale by the suns of a hundred years; but unlike many of these Italian towns perched out of harm's way on a rocky eminence it does not offer you at one delightful glance all it has to give. It has quaint streets that zig-zag up the hill, and battered, painted houses in the baroque style, but very late, in which Neapolitan noblemen led for a season lives of penurious grandeur. It is indeed almost excessively picturesque and in winter its two or three modest hotels are crowded with painters, male and female, who in their different ways acknowledge by their daily labours the emotion it has excited in them. Some take infinite pains to place on canvas every window and every tile their peering eyes can discover and doubtless achieve the satisfaction that rewards honest industry. 'At all events it's sincere,' they say modestly when they show you their work. Some, rugged and dashing, in a fine frenzy attack their canvas with a pallet knife charged with a wad of paint, and they say: 'You see, what I was trying to bring out was my personality.' They slightly close their eyes and tentatively murmur: 'I think it's rather me, don't you?' And there are some who give you highly entertaining arrangements of spheres and cubes and utter sombrely: 'That's how I see it!' These for the most part are strong silent men who waste no words.

But Positano looks full south and the chances are that in summer you will have it to yourself. The hotel is clean and cool and there is a terrace, overhung with vines, where you can sit at night and look at the sea bespangled with dim stars. Down at the Marina, on the quay, is a little tavern where you can dine under an archway off anchovies and ham, macaroni and fresh-caught mullet, and drink cold wine. Once a day the steamer from Naples comes in, bringing the mail, and for a quarter of an hour gives the beach (there is no port and the passengers are landed in small boats) an air of animation.

One August, tiring of Capri where I had been staying, I made up my mind to spend a few days at Positano, so I hired a fishing-boat and rowed over. I stopped on the way in a shady cove to bathe and lunch and sleep, and did not arrive till evening. I strolled up the hill, my two bags following me on the heads of two sturdy women, to the hotel, and was surprised to learn that I was not its only guest. The waiter, whose name was Giuseppe, was an old friend of mine, and at that season he was boots, porter, chambermaid, and cook as well. He told me that an American signore had been staying there for three months.

'Is he a painter or a writer or something?' I asked.

'No, *Signore*, he's a gentleman.'

Odd, I thought. No foreigners came to Positano at that time of year but German *Wandervogel*, looking hot and dusty, with satchels on their backs, and they only stayed overnight. I could not imagine anyone wishing to spend three months there; unless of course he were hiding. And since all London had been excited by the flight earlier in the year of an eminent, but dishonest, financier, the amusing thought occurred to me that this mysterious stranger was perhaps he. I knew him slightly and trusted that my sudden arrival would not disconcert him.

'You'll see the *Signore* at the Marina,' said Giuseppe, as I was setting out to go down again. 'He always dines there.'

He was certainly not there when I arrived. I asked what there was for dinner and drank an americano, which is by no means a bad substitute for a cocktail. In a few minutes, however, a man walked in who could be no other than my fellow-guest at the hotel and I had a moment's disappointment when I saw that it was not the absconding financier. A tall, elderly man, bronzed after his summer on the Mediterranean, with a handsome, thin face. He wore a very neat, even smart, suit of cream-coloured silk and no hat. His grey hair was cut very short, but was still thick. There was ease in his bearing, and elegance. He looked round the half-dozen tables under the archway at which the natives of the place were playing cards or dominoes and his eyes rested on me. They smiled pleasantly. He came up.

'I hear you have just arrived at the hotel. Giuseppe suggested that as he couldn't come down here to effect an introduction you wouldn't mind if I introduced myself. Would it bore you to dine with a total stranger?'

'Of course not. Sit down.'

He turned to the maid who was laying a cover for me and in beautiful Italian told her that I would eat with him. He looked at my americano.

'I have got them to stock a little gin and French vermouth for me. Would you allow me to mix you a very dry Martini?'

'Without hesitation.'

'It gives an exotic note to the surroundings which brings out the local colour.'

He certainly made a very good cocktail and with added appetite we ate the ham and anchovies with which our dinner began. My host had a pleasant humour and his fluent conversation was agreeable.

'You must forgive me if I talk too much,' he said presently. 'This is the first chance I've had to speak English for three months. I don't suppose you will stay here long and I mean to make the most of it.'

'Three months is a long time to stay at Positano.'

'I've hired a boat and I bathe and fish. I read a great deal. I have a good many books here and if there's anything I can lend you I shall be very glad.'

'I think I have enough reading matter. But I should love to look at what you have. It's always fun looking at other people's books.'

He gave me a sharp look and his eyes twinkled.

'It also tells you a good deal about them,' he murmured.

When we finished dinner we went on talking. The stranger was well-read and interested in a diversity of topics. He spoke with so much knowledge of painting that I wondered if he was an art critic or a dealer. But then it appeared that he had been reading Suetonius and I came to the conclusion that he was a college professor. I asked him his name.

'Barnaby,' he answered.

'That's a name that has recently acquired an amazing celebrity.'

'Oh, how so?'

'Have you never heard of the celebrated Mrs Barnaby? She's a compatriot of yours.'

'I admit that I've seen her name in the papers rather frequently of late. Do you know her?'

'Yes, quite well. She gave the grandest parties all last season and I went to them whenever she asked me. Everyone did. She's an astounding woman. She came to London to do the season, and, by George, she did it. She just swept everything before her.'

'I understand she's very rich?'

'Fabulously, I believe, but it's not that that has made her success. Plenty of American women have money. Mrs Barnaby has got where she has by sheer force of character. She never pretends to be anything but what she is. She's natural. She's priceless. You know her history, of course?'

My friend smiled.

'Mrs Barnaby may be a great celebrity in London, but to the best of my belief in America she is almost inconceivably unknown.'

I smiled also, but within me; I could well imagine how shocked this distinguished and cultured man would be by the rollicking humour, the frankness, with its tang of the soil, and the rich and vital experience of the amazing Mrs Barnaby.

'Well, I'll tell you about her. Her husband appears to be a very rough diamond; he's a great hulking fellow, she says, who could fell a steer with his fist. He's known in Arizona as One-Bullet Mike.'

'Good gracious! Why?'

'Well, years ago in the old days he killed two men with a single shot. She says he's handier with his gun even now than any man West of the Rockies. He's a miner, but he's been a cowpuncher, a gun-runner, and God knows what in his day.'

'A thoroughly Western type,' said my professor a trifle acidly, I thought.

'Something of a desperado, I imagine. Mrs Barnaby's stories about him are a real treat. Of course everyone's been begging her to let him come over, but she says he'd never leave the wide open spaces. He struck oil a year or two ago and now he's got all the money in the world. He must be a great character. I've heard her keep the whole dinner-table spellbound when she's talked of the old days when they roughed it together. It gives you quite a thrill when you see this grey-haired woman, not at all pretty, but exquisitely dressed, with the most wonderful pearls, and hear her tell how she washed the miners' clothes and cooked for the camp. Your American women have an adaptability that's really stupendous. When you see Mrs Barnaby sitting at the head of her table, perfectly at home with princes of the blood, ambassadors, cabinet ministers, and the duke of this and the duke of that, it seems almost incredible that only a few years ago she was cooking the food of seventy miners.'

'Can she read or write?'

'I suppose her invitations are written by her secretary, but she's by no means an ignorant woman. She told me she used to make a point of reading for an hour every night after the fellows in camp had gone to bed.'

'Remarkable!'

'On the other hand One-Bullet Mike only learnt to write his

name when he suddenly found himself under the necessity of signing cheques.'

We walked up the hill to our hotel and before separating for the night arranged to take our luncheon with us next day and row over to a cove that my friend had discovered. We spent a charming day bathing, reading, eating, sleeping, and talking, and we dined together in the evening. The following morning, after breakfast on the terrace, I reminded Barnaby of his promise to show me his books.

'Come right along.'

I accompanied him to his bedroom, where Giuseppe, the waiter, was making his bed. The first thing I caught sight of was a photograph in a gorgeous frame of the celebrated Mrs Barnaby. My friend caught sight of it too and suddenly turned pale with anger.

'You fool, Giuseppe. Why have you taken that photograph out of my wardrobe? Why the devil did you think I put it away?'

'I didn't know, Signore. That's why I put it back on the Signore's table. I thought he liked to see the portrait of his *signora*.'

I was staggered.

'Is my Mrs Barnaby your wife?' I cried.

'She is.'

'Good Lord, are you One-Bullet Mike?'

'Do I look it?'

I began to laugh.

'I'm bound to say you don't.'

I glanced at his hands. He smiled grimly and held them out.

'No, sir, I have never felled a steer with my naked fist.'

For a moment we stared at one another in silence.

'She'll never forgive me,' he moaned. 'She wanted me to take a false name, and when I wouldn't she was quite vexed with me. She said it wasn't safe. I said it was bad enough to hide myself in Positano for three months, but I'd be damned if I'd use any other name than my own.' He hesitated. 'I throw myself on your mercy. I can do nothing but trust to your generosity not to disclose a secret that you have discovered by the most unlikely chance.'

'I will be as silent as the grave, but honestly I don't understand. What does it all mean?'

'I am a doctor by profession and for the last thirty years my wife and I have lived in Pennsylvania. I don't know if I have struck you as a roughneck, but I venture to say that Mrs Barnaby is one of the most cultivated women I have ever known. Then a cousin of hers died and left her a very large fortune. There's no mistake about that. My wife is a very, very rich women. She has always read a great deal of English fiction and her one desire was to have a London season and entertain and do all the grand things she had read about in books. It was her money and although the prospect did not particularly tempt me, I was very glad that she should gratify her wish. We sailed last April. The young Duke and Duchess of Hereford happened to be on board.'

'I know. It was they who first launched Mrs Barnaby. They were crazy about her. They've boomed her like an army of press-agents.'

'I was ill when we sailed, I had a carbuncle which confined me to my stateroom, and Mrs Barnaby was left to look after herself. Her deck-chair happened to be next the duchess's, and from a remark she overheard it occurred to her that the English aristocracy were not so wrapped up in our social leaders as one might have expected. My wife is a quick little woman and she remarked to me that if you had an ancestor who signed Magna Carta perhaps you were not excessively impressed because the grandfather of one of your acquaintances sold skunks and the grandfather of another ran ferryboats. My wife has a very keen sense of humour. Getting into conversation with the duchess, she told her a little Western anecdote, and to make it more interesting told it as having happened to herself. Its success was immediate. The duchess begged for another and my wife ventured a little further. Twenty-four hours later she had the duke and duchess eating out of her hand. She used to come down to my stateroom at intervals and tell me of her progress. In the innocence of my heart, I was tickled to death and since I had nothing else to do, I sent to the library for the works of Bret Harte and primed her with effective touches.'

I slapped my forehead.

'We said she was as good as Bret Harte,' I cried.

'I had a grand time thinking of the consternation of my wife's friends when at the end of the voyage I appeared and we told them the truth. But I reckoned without my wife. The day before we reached Southampton Mrs Barnaby told me that the Herefords were arranging parties for her. The duchess was crazy to introduce her to all sorts of wonderful people. It was a chance in a thousand; but of course I should spoil everything, she admitted that she had been forced by the course of events to represent me as very different from what I was. I did not know that she had already transformed me into One-Bullet Mike, but I had a shrewd suspicion that she had forgotten to mention that I was on board. Well, to make a long story short, she asked me to go to Paris for a week or two till she had consolidated her position. I didn't mind that. I was much more inclined to do a little work at the Sorbonne than to go to parties in Mayfair, and so leaving her to go on to Southampton, I got off at Cherbourg. But when I had been in Paris ten days she flew over to see me. She told me that her success had exceeded her wildest dreams: it was ten times more wonderful than any of the novels; but my appearance would ruin it all. Very well, I said, I would stay in Paris. She didn't like the idea of that; she said she'd never have a moment's peace so long as I was so near and I might run across someone who knew me. I suggested Vienna or Rome. They wouldn't do either, and at last I came here and here have I been hiding like a criminal for three interminable months.'

'Do you mean to say you never killed the two gamblers, shooting one with your right hand and the other with your left?'

'Sir, I have never fired a pistol in my life.'

'And what about the attack on your log-cabin by the Mexican bandits when your wife loaded your guns for you and you stood the siege for three days till the Federal troops rescued you?'

Mr Barnaby smiled grimly.

'I never heard that one. Isn't it a trifle crude?'

'Crude! It was as good as any Wild West picture.'

'If I may venture a guess, that is where my wife in all probability got the idea.'

'But the wash-tub. Washing the miners' clothes and all that. You don't know how she made us roar with that story. Why, she swam into London Society in her wash-tub.'

I began to laugh.

'She's made the most gorgeous fools of us all,' I said.

'She's made a pretty considerable fool of me, I would have you observe,' remarked Mr Barnaby.

'She's a marvellous woman and you're right to be proud of her. I always said she was priceless. She realized the passion for romance that beats in every British heart and she's given us exactly what we wanted. I wouldn't betray her for worlds.'

'It's all very fine for you, sir. London may have gained a wonderful hostess, but I'm beginning to think that I have lost a perfectly good wife.'

'The only place for One-Bullet Mike is the great open West. My dear Mr Barnaby, there is only one course open to you now. You must continue to disappear.'

'I'm very much obliged to you.'

I thought he replied with a good deal of acidity.

A MAN WITH A CONSCIENCE

St Laurent de Maroni is a pretty little place. It is neat and clean. It has an Hôtel de Ville and a Palais de Justice of which many a town in France would be proud. The streets are wide, and the fine trees that border them give a grateful shade. The houses look as though they had just had a coat of paint. Many of them nestle in little gardens, and in the gardens are palm trees and flame of the forest; cannas flaunt their bright colours and crotons their variety; the bougainvilleas, purple or red, riot profusely, and the elegant hibiscus offers its gorgeous flowers with a negligence that seems almost affected. St Laurent de Maroni is the centre of the French penal settlements of Guiana, and a hundred yards from the quay at which you land is the great gateway of the prison camp. These pretty little houses in their tropical gardens are the residence of the prison officials, and if the streets are neat and clean it is because there is no lack of convicts to keep them so. One day, walking with a casual acquaintance, I came upon a young man, in the round straw hat and the pink and white stripes of the convict's uniform, who was standing by the road-side with a pick. He was doing nothing.

'Why are you idling?' my companion asked him.

The man gave his shoulders a scornful shrug.

'Look at the blade of grass there,' he answered. 'I've got twenty years to scratch it away.'

St Laurent de Maroni exists for the group of prison camps of which it is the centre. Such trade as it has depends on them; its shops, kept by Chinese, are there to satisfy the wants of the warders, the doctors, and the numerous officials who are connected with the penal settlements. The streets are silent and deserted. You pass a convict with a dispatch-case under his arm; he has some job in the administration; or another with a basket; he is a servant in somebody's house. Sometimes you come upon a little group in the charge of a warder; often you see them strolling to or from the prison unguarded. The prison gates are open all day long and the prisoners freely saunter in and out. If you see a man not in the prison uniform he is probably a freed man who is condemned to spend a number of years in the colony and who, unable to get work, living on the edge of starvation, is drinking himself to death on the cheap strong rum which is called tafia.

There is an hotel at St Laurent de Maroni and here I had my meals. I soon got to know by sight the habitual frequenters. They came in and sat each at his little table, ate their meals in silence, and went out again. The hotel was kept by a coloured woman, and the man she lived with, an ex-convict, was the only waiter. But the Governor of the colony, who lives at Cayenne, had put at my disposal his own bungalow and it was there I slept. An old Arab looked after it; he was a devout Mahommedan, and at intervals during the day I heard him say his prayers. To make my bed, keep my rooms tidy, and run errands for me, the commandant of the prison had assigned me another convict. Both were serving life sentences for murder; the commandant told me that I could place entire confidence in them; they were as honest as the day, and I could leave anything about without the slightest risk. But I will not conceal from the reader that when I went to bed at night I took the precaution to lock my door and to bolt my shutters. It was foolish no doubt, but I slept more comfortably.

I had come with letters of introduction, and both the governor of the prison settlements and the commandant of the camp at St Laurent did everything they could to make my visit agreeable and instructive. I will not here narrate all I heard and saw. I am not a reporter. It is not my business to attack or to defend the system which the French have thought fit to adopt in regard to their criminals. Besides, the system is now condemned; prisoners will soon cease to be sent out to French Guiana, to suffer the illnesses incidental to the climate and the work in malarial jungles to which so many are relegated, to endure nameless degradations, to lose hope, to rot, to die. I will only say that I saw no physical cruelty. On the other hand I saw no attempt to make the criminal on the expiration of his sentence a useful citizen. I saw nothing done for his spiritual welfare. I heard nothing of classes that he could attend in order to improve his education or organized games that might distract his mind. I saw no library where he could get books to read when his day's work was done. I saw a condition of affairs that only the strongest character could hope to surmount. I saw a brutishness that must reduce all but a very few to apathy and despair.

All this has nothing to do with me. It is vain to torment oneself over sufferings that one cannot alleviate. My object here is to tell a story. As I am well aware, one can never know everything there is to be known about human nature. One can be sure only of one thing, and that is that it will never cease to have a surprise in store for you. When I had got over the impression of bewilderment, surprise, and horror to which my first visit to the prison camp gave rise, I bethought myself that there were certain matters that I was interested to inquire into. I should inform the reader that three-quarters of the convicts at St Laurent de Maroni are there for murder. This is not official information and it may be that I exaggerate; every prisoner has a little book in which are set down his crime, his sentence, his punishments, and whatever else the authorities think necessary to keep note of; and it was from an examination of a considerable number of these that I formed my estimate. It gave me something of a shock to realize that in England far, far the greater number of these men whom I saw working in shops, lounging about the verandas of their dormitories, or sauntering through the streets would have suffered capital punishment. I found them not at all disinclined to speak of the crime for which they had been convicted, and in pursuance of my purpose I spent the better part of one day inquiring into crimes of passion. I wanted to know exactly what was the motive that had made a man kill his wife or his girl. I had a notion that jealousy and wounded honour might not perhaps tell the whole story. I got some curious replies, and among them one that was not to my mind lacking in humour. This was from a man working in the carpenter's shop who had cut his wife's throat; when I asked him why he had done it, he answered with a shrug of the shoulders: *Manque d'entente*. His casual tone made the best translation of this: We didn't get on very well. I could not help observing that if men in general looked upon this as an adequate reason for murdering their wives, the mortality in the female sex would be alarming. But after putting a good many questions to a good many men I arrived at the conclusion that at the bottom of nearly all these crimes was an economic motive; they had killed their wives or mistresses not only from jealousy, because they were unfaithful to them, but also because somehow it affected their pockets. A woman's infidelity was sometimes an occasion of financial loss, and it was this in the end that drove a man to his desperate act; or, himself in need of money to gratify other passions, he murdered because his victim was an obstacle to his exclusive possession of it. I do not conclude that a man never kills his woman because his love is spurned or his honour tarnished, I only offer my observation on these particular cases as a curious sidelight on human nature. I should not venture to deduce from it a general rule.

I spent another day inquiring into the matter of conscience. Moralists have sought to persuade us that it is one of the most powerful agents in human behaviour. Now that reason and pity have agreed to regard hell-fire as a hateful myth, many good men have seen in conscience the chief safeguard that shall induce the human race to walk in the way of righteousness. Shakespeare has told us that it makes cowards of us all. Novelists and playwrights have described for us the pangs that assail the wicked; they have vividly pictured the anguish of a stricken conscience and the sleepless nights it occasions; they have shown it poisoning every pleasure till life is so intolerable that discovery and punishment come as a welcome relief. I had often wondered how much of all this was true. Moralists have an axe to grind; they must draw a moral. They think that if they say a thing often enough people will believe it. They are apt to state that a thing is so when they consider it desirable that it should be. They tell us that the wages of sin is death; we know very well that it is not always. And so far as the authors of fiction are concerned, the playwrights and the novelists, when they get hold of an effective theme they are disposed to make use of it without bothering very much whether it agrees with the facts of life. Certain statements about human nature become, as it were, common property, and so are accepted as self-evident. In the same way painters for ages painted shadows black, and it was not till the impressionists looked at them with unprejudiced eyes and painted what they saw that we discovered that shadows were coloured. It had sometimes struck me that perhaps conscience was the expression of a high moral development, so that its influence was strong only in those whose virtue was so shining that they were unlikely to commit any action for which they could seriously reproach themselves. It is generally accepted that murder is a shocking crime, and it is the murderer above all other criminals who is supposed to suffer remorse. His victim, we have been led to believe, haunts his dreams in horrifying nightmares, and the recollection of his dreadful deed tortures his waking hours. I could not miss the opportunity to inquire into the truth of this. I had no intention of insisting if I encountered reticence or distress, but I found in none of those with whom I talked any such thing. Some said that in the same circumstances they would do as they had done before. Determinists without knowing it, they seemed to look upon their action as ordained by a fate over which they had no control. Some appeared to think that their crime was committed by someone with whom they had no connexion.

'When's one's young, one's foolish,' they said, with a careless gesture or a deprecating smile.

Others told me that if they had known what the punishment was they would suffer, they would certainly have held their hands. I found in none any regret for the human being they had violently bereft of life. It seemed to me that they had no more feeling for the creature they had killed than if it had been a pig whose throat they had cut in the way of business. Far from feeling pity for their victim, they were more inclined to feel anger because he had been the occasion of their imprisonment in that distant land. In only one man did I discern anything that might appropriately be called a conscience, and his story was so remarkable that I think it well worth narrating. For in this case it was, so far as I can understand, remorse that was the motive of the crime. I noticed the man's number, which was printed on the chest of the pink and white pyjamas of his prison uniform, but I have forgotten it. Anyhow it is of no consequence. I never knew his name. He did not offer to tell me and I did not like to ask it. I will call him Jean Charvin.

I met him on my first visit to the camp with the commandant. We were walking through a courtyard round which were cells, not punishment cells, but individual cells which are given to well-behaved prisoners who ask for them. They are sought after by those to whom the promiscuity of the dormitories is odious. Most of them were empty, for their occupants were engaged in their various employments. Jean Charvin was at work in his cell, writing at a small table, and the door was open. The commandant called him and he came out. I looked into the cell. It contained a fixed hammock, with a dingy mosquito-net; by the side of this was a small table on which were his bits and pieces, a shaving-mop and a razor, a hairbrush and two or three battered books. On the walls were photographs of persons of respectable appearance and illustrations from picture papers. He had been sitting on his bed to write and the table on which he had been writing was covered with papers. They looked like accounts. He was a handsome man, tall, erect, and lean, with flashing dark eyes and clean-cut, strong features. The first thing I noticed about him was that he had a fine head of long, naturally-waving dark brown hair. This at once made him look different from the rest of the prisoners, whose hair is close-cropped, but cropped so badly, in ridges, that it gives them a sinister look. The commandant spoke to him of some official business, and then as we were leaving added in a friendly way:

'I see your hair is growing well.'

Jean Charvin reddened and smiled. His smile was boyish and engaging.

'It'll be some time yet before I get it right again.'

The commandant dismissed him and we went on.

'He's a very decent fellow,' he said. 'He's in the accountant's department, and he's had leave to let his hair grow. He's delighted.'

'What is he here for?' I asked.

'He killed his wife. But he's only got six years. He's clever and a good worker. He'll do well. He comes from a very decent family and he's had an excellent education.'

I thought no more of Jean Charvin, but by chance I met him next day on the road. He was coming towards me. He carried a black dispatch-case under his arm, and except for the pink and white stripes of his uniform and the ugly round straw hat that concealed his handsome head of hair, you might have taken him for a young lawyer on his way to court. He walked with a long, leisurely stride, and he had an easy, you might almost say a gallant, bearing. He recognized me, and taking off his hat bade me good morning. I stopped, and for something to say asked him where he was going. He told me he was taking some papers from the governor's office to the bank. There was a pleasing frankness in his face, and his eyes, his really beautiful eyes, shone with good will. I supposed that the vigour of his youth was such that it made life, notwithstanding his position and his surroundings, more than tolerable, even pleasant. You would have said that here was a young man without a care in the world.

'I hear you're going to St Jean tomorrow,' he said.

'Yes. It appears I must start at dawn.'

St Jean is a camp seventeen kilometres from St Laurent, and it is here that are interned the habitual criminals who have been sentenced to transportation after repeated terms of imprisonment. They are petty thieves, confidence men, forgers, tricksters, and suchlike; the prisoners of St Laurent, condemned for more serious offences, look upon them with contempt.

'You should find it an interesting experience,' Jean Charvin said, with his frank and engaging smile. 'But keep your pocket-book buttoned up, they'd steal the shirt off your back if they had half a chance. They're a dirty lot of scoundrels!'

That afternoon, waiting till the heat of the day was less, I sat on the veranda outside my bedroom and read: I had drawn the jalousies and it was tolerably cool. My old Arab came up the stairs on his bare feet, and in his halting French told me that there was a man from the commandant who wanted to see me.

'Send him up,' I said.

In a moment the man came, and it was Jean Charvin. He told me that the commandant had sent him to give me a message about my excursion next day to St Jean. When he had delivered it I asked him if he would not sit down and have a cigarette with me. He wore a cheap wrist-watch and he looked at it.

'I have a few minutes to spare. I should be glad to.' He sat down and lit the cigarette I offered him. He gave me a smiling look of his soft eyes. 'Do you know, this is the first time I've ever been asked to sit down since I was sentenced.' He inhaled a long whiff of his cigarette. 'Egyptian. I haven't smoked an Egyptian cigarette for three years.'

The convicts make their own cigarettes out of a coarse, strong tobacco that is sold in square blue packets. Since one is not allowed to pay them for the services they may render you, but may give them tobacco, I had bought a good many packets of this.

'How does it taste?'

'One gets accustomed to everything and, to tell you the truth, my palate is so vitiated, I prefer the stuff we get here.'

'I'll give you a couple of packets.'

I went into my room and fetched them. When I returned he was looking at some books that were lying on the table.

'Are you fond of reading?' I asked.

'Very. I think the want of books is what I most suffer from now. The few I can get hold of I'm forced to read over and over again.'

To so great a reader as myself no deprivation seems more insupportable than the lack of books.

'I have several French ones in my bag. I'll look them out and if you care to have them I'll give them to you if you can come along again.'

My offer was due only in part to kindness; I wanted to have another chance of a talk with him.

'I should have to show them to the commandant. He would only let me keep them if there was no doubt they couldn't possibly corrupt my morals. But he's a good-natured man, I don't think he'll make any difficulties.'

There was a hint of slyness in the smile with which he said this, and I suspected that he had taken the measure of the well-meaning conscientious chief of the camp and knew pretty well how to get on the right side of him. It would have been unjust to blame him if he exercised tact, and even cunning, to render his lot as tolerable as might be.

'The commandant has a very good opinion of you.'

'He's a fine man. I'm very grateful to him, he's done a great deal for me. I'm an accountant by profession and he's put me in the accountant's department. I love figures, it gives me an intense satisfaction to deal with them, they're living things to me, and now that I can handle them all day long I feel myself again.'

'And are you glad to have a cell of your own?'

'It's made all the difference. To be herded with fifty men, the scum of the earth, and never to be alone for a minute – it was awful. That was the worst of all. At home, at Le Havre, that is where I lived, I had an apartment, modest of course, but my own, and we had a maid who came in by the day. We lived decently. It made it ten times harder for me than for the rest, most of them, who have never known anything but squalor, filth, and promiscuity.'

I had asked him about the cell in the hope that I could get him to talk about the life that is led in those vast dormitories in which the men are locked from five in the evening till five next morning. During these twelve hours they are their own masters. A warder can enter, they told me, only at the risk of his life. They have no light after eight o'clock, but from sardine-tins, a little oil, and a rag they make lamps by the light of which they can see enough to play cards. They gamble furiously, not for love, but for the money they keep secreted on their bodies; they are unscrupulous ruthless men, and naturally enough bitter quarrels often arise. They are settled with knives. Often in the morning, when the dormitory is opened, a man is found dead, but no threats, no promises, will induce anyone to betray the slayer. Other things Jean Charvin told me which I cannot narrate. He told me of one young fellow who had come out from France on the same ship with himself and with whom he had made friends. He was a good-looking boy. One day he went to the commandant and asked him if he could have a cell to himself. The commandant asked him why he wanted one. He explained. The commandant looked through his list and told him that at the moment all were occupied, but that as soon as there was a vacancy he should have one. Next morning when the dormitory was opened, he was found dead on his hammock with his belly ripped open to the breast-bone.

'They're savage brutes, and if one isn't a brute by the time one arrives only a miracle can save one from becoming as brutal as the rest.'

Jean Charvin looked at his watch and got up. He walked away from me and then, with his charming smile, turned and faced me.

'I must go now. If the commandant gives me permission I will come and get the books you were kind enough to offer me.'

In Guiana you do not shake hands with a convict, and a tactful man, taking leave of you, puts himself in such a position that there can be no question of your offering him your hand or of refusing his should he, forgetting for a moment, instinctively tender it. Heaven knows, it would have meant nothing to me to shake hands with Jean Charvin; it gave me a pang to see the care he had taken to spare me embarrassment.

I saw him twice more during my stay at St Laurent. He told me his story, but I will tell it now in my words rather than in his, for I had to piece it together from what he said at one time and another, and what he left out I have had to supply out of my own imagination. I do not believe it has led me astray. It was as though he had given me three letters out of a number of five-letter words; the chances are that I have guessed most of the words correctly.

Jean Charvin was born and bred in the great seaport of Le Havre. His father had a good post in the Customs. Having finished his education, he did his military service, and then looked about for a job. Like a great many other young Frenchmen he was prepared to sacrifice the hazardous chance of wealth for a respectable security. His natural gift for figures made it easy for him to get a place in the accountant's department of a large exporting house. His future was assured. He could look forward to earning a sufficient income to live in the modest comfort of the class to which he belonged. He was industrious and well-behaved. Like most young Frenchmen of his generation he was athletic. He swam and played tennis in summer, and in winter he bicycled. On two evenings a week to keep himself fit he spent a couple of hours in a gymnasium. Through his childhood, his adolescence, and his young manhood, he lived in the constant companionship of a boy called, shall we say for the purposes of this narrative, Henri Renard, whose father was also an official in the Customs. Jean and Riri went to school together, played together, worked for their examinations together, spent their holidays together, for the two families were intimate, had their first affairs with girls together, partnered one another in the local tennis tournaments, and did their military service together. They never quarrelled. They were never so happy as in one another's society. They were inseparable. When the time came for them to start working they decided that they would go into the same firm; but that was not so easy; Jean tried to get Riri a job in the exporting house that had engaged him, but could not manage it, and it was not till a year later that Riri got something to do. But by then trade was as bad at Le Havre as everywhere else, and in a few months he found himself once more without employment.

Riri was a light-hearted youth, and he enjoyed his leisure. He danced, bathed, and played tennis. It was thus that he made the acquaintance of a girl who had recently come to live at Le Havre. Her father had been a captain in the colonial army and on his death her mother had returned to Le Havre, which was her native place. Marie-Louise was then eighteen. She had spent almost all her life in Tonkin. This gave her an exotic attraction for the young men who had never been out of France in their lives, and first Riri, then Jean, fell in love with her. Perhaps that was inevitable; it was certainly unfortunate. She was a well-brought-up girl, an only child, and her mother, besides her pension, had a little money of her own. It was evident that she could be pursued only with a view to marriage. Of course Riri, dependent for the while entirely on his father, could not make an offer that there was the least chance of Madame Meurice, Marie-Louise's mother, accepting; but having the whole day to himself he was able to see a great deal more of Marie-Louise than Jean could. Madame Meurice was something of an invalid, so that Marie-Louise had more liberty than most French girls of her age and station. She knew that both Riri and Jean were in love with her, she liked them both and was pleased by their attentions, but she gave no sign that she was in love with either. It was impossible to tell which she preferred. She was well aware that Riri was not in a position to marry her.

'What did she look like?' I asked Jean Charvin.

'She was small, with a pretty little figure, with large grey eyes, a pale skin, and soft, mouse-coloured hair. She was rather like a little mouse. She was not beautiful, but pretty, in a quaint demure way; there was something very appealing about her. She was easy to get on with. She was simple and unaffected. You couldn't help feeling that she was reliable and would make anyone a good wife.'

Jean and Riri hid nothing from one another and Jean made no secret of the fact that he was in love with Marie-Louise, but Riri had met her first and it was an understood thing between them that Jean should not stand in his way. At length she made her choice. One day Riri waited for Jean to come away from his office and told him that Marie-Louise had consented to marry him. They had arranged that as soon as he got a job his father should go to her mother and make the formal offer. Jean was hard hit. It was not easy to listen with eager sympathy to the plans that the excitable and enchanted Riri made for the future. But he was too much attached to Riri to feel sore with him; he knew how lovable he was and he could not blame Marie-Louise. He tried with all his might to accept honestly the sacrifice he made on the altar of friendship.

'Why did she choose him rather than you?' I asked.

'He had immense vitality. He was the gayest, most amusing lad you ever met. His high spirits were infectious. You couldn't be dull in his company.'

'He had pep,' I smiled.

'And an incredible charm.'

'Was he good-looking?'

'No, not very. He was shorter than me, slight and wiry; but he had a nice, good-humoured face.' Jean Charvin smiled rather pleasantly. 'I think without any vanity I can say that I was better-looking than Riri.'

But Riri did not get a job. His father, tired of keeping him in idleness, wrote to everyone he could think of, the members of his family and his friends in various parts of France, asking them if they could not find something, however modest, for Riri to do; and at last he got a letter from a cousin in Lyons who was in the silk business to say that his firm were looking for a young man to go out to Phnom-Penh, in Cambodia, where they had a branch, to buy native silk for them. If Riri was willing to take the job he could get it for him.

Though like all French parents Riri's hated him to emigrate, there seemed no help for it, and it was determined, although the salary was small, that he must go. He was not disinclined. Cambodia was not so far from Tonkin, and Marie-Louise must be familiar with the life. She had so often talked of it that he had come to the conclusion that she would be glad to go back to the East. To his dismay she told him that nothing would induce her to. In the first place she could not desert her mother, whose health was obviously declining; and then, after having at last settled down in France, she was determined never again to leave it. She was sympathetic to Riri, but resolute. With nothing else in prospect his father would not hear of his refusing the offer; there was no help for it, he had to go. Jean hated losing him, but from the moment Riri told him his bad news, he had realized with an exulting heart that fate was playing into his hands. With Riri out of his way for five years at least, and unless he were incompetent with the probability that he would settle in the East for good, Jean could not doubt that after a while Marie-Louise would marry him. His circumstances, his settled, respectable position in Le Havre, where she could be near her mother, would make her think it very sensible; and when she was no longer under the spell of Riri's charm there was no reason why her great liking for him should not turn to love. Life changed for him. After months of misery he was happy again, and though he kept them to himself he too now made great plans for the future. There was no need any longer to try not to love Marie-Louise.

Suddenly his hopes were shattered. One of the shipping firms at Le Havre had a vacancy, and it looked as though the application that Riri had quickly made would be favourably considered. A friend in the office told him that it was a certainty. It would settle everything. It was an old and conservative house, and it was well known that when you once got into it you were there for life. Jean Charvin was in despair, and the worst of it was that he had to keep his anguish to himself. One day the director of his own firm sent for him.

When he reached this point Jean stopped. A harassed look came into his eyes.

'I'm going to tell you something now that I've never told to anyone before. I'm an honest man, a man of principle; I'm going to tell you of the only discreditable action I've ever done in my life.'

I must remind the reader here that Jean Charvin was wearing the pink and white stripes of the convict's uniform, with his number stencilled on his chest, and that he was serving a term of imprisonment for the murder of his wife.

'I couldn't imagine what the director wanted with me. He was sitting at his desk when I went into his office, and he gave me a searching look.

' "I want to ask you a question of great importance," he said. "I wish you to treat it as confidential. I shall of course treat your answer as equally so."

'I waited. He went on:

' "You've been with us for a considerable time. I am very well satisfied with you, there is no reason why you shouldn't reach a very good position in the firm. I put implicit confidence in you."

' "Thank you, sir," I said. "I will always try to merit your good opinion."

' "The question at issue is this. Monsieur Untel is proposing to engage Henri Renard. He is very particular about the character of his employees, and in this case it is essential that he shouldn't make a mistake. Part of Henri Renard's duties would be to pay the crews of the firm's ships, and many hundreds of thousand francs will pass through his hands. I know that Henri Renard is your great friend and that your families have always been very intimate. I put you on your honour to tell me whether Monsieur Untel would be justified in engaging this young man."

'I saw at once what the question meant. If Riri got the job he would stay and marry Marie-Louise, if he didn't he would go out to Cambodia and I should marry her. I swear to you it was not I who answered, it was someone who stood in my shoes and spoke with my voice, I had nothing to do with the words that came from my mouth.

' "*Monsieur le directeur*," I said, "Henri and I have been friends all our lives. We have never been separated for a week. We went to school together; we shared our pocket-money and our mistresses when we were old enough to have them; we did our military service together."

' "I know. You know him better than anyone in the world. That is why I ask you these questions."

' "It is not fair, *Monsieur le directeur*. You are asking me to betray my friend. I cannot, and I will not answer your questions."

'The director gave me a shrewd smile. He thought himself much cleverer than he really was.

' "Your answer does you credit, but it has told me all I wished to know." Then he smiled kindly. I suppose I was pale, I dare say I was trembling a little. "Pull yourself together, my dear boy; you're upset and I can understand it. Sometimes in life one is faced by a situation where honesty stands on the one side and loyalty on the other. Of course one mustn't hesitate, but the choice is bitter. I shall not forget your behaviour in this case and on behalf of Monsieur Untel I thank you."

'I withdrew. Next morning Riri received a letter informing him that his services were not required, and a month later he sailed for the Far East.'

Six months after this Jean Charvin and Marie-Louise were married. The marriage was hastened by the increasing gravity of Madame Meurice's illness. Knowing that she could not live long, she was anxious to see her daughter settled before she died. Jean wrote to Riri telling him the facts and Riri wrote back warmly congratulating him. He assured him that he need have no compunctions on his behalf; when he had left France he realized that *he* could never marry Marie-Louise, and he was glad that Jean was going to. He was finding consolation at Phnom-Penh. His letter was very cheerful. From the beginning Jean had told himself that Riri, with his mercurial temperament, would soon forget Marie-Louise, and his letter looked as if he had already done so. He had done him no irreparable injury. It was a justification. For if *he* had lost Marie-Louise he would have died; with him it was a matter of life and death.

For a year Jean and Marie-Louise were extremely happy. Madame Meurice died, and Marie-Louise inherited a couple of hundred thousand francs; but with the depression and the unstable currency they decided not to have a child till the economic situation was less uncertain. Marie-Louise was a good and frugal housekeeper. She was an affectionate, amiable, and satisfactory wife. She was placid. This before he married her had seemed to Jean a rather charming trait, but as time wore on it was borne in upon him that her placidity came from a certain lack of emotional ardour. It concealed no depth. He had always thought she was like a little mouse; there was something mouse-like in her furtive reticences; she was oddly serious about trivial matters and could busy herself indefinitely with things that were of no consequence. She had her own little set of interests and they left no room in her pretty sleek head for any others. She sometimes began a novel, but seldom cared to finish it. Jean was obliged to admit to himself that she was rather dull. The uneasy thought came to him that perhaps it had not been worth while to do a dirty trick for her sake. It began to worry him. He missed Riri. He tried to persuade himself that what was done was done and that he had really not been a free agent, but he could not quite still the prickings of his conscience. He wished now that when the director of his firm spoke to him he had answered differently.

Then a terrible thing happened. Riri contracted typhoid fever and died. It was a frightful shock for Jean. It was a shock to Marie-Louise too; she paid Riri's parents the proper visit of condolence, but she neither ate less heartily nor slept less soundly. Jean was exasperated by her composure.

'Poor chap, he was always so gay,' she said, 'he must have hated dying. But why did he go out there? I told him the climate was bad; it killed my father and I knew what I was talking about.'

Jean felt that he had killed him. If he had told the director all the good he knew of Riri, knew as no one else in the world did, he would have got the post and would now be alive and well.

'I shall never forgive myself,' he thought. 'I shall never be happy again. Oh, what a fool I was, and what a cad!'

He wept for Riri. Marie-Louise sought to comfort him. She was a kind little thing and she loved him.

'You mustn't take it too hardly. After all, you wouldn't have seen him for five years, and you'd have found him so changed that there wouldn't have been anything between you any more. He would have been a stranger to you. I've seen that sort of thing happen so often. You'd have been delighted to see him, and in half an hour you'd have discovered that you had nothing to say to one another.'

'I dare say you're right,' he sighed.

'He was too scatter-brained ever to have amounted to anything very much. He never had your firmness of character and your clear, solid intellect.'

He knew what she was thinking. What would have been her position now if she had followed Riri to Indo-China and found herself at twenty-one a widow with nothing but her own two hundred thousand francs to live on? It was a lucky escape and she congratulated herself on her good sense. Jean was a husband of whom she could be proud. He was earning good money. Jean was tortured by remorse. What he had suffered before was nothing to what he suffered now. The anguish that the recollection of his treachery caused him was worse than a physical pain gnawing at his vitals. It would assail him suddenly when he was in the middle of his work and twist his heartstrings with a violent pang. His agony was such that he craved for relief, and it was only by an effort of all his will that he prevented himself from making a full confession to Marie-Louise. But he knew how she would take it; she would not be shocked, she would think it rather a clever trick and be even subtly flattered that for her sake he had been guilty of a despicable act. She could not help him. He began to dislike her. For it was for her that he had done the shameful thing, and what was she? An ordinary, commonplace, rather calculating little woman.

'What a fool I've been,' he repeated.

He did not even find her pretty any more. He knew now that she was terribly stupid. But of course she was not to blame for that, she was not to blame because he had been false to his friend; and he forced himself to be as sweet and tender to her as he had always been. He did whatever she wanted. She had only to express a wish for him to fulfil it if it was in his power. He tried to pity her, he tried to be tolerant; he told himself that from her own petty standpoint she was a good wife, methodical, saving, and in her manner, dress, and appearance a credit to a respectable young man. All that was true; but it was on her account that Riri had died, and he loathed her. She bored him to distraction. Though he said nothing, though he was kind, amiable, and indulgent, he could often have killed her. When he did, however, it was almost without meaning to. It was ten months after Riri's death, and Riri's parents, Monsieur and Madame Renard, gave a party to celebrate the engagement of their daughter. Jean had seen little of them since Riri's death and he did not want to go. But Marie-Louise said they must; he had been Riri's greatest friend and it would be a grave lack of politeness on Jean's part not to attend an important celebration in the family. She had a keen sense of social obligation.

'Besides, it'll be a distraction for you. You've been in poor spirits for so long, a little amusement will do you good. There'll be champagne, won't there? Madame Renard doesn't like spending money, but on an occasion like this she'll have to sacrifice herself.'

Marie-Louise chuckled slyly when she thought what a wrench it would be to Madame Renard to unloose her purse-strings.

The party had been very gay. It gave Jean a nasty turn when he found that they were using Riri's old room for the women to put their wraps in and the men their coats. There was plenty of champagne. Jean drank a great deal to drown the bitter remorse that tormented him. He wanted to deaden the sound in his ears of Riri's laugh and to shut his eyes to the good-humour of his shining glance. It was three o'clock when they got home. Next day was Sunday, so Jean had no work to go to. They slept late. The rest I can tell in Jean Charvin's own words.

'I had a headache when I woke. Marie-Louise was not in bed. She was sitting at the dressing-table brushing her hair. I've always been very keen on physical culture, and I was in the habit of doing exercises every morning. I didn't feel very much inclined to do them that morning, but after all that champagne I thought I'd better. I got out of bed and took up my Indian clubs. Our bedroom was fairly large and there was plenty of room to swing them between the bed and the dressing-table where Marie-Louise was sitting. I did my usual exercises. Marie-Louise had started a little while before having her hair cut differently, quite short, and I thought it repulsive. From the back she looked like a boy, and the stubble of cropped hair on her neck made me feel rather sick. She put down her brushes and began to powder her face. She gave a nasty little laugh.

' "What are you laughing at?" I asked.

' "Madame Renard. That was the same dress she wore at our wedding, she'd had it dyed and done over; but it didn't deceive me. I'd have known it anywhere."

'It was such a stupid remark, it infuriated me. I was seized with rage, and with all my might I hit her over the head with my Indian club. I broke her skull, apparently, and she died two days later in hospital without recovering consciousness.'

He paused for a moment. I handed him a cigarette and lit another myself.

'I was glad she did. We could never have lived together again, and it would have been very hard to explain my action.'

'Very.'

'I was arrested and tried for murder. Of course I swore it was an accident, I said the club had slipped out of my hand, but the medical evidence was against me. The prosecution proved that such an injury as Marie-Louise had suffered could only have been caused by a violent and deliberate blow. Fortunately for me they could find no motive. The public prosecutor tried to make out that I had been jealous of the attentions some man had paid her at the party and that we had quarrelled on that account, but the man he mentioned swore that he had done nothing to arouse my suspicions and others at the party testified that we had left the best of friends. They found on the dressing-table an unpaid dressmaker's bill and the prosecutor suggested that we had quarrelled about that, but I was able to prove that Marie-Louise paid for her

clothes out of her own money, so that the bill could not possibly
have been the cause of a dispute. Witnesses came forward and
said that I had always been kind to Marie-Louise. We were
generally looked upon as a devoted couple. My character was
excellent and my employer spoke in the highest terms of me. I
was never in danger of losing my head, and at one moment I
thought I had a chance of getting off altogether. In the end I was
sentenced to six years. I don't regret what I did, for from that day,
all the time I was in prison awaiting my trial, and since, while I've
been here, I've ceased to worry about Riri. If I believed in ghosts
I'd be inclined to say that Marie-Louise's death has laid Riri's.
Anyhow, my conscience is at rest, and after all the torture I
suffered I can assure you that everything I've gone through since
is worth it; I feel I can now look the world in the face again.'

I know that this is a fantastic story; I am by way of being a
realist, and in the stories I write I seek verisimilitude. I eschew
the bizarre as scrupulously as I avoid the whimsical. If this had
been a tale that I was inventing I would certainly have made it
more probable. As it is, unless I had heard it with my own ears
I am not sure that I should believe it. I do not know whether Jean
Charvin told me the truth, and yet the words with which he closed
his final visit to me had a convincing ring. I had asked him what
were his plans for the future.

'I have friends working for me in France,' he answered. 'A
great many people thought at the time that I was the victim of a
grave miscarriage of justice; the director of my firm is convinced
that I was unjustly condemned; and I may get a reduction of my
sentence. Even if I don't, I think I can count upon getting back
to France at the end of my six years. You see, I'm making myself
useful here. The accounts were very badly kept when I took them
over, and I've got them in apple-pie order. There have been
leakages, and I'm convinced that if they'll give me a free hand,
I can stop them. The commandant likes me and I'm certain that
he'll do everything he can for me. At the worst I shan't be much
over thirty when I get back.'

'But won't you find it rather difficult to get work?'

'A clever accountant like me, and a man who's honest and
industrious, can always get work. Of course I shan't be able to
live in Le Havre, but the director of my firm has business con-
nexons at Lille and Lyons and Marseilles. He's promised to do
something for me. No, I look forward to the years to come with a
good deal of confidence. I shall settle down somewhere, and as

soon as I'm comfortably fixed up I shall marry. After what I've been through I want a home.'

We were sitting in one of the corners of the veranda that surrounded my house in order to get any draught there might be, and on the north side I had left a jalousie undrawn. The strip of sky you saw with a single coconut tree on one side, its green foliage harsh against the blue, looked like an advertisement for a tropical cruise. Jean Charvin's eyes searched the distance as though he sought to see the future.

'But next time I marry,' he said thoughtfully, 'I shan't marry for love, I shall marry for money.'

AN OFFICIAL POSITION

HE was a sturdy broad-shouldered fellow, of the middle height; though his bones were well covered as became his age, which was fifty, he was not fat; he had a ruddy complexion which neither the heat of the sun nor the unwholesomeness of the climate had affected. It was good rich blood that ran through his veins. His hair was brown and thick, and only at the temples touched with grey; he was very proud of his fair, handsome moustache and he kept it carefully brushed. There was a pleasant twinkle in his blue eyes. You would have said that this was a man whom life had treated well. There was in his appearance an air of good nature and in his vigour a glow of health that gave you confidence. He reminded you of one of those well-fed, rubicund burghers in an old Dutch picture, with their pink-cheeked wives, who made money and enjoyed the good things with which their industry provided them. He was, however, a widower. His name was Louis Remire, and his number 68763. He was serving a twelve-year sentence at St Laurent de Maroni, the great penal settlement of French Guiana, for killing his wife, but partly because he had served in the police force at Lyons, his native town, and partly on account of his good character, he had been given an official position. He had been chosen among nearly two hundred applicants to be the public executioner.

That was why he was allowed to sport the handsome moustache of which he took so much care. He was the only convict who wore one. It was in a manner of speaking his badge of office. That also was why he was allowed to wear his own clothes. The convicts wear pyjamas in pink and white stripes, round straw hats, and clumsy boots with wooden soles and leather tops. Louis Remire wore espadrilles on his bare feet, blue cotton trousers, and a khaki shirt the open neck of which exposed to view his hairy and virile chest. When you saw him strolling about the public garden, with a kindly eye looking at the children, black or half-caste, who played there, you would have taken him for a respectable shopkeeper who was enjoying an hour's leisure. He had his own house. That was not only one of the perquisites of his office, but it was a necessity, since if he had lodged in the prison camp the convicts would have made short work of him. One morning he would have been found with his belly ripped open. It was true that the house was small, it was just a wooden shack of one room, with a lean-to that served as a kitchen; but it was surrounded by a tiny garden, within a palisade, and in the garden grew bananas, papaias, and such vegetables as the climate allowed him to raise. The garden faced the sea and was surrounded by a coconut grove. The situation was charming. It was only a quarter of a mile from the prison, which was convenient for his rations. They were fetched by his assistant, who lived with him. The assistant, a tall, gawky, ungainly fellow, with deep-set, staring eyes and cavernous jaws, was serving a life sentence for rape and murder; he was not very intelligent, but in civil life he had been a cook and it was wonderful what, with the help of the vegetables they grew and such condiments as Louis Remire could afford to buy at the Chinese grocer's, he managed to do with the soup, potatoes and cabbage, and eternal beef, beef for three hundred and sixty-five days of the year, which the prison kitchens provided. It was on this account that Louis Remire had pressed his claim on the commandant when it had been found necessary to get a new assistant. The last one's nerves had given way and, absurdly enough, thought Louis Remire with a good-natured laugh, he had developed scruples about capital punishment; now, suffering from neurasthenia, he was on the Ile St Joseph, where the insane were confined.

His present assistant happened to be ill. He had high fever, and looked very much as if he were going to die. It had been necessary to send him to hospital. Louis Remire was sorry; he would not easily find so good a cook again. It was bad luck that this should have happened just now, for next day there was a job of work to be done. Six men were to be executed. Two were Algerians, one was a Pole, another a Spaniard from the mainland, and only two were French. They had escaped from prison in a band and gone up the river. For nearly twelve months, stealing, raping, and killing they had spread terror through the colony. People scarcely dared move from their homesteads. Recaptured at last, they had all been sentenced to death, but the sentence had to be confirmed by the Minister of the Colonies, and the confirmation had only just arrived. Louis Remire could not manage without help, and besides there was a lot to arrange beforehand; it was particularly unfortunate that on this occasion of all others he should have to depend on an inexperienced man. The commandant had assigned to him one of the turnkeys. The turnkeys are convicts like the others, but they have been given their places for good behaviour and they live in separate quarters. They are on the side of the authorities and so are disliked by the other prisoners. Louis

Remire was a conscientious fellow, and he was anxious that everything next day should go without a hitch. He arranged that his temporary assistant should come that afternoon to the place where the guillotine was kept so that he might explain to him thoroughly how it worked and show him exactly what he would have to do.

The guillotine, when not in use, stood in a small room which was part of the prison building, but which was entered by a separate door from the outside. When he sauntered along there at the appointed hour he found the man already waiting. He was a large-limbed, coarse-faced fellow. He was dressed in the pink and white stripes of the prison garb, but as turnkey he wore a felt hat instead of the straw of common convicts.

'What are you here for?'

The man shrugged his shoulders.

'I killed a farmer and his wife.'

'H'm. How long have you got?'

'Life.'

He looked a brute, but you could never be sure of people. He had himself seen a warder, a big, powerful man, faint dead away at an execution. He did not want his assistant to have an attack of nerves at the wrong moment. He gave him a friendly smile, and with his thumb pointed to the closed door behind which stood the guillotine.

'This is another sort of job,' he said. 'There are six of them, you know. They're a bad lot. The sooner they're out of the way the better.'

'Oh, that's all right. After what I've seen in this place I'm scared of nothing. It means no more to me than cutting the head off a chicken.'

Louis Remire unlocked the door and walked in. His assistant followed him. The guillotine in that small room, hardly larger than a cell, seemed to take up a great deal of space. It stood grim and sinister. Louis Remire heard a slight gasp and turning round saw that the turnkey was staring at the instrument with terrified eyes. His face was sallow and drawn from the fever and the hookworm from which all the convicts intermittently suffered, but now its pallor was ghastly. The executioner smiled good-naturedly.

'Gives you a turn, does it? Have you never seen it before?'

'Never.'

Louis Remire gave a little throaty chuckle.

'If you had, I suppose you wouldn't have survived to tell the tale. How did you escape it?'

'I was starving when I did my job. I'd asked for something to eat and they set the dogs on me. I was condemned to death. My lawyer went to Paris and he got the President to reprieve me.'

'It's better to be alive than dead, there's no denying that,' said Louis Remire, with that agreeable twinkle in his eyes.

He always kept his guillotine in perfect order. The wood, a dark hard native wood somewhat like mahogany, was highly polished; but there was a certain amount of brass, and it was Louis Remire's pride that this should be as bright and clean as the brass-work on a yacht. The knife shone as though it had just come out of the workshop. It was necessary not only to see that everything functioned properly, but to show his assistant how it functioned. It was part of the assistant's duty to refix the rope when the knife had dropped, and to do this he had to climb a short ladder.

It was with the satisfaction of a competent workman who knows his job from A to Z that Remire entered upon the necessary explanations. It gave him a certain quiet pleasure to point out the ingenuity of the apparatus. The condemned man was strapped to the bascule, a sort of shelf, and this by a simple mechanism was precipitated down and forwards so that the man's neck was conveniently under the knife. The conscientious fellow had brought with him a banana stem, about five feet long, and the turnkey wondered why. He was now to learn. The stem was of about the same circumference and consistency as the human neck, so that it afforded a very good way, not only of showing a novice how the apparatus worked, but of making sure beforehand that it was in perfect order. Louis Remire placed the banana stem in position. He released the knife. It fell with incredible speed and with a great bang. From the time the man was attached to the bascule to the time his head was off only thirty seconds elapsed. The head fell in the basket. The executioner took it up by the ears and exhibited it to those whose duty it was to watch the execution. He uttered the solemn words:

'*Au nom du peuple français justice est faite.* In the name of the French people justice is done.'

Then he dropped the head into the basket. Tomorrow, with six to be dispatched, the trunk would have to be unstrapped from the bascule and placed with the head on a stretcher, and the next man brought forward. They were taken in order of their guilt. The least guilty, executed first, were spared the horror of seeing the death of their mates.

'We shall have to be careful that the right head goes with the right body,' said Louis Remire, in that rather jovial manner of his, 'or there may be no end of confusion at the Resurrection.'

He let down the knife two or three times in order to make quite sure that the assistant understood how to fix it, and then getting his cleaning-materials from the shelf on which he kept them set him to work on the brass. Though it was spotless he thought that a final polish would do no harm. He leaned against the wall and idly smoked cigarettes.

Finally everything was in order and Louis Remire dismissed the assistant till midnight. At midnight they were moving the guillotine from the room in which it stood to the prison yard. It was always a bit of a job to set it up again, but it had to be in place an hour before dawn, at which time the execution took place. Louis Remire strolled slowly home to his shack. The afternoon was drawing to its close, and as he walked along he passed a working party who were returning to the prison. They spoke to one another in undertones and he guessed that they spoke of him; some looked down, two or three threw him a glance of hatred, and one spat on the ground. Louis Remire, the end of a cigarette sticking to his lip, looked at them with irony. He was indifferent to the loathing, mingled with fear, with which they regarded him. It did not matter to him that not one of them would speak to him, and it only amused him to think that there was hardly one who would not gladly have thrust a knife into his guts. He had a supreme contempt for them all. He could take care of himself. He could use a knife as well as any of them, and he had confidence in his strength. The convicts knew that men were to be executed next day, and as always before an execution they were depressed and nervous. They went about their work in sullen silence, and the warders had to be more than usually on the alert.

'They'll settle down when it's all over,' said Louis Remire as he let himself into his little compound.

The dogs barked as he came along, and brave though he was, he listened to their uproar with satisfaction. With his own assistant ill, so that he was alone in the house, he was not sorry that he had the protection of those two savage mongrels. They prowled about the coconut grove outside his compound all night and they would give him good warning if anyone lurked there. They could be relied on to spring at the throat of any stranger who ventured too near. If his predecessor had had these dogs he wouldn't have come to his end.

The man who had been executioner before Louis Remire had

only held the job a couple of years when one day he disappeared. The authorities thought he had run away; he was known to have a bit of money, and it was very probable that he had managed to make arrangements with the captain of a schooner to take him to Brazil. His nerves had given way. He had gone two or three times to the governor of the prison and told him that he feared for his life. He was convinced that the convicts were out to kill him. The governor felt pretty sure that his fears were groundless and paid no attention, but when the man was nowhere to be found he concluded that his terror had got the better of him and he had preferred to run the danger of escape, and the danger of being recaptured and put back into prison, rather than face the risk of an avenging convict's knife. About three weeks later the warder in charge of a working party in the jungle noticed a great flock of vultures clustered round a tree. These vultures, called urubus, are large black birds, of a horrible aspect, and they fly about the market-place of St Laurent, picking up the offal that is left there by the starving liberated convicts, and flit heavily from tree to tree in the neat, well-kept streets of the town. They fly in the prison yard to remind the convicts that if they attempt an escape into the jungle their end, ten to one, will be to have their bones picked clean by these loathsome creatures. They were fighting and screaming in such a mass round the tree that the warder thought there was something strange there. He reported it and the commandant sent a party to see. They found a man hanging by the neck from one of the branches, and when they cut him down discovered that he was the executioner. It was given out that he had committed suicide, but there was a knife-thrust in his back, and the convicts knew that he had been stabbed and then, still alive, taken to the jungle and hanged.

Louis Remire had no fear that anything of that sort would happen to him. He knew how his predecessor had been caught. The job had not been done by the convicts. By the French law when a man is sentenced to hard labour for a certain number of years he has at the expiration of his sentence to remain in the colony for the same number of years. He is free, but he may not stir from the spot that is assigned to him as a residence. In certain circumstances he can get a concession and if he works hard he manages to scrape a bare living from it, but after a long term of penal servitude, during which he has lost all power of initiative, what with the debilitating effect of fever, hookworm, and so on, he is unfit for heavy and continuous labour, and so most of the liberated men subsist on begging, larceny, smuggling tobacco or money to the prisoners, and loading and unloading cargoes when two or three times a month a steamer comes into the harbour. It was the wife of one of these freed men that had been the means of the undoing of Louis Remire's predecessor. She was a coloured woman, young and pretty, with a neat little figure and mischievous eyes. The plot was well-considered. The executioner was a burly, sanguine man, of ardent passions. She had thrown herself in his way, and when she caught his approving glance, had cast him a saucy look. He saw her a day or two later in the public garden. He did not venture to speak to her (no one, man, woman, or child, would be seen speaking to him), but when he winked at her she smiled. One evening he met her walking through the coconut grove that surrounded his compound. No one was about. He got into conversation with her. They only exchanged a few words, for she was evidently terrified of being seen with him. But she came again to the coconut grove. She played him carefully till his suspicions were allayed; she teased his desires; she made him give her little presents, and at last on the promise of what was for both of them quite a sum of money she agreed to come one dark night to the compound. A ship had just come in and her husband would be working till dawn. It was when he opened the door for her and she hesitated to come in as though at the last moment she could not make up her mind, that he stepped outside to draw her in, and fell to the ground with the violence of the knife-thrust in his back.

'The fool,' muttered Louis Remire. 'He only got what he deserved. He should have smelt a rat. The eternal vanity of man.'

For his part he was through with women. It was on account of women that he found himself in the situation he was in now, at least on account of one woman; and besides, at his time of life, his passions were assuaged. There were other things in life and after a certain age a man, if he was sensible, turned his attention to them. He had always been a great fisherman. In the old days, at home in France before he had had his misfortune, as soon as he came off duty, he took his rod and line and went down to the Rhône. He got a lot of fishing now. Every morning, till the sun grew hot, he sat on his favourite rock and generally managed to get enough for the prison governor's table. The governor's wife knew the value of things and beat him down on the price he asked, but he did not blame her for that; she knew that he had to take what she was prepared to give and it would have been stupid of her to pay a penny more than she had to. In any case it brought in a little money useful for tobacco and rum and other odds and ends. But this evening he was going to fish for himself. He got his bait from the lean-to, and his rod, and settled down on his rock. No fish was so good as the fish you caught yourself, and by now he knew which were those that were good to eat and which were so tough and flavourless that you could only throw them back into the sea. There was one sort that, fried in real olive oil, was as good as mullet. He had not been sitting there five minutes when his float gave a sudden jerk, and when he pulled up his line, there, like an answer to prayer, was one of those very fish wriggling on the hook. He took it off, banged its head on the rock, and putting it down, replaced his bait. Four of them would make a good supper, the best a man could have, and with a night's hard work before him he needed a hearty meal. He would not have time to fish tomorrow morning. First of all the scaffold would have to be taken down and the pieces brought back to the room in which it was kept, and there would be a lot of cleaning to do. It was a bloody business; last time he had had his pants so soaked that he had been able to do nothing with them and had had to throw them away. The brass would have to be polished, the knife would have to be honed. He was not a man to leave a job half finished, and by the time it was through he would be pretty peckish. It would be worth while to catch a few more fish and put them in a cool place so that he could have a substantial breakfast. A cup of coffee, a couple of eggs, and a bit of fried fish; he could do with that. Then he would have a good sleep; after a night on his feet, the anxiety of an inexperienced assistant, and the clearing away of all the mess, God knew he would deserve it.

In front of him was spread the bay in a noble sweep, and in the distance was a little island green with trees. The afternoon was exquisitely still. Peace descended on the fisherman's soul. He watched his float idly. When you came to think of it, he reflected, he might be a great deal worse off; some of them, the convicts he meant, the convicts who swarmed in the prison a few hundred yards away from him, some of them had such a nostalgia for France that they went mad with melancholy; but he was a bit of a philosopher, so long as he could fish he was content; and did it really matter if he watched his float on the southern sea or in the Rhône? His thoughts wandered back to the past. His wife was an intolerable woman and he did not regret that he had killed her. He had never meant to marry her. She was a dressmaker, and he had taken a fancy to her because she was always neatly and smartly dressed. She seemed respectable and ladylike. He would not have been surprised if she had looked upon herself as a cut above a policeman. But he had a way with him. She soon gave him to understand that she was no snob, and when he made the customary advances he discovered to his relief, for he was not a man who considered that resistance added a flavour to conquest, that she was no prude. He liked to be seen with her when he took her out to dinner. She talked intelligently, and she was economical. She knew where they could dine well at the cheapest price. His situation was enviable. It added to his satisfaction that he could gratify the sexual desires natural to his healthy temperament at so moderate an expense. When she came to him and said she was going to have a baby it seemed natural enough that they should get married. He was earning good wages, and it was time that he should settle down. He often grew tired of eating, *en pension*, at a restaurant, and he looked forward to having his own home and home cooking. Well, it turned out that it had been a mistake about the baby, but Louis Remire was a good-natured fellow, and he didn't hold it up against Adèle. But he found, as many men have found before, that the wife was a very different woman from the mistress. She was jealous and possessive. She seemed to think that on a Sunday afternoon he ought to take her for a walk instead of going fishing, and she made it a grievance that, on coming off duty, he would go to the café. There was one café he frequented where other fishermen went and where he met men with whom he had a lot in common. He found it much pleasanter to spend his free evenings there over a glass or two of beer, whiling away the time with a game of cards, than to sit at home with his wife. She began to make scenes. Though sociable and jovial by nature he had a quick temper. There was a rough crowd at Lyons, and sometimes you could not manage them unless you were prepared to show a certain amount of firmness. When his wife began to make a nuisance of herself it never occurred to him that there was any other way of dealing with her than that he adopted. He let her know the strength of his hand. If she had been a sensible woman she would have learnt her lesson, but she was not a sensible woman. He found occasion more and more often to apply a necessary correction; she revenged herself by screaming the place down and by telling the neighbours – they lived in a two-roomed apartment on the fifth floor of a big house – what a brute he was. She told them that she was sure he would kill her one day. And yet never was there a more good-natured man than Louis

Remire; she blamed him for the money he spent at the café, she accused him of wasting it on other women; well, in his position he had opportunities now and then, and as any man would he took them, and he was easy with his money, he never minded paying a round of drinks for his friends, and when a girl who had been nice to him wanted a new hat or a pair of silk stockings he wasn't the man to say no. His wife looked upon money that he did not spend on her as money stolen from her; she tried to make him account for every penny he spent, and when in his jovial way he told her he had thrown it out of the window, she was infuriated. Her tongue grew bitter and her voice was rasping. She was in a sullen rage with him all the time. She could not speak without saying something disagreeable. They led a cat-and-dog life. Louis Remire used to tell his friends what a harridan she was, he used to tell them that he wished ten times a day that he had never married her, and sometimes he would add that if an epidemic of influenza did not carry her off he would really have to kill her.

It was these remarks, made merely in jest, and the fact that she had so often told the neighbours that she knew he would murder her, that had sent him to St Laurent de Maroni with a twelve-year sentence. Otherwise he might very well have got off with three or four years in a French prison. The end had come one hot summer's day. He was, which was rare for him, in a bad temper. There was a strike in progress and the strikers had been violent. The police had had to make a good many arrests and the men had not submitted to this peaceably. Louis Remire had got a nasty blow on the jaw and he had had to make free use of his truncheon. To get the arrested men to the station had been a hot and tiring job. On coming off duty he had gone home to get out of his uniform and was intending to go to the café and have a glass of beer and a pleasant game of cards. His jaw was hurting him. His wife chose that moment to ask him for money and when he told her that he had none to give her she made a scene. He had plenty of money to go to the café, but none for her to buy a scrap of food with, she could starve for all he cared. He told her to shut up, and then the row began. She got in front of the door and swore that he should not pass till he gave her money. He told her to get out of the way, and took a step towards her. She whipped out his service revolver which he had taken off when he removed his uniform and threatened that she would shoot him if he moved a step. He was used to dealing with dangerous criminals, and the words were hardly out of her mouth before he had sprung upon her and snatched the revolver out of her hand. She screamed and hit him in the face. She hit him exactly where his jaw most hurt him. Blind with rage and mad with pain, he fired, he fired twice and she fell to the floor. For a moment he stood and stared at her. He was dazed. She looked as if she were dead. His first feeling was one of indescribable relief. He listened. No one seemed to have heard the sound of the shot. The neighbours must be out. That was a bit of luck, for it gave him time to do what he had to do in his own way. He changed back into his uniform, went out, locking the door behind him and putting the key in his pocket; he stopped for five minutes at his familiar café to have a glass of beer and then returned to the police-station he had lately left. On account of the day's disturbances the chief inspector was still there. Louis Remire went to his room and told him what had happened. He spent the night in a cell adjoining those of the strikers he had so recently himself arrested. Even at that tragic moment he was struck by the irony of the situation.

Louis Remire had on frequent occasions appeared as a police witness in criminal cases and he knew how eager are a man's companions to give any information that may damage him when he gets into trouble. It had caused him a certain grim amusement to realize how often it happened that a conviction was obtained only by the testimony of a prisoner's best friends. But notwithstanding his experience he was amazed, when his own case came up for trial, to listen to the evidence given by the proprietor of the little café he had so much frequented, and to that of the men who for years had fished with him, played cards with him, and drunk with him. They seemed to have treasured every careless word he had ever uttered, the complaints he had made about his wife and the joking threats he had from time to time made that he would get even with her. He knew that at the time they had taken them no more seriously than he meant them. If he was able to do them a small service, and a man in the force often has it in his power to do one, he never hesitated. He had never been ungenerous with his money. You would have thought as you listened to them in the witness-box that it gave them the most intense satisfaction to disclose every trivial detail that could damage him.

From what appeared at the trial you would have thought that he was a bad man, dissolute, of violent temper, extravagant, idle, and corrupt. He knew that he was nothing of the kind. He was just an ordinary, good-natured, easy-going fellow, who was willing to let you go your way if you would let him go his. It was true that he liked his game of cards and his glass of beer, it was true that he liked a pretty girl, but what of it? When he looked at the jury he wondered how many of them would come out of it any better than he if all their errors, all their rash words, all their follies were thus laid bare. He did not resent the long term of penal servitude to which he was sentenced. He was an officer of the law; he had committed a crime and it was right that he should be punished. But he was not a criminal; he was the victim of an unfortunate accident.

At St Laurent de Maroni, in the prison camp, wearing the pink and white stripe of the prison garb and the ugly straw hat, he remembered still that he had been a policeman and that the convicts with whom he must now consort had always been his natural enemies. He despised and disliked them. He had as little to do with them as he could. And he was not frightened of them. He knew them too well. Like all the rest he had a knife and he showed that he was prepared to use it. He did not want to interfere with anybody, but he was not going to allow anyone to interfere with him.

The chief of the Lyons police had liked him, his character while in the force had been exemplary, and the *fiche* which accompanied every prisoner spoke well of him. He knew that what officials like is a prisoner who gives no trouble, who accepts his position with cheerfulness, and who is willing. He got a soft job; very soon he got a cell of his own and so escaped the horrible promiscuity of the dormitories; he got on well with the warders, they were decent chaps, most of them, and knowing that he had formerly been in the police they treated him more as a comrade than as a convict. The commandant of the prison trusted him. Presently he got the job of servant to one of the prison officials. He slept in the prison, but otherwise enjoyed complete freedom. He took the children of his master to school every day and fetched them at the end of their school hours. He made toys for them. He accompanied his mistress to market and carried back the provisions she bought. He spent long hours gossiping with her. The family liked him. They liked his chaffing manner and his good-natured smile. He was industrious and trustworthy. Life once more was tolerable.

But after three years his master was transferred to Cayenne. It was a blow. But it happened just then that the post of executioner fell free and he obtained it. Now once more he was in the service of the state. He was an official. However humble his residence it was his own. He need no longer wear the prison uniform. He could grow his hair and his moustache. He cared little if the convicts looked upon him with horror and contempt. That was how he looked upon them. Scum. When he took the bleeding head of an executed man from the basket and holding it by the ears pronounced those solemn words: *Au nom du peuple français justice est faite*, he felt that he did represent the Republic. He stood for law and order. He was the protector of society against that vast horde of ruthless criminals.

He got a hundred francs for each execution. That and what the governor's wife paid him for his fish provided him with many a pleasant comfort and not a few luxuries. And now as he sat on his rock in the peace of eventide he considered what he would do with the money he would earn next day. Occasionally he got a bite, now and then a fish; he drew it out of the water, took it off the hook, and put on fresh bait; but he did this mechanically, and it did not disturb the current of his thoughts. Six hundred francs. It was a respectable sum. He scarcely knew what to do with it. He had everything he wanted in his little house, he had a good store of groceries, and plenty of rum for one who was as little of a drinker as he was; he needed no fishing tackle; his clothes were good enough. The only thing was to put it aside. He already had a tidy little sum hidden in the ground at the root of a papaia tree. He chuckled when he thought how Adèle would have stared had she known that he was actually saving. It would have been balm to her avaricious soul. He was saving up gradually for when he was released. That was the difficult moment for the convicts. So long as they were in prison they had a roof over their heads and food to eat, but when they were released, with the obligation of staying for so many years more in the colony, they had to shift for themselves. They all said the same thing: it was at the expiration of their term that their real punishment began. They could not get work. Employers mistrusted them. Contractors would not engage them because the prison authorities hired out convict labour at a price that defied competition. They slept in the open, in the market-place, and for food were often glad to go to the Salvation Army. But the Salvation Army made them work hard for what they gave and besides forced them to listen to their services. Sometimes they committed a violent crime merely to get back to the safety of prison. Louis Remire was not going to take any risks. He meant to amass a sufficient capital to start in business. He ought to be able to get permission to settle in Cayenne, and there he might open a bar. People might hesitate to come at first because he had been the executioner, but if he provided good liquor they would get over their prejudice, and with his jovial manner, with his experience in keeping order, he ought to be able to make a go of it. Visitors came to Cayenne now and then and they would come out of curiosity. It would be something interesting to tell their friends when they got home that the best rum punch they had had in Cayenne was at the executioner's. But he had a good many years to go yet, and if there really was something he needed there was no reason why he shouldn't get it. He racked his brains. No, there wasn't a thing in the world he wanted. He was surprised. He allowed his eyes to wander from his float. The sea was wonderfully calm and now it was rich with all the colour of the setting sun. In the sky already a solitary star twinkled. A thought came to him that filled him with an extraordinary sensation.

'But if there's nothing in the world you want, surely that's happiness.' He stroked his handsome moustache and his blue eyes shone softly. 'There are no two ways about it, I'm a happy man and till this moment I never knew it.'

The notion was so unexpected that he did not know what to make of it. It was certainly a very odd one. But there it was, as obvious to anyone with a logical mind as a proposition of Euclid.

'Happy, that's what I am. How many men can say the same? In St Laurent de Maroni of all places, and for the first time in my life.'

The sun was setting. He had caught enough fish for his supper and enough for his breakfast. He drew in his line, gathered up his fish, and went back to his house. It stood but a few yards from the sea. It did not take him long to light his fire and in a little while he had four little fish cheerfully frizzling in a pan. He was always very particular about the oil he used. The best olive oil was expensive, but it was worth the money. The prison bread was good, and after he had fried his fish, he fried a couple of pieces of bread in the rest of the oil. He sniffed the savoury smell with satisfaction. He lit a lamp, washed a lettuce grown in his own garden, and mixed himself a salad. He had a notion that no one in the world could mix a salad better than he. He drank a glass of rum and ate his supper with appetite. He gave a few odds and ends to the two mongrel dogs who were lying at his feet, and then, having washed up, for he was by nature a tidy man and when he came in to breakfast next morning did not want to find things in a mess, let the dogs out of the compound to wander about the coconut grove. He took the lamp into the house, made himself comfortable in his deck-chair, and smoking a cigar smuggled in from the neighbouring Dutch Colony settled down to read one of the French papers that had arrived by the last mail. Replete, his mind at ease, he could not but feel that life, with all its disadvantages, was good to live. He was still affected by the amused surprise that had overcome him when it suddenly occurred to him that he was a happy man. When you considered that men spent their lives seeking for happiness, it seemed hardly believable that he had found it. Yet the fact stared him in the face. A man who has everything he wants is happy, he had everything he wanted; therefore he was happy. He chuckled as a new thought crossed his mind.

'There's no denying it, I owe it to Adèle.'

Old Adèle. What a foul woman!

Presently he decided that he had better have a nap; he set his alarm clock for a quarter to twelve and lying down on his bed in a few minutes was fast asleep. He slept soundly and no dreams troubled him. He woke with a start when the alarm sounded, but in a moment remembered why he had set it. He yawned and stretched himself lazily.

'Ah, well, I suppose I must get to work. Every job has its inconveniences.'

He slipped from under his mosquito-net and relit his lamp. To freshen himself he washed his hands and face, and then as a protection against the night air drank a glass of rum. He thought for a moment of his inexperienced assistant and wondered whether it would be wise to take some rum in a flask with him.

'It would be a pretty business if his nerves went back on him.'

It was unfortunate that so many as six men had to be executed. If there had been only one, it wouldn't have mattered so much his assistant being new to the game; but with five others waiting there, it would be awkward if there were a hitch. He shrugged his shoulders. They would just have to do the best they could. He passed a comb through his tousled hair and carefully brushed his handsome moustache. He lit a cigarette. He walked through his compound, unlocked the door in the stout palisade that surrounded it, and locked it again behind him. There was no moon. He whistled for his dogs. He was surprised that they did not come. He whistled again. The brutes. They'd probably caught a rat and were fighting over it. He'd give them a good hiding for that; he'd teach them not to come when he whistled. He set out to walk in the direction of the prison. It was dark under the coconut trees and he would just as soon have had the dogs with him. Still there were only fifty yards to go and then he would be out in the open. There were lights in the governor's house, and it gave him confidence to see them. He smiled, for he guessed what those lights at that late hour meant: the governor, with the execution before him at dawn, was finding it hard to sleep. The anxiety, the malaise, that affected convicts and ex-convicts alike on the eve of an execution, had got on his nerves. It was true that there was always the chance of an outbreak then, and the warders went around with their eyes skinned and their hands ready to draw their guns at a suspicious movement.

Louis Remire whistled for his dogs once more, but they did not come. He could not understand it. It was a trifle disquieting. He was a man who habitually walked slowly, strolling along with a sort of roll, but now he hastened his pace. He spat the cigarette out of his mouth. It had struck him that it was prudent not to betray his whereabouts by the light it gave. Suddenly he stumbled against something. He stopped dead. He was a brave man, with nerves of steel, but on a sudden he felt sick with terror. It was something soft and rather large that he had stumbled against, and he was pretty sure what it was. He wore espadrilles, and with one foot he cautiously felt the object on the ground before him. Yes, he was right. It was one of his dogs. It was dead. He took a step backwards and drew his knife. He knew it was no good to shout. The only house in the neighbourhood was the prison governor's, it faced the clearing just beyond the coconut grove; but they would not hear him, or if they did would not stir. St Laurent de Maroni was not a place where you went out in the dead of night when you heard a man calling for help. If next day one of the freed convicts was found lying dead, well, it was no great loss. Louis Remire saw in a flash what had happened.

He thought rapidly. They had killed his dogs while he was sleeping. They must have got them when he had put them out of his compound after supper. They must have thrown them some poisoned meat and the brutes had snatched at it. If the one he had stumbled over was near his house it was because it tried to crawl home to die. Louis Remire strained his eyes. He could see nothing. The night was pitch black. He could hardly see the trunks of the coconut trees a yard away from him. His first thought was to make a rush for his shack. If he got back to the safety of that he could wait till the prison people, wondering why he did not come, sent to fetch him. But he knew he could never get back. He knew they were there in the darkness, the men who had killed his dogs; he would have to fumble with the key to find the lock and before he found it he would have a knife plunged in his back. He listened intently. There was not a sound. And yet he felt that there were men there, lurking behind the trees, and they were there to kill him. They would kill him as they had killed his dogs. And he would die like a dog. There was more than one certainly. He knew them, there were three or four of them at least, there might be more, convicts in service in private houses who were not obliged to get back to the camp till a late hour, or desperate and starving freed men who had nothing to lose. For a moment he hesitated what to do. He dared not make a run for it, they might easily have put a rope across the pathway that led from his house to the open, and if he tripped he was done for. The coconut trees were loosely planted and among them his enemies would see him as little as he saw them. He stepped over the dead dog and plunged into the grove. He stood with his back to a tree to decide how he should proceed. The silence was terrifying. Suddenly he heard a whisper and the horror of it was frightful. Again a dead silence. He felt he must move on, but his feet seemed rooted to the ground. He felt that they were peering at him out of the darkness and it seemed to him that he was as visible to them as though he stood in the broad light of day. Then from the other side was a little cough. It came as such a shock that Louis Remire nearly screamed. He was conscious now that they were all round him. He could expect no mercy from those robbers and murderers. He remembered the other executioner, his predecessor, whom they had carried still alive into the jungle, whose eyes they had gouged out, and whom they had left hanging for the vultures to devour. His knees began to tremble. What a fool he had been to take on the job! There were soft jobs he could have found in which you ran no risk. It was too late to think of that. He pulled himself together. He had no chance of getting out of the coconut grove alive, he knew that; he wanted to be sure that he would be dead. He tightened his grip on his knife. The awful part was that he could hear no one, he could see no one, and yet he knew that they were lurking there waiting to strike. For one moment he had a mad idea, he would throw his knife away and shout out to them that he was unarmed and they could come and kill him in safety. But he knew them; they would never be satisfied merely to kill him. Rage seized him. He was not the man to surrender tamely to a pack of criminals. He was an honest man and an official of the state; it was his duty to defend himself. He could not stay there all night. It was better to get it over quickly. Yet that tree at his back seemed to offer a sort of security, he could not bring himself to move. He stared at the trunk of a tree in front of him and suddenly it moved and he realized with horror that it was a man. That made up his mind for him and with a huge effort he stepped forwards. He advanced slowly and cautiously. He could hear nothing, he could see nothing. But he knew that as he advanced they advanced too. It was as though he were accompanied by an invisible bodyguard. He thought he could hear the sound of their naked feet on the ground. His fear had left him. He walked on, keeping as close to the trees as he could, so that they should have less chance of attacking him from behind; a wild hope sprang up in his breast that they would be afraid to strike, they knew him, they all knew him, and whoever struck the first blow would be lucky if he escaped a knife in his own guts; he had only another thirty yards to go, and once in the open, able to see, he could make a fight for it. A few yards more and then he would run for his life. Suddenly something happened that made him start out of his skin, and he stopped dead. A light was flashed and in that heavy darkness the sudden glare was terrifying. It was an electric torch. Instinctively he sprang to a tree and stood with his back to it. He could not see who held the light. He was blinded by it. He did not speak. He held his knife low, he knew that when they struck it was in the belly, and if someone flung himself at him he was prepared to strike back. He was going to sell his life dearly. For half a minute perhaps the light shone on his face, but it seemed to him an eternity. He thought now that he discerned dimly the faces of men. Then a word broke the horrible silence.

'Throw.'

At the same instant a knife came flying through the air and struck him on the breast-bone. He threw up his hands and as he did so someone sprang at him and with a great sweep of the knife ripped up his belly. The light was switched off. Louis Remire sank to the ground with a groan, a terrible groan of pain. Five, six men gathered out of the gloom and stood over him. With his fall the knife that had stuck in his breast-bone was dislodged. It lay on the ground. A quick flash of the torch showed where it was. One of the men took it and with a single, swift motion cut Remire's throat from ear to ear.

'*Au nom du peuple français justice est faite,*' he said.

They vanished into the darkness and in the coconut grove was the immense silence of death.

WINTER CRUISE

CAPTAIN ERDMANN knew Miss Reid very little till the *Friedrich Weber* reached Haiti. She came on board at Plymouth, but by then he had taken on a number of passengers, French, Belgian, and Haitian, many of whom had travelled with him before, and she was placed at the chief engineer's table. The *Friedrich Weber* was a freighter sailing regularly from Hamburg to Cartagena on the Colombian coast and on the way touching at a number of islands in the West Indies. She carried phosphates and cement from Germany and took back coffee and timber; but her owners, the Brothers Weber, were always willing to send her out of her route if a cargo of any sort made it worth their while. The *Friedrich Weber* was prepared to take cattle, mules, potatoes, or anything else that offered the chance of earning an honest penny. She carried passengers. There were six cabins on the upper deck and six below. The accommodation was not luxurious, but the food was good, plain, and abundant, and the fares were cheap. The round trip took nine weeks and was not costing Miss Reid more than forty-five pounds. She looked forward not only to seeing many interesting places, with historical associations, but also to acquiring a great deal of information that would enrich her mind.

The agent had warned her that till the ship reached Port au Prince in Haiti she would have to share a cabin with another woman. Miss Reid did not mind that, she liked company, and when the steward told her that her companion was Madame Bollin she thought at once that it would be a very good opportunity to rub up her French. She was only very slightly disconcerted when she found that Madame Bollin was coal-black. She told herself that one had to accept the rough with the smooth and that it takes all sorts to make a world. Miss Reid was a good sailor, as indeed was only to be expected since her grandfather had been a naval officer, but after a couple of roughish days the weather was fine and in a very short while she knew all her fellow-passengers. She was a good mixer. That was one of the reasons why she had made a success of her business; she owned a tea-room at a celebrated beauty spot in the west of England and she always had a smile and a pleasant word for every customer who came in; she closed down in the winter and for the last four years had taken a cruise. You met such interesting people, she said, and you always learnt something. It was true that the passengers on the *Friedrich Weber* weren't of quite so good a class as those she had met the year before on her Mediterranean cruise, but Miss Reid was not a snob, and though the table manners of some of them shocked her somewhat, determined to look upon the bright side of things she decided to make the best of them. She was a great reader and she was glad, on looking at the ship's library, to find that there were a lot of books by Phillips Oppenheim, Edgar Wallace, and Agatha Christie; but with so many people to talk to she had no time for reading and she made up her mind to leave them till the ship emptied herself at Haiti.

'After all,' she said, 'human nature is more important than literature.'

Miss Reid had always had the reputation of being a good talker and she flattered herself that not once during the many days they were at sea had she allowed the conversation at table to languish. She knew how to draw people out, and whenever a topic seemed to be exhausted she had a remark ready to revive it or another topic waiting on the tip of her tongue to set the conversation off again. Her friend Miss Prince, daughter of the late Vicar of Campden, who had come to see her off at Plymouth, for she lived there, had often said to her:

'You know, Venetia, you have a mind like a man. You're never at a loss for something to say.'

'Well, I think if you're interested in everyone, everyone will be interested in you,' Miss Reid answered modestly. 'Practice makes perfect, and I have the infinite capacity for taking pains which Dickens said was genius.'

Miss Reid was not really called Venetia, her name was Alice, but disliking it she had, when still a girl, adopted the poetic name which she felt so much better suited to her personality.

Miss Reid had a great many interesting talks with her fellow-passengers and she was really sorry when the ship at length reached Port au Prince and the last of them disembarked. The *Friedrich Weber* stopped two days there, during which she visited the town and the neighbourhood. When they sailed she was the only passenger. The ship was skirting the coast of the island stopping off at a variety of ports to discharge or to take on cargo.

'I hope you will not feel embarrassed alone with so many men, Miss Reid,' said the captain heartily as they sat down to midday dinner.

She was placed on his right hand and at table besides sat the first mate, the chief engineer, and the doctor.

'I'm a woman of the world, Captain. I always think if a lady is a lady gentlemen will be gentlemen.'

'We're only rough sailor men, madam, you mustn't expect too much.'

'Kind hearts are more than coronets and simple faith than Norman blood, Captain,' answered Miss Reid.

He was a short, thick-set man, with a clean-shaven head and a red, clean-shaven face. He wore a white stengah-shifter, but except at meal-times unbuttoned at the neck and showing his hairy chest. He was a jovial fellow. He could not speak without bellowing. Miss Reid thought him quite an eccentric, but she had a keen sense of humour and was prepared to make allowances for that. She took the conversation in hand. She had learnt a great deal about Haiti on the voyage out and more during the two days she had spent there, but she knew that men liked to talk rather than to listen, so she put them a number of questions to which she already knew the answers; oddly enough they didn't. In the end she found herself obliged to give quite a little lecture, and before dinner was over, *Mittag Essen* they called it in their funny way, she had imparted to them a great deal of interesting information about the history and economic situation of the Republic, the problems that confronted it, and its prospects for the future. She talked rather slowly, in a refined voice, and her vocabulary was extensive.

At nightfall they put in at a small port where they were to load three hundred bags of coffee, and the agent came on board. The captain asked him to stay to supper and ordered cocktails. As the steward brought them Miss Reid swam into the saloon. Her movements were deliberate, elegant, and self-assured. She always said that you could tell at once by the way she walked if a woman was a lady. The captain introduced the agent to her and she sat down.

'What is that you men are drinking?' she asked.

'A cocktail. Will you have one, Miss Reid?'

'I don't mind if I do.'

She drank it and the captain somewhat doubtfully asked her if she would have another.

'Another? Well, just to be matey.'

The agent, much whiter than some, but a good deal darker than many, was the son of a former minister of Haiti to the

German court, and having lived for many years in Berlin spoke good German. It was indeed on this account that he had got a job with a German shipping firm. On the strength of this Miss Reid, during supper, told them all about a trip down the Rhine that she had once taken. Afterwards she and the agent, the skipper, the doctor, and the mate sat round a table and drank beer. Miss Reid made it her business to draw the agent out. The fact that they were loading coffee suggested to her that he would be interested in learning how they grew tea in Ceylon, yes, she had been to Ceylon on a cruise, and the fact that his father was a diplomat made it certain that he would be interested in the royal family of England. She had a very pleasant evening. When she at last retired to rest, for she would never have thought of saying she was going to bed, she said to herself:

'There's no doubt that travel is a great education.'

It was really an experience to find herself alone with all those men. How they would laugh when she told them all about it when she got home! They would say that things like that only happened to Venetia. She smiled when she heard the captain on deck singing with that great booming voice of his. Germans were so musical. He had a funny way of strutting up and down on his short legs singing Wagner tunes to words of his own invention. It was *Tannhäuser* he was singing now (that lovely thing about the evening star) but knowing no German Miss Reid could only wonder what absurd words he was putting to it. It was as well.

'Oh, what a bore that woman is, I shall certainly kill her if she goes on much longer.' Then he broke into Siegfried's martial strain. 'She's a bore, she's a bore, she's a bore. I shall throw her into the sea.'

And that of course is what Miss Reid was. She was a crashing, she was a stupendous, she was an excruciating bore. She talked in a steady monotone, and it was no use to interrupt her because then she started again from the beginning. She had an insatiable thirst for information and no casual remark could be thrown across the table without her asking innumerable questions about it. She was a great dreamer and she narrated her dreams at intolerable length. There was no subject upon which she had not something prosy to say. She had a truism for every occasion. She hit on the commonplace like a hammer driving a nail into the wall. She plunged into the obvious like a clown in a circus jumping through a hoop. Silence did not abash her. Those poor men far away from their homes and the patter of little feet, and with

Christmas coming on, no wonder they felt low; she redoubled her efforts to interest and amuse them. She was determined to bring a little gaiety into their dull lives. For that was the awful part of it: Miss Reid meant well. She was not only having a good time herself, but she was trying to give all of them a good time. She was convinced that they liked her as much as she liked them. She felt that she was doing her bit to make the party a success and she was naïvely happy to think that she was succeeding. She told them all about her friend Miss Price and how often she had said to her: Venetia, no one ever has a dull moment in your company. It was the captain's duty to be polite to a passenger and however much he would have liked to tell her to hold her silly tongue he could not, but even if he had been free to say what he liked, he knew that he could not have brought himself to hurt her feelings. Nothing stemmed the torrent of her loquacity. It was as irresistible as a force of nature. Once in desperation they began talking German, but Miss Reid stopped this at once.

'Now I won't have you saying things I don't understand. You ought all to make the most of your good luck in having me all to yourselves and practise your English.'

'We were talking of technical matters that would only bore you, Miss Reid,' said the captain.

'I'm never bored. That's why, if you won't think me a wee bit conceited to say so, I'm never boring. You see, I like to know things. Everything interests me and you never know when a bit of information won't come in useful.'

The doctor smiled dryly.

'The captain was only saying that because he was embarrassed. In point of fact he was telling a story that was not fit for the ears of a maiden lady.'

'I may be a maiden lady but I'm also a woman of the world, I don't expect sailors to be saints. You need never be afraid of what you say before me, Captain, I shan't be shocked. I should love to hear your story.'

The doctor was a man of sixty with thin grey hair, a grey moustache, and small bright blue eyes. He was a silent, bitter man, and however hard Miss Reid tried to bring him into the conversation it was almost impossible to get a word out of him. But she wasn't a woman who would give in without a struggle, and one morning when they were at sea and she saw him sitting on deck with a book, she brought her chair next to his and sat down beside him.

'Are you fond of reading, Doctor?' she said brightly.

'Yes.'

'So am I. And I suppose like all Germans you're musical.'

'I'm fond of music.'

'So am I. The moment I saw you I thought you looked clever.'

He gave her a brief look and pursing his lips went on reading. Miss Reid was not disconcerted.

'But of course one can always read. I always prefer a good talk to a good book. Don't you?'

'No.'

'How very interesting. Now do tell me why?'

'I can't give you a reason.'

'That's very strange, isn't it? But then I always think human nature is strange. I'm terribly interested in people, you know. I always like doctors, they know so much about human nature, but I could tell you some things that would surprise even you. You learn a great deal about people if you run a tea-shop like I do, that's to say if you keep your eyes open.'

The doctor got up.

'I must ask you to excuse me, Miss Reid. I have to go and see a patient.'

'Anyhow I've broken the ice now,' she thought, as he walked away. 'I think he was only shy.'

But a day or two later the doctor was not feeling at all well. He had an internal malady that troubled him now and then, but he was used to it and disinclined to talk about it. When he had one of his attacks he only wanted to be left alone. His cabin was small and stuffy, so he settled himself on a long chair on deck and lay with his eyes closed. Miss Reid was walking up and down to get the half-hour's exercise she took morning and evening. He thought that if he pretended to be asleep she would not disturb him. But when she had passed him half a dozen times she stopped in front of him and stood quite still. Though he kept his eyes closed he knew that she was looking at him.

'Is there anything I can do, Doctor?' she said.

He started.

'Why, what should there be?'

He gave her a glance and saw that her eyes were deeply troubled.

'You look dreadfully ill,' she said.

'I'm in great pain.'

'I know. I can see that. Can't something be done?'

'No, it'll pass off presently.'

She hesitated for a moment then went away. Presently she returned.

'You look so uncomfortable with no cushions or anything. I've brought you my own pillow that I always travel with. Do let me put it behind your head.'

He felt at that moment too ill to remonstrate. She lifted his head gently and put the soft pillow behind it. It really did make him feel more comfortable. She passed her hand across his forehead and it was cool and soft.

'Poor dear,' she said. 'I know what doctors are. They haven't the first idea how to take care of themselves.'

She left him, but in a minute or two returned with a chair and a bag. The doctor when he saw her gave a twitch of anguish.

'Now I'm not going to let you talk, I'm just going to sit beside you and knit. I always think it's a comfort when one isn't feeling very well to have someone near.'

She sat down and taking an unfinished muffler out of her bag began busily to ply her needles. She never said a word. And strangely enough the doctor found her company a solace. No one else on board had even noticed that he was ill, he had felt lonely, and the sympathy of that crashing bore was grateful to him. It soothed him to see her silently working and presently he fell asleep. When he awoke she was still working. She gave him a little smile, but did not speak. His pain had left him and he felt much better.

He did not go into the saloon till late in the afternoon. He found the captain and Hans Krause, the mate, having a glass of beer together.

'Sit down, Doctor,' said the captain. 'We're holding a council of war. You know that the day after tomorrow is Sylvester Abend.'

'Of course.'

Sylvester Abend, New Year's Eve, is an occasion that means a great deal to a German, and they had all been looking forward to it. They had brought a Christmas tree all the way from Germany with them.

'At dinner today Miss Reid was more talkative than ever. Hans and I have decided that something must be done about it.'

'She sat with me for two hours this morning in silence. I suppose she was making up for lost time.'

'It's bad enough to be away from one's home and family just now anyway and all we can do is to make the best of a bad job.

We want to enjoy our Sylvester Abend, and unless something is done about Miss Reid we haven't a chance.'

'We can't have a good time if she's with us,' said the mate. 'She'll spoil it as sure as eggs is eggs.'

'How do you propose to get rid of her, short of throwing her overboard?' smiled the doctor. 'She's not a bad old soul; all she wants is a lover.'

'At her age?' cried Hans Krause.

'Especially at her age. That inordinate loquacity, that passion for information, the innumerable questions she asks, her prosiness, the way she goes on and on – it is all a sign of her clamouring virginity. A lover would bring her peace. Those jangled nerves of hers would relax. At least for an hour she would have lived. The deep satisfaction which her being demands would travel through those exacerbated centres of speech, and we should have quiet.'

It was always a little difficult to know how much the doctor meant what he said and when he was having a joke at your expense. The captain's blue eyes, however, twinkled mischievously.

'Well, Doctor, I have great confidence in your powers of diagnosis. The remedy you suggest is evidently worth trying, and since you are a bachelor it is clear that it is up to you to apply it.'

'Pardon me, Captain, it is my professional duty to prescribe remedies for the patients under my charge in this ship, but not to administer them personally. Besides, I am sixty.'

'I am a married man with grown-up children,' said the captain. 'I am old and fat and asthmatic, it is obvious that I cannot be expected to undertake a task of this kind. Nature cut me out for the role of a husband and father, not for that of a lover.'

'Youth in these matters is essential and good looks are advantageous,' said the doctor gravely.

The captain gave a great bang on the table with his fist.

'You are thinking of Hans. You're quite right. Hans must do it.'

The mate sprang to his feet.

'Me? Never.'

'Hans, you are tall, handsome, strong as a lion, brave, and young. We have twenty-three days more at sea before we reach Hamburg, you wouldn't desert your trusted old captain in an emergency or let down your good friend the doctor?'

'No, Captain, it's asking too much of me. I have been married less than a year and I love my wife. I can hardly wait to get back

to Hamburg. She is yearning for me as I am yearning for her.
I will not be unfaithful to her, especially with Miss Reid.'

'Miss Reid's not so bad,' said the doctor.

'Some people might call her even nice-looking,' said the captain.

And indeed when you took Miss Reid feature by feature she
was not in fact a plain women. True, she had a long, stupid face,
but her brown eyes were large and she had very thick lashes; her
brown hair was cut short and curled rather prettily over her neck;
she hadn't a bad skin, and she was neither too fat nor too thin.
She was not old as people go nowadays, and if she had told you
that she was forty you would have been quite willing to believe
it. The only thing against her was that she was drab and
dull.

'Must I then for twenty-three mortal days endure the prolixity
of that tedious woman? Must I for twenty-three mortal days
answer her inane questions and listen to her fatuous remarks?
Must I, an old man, have my Sylvester Abend, the jolly evening
I was looking forward to, ruined by the unwelcome company of
that intolerable virgin? And all because no one can be found to
show a little gallantry, a little human kindness, a spark of charity
to a lonely woman. I shall wreck the ship.'

'There's always the radio-operator,' said Hans.

The captain gave a loud shout.

'Hans, let the ten thousand virgins of Cologne arise and call
you blessed. Steward,' he bellowed, 'tell the radio-operator that
I want him.'

The radio-operator came into the saloon and smartly clicked
his heels together. The three men looked at him in silence. He
wondered uneasily whether he had done something for which he
was to be hauled over the coals. He was above the middle height,
with square shoulders and narrow hips, erect and slender, his
tanned, smooth skin looked as though a razor had never touched
it, he had large eyes of a startling blue and a mane of curling
golden hair. He was a perfect specimen of young Teutonic manhood. He was so healthy, so vigorous, so much alive that even
when he stood some way from you, you felt the glow of his
vitality.

'Aryan, all right,' said the captain. 'No doubt about that. How
old are you, my boy?'

'Twenty-one, sir.'

'Married?'

'No, sir.'

247

'Engaged?'

The radio-operator chuckled. There was an engaging boyish-ness in his laugh.

'No, sir.'

'You know that we have a female passenger on board?'

'Yes, sir.'

'Do you know her?'

'I've said good morning to her when I've seen her on deck.'

The captain assumed his most official manner. His eyes, which generally twinkled with fun, were stern and he got a sort of bark into his rich, fruity voice.

'Although this is a cargo-boat and we carry valuable freight, we also take such passengers as we can get, and this is a branch of our business that the company is anxious to encourage. My instructions are to do everything possible to promote the happiness and comfort of the passengers. Miss Reid needs a lover. The doctor and I have come to the conclusion that you are well suited to satisfy Miss Reid's requirements.'

'Me, sir?'

The radio-operator blushed scarlet and then began to giggle, but quickly composed himself when he saw the set faces of the three men who confronted him.

'But she's old enough to be my mother.'

'That at your age is a matter of no consequence. She is a woman of the highest distinction and allied to all the great families of England. If she were German she would be at least a countess. That you should have been chosen for this responsible position is an honour that you should greatly appreciate. Furthermore, your English is halting and this will give you an excellent opportunity to improve it.'

'That of course is something to be thought of,' said the radio-operator. 'I know that I want practice.'

'It is not often in this life that it is possible to combine pleasure with intellectual improvement, and you must congratulate yourself on your good fortune.'

'But if I may be allowed to put the question, sir, why does Miss Reid want a lover?'

'It appears to be an old English custom for unmarried women of exalted rank to submit themselves to the embraces of a lover at this time of year. The company is anxious that Miss Reid should be treated exactly as she would be on an English ship, and we trust that if she is satisfied, with her aristocratic connexions she will be able to persuade many of her friends to take cruises in the line's ships.'

'Sir, I must ask to be excused.'

'It is not a request that I am making, it is an order. You will present yourself to Miss Reid, in her cabin, at eleven o'clock tonight.'

'What shall I do when I get there?'

'Do?' thundered the captain. 'Do? Act naturally.'

With a wave of the hand he dismissed him. The radio-operator clicked his heels, saluted, and went out.

'Now let us have another glass of beer,' said the captain.

At supper that evening Miss Reid was at her best. She was verbose. She was playful. She was refined. There was not a truism that she failed to utter. There was not a commonplace that she forebore to express. She bombarded them with foolish questions. The captain's face grew redder and redder as he sought to contain his fury; he felt that he could not go on being polite to her any longer and if the doctor's remedy did not help, one day he would forget himself and give her, not a piece, but the whole of his mind.

'I shall lose my job,' he thought, 'but I'm not sure that it wouldn't be worth it.'

Next day they were already sitting at table when she came in to dinner.

'Sylvester Abend tomorrow,' she said, brightly. That was the sort of thing she would say. She went on: 'Well, what have you all been up to this morning?'

Since they did exactly the same thing every day, and she knew very well what that was, the question was enraging. The captain's heart sank. He briefly told the doctor what he thought of him.

'Now, no German, please,' said Miss Reid archly. 'You know I don't allow that, and why, Captain, did you give the poor doctor that sour look? It's Christmas time, you know; peace and good-will to all men. I'm so excited about tomorrow evening, and will there be candles on the Christmas tree?'

'Naturally.'

'How thrilling! I always think a Christmas tree without candles isn't a Christmas tree. Oh, d'you know, I had such a funny experience last night. I can't understand it at all.'

A startled pause. They all looked intently at Miss Reid. For once they hung on her lips.

'Yes,' she went on in that monotonous, rather finicking way of hers, 'I was just getting into bed last night when there was a

knock at my door. "Who is it?" I said. "It's the radio-operator,"
was the answer. "What is it?" I said. "Can I speak to you?" he
said.'

They listened with rapt attention.

'"Well, I'll just pop on a dressing-gown," I said, "and open the
door." So I popped on a dressing-gown and opened the door.
The radio-operator said: "Excuse me, miss, but do you want to
send a radio?" Well, I did think it was funny his coming at that
hour to ask me if I wanted to send a radio, I just laughed in his
face, it appealed to my sense of humour if you understand what I
mean, but I didn't want to hurt his feelings so I said: "Thank you
so much, but I don't think I want to send a radio." He stood there,
looking so funny, as if he was quite embarrassed, so I said:
"Thank you all the same for asking me," and then I said "Good
night, pleasant dreams", and shut the door.'

'The damned fool,' cried the captain.

'He's young, Miss Reid,' the doctor put in. 'It was excess of
zeal. I suppose he thought you would want to send a New Year's
greeting to your friends and he wished you to get the advantage of
the special rate.'

'Oh, I didn't mind at all. I like these queer little things that
happen to one when one's travelling. I just get a good laugh out
of them.'

As soon as dinner was over and Miss Reid had left them the
captain sent for the radio-operator.

'You idiot, what in heaven's name made you ask Miss Reid
last night whether she wanted to send a radio?'

'Sir, you told me to act naturally. I am a radio-operator. I
thought it natural to ask her if she wanted to send a radio. I
didn't know what else to say.'

'God in heaven,' shouted the captain, 'when Siegfried saw
Brunhilde lying on her rock and cried: *Das ist kein Mann,*' (the
captain sang the words, and being pleased with the sound of his
voice, repeated the phrase two or three times before he continued), 'did Siegfried when she awoke ask her if she wished to
send a radio, to announce to her papa, I suppose, that she was
sitting up after her long sleep and taking notice?'

'I beg most respectfully to draw your attention to the fact that
Brunhilde was Siegfried's aunt. Miss Reid is a total stranger to
me.'

'He did not reflect that she was his aunt. He knew only that
she was a beautiful and defenceless woman of obviously good

family and he acted as any gentleman would have done. You are young, handsome, Aryan to the tips of your fingers, the honour of Germany is in your hands.'

'Very good sir. I will do my best.'

That night there was another knock on Miss Reid's door.

'Who is it?'

'The radio-operator. I have a radio for you, Miss Reid.'

'For me?' She was surprised, but it at once occurred to her that one of her fellow-passengers who had got off at Haiti had sent her New Year's greetings. 'How very kind people are,' she thought. 'I'm in bed. Leave it outside the door.'

'It needs an answer. Ten words prepaid.'

Then it couldn't be a New Year's greeting. Her heart stopped beating. It could only mean one thing; her shop had been burned to the ground. She jumped out of bed.

'Slip it under the door and I'll write the answer and slip it back to you.'

The envelope was pushed under the door and as it appeared on the carpet it had really a sinister look. Miss Reid snatched it up and tore the envelope open. The words swam before her eyes and she couldn't for a moment find her spectacles. This is what she read:

'Happy New Year. Stop. Peace and goodwill to all men. Stop. You are very beautiful. Stop. I love you. Stop. I must speak to you. Stop. Signed: Radio Operator.'

Miss Reid read this through twice. Then she slowly took off her spectacles and hid them under a scarf. She opened the door.

'Come in,' she said.

Next day was New Year's Eve. The officers were cheerful and a little sentimental when they sat down to dinner. The stewards had decorated the saloon with tropical creepers to make up for holly and mistletoe, and the Christmas tree stood on a table with the candles ready to be lit at supper time. Miss Reid did not come in till the officers were seated, and when they bade her good morning she did not speak but merely bowed. They looked at her curiously. She ate a good dinner, but uttered never a word. Her silence was uncanny. At last the captain could stand it no longer, and he said:

'You're very quiet today, Miss Reid.'

'I'm thinking,' she remarked.

'And will you not tell us your thoughts, Miss Reid?' the doctor asked playfully.

251

She gave him a cool, you might almost have called it a supercilious, look.

'I prefer to keep them to myself, Doctor. I will have a little more of that hash, I've got a very good appetite.'

They finished the meal in a blessed silence. The captain heaved a sigh of relief. That was what meal-time was for, to eat, not to chatter. When they had finished he went up to the doctor and wrung his hand.

'Something has happened, Doctor.'

'It has happened. She's a changed woman.'

'But will it last?'

'One can only hope for the best.'

Miss Reid put on an evening dress for the evening's celebration, a very quiet black dress, with artificial roses at her bosom and a long string of imitation jade round her neck. The lights were dimmed and the candles on the Christmas tree were lit. It felt a little like being in church. The junior officers were supping in the saloon that evening and they looked very smart in their white uniforms. Champagne was served at the company's expense and after supper they had a *Maibowle*. They pulled crackers. They sang songs to the gramophone, *Deutschland, Deutschland über Alles, Alt Heidelberg*, and *Auld Lang Syne*. They shouted out the tunes lustily, the captain's voice rising loud above the others, and Miss Reid joining in with a pleasing contralto. The doctor noticed that Miss Reid's eyes from time to time rested on the radio-operator, and in them he read an expression of some bewilderment.

'He's a good-looking fellow, isn't he?' said the doctor.

Miss Reid turned round and looked at the doctor coolly.

'Who?'

'The radio-operator. I thought you were looking at him.'

'Which is he?'

'The duplicity of women,' the doctor muttered, but with a smile he answered: 'He's sitting next to the chief engineer.'

'Oh, of course, I recognize him now. You know, I never think it matters what a man looks like. I'm so much more interested in a man's brains than in his looks.'

'Ah,' said the doctor.

They all got a little tight, including Miss Reid, but she did not lose her dignity and when she bade them good night it was in her best manner.

'I've had a very delightful evening. I shall never forget my New

Year's Eve on a German boat. It's been very interesting. Quite an experience.'

She walked steadily to the door, and this was something of a triumph, for she had drunk drink for drink with the rest of them through the evening.

They were all somewhat jaded next day. When the captain, the mate, the doctor, and the chief engineer came down to dinner they found Miss Reid already seated. Before each place was a small parcel tied up in pink ribbon. On each was written: Happy New Year. They gave Miss Reid a questioning glance.

'You've all been so very kind to me I thought I'd like to give each of you a little present. There wasn't much choice at Port au Prince, so you mustn't expect too much.'

There was a pair of briar pipes for the captain, half a dozen silk handkerchiefs for the doctor, a cigar-case for the mate, and a couple of ties for the chief engineer. They had dinner and Miss Reid retired to her cabin to rest. The officers looked at one another uncomfortably. The mate fiddled with the cigar-case she had given him.

'I'm a little ashamed of myself,' he said at last.

The captain was pensive and it was plain that he too was a trifle uneasy.

'I wonder if we ought to have played that trick on Miss Reid,' he said. 'She's a good old soul and she's not rich; she's a woman who earns her own living. She must have spent the best part of a hundred marks on these presents. I almost wish we'd left her alone.'

The doctor shrugged his shoulders.

'You wanted her silenced and I've silenced her.'

'When all's said and done, it wouldn't have hurt us to listen to her chatter for three weeks more,' said the mate.

'I'm not happy about her,' added the captain. 'I feel there's something ominous in her quietness.'

She had spoken hardly a word during the meal they had just shared with her. She seemed hardly to listen to what they said.

'Don't you think you ought to ask her if she's feeling quite well, doctor?' suggested the captain.

'Of course she's feeling quite well. She's eating like a wolf. If you want inquiries made you'd much better make them of the radio-operator.'

'You may not be aware of it, Doctor, but I am a man of great delicacy.'

'I am a man of heart myself,' said the doctor.

For the rest of the journey those men spoilt Miss Reid outrageously. They treated her with the consideration they would have shown to someone who was convalescent after a long and dangerous illness. Though her appetite was excellent they sought to tempt her with new dishes. The doctor ordered wine and insisted on her sharing his bottle with him. They played dominoes with her. They played chess with her. They played bridge with her. They engaged her in conversation. But there was no doubt about it, though she responded to their advances with politeness, she kept herself to herself. She seemed to regard them with something very like disdain; you might almost have thought that she looked upon those men and their efforts to be amiable as pleasantly ridiculous. She seldom spoke unless spoken to. She read detective stories and at night sat on deck looking at the stars. She lived a life of her own.

At last the journey drew to its close. They sailed up the English Channel on a still grey day; they sighted land. Miss Reid packed her trunk. At two o'clock in the afternoon they docked at Plymouth. The captain, the mate, and the doctor came along to say good-bye to her.

'Well, Miss Reid,' said the captain in his jovial way, 'we're sorry to lose you, but I suppose you're glad to be getting home.'

'You've been very kind to me, you've all been very kind to me, I don't know what I've done to deserve it. I've been very happy with you. I shall never forget you.'

She spoke rather shakily, she tried to smile, but her lips quivered, and tears ran down her cheeks. The captain got very red. He smiled awkwardly.

'May I kiss you, Miss Reid?'

She was taller than he by half a head. She bent down and he planted a fat kiss on one wet cheek and a fat kiss on the other. She turned to the mate and the doctor. They both kissed her.

'What an old fool I am,' she said. 'Everybody's so good.'

She dried her eyes and slowly, in her graceful, rather absurd way, walked down the companion. The captain's eyes were wet. When she reached the quay she looked up and waved to someone on the boat deck.

'Who's she waving to?' asked the captain.

'The radio-operator.'

Miss Price was waiting on the quay to welcome her. When they had passed the Customs and got rid of Miss Reid's heavy luggage they went to Miss Price's house and had an early cup of tea. Miss Reid's train did not start till five. Miss Price had much to tell Miss Reid.

'But it's too bad of me to go on like this when you've just come home. I've been looking forward to hearing all about your journey.'

'I'm afraid there's not very much to tell.'

'I can't believe that. Your trip was a success, wasn't it?'

'A distinct success. It was very nice.'

'And you didn't mind being with all those Germans?'

'Of course they're not like English people. One has to get used to their ways. They sometimes do things that – well, that English people wouldn't do, you know. But I always think that one has to take things as they come.'

'What sort of things do you mean?'

Miss Reid looked at her friend calmly. Her long, stupid face had a placid look, and Miss Price never noticed that in the eyes was a strangely mischievous twinkle.

'Things of no importance really. Just funny, unexpected, rather nice things. There's no doubt that travel is a wonderful education.'

MABEL

I was at Pagan, in Burma, and from there I took the steamer to Mandalay, but a couple of days before I got there, when the boat tied up for the night at a riverside village, I made up my mind to go ashore. The skipper told me that there was there a pleasant little club in which I had only to make myself at home; they were quite used to having strangers drop off like that from the steamer, and the secretary was a very decent chap; I might even get a game of bridge. I had nothing in the world to do, so I got into one of the bullock-carts that were waiting at the landing-stage and was driven to the club. There was a man sitting on the veranda and as I walked up he nodded to me and asked whether I would have a whisky and soda or a gin and bitters. The possibility that I would have nothing at all did not even occur to him. I chose the longer drink and sat down. He was a tall, thin, bronzed man, with a big moustache, and he wore khaki shorts and a khaki shirt. I never knew his name, but when we had been chatting a little while another man came in who told me he was the secretary, and he addressed my friend as George.

'Have you heard from your wife yet?' he asked him.

The other's eyes brightened.

'Yes, I had letters by this mail. She's having no end of a time.'

'Did she tell you not to fret?'

George gave a little chuckle, but was I mistaken in thinking that there was in it the shadow of a sob?

'In point of fact she did. But that's easier said than done. Of course I know she wants a holiday, and I'm glad she should have it, but it's devilish hard on a chap.' He turned to me. 'You see, this is the first time I've ever been separated from my missus, and I'm like a lost dog without her.'

'How long have you been married?'

'Five minutes.'

The secretary of the club laughed.

'Don't be a fool, George. You've been married eight years.'

After we had talked for a little, George, looking at his watch, said he must go and change his clothes for dinner and left us. The secretary watched him disappear into the night with a smile of not unkindly irony.

'We all ask him as much as we can now that he's alone,' he told me. 'He mopes so terribly since his wife went home.'

'It must be very pleasant for her to know that her husband is as devoted to her as all that.'

'Mabel is a remarkable woman.'

He called the boy and ordered more drinks. In this hospitable place they did not ask you if you would have anything; they took it for granted. Then he settled himself in his long chair and lit a cheroot. He told me the story of George and Mabel.

They became engaged when he was home on leave, and when he returned to Burma it was arranged that she should join him in six months. But one difficulty cropped up after another; Mabel's father died, the war came, George was sent to a district unsuitable for a white woman; so that in the end it was seven years before she was able to start. He made all arrangements for the marriage, which was to take place on the day of her arrival, and went down to Rangoon to meet her. On the morning on which the ship was due he borrowed a motor-car and drove along to the dock. He paced the quay.

Then, suddenly, without warning, his nerve failed him. He had not seen Mabel for seven years. He had forgotten what she was like. She was a total stranger. He felt a terrible sinking in the pit of his stomach and his knees began to wobble. He couldn't go through with it. He must tell Mabel that he was very sorry, but he couldn't, he really couldn't marry her. But how could a man tell a girl a thing like that when she had been engaged to him for seven years and had come six thousand miles to marry him? He hadn't the nerve for that either. George was seized with the courage of despair. There was a boat at the quay on the very point of starting for Singapore; he wrote a hurried letter to Mabel, and without a stick of luggage, just in the clothes he stood up in, leaped on board.

The letter Mabel received ran somewhat as follows:

Dearest Mabel,

I have been suddenly called away on business and do not know when I shall be back. I think it would be much wiser if you returned to England. My plans are very uncertain. Your loving George.

But when he arrived at Singapore he found a cable waiting for him.

Quite understand. Don't worry. Love. Mabel.

Terror made him quick-witted.

'By Jove, I believe she's following me,' he said.

He telegraphed to the shipping-office at Rangoon and sure enough her name was on the passenger list of the ship that was now on its way to Singapore. There was not a moment to lose. He jumped on the train to Bangkok. But he was uneasy; she would have no difficulty in finding out that he had gone to Bangkok and it was just as simple for her to take the train as it had been for him. Fortunately there was a French tramp sailing next day for Saigon. He took it. At Saigon he would be safe; it would never occur to her that he had gone there; and if it did, surely by now she would have taken the hint. It is five day's journey from Bangkok to Saigon and the boat is dirty, cramped, and uncomfortable. He was glad to arrive and took a rickshaw to the hotel. He signed his name in the visitors' book and a telegram was immediately handed to him. It contained but two words: *Love. Mabel.* They were enough to make him break into a cold sweat.

'When is the next boat for Hong-Kong?' he asked.

Now his flight grew serious. He sailed to Hong-Kong, but dared not stay there; he went to Manila; Manila was ominous; he went on to Shanghai: Shanghai was nerve-racking; every time he went out of the hotel he expected to run straight into Mabel's arms; no, Shanghai would never do. The only thing was to go to Yokohama. At the Grand Hotel at Yokohama a cable awaited him:

So sorry to have missed you at Manila. Love. Mabel.

He scanned the shipping intelligence with a fevered brow. Where was she now? He doubled back to Shanghai. This time he went straight to the club and asked for a telegram. It was handed to him:

Arriving shortly. Love. Mabel.

No, no, he was not so easy to catch as all that. He had already made his plans. The Yangtse is a long river and the Yangtse was falling. He could just about catch the last steamer that could get up to Chungking and then no one could travel till the following spring except by junk. Such a journey was out of the question for a woman alone. He went to Hankow and from Hankow to Ichang, he changed boats here and from Ichang through the rapids went to Chungking. But he was desperate now, he was not going to take any risks: there was a place called Cheng-tu, the capital of Szechuan, and it was four hundred miles away. It could only be reached by road, and the road was infested with brigands. A man would be safe there.

George collected chair-bearers and coolies and set out. It was with a sigh of relief that he saw at last the crenellated walls of the lonely Chinese city. From those walls at sunset you could see the snowy mountains of Tibet.

He could rest at last: Mabel would never find him there. The consul happened to be a friend of his and he stayed with him. He enjoyed the comfort of a luxurious house, he enjoyed his idleness after that strenuous escape across Asia, and above all he enjoyed his divine security. The weeks passed lazily one after the other.

One morning George and the consul were in the courtyard looking at some curios that a Chinese had brought for their inspection when there was a loud knocking at the great door of the Consulate. The door-man flung it open. A chair borne by four coolies entered, advanced, and was set down. Mabel stepped out. She was neat and cool and fresh. There was nothing in her appearance to suggest that she had just come in after a fortnight on the road. George was petrified. He was as pale as death. She went up to him.

'Hullo, George, I was so afraid I'd missed you again.'

'Hullo, Mabel,' he faltered.

He did not know what to say. He looked this way and that: she stood between him and the doorway. She looked at him with a smile in her blue eyes.

'You haven't altered at all,' she said. 'Men can go off so dreadfully in seven years and I was afraid you'd got fat and bald. I've been so nervous. It would have been terrible if after all these years I simply hadn't been able to bring myself to marry you after all.'

She turned to George's host.

'Are you the consul?' she asked.

'I am.'

'That's all right. I'm ready to marry him as soon as I've had a bath.'

And she did.

MASTERSON

When I left Colombo I had no notion of going to Keng Tung, but on the ship I met a man who told me he had spent five years there. He said it had an important market, held every five days, whither came natives of half a dozen countries and members of half a hundred tribes. It had pagodas darkly splendid and a remoteness that liberated the questing spirit from its anxiety. He said he would sooner live there than anywhere in the world. I asked him what it had offered him and he said, contentment. He was a tall, dark fellow with the aloofness of manner you often find in those who have lived much alone in unfrequented places. Men like this are a little restless in the company of others and though in the smoking-room of a ship or at the club bar they may be talkative and convivial, telling their story with the rest, joking and glad sometimes to narrate their unusual experiences, they seem always to hold something back. They have a life in themselves that they keep apart, and there is a look in their eyes, as it were turned inwards, that informs you that this hidden life is the only one that signifies to them. And now and then their eyes betray their weariness with the social round into which hazard or the fear of seeming odd has for a moment forced them. They seem then to long for the monotonous solitude of some place of their predilection where they can be once more alone with the reality they have found.

It was as much the manner of this chance acquaintance as what he told me that persuaded me to make the journey across the Shan States on which I now set out. From the rail-head in Upper Burma to the rail-head in Siam, whence I could get down to Bangkok, it was between six and seven hundred miles. Kind people had done everything possible to render the excursion easy for me and the Resident at Taunggyi had wired to me that he had made arrangements for mules and ponies to be ready for me on my arrival. I had bought in Rangoon such stores as seemed necessary, folding chairs and a table, a filter, lamps, and I know not what. I took the train from Mandalay to Thazi, intending there to hire a car for Taunggyi, and a man I had met at the club at Mandalay and who lived at Thazi asked me to have brunch (the pleasant meal of Burma that combines breakfast and lunch) with him before I started. His name was Masterson. He was a man in the early thirties, with a pleasant friendly face, curling dark hair speckled with grey, and handsome dark eyes. He spoke with a singularly musical voice, very slowly, and this, I hardly know why, inspired you with confidence. You felt that a man who took such a long time to say what he had to say and had found the world with sufficient leisure to listen to him must have qualities that made him sympathetic to his fellows. He took the amiability of mankind for granted and I suppose he could only have done this because he was himself amiable. He had a nice sense of humour, without of course a quick thrust and parry, but agreeably sarcastic; it was of that agreeable type that applies common sense to the accidents of life and so sees them in a faintly ridiculous aspect. He was engaged in a business that kept him travelling up and down Burma most of the year, and in his journeyings he had acquired the collector's habit. He told me that he spent all his spare money on buying Burmese curiosities and it was especially to see them that he asked me to have a meal with him.

The train got in early in the morning. He had warned me that, having to be at his office, he could not meet me; but brunch was at ten and he told me to go to his house as soon as I was finished with the one or two things I had to do in the town.

'Make yourself at home,' he said, 'and if you want a drink ask the boy for it. I'll get back as soon as I've got through with my business.'

I found out where there was a garage and made a bargain with the owner of a very dilapidated Ford to take me and my baggage to Taunggyi. I left my Madrassi servant to see that everything was stowed in it that was possible and the rest tied on to the footboards, and strolled along to Masterson's house. It was a neat little bungalow in a road shaded by tall trees, and in the early light of a sunny day looked pretty and homelike. I walked up the steps and was hailed by Masterson.

'I got done more quickly than I expected. I shall have time to show you my things before brunch is ready. What will you have? I'm afraid I can only offer you a whisky and soda.'

'Isn't it rather early for that?'

'Rather. But it's one of the rules of the house that nobody crosses the threshold without having a drink.'

'What can I do but submit to the rule?'

He called the boy and in a moment a trim Burmese brought in a decanter, a syphon, and glasses. I sat down and looked about the room. Though it was still so early the sun was hot outside and the jalousies were drawn. The light was pleasant and cool after the glare of the road. The room was comfortably furnished with rattan chairs and on the walls were water-colour paintings of English scenes. They were a little prim and old-fashioned and I guessed that they had been painted in her youth by the maiden and elderly aunt of my host. There were two of a cathedral I did not know, two or three of a rose garden, and one of a Georgian house. When he saw my eyes for an instant rest upon this, he said:

'That was our house at Cheltenham.'

'Oh, is that where you come from?'

Then there was his collection. The room was crowded with Buddhas and with figures, in bronze or wood, of the Buddha's disciples; there were boxes of all shapes, utensils of one kind and another, curiosities of every sort, and although there were far too many they were arranged with a certain taste so that the effect was pleasing. He had some lovely things. He showed them to me with pride, telling me how he had got this object and that, and how he had heard of another and hunted it down and the incredible astuteness he had employed to induce an unwilling owner to part with it. His kindly eyes shone when he described a great bargain and they flashed darkly when he inveighed against the unreasonableness of a vendor who rather than accept a fair price for a bronze dish had taken it away. There were flowers in the room, and it had not the forlorn look that so many bachelors' houses have in the East.

'You've made the place very comfortable,' I said.

He gave the room a sweeping glance.

'It *was* all right. It's not much now.'

I did not quite know what he meant. Then he showed me a long wooden gilt box, decorated with the glass mosaic that I had admired in the palace at Mandalay, but the workmanship was more delicate than anything I had seen there, and this with its gem-like richness had really something of the ornate exquisiteness of the Italian Renaissance.

'They tell me it's about a couple of hundred years old,' he said. 'They've not been able to turn out anything like this for a long time.'

It was a piece made obviously for a king's palace and you wondered to what uses it had been put and what hands it had passed through. It was a jewel.

'What is the inside like?' I asked.

'Oh, nothing much. It's just lacquered.'

He opened it and I saw that it contained three or four framed photographs.

'Oh, I'd forgotten those were there,' he said.

His soft, musical voice had a queer sound in it, and I gave him a sidelong look. He was bronzed by the sun, but his face notwithstanding flushed a deeper red. He was about to close the box, and then he changed his mind. He took out one of the photographs and showed it to me.

'Some of these Burmese girls are rather sweet when they're young, aren't they?' he said.

The photograph showed a young girl standing somewhat self-consciously against the conventional background of a photographer's studio, a pagoda and a group of palm-trees. She was wearing her best clothes and she had a flower in her hair. But the embarrassment you saw she felt at having her picture taken did not prevent a shy smile from trembling on her lips and her large solemn eyes had nevertheless a roguish twinkle. She was very small and very slender.

'What a ravishing little thing,' I said.

Then Masterson took out another photograph in which she sat with a child standing by her side, his hand timidly on her knee, and a baby in her arms. The child stared straight in front of him with a look of terror on his face; he could not understand what that machine and the man behind it, his head under a black cloth, were up to.

'Are those her children?' I asked.

'And mine,' said Masterson.

At that moment the boy came in to say that brunch was ready. We went into the dining-room and sat down.

'I don't know what you'll get to eat. Since my girl went away everything in the house has gone to blazes.'

A sulky look came into his red honest face and I did not know what to reply.

'I'm so hungry that whatever I get will seem good,' I hazarded.

He did not say anything and a plate of thin porridge was put before us. I helped myself to milk and sugar. Masterson ate a spoonful or two and pushed his plate aside.

'I wish I hadn't looked at those damned photographs,' he said. 'I put them away on purpose.'

I did not want to be inquisitive or to force a confidence my host had no wish to give, but neither did I desire to seem so unconcerned as to prevent him from telling me something he had in his heart. Often in some lonely post in the jungle or in a stiff grand house, solitary in the midst of a teeming Chinese city, a man has told me stories about himself that I was sure he had never told to a living soul. I was a stray acquaintance whom he had never seen before and would never see again, a wanderer for a moment through his monotonous life, and some starved impulse led him to lay bare his soul. I have in this way learned more about men in a night (sitting over a syphon or two and a bottle of whisky, the hostile, inexplicable world outside the radius of an acetylene lamp) than I could have if I had known them for ten years. If you are interested in human nature it is one of the great pleasures of travel. And when you separate (for you have to be up betimes) sometimes they will say to you:

'I'm afraid I've bored you to death with all this nonsense. I haven't talked so much for six months. But it's done me good to get it off my chest.'

The boy removed the porridge plates and gave each of us a piece of pale fried fish. It was rather cold.

'The fish is beastly, isn't it?' said Masterson. 'I hate river fish, except trout; the only thing is to smother it with Worcester sauce.'

He helped himself freely and passed me the bottle.

'She was a damned good housekeeper, my girl; I used to feed like a fighting-cock when she was here. She'd have had the cook out of the house in a quarter of an hour if he'd sent in muck like this.'

He gave me a smile, and I noticed that his smile was very sweet. It gave him a peculiarly gentle look.

'It was rather a wrench parting with her, you know.'

It was quite evident now that he wished to talk and I had no hesitation in giving him a lead.

'Did you have a row?'

'No. You could hardly call it a row. She lived with me five years and we never had a tiff even. She was the best-tempered little thing that ever was. Nothing seemed to put her out. She was always as merry as a cricket. You couldn't look at her without her lips breaking into a smile. She was always happy. And there was no reason why she shouldn't be. I was very good to her.'

'I'm sure you were,' I answered.

'She was mistress here. I gave her everything she wanted. Perhaps if I'd been more of a brute she wouldn't have gone away.'

'Don't make me say anything so obvious as that women are incalculable.'

He gave me a deprecating glance and there was a trace of shyness in the smile that just flickered in his eyes.

'Would it bore you awfully if I told you about it?'

'Of course not.'

'Well, I saw her one day in the street and she rather took my fancy. I showed you her photograph, but the photograph doesn't begin to do her justice. It sounds silly to say about a Burmese girl, but she was like a rose-bud, not an English rose, you know, she was as little like that as the glass flowers on that box I showed you are like real flowers, but a rose grown in an Eastern garden that had something strange and exotic about it. I don't know how to make myself plain.'

'I think I understand what you mean all the same,' I smiled.

'I saw her two or three times and found out where she lived. I sent my boy to make inquiries about her, and he told me that her parents were quite willing that I should have her if we could come to an arrangement. I wasn't inclined to haggle and everything was settled in no time. Her family gave a party to celebrate the occasion and she came to live here. Of course I treated her in every way as my wife and put her in charge of the house. I told the boys that they'd got to take their orders from her and if she complained of any of them out they went. You know, some fellows keep their girls in the servants' quarters and when they go away on tour the girls have a rotten time. Well, I think that's a filthy thing to do. If you are going to have a girl to live with you the least you can do is to see that she has a good time.

'She was a great success and I was as pleased as Punch. She kept the house spotless. She saved me money. She wouldn't let the boys rob me. I taught her to play bridge and, believe me, she learned to play a damned good game.'

'Did she like it?'

'Loved it. When people came here she couldn't have received them better if she'd been a duchess. You know, these Burmese have beautiful manners. Sometimes it would make me laugh to see the assurance with which she would receive my guests, government officials, you know, and soldiers who were passing through. If some young subaltern was rather shy she'd put him at his ease at once. She was never pushing or obtrusive, but just there when she was wanted and doing her best to see that everything went well and everyone had a good time. And I'll tell you what, she could mix the best cocktail you'd get anywhere between Rangoon and Bhamo. People used to say I was lucky.'

'I'm bound to say I think you were,' I said.

The curry was served and I piled my plate with rice and helped myself to chicken and then chose from a dozen little dishes the condiments I fancied. It was a good curry.

'Then she had her babies, three in three years, but one died when it was six weeks old. I showed you a photograph of the two that are living. Funny-looking little things, aren't they? Are you fond of children?'

'Yes. I have a strange and almost unnatural passion for new-born babies.'

'I don't think I am, you know. I couldn't even feel very much about my own. I've often wondered if it showed that I was rather a rotter.'

'I don't think so. I think the passion many people affect for children is merely a fashionable pose. I have a notion that children are all the better for not being burdened with too much parental love.'

'Then my girl asked me to marry her, legally I mean, in the English way. I treated it as a joke. I didn't know how she'd got such an idea in her head. I thought it was only a whim and I gave her a gold bracelet to keep her quiet. But it wasn't a whim. She was quite serious about it. I told her there was nothing doing. But you know what women are, when they once set their mind on getting something they never give you a moment's peace. She wheedled and sulked, she cried, she appealed to my compassion, she tried to extract a promise out of me when I was rather tight, she was on the watch for me when I was feeling amorous, she nearly tripped me when she was ill. She watched me more carefully, I should think, than a stockbroker ever watched the market, and I knew that, however natural she seemed, however occupied with something else, she was always warily alert for the unguarded moment when she could pounce on me and gain her point.'

Masterson gave me once more his slow, ingenuous smile.

'I suppose women are pretty much the same all the world over,' he said.

'I expect so,' I answered.

'A thing I've never been able to understand is why a woman thinks it worth while to make you do something you don't want to. She'd rather you did a thing against the grain than not do it at all. I don't see what satisfaction it can be to them.'

'The satisfaction of triumph. A man convinced against his will may be of the same opinion still, but a woman doesn't mind that. She has conquered. She has proved her power.'

Masterson shrugged his shoulders. He drank a cup of tea.

'You see, she said that sooner or later I was bound to marry an English girl and turn her out. I said I wasn't thinking of marrying. She said she knew all about that. And even if I didn't I should retire some day and go back to England. And where would she be then? It went on for a year. I held out. Then she said that if I wouldn't marry her she'd go and take the kids with her. I told her not to be a silly little fool. She said that if she left me now she could marry a Burman, but in a few years nobody would want her. She began to pack her things. I thought it was only a bluff and I called it: I said: "Well, go if you want to, but if you do you won't come back." I didn't think she'd give up a house like this, and the presents I made her, and all the pickings, to go back to her own family. They were as poor as church mice. Well, she went on packing her things. She was just as nice as ever to me, she was gay and smiling; when some fellows came to spend the night here she was just as cordial as usual, and she played bridge with us till two in the morning. I couldn't believe she meant to go and yet I was rather scared. I was very fond of her. She was a damned good sort.'

'But if you were fond of her why on earth didn't you marry her? It had been a great success.'

'I'll tell you. If I married her I'd have to stay in Burma for the rest of my life. Sooner or later I shall retire and then I want to go back to my old home and live there. I don't want to be buried out here. I want to be buried in an English churchyard. I'm happy enough here, but I don't want to live here always. I couldn't. I want England. Sometimes I get sick of this hot sunshine and these garish colours. I want grey skies and a soft rain falling and the smell of the country. I shall be a funny fat elderly man when I go back, too old to hunt even if I could afford it, but I can fish. I don't want to shoot tigers, I want to shoot rabbits. And I can play golf on a proper course. I know I shall be out of it, we fellows who've spent our lives out here always are, but I can potter about the local club and talk to retired Anglo-Indians. I want to feel under my feet the grey pavement of an English country town, I want to be able to go and have a row with the butcher because the steak he sent me in yesterday was tough, and I want to browse about second-hand bookshops. I want to be said how d'you do to in the street by people who knew me when I was a boy. And I want to have a walled garden at the back of my house and grow roses. I dare say it all sounds very humdrum and provincial and dull to you, but that's the sort of life my people have always lived and that's the sort of life I want to live myself. It's a dream if you like, but it's all I have, it means everything in the world to me, and I can't give it up.'

He paused for a moment and looked into my eyes.

'Do you think me an awful fool?'

'No.'

'Then one morning she came to me and said that she was off. She had her things put on a cart and even then I didn't think she meant it. Then she put the two children in a rickshaw and came to say good-bye to me. She began to cry. By George, that pretty well broke me up. I asked her if she really meant to go and she said yes, unless I married her. I shook my head. I very nearly yielded. I'm afraid I was crying too. Then she gave a great sob and ran out of the house. I had to drink about half a tumbler of whisky to steady my nerves.'

'How long ago did this happen?'

'Four months. At first I thought she'd come back and then because I thought she was ashamed to make the first step I sent my boy to tell her that if she wanted to come I'd take her. But she refused. The house seemed awfully empty without her. At first I thought I'd get used to it, but somehow it doesn't seem to get any less empty. I didn't know how much she meant to me. She'd twined herself round my heart.'

'I suppose she'll come back if you agree to marry her.'

'Oh, yes, she told the boy that. Sometimes I ask myself if it's worth while to sacrifice my happiness for a dream. It is only a dream, isn't it? It's funny, one of the things that holds me back is the thought of a muddy lane I know, with great clay banks on both sides of it, and above, beech trees bending over. It's got a sort of cold, earthy smell that I can never quite get out of my nostrils. I don't blame her, you know. I rather admire her. I had no idea she had so much character. Sometimes I'm awfully inclined to give way.' He hesitated for a little while. 'I think, perhaps, if I thought she loved me I would. But of course, she doesn't; they never do, these girls who go and live with white men. I think she liked me, but that's all. What would you do in my place?'

'Oh, my dear fellow, how can I tell? Would you ever forget that dream?'

'Never.'

At that moment the boy came in to say that my Madrassi servant with the Ford car had just come up. Masterson looked at his watch.

'You'll want to be getting off, won't you? And I must get back to my office. I'm afraid I've rather bored you with my domestic affairs.'

'Not at all,' I said.

We shook hands, I put on my topee, and he waved to me as the car drove off.

FIRST the King of Siam had two daughters and he called them Night and Day. Then he had two more, so he changed the names of the first ones and called the four of them after the seasons, Spring and Autumn, Winter and Summer. But in course of time he had three others and he changed their names again and called all seven by the days of the week. But when his eighth daughter was born he did not know what to do till he suddenly thought of the months of the year. The Queen said there were only twelve and it confused her to have to remember so many new names, but the King had a methodical mind and when he made it up he never could change it if he tried. He changed the names of all his daughters and called them January, February, March (though of course in Siamese) till he came to the youngest, who was called August, and the next one was called September.

'That only leaves October, November, and December,' said the Queen. 'And after that we shall have to begin all over again.'

'No, we shan't,' said the King, 'because I think twelve daughters are enough for any man and after the birth of dear little December I shall be reluctantly compelled to cut off your head.'

He cried bitterly when he said this, for he was extremely fond of the Queen. Of course it made the Queen very uneasy because she knew that it would distress the King very much if he had to cut off her head. And it would not be very nice for her. But it so happened that there was no need for either of them to worry because September was the last daughter they ever had. The Queen only had sons after that and they were called by the letters of the alphabet, so there was no cause for anxiety there for a long time, since she had only reached the letter J.

Now the King of Siam's daughters had had their characters permanently embittered by having to change their names in this way, and the older ones, whose names of course had been changed oftener than the others, had their characters more permanently embittered. But September, who had never known what it was to be called anything but September (except of course by her sisters, who because their characters were embittered called her all sorts of names), had a very sweet and charming nature.

The King of Siam had a habit which I think might be usefully imitated in Europe. Instead of receiving presents on his birthday he gave them and it looks as though he liked it, for he used often to say he was sorry he had only been born on one day and so only had one birthday in the year. But in this way he managed in course of time to give away all his wedding presents and the loyal addresses which the mayors of the cities in Siam presented him with and all his own crowns which had gone out of fashion. One year on his birthday, not having anything else handy, he gave each of his daughters a beautiful green parrot in a beautiful golden cage. There were nine of them and on each cage was written the name of the month which was the name of the princess it belonged to. The nine princesses were very proud of their parrots and they spent an hour every day (for like their father they were of a methodical turn of mind) in teaching them to talk. Presently all the parrots could say God Save the King (in Siamese, which is very difficult) and some of them could say Pretty Polly in no less than seven oriental languages. But one day when the Princess September went to say good morning to her parrot she found it lying dead at the bottom of its golden cage. She burst into a flood of tears, and nothing that her Maids of Honour could say comforted her. She cried so much that the Maids of Honour, not knowing what to do, told the Queen, and the Queen said it was stuff and nonsense and the child had better go to bed without any supper. The Maids of Honour wanted to go to a party, so they put the Princess September to bed as quickly as they could and left her by herself. And while she lay in her bed, crying still even though she felt rather hungry, she saw a little bird hop into her room. She took her thumb out of her mouth and sat up. Then the little bird began to sing and he sang a beautiful song all about the lake in the King's garden and the willow trees that looked at themselves in the still water and the goldfish that glided in and out of the branches that were reflected in it. When he had finished, the Princess was not crying any more and she quite forgot that she had had no supper.

'That was a very nice song,' she said.

The little bird gave her a bow, for artists have naturally good manners, and they like to be appreciated.

'Would you care to have me instead of your parrot?' said the little bird. 'It's true that I'm not so pretty to look at, but on the other hand I have a much better voice.'

The Princess September clapped her hands with delight and then the little bird hopped on to the end of her bed and sang her to sleep.

When she awoke next day the little bird was still sitting there, and as she opened her eyes he said good morning. The Maids of Honour brought in her breakfast, and he ate rice out of her hand and he had his bath in her saucer. He drank out of it too. The Maids of Honour said they didn't think it was very polite to drink one's bath water, but the Princess September said that was the artistic temperament. When he had finished his breakfast he began to sing again so beautifully that the Maids of Honour were quite surprised, for they had never heard anything like it, and the Princess September was very proud and happy.

'Now I want to show you to my eight sisters,' said the Princess. She stretched out the first finger of her right hand so that it served as a perch and the little bird flew down and sat on it. Then, followed by her Maids of Honour, she went through the palace and called on each of the Princesses in turn, starting with January, for she was mindful of etiquette, and going all the way down to August. And for each of the Princesses the little bird sang a different song. But the parrots could only say God Save the King and Pretty Polly. At last she showed the little bird to the King and Queen. They were surprised and delighted.

'I knew I was right to send you to bed without any supper,' said the Queen.

'This bird sings much better than the parrots,' said the King.

'I should have thought you got quite tired of hearing people say God Save the King,' said the Queen. 'I can't think why those girls wanted to teach their parrots to say it too.'

'The sentiment is admirable,' said the King, 'and I never mind how often I hear it. But I do get tired of hearing those parrots say Pretty Polly.'

'They say it in seven different languages,' said the Princesses.

'I dare say they do,' said the King, 'but it reminds me too much of my councillors. They say the same thing in seven different ways and it never means anything in any way they say it.'

The Princesses, their characters as I have already said being naturally embittered, were vexed at this, and the parrots looked very glum indeed. But the Princess September ran through all the rooms of the palace, singing like a lark, while the little bird flew round and round her, singing like a nightingale, which indeed it was.

Things went on like this for several days and then the eight Princesses put their heads together. They went to September and sat down in a circle round her, hiding their feet as is proper for Siamese princesses to do.

'My poor September,' they said. 'We are sorry for the death of your beautiful parrot. It must be dreadful for you not to have a pet bird as we have. So we have all put our pocket-money together and we are going to buy you a lovely green and yellow parrot.'

'Thank you for nothing,' said September. (This was not very civil of her, but Siamese princesses are sometimes a little short with one another.) 'I have a pet bird which sings the most charming songs to me and I don't know what on earth I should do with a green and yellow parrot.'

January sniffed, then February sniffed, then March sniffed; in fact all the Princesses sniffed, but in their proper order of precedence. When they had finished September asked them:

'Why do you sniff? Have you all got colds in the head?'

'Well, my dear,' they said, 'it's absurd to talk of *your* bird when the little fellow flies in and out just as he likes.' They looked round the room and raised their eyebrows so high that their foreheads entirely disappeared.

'You'll get dreadful wrinkles,' said September.

'Do you mind our asking where your bird is now?' they said.

'He's gone to pay a visit to his father-in-law,' said the Princess September.

'And what makes you think he'll come back?' asked the Princesses.

'He always does come back,' said September.

'Well, my dear,' said the eight Princesses, 'if you'll take our advice you won't run any risks like that. If he comes back, and mind you, if he does you'll be lucky, pop him into the cage and keep him there. That's the only way you can be sure of him.'

'But I like to have him fly about the room,' said the Princess September.

'Safety first,' said her sisters ominously.

They got up and walked out of the room, shaking their heads, and they left September very uneasy. It seemed to her that her little bird was away a long time and she could not think what he was doing. Something might have happened to him. What with hawks and men with snares you never knew what trouble he might get into. Besides, he might forget her, or he might take a fancy to somebody else; that would be dreadful; oh, she wished he were safely back again, and in the golden cage that stood there empty and ready. For when the Maids of Honour had buried the dead parrot they had left the cage in its old place.

Suddenly September heard a tweet-tweet just behind her ear and she saw the little bird sitting on her shoulder. He had come in so quietly and alighted so softly that she had not heard him.

'I wondered what on earth had become of you,' said the Princess.

'I thought you'd wonder that,' said the little bird. 'The fact is I very nearly didn't come back tonight at all. My father-in-law was giving a party and they all wanted me to stay, but I thought you'd be anxious.'

Under the circumstances this was a very unfortunate remark for the little bird to make.

September felt her heart go thump, thump against her chest, and she made up her mind to take no more risks. She put up her hand and took hold of the bird. This he was quite used to, she liked feeling his heart go pit-a-pat, so fast, in the hollow of her hand, and I think he liked the soft warmth of her little hand. So the bird suspected nothing and he was so surprised when she carried him over to the cage, popped him in, and shut the door on him for a moment he could think of nothing to say. But in a moment or two he hopped up on the ivory perch and said:

'What is the joke?'

'There's no joke,' said September, 'but some of mamma's cats are prowling about tonight, and I think you're much safer in there.'

'I can't think why the Queen wants to have all those cats,' said the little bird, rather crossly.

'Well, you see, they're very special cats,' said the Princess, 'they have blue eyes and a kink in their tails, and they're a speciality of the royal family, if you understand what I mean.'

'Perfectly,' said the little bird, 'but why did you put me in this cage without saying anything about it? I don't think it's the sort of place I like.'

'I shouldn't have slept a wink all night if I hadn't known you were safe.'

'Well, just for this once I don't mind,' said the little bird, 'so long as you let me out in the morning.'

He ate a very good supper and then began to sing. But in the middle of his song he stopped.

'I don't know what is the matter with me,' he said, 'but I don't feel like singing tonight.'

'Very well,' said September, 'go to sleep instead.'

So he put his head under his wing and in a minute was fast asleep. September went to sleep too. But when the dawn broke she was awakened by the little bird calling her at the top of his voice:

'Wake up, wake up,' he said. 'Open the door of this cage and let me out. I want to have a good fly while the dew is still on the ground.'

'You're much better off where you are,' said September. 'You have a beautiful golden cage. It was made by the best workman in my papa's kingdom, and my papa was so pleased with it that he cut off his head so that he should never make another.'

'Let me out, let me out,' said the little bird.

'You'll have three meals a day served by my Maids of Honour; you'll have nothing to worry you from morning till night, and you can sing to your heart's content.'

'Let me out, let me out,' said the little bird. And he tried to slip through the bars of the cage, but of course he couldn't, and he beat against the door but of course he couldn't open it. Then the eight Princesses came in and looked at him. They told September she was very wise to take their advice. They said he would soon get used to the cage and in a few days would quite forget that he had ever been free. The little bird said nothing at all while they were there, but as soon as they were gone he began to cry again: 'Let me out, let me out.'

'Don't be such an old silly,' said September. 'I've only put you in the cage because I'm so fond of you. *I* know what's good for you much better than you do yourself. Sing me a little song and I'll give you a piece of brown sugar.'

But the little bird stood in the corner of his cage, looking out at the blue sky, and never sang a note. He never sang all day.

'What's the good of sulking?' said September. 'Why don't you sing and forget your troubles?'

'How can I sing?' answered the bird. 'I want to see the trees and the lake and the green rice growing in the fields.'

'If that's all you want I'll take you for a walk,' said September.

She picked up the cage and went out and she walked down to the lake round which grew the willow trees, and she stood at the edge of the rice-fields that stretched as far as the eye could see.

'I'll take you out every day,' she said. 'I love you and I only want to make you happy.'

274

'It's not the same thing,' said the little bird. 'The rice-fields and the lake and the willow trees look quite different when you see them through the bars of a cage.'

So she brought him home again and gave him his supper. But he wouldn't eat a thing. The Princess was a little anxious at this, and asked her sisters what they thought about it.

'You must be firm,' they said.

'But if he won't eat, he'll die,' she answered.

'That would be very ungrateful of him,' they said. 'He must know that you're only thinking of his own good. If he's obstinate and dies it'll serve him right and you'll be well rid of him.'

September didn't see how that was going to do *her* very much good, but they were eight to one and all older than she, so she said nothing.

'Perhaps he'll have got used to his cage by tomorrow,' she said.

And next day when she awoke she cried out good morning in a cheerful voice. She got no answer. She jumped out of bed and ran to the cage. She gave a startled cry, for there the little bird lay, at the bottom, on his side, with his eyes closed, and he looked as if he were dead. She opened the door and putting her hand in lifted him out. She gave a sob of relief, for she felt that his little heart was beating still.

'Wake up, wake up, little bird,' she said.

She began to cry and her tears fell on the little bird. He opened his eyes and felt that the bars of the cage were no longer round him.

'I cannot sing unless I'm free and if I cannot sing, I die,' he said.

The Princess gave a great sob.

'Then take your freedom,' she said, 'I shut you in a golden cage because I loved you and wanted to have you all to myself. But I never knew it would kill you. Go. Fly away among the trees that are round the lake and fly over the green rice-fields. I love you enough to let you be happy in your own way.'

She threw open the window and gently placed the little bird on the sill. He shook himself a little.

'Come and go as you will, little bird,' she said. 'I will never put you in a cage any more.'

'I will come because I love you, little Princess,' said the bird. 'And I will sing you the loveliest songs I know. I shall go far away, but I shall always come back, and I shall never forget you.' He gave himself another shake. 'Good gracious me, how stiff I am,' he said.

Then he opened his wings and flew right away into the blue. But the little Princess burst into tears, for it is very difficult to put the happiness of someone you love before your own, and with her little bird far out of sight she felt on a sudden very lonely. When her sisters knew what had happened they mocked her and said that the little bird would never return. But he did at last. And he sat on September's shoulder and ate out of her hand and sang her the beautiful songs he had learned while he was flying up and down the fair places of the world. September kept her window open day and night so that the little bird might come into her room whenever he felt inclined, and this was very good for her; so she grew extremely beautiful. And when she was old enough she married the King of Cambodia and was carried all the way to the city in which he lived on a white elephant. But her sisters never slept with their windows open, so they grew extremely ugly as well as disagreeable, and when the time came to marry them off they were given away to the King's councillors with a pound of tea and a Siamese cat.

A MARRIAGE OF CONVENIENCE

I LEFT Bangkok on a shabby little ship of four or five hundred tons. The dingy saloon, which served also as dining-room, had two narrow tables down its length with swivel chairs on both sides of them. The cabins were in the bowels of the ship and they were extremely dirty. Cockroaches walked about on the floor and however placid your temperament it is difficult not to be startled when you go to the wash-basin to wash your hands and a huge cockroach stalks leisurely out.

We dropped down the river, broad and lazy and smiling, and its green banks were dotted with little huts on piles standing at the water's edge. We crossed the bar; and the open sea, blue and still, spread before me. The look of it and the smell of it filled me with elation.

I had gone on board early in the morning and soon discovered that I was thrown amid the oddest collection of persons I had ever encountered. There were two French traders and a Belgian colonel, an Italian tenor, the American proprietor of a circus with his wife, and a retired French official with his. The circus proprietor was what is termed a good mixer, a type which according to your mood you fly from or welcome, but I happened to be feeling much pleased with life and before I had been on board an hour we had shaken for drinks, and he had shown me his animals. He was a very short fat man, and his stengah-shifter, white but none too clean, outlined the noble proportions of his abdomen, but the collar was so tight that you wondered he did not choke. He had a red, clean-shaven face, a merry blue eye, and short, untidy sandy hair. He wore a battered topee well on the back of his head. His name was Wilkins and he was born in Portland, Oregon. It appears that the Oriental has a passion for the circus and Mr Wilkins for twenty years had been travelling up and down the East from Port Said to Yokohama (Aden, Bombay, Madras, Calcutta, Rangoon, Singapore, Penang, Bangkok, Saigon, Huë, Hanoi, Hong-Kong, Shanghai, their names roll on the tongue savourily, crowding the imagination with sunshine and strange sounds and a multicoloured activity) with his menagerie and his merry-go-rounds. It was a strange life he led, unusual, and one that, one would have thought, must offer the occasion for all sorts of curious experiences, but the odd thing about him was that he

277

was a perfectly commonplace little man and you would have been prepared to find him running a garage or keeping a third-rate hotel in a second-rate town in California. The fact is, and I have noticed it so often that I do not know why it should always surprise me, that the extraordinariness of a man's life does not make him extraordinary, but contrariwise if a man is extraordinary he will make extraordinariness out of a life as humdrum as that of a country curate. I wish I could feel it reasonable to tell here the story of the hermit I went to see on an island in the Torres Straits, a shipwrecked mariner who had lived there alone for thirty years, but when you are writing a book you are imprisoned by the four walls of your subject and though for the entertainment of my own digressing mind I set it down now I should be forced in the end, by my sense of what is fit to go between two covers and what is not, to cut it out. Anyhow, the long and short of it is that notwithstanding his long and intimate communion with nature and his thoughts the man was as dull, insensitive, and vulgar an oaf at the end of this experience as he must have been at the beginning.

The Italian singer passed us, and Mr Wilkins told me that he was a Neapolitan who was on his way to Hong-Kong to rejoin his company, which he had been forced to leave owing to an attack of malaria in Bangkok. He was an enormous fellow, and very fat, and when he flung himself into a chair it creaked with dismay. He took off his topee, displayed a great head of long, curly, greasy hair, and ran podgy and beringed fingers through it.

'He ain't very sociable,' said Mr Wilkins. 'He took the cigar I gave him, but he wouldn't have a drink. I shouldn't wonder if there wasn't somethin' rather queer about him. Nasty-lookin' guy, ain't he?'

Then a little fat woman in white came on deck holding by the hand a Wa-Wa monkey. It walked solemnly by her side.

'This is Mrs Wilkins,' said the circus proprietor, 'and our youngest son. Draw up a chair, Mrs Wilkins, and meet this gentleman. I don't know his name, but he's already paid for two drinks for me and if he can't shake any better than he has yet he'll pay for one for you too.'

Mrs Wilkins sat down with an abstracted, serious look, and with her eyes on the blue sea suggested that she did not see why she shouldn't have a lemonade.

'My, it's hot,' she murmured, fanning herself with the topee which she took off.

'Mrs Wilkins feels the heat,' said her husband. 'She's had twenty years of it now.'

'Twenty-two and a half,' said Mrs Wilkins, still looking at the sea.

'And she's never got used to it yet.'

'Nor never shall and you know it,' said Mrs Wilkins.

She was just the same size as her husband and just as fat, and she had a round red face like his and the same sandy, untidy hair. I wondered if they had married because they were so exactly alike, or if in the course of years they had acquired this astonishing resemblance. She did not turn her head but continued to look absently at the sea.

'Have you shown him the animals?' she asked.

'You bet your life I have.'

'What did he think of Percy?'

'Thought him fine.'

I could not but feel that I was being unduly left out of a conversation of which I was at all events partly the subject, so I asked:

'Who's Percy?'

'Percy's our eldest son. There's a flyin'-fish, Elmer. He's the orang-utan. Did he eat his food well this morning?'

'Fine. He's the biggest orang-utan in captivity. I wouldn't take a thousand dollars for him.'

'And what relation is the elephant?' I asked.

Mrs Wilkins did not look at me, but with her blue eyes still gazed indifferently at the sea.

'He's no relation,' she answered. 'Only a friend.'

The boy brought lemonade for Mrs Wilkins, a whisky and soda for her husband, and a gin and tonic for me. We shook dice and I signed the chit.

'It must come expensive if he always loses when he shakes,' Mrs Wilkins murmured to the coast-line.

'I guess Egbert would like a sip of your lemonade, my dear,' said Mr Wilkins.

Mrs Wilkins slightly turned her head and looked at the monkey sitting on her lap.

'Would you like a sip of mother's lemonade, Egbert?'

The monkey gave a little squeak and putting her arm round him she handed him a straw. The monkey sucked up a little lemonade and having drunk enough sank back against Mrs Wilkins's ample bosom.

'Mrs Wilkins thinks the world of Egbert,' said her husband. 'You can't wonder at it, he's her youngest.'

Mrs Wilkins took another straw and thoughtfully drank her lemonade.

'Egbert's all right,' she remarked. 'There's nothin' wrong with Egbert.'

Just then the French official, who had been sitting down, got up and began walking up and down. He had been accompanied on board by the French minister at Bangkok, one or two secretaries, and a prince of the royal family. There had been a great deal of bowing and shaking of hands and as the ship slipped away from the quay much waving of hats and handkerchiefs. He was evidently a person of consequence. I had heard the captain address him as Monsieur le Gouverneur.

'That's the big noise on this boat,' said Mr Wilkins. 'He was Governor of one of the French colonies and now he's makin' a tour of the world. He came to see my circus at Bangkok. I guess I'll ask him what he'll have. What shall I call him, my dear?'

Mrs Wilkins slowly turned her head and looked at the Frenchman, with the rosette of the Legion of Honour in his buttonhole, pacing up and down.

'Don't call him anythin',' she said. 'Show him a hoop and he'll jump right through it.'

I could not but laugh. Monsieur le Gouverneur was a little man, well below the average height, and smally made, with a very ugly little face and thick, almost negroid features; and he had a bushy grey head, bushy grey eyebrows, and a bushy grey moustache. He did look a little like a poodle and he had the poodle's soft, intelligent and shining eyes. Next time he passed us Mr Wilkins called out:

'*Monsoo. Qu'est-ce que vous prenez?*' I cannot reproduce the eccentricities of his accent. '*Une petite verre de porto.*' He turned to me. 'Foreigners, they all drink porto. You're always safe with that.'

'Not the Dutch,' said Mrs Wilkins, with a look at the sea. 'They won't touch nothin' but Schnapps.'

The distinguished Frenchman stopped and looked at Mr Wilkins with some bewilderment. Whereupon Mr Wilkins tapped his breast and said:

'*Moa, proprietarre Cirque. Vous avez visité.*'

Then, for a reason that escaped me, Mr Wilkins made his arms into a hoop and outlined the gestures that represented a poodle jumping through it. Then he pointed at the Wa-Wa that Mrs Wilkins was still holding on her lap.

'*La petit fils de mon femme,*' he said.

Light broke upon the Governor and he burst into a peculiarly musical and infectious laugh. Mr Wilkins began laughing too.

'*Oui, oui,*' he cried. '*Moa,* circus proprietor. *Une petite verre de porto. Oui. Oui. N'est-ce pas?*'

'Mr Wilkins talks French like a Frenchman,' Mrs Wilkins informed the passing sea.

'*Mais très volontiers,*' said the Governor, still smiling. I drew him up a chair and he sat down with a bow to Mrs Wilkins.

'Tell poodle-face his name's Egbert,' she said, looking at the sea.

I called the boy and we ordered a round of drinks.

'You sign the chit, Elmer,' she said. 'It's not a bit of good Mr What's-his-name shakin' if he can't shake nothin' better than a pair of treys.'

'*Vous comprenez le français, madame?*' asked the Governor politely.

'He wants to know if you speak French, my dear.'

'Where does he think I was raised? Naples?'

Then the Governor, with exuberant gesticulation, burst into a torrent of English so fantastic that it required all my knowledge of French to understand what he was talking about.

Presently Mr Wilkins took him down to look at his animals and a little later we assembled in the stuffy saloon for luncheon. The Governor's wife appeared and was put on the captain's right. The Governor explained to her who we all were and she gave us a gracious bow. She was a large woman, tall and of a robust build, of fifty-five perhaps, and she was dressed somewhat severely in black silk. On her head she wore a huge round topee. Her features were so large and regular, her form so statuesque, that you were reminded of the massive females who take part in processions. She would have admirably suited the role of Columbia or Britannia in a patriotic demonstration. She towered over her diminutive husband like a skyscraper over a shack. He talked incessantly, with vivacity and wit, and when he said anything amusing her heavy features relaxed into a large fond smile.

'*Que tu es bête, mon ami,*' she said. She turned to the captain. 'You must not pay any attention to him. He is always like that.'

We had indeed a very amusing meal and when it was over we separated to our various cabins to sleep away the heat of the afternoon. In such a small ship having once made the acquaintance of my fellow passengers, it would have been impossible, even had I wished it, not to pass with them every moment of the day that

I was not in my cabin. The only person who held himself aloof was the Italian tenor. He spoke to no one, but sat by himself as far forward as he could get, twanging a guitar in an undertone so that you had to strain your ears to catch the notes. We remained in sight of land and the sea was like a pail of milk. Talking of one thing and another we watched the day decline, we dined, and then we sat out again on deck under the stars. The two traders played picquet in the hot saloon, but the Belgian colonel joined our little group. He was shy and fat and opened his mouth only to utter a civility. Soon, influenced perhaps by the night and encouraged by the darkness that gave him, up there in the bows, the sensation of being alone with the sea, the Italian tenor, accompanying himself on his guitar, began to sing, first in a low tone, and then a little louder, till presently, his music captivating him, he sang with all his might. He had the real Italian voice, all macaroni, olive oil, and sunshine, and he sang the Neapolitan songs that I had heard in my youth in the Piazza San Ferdinando, and fragments from *La Bohème*, and *Traviata*, and *Rigoletto*. He sang with emotion and false emphasis and his tremolo reminded you of every third-rate Italian tenor you had ever heard, but there in the openness of that lovely night his exaggerations only made you smile and you could not but feel in your heart a lazy sensual pleasure. He sang for an hour, perhaps, and we all fell silent; then he was still, but he did not move and we saw his huge bulk dimly outlined against the luminous sky.

I saw that the little French Governor had been holding the hand of his large wife and the sight was absurd and touching.

'Do you know that this is the anniversary of the day on which I first saw my wife?' he said, suddenly breaking the silence which had certainly weighed on him, for I had never met a more loquacious creature. 'It is also the anniversary of the day on which she promised to be my wife. And, which will surprise you, they were one and the same.'

'*Voyons, mon ami,*' said the lady, 'you are not going to bore our friends with that old story. You are really quite insupportable.'

But she spoke with a smile on her large, firm face, and in a tone that suggested that she was quite willing to hear it again.

'But it will interest them, *mon petit chou.*' It was in this way that he always addressed his wife and it was funny to hear this imposing and even majestic lady thus addressed by her small husband. 'Will it not, *monsieur?*' he asked me. 'It is a romance, and who does not like romance, especially on such a night as this?'

I assured the Governor that we were all anxious to hear and the Belgian colonel took the opportunity once more to be polite.

'You see, ours was a marriage of convenience pure and simple.'

'*C'est vrai*,' said the lady. 'It would be stupid to deny it. But sometimes love comes after marriage and not before, and then it is better. It lasts longer.'

I could not but notice that the Governor gave her hand an affectionate little squeeze.

'You see, I had been in the navy, and when I retired I was forty-nine. I was strong and active and I was very anxious to find an occupation. I looked about; I pulled all the strings I could. Fortunately I had a cousin who had some political importance. It is one of the advantages of democratic government that if you have sufficient influence, merit, which otherwise might pass unnoticed, generally receives its due reward.'

'You are modesty itself, *mon pauvre ami*,' said she.

'And presently I was sent for by the Minister to the Colonies and offered the post of Governor in a certain colony. It was a very distant spot that they wished to send me to and a lonely one, but I had spent my life wandering from port to port, and that was not a matter that troubled me. I accepted with joy. The minister told me that I must be ready to start in a month. I told him that would be easy for an old bachelor who had nothing much in the world but a few clothes and a few books.

' "*Comment, mon lieutenant*," he cried. "You are a bachelor?"

' "Certainly," I answered. "And I have every intention of remaining one."

' "In that case I am afraid I must withdraw my offer. For this position it is essential that you should be married." '

'It is too long a story to tell you, but the gist of it was that owing to the scandal my predecessor, a bachelor, had caused by having native girls to live in the Residency and the consequent complaints of the white people, planters and the wives of functionaries, it had been decided that the next Governor must be a model of respectability. I expostulated. I argued. I recapitulated my services to the country and the services my cousin could render at the next elections. Nothing would serve. The minister was adamant.

' "But what can I do?" I cried with dismay.

' "You can marry," said the minister.

' "*Mais voyons, monsieur le ministre*, I do not know any women. I am not a lady's man and I am forty-nine. How do you expect me to find a wife?" '

' "Nothing is more simple. Put an advertisement in the paper."

'I was confounded. I did not know what to say.

' "Well, think it over," said the minister. "If you can find a wife in a month you can go, but no wife no job. That is my last word." He smiled a little, to him the situation was not without humour. "And if you think of advertising I recommend the *Figaro*."

'I walked away from the ministry with death in my heart. I knew the place to which they desired to appoint me and I knew it would suit me very well to live there; the climate was tolerable and the Residency was spacious and comfortable. The notion of being a Governor was far from displeasing me and, having nothing much but my pension as a naval officer, the salary was not to be despised. Suddenly I made up my mind. I walked to the offices of the *Figaro*, composed an advertisement, and handed it in for insertion. But I can tell you, when I walked up the Champs Élysées afterwards my heart was beating much more furiously than it had ever done when my ship was stripped for action.'

The Governor leaned forward and put his hand impressively on my knee.

'*Mon cher monsieur*, you will never believe it, but I had four thousand three hundred and seventy-two replies. It was an avalanche. I had expected half-a-dozen; I had to take a cab to take the letters to my hotel. My room was swamped with them. There were four thousand three hundred and seventy-two women who were willing to share my solitude and be a Governor's lady. It was staggering. They were of all ages from seventeen to seventy. There were maidens of irreproachable ancestry and the highest culture, there were unmarried ladies who had made a little slip at one period of their career and now desired to regularize their situation; there were widows whose husbands had died in the most harrowing circumstances; and there were widows whose children would be a solace to my old age. They were blonde and dark, tall and short, fat and thin; some could speak five languages and others could play the piano. Some offered me love and some craved for it; some could only give me a solid friendship but mingled with esteem; some had a fortune and others golden prospects. I was overwhelmed. I was bewildered. At last I lost my temper, for I am a passionate man, and I got up and I stamped on all those letters and all those photographs and I cried; I will marry none of them. It was hopeless, I had less than a month now and I could not see over four thousand aspirants to my hand in that time. I felt that if I did not see them all, I should be tortured for the rest of my life by the thought that I had missed the one woman the fates had destined to make me happy. I gave it up as a bad job.

'I went out of my room hideous with all those photographs and littered papers and to drive care away went on to the boulevard and sat down at the Café de la Paix. After a time I saw a friend passing and he nodded to me and smiled. I tried to smile but my heart was sore. I realized that I must spend the years that remained to me in a cheap *pension* at Toulon or Brest as an *officier de marine en retraite. Zut*! My friend stopped and coming up to me sat down.

' "What is making you look so glum, *mon cher?*" he asked me. "You who are the gayest of mortals."

'I was glad to have someone in whom I could confide my troubles and told him the whole story. He laughed consumedly. I have thought since that perhaps the incident had its comic side, but at the time, I assure you, I could see in it nothing to laugh at. I mentioned the fact to my friend not without asperity and then, controlling his mirth as best he could, he said to me: "But, my dear fellow, do you really want to marry?" At this I entirely lost my temper.

' "You are completely idiotic," I said. "If I did not want to marry, and what is more marry at once, within the next fortnight, do you imagine that I should have spent three days reading love letters from women I have never set eyes on?"

' "Calm yourself and listen to me," he replied. "I have a cousin who lives in Geneva. She is Swiss, *du reste*, and she belongs to a family of the greatest respectability in the republic. Her morals are without reproach, she is of a suitable age, a spinster, for she has spent the last fifteen years nursing an invalid mother who has lately died, she is well educated and *pardessus le marché* she is not ugly."

' "It sounds as though she were a paragon," I said.

' "I do not say that, but she has been well brought up and would become the position you have to offer her."

' "There is one thing you forget. What inducement would there be for her to give up her friends and her accustomed life to accompany in exile a man of forty-nine who is by no means a beauty?" '

Monsieur le Gouverneur broke off his narrative and shrugging his shoulders so emphatically that his head almost sank between them, turned to us.

'I am ugly. I admit it. I am of an ugliness that does not inspire terror or respect, but only ridicule, and that is the worst ugliness of all. When people see me for the first time they do not shrink with horror, there would evidently be something flattering in that, they burst out laughing. Listen, when the admirable Mr Wilkins showed me his animals this morning, Percy, the orang-utan, held out his arms and but for the bars of the cage would have clasped me to to his bosom as a long lost brother. Once indeed when I was at the Jardin des Plantes in Paris and was told that one of the anthropoid apes had escaped I made my way to the exit as quickly as I could in fear that, mistaking me for the refugee, they would seize me and, notwithstanding my expostulations, shut me up in the monkey house.'

'*Voyons, mon ami*,' said Madame his wife, in her deep slow voice, 'you are talking even greater nonsense than usual. I do not say that you are an Apollo, in your position it is unnecessary that you should be, but you have dignity, you have poise, you are what any woman would call a fine man.'

'I will resume my story. When I made this remark to my friend he replied: "One can never tell with women. There is something about marriage that wonderfully attracts them. There would be no harm in asking her. After all it is regarded as a compliment by woman to be asked in marriage. She can but refuse."

' "But I do not know your cousin and I do not see how I am to make her acquaintance. I cannot go to her house, ask to see her and when I am shown into the drawing-room say: *Voilà*, I have come to ask you to marry me. She would think I was a lunatic and scream for help. Besides, I am a man of an extreme timidity, and I could never take such a step."

' "I will tell you what to do," said my friend. "Go to Geneva and take her a box of chocolates from me. She will be glad to have news of me and will receive you with pleasure. You can have a little talk and then if you do not like the look of her you take your leave and no harm is done. If on the other hand you do, we can go into the matter and you can make a formal demand for her hand."

'I was desperate. It seemed the only thing to do. We went to a shop at once and bought an enormous box of chocolates and that night I took the train to Geneva. No sooner had I arrived than I sent her a letter to say that I was the bearer of a gift from her cousin and much wished to give myself the pleasure of delivering it in person. Within an hour I received her reply to the effect that she would be pleased to receive me at four o'clock in the afternoon. I spent the interval before my mirror and seventeen times I tied and retied my tie. As the clock struck four I presented myself at the door of her house and was immediately ushered into the drawing-room. She was waiting for me. Her cousin said she was not ugly. Imagine my surprise to see a young woman, *enfin* a woman still young, of a noble presence, with the dignity of Juno, the features of Venus, and in her expression the intelligence of Minerva.'

'You are too absurd,' said Madame. 'But by now these gentlemen know that one cannot believe all you say.'

'I swear to you that I do not exaggerate. I was so taken aback that I nearly dropped the box of chocolates. But I said to myself: *La garde meurt mais ne se rend pas.* I presented the box of chocolates. I gave her news of her cousin. I found her amiable. We talked for a quarter of an hour. And then I said to myself: *Allons-y.* I said to her:

'"Mademoiselle, I must tell you that I did not come here merely to give you a box of chocolates."

'She smiled and remarked that evidently I must have had reasons to come to Geneva of more importance than that.

'"I came to ask you to do me the honour of marrying me." She gave a start.

'"But, *monsieur*, you are mad," she said.

'"I beseech you not to answer till you have heard the facts," I interrupted, and before she could say another word I told her the whole story. I told her about my advertisement in the *Figaro* and she laughed till the tears ran down her face. Then I repeated my offer.

'"You are serious?" she asked.

'"I have never been more serious in my life."

'"I will not deny that your offer has come as a surprise. I had not thought of marrying, I have passed the age; but evidently your offer is not one that a woman should refuse without consideration. I am flattered. Will you give me a few days to reflect?"

'"*Mademoiselle*, I am absolutely desolated," I replied. "But I have not time. If you will not marry me I must go back to Paris and resume my perusal of the fifteen or eighteen hundred letters that still await my attention."

'"It is quite evident that I cannot possibly give you an answer at once. I had not set eyes on you a quarter of an hour ago. I must consult my friends and my family."

'"What have they got to do with it? You are of full age. The matter is pressing. I cannot wait. I have told you everything. You are an intelligent woman. What can prolonged reflection add to the impulse of the moment?"

' "You are not asking me to say yes or no this very minute? That is outrageous."

' "That is exactly what I am asking. My train goes back to Paris in a couple of hours."

'She looked at me reflectively.

' "You are quite evidently a lunatic. You ought to be shut up both for your own safety and that of the public."

' "Well, which is it to be?" I said. "Yes or no?"

'She shrugged her shoulders.

' "*Mon Dieu*." She waited a minute and I was on tenterhooks. "Yes."

The Governor waved his hand towards his wife.

'And there she is. We were married in a fortnight and I became Governor of a colony. I married a jewel, my dear sirs, a woman of the most charming character, one in a thousand, a woman of a masculine intelligence and a feminine sensibility, an admirable woman.'

'But hold your tongue, *mon ami*,' his wife said. 'You are making me as ridiculous as yourself.'

He turned to the Belgian colonel.

'Are you a bachelor, *mon colonel*? If so I strongly recommend you to go to Geneva. It is a nest (*une pépinière* was the word he used) of the most adorable young women. You will find a wife there as nowhere else. Geneva is besides a charming city. Do not waste a minute, but go there and I will give you a letter to my wife's nieces.'

It was she who summed up the story.

'The fact is that in a marriage of convenience you expect less and so you are less likely to be disappointed. As you do not make senseless claims on one another there is no reason for exasperation. You do not look for perfection and so you are tolerant to one another's faults. Passion is all very well, but it is not a proper foundation for marriage. *Voyez-vous*, for two people to be happy in marriage they must be able to respect one another, they must be of the same condition, and their interests must be alike; then if they are decent people and are willing to give and take, to live and let live, there is no reason why their union should not be as happy as ours.' She paused. 'But, of course, my husband is a very, very remarkable man.'

MIRAGE

I HAD been wandering about the East for months and at last reached Haiphong. It is a commercial town and a dull one, but I knew that from there I could find a ship of sorts to take me to Hong-Kong. I had some days to wait and nothing to do. It is true that from Haiphong you can visit the Bay of Along, which is one of the *Sehenswurdigkeiten* of Indo-China, but I was tired of sights. I contented myself with sitting in the cafés, for here it was none too warm and I was glad to get out of tropical clothes, and reading back numbers of *L'Illustration*, or for the sake of exercise taking a brisk walk along straight, wide streets. Haiphong is traversed by canals and sometimes I got a glimpse of a scene which in its varied life, with all the native craft on the water, was multi-coloured and charming. There was one canal, with tall Chinese houses on each side of it, that had a pleasant curve. The houses were whitewashed, but the whitewash was discoloured and stained; with their grey roofs they made an agreeable composition against the pale sky. The picture had the faded elegance of an old water-colour. There was nowhere an emphatic note. It was soft and a little weary and inspired one with a faint melancholy. I was reminded I scarcely know why of an old maid I knew in my youth, a relic of the Victorian age, who wore black silk mittens and made crochet shawls for the poor, black for widows and white for married women. She had suffered in her youth, but whether from ill-health or unrequited love, no one exactly knew.

But there was a local paper at Haiphong, a small dingy sheet with stubby type the ink of which came off on your fingers, and it gave you a political article, the wireless news, advertisements, and local intelligence. The editor, doubtless hard pressed for matter, printed the names of the persons, Europeans, natives of the country, and Chinese, who had arrived at Haiphong or left it, and mine was put in with the rest. On the morning of the day before that on which the old tub I was taking was to sail for Hong-Kong I was sitting in the café of the hotel drinking a Dubonnet before luncheon when the boy came in and said that a gentleman wished to see me. I did not know a soul in Haiphong and asked who it was. The boy said he was an Englishman and lived there, but he could not tell me his name. The boy spoke very little French and it was hard for me to understand what he said.

I was mystified, but told him to show the visitor in. A moment later he came back followed by a white man and pointed me out to him. The man gave me a look and walked towards me. He was a very tall fellow, well over six feet high, rather fat and bloated, with a red, clean-shaven face and extremely pale blue eyes. He wore very shabby khaki shorts and a stengah-shifter unbuttoned at the neck, and a battered helmet. I concluded at once that he was a stranded beachcomber who was going to touch me for a loan and wondered how little I could hope to get off for.

He came up to me and held out a large red hand with broken, dirty nails.

'I don't suppose you remember me,' he said. 'My name's Grosely. I was at St Thomas's Hospital with you. I recognized your name as soon as I saw it in the paper and I thought I'd look you up.'

I had not the smallest recollection of him, but I asked him to sit down and offered him a drink. By his appearance I had first thought he would ask me for ten piastres and I might have given him five, but now it looked more likely that he would ask for a hundred and I should have to think myself lucky if I could content him with fifty. The habitual borrower always asks twice what he expects to get and it only dissatisfies him to give him what he has asked since then he is vexed with himself for not having asked more. He feels you have cheated him.

'Are you a doctor?' I asked.

'No, I was only at the bloody place a year.'

He took off his sun-helmet and showed me a mop of grey hair, which much needed a brush. His face was curiously mottled and he did not look healthy. His teeth were badly decayed and at the corners of his mouth were empty spaces. When the boy came to take the orders he asked for brandy.

'Bring the bottle,' he said. '*La bouteille.* Savvy?' He turned to me. 'I've been living here for the last five years, but I can't get along with French somehow. I talk Tonkinese.' He leaned his chair back and looked at me. 'I remember you, you know. You used to go about with those twins. What was their name? I expect I've changed more than you have. I've spent the best part of my life in China. Rotten climate, you know. It plays hell with a man.'

I still had not the smallest recollection of him. I thought it best to say so.

'Were you the same year as I was?' I asked.

'Yes. '92.'

290

'It's a devil of a long time ago.'

About sixty boys and young men entered the hospital every year; they were most of them shy and confused by the new life they were entering upon; many had never been in London before; and to me at least they were shadows that passed without any particular rhyme or reason across a white sheet. During the first year a certain number for one reason or another dropped out, and in the second year those that remained gained by degrees the beginnings of a personality. They were not only themselves, but the lectures one had attended with them, the scone and coffee one had eaten at the same table for luncheon, the dissection one had done at the same board in the same dissecting room, and *The Belle of New York* one had seen together from the pit of the Shaftesbury Theatre.

The boy brought the bottle of brandy, and Grosely, if that was really his name, pouring himself out a generous helping drank it down at a gulp without water or soda.

'I couldn't stand doctoring,' he said. 'I chucked it. My people got fed up with me and I went out to China. They gave me a hundred pounds and told me to shift for myself. I was damned glad to get out, I can tell you. I guess I was just about as much fed up with them as they were with me. I haven't troubled them much since.'

Then from somewhere in the depths of my memory a faint hint crept into the rim, as it were, of consciousness, as on a rising tide the water slides up the sand and then withdraws to advance with the next wave in a fuller volume. I had first an inkling of some shabby little scandal that had got into the papers. Then I saw a boy's face, and so gradually the facts recurred to me; I remembered him now. I didn't believe he was called Grosely then, I think he had a one-syllabled name, but that I was uncertain of. He was a very tall lad (I began to see him quite well), thin, with a slight stoop, he was only eighteen and had grown too fast for his strength, he had curly, shining brown hair, rather large features (they did not look so large now, perhaps because his face was fat and puffy) and a peculiarly fresh complexion, very pink and white, like a girl's. I imagine people, women especially, would have thought him a very handsome boy, but to us he was only a clumsy, shuffling lout. Then I remembered that he did not often come to lectures, no, it wasn't that I remembered, there were too many students in the theatre to recollect who was there and who wasn't. I remembered the dissecting room. He had a leg at the next table to the one I was working at and he hardly ever touched it; I forget why the men who had other parts of the body complained of his neglecting the work, I suppose somehow it interfered with them. In those days a good deal of gossip went on over the dissection of a 'part' and out of the distance of thirty years some of it came back to me. Someone started the story that Grosely was a very gay dog. He drank like a fish and was an awful womanizer. Most of those boys were very simple, and they had brought to the hospital the notions they had acquired at home and at school. Some were prudish and they were shocked; others, those who worked hard, sneered at him and asked how he could hope to pass his exams; but a good many were excited and impressed, he was doing what they would have liked to do if they had had the courage. Grosely had his admirers and you could often see him surrounded by a little band listening open-mouthed to stories of his adventures. Recollections now were crowding upon me. In a very little while he lost his shyness and assumed the airs of a man of the world. They must have looked absurd on this smooth-cheeked boy with his pink and white skin. Men (so they called themselves) used to tell one another of his escapades. He became quite a hero. He would make caustic remarks as he passed the museum and saw a pair of earnest students going over their anatomy together. He was at home in the public-houses of the neighbourhood and was on familiar terms with the barmaids. Looking back, I imagine that, newly arrived from the country and the tutelage of parents and schoolmasters, he was captivated by his freedom and the thrill of London. His dissipations were harmless enough. They were due only to the urge of youth. He lost his head.

But we were all very poor and we did not know how Grosely managed to pay for his garish amusements. We knew his father was a country doctor and I think we knew exactly how much he gave his son a month. It was not enough to pay for the harlots he picked up on the promenade at the Pavilion and for the drinks he stood his friends in the Criterion Bar. We told one another in awe-struck tones that he must be getting fearfully into debt. Of course he could pawn things, but we knew by experience that you could not get more than three pounds for a microscope and thirty shillings for a skeleton. We said he must be spending at least ten pounds a week. Our ideas were not very grand and this seemed to us the wildest pitch of extravagance. At last one of his friends disclosed the mystery: Grosely had discovered a wonderful system for making money. It amused and impressed us. None of us would have thought of anything so ingenious or have had the nerve to attempt it if he had. Grosely went to auctions, not Christie's, of course, but auctions in the Strand and Oxford Street, and in private houses, and bought anything portable that was going cheap. Then he took his purchase to a pawnbroker's and pawned it for ten shillings or a pound more than he had paid. He was making money, four or five pounds a week, and he said he was going to give up medicine and make a regular business of it. Not one of us had ever made a penny in his life and we regarded Grosely with admiration.

'By Jove, he's clever,' we said.

'He's just about as sharp as they make them.'

'That's the sort that ends up as a millionaire.'

We were all very worldly-wise and what we didn't know about life at eighteen we were pretty sure wasn't worth knowing. It was a pity that when an examiner asked us a question we were so nervous that the answer often flew straight out of our head and when a nurse asked us to post a letter we blushed scarlet. It became known that the Dean had sent for Grosely and hauled him over the coals. He had threatened him with sundry penalties if he continued systematically to neglect his work. Grosely was indignant. He'd had enough of that sort of thing at school, he said, he wasn't going to let a horse-faced eunuch treat him like a boy. Damn it all, he was getting on for nineteen and there wasn't much you could teach him. The Dean had said he heard he was drinking more than was good for him. Damned cheek. He could carry his liquor as well as any man of his age, he'd been blind last Saturday and he meant to get blind next Saturday, and if anyone didn't like it he could do the other thing. Grosely's friends quite agreed with him that a man couldn't let himself be insulted like that.

But the blow fell at last and now I remembered quite well the shock it gave us all. I suppose we had not seen Grosely for two or three days, but he had been in the habit of coming to the hospital more and more irregularly, so if we thought anything about it, I imagine we merely said that he was off on one of his bats. He would turn up again in a day or so, rather pale, but with a wonderful story of some girl he had picked up and the time he had had with her. The anatomy lecture was at nine in the morning and it was a rush to get there in time. On this particular day little attention was paid to the lecturer, who, with a visible pleasure in his limpid English and admirable elocution, was describing I know not what part of the human skeleton, for there was much excited whispering along the benches and a newspaper was surreptitiously passed from hand to hand. Suddenly the lecturer stopped. He had a pedagogic sarcasm. He affected not to know the names of his students.

'I am afraid I am disturbing the gentleman who is reading the paper. Anatomy is a very tedious science and I regret that the regulations of the Royal College of Surgeons oblige me to ask you to give it enough of your attention to pass an examination in it. Any gentleman, however, who finds this impossible is at liberty to continue his perusal of the paper outside.'

The wretched boy to whom this reproof was addressed reddened to the roots of his hair and in his embarrassment tried to stuff the newspaper in his pocket. The professor of anatomy observed him coldly.

'I am afraid, sir, that the paper is a little too large to go into your pocket,' he remarked. 'Perhaps you would be good enough to hand it down to me?'

The newspaper was passed from row to row to the well of the theatre, and, not content with the confusion to which he had put the poor lad, the eminent surgeon, taking it, asked:

'May I inquire what it is in the paper that the gentleman in question found of such absorbing interest?'

The student who gave it to him without a word pointed out the paragraph that we had all been reading. The professor read it and we watched him in silence. He put the paper down and went on with his lecture. The headline ran *Arrest of a Medical Student.* Grosely had been brought before the police-court magistrate for getting goods on credit and pawning them. It appears that this is an indictable offence and the magistrate had remanded him for a week. Bail was refused. It looked as though his method of making money by buying things at auctions and pawning them had not in the long run proved as steady a source of income as he expected and he had found it more profitable to pawn things that he was not at the expense of paying for. We talked the matter over excitedly as soon as the lecture was over and I am bound to say that, having no property ourselves, so deficient was our sense of its sanctity we could none of us look upon his crime as a very serious one; but with the natural love of the young for the terrible there were few who did not think he would get anything from two years hard labour to seven years penal servitude.

I do not know why, but I did not seem to have any recollection of what happened to Grosely. I think he may have been arrested towards the end of a session and his case may have come on again when we had all separated for holidays. I did not know if it was disposed of by the police-court magistrate or whether it went up for trial. I had a sort of feeling that he was sentenced to a short term of imprisonment, six weeks perhaps, for his operations had been pretty extensive; but I knew that he had vanished from our midst and in a little while was thought of no more. It was strange to me that after all these years I should recollect so much of the incident so clearly. It was as though, turning over an album of old snapshots, I saw all at once the photograph of a scene I had quite forgotten.

But of course in that gross elderly man with grey hair and mottled red face I should never have recognised the lanky pink-cheeked boy. He looked sixty, but I knew he must be much less than that. I wondered what he had done with himself in the intervening time. It did not look as though he had excessively prospered.

'What were you doing in China?' I asked him.

'I was a tide-waiter.'

'Oh, were you?'

It is not a position of great importance and I took care to keep out of my tone any note of surprise. The tide-waiters are employees of the Chinese Customs whose duty it is to board the ships and junks at the various treaty ports and I think their chief business is to prevent opium-smuggling. They are mostly retired A.B.s from the Royal Navy and non-commissioned officers who have finished their time. I have seen them come on board at various places up the Yangtse. They hobnob with the pilot and the engineer, but the skipper is a trifle curt with them. They learn to speak Chinese more fluently than most Europeans and often marry Chinese women.

'When I left England I swore I wouldn't go back till I'd made my pile. And I never did. They were glad enough to get anyone to be a tide-waiter in those days, any white man I mean, and they didn't ask questions. They didn't care who you were. I was damned glad to get the job, I can tell you, I was about broke to the wide when they took me on. I only took it till I could get something better, but I stayed on, it suited me, I wanted to make money and I found out that a tide-waiter could make a packet if he knew the right way to go about it. I was with the Chinese

Customs for the best part of twenty-five years and when I came away I wouldn't mind betting that lots of commissioners would have been glad to have the money I had.'

He gave me a sly, mean look. I had an inkling of what he meant. But there was a point on which I was willing to be reassured; if he was going to ask me for a hundred piastres (I was resigned to that sum now) I thought I might just as well take the blow at once.

'I hope you kept it,' I said.

'You bet I did. I invested all my money in Shanghai and when I left China I put it all in American railway bonds. Safety first is my motto. I know too much about crooks to take any risks myself.'

I liked that remark, so I asked him if he wouldn't stay and have luncheon with me.

'No, I don't think I will. I don't eat much tiffin and anyway my chow's waiting for me at home. I think I'll be getting along.' He got up and he towered over me. 'But look here, why don't you come along this evening and see my place? I've married a Haiphong girl. Got a baby too. It's not often I get a chance of talking to anyone about London. You'd better not come to dinner. We only eat native food and I don't suppose you'd care for that. Come along about nine, will you?'

'All right,' I said.

I had already told him that I was leaving Haiphong next day. He asked the boy to bring him a piece of paper so that he might write down his address. He wrote laboriously in the hand of a boy of fourteen.

'Tell the porter to explain to your rickshaw boy where it is. I'm on the second floor. There's no bell. Just knock. Well, see you later.'

He walked out and I went in to luncheon.

After dinner I called a rickshaw and with the porter's help made the boy understand where I wanted to go. I found presently that he was taking me along the curved canal the houses of which had looked to me so like a faded Victorian water-colour; he stopped at one of them and pointed to the door. It looked so shabby and the neighbourhood was so squalid that I hesitated, thinking he had made a mistake. It seemed unlikely that Grosely could live so far in the native quarter and in a house so bedraggled. I told the rickshaw boy to wait and pushing open the door saw a dark staircase in front of me. There was no one about and the street was empty. It might have been the small hours of the morning. I struck a match and fumbled my way upstairs; on the second floor I struck another match and saw a large brown door in front of me. I knocked and in a moment it was opened by a little Tonkinese woman holding a candle. She was dressed in the earth-brown of the poorer classes, with a tight little black turban on her head; her lips and the skin round them were stained red with betel and when she opened her mouth to speak I saw that she had the black teeth and black gums that so disfigure these people. She said something in her native language and then I heard Grosely's voice:

'Come along in. I was beginning to think you weren't going to turn up.'

I passed through a little dark ante-chamber and entered a large room that evidently looked on the canal. Grosely was lying on a long chair and he raised his length from it as I came in. He was reading the Hong-Kong papers by the light of a paraffin-lamp that stood on a table by his side.

'Sit down,' he said, 'and put your feet up.'

'There's no reason I should take your chair.'

'Go on. I'll sit on this.'

He took a kitchen chair and sitting on it put his feet on the end of mine.

'That's my wife,' he said pointing with his thumb at the Tonkinese woman who had followed me into the room. 'And over there in the corner's the kid.'

I followed his eyes and against the wall, lying on bamboo mats and covered with a blanket, I saw a child sleeping.

'Lively little beggar when he's awake. I wish you could have seen him. She's going to have another soon.'

I glanced at her and the truth of what he said was apparent. She was very small, with tiny hands and feet, but her face was flat and the skin muddy. She looked sullen, but may only have been shy. She went out of the room and presently came back with a bottle of whisky, two glasses, and a syphon. I looked round. There was a partition at the back of dark unpainted wood, which I suppose shut off another room, and pinned against the middle of this was a portrait cut out of an illustrated paper of John Galsworthy. He looked austere, mild, and gentlemanly, and I wondered what he did there. The other walls were whitewashed, but the whitewash was dingy and stained. Pinned on to them were pages of pictures from the *Graphic* or the *Illustrated London News*.

'I put them up,' said Grosely, 'I thought they made the place look homelike.'

'What made you put up Galsworthy? Do you read his books?'

'No, I didn't know he wrote books. I liked his face.'

There were one or two torn and shabby rattan mats on the floor and in a corner a great pile of the *Hong-Kong Times*. The only furniture consisted of a wash-hand stand, two or three kitchen chairs, a table or two, and a large teak native bed. It was cheerless and sordid.

'Not a bad little place, is it?' said Grosely. 'Suits me all right. Sometimes I've thought of moving, but I don't suppose I ever shall now.' He gave a little chuckle. 'I came to Haiphong for forty-eight hours and I've been here five years. I was on my way to Shanghai really.'

He was silent. Having nothing to say I said nothing. Then the little Tonkinese woman made a remark to him, which I could not of course understand, and he answered her. He was silent again for a minute or two, but I thought he looked at me as though he wanted to ask me something. I did not know why he hesitated.

'Have you ever tried smoking opium on your travels in the East?' he inquired at last, casually.

'Yes, I did once, at Singapore. I thought I'd like to see what it was like.'

'What happened?'

'Nothing very thrilling, to tell you the truth. I thought I was going to have the most exquisite emotions. I expected visions, like de Quincey's, you know. The only thing I felt was a kind of physical well-being, the same sort of feeling that you get when you've had a Turkish bath and are lying in the cooling room, and then a peculiar activity of mind so that everything I thought of seemed extremely clear.'

'I know.'

'I really felt that two and two are four and there could not be the smallest doubt about it. But next morning – oh God! My head reeled. I was as sick as a dog, I was sick all day, I vomited my soul out, and as I vomited I said to myself miserably: And there are people who call this fun.'

Grosely leaned back in his chair and gave a low mirthless laugh.

'I expect it was bad stuff. Or you went at it too hard. They saw you were a mug and gave you dregs that had been smoked already. They're enough to turn anybody up. Would you like to have another try now? I've got some stuff here that I know's good.'

'No, I think once was enough for me.'

'D'you mind if I have a pipe or two? You want it in a climate like this. It keeps you from getting dysentery. And I generally have a bit of a smoke about this time.'

'Go ahead,' I said.

He spoke again to the woman and she, raising her voice, called out something in a raucous tone. An answer came from the room behind the wooden partition and after a minute or two an old woman came out carrying a little round tray. She was shrivelled and old and when she entered gave me an ingratiating smile of her stained mouth. Grosely got up and crossed over to the bed and lay on it. The old woman set the tray down on the bed; on it was a spirit-lamp, a pipe, a long needle, and a little round box of opium. She squatted on the bed and Grosely's wife got on it too and sat, her feet tucked up under her, with her back against the wall. Grosely watched the old woman while she put a little pellet of the drug on the needle, held it over the flame till it sizzled, and then plugged it into the pipe. She handed it to him and with a great breath he inhaled it, he held the smoke for a little while and then blew it out in a thick grey cloud. He handed her back the pipe and she started to make another. Nobody spoke. He smoked three pipes in succession and then sank back.

'By George, I feel better now. I was feeling all in. She makes a wonderful pipe, this old hag. Are you sure you won't have one?'

'Quite.'

'Please yourself. Have some tea then.'

He spoke to his wife, who scrambled off the bed and went out of the room. Presently she came back with a little china pot of tea and a couple of Chinese bowls.

'A lot of people smoke here, you know. It does you no harm if you don't do it to excess. I never smoke more than twenty to twenty-five pipes a day. You can go on for years if you limit yourself to that. Some of the Frenchmen smoke as many as forty or fifty a day. That's too much. I never do that, except now and then when I feel I want a binge. I'm bound to say it's never done me any harm.'

We drank our tea, pale and vaguely scented and clean on the palate. Then the old woman made him another pipe and then another. His wife had got back on to the bed and soon curling herself up at his feet went to sleep. Grosely smoked two or three pipes at a time, and while he was smoking seemed intent upon nothing else, but in the intervals he was loquacious. Several times I suggested going, but he would not let me. The hours wore on. Once or twice while he smoked I dozed. He told me all about himself. He went on and on. I spoke only to give him a cue. I cannot relate what he told me in his own words. He repeated himself. He was very long-winded and he told me his story confusedly, first a late bit, then an early bit, so that I had to arrange the sequence for myself; sometimes I saw that, afraid he had said too much, he held something back; sometimes he lied and I had to make a guess at the truth from the smile he gave me or the look in his eyes. He had not the words to describe what he had felt, and I had to conjecture his meaning from slangy metaphors and hackneyed, vulgar phrases. I kept on asking myself what his real name was, it was on the tip of my tongue and it irritated me not to be able to recall it, though why it should in the least matter to me I did not know. He was somewhat suspicious of me at first and I saw that this escapade of his in London and his imprisonment had been all these years a tormenting secret. He had always been haunted by the fear that sooner or later someone would find out.

'It's funny that even now you shouldn't remember me at the hospital,' he said, looking at me shrewdly. 'You must have a rotten memory.'

'Hang it all, it's nearly thirty years ago. Think of the thousands of people I've met since then. There's no reason why I should remember you any more than you remember me.'

'That's right. I don't suppose there is.'

It seemed to reassure him. At last he had smoked enough and the old woman made herself a pipe and smoked it. Then she went over to the mat on which the child was lying and huddled down beside it. She lay so still that I supposed she had fallen directly asleep. When at last I went I found my boy curled up on the foot-board of the rickshaw in so deep a slumber that I had to shake him. I knew where I was and I wanted air and exercise, so I gave him a couple of piastres and told him I would walk.

It was a strange story I carried away with me.

It was with a sort of horror that I had listened to Grosely, telling me of those twenty years he had spent in China. He had made money, I do not know how much, but from the way he talked I should think something between fifteen and twenty thousand pounds, and for a tide-waiter it was a fortune. He could not have come by it honestly, and little as I knew of the details of his trade, by his sudden reticences, by his leers and hints I guessed that there was no base transaction that, if it was made worth his while, he jibbed at. I suppose that nothing paid him better than smuggling opium, and his position gave him the opportunity to do this with safety and profit. I understood that his superior officers had often had their suspicions of him, but had never been able to get such proof of his malpractices as to justify them in taking any steps. They contented themselves with moving him from one port to another, but that did not disturb him; they watched him, but he was too clever for them. I saw that he was divided between the fear of telling me too much to his discredit and the desire to boast of his own astuteness. He prided himself on the confidence the Chinese had placed in him.

'They knew they could trust me,' he said, 'and it gave me a pull. I never double-crossed a Chinaman once.'

The thought filled him with the complacency of the honest man. The Chinese discovered that he was keen on curios and they got in the habit of giving him bits or bringing him things to buy; he never made inquiries how they had come by them and he bought them cheap. When he had got a good lot he sent them to Peking and sold them at a handsome profit. I remembered how he had started his commercial career by buying things at auctions and pawning them. For twenty years by shabby shift and petty dishonesty he added pound to pound, and everything he made he invested in Shanghai. He lived penuriously, saving half his pay; he never went on leave because he did not want to waste his money, he would not have anything to do with the Chinese women, he wanted to keep himself free from any entanglement; he did not drink. He was consumed by one ambition, to save enough to be able to go back to England and live the life from which he had been snatched as a boy. That was the only thing he wanted. He lived in China as though in a dream; he paid no attention to the life around him; its colour and strangeness, its possibilities of pleasure, meant nothing to him. There was always before him the mirage of London, the Criterion Bar, himself standing with his foot on the rail, the promenade at the Empire and the Pavilion, the picked-up harlot, the serio-comic at the music-hall, and the musical comedy at the Gaiety. This was life and love and adventure. This was romance. This was what he yearned for with all his heart. There was surely something impressive in the way in which during all those years he had lived like an anchorite with that one end in view of leading again a life that was so vulgar. It showed character.

'You see,' he said to me, 'even if I'd been able to get back to England on leave I wouldn't have gone. I didn't want to go till I could go for good. And then I wanted to do the thing in style.'

He saw himself putting on evening clothes every night and going out with a gardenia in his buttonhole, and he saw himself going to the Derby in a long coat and a brown hat and a pair of opera glasses slung over his shoulder. He saw himself giving the girls a look over and picking out the one he fancied. He made up his mind that on the night he arrived in London he would get blind, he hadn't been drunk for twenty years; he couldn't afford to in his job, you had to keep your wits about you. He'd take care not to get drunk on the ship on the way home. He'd wait till he got to London. What a night he'd have! He thought of it for twenty years.

I do not know why Grosely left the Chinese Customs, whether the place was getting too hot for him, whether he had reached the end of his service, or whether he had amassed the sum he had fixed. But at last he sailed. He went second class; he did not intend to start spending money till he reached London. He took rooms in Jermyn Street, he had always wanted to live there, and he went straight to a tailor's and ordered himself an outfit. Slap up. Then he had a look round the town. It was different from how he remembered it, there was much more traffic and he felt confused and a little at sea. He went to the Criterion and found there was no longer a bar where he had been used to lounge and drink. There was a restaurant in Leicester Square where he had been in the habit of dining when he was in funds, but he could not find it; he supposed it had been torn down. He went to the Pavilion, but there were no women there; he was rather disgusted and went on to the Empire, he found they had done away with the Promenade. It was rather a blow. He could not quite make it out. Well, anyhow, he must be prepared for changes in twenty years, and if he couldn't do anything else he could get drunk. He had had fever several times in China and the change of climate had brought it on again, he wasn't feeling any too well, and after four or five drinks he was glad to go to bed.

That first day was only a sample of many that followed it. Everything went wrong. Grosely's voice grew peevish and bitter as he told me how one thing and another had failed him. The old places were gone, the people were different, he found it hard to make friends, he was strangely lonely; he had never expected that in a great city like London. That's what was wrong with it, London had become too big, it wasn't the jolly, intimate place it had been in the early nineties. It had gone to pieces. He picked up a few girls, but they weren't as nice as the girls he had known before, they weren't the fun they used to be, and he grew dimly conscious that they thought him a rum sort of cove. He was only just over forty and they looked upon him as an old man. When he tried to cotton on to a lot of young fellows standing round a bar they gave him the cold shoulder. Anyway, these young fellows didn't know how to drink. He'd show them. He got soused every night, it was the only thing to do in that damned place, but, by Jove, it made him feel rotten next day. He supposed it was the climate of China. When he was a medical student he could drink a bottle of whisky every night and be as fresh as a daisy in the morning. He began to think more about China. All sorts of things that he never knew he had noticed came back to him. It wasn't a bad life he'd led there. Perhaps he'd been a fool to keep away from those Chinese girls, they were pretty little things some of them, and they didn't put on the airs these English girls did. One could have a damned good time in China if one had the money he had. One could keep a Chinese girl and get into the club, and there'd be a lot of nice fellows to drink with and play bridge with and billiards. He remembered the Chinese shops and all the row in the streets and the coolies carrying loads and the ports with the junks in them and the rivers with pagodas on the banks. It was funny, he never thought much of China while he was there and now – well, he couldn't get it out of his mind. It obsessed him. He began to think that London was no place for a white man. It had just gone to the dogs, that was the long and short of it, and one day the thought came to him that perhaps it would be a good thing if he went back to China. Of course it was silly, he'd worked like a slave for twenty years to be able to have a good time in London, and it was absurd to go and live in China. With his money he ought to be able to have a good time anywhere. But somehow he couldn't think of anything else but China. One day he went to the pictures and saw a scene at Shanghai. That settled it. He was fed up with London. He hated it. He was going to get out and this time he'd get out for good. He had been home a year and a half, and it seemed longer to him than all his twenty years in the East. He took a passage on a

French boat sailing from Marseilles, and when he saw the coast of Europe sink into the sea he heaved a great sigh of relief. When they got to Suez and he felt the first touch of the East he knew he had done the right thing. Europe was finished. The East was the only place.

He went ashore at Djibouti and again at Colombo and Singapore, but though the ship stopped for two days at Saigon he remained on board there. He'd been drinking a good deal and he was feeling a bit under the weather. But when they reached Haiphong, where they were staying for forty-eight hours, he thought he might just as well have a look at it. That was the last stopping-place before they got to China. He was bound for Shanghai. When he got there he meant to go to a hotel and look around a bit and then get hold of a girl and a place of his own. He would buy a pony or two and race. He'd soon make friends. In the East they weren't so stiff and stand-offish as they were in London. Going ashore, he dined at the hotel and after dinner got into a rickshaw and told the boy he wanted a woman. The boy took him to the shabby tenement in which I had sat for so many hours and there were the old woman and the girl who was now the mother of his child. After a while the old woman asked him if he wouldn't like a smoke. He had never tried opium, he had always been frightened of it, but now he didn't see why he shouldn't have a go. He was feeling good that night and the girl was a jolly cuddlesome little thing; she was rather like a Chinese girl, small and pretty, like an idol. Well, he had a pipe or two, and he began to feel very happy and comfortable. He stayed all night. He didn't sleep. He just lay, feeling very restful, and thought about things.

'I stopped there till my ship went on to Hong-Kong,' he said. 'And when she left I just stopped on.'

'How about your luggage?' I asked.

For I am perhaps unworthily interested in the manner people combine practical details with the ideal aspects of life. When in a novel penniless lovers drive in a long, swift racing car over the distant hills I have always a desire to know how they managed to pay for it; and I have often asked myself how the characters of Henry James in the intervals of subtly examining their situation coped with the physiological necessities of their bodies.

'I only had a trunk full of clothes, I was never one to want much more than I stood up in, and I went down with the girl in a rickshaw to fetch it. I only meant to stay on till the next boat came through. You see, I was so near China here I thought I'd wait a bit and get used to things, if you understand what I mean, before I went on.'

I did. Those last words of his revealed him to me. I knew that on the threshold of China his courage had failed him. England had been such a terrible disappointment that now he was afraid to put China to the test too. If that failed him he had nothing. For years England had been like a mirage in the desert. But when he had yielded to the attraction, those shining pools and the palm trees and the green grass were nothing but the rolling sandy dunes. He had China, and so long as he never saw it again he kept it.

'Somehow I stayed on. You know, you'd be surprised how quickly the days pass. I don't seem to have time to do half the things I want to. After all I'm comfortable here. The old woman makes a damned good pipe, and she's a jolly little girl, my girl, and then there's the kid. A lively young beggar. If you're happy somewhere what's the good of going somewhere else?'

I looked round that large bare sordid room. There was no comfort in it and not one of the little personal things that one would have thought might have given him the feeling of home. Grosely had taken on this equivocal little apartment, which served as a house of assignation and as a place for Europeans to smoke opium in, with the old woman who kept it, just as it was, and he camped, rather than lived, there still as though next day he would pack his traps and go. After a little while he answered my question.

'I've never been so happy in my life. I often think I'll go on to Shanghai some day, but I don't suppose I ever shall. And God knows, I never want to see England again.'

'Aren't you awfully lonely sometimes for people to talk to?'

'No. Sometimes a Chinese tramp comes in with an English skipper or a Scotch engineer, and then I go on board and we have a talk about old times. There's an old fellow here, a Frenchman who was in the Customs, and he speaks English; I go and see him sometimes. But the fact is I don't want anybody very much. I think a lot. It gets on my nerves when people come between me and my thoughts. I'm not a big smoker, you know, I just have a pipe or two in the morning to settle my stomach, but I don't really smoke till night. Then I think.'

'What d'you think about?'

'Oh, all sorts of things. Sometimes about London and what it was like when I was a boy. But mostly about China. I think of the good times I had and the way I made my money, and I remember the fellows I used to know, and the Chinese. I had some narrow squeaks now and then, but I always came through all right. And I wonder what the girls would have been like that I might have had. Pretty little things. I'm sorry now I didn't keep one or two. It's a great country, China; I love those shops, with an old fellow sitting on his heels smoking a water-pipe, and all the shop-signs. And the temples. By George, that's the place for a man to live in. There's life.'

The mirage shone before his eyes. The illusion held him. He was happy. I wondered what would be his end. Well, that was not yet. For the first time in his life perhaps he held the present in his hand.

THE LETTER

OUTSIDE on the quay the sun beat fiercely. A stream of motors, lorries and buses, private cars and hirelings, sped up and down the crowded thoroughfare, and every chauffeur blew his horn; rickshaws threaded their nimble path amid the throng, and the panting coolies found breath to yell at one another; coolies, carrying heavy bales, sidled along with their quick jog-trot and shouted to the passer-by to make way; itinerant vendors proclaimed their wares. Singapore is the meeting-place of a hundred peoples; and men of all colours, black Tamils, yellow Chinks, brown Malays, Armenians, Jews, and Bengalis, called to one another in raucous tones. But inside the office of Messrs Ripley, Joyce, and Naylor it was pleasantly cool; it was dark after the dusty glitter of the street and agreeably quiet after its unceasing din. Mr Joyce sat in his private room, at the table, with an electric fan turned full on him. He was leaning back, his elbows on the arms of the chair, with the tips of the outstretched fingers of one hand resting neatly against the tips of the outstretched fingers of the other. His gaze rested on the battered volumes of the Law Reports which stood on a long shelf in front of him. On the top of a cupboard were square boxes of japanned tin, on which were painted the names of various clients.

There was a knock at the door.

'Come in.'

A Chinese clerk, very neat in his white ducks, opened it.

'Mr Crosbie is here, sir.'

He spoke beautiful English, accenting each word with precision, and Mr Joyce had often wondered at the extent of his vocabulary. Ong Chi Seng was a Cantonese, and he had studied law at Gray's Inn. He was spending a year or two with Messrs Ripley, Joyce, and Naylor in order to prepare himself for practice on his own account. He was industrious, obliging, and of exemplary character.

'Show him in,' said Mr Joyce.

He rose to shake hands with his visitor and asked him to sit down. The light fell on him as he did so. The face of Mr Joyce remained in shadow. He was by nature a silent man, and now he looked at Robert Crosbie for quite a minute without speaking. Crosbie was a big fellow, well over six feet high, with broad

307

shoulders, and muscular. He was a rubber-planter, hard with the constant exercise of walking over the estate, and with the tennis which was his relaxation when the day's work was over. He was deeply sunburned. His hairy hands, his feet in clumsy boots were enormous, and Mr Joyce found himself thinking that a blow of that great fist would easily kill the fragile Tamil. But there was no fierceness in his blue eyes; they were confiding and gentle; and his face, with its big, undistinguished features, was open, frank, and honest. But at this moment it bore a look of deep distress. It was drawn and haggard.

'You look as though you hadn't had much sleep the last night or two,' said Mr Joyce.

'I haven't.'

Mr Joyce noticed now the old felt hat, with its broad double brim, which Crosbie had placed on the table; and then his eyes travelled to the khaki shorts he wore, showing his red hairy thighs, the tennis shirt open at the neck, without a tie, and the dirty khaki jacket with the ends of the sleeves turned up. He looked as though he had just come in from a long tramp among the rubber trees. Mr Joyce gave a slight frown.

'You must pull yourself together, you know. You must keep your head.'

'Oh, I'm all right.'

'Have you seen your wife today?'

'No, I'm to see her this afternoon. You know, it is a damned shame that they should have arrested her.'

'I think they had to do that,' Mr Joyce answered in his level, soft tone.

'I should have thought they'd have let her out on bail.'

'It's a very serious charge.'

'It is damnable. She did what any decent woman would do in her place. Only, nine women out of ten wouldn't have the pluck. Leslie's the best woman in the world. She wouldn't hurt a fly. Why, hang it all, man, I've been married to her for twelve years, do you think I don't know her? God, if I'd got hold of the man I'd have wrung his neck, I'd have killed him without a moment's hesitation. So would you.'

'My dear fellow, everybody's on your side. No one has a good word to say for Hammond. We're going to get her off. I don't suppose either the assessors or the judge will go into court without having already made up their minds to bring in a verdict of not guilty.'

'The whole thing's a farce,' said Crosbie violently. 'She ought never to have been arrested in the first place, and then it's terrible, after all the poor girl's gone through, to subject her to the ordeal of a trial. There's not a soul I've met since I've been in Singapore, man or woman, who hasn't told me that Leslie was absolutely justified. I think it's awful to keep her in prison all these weeks.'

'The law is the law. After all, she confesses that she killed the man. It is terrible, and I'm dreadfully sorry for both you and her.'

'I don't matter a hang,' interrupted Crosbie.

'But the fact remains that murder has been committed, and in a civilized community a trial is inevitable.'

'Is it murder to exterminate noxious vermin? She shot him as she would have shot a mad dog.'

Mr Joyce leaned back again in his chair and once more placed the tips of his ten fingers together. The little construction he formed looked like the skeleton of a roof. He was silent for a moment.

'I should be wanting in my duty as your legal adviser,' he said at last, in an even voice, looking at his client with his cool, brown eyes, 'if I did not tell you that there is one point which causes me just a little anxiety. If your wife had only shot Hammond once, the whole thing would be absolutely plain sailing. Unfortunately she fired six times.'

'Her explanation is perfectly simple. In the circumstances anyone would have done the same.'

'I dare say,' said Mr Joyce, 'and of course I think the explanation is very reasonable. But it's no good closing our eyes to the facts. It's always a good plan to put yourself in another man's place, and I can't deny that if I were prosecuting for the Crown that is the point on which I should centre my inquiry.'

'My dear fellow, that's perfectly idiotic.'

Mr Joyce shot a sharp glance at Robert Crosbie. The shadow of a smile hovered over his shapely lips. Crosbie was a good fellow, but he could hardly be described as intelligent.

'I dare say it's of no importance,' answered the lawyer, 'I just thought it was a point worth mentioning. You haven't got very long to wait now, and when it's all over I recommend you to go off somewhere with your wife on a trip, and forget all about it. Even though we are almost dead certain to get an acquittal, a trial of that sort is anxious work, and you'll both want a rest.'

For the first time Crosbie smiled, and his smile strangely changed his face. You forgot the uncouthness and saw only the goodness of his soul.

'I think I shall want it more than Leslie. She's borne up wonderfully. By God, there's a plucky little woman for you.'

'Yes, I've been very much struck by her self-control,' said the lawyer. 'I should never have guessed that she was capable of such determination.'

His duties as her counsel had made it necessary for him to have a good many interviews with Mrs Crosbie since her arrest. Though things had been made as easy as could be for her, the fact remained that she was in gaol, awaiting her trial for murder, and it would not have been surprising if her nerves had failed her. She appeared to bear her ordeal with composure. She read a great deal, took such exercise as was possible, and by favour of the authorities worked at the pillow lace which had always formed the entertainment of her long hours of leisure. When Mr Joyce saw her, she was neatly dressed in cool, fresh, simple frocks, her hair was carefully arranged, and her nails were manicured. Her manner was collected. She was able even to jest upon the little inconveniences of her position. There was something casual about the way in which she spoke of the tragedy, which suggested to Mr Joyce that only her good breeding prevented her from finding something a trifle ludicrous in a situation which was eminently serious. It surprised him, for he had never thought that she had a sense of humour.

He had known her off and on for a good many years. When she paid visits to Singapore she generally came to dine with his wife and himself, and once or twice she had passed a week-end with them at their bungalow by the sea. His wife had spent a fortnight with her on the estate, and had met Geoffrey Hammond several times. The two couples had been on friendly, if not on intimate, terms, and it was on this account that Robert Crosbie had rushed over to Singapore immediately after the catastrophe and begged Mr Joyce to take charge personally of his unhappy wife's defence.

The story she told him the first time he saw her she had never varied in the smallest detail. She told it as coolly then, a few hours after the tragedy, as she told it now. She told it connectedly, in a level, even voice, and her only sign of confusion was when a slight colour came into her cheeks as she described one or two of its incidents. She was the last women to whom one would have expected such a thing to happen. She was in the early thirties, a fragile creature, neither short nor tall, and graceful rather than pretty. Her wrists and ankles were very delicate, but she was extremely thin, and you could see the bones of her hands through the white skin, and the veins were large and blue. Her face was colourless, slightly sallow, and her lips were pale. You did not notice the colour of her eyes. She had a great deal of light brown hair, and it had a slight natural wave; it was the sort of hair that with a little touching-up would have been very pretty, but you could not imagine that Mrs Crosbie would think of resorting to any such device. She was a quiet, pleasant, unassuming woman. Her manner was engaging, and if she was not very popular it was because she suffered from a certain shyness. This was comprehensible enough, for the planter's life is lonely, and in her own house, with people she knew, she was in her quiet way charming. Mrs Joyce, after her fortnight's stay, had told her husband that Leslie was a very agreeable hostess. There was more in her, she said, than people thought; and when you came to know her you were surprised how much she had read and how entertaining she could be.

She was the last woman in the world to commit murder.

Mr Joyce dismissed Robert Crosbie with such reassuring words as he could find and, once more alone in his office, turned over the pages of the brief. But it was a mechanical action, for all its details were familiar to him. The case was the sensation of the day, and it was discussed in all the clubs, at all the dinner tables, up and down the Peninsula, from Singapore to Penang. The facts that Mrs Crosbie gave were simple. Her husband had gone to Singapore on business, and she was alone for the night. She dined by herself, late, at a quarter to nine, and after dinner sat in the sitting-room working at her lace. It opened on the veranda. There was no one in the bungalow, for the servants had retired to their own quarters at the back of the compound. She was surprised to hear a step on the gravel path in the garden, a booted step, which suggested a white man rather than a native, for she had not heard a motor drive up, and she could not imagine who could be coming to see her at that time of night. Someone ascended the few stairs that led up to the bungalow, walked across the veranda, and appeared at the door of the room in which she sat. At the first moment she did not recognize the visitor. She sat with a shaded lamp, and he stood with his back to the darkness.

'May I come in?' he said.

She did not even recognize the voice.

'Who is it?' she asked.

She worked with spectacles, and she took them off as she spoke.

'Geoff Hammond.'

'Of course. Come in and have a drink.'

She rose and shook hands with him cordially. She was a little surprised to see him, for though he was a neighbour neither she nor Robert had been lately on very intimate terms with him, and she had not seen him for some weeks. He was the manager of a rubber estate nearly eight miles from theirs, and she wondered why he had chosen this late hour to come and see them.

'Robert's away,' she said. 'He had to go to Singapore for the night.'

Perhaps he thought his visit called for some explanation, for he said:

'I'm sorry. I felt rather lonely tonight, so I thought I'd just come along and see how you were getting on.'

'How on earth did you come? I never heard a car.'

'I left it down the road. I thought you might both be in bed and asleep.'

This was natural enough. The planter gets up at dawn in order to take the roll-call of the workers, and soon after dinner he is glad to go to bed. Hammond's car was in point of fact found next day a quarter of a mile from the bungalow.

Since Robert was away there was no whisky and soda in the room. Leslie did not call the boy, who was probably asleep, but fetched it herself. Her guest mixed himself a drink and filled his pipe.

Geoff Hammond had a host of friends in the colony. He was at this time in the late thirties, but he had come out as a lad. He had been one of the first to volunteer on the outbreak of war, and had done very well. A wound in the knee caused him to be invalided out of the army after two years, but he returned to the Federated Malay States with a D.S.O. and an M.C. He was one of the best billiard-players in the colony. He had been a beautiful dancer and a fine tennis-player, but though able no longer to dance, and his tennis, with a stiff knee, was not so good as it had been, he had the gift of popularity and was universally liked. He was a tall, good-looking fellow, with attractive blue eyes and a fine head of black, curling hair. Old stagers said his only fault was that he was too fond of the girls, and after the catastrophe they shook their heads and vowed that they had always known this would get him into trouble.

He began now to talk to Leslie about the local affairs, the forthcoming races in Singapore, the price of rubber, and his chances of killing a tiger which had been lately seen in the neighbourhood. She was anxious to finish by a certain date a piece of lace on which she was working, for she wanted to send it home for her mother's birthday, and so put on her spectacles again, and drew towards her chair the little table on which stood the pillow.

'I wish you wouldn't wear those great horn-spectacles,' he said. 'I don't know why a pretty woman should do her best to look plain.'

She was a trifle taken aback at this remark. He had never used that tone with her before. She thought the best thing was to make light of it.

'I have no pretensions to being a raving beauty, you know, and if you ask me point-blank, I'm bound to tell you that I don't care two pins if you think me plain or not.'

'I don't think you're plain. I think you're awfully pretty.'

'Sweet of you,' she answered, ironically. 'But in that case I can only think you half-witted.'

He chuckled. But he rose from his chair and sat down in another by her side.

'You're not going to have the face to deny that you have the prettiest hands in the world,' he said.

He made a gesture as though to take one of them. She gave him a little tap.

'Don't be an idiot. Sit down where you were before and talk sensibly, or else I shall send you home.'

He did not move.

'Don't you know that I'm awfully in love with you?' he said.

She remained quite cool.

'I don't. I don't believe it for a minute, and even if it were true I don't want you to say it.'

She was the more surprised at what he was saying, since during the seven years she had known him he had never paid her any particular attention. When he came back from the war they had seen a good deal of one another, and once when he was ill Robert had gone over and brought him back to their bungalow in his car. He had stayed with them for a fortnight. But their interests were dissimilar, and the acquaintance had never ripened into friendship. For the last two or three years they had seen little of him.

Now and then he came over to play tennis, now and then they met him at some planter's who was giving a party, but it often happened that they did not set eyes on him for a month at a time.

Now he took another whisky and soda. Leslie wondered if he had been drinking before. There was something odd about him, and it made her a trifle uneasy. She watched him help himself with disapproval.

'I wouldn't drink any more if I were you,' she said, good-humouredly still.

He emptied his glass and put it down.

'Do you think I'm talking to you like this because I'm drunk?' he asked abruptly.

'That is the most obvious explanation, isn't it?'

'Well, it's a lie. I've loved you ever since I first knew you. I've held my tongue as long as I could, and now it's got to come out. I love you, I love you, I love you.'

She rose and carefully put aside the pillow.

'Good night,' she said.

'I'm not going now.'

At last she began to lose her temper.

'But, you poor fool, don't you know that I've never loved anyone but Robert, and even if I didn't love Robert you're the last man I should care for.'

'What do I care? Robert's away.'

'If you don't go away this minute I shall call the boys, and have you thrown out.'

'They're out of earshot.'

She was very angry now. She made a movement as though to go on to the veranda, from which the house-boy would certainly hear her, but he seized her arm.

'Let me go,' she cried furiously.

'Not much. I've got you now.'

She opened her mouth and called 'Boy, boy,' but with a quick gesture he put his hand over it. Then before she knew what he was about he had taken her in his arms and was kissing her passionately. She struggled, turning her lips away from his burning mouth.

'No, no, no,' she cried. 'Leave me alone. I won't.'

She grew confused about what happened then. All that had been said before she remembered accurately, but now his words assailed her ears through a mist of horror and fear. He seemed to plead for her love. He broke into violent protestations of passion.

And all the time he held her in his tempestuous embrace. She was helpless, for he was a strong, powerful man, and her arms were pinioned to her sides; her struggles were unavailing, and she felt herself grow weaker; she was afraid she would faint, and his hot breath on her face made her feel desperately sick. He kissed her mouth, her eyes, her cheeks, her hair. The pressure of his arms was killing her. He lifted her off her feet. She tried to kick him, but he only held her more closely. He was carrying her now. He wasn't speaking any more, but she knew that his face was pale and his eyes hot with desire. He was taking her into the bedroom. He was no longer a civilized man, but a savage. And as he ran he stumbled against a table which was in the way. His stiff knee made him a little awkward on his feet, and with the burden of the woman in his arms he fell. In a moment she had snatched herself away from him. She ran round the sofa. He was up in a flash, and flung himself towards her. There was a revolver on the desk. She was not a nervous woman, but Robert was to be away for the night, and she had meant to take it into her room when she went to bed. That was why it happened to be there. She was frantic with terror now. She did not know what she was doing. She heard a report. She saw Hammond stagger. He gave a cry. He said something, she didn't know what. He lurched out of the room on to the veranda. She was in a frenzy now, she was beside herself, she followed him out, yes, that was it, she must have followed him out, though she remembered nothing of it, she followed firing automatically, shot after shot, till the six chambers were empty. Hammond fell down on the floor of the veranda. He crumbled up into a bloody heap.

When the boys, startled by the reports, rushed up, they found her standing over Hammond with the revolver still in her hand and Hammond lifeless. She looked at them for a moment without speaking. They stood in a frightened, huddled bunch. She let the revolver fall from her hand, and without a word turned and went into the sitting-room. They watched her go into her bedroom and turn the key in the lock. They dared not touch the dead body, but looked at it with terrified eyes, talking excitedly to one another in undertones. Then the head-boy collected himself; he had been with them for many years, he was Chinese and a level-headed fellow. Robert had gone into Singapore on his motor-cycle, and the car stood in the garage. He told the seis to get it out; they must go at once to the Assistant District Officer and tell him what had happened. He picked up the revolver and put it in his pocket. The A.D.O., a man called Withers, lived on the outskirts of the nearest town, which was about thirty-five miles away. It took them an hour and a half to reach him. Everyone was asleep, and they had to rouse the boys. Presently Withers came out and they told him their errand. The head-boy showed him the revolver in proof of what he said. The A.D.O. went into his room to dress, sent for his car, and in a little while was following them back along the deserted road. The dawn was just breaking as he reached the Crosbies' bungalow. He ran up the steps of the veranda, and stopped short as he saw Hammond's body lying where he fell. He touched the face. It was quite cold.

'Where's mem?' he asked the house-boy.

The Chinese pointed to the bedroom. Withers went to the door and knocked. There was no answer. He knocked again.

'Mrs Crosbie,' he called.

'Who is it?'

'Withers.'

There was another pause. Then the door was unlocked and slowly opened. Leslie stood before him. She had not been to bed, and wore the tea-gown in which she had dined. She stood and looked silently at the A.D.O.

'Your house-boy fetched me,' he said. 'Hammond. What have you done?'

'He tried to rape me, and I shot him.'

'My God. I say, you'd better come out here. You must tell me exactly what happened.'

'Not now. I can't. You must give me time. Send for my husband.'

Withers was a young man, and he did not know exactly what to do in an emergency which was so out of the run of his duties. Leslie refused to say anything till at last Robert arrived. Then she told the two men the story, from which since then, though she had repeated it over and over again, she had never in the slightest degree diverged.

The point to which Mr Joyce recurred was the shooting. As a lawyer he was bothered that Leslie had fired not once, but six times, and the examination of the dead man showed that four of the shots had been fired close to the body. One might almost have thought that when the man fell she stood over him and emptied the contents of the revolver into him. She confessed that her memory, so accurate for all that had preceded, failed her here. Her mind was blank. It pointed to an uncontrollable fury; but uncontrollable fury was the last thing you would have expected from this quiet and demure woman. Mr Joyce had known her a good many years, and had always thought her an unemotional person; during the weeks that had passed since the tragedy her composure had been amazing.

Mr Joyce shrugged his shoulders.

'The fact is, I suppose,' he reflected, 'that you can never tell what hidden possibilities of savagery there are in the most respectable of women.'

There was a knock at the door.

'Come in.'

The Chinese clerk entered and closed the door behind him. He closed it gently, with deliberation, but decidedly, and advanced to the table at which Mr Joyce was sitting.

'May I trouble you, sir, for a few words' private conversation?' he said.

The elaborate accuracy with which the clerk expressed himself always faintly amused Mr Joyce, and now he smiled.

'It's no trouble, Chi Seng,' he replied.

'The matter on which I desire to speak to you, sir, is delicate and confidential.'

'Fire away.'

Mr Joyce met his clerk's shrewd eyes. As usual Ong Chi Seng was dressed in the height of local fashion. He wore very shiny patent-leather shoes and gay silk socks. In his black tie was a pearl and ruby pin, and on the fourth finger of his left hand a diamond ring. From the pocket of his neat white coat protruded a gold fountain pen and a gold pencil. He wore a gold wrist-watch, and on the bridge of his nose invisible prince-nez. He gave a little cough.

'The matter has to do with the case R. *v.* Crosbie, sir.'

'Yes?'

'A circumstance has come to my knowledge, sir, which seems to me to put a different complexion on it.'

'What circumstance?'

'It has come to my knowledge, sir, that there is a letter in existence from the defendant to the unfortunate victim of the tragedy.'

'I shouldn't be at all surprised. In the course of the last seven years I have no doubt that Mrs Crosbie often had occasion to write to Mr Hammond.'

Mr Joyce had a high opinion of his clerk's intelligence and his words were designed to conceal his thoughts.

'That is very probable, sir. Mrs Crosbie must have communicated with the deceased frequently, to invite him to dine with her for example, or to propose a tennis game. That was my first thought when the matter was brought to my notice. This letter, however, was written on the day of the late Mr Hammond's death.'

Mr Joyce did not flicker an eyelash. He continued to look at Ong Chi Seng with the smile of faint amusement with which he generally talked to him.

'Who has told you this?'

'The circumstances were brought to my knowledge, sir, by a friend of mine.'

Mr Joyce knew better than to insist.

'You will no doubt recall, sir, that Mrs Crosbie has stated that until the fatal night she had had no communication with the deceased for several weeks.'

'Have you got the letter?'

'No, sir.'

'What are its contents?'

'My friend gave me a copy. Would you like to peruse it, sir?'

'I should.'

Ong Chi Seng took from an inside pocket a bulky wallet. It was filled with papers, Singapore dollar notes and cigarette cards. From the confusion he presently extracted a half-sheet of thin notepaper and placed it before Mr Joyce. The letter read as follows:

R. will be away for the night. I absolutely must see you. I shall expect you at eleven. I am desperate, and if you don't come I won't answer for the consequences. Don't drive up. – L.

It was written in the flowing hand which the Chinese were taught at the foreign schools. The writing, so lacking in character, was oddly incongruous with the ominous words.

'What makes you think that this note was written by Mrs Crosbie?'

'I have every confidence in the veracity of my informant, sir,' replied Ong Chi Seng. 'And the matter can very easily be put to the proof. Mrs Crosbie will, no doubt, be able to tell you at once whether she wrote such a letter or not.'

Since the beginning of the conversation Mr Joyce had not taken his eyes off the respectable countenance of his clerk. He wondered now if he discerned in it a faint expression of mockery.

'It is inconceivable that Mrs Crosbie should have written such a letter,' said Mr Joyce.

'If that is your opinion, sir, the matter is of course ended. My friend spoke to me on the subject only because he thought, as I was in your office, you might like to know of the existence of this letter before a communication was made to the Deputy Public Prosecutor.'

'Who has the original?' asked Mr Joyce sharply.

Ong Chi Seng made no sign that he perceived in this question and its manner a change of attitude.

'You will remember, sir, no doubt, that after the death of Mr Hammond it was discovered that he had had relations with a Chinese woman. The letter is at present in her possession.'

That was one of the things which had turned public opinion most vehemently against Hammond. It came to be known that for several months he had had a Chinese woman living in his house.

For a moment neither of them spoke. Indeed everything had been said and each understood the other perfectly.

'I'm obliged to you, Chi Seng. I will give the matter my consideration.'

'Very good, sir. Do you wish me to make a communication to that effect to my friend?'

'I dare say it would be as well if you kept in touch with him,' Mr Joyce answered with gravity.

'Yes, sir.'

The clerk noiselessly left the room, shutting the door again with deliberation, and left Mr Joyce to his reflections. He stared at the copy, in its neat, impersonal writing, of Leslie's letter. Vague suspicions troubled him. They were so disconcerting that he made an effort to put them out of his mind. There must be a simple explanation of the letter, and Leslie without doubt could give it at once, but, by heaven, an explanation was needed. He rose from his chair, put the letter in his pocket, and took his topee. When he went out Ong Chi Seng was busily writing at his desk.

'I'm going out for a few minutes, Chi Seng,' he said.

'Mr George Reed is coming by appointment at twelve o'clock, sir. Where shall I say you've gone?'

Mr Joyce gave him a thin smile.

'You can say that you haven't the least idea.'

But he knew perfectly well that Ong Chi Seng was aware that he was going to the gaol. Though the crime had been committed in Belanda and the trial was to take place at Belanda Bharu, since there was in the gaol no convenience for the detention of a white woman Mrs Crosbie had been brought to Singapore.

When she was led into the room in which he waited she held out her thin, distinguished hand, and gave him a pleasant smile. She was as ever neatly and simply dressed, and her abundant, pale hair was arranged with care.

'I wasn't expecting to see you this morning,' she said, graciously.

She might have been in her own house, and Mr Joyce almost expected to hear her call the boy and tell him to bring the visitor a gin pahit.

'How are you?' he asked.

'I'm in the best of health, thank you.' A flicker of amusement flashed across her eyes. 'This is a wonderful place for a rest cure.'

The attendant withdrew and they were left alone.

'Do sit down,' said Leslie.

He took a chair. He did not quite know how to begin. She was so cool that it seemed almost impossible to say to her the thing he had come to say. Though she was not pretty there was something agreeable in her appearance. She had elegance, but it was the elegance of good breeding in which there was nothing of the artifice of society. You had only to look at her to know what sort of people she had and what kind of surroundings she had lived in. Her fragility gave her a singular refinement. It was impossible to associate her with the vaguest idea of grossness.

'I'm looking forward to seeing Robert this afternoon,' she said, in her good-humoured, easy voice. (It was a pleasure to hear her speak, her voice and her accent were so distinctive of her class.) 'Poor dear, it's been a great trial to his nerves. I'm thankful it'll all be over in a few days.'

'It's only five days now.'

'I know. Each morning when I awake I say to myself, "one less."' She smiled then. 'Just as I used to do at school and the holidays were coming.'

'By the way, am I right in thinking that you had no communication whatever with Hammond for several weeks before the catastrophe?'

'I'm quite positive of that. The last time we met was at a tennis-party at the MacFarrens. I don't think I said more than two words to him. They have two courts, you know, and we didn't happen to be in the same sets.'

'And you haven't written to him?'

'Oh, no.'

'Are you quite sure of that?'

'Oh, quite,' she answered, with a little smile. 'There was nothing I should write to him for except to ask him to dine or to play tennis, and I hadn't done either for months.'

'At one time you'd been on fairly intimate terms with him. How did it happen that you had stopped asking him to anything?'

Mrs Crosbie shrugged her thin shoulders.

'One gets tired of people. We hadn't anything very much in common. Of course, when he was ill Robert and I did everything we could for him, but the last year or two he'd been quite well, and he was very popular. He had a good many calls on his time, and there didn't seem to be any need to shower invitations upon him.'

'Are you quite certain that was all?'

Mrs Crosbie hesitated for a moment.

'Well, I may just as well tell you. It had come to our ears that he was living with a Chinese woman, and Robert said he wouldn't have him in the house. I had seen her myself.'

Mr Joyce was sitting in a straight-backed arm-chair, resting his chin on his hand, and his eyes were fixed on Leslie. Was it his fancy that, as she made this remark, her black pupils were filled on a sudden, for the fraction of a second, with a dull red light? The effect was startling. Mr Joyce shifted in his chair. He placed the tips of his ten fingers together. He spoke very slowly, choosing his words.

'I think I should tell you that there is in existence a letter in your handwriting to Geoff Hammond.'

He watched her closely. She made no movement, nor did her face change colour, but she took a noticeable time to reply.

'In the past I've often sent him little notes to ask him to something or other, or to get me something when I knew he was going to Singapore.'

'This letter asks him to come and see you because Robert was going to Singapore.'

'That's impossible. I never did anything of the kind.'

'You'd better read it for yourself.'

He took it out of his pocket and handed it to her. She gave it a glance and with a smile of scorn handed it back to him.

'That's not my handwriting.'

'I know, it's said to be an exact copy of the original.'

321

She read the words now, and as she read a horrible change came over her. Her colourless face grew dreadful to look at. It turned green. The flesh seemed on a sudden to fall away and her skin was tightly stretched over the bones. Her lips receded, showing her teeth, so that she had the appearance of making a grimace. She stared at Mr Joyce with eyes that started from their sockets. He was looking now at a gibbering death's head.

'What does it mean?' she whispered.

Her mouth was so dry that she could utter no more than a hoarse sound. It was no longer a human voice.

'That is for you to say,' he answered.

'I didn't write it. I swear I didn't write it.'

'Be very careful what you say. If the original is in your hand-writing it would be useless to deny it.'

'It would be a forgery.'

'It would be difficult to prove that. It would be easy to prove that it was genuine.'

A shiver passed through her lean body. But great beads of sweat stood on her forehead. She took a handkerchief from her bag and wiped the palms of her hands. She glanced at the letter again and gave Mr Joyce a sidelong look.

'It's not dated. If I had written it and forgotten all about it, it might have been written years ago. If you'll give me time, I'll try and remember the circumstances.'

'I noticed there was no date. If this letter were in the hands of the prosecution they would cross-examine the boys. They would soon find out whether someone took a letter to Hammond on the day of his death.'

Mrs Crosbie clasped her hands violently and swayed in her chair so that he thought she would faint.

'I swear to you that I didn't write that letter.'

Mr Joyce was silent for a little while. He took his eyes from her distraught face, and looked down on the floor. He was reflecting.

'In these circumstances we need not go into the matter further,' he said slowly, at last breaking the silence. 'If the possessor of this letter sees fit to place it in the hands of the prosecution you will be prepared.'

His words suggested that he had nothing more to say to her, but he made no movement of departure. He waited. To himself he seemed to wait a very long time. He did not look at Leslie, but he was conscious that she sat very still. She made no sound. At last it was he who spoke.

'If you have nothing more to say to me I think I'll be getting back to my office.'

'What would anyone who read the letter be inclined to think that it meant?' she asked then.

'He'd know that you had told a deliberate lie,' answered Mr Joyce sharply.

'When?'

'You have stated definitely that you had had no communication with Hammond for at least three months.'

'The whole thing has been a terrible shock to me. The events of that dreadful night have been a nightmare. It's not very strange if one detail has escaped my memory.'

'It would be unfortunate, when your memory has reproduced so exactly every particular of your interview with Hammond, that you should have forgotten so important a point as that he came to see you in the bungalow on the night of his death at your express desire.'

'I hadn't forgotten. After what happened I was afraid to mention it. I thought you'd none of you believe my story if I admitted that he'd come at my invitation. I dare say it was stupid of me; but I lost my head, and after I'd said once that I'd had no communication with Hammond I was obliged to stick to it.'

By now Leslie had recovered her admirable composure, and she met Mr Joyce's appraising glance with candour. Her gentleness was very disarming.

'You will be required to explain, then, *why* you asked Hammond to come and see you when Robert was away for the night.'

She turned her eyes full on the lawyer. He had been mistaken in thinking them insignificant, they were rather fine eyes, and unless he was mistaken they were bright now with tears. Her voice had a little break in it.

'It was a surprise I was preparing for Robert. His birthday is next month. I knew he wanted a new gun and you know I'm dreadfully stupid about sporting things. I wanted to talk to Geoff about it. I thought I'd get him to order it for me.'

'Perhaps the terms of the letter are not very clear to your recollection. Will you have another look at it?'

'No, I don't want to,' she said quickly.

'Does it seem to you the sort of letter a woman would write to a somewhat distant acquaintance because she wanted to consult him about buying a gun?'

'I dare say it's rather extravagant and emotional. I do express myself like that, you know. I'm quite prepared to admit it's very silly.' She smiled. 'And after all, Geoff Hammond wasn't quite a distant acquaintance. When he was ill I'd nursed him like a mother. I asked him to come when Robert was away, because Robert wouldn't have him in the house.'

Mr Joyce was tired of sitting so long in the same position. He rose and walked once or twice up and down the room, choosing the words he proposed to say; then he leaned over the back of the chair in which he had been sitting. He spoke slowly in a tone of deep gravity.

'Mrs Crosbie, I want to talk to you very, very seriously. This case was comparatively plain sailing. There was only one point which seemed to me to require explanation: as far as I could judge, you had fired no less than four shots into Hammond when he was lying on the ground. It was hard to accept the possibility that a delicate, frightened, and habitually self-controlled woman, of gentle nature and refined instincts, should have surrendered to an absolutely uncontrolled frenzy. But of course it was admissible. Although Geoffrey Hammond was much liked and on the whole thought highly of, I was prepared to prove that he was the sort of man who might be guilty of the crime which in justification of your act you accused him of. The fact, which was discovered after his death, that he had been living with a Chinese woman gave us something very definite to go upon. That robbed him of any sympathy which might have been felt for him. We made up our minds to make use of the odium which such a connexion cast upon him in the minds of all respectable people. I told your husband this morning that I was certain of an acquittal, and I wasn't just telling him that to give him heart. I do not believe the assessors would have left the court.'

They looked into one another's eyes. Mrs Crosbie was strangely still. She was like a little bird paralysed by the fascination of a snake. He went on in the same quiet tones.

'But this letter has thrown an entirely different complexion on the case. I am your legal adviser, I shall represent you in court. I take your story as you tell it me, and I shall conduct your defence according to its terms. It may be that I believe your statements, and it may be that I doubt them. The duty of counsel is to persuade the court that the evidence placed before it is not such as to justify it in bringing in a verdict of guilty, and any private opinion he may have of the guilt or innocence of his client is entirely beside the point.'

He was astonished to see in Leslie's eyes the flicker of a smile. Piqued, he went on somewhat dryly:

'You're not going to deny that Hammond came to your house at your urgent, and I may even say, hysterical invitation?'

Mrs Crosbie, hesitating for an instant, seemed to consider.

'They can prove that the letter was taken to his bungalow by one of the house-boys. He rode over on his bicycle.'

'You mustn't expect other people to be stupider than you. The letter will put them on the track of suspicions which have entered nobody's head. I will not tell you what I personally thought when I saw the copy. I do not wish you to tell me anything but what is needed to save your neck.'

Mrs Crosbie gave a shrill cry. She sprang to her feet, white with terror.

'You don't think they'd hang me?'

'If they came to the conclusion that you hadn't killed Hammond in self-defence, it would be the duty of the assessors to bring in a verdict of guilty. The charge is murder. It would be the duty of the judge to sentence you to death.'

'But what can they prove?' she gasped.

'I don't know what they can prove. You know. I don't want to know. But if their suspicions are aroused, if they begin to make inquiries, if the natives are questioned – what is it that can be discovered?'

She crumpled up suddenly. She fell on the floor before he could catch her. She had fainted. He looked round the room for water, but there was none there, and he did not want to be disturbed. He stretched her out on the floor, and kneeling beside her waited for her to recover. When she opened her eyes he was disconcerted by the ghastly fear that he saw in them.

'Keep quite still,' he said. 'You'll be better in a moment.'

'You won't let them hang me,' she whispered.

She began to cry, hysterically, while in undertones he sought to quieten her.

'For goodness sake pull yourself together,' he said.

'Give me a minute.'

Her courage was amazing. He could see the effort she made to regain her self-control, and soon she was once more calm.

'Let me get up now.'

He gave her his hand and helped her to her feet. Taking her arm, he led her to the chair. She sat down wearily.

'Don't talk to me for a minute or two,' she said.

'Very well.'

When at last she spoke it was to say something which he did not expect. She gave a little sigh.

'I'm afraid I've made rather a mess of things,' she said.

He did not answer, and once more there was a silence.

'Isn't it possible to get hold of the letter?' she said at last.

'I do not think anything would have been said to me about it if the person in whose possession it is was not prepared to sell it.'

'Who's got it?'

'The Chinese woman who was living in Hammond's house.'

A spot of colour flickered for an instant on Leslie's cheek-bones.

'Does she want an awful lot for it?'

'I imagine that she has a very shrewd idea of its value. I doubt if it would be possible to get hold of it except for a very large sum.'

'Are you going to let me be hanged?'

'Do you think it's so simple as all that to secure possession of an unwelcome piece of evidence? It's no different from suborning a witness. You have no right to make any such suggestion to me.'

'Then what is going to happen to me?'

'Justice must take its course.'

She grew very pale. A little shudder passed through her body.

'I put myself in your hands. Of course I have no right to ask you to do anything that isn't proper.'

Mr Joyce had not bargained for the little break in her voice which her habitual self-restraint made quite intolerably moving. She looked at him with humble eyes, and he thought that if he rejected their appeal they would haunt him for the rest of his life. After all, nothing could bring poor Hammond back to life again. He wondered what really was the explanation of that letter. It was not fair to conclude from it that she had killed Hammond without provocation. He had lived in the East a long time and his sense of professional honour was not perhaps so acute as it had been twenty years before. He stared at the floor. He made up his mind to do something which he knew was unjustifiable, but it stuck in his throat and he felt dully resentful towards Leslie. It embarrassed him a little to speak.

'I don't know exactly what your husband's circumstances are?'

Flushing a rosy red, she shot a swift glance at him.

'He has a good many tin shares and a small share in two or three rubber estates. I suppose he could raise money.'

'He would have to be told what it was for.'

She was silent for a moment. She seemed to think.

'He's in love with me still. He would make any sacrifice to save me. Is there any need for him to see the letter?'

Mr Joyce frowned a little, and, quick to notice, she went on.

'Robert is an old friend of yours. I'm not asking you to do anything for me, I'm asking you to save a rather simple, kind man who never did you any harm from all the pain that's possible.'

Mr Joyce did not reply. He rose to go and Mrs Crosbie, with the grace that was natural to her, held out her hand. She was shaken by the scene, and her look was haggard, but she made a brave attempt to speed him with courtesy.

'It's so good of you to take all this trouble for me. I can't begin to tell you how grateful I am.'

Mr Joyce returned to his office. He sat in his own room, quite still, attempting to do no work, and pondered. His imagination brought him many strange ideas. He shuddered a little. At last there was the discreet knock on the door which he was expecting. Ong Chi Seng came in.

'I was just going out to have my tiffin, sir,' he said.

'All right.'

'I didn't know if there was anything you wanted before I went, sir.'

'I don't think so. Did you make another appointment for Mr Reed?'

'Yes, sir. He will come at three o'clock.'

'Good.'

Ong Chi Seng turned away, walked to the door, and put his long slim fingers on the handle. Then, as though on an afterthought, he turned back.

'Is there anything you wish me to say to my friend, sir?'

Although Ong Chi Seng spoke English so admirably he had still a difficulty with the letter R, and he pronounced it "fliend".

'What friend?'

'About the letter Mrs Crosbie wrote to Hammond deceased, sir.'

'Oh! I'd forgotten about that. I mentioned it to Mrs Crosbie and she denies having written anything of the sort. It's evidently a forgery.'

Mr Joyce took the copy from his pocket and handed it to Ong Chi Seng. Ong Chi Seng ignored the gesture.

'In that case, sir, I suppose there would be no objection if my fliend delivered the letter to the Deputy Public Prosecutor.'

'None. But I don't quite see what good that would do your friend.'

'My fliend, sir, thought it was his duty in the interests of justice.'

'I am the last man in the world to interfere with anyone who wishes to do his duty, Chi Seng.'

The eyes of the lawyer and of the Chinese clerk met. Not the shadow of a smile hovered on the lips of either, but they understood each other perfectly.

'I quite understand, sir,' said Ong Chi Seng, 'but from my study of the case R. *v.* Crosbie I am of opinion that the production of such a letter would be damaging to our client.'

'I have always had a very high opinion of your legal acumen, Chi Seng.'

'It had occurred to me, sir, that if I could persuade my fliend to induce the Chinese woman who has the letter to deliver it into our hands it would save a great deal of trouble.'

Mr Joyce idly drew faces on his blotting-paper.

'I suppose your friend is a business man. In what circumstances do you think he would be induced to part with the letter?'

'He has not got the letter. The Chinese woman has the letter. He is only a relation of the Chinese woman. She is an ignorant woman; she did not know the value of that letter till my fliend told her.'

'What value did he put on it?'

'Ten thousand dollars, sir.'

'Good God! Where on earth do you suppose Mrs Crosbie can get ten thousand dollars! I tell you the letter's a forgery.'

He looked up at Ong Chi Seng as he spoke. The clerk was unmoved by the outburst. He stood at the side of the desk, civil, cool, and observant.

'Mr Crosbie owns an eighth share of the Betong Rubber Estate and a sixth share of the Selantan River Rubber Estate. I have a fliend who will lend him the money on the security of his property.'

'You have a large circle of acquaintance, Chi Seng.'

'Yes sir.'

'Well, you can tell them all to go to hell. I would never advise Mr Crosbie to give a penny more than five thousand for a letter that can be very easily explained.'

'The Chinese woman does not want to sell the letter, sir. My fliend took a long time to persuade her. It is useless to offer her less than the sum mentioned.'

Mr Joyce looked at Ong Chi Seng for at least three minutes. The clerk bore the searching scrutiny without embarrassment. He stood in a respectful attitude with downcast eyes. Mr Joyce knew his man. Clever fellow, Chi Seng, he thought, I wonder how much he's going to get out of it.

'Ten thousand dollars is a very large sum.'

'Mr Crosbie will certainly pay it rather than see his wife hanged, sir.'

Again Mr Joyce paused. What more did Chi Seng know than he had said? He must be pretty sure of his ground if he was obviously so unwilling to bargain. That sum had been fixed because whoever it was that was managing the affair knew it was the largest amount that Robert Crosbie could raise.

'Where is the Chinese woman now?' asked Mr Joyce.

'She is staying at the house of my fliend, sir.'

'Will she come here?'

'I think it more better if you go to her, sir. I can take you to the house tonight and she will give you the letter. She is a very ignorant woman, sir, and she does not understand cheques.'

'I wasn't thinking of giving her a cheque. I will bring bank notes with me.'

'It would only be waste of valuable time to bring less than ten thousand dollars, sir.'

'I quite understand.'

'I will go and tell my fliend after I have had my tiffin, sir.'

'Very good. You'd better meet me outside the club at ten o'clock tonight.'

'With pleasure, sir,' said Ong Chi Seng.

He gave Mr Joyce a little bow and left the room. Mr Joyce went out to have luncheon, too. He went to the club and here, as he had expected, he saw Robert Crosbie. He was sitting at a crowded table, and as he passed him, looking for a place, Mr Joyce touched him on the shoulder.

'I'd like a word or two with you before you go,' he said.

'Right you are. Let me know when you're ready.'

Mr Joyce had made up his mind how to tackle him. He played a rubber of bridge after luncheon in order to allow time for the club to empty itself. He did not want on this particular matter to see Crosbie in his office. Presently Crosbie came into the card-room and looked on till the game was finished. The other players went on their various affairs, and the two were left alone.

'A rather unfortunate thing has happened, old man,' said Mr Joyce, in a tone which he sought to render as casual as possible. 'It appears that your wife sent a letter to Hammond asking him to come to the bungalow on the night he was killed.'

'But that's impossible,' cried Crosbie. 'She's always stated that she had had no communication with Hammond. I know from my own knowledge that she hadn't set eyes on him for a couple of months.'

'The fact remains that the letter exists. It's in the possession of the Chinese woman Hammond was living with. Your wife meant to give you a present on your birthday, and she wanted Hammond to help her to get it. In the emotional excitement that she suffered from after the tragedy, she forgot all about it, and having once denied having any communication with Hammond she was afraid to say that she had made a mistake. It was, of course, very unfortunate, but I dare say it was not unnatural.'

Crosbie did not speak. His large, red face bore an expression of complete bewilderment, and Mr Joyce was at once relieved and exasperated by his lack of comprehension. He was a stupid man, and Mr Joyce had no patience with stupidity. But his distress since the catastrophe had touched a soft spot in the lawyer's heart; and Mrs Crosbie had struck the right note when she asked him to help her, not for her sake, but for her husband's.

'I need not tell you that it would be very awkward if this letter found its way into the hands of the prosecution. Your wife has lied, and she would be asked to explain the lie. It alters things a little if Hammond did not intrude, an unwanted guest, but came to your house by invitation. It would be easy to arouse in the assessors a certain indecision of mind.'

Mr Joyce hesitated. He was face to face now with his decision. If it had been a time for humour, he could have smiled at the reflection that he was taking so grave a step, and that the man for whom he was taking it had not the smallest conception of its gravity. If he gave the matter a thought, he probably imagined that what Mr Joyce was doing was what any lawyer did in the ordinary run of business.

'My dear Robert, you are not only my client, but my friend. I think we must get hold of that letter. It'll cost a good deal of money. Except for that I should have preferred to say nothing to you about it.'

'How much?'

'Ten thousand dollars.'

'That's a devil of a lot. With the slump and one thing and another it'll take just about all I've got.'

'Can you get it at once?'

'I suppose so. Old Charlie Meadows will let me have it on my tin shares and on those two estates I'm interested in.'

'Then will you?'

'Is it absolutely necessary?'

'If you want your wife to be acquitted.'

Crosbie grew very red. His mouth sagged strangely.

'But . . .' he could not find words, his face now was purple. 'But I don't understand. She can explain. You don't mean to say they'd find her guilty? They couldn't hang her for putting a noxious vermin out of the way.'

'Of course they wouldn't hang her. They might only find her guilty of manslaughter. She'd probably get off with two or three years.'

Crosbie started to his feet and his red face was distraught with horror.

'Three years.'

Then something seemed to dawn in that slow intelligence of his. His mind was darkness across which shot suddenly a flash of lightning, and though the succeeding darkness was as profound, there remained the memory of something not seen but perhaps just descried. Mr Joyce saw that Crosbie's big red hands, coarse and hard with all the odd jobs he had set them to, trembled.

'What was the present she wanted to make me?'

'She says she wanted to give you a new gun.'

Once more that great red face flushed a deeper red.

'When have you got to have the money ready?'

There was something odd in his voice now. It sounded as though he spoke with invisible hands clutching at his throat.

'At ten o'clock tonight. I thought you could bring it to my office at about six.'

'Is the woman coming to you?'

'No, I'm going to her.'

'I'll bring the money. I'll come with you.'

Mr Joyce looked at him sharply.

'Do you think there's any need for you to do that? I think it would be better if you left me to deal with this matter by myself.'

'It's my money, isn't it? I'm going to come.'

Mr Joyce shrugged his shoulders. They rose and shook hands. Mr Joyce looked at him curiously.

At ten o'clock they met in the empty club.

'Everything all right?' asked Mr Joyce.

'Yes. I've got the money in my pocket.'

'Let's go then.'

They walked down the steps. Mr Joyce's car was waiting for them in the square, silent at that hour, and as they came to it Ong Chi Seng stepped out of the shadow of a house. He took his seat beside the driver and gave him a direction. They drove past the Hotel de l'Europe and turned up by the Sailor's Home to get into Victoria Street. Here the Chinese shops were still open, idlers lounged about, and in the roadway rickshaws and motor-cars and gharries gave a busy air to the scene. Suddenly their car stopped and Chi Seng turned round.

'I think it more better if we walk here, sir,' he said.

They got out and he went on. They followed a step or two behind. Then he asked them to stop.

'You wait here, sir. I go in and speak to my fliend.'

He went into a shop, open to the street, where three or four Chinese were standing behind the counter. It was one of those strange shops where nothing was on view, and you wondered what it was they sold there. They saw him address a stout man in a duck suit with a large gold chain across his breast, and the man shot a quick glance out into the night. He gave Chi Seng a key and Chi Seng came out. He beckoned to the two men waiting and slid into a doorway at the side of the shop. They followed him and found themselves at the foot of a flight of stairs.

'If you wait a minute I will light a match,' he said, always resourceful. 'You come upstairs, please.'

He held a Japanese match in front of them, but it scarcely dispelled the darkness and they groped their way up behind him. On the first floor he unlocked a door and going in lit a gas-jet.

'Come in, please,' he said.

It was a small square room, with one window, and the only furniture consisted of two low Chinese beds covered with matting. In one corner was a large chest, with an elaborate lock, and on this stood a shabby tray with an opium pipe on it and a lamp. There was in the room the faint, acrid scent of the drug. They sat down and Ong Chi Seng offered them cigarettes. In a moment the door was opened by the fat Chinaman whom they had seen behind the counter. He bade them good evening in very good English, and sat down by the side of his fellow-countryman.

'The Chinese woman is just coming,' said Chi Seng.

A boy from the shop brought in a tray with a teapot and cups and the Chinaman offered them a cup of tea. Crosbie refused. The Chinese talked to one another in undertones, but Crosbie and Mr Joyce were silent. At last there was the sound of a voice outside; someone was calling in a low tone; and the Chinaman went to the door. He opened it, spoke a few words, and ushered a woman in. Mr Joyce looked at her. He had heard much about her since Hammond's death, but he had never seen her. She was a stoutish person, not very young, with a broad, phlegmatic face, she was powdered and rouged and her eyebrows were a thin black line, but she gave you the impression of a woman of character. She wore a pale blue jacket and a white skirt, her costume was not quite European nor quite Chinese, but on her feet were little Chinese silk slippers. She wore heavy gold chains round her neck, gold bangles on her wrists, gold ear-rings, and elaborate gold pins in her black hair. She walked in slowly, with the air of a woman sure of herself, but with a certain heaviness of tread, and sat down on the bed beside Ong Chi Seng. He said something to her and nodding she gave an incurious glance at the two white men.

'Has she got the letter?' asked Mr Joyce.

'Yes, sir.'

Crosbie said nothing, but produced a roll of five-hundred-dollar notes. He counted out twenty and handed them to Chi Seng.

'Will you see if that is correct?'

The clerk counted them and gave them to the fat Chinaman.

'Quite correct, sir.'

The Chinaman counted them once more and put them in his pocket. He spoke again to the woman and she drew from her bosom a letter. She gave it to Chi Seng who cast his eyes over it.

'This is the right document, sir,' he said, and was about to give it to Mr Joyce when Crosbie took it from him.

'Let me look at it,' he said.

Mr Joyce watched him read and then held out his hand for it.

'You'd better let me have it.'

Crosbie folded it up deliberately and put it in his pocket.

'No, I'm going to keep it myself. It's cost me enough money.'

Mr Joyce made no rejoinder. The three Chinese watched the little passage, but what they thought about it, or whether they thought, it was impossible to tell from their impassive countenances. Mr Joyce rose to his feet.

'Do you want me any more tonight, sir?' said Ong Chi Seng.

'No.' He knew that the clerk wished to stay behind in order to get his agreed share of the money, and he turned to Crosbie. 'Are you ready?'

Crosbie did not answer, but stood up. The Chinaman went to the door and opened it for them. Chi Seng found a bit of candle and lit it in order to light them down, and the two Chinese accompanied them to the street. They left the woman sitting quietly on the bed smoking a cigarette. When they reached the street the Chinese left them and went once more upstairs.

'What are you going to do with that letter?' asked Mr Joyce.

'Keep it.'

They walked to where the car was waiting for them and here Mr Joyce offered his friend a lift. Crosbie shook his head.

'I'm going to walk.' He hesitated a little and shuffled his feet. 'I went to Singapore on the night of Hammond's death partly to buy a new gun that a man I knew wanted to dispose of. Good night.'

He disappeared quickly into the darkness.

Mr Joyce was quite right about the trial. The assessors went into court fully determined to acquit Mrs Crosbie. She gave evidence on her own behalf. She told her story simply and with straightforwardness. The D.P.P. was a kindly man and it was plain that he took no great pleasure in his task. He asked the necessary questions in a deprecating manner. His speech for the prosecution might really have been a speech for the defence, and the assessors took less than five minutes to consider their popular verdict. It was impossible to prevent the great outburst of applause with which it was received by the crowd that packed the courthouse. The judge congratulated Mrs Crosbie and she was a free woman.

No one had expressed a more violent disapprobation of Hammond's behaviour than Mrs Joyce; she was a woman loyal to her friends and she had insisted on the Crosbies staying with her after the trial, for she in common with everyone else had no doubt of the result, till they could make arrangements to go away. It was out of the question for poor, dear, brave Leslie to return to the bungalow at which the horrible catastrophe had taken place. The trial was over by half past twelve and when they reached the Joyces' house a grand luncheon was awaiting them. Cocktails were ready, Mrs Joyce's million-dollar cocktail was celebrated through all the Malay States, and Mrs Joyce drank Leslie's health. She was a talkative, vivacious woman, and now she was in the highest spirits. It was fortunate, for the rest of them were silent. She did not wonder; her husband never had much to say, and the other two were naturally exhausted from the long strain to which they had been subjected. During luncheon she carried on a bright and spirited monologue. Then coffee was served.

'Now, children,' she said in her gay, bustling fashion, 'you must have a rest and after tea I shall take you both for a drive to the sea.'

Mr Joyce, who lunched at home only by exception, had of course to go back to his office.

'I'm afraid I can't do that, Mrs Joyce,' said Crosbie. 'I've got to get back to the estate at once.'

'Not today?' she cried.

'Yes, now. I've neglected it for too long and I have urgent business. But I shall be very grateful if you will keep Leslie until we have decided what to do.'

Mrs Joyce was about to expostulate, but her husband prevented her.

'If he must go, he must, and there's an end of it.'

There was something in the lawyer's tone which made her look at him quickly. She held her tongue and there was a moment's silence. Then Crosbie spoke again.

'If you'll forgive me, I'll start at once so that I can get there before dark.' He rose from the table. 'Will you come and see me off, Leslie?'

'Of course.'

They went out of the dining-room together.

'I think that's rather inconsiderate of him,' said Mrs Joyce. 'He must know that Leslie wants to be with him just now.'

'I'm sure he wouldn't go if it wasn't absolutely necessary.'

'Well, I'll just see that Leslie's room is ready for her. She wants a complete rest, of course, and then amusement.'

Mrs Joyce left the room and Joyce sat down again. In a short time he heard Crosbie start the engine of his motor-cycle and then noisily scrunch over the gravel of the garden path. He got up and went into the drawing-room. Mrs Crosbie was standing in the middle of it, looking into space, and in her hand was an open letter. He recognized it. She gave him a glance as he came in and he saw that she was deathly pale.

'He knows,' she whispered.

Mr Joyce went up to her and took the letter from her hand. He lit a match and set the paper afire. She watched it burn. When he could hold it no longer he dropped it on the tiled floor and they both looked at the paper curl and blacken. Then he trod it into ashes with his foot.

'What does he know?'

She gave him a long, long stare and into her eyes came a strange look. Was it contempt or despair? Mr Joyce could not tell.

'He knows that Geoff was my lover.'

Mr Joyce made no movement and uttered no sound.

'He'd been my lover for years. He became my lover almost immediately after he came back from the war. We knew how careful we must be. When we became lovers I pretended I was tired of him, and he seldom came to the house when Robert was there. I used to drive out to a place we knew and he met me, two or three times a week, and when Robert went to Singapore he used to come to the bungalow late, when the boys had gone for the night. We saw one another constantly, all the time, and not a soul had the smallest suspicion of it. And then lately, a year ago, he began to change. I didn't know what was the matter. I couldn't believe that he didn't care for me any more. He always denied it. I was frantic. I made him scenes. Sometimes I thought he hated me. Oh, if you knew what agonies I endured. I passed through hell. I knew he didn't want me any more and I wouldn't let him go. Misery! Misery! I loved him. I'd given him everything. He was my life. And then I heard he was living with a Chinese woman. I couldn't believe it. I wouldn't believe it. At last I saw her, I saw her with my own eyes, walking in the village, with her gold bracelets and her necklaces, an old, fat Chinese woman. She was older than I was. Horrible! They all knew in the kampong that she was his mistress. And when I passed her, she looked at me and I knew that she knew I was his mistress too. I sent for him. I told him I must see him. You've read the letter. I was mad to write it. I didn't know what I was doing. I didn't care. I hadn't seen him for ten days. It was a lifetime. And when last we'd parted he took me in his arms and kissed me, and told me not to worry. And he went straight from my arms to hers.'

She had been speaking in a low voice, vehemently, and now she stopped and wrung her hands.

'That damned letter. We'd always been so careful. He always tore up any word I wrote to him the moment he'd read it. How was I to know he'd leave that one? He came, and I told him I knew about the Chinawoman. He denied it. He said it was only scandal. I was beside myself. I don't know what I said to him. Oh, I hated him then. I tore him limb from limb. I said everything I could to wound him. I insulted him. I could have spat in his face. And at last he turned on me. He told me he was sick and tired of me and never wanted to see me again. He said I bored him to death. And then he acknowledged that it was true about the Chinawoman. He said he'd known her for years, before the war, and she was the only woman who really meant anything to him, and the rest was just pastime. And he said he was glad I knew and now at last I'd leave him alone. And then I don't know what happened, I was beside myself, I saw red. I seized the revolver and I fired. He gave a cry and I saw I'd hit him. He staggered and rushed for the veranda. I ran after him and fired again. He fell and then I stood over him and I fired till the revolver went click, click, and I knew there were no more cartridges.'

At last she stopped, panting. Her face was no longer human, it was distorted with cruelty, and rage and pain. You would never have though that this quiet, refined woman was capable of such fiendish passion. Mr Joyce took a step backwards. He was absolutely aghast at the sight of her. It was not a face, it was a gibbering, hideous mask. Then they heard a voice calling from another room, a loud, friendly, cheerful voice. It was Mrs Joyce.

'Come along, Leslie darling, your room's ready. You must be dropping with sleep.'

Mrs Crosbie's features gradually composed themselves. Those passions, so clearly delineated, were smoothed away as with your hand you would smooth crumpled paper, and in a minute the face was cool and calm and unlined. She was a trifle pale, but her lips broke into a pleasant, affable smile. She was once more the well-bred and even distinguished woman.

'I'm coming, Dorothy dear. I'm sorry to give you so much trouble.'

THE OUTSTATION

The new assistant arrived in the afternoon. When the Resident, Mr Warburton, was told that the prahu was in sight he put on his solar topee and went down to the landing-stage. The guard, eight little Dyak soldiers, stood to attention as he passed. He noted with satisfaction that their bearing was martial, their uniforms neat and clean, and their guns shining. They were a credit to him. From the landing-stage he watched the bend of the river round which in a moment the boat would sweep. He looked very smart in his spotless ducks and white shoes. He held under his arm a gold-headed Malacca cane which had been given him by the Sultan of Perak. He awaited the newcomer with mingled feelings. There was more work in the district than one man could properly do, and during his periodical tours of the country under his charge it had been inconvenient to leave the station in the hands of a native clerk, but he had been so long the only white man there that he could not face the arrival of another without misgiving. He was accustomed to loneliness. During the war he had not seen an English face for three years; and once when he was instructed to put up an afforestation officer he was seized with panic, so that when the stranger was due to arrive, having arranged everything for his reception, he wrote a note telling him he was obliged to go up-river, and fled; he remained away till he was informed by a messenger that his guest had left.

Now the prahu appeared in the broad reach. It was manned by prisoners, Dyaks under various sentences, and a couple of warders were waiting on the landing-stage to take them back to gaol. They were sturdy fellows, used to the river, and they rowed with a powerful stroke. As the boat reached the side a man got out from under the attap awning and stepped on shore. The guard presented arms.

'Here we are at last. By God, I'm as cramped as the devil. I've brought you your mail.'

He spoke with exuberant joviality. Mr Warburton politely held out his hand.

'Mr Cooper, I presume?'

'That's right. Were you expecting anyone else?'

The question had a facetious intent, but the Resident did not smile.

'My name is Warburton. I'll show you your quarters. They'll bring your kit along.'

He preceded Cooper along the narrow pathway and they entered a compound in which stood a small bungalow.

'I've had it made as habitable as I could, but of course no one has lived in it for a good many years.'

It was built on piles. It consisted of a long living-room which opened on to a broad veranda, and behind, on each side of a passage, were two bedrooms.

'This'll do me all right,' said Cooper.

'I dare say you want to have a bath and a change. I shall be very much pleased if you'll dine with me tonight. Will eight o'clock suit you?'

'Any old time will do for me.'

The Resident gave a polite, but slightly disconcerted smile, and withdrew. He returned to the Fort where his own residence was. The impression which Allen Cooper had given him was not very favourable, but he was a fair man, and he knew that it was unjust to form an opinion on so brief a glimpse. Cooper seemed to be about thirty. He was a tall, thin fellow, with a sallow face in which there was not a spot of colour. It was a face all in one tone. He had a large, hooked nose and blue eyes. When, entering the bungalow, he had taken off his topee and flung it to a waiting boy, Mr Warburton noticed that his large skull, covered with short, brown hair, contrasted somewhat oddly with a weak, small chin. He was dressed in khaki shorts and a khaki shirt, but they were shabby and soiled; and his battered topee had not been cleaned for days. Mr Warburton reflected that the young man had spent a week on a coasting steamer and had passed the last forty-eight hours lying in the bottom of a prahu.

'We'll see what he looks like when he comes in to dinner.'

He went into his room, where his things were as neatly laid out as if he had an English valet, undressed, and, walking down the stairs to the bath-house, sluiced himself with cool water. The only concession he made to the climate was to wear a white dinner jacket; but otherwise, in a boiled shirt and a high collar, silk socks and patent-leather shoes, he dressed as formally as though he were dining at his club in Pall Mall. A careful host, he went into the dining-room to see that the table was properly laid. It was gay with orchids, and the silver shone brightly. The napkins were folded into elaborate shapes. Shaded candles in silver candlesticks shed a soft light. Mr Warburton smiled his approval and returned to the sitting-room to await his guest. Presently he appeared. Cooper was wearing the khaki shorts, the khaki shirt, and the ragged jacket in which he had landed. Mr Warburton's smile of greeting froze on his face.

'Hullo, you're all dressed up,' said Cooper. 'I didn't know you were going to do that. I very nearly put on a sarong.'

'It doesn't matter at all. I dare say your boys were busy.'

'You needn't have bothered to dress on my account, you know.'

'I didn't. I always dress for dinner.'

'Even when you're alone?'

'Especially when I'm alone,' replied Mr Warburton, with a frigid stare.

He saw a twinkle of amusement in Cooper's eyes, and he flushed an angry red. Mr Warburton was a hot-tempered man; you might have guessed that from his red face with its pugnacious features and from his red hair now growing white; his blue eyes, cold as a rule and observing, could flash with sudden wrath; but he was a man of the world and he hoped a just one. He must do his best to get on with this fellow.

'When I lived in London I moved in circles in which it would have been just as eccentric not to dress for dinner every night as not to have a bath every morning. When I came to Borneo I saw no reason to discontinue so good a habit. For three years during the war I never saw a white man. I never omitted to dress on a single occasion on which I was well enough to come in to dinner. You have not been very long in this country; believe me, there is no better way to maintain the proper pride which you should have in yourself. When a white man surrenders in the slightest degree to the influences that surround him he very soon loses his self-respect, and when he loses his self-respect you may be quite sure the natives will soon cease to respect him.'

'Well, if you expect me to put on a boiled shirt and a stiff collar in this heat I'm afraid you'll be disappointed.'

'When you are dining in your own bungalow you will, of course, dress as you think fit, but when you do me the pleasure of dining with me, perhaps you will come to the conclusion that it is only polite to wear the costume usual in civilized society.'

Two Malay boys, in sarongs and songkoks, with smart white coats and brass buttons, came in, one bearing gin pahits, and the other a tray on which were olives and anchovies. Then they went in to dinner. Mr Warburton flattered himself that he had the best cook, a Chinese, in Borneo, and he took great trouble to have as good food as in the difficult circumstances was possible. He exercised much ingenuity in making the best of his materials.

'Would you care to look at the menu?' he said, handing it to Cooper.

It was written in French and the dishes had resounding names. They were waited on by the two boys. In opposite corners of the room two more waved immense fans, and so gave movement to the sultry air. The fare was sumptuous and the champagne excellent.

'Do you do yourself like this every day?' said Cooper.

Mr Warburton gave the menu a careless glance.

'I have not noticed that the dinner is any different from usual,' he said. 'I eat very little myself, but I make a point of having a proper dinner served to me every night. It keeps the cook in practice and it's good discipline for the boys.'

The conversation proceeded with effort. Mr Warburton was elaborately courteous and, it may be, found a slightly malicious amusement in the embarrassment which he thereby occasioned in his companion. Cooper had not been more than a few months in Sembulu, and Mr Warburton's inquiries about friends of his in Kuala Solor were soon exhausted.

'By the way,' he said presently, 'did you meet a lad called Hennerley? He's come out recently, I believe.'

'Oh yes, he's in the police. A rotten bounder.'

'I should hardly have expected him to be that. His uncle is my friend Lord Barraclough. I had a letter from Lady Barraclough only the other day asking me to look out for him.'

'I heard he was related to somebody or other. I suppose that's how he got the job. He's been to Eton and Oxford and he doesn't forget to let you know it.'

'You surprise me,' said Mr Warburton. 'All his family have been at Eton and Oxford for a couple of hundred years. I should have expected him to take it as a matter of course.'

'I thought him a damned prig.'

'To what school did you go?'

'I was born in Barbados. I was educated there.'

'Oh, I see.'

Mr Warburton managed to put so much offensiveness into his brief reply that Cooper flushed. For a moment he was silent.

'I've had two or three letters from Kuala Solor,' continued Mr

Warburton, 'and my impression was that young Hennerley was a great success. They say he's a first-rate sportsman.'

'Oh, yes, he's very popular. He's just the sort of fellow they would like in K.S. I haven't got much use for the first-rate sportsman myself. What does it amount to in the long run that a man can play golf and tennis better than other people? And who cares if he can make a break of seventy-five at billiards? They attach a damned sight too much importance to that sort of thing in England.'

'Do you think so? I was under the impression that the first-rate sportsman had come out of the war certainly no worse than anyone else.'

'Oh, if you're going to talk of the war then I do know what I'm talking about. I was in the same regiment as Hennerley and I can tell you that the men couldn't stick him at any price.'

'How do you know?'

'Because I was one of the men.'

'Oh, you hadn't got a commission.'

'A fat chance I had of getting a commission. I was what was called a Colonial. I hadn't been to a public school and I had no influence. I was in the ranks the whole damned time.'

Cooper frowned. He seemed to have difficulty in preventing himself from breaking out into violent invective. Mr Warburton watched him, his little blue eyes narrowed, watched him and formed his opinion. Changing the conversation, he began to speak to Cooper about the work that would be required of him, and as the clock struck ten he rose.

'Well, I won't keep you any more. I dare say you're tired by your journey.'

They shook hands.

'Oh, I say, look here,' said Cooper, 'I wonder if you can find me a boy. The boy I had before never turned up when I was starting from K.S. He took my kit on board and all that, and then disappeared. I didn't know he wasn't there till we were out of the river.'

'I'll ask my head-boy. I have no doubt he can find you some-one.'

'All right. Just tell him to send the boy along and if I like the look of him I'll take him.'

There was a moon, so that no lantern was needed. Cooper walked across from the Fort to his bungalow.

'I wonder why on earth they've sent me a fellow like that?'

reflected Mr Warburton. 'If that's the kind of man they're going to get out now I don't think much of it.'

He strolled down his garden. The Fort was built on the top of a little hill and the garden ran down to the river's edge; on the bank was an arbour, and hither it was his habit to come after dinner to smoke a cheroot. And often from the river that flowed below him a voice was heard, the voice of some Malay too timorous to venture into the light of day, and a complaint or an accusation was softly wafted to his ears, a piece of information was whispered to him or a useful hint, which otherwise would never have come into his official ken. He threw himself heavily into a long rattan chair. Cooper! An envious, ill-bred fellow, bumptious, self-assertive, and vain. But Mr Warburton's irritation could not withstand the silent beauty of the night. The air was scented with the sweet-smelling flowers of a tree that grew at the entrance to the arbour, and the fire-flies, sparkling dimly, flew with their slow and silvery flight. The moon made a pathway on the broad river for the light feet of Sila's bride, and on the further bank a row of palm trees was delicately silhouetted against the sky. Peace stole into the soul of Mr Warburton.

He was a queer creature and he had had a singular career. At the age of twenty-one he had inherited a considerable fortune, a hundred thousand pounds, and when he left Oxford he threw himself into the gay life, which in those days (now Mr Warburton was a man of four-and-fifty) offered itself to the young man of good family. He had his flat in Mount Street, his private hansom, and his hunting-box in Warwickshire. He went to all the places where the fashionable congregate. He was handsome, amusing, and generous. He was a figure in the society of London in the early nineties, and society then had not lost its exclusiveness nor its brilliance. The Boer War which shook it was unthought of; the Great War which destroyed it was prophesied only by the pessimists. It was no unpleasant thing to be a rich young man in those days, and Mr Warburton's chimney-piece during the season was packed with cards for one great function after another. Mr Warburton displayed them with complacency. For Mr Warburton was a snob. He was not a timid snob, a little ashamed of being impressed by his betters, nor a snob who sought the intimacy of persons who had acquired celebrity in politics or notoriety in the arts, nor the snob who was dazzled by riches; he was the naked, unadulterated common snob who dearly loved a lord. He was touchy and quick-tempered, but he would much rather have been snubbed by a person of quality than flattered by a commoner. His name figured insignificantly in Burke's Peerage, and it was marvellous to watch the ingenuity he used to mention his distant relationship to the noble family he belonged to; but never a word did he say of the honest Liverpool manufacturer from whom, through his mother, a Miss Gubbins, he had come by his fortune. It was the terror of his fashionable life that at Cowes, maybe, or at Ascot, when he was with a duchess or even with a prince of the blood, one of these relatives would claim acquaintance with him.

His failing was too obvious not soon to become notorious, but its extravagance saved it from being merely despicable. The great whom he adored laughed at him, but in their hearts felt his adoration not unnatural. Poor Warburton was a dreadful snob, of course, but after all he was a good fellow. He was always ready to back a bill for an impecunious nobleman, and if you were in a tight corner you could safely count on him for a hundred pounds. He gave good dinners. He played whist badly, but never minded how much he lost if the company was select. He happened to be a gambler, an unlucky one, but he was a good loser, and it was impossible not to admire the coolness with which he lost five hundred pounds at a sitting. His passion for cards, almost as strong as his passion for titles, was the cause of his undoing. The life he led was expensive and his gambling losses were formidable. He began to plunge more heavily, first on horses, and then on the Stock Exchange. He had a certain simplicity of character, and the unscrupulous found him an ingenuous prey. I do not know if he ever realized that his smart friends laughed at him behind his back, but I think he had an obscure instinct that he could not afford to appear other than careless of his money. He got into the hands of money-lenders. At the age of thirty-four he was ruined.

He was too much imbued with the spirit of his class to hesitate in the choice of his next step. When a man in his set had run through his money, he went out to the colonies. No one heard Mr Warburton repine. He made no complaint because a noble friend had advised a disastrous speculation, he pressed nobody to whom he had lent money to repay it, he paid his debts (if he had only known it, the despised blood of the Liverpool manufacturer came out in him there), sought help from no one, and, never having done a stroke of work in his life, looked for a means of livelihood. He remained cheerful, unconcerned, and full of humour. He had no wish to make anyone with whom he happened to be uncomfortable by the recital of his misfortune. Mr Warburton was a snob, but he was also a gentleman.

The only favour he asked of any of the great friends in whose daily company he had lived for years was a recommendation. The able man who was at that time Sultan of Sembulu took him into his service. The night before he sailed he dined for the last time at his club.

'I hear you're going away, Warburton,' the old Duke of Hereford said to him.

'Yes, I'm going to Borneo.'

'Good God, what are you going there for?'

'Oh, I'm broke.'

'Are you? I'm sorry. Well, let us know when you come back. I hope you have a good time.'

'Oh yes. Lots of shooting, you know.'

The Duke nodded and passed on. A few hours later Mr Warburton watched the coast of England recede into the mist, and he left behind everything which to him made life worth living.

Twenty years had passed since then. He kept up a busy correspondence with various great ladies and his letters were amusing and chatty. He never lost his love for titled persons and paid careful attention to the announcements in *The Times* (which reached him six weeks after publication) of their comings and goings. He perused the column which records births, deaths, and marriages, and he was always ready with his letter of congratulation or condolence. The illustrated papers told him how people looked and on his periodical visits to England, able to take up the threads as though they had never been broken, he knew all about any new person who might have appeared on the social surface. His interest in the world of fashion was as vivid as when himself had been a figure in it. It still seemed to him the only thing that mattered.

But insensibly another interest had entered into his life. The position he found himself in flattered his vanity; he was no longer the sycophant craving the smiles of the great, he was the master whose word was law. He was gratified by the guard of Dyak soldiers who presented arms as he passed. He liked to sit in judgement on his fellow men. It pleased him to compose quarrels between rival chiefs. When the head-hunters were troublesome in the old days he set out to chastise them with a thrill of pride in his own behaviour. He was too vain not to be of dauntless courage, and a pretty story was told of his coolness in adventuring single-handed into a stockaded village and demanding the surrender of a bloodthirsty pirate. He became a skilful administrator. He was strict, just, and honest.

And little by little he conceived a deep love for the Malays. He interested himself in their habits and customs. He was never tired of listening to their talk. He admired their virtues, and with a smile and a shrug of the shoulders condoned their vices.

'In my day,' he would say, 'I have been on intimate terms with some of the greatest gentlemen in England, but I have never known finer gentlemen than some well-born Malays whom I am proud to call my friends.'

He liked their courtesy and their distinguished manners, their gentleness and their sudden passions. He knew by instinct exactly how to treat them. He had a genuine tenderness for them. But he never forgot that he was an English gentleman, and he had no patience with the white men who yielded to native customs. He made no surrenders. And he did not imitate so many of the white men in taking a native woman to wife, for an intrigue of this nature, however sanctified by custom, seemed to him not only shocking but undignified. A man who had been called George by Albert Edward, Prince of Wales, could hardly be expected to have any connexion with a native. And when he returned to Borneo from his visits to England it was now with something like relief. His friends, like himself, were no longer young, and there was a new generation which looked upon him as a tiresome old man. It seemed to him that the England of today had lost a good deal of what he had loved in the England of his youth. But Borneo remained the same. It was home to him now. He meant to remain in service as long as was possible, and the hope in his heart was that he would die before at last he was forced to retire. He had stated in his will that wherever he died he wished his body to be brought back to Sembulu, and buried among the people he loved within the sound of the softly flowing river.

But these emotions he kept hidden from the eyes of men; and no one, seeing this spruce, stout, well-set-up man, with his clean-shaven strong face and his whitening hair, would have dreamed that he cherished so profound a sentiment.

He knew how the work of the station should be done, and during the next few days he kept a suspicious eye on his assistant. He saw very soon that he was painstaking and competent. The only fault he had to find with him was that he was brusque with the natives.

'The Malays are shy and very sensitive,' he said to him. 'I think you will find that you will get much better results if you take care always to be polite, patient, and kindly.'

Cooper gave a short, grating laugh.

'I was born in Barbados and I was in Africa in the war. I don't think there's much about niggers that I don't know.'

'I know nothing,' said Mr Warburton acidly. 'But we were not talking of them. We were taking of Malays.'

'Aren't they niggers?'

'You are very ignorant,' replied Mr Warburton.

He said no more.

On the first Sunday after Cooper's arrival he asked him to dinner. He did everything ceremoniously, and though they had met on the previous day in the office and later, on the Fort veranda where they drank a gin and bitters together at six o'clock, he sent a polite note across to the bungalow by a boy. Cooper, however unwillingly, came in evening dress and Mr Warburton, though gratified that his wish was respected, noticed with disdain that the young man's clothes were badly cut and his shirt ill-fitting. But Mr Warburton was in a good temper that evening.

'By the way,' he said to him, as he shook hands, 'I've talked to my head-boy about finding you someone and he recommends his nephew. I've seen him and he seems a bright and willing lad. Would you like to see him?'

'I don't mind.'

'He's waiting now.'

Mr Warburton called his boy and told him to send for his nephew. In a moment a tall, slender youth of twenty appeared. He had large dark eyes and a good profile. He was very neat in his sarong, a little white coat, and a fez, without a tassel, of plum-coloured velvet. He answered to the name of Abas. Mr Warburton looked on him with approval, and his manner insensibly soft-ened as he spoke to him in fluent and idomatic Malay. He was inclined to be sarcastic with white people, but with the Malays he had a happy mixture of condescension and kindliness. He stood in the place of the Sultan. He knew perfectly how to preserve his own dignity and at the same time put a native at his ease.

'Will he do?' said Mr Warburton, turning to Cooper.

'Yes, I dare say he's no more of a scoundrel than any of the rest of them.'

Mr Warburton informed the boy that he was engaged, and dismissed him.

'You're very lucky to get a boy like that,' he told Cooper. 'He belongs to a very good family. They came over from Malacca nearly a hundred years ago.'

'I don't much mind if the boy who cleans my shoes and brings me a drink when I want it has blue blood in his veins or not. All I ask is that he should do what I tell him and look sharp about it.'

Mr Warburton pursed his lips, but made no reply.

They went in to dinner. It was excellent, and the wine was good. Its influence presently had its effect on them, and they talked not only without acrimony, but even with friendliness. Mr Warburton liked to do himself well, and on Sunday night he made it a habit to do himself even a little better than usual. He began to think he was unfair to Cooper. Of course he was not a gentleman, but that was not his fault, and when you got to know him it might be that he would turn out a very good fellow. His faults, perhaps, were faults of manner. And he was certainly good at his work, quick, conscientious, and thorough. When they reached the dessert Mr Warburton was feeling kindly disposed towards all mankind.

'This is your first Sunday, and I'm going to give you a very special glass of port. I've only got about two dozen of it left and I keep it for special occasions.'

He gave his boy instructions and presently the bottle was brought. Mr Warburton watched the boy open it.

'I got this port from my old friend Charles Hollington. He'd had it for forty years, and I've had it for a good many. He was well-known to have the best cellar in England.'

'Is he a wine merchant?'

'Not exactly,' smiled Mr Warburton. 'I was speaking of Lord Hollington of Castle Reagh. He's one of the richest peers in England. A very old friend of mine. I was at Eton with his brother.'

This was an opportunity that Mr Warburton could never resist, and he told a little anecdote of which the only point seemed to be that he knew an Earl. The port was certainly very good; he drank a glass and then a second. He lost all caution. He had not talked to a white man for months. He began to tell stories. He showed himself in the company of the great. Hearing him, you would have thought that at one time ministries were formed and policies decided on his suggestion whispered into the ear of a duchess or thrown over the dinner-table to be gratefully acted on by the confidential adviser of the Sovereign. The old days at Ascot,

Goodwood, and Cowes lived again for him. Another glass of port. There were the great house-parties in Yorkshire and in Scotland to which he went every year.

'I had a man called Foreman then, the best valet I ever had, and why do you think he gave me notice? You know in the House-keeper's Room the ladies' maids and the gentlemen's gentlemen sit according to the precedence of their masters. He told me he was sick of going to party after party at which I was the only commoner. It meant that he always had to sit at the bottom of the table, and all the best bits were taken before a dish reached him. I told the story to the old Duke of Hereford, and he roared. "By God, sir," he said, "if I were King of England, I'd make you a viscount just to give your man a chance." "Take him yourself, Duke," I said. "He's the best valet I've ever had." "Well, War-burton," he said, "if he's good enough for you he's good enough for me. Send him along."'

Then there was Monte Carlo, where Mr Warburton and the Grand Duke Fyodor, playing in partnership, had broken the bank one evening; and there was Marienbad. At Marienbad Mr Warburton had played baccarat with Edward VII.

'He was only Prince of Wales then, of course. I remember him saying to me, "George, if you draw on a five you'll lose your shirt." He was right; I don't think he ever said a truer word in his life. He was a wonderful man. I always said he was the greatest diplomatist in Europe. But I was a young fool in those days, I hadn't the sense to take his advice. If I had, if I'd never drawn on a five, I dare say I shouldn't be here today.'

Cooper was watching him. His brown eyes, deep in their sockets, were hard and supercilious, and on his lips was a mocking smile. He had heard a good deal about Mr Warburton in Kuala Solor, not a bad sort, and he ran his district like clockwork, they said, but by heaven, what a snob! They laughed at him good-naturedly, for it was impossible to dislike a man who was so generous and so kindly, and Cooper had already heard the story of the Prince of Wales and the game of baccarat. But Cooper listened without indulgence. From the beginning he had resented the Resident's manner. He was very sensitive, and he writhed under Mr Warburton's polite sarcasms. Mr Warburton had a knack of receiving a remark of which he disapproved with a devastating silence. Cooper had lived little in England and he had a peculiar dislike of the English. He resented especially the public-school boy since he always feared that he was going to patronize him. He was so much afraid of others putting on airs with him that, in order as it were to get in first, he put on such airs as to make everyone think him insufferably conceited.

'Well, at all events the war has done one good thing for us,' he said at last. 'It's smashed up the power of the aristocracy. The Boer War started it, and 1914 put the lid on.'

'The great families of England are doomed,' said Mr Warburton with the complacent melancholy of an *émigré* who remembered the court of Louis XV. 'They cannot afford any longer to live in their splendid palaces and their princely hospitality will soon be nothing but a memory.'

'And a damned good job too in my opinion.'

'My poor Cooper, what can you know of the glory that was Greece and the grandeur that was Rome?'

Mr Warburton made an ample gesture. His eyes for an instant grew dreamy with a vision of the past.

'Well, believe me, we're fed up with all that rot. What we want is a business government by business men. I was born in a Crown Colony, and I've lived practically all my life in the colonies. I don't give a row of pins for a lord. What's wrong with England is snobbishness. And if there's anything that gets my goat it's a snob.'

A snob! Mr Warburton's face grew purple and his eyes blazed with anger. That was a word that had pursued him all his life. The great ladies whose society he had enjoyed in his youth were not inclined to look upon his appreciation of themselves as unworthy, but even great ladies are sometimes out of temper and more than once Mr Warburton had had the dreadful word flung in his teeth. He knew, he could not help knowing, that there were odious people who called him a snob. How unfair it was! Why, there was no vice he found so detestable as snobbishness. After all, he liked to mix with people of his own class, he was only at home in their company, and how in heaven's name could anyone say that was snobbish? Birds of a feather.

'I quite agree with you,' he answered. 'A snob is a man who admires or despises another because he is of a higher social rank than his own. It is the most vulgar failing of our English middle-class.'

He saw a flicker of amusement in Cooper's eyes. Cooper put up his hand to hide the broad smile that rose to his lips, and so made it more noticeable. Mr Warburton's hands trembled a little.

Probably Cooper never knew how greatly he had offended his chief. A sensitive man himself he was strangely insensitive to the feelings of others.

Their work forced them to see one another for a few minutes now and then during the day, and they met at six to have a drink on Mr Warburton's veranda. This was an old-established custom of the country which Mr Warburton would not for the world have broken. But they ate their meals separately, Cooper in his bungalow and Mr Warburton at the Fort. After the office work was over they walked till dusk fell, but they walked apart. There were but few paths in this country where the jungle pressed close upon the plantations of the village, and when Mr Warburton caught sight of his assistant passing along with his loose stride, he would make a circuit in order to avoid him. Cooper, with his bad manners, his conceit in his own judgement, and his intolerance, had already got on his nerves; but it was not till Cooper had been on the station for a couple of months that an incident happened which turned the Resident's dislike into bitter hatred.

Mr Warburton was obliged to go up-country on a tour of inspection, and he left the station in Cooper's charge with more confidence, since he had definitely come to the conclusion that he was a capable fellow. The only thing he did not like was that he had no indulgence. He was honest, just, and painstaking, but he had no sympathy for the natives. It bitterly amused Mr Warburton to observe that this man who looked upon himself as every man's equal should look upon so many men as his own inferiors. He was hard, he had no patience with the native mind, and he was a bully. Mr Warburton very quickly realized that the Malays disliked and feared him. He was not altogether displeased. He would not have liked it very much if his assistant had enjoyed a popularity which might rival his own. Mr Warburton made his elaborate preparations, set out on his expedition, and in three weeks returned. Meanwhile the mail had arrived. The first thing that struck his eyes when he entered his sitting-room was a great pile of open newspapers. Cooper had met him, and they went into the room together. Mr Warburton turned to one of the servants who had been left behind, and sternly asked him what was the meaning of those open papers. Cooper hastened to explain.

'I wanted to read all about the Wolverhampton murder, and so I borrowed your *Times*. I brought them back again. I knew you wouldn't mind.'

Mr Warburton turned on him, white with anger.

'But I do mind. I mind very much.'

'I'm sorry,' said Cooper, with composure. 'The fact is, I simply couldn't wait till you came back.'

'I wonder you didn't open my letters as well.'

Cooper, unmoved, smiled at his chief's exasperation.

'Oh, that's not quite the same thing. After all, I couldn't imagine you'd mind my looking at your newspapers. There's nothing private in them.'

'I very much object to anyone reading my paper before me.' He went up to the pile. There were nearly thirty numbers there. 'I think it extremely impertinent of you. They're all mixed up.'

'We can easily put them in order,' said Cooper, joining him at the table.

'Don't touch them,' cried Mr Warburton.

'I say, it's childish to make a scene about a little thing like that.'

'How dare you speak to me like that?'

'Oh, go to hell,' said Cooper, and he flung out of the room.

Mr Warburton, trembling with passion, was left contemplating his papers. His greatest pleasure in life had been destroyed by those callous, brutal hands. Most people living in out-of-the-way places when the mail comes tear open impatiently their papers and taking the last ones first glance at the latest news from home. Not so Mr Warburton. His newsagent had instructions to write on the outside of the wrapper the date of each paper he dispatched, and when the great bundle arrived Mr Warburton looked at these dates and with his blue pencil numbered them. His head-boy's orders were to place one on the table every morning in the veranda with the early cup of tea and it was Mr Warburton's especial delight to break the wrapper as he sipped his tea, and read the morning paper. It gave him the illusion of living at home. Every Monday morning he read the Monday *Times* of six weeks back, and so went through the week. On Sunday he read the *Observer*. Like his habit of dressing for dinner it was a tie to civilization. And it was his pride that no matter how exciting the news was he had never yielded to the temptation of opening a paper before its allotted time. During the war the suspense sometimes had been intolerable, and when he read one day that a push was begun he had undergone agonies of suspense which he might have saved himself by the simple expedient of opening a later paper which lay waiting for him on a shelf. It had been the severest trial to which he had ever exposed himself, but he victoriously surmounted it. And that clumsy fool had broken open those neat tight packages because he wanted to know whether some horrid woman had murdered her odious husband.

Mr Warburton sent for his boy and told him to bring wrappers. He folded up the papers as neatly as he could, placed a wrapper round each and numbered it. But it was a melancholy task.

'I shall never forgive him,' he said. 'Never.'

Of course his boy had been with him on his expedition; he never travelled without him, for his boy knew exactly how he liked things, and Mr Warburton was not the kind of jungle traveller who was prepared to dispense with his comforts; but in the interval since their arrival he had been gossiping in the servants' quarters. He had learnt that Cooper had had trouble with his boys. All but the youth Abas had left him. Abas had desired to go too, but his uncle had placed him there on the instructions of the Resident, and he was afraid to leave without his uncle's permission.

'I told him he had done well, Tuan,' said the boy. 'But he is unhappy. He says it is not a good house, and he wishes to know if he may go as the others have gone.'

'No, he must stay. The Tuan must have servants. Have those who went been replaced?'

'No, Tuan, no one will go.'

Mr Warburton frowned. Cooper was an insolent fool, but he had an official position and must be suitably provided with servants. It was not seemly that his house should be improperly conducted.

'Where are the boys who ran away?'

'They are in the kampong, Tuan.'

'Go and see them tonight, and tell them that I expect them to be back in Tuan Cooper's house at dawn tomorrow.'

'They say they will not go, Tuan.'

'On my order?'

The boy had been with Mr Warburton for fifteen years, and he knew every intonation of his master's voice. He was not afraid of him, they had gone through too much together, once in the jungle the Resident had saved his life, and once, upset in some rapids, but for him the Resident would have been drowned; but he knew when the Resident must be obeyed without question.

'I will go to the kampong,' he said.

Mr Warburton expected that his subordinate would take the first opportunity to apologize for his rudeness, but Cooper had the ill-bred man's inability to express regret; and when they met next morning in the office he ignored the incident. Since Mr Warburton had been away for three weeks it was necessary for them to have a somewhat prolonged interview. At the end of it, Mr Warburton dismissed him.

'I don't think there's anything else, thank you.' Cooper turned to go, but Mr Warburton stopped him. 'I understand you've been having some trouble with your boys.'

Cooper gave a harsh laugh.

'They tried to blackmail me. They had the damned cheek to run away, all except that incompetent fellow Abas – he knew when he was well off – but I just sat tight. They've all come to heel again.'

'What do you mean by that?'

'This morning they were all back on their jobs, the Chinese cook and all. There they were, as cool as cucumbers; you would have thought they owned the place. I suppose they'd come to the conclusion that I wasn't such a fool as I looked.'

'By no means. They came back on my express order.'

Cooper flushed slightly.

'I should be obliged if you wouldn't interfere with my private concerns.'

'They're not your private concerns. When your servants run away it makes you ridiculous. You are perfectly free to make a fool of yourself, but I cannot allow you to be made a fool of. It is unseemly that your house should not be properly staffed. As soon as I heard that your boys had left you, I had them told to be back in their places at dawn. That'll do.'

Mr Warburton nodded to signify that the interview was at an end. Cooper took no notice.

'Shall I tell you what I did? I called them and gave the whole bally lot the sack. I gave them ten minutes to get out of the compound.'

Mr Warburton shrugged his shoulders.

'What makes you think you can get others?'

'I've told my own clerk to see about it.'

Mr Warburton reflected for a moment.

'I think you behaved very foolishly. You will do well to remember in future that good masters make good servants.'

'Is there anything else you want to teach me?'

'I should like to teach you manners, but it would be an arduous task, and I have not the time to waste. I will see that you get boys.'

'Please don't put yourself to any trouble on my account. I'm quite capable of getting them for myself.'

Mr Warburton smiled acidly. He had an inkling that Cooper disliked him as much as he disliked Cooper, and he knew that nothing is more galling than to be forced to accept the favours of a man you detest.

'Allow me to tell you that you have no more chance of getting Malay or Chinese servants here now than you have of getting an English butler or a French chef. No one will come to you except on an order from me. Would you like me to give it?'

'No.'

'As you please. Good morning.'

Mr Warburton watched the development of the situation with acrid humour. Cooper's clerk was unable to persuade Malay, Dyak, or Chinese to enter the house of such a master. Abas, the boy who remained faithful to him, knew how to cook only native food, and Cooper, a coarse feeder, found his gorge rise against the everlasting rice. There was no water-carrier, and in that great heat he needed several baths a day. He cursed Abas, but Abas opposed him with sullen resistance and would not do more than he chose. It was galling to know that the lad stayed with him only because the Resident insisted. This went on for a fortnight and then, one morning, he found in his house the very servants whom he had previously dismissed. He fell into a violent rage, but he had learnt a little sense, and this time, without a word, he let them stay. He swallowed his humiliation, but the impatient contempt he had felt for Mr Warburton's idiosyncrasies changed into a sullen hatred: the Resident with this malicious stroke had made him the laughing-stock of all the natives.

The two men now held no communication with one another. They broke the time-honoured custom of sharing, notwithstanding personal dislike, a drink at six o'clock with any white man who happened to be at the station. Each lived in his own house as though the other did not exist. Now that Cooper had fallen into the work, it was necessary for them to have little to do with one another in the office. Mr Warburton used his orderly to send any message he had to give his assistant, and his instructions he sent by formal letter. They saw one another constantly, that was inevitable, but did not exchange half a dozen words in a week. The fact that they could not avoid catching sight of one another got on their nerves. They brooded over their antagonism, and Mr Warburton, taking his daily walk, could think of nothing but how much he detested his assistant.

And the dreadful thing was that in all probability they would remain thus, facing each other in deadly enmity, till Mr Warburton went on leave. It might be three years. He had no reason to send in a complaint to headquarters: Cooper did his work very well, and at that time men were hard to get. True, vague complaints reached him and hints that the natives found Cooper harsh. There was certainly a feeling of dissatisfaction among them. But when Mr Warburton looked into specific cases, all he could say was that Cooper had shown severity where mildness would not have been misplaced, and had been unfeeling when himself would have been sympathetic. He had done nothing for which he could be taken to task. But Mr Warburton watched him. Hatred will often make a man clear-sighted, and he had a suspicion that Cooper was using the natives without consideration, yet keeping within the law, because he felt that thus he could exasperate his chief. One day perhaps he would go too far. None knew better than Mr Warburton how irritable the incessant heat could make a man and how difficult it was to keep one's self-control after a sleepless night. He smiled softly to himself. Sooner or later Cooper would deliver himself into his hand.

When at last the opportunity came, Mr Warburton laughed aloud. Cooper had charge of the prisoners; they made roads, built sheds, rowed when it was necessary to send the prahu up or down stream, kept the town clean, and otherwise usefully employed themselves. If well-behaved they even on occasion served as house-boys. Cooper kept them hard at it. He liked to see them work. He took pleasure in devising tasks for them; and seeing quickly enough that they were being made to do useless things the prisoners worked badly. He punished them by lengthening their hours. This was contrary to the regulations, and as soon as it was brought to the attention of Mr Warburton, without referring the matter back to his subordinate, he gave instructions that the old hours should be kept; Cooper, going out for his walk, was astounded to see the prisoners strolling back to the gaol; he had given instructions that they were not to knock off till dusk. When he asked the warder in charge why they had left off work he was told that it was the Resident's bidding.

White with rage he strode to the Fort. Mr Warburton, in his spotless white ducks and his neat topee, with a walking-stick in his hand, followed by his dogs, was on the point of starting out on his afternoon stroll. He had watched Cooper go, and knew that he had taken the road by the river. Cooper jumped up the steps and went straight up to the Resident.

'I want to know what the hell you mean by countermanding my order that the prisoners were to work till six,' he burst out, beside himself with fury.

Mr Warburton opened his cold blue eyes very wide and assumed an expression of great surprise.

'Are you out of your mind? Are you so ignorant that you do not know that that is not the way to speak to your official superior?'

'Oh, go to hell. The prisoners are my pidgin, and you've got no right to interfere. You mind your business and I'll mind mine. I want to know what the devil you mean by making a damned fool of me. Everyone in the place will know that you've countermanded my order.'

Mr Warburton kept very cool.

'You had no power to give the order you did. I countermanded it because it was harsh and tyrannical. Believe me, I have not made half such a damned fool of you as you have made of yourself.'

'You disliked me from the first moment I came here. You've done everything you could to make the place impossible for me because I wouldn't lick your boots for you. You got your knife into me because I wouldn't flatter you.'

Cooper, spluttering with rage, was nearing dangerous ground, and Mr Warburton's eyes grew on a sudden colder and more piercing.

'You are wrong. I thought you were a cad, but I was perfectly satisfied with the way you did your work.'

'You snob. You damned snob. You thought me a cad because I hadn't been to Eton. Oh, they told me in K.S. what to expect. Why, don't you know that you're the laughing-stock of the whole country? I could hardly help bursting into a roar of laughter when you told your celebrated story about the Prince of Wales. My God, how they shouted at the club when they told it. By God, I'd rather be the cad I am than the snob you are.'

He got Mr Warburton on the raw.

'If you don't get out of my house this minute I shall knock you down,' he cried.

The other came a little a closer to him and put his face in his.

'Touch me, touch me,' he said. 'By God, I'd like to see you hit me. Do you want me to say it again? Snob. Snob.'

Cooper was three inches taller than Mr Warburton, a strong, muscular young man. Mr Warburton was fat and fifty-four. His clenched fist shot out. Cooper caught him by the arm and pushed him back.

'Don't be a damned fool. Remember I'm not a gentleman. I know how to use my hands.'

He gave a sort of hoot, and grinning all over his pale, sharp face jumped down the veranda steps. Mr Warburton, his heart in his anger pounding against his ribs, sank exhausted into a chair. His body tingled as though he had prickly heat. For one horrible moment he thought he was going to cry. But suddenly he was conscious that his head-boy was on the veranda and instinctively regained control of himself. The boy came forward and filled him a glass of whisky and soda. Without a word Mr Warburton took it and drank it to the dregs.

'What do you want to say to me?' asked Mr Warburton, trying to force a smile on to his strained lips.

'Tuan, the assistant Tuan is a bad man. Abas wishes again to leave him.'

'Let him wait a little. I shall write to Kuala Solor and ask that Tuan Cooper should go elsewhere.'

'Tuan Cooper is not good with the Malays.'

'Leave me.'

The boy silently withdrew. Mr Warburton was left alone with his thoughts. He saw the club at Kuala Solor, the men sitting round the table in the window in their flannels, when the night had driven them in from golf and tennis, drinking whiskies and gin pahits, and laughing when they told the celebrated story of the Prince of Wales and himself at Marienbad. He was hot with shame and misery. A snob! They all thought him a snob. And he had always thought them very good fellows, he had always been gentleman enough to let it make no difference to him that they were of very second-rate position. He hated them now. But his hatred for them was nothing compared with his hatred for Cooper. And if it had come to blows Cooper could have thrashed him. Tears of mortification ran down his red, fat face. He sat there for a couple of hours smoking cigarette after cigarette, and he wished he were dead.

At last the boy came back and asked him if he would dress for dinner. Of course! He always dressed for dinner. He rose wearily from his chair and put on his stiff shirt and the high collar. He sat down at the prettily decorated table, and was waited on as usual by the two boys while two others waved their great fans. Over there in the bungalow, two hundred yards away, Cooper was eating a filthy meal clad only in a sarong and a baju. His feet were bare and while he ate he probably read a detective story. After dinner Mr Warburton sat down to write a letter. The Sultan was away, but he wrote, privately and confidentially, to his representative. Cooper did his work very well, he said, but the fact was that he couldn't get on with him. They were getting dreadfully on each other's nerves and he would look upon it as a very great favour if Cooper could be transferred to another post.

He dispatched the letter next morning by special messenger. The answer came a fortnight later with the month's mail. It was a private note, and ran as follows:

My dear Warburton,

I do not want to answer your letter officially, and so I am writing you a few lines myself. Of course if you insist I will put the matter up to the Sultan, but I think you would be much wiser to drop it. I know Cooper is a rough diamond, but he is capable, and he had a pretty thin time in the war, and I think he should be given every chance. I think you are a little too much inclined to attach importance to a man's social position. You must remember that times have changed. Of course it's a very good thing for a man to be a gentleman, but it's better that he should be competent and hard-working. I think if you'll exercise a little tolerance you'll get on very well with Cooper.

Yours very sincerely,

Richard Temple

The letter dropped from Mr Warburton's hand. It was easy to read between the lines. Dick Temple, whom he had known for twenty years, Dick Temple who came from quite a good county family, thought him a snob, and for that reason had no patience with his request. Mr Warburton felt on a sudden discouraged with life. The world of which he was a part had passed away and the future belonged to a meaner generation. Cooper represented it and Cooper he hated with all his heart. He stretched out his hand to fill his glass, and at the gesture his head-boy stepped forward.

'I didn't know you were there.'

The boy picked up the official letter. Ah, that was why he was waiting.

'Does Tuan Cooper go, Tuan?'

'No.'

'There will be a misfortune.'

For a moment the words conveyed nothing to his lassitude.

But only for a moment. He sat up in his chair and looked at the boy. He was all attention.

'What do you mean by that?'

'Tuan Cooper is not behaving rightly with Abas.'

Mr Warburton shrugged his shoulders. How should a man like Cooper know how to treat servants? Mr Warburton knew the type: he would be grossly familiar with them at one moment and rude and inconsiderate the next.

'Let Abas go back to his family.'

'Tuan Cooper holds back his wages so that he may not run away. He has paid him nothing for three months. I tell him to be patient. But he is angry, he will not listen to reason. If the Tuan continues to use him ill there will be a misfortune.'

'You were right to tell me.'

The fool! Did he know so little of the Malays as to think he could safely injure them? It would serve him damned well right if he got a kris in his back. A kris. Mr Warburton's heart seemed on a sudden to miss a beat. He had only to let things take their course and one fine day he would be rid of Cooper. He smiled faintly as the phrase, a masterly inactivity, crossed his mind. And now his heart beat a little quicker, for he saw the man he hated lying on his face in a pathway of the jungle with a knife in his back. A fit end for the cad and the bully. Mr Warburton sighed. It was his duty to warn him, and of course he must do it. He wrote a brief and formal note to Cooper asking him to come to the Fort at once.

In ten minutes Cooper stood before him. They had not spoken to one another since the day when Mr Warburton had nearly struck him. He did not now ask him to sit down.

'Did you wish to see me?' asked Cooper.

He was untidy and none too clean. His face and hands were covered with little red blotches where mosquitoes had bitten him and he had scratched himself till the blood came. His long, thin face bore a sullen look.

'I understand that you are again having trouble with your servants. Abas, my head-boy's nephew, complains that you have held back his wages for three months. I consider it a most arbitrary proceeding. The lad wishes to leave you, and I certainly do not blame him. I must insist on your paying what is due to him.'

'I don't choose that he should leave me. I am holding back his wages as a pledge of his good behaviour.'

'You do not know the Malay character. The Malays are very sensitive to injury and ridicule. They are passionate and revengeful. It is my duty to warn you that if you drive this boy beyond a certain point you run a great risk.'

Cooper gave a contemptuous chuckle.

'What do you think he'll do?'

'I think he'll kill you.'

'Why should you mind?'

'Oh, I wouldn't,' replied Mr Warburton, with a faint laugh. 'I should bear it with the utmost fortitude. But I feel the official obligation to give you a proper warning.'

'Do you think I'm afraid of a damned nigger?'

'It's a matter of entire indifference to me.'

'Well, let me tell you this, I know how to take care of myself; that boy Abas is a dirty, thieving rascal, and if he tries any monkey tricks on me, by God, I'll wring his bloody neck.'

'That was all I wished to say to you,' said Mr Warburton. 'Good evening.'

Mr Warburton gave him a little nod of dismissal. Cooper flushed, did not for a moment know what to say or do, turned on his heel, and stumbled out of the room. Mr Warburton watched him go with an icy smile on his lips. He had done his duty. But what would he have thought had he known that when Cooper got back to his bungalow, so silent and cheerless, he threw himself down on his bed and in his bitter loneliness on a sudden lost all control of himself? Painful sobs tore his chest and heavy tears rolled down his thin cheeks.

After this Mr Warburton seldom saw Cooper, and never spoke to him. He read his *Times* every morning, did his work at the office, took his exercise, dressed for dinner, dined, and sat by the river smoking his cheroot. If by chance he ran across Cooper he cut him dead. Each, though never for a moment unconscious of the propinquity, acted as though the other did not exist. Time did nothing to assuage their animosity. They watched one another's actions and each knew what the other did. Though Mr Warburton had been a keen shot in his youth, with age he had acquired a distaste for killing the wild things of the jungle, but on Sundays and holidays Cooper went out with his gun: if he got something it was a triumph over Mr Warburton; if not, Mr Warburton shrugged his shoulders and chuckled. These counter-jumpers trying to be sportsmen! Christmas was a bad time for both of them: they ate their dinners alone, each in his own quarters, and they got deliberately drunk. They were the only white men within two hundred miles and they lived within shouting distance of each other. At the beginning of the year Cooper went down with fever, and when Mr Warburton caught sight of him again he was surprised to see how thin he had grown. He looked ill and worn. The solitude, so much more unnatural because it was due to no necessity, was getting on his nerves. It was getting on Mr Warburton's too, and often he could not sleep at night. He lay awake brooding. Cooper was drinking heavily and surely the breaking point was near; but in his dealings with the natives he took care to do nothing that might expose him to his chief's rebuke. They fought a grim and silent battle with one another. It was a test of endurance. The months passed, and neither gave sign of weakening. They were like men dwelling in regions of eternal night, and their souls were oppressed with the knowledge that never would the day dawn for them. It looked as though their lives would continue for ever in this dull and hideous monotony of hatred.

And when at last the inevitable happened it came upon Mr Warburton with all the shock of the unexpected. Cooper accused the boy Abas of stealing some of his clothes, and when the boy denied the theft took him by the scruff of the neck and kicked him down the steps of the bungalow. The boy demanded his wages and Cooper flung at his head every word of abuse he knew. If he saw him in the compound in an hour he would hand him over to the police. Next morning the boy waylaid him outside the Fort when he was walking over to his office, and again demanded his wages. Cooper struck him in the face with his clenched fist. The boy fell to the ground and got up with blood streaming from his nose.

Cooper walked on and set about his work. But he could not attend to it. The blow had calmed his irritation, and he knew that he had gone too far. He was worried. He felt ill, miserable, and discouraged. In the adjoining office sat Mr Warburton, and his impulse was to go and tell him what he had done; he made a movement in his chair, but he knew with what icy scorn he would listen to the story. He could see his patronizing smile. For a moment he had an uneasy fear of what Abas might do. Warburton had warned him all right. He sighed. What a fool he had been! But he shrugged his shoulders impatiently. He did not care; a fat lot he had to live for. It was all Warburton's fault; if he hadn't put his back up nothing like this would have happened. Warburton had made life a hell for him from the start. The snob. But they were all like that: it was because he was a Colonial. It was a damned shame that he had never got his commission in the war; he was as good as anyone else. They were a lot of dirty snobs. He was damned if he was going to knuckle under now. Of course Warburton would hear of what had happened; the old devil knew everything. He wasn't afraid. He wasn't afraid of any Malay in Borneo, and Warburton could go to blazes.

He was right in thinking that Mr Warburton would know what had happened. His head-boy told him when he went in to tiffin.

'Where is your nephew now?'

'I do not know, Tuan. He has gone.'

Mr Warburton remained silent. After luncheon as a rule he slept a little, but today he found himself very wide awake. His eyes involuntarily sought the bungalow where Cooper was now resting.

The idiot! Hesitation for a little was in Mr Warburton's mind. Did the man know in what peril he was? He supposed he ought to send for him. But each time he had tried to reason with Cooper, Cooper had insulted him. Anger, furious anger welled up suddenly in Mr Warburton's heart, so that the veins on his temples stood out and he clenched his fists. The cad had had his warning. Now let him take what was coming to him. It was no business of his, and if anything happened it was not his fault. But perhaps they would wish in Kuala Solor that they had taken his advice and transferred Cooper to another station.

He was strangely restless that night. After dinner he walked up and down the veranda. When the boy went away to his own quarters, Mr Warburton asked him whether anything had been seen of Abas.

'No, Tuan, I think maybe he has gone to the village of his mother's brother.'

Mr Warburton gave him a sharp glance, but the boy was looking down, and their eyes did not meet. Mr Warburton went down to the river and sat in his arbour. But peace was denied him. The river flowed ominously silent. It was like a great serpent gliding with sluggish movement towards the sea. And the trees of the jungle over the water were heavy with a breathless menace. No bird sang. No breeze ruffled the leaves of the cassias. All around him it seemed as though something waited.

He walked across the garden to the road. He had Cooper's bungalow in full view from there. There was a light in his sitting-room, and across the road floated the sound of rag-time. Cooper was playing his gramophone. Mr Warburton shuddered; he had never got over his instinctive dislike of that instrument. But for that he would have gone over and spoken to Cooper. He turned and went back to his own house. He read late into the night, and at last he slept. But he did not sleep very long, he had terrible dreams, and he seemed to be awakened by a cry. Of course that was a dream too, for no cry – from the bungalow for instance – could be heard in his room. He lay awake till dawn. Then he heard hurried steps and the sound of voices, his head-boy burst suddenly into the room without his fez, and Mr Warburton's heart stood still.

'Tuan, Tuan.'

Mr Warburton jumped out of bed.

'I'll come at once.'

He put on his slippers, and in his sarong and pyjama-jacket walked across his compound and into Cooper's. Cooper was lying in bed, with his mouth open, and a kris sticking in his heart. He had been killed in his sleep. Mr Warburton started, but not because he had not expected to see just such a sight, he started because he felt in himself a sudden glow of exultation. A great burden had been lifted from his shoulders.

Cooper was quite cold. Mr Warburton took the kris out of the wound, it had been thrust in with such force that he had to use an effort to get it out, and looked at it. He recognized it. It was a kris that a dealer had offered him some weeks before, and which he knew Cooper had bought.

'Where is Abas?' he asked sternly.

'Abas is at the village of his mother's brother.'

The sergeant of the native police was standing at the foot of the bed.

'Take two men and go to the village and arrest him.'

Mr Warburton did what was immediately necessary. With set face he gave orders. His words were short and peremptory. Then he went back to the Fort. He shaved and had his bath, dressed, and went into the dining-room. By the side of his plate *The Times* in its wrapper lay waiting for him. He helped himself to some fruit. The head-boy poured out his tea while the second handed him a dish of eggs. Mr Warburton ate with a good appetite. The head-boy waited.

'What is it?' asked Mr Warburton.

'Tuan, Abas, my nephew, was in the house of his mother's

brother all night. It can be proved. His uncle will swear that he did not leave the kampong.'

Mr Warburton turned upon him with a frown.

'Tuan Cooper was killed by Abas. You know it as well as I know it. Justice must be done.'

'Tuan, you would not hang him?'

Mr Warburton hesitated an instant, and though his voice remained set and stern a change came into his eyes. It was a flicker which the Malay was quick to notice and across his own eyes flashed an answering look of understanding.

'The provocation was very great. Abas will be sentenced to a term of imprisonment.' There was a pause while Mr Warburton helped himself to marmalade. 'When he has served a part of his sentence in prison I will take him into this house as a boy. You can train him in his duties. I have no doubt that in the house of Tuan Cooper he got into bad habits.'

'Shall Abas give himself up, Tuan?'

'It would be wise of him.'

The boy withdrew. Mr Warburton took his *Times* and neatly slit the wrapper. He loved to unfold the heavy, rustling pages. The morning, so fresh and cool, was delicious and for a moment his eyes wandered out over the garden with a friendly glance. A great weight had been lifted from his mind. He turned to the columns in which were announced the births, deaths, and marriages. That was what he always looked at first. A name he knew caught his attention. Lady Ormskirk had had a son at last. By George, how pleased the old dowager must be! He would write her a note of congratulation by the next mail.

Abas would make a very good house-boy.

That fool Cooper!

THE PORTRAIT OF A GENTLEMAN

I ARRIVED in Seoul towards evening and after dinner, tired by the long railway journey from Peking, to stretch my cramped legs I went for a walk. I wandered at random along a narrow and busy street. The Koreans in their long white gowns and their little white top-hats were amusing to look at and the open shops displayed wares that arrested my foreign eyes. Presently I came to a second-hand bookseller's and catching sight of shelves filled with English books went in to have a look at them. I glanced at the titles and my heart sank. They were commentaries on the Old Testament, treatises on the Epistles of St Paul, sermons and lives of divines doubtless eminent, but whose names were unfamiliar to me; I am an ignorant person. I supposed that this was the library of some missionary whom death had claimed in the midst of his labours and whose books then had been purchased by a Japanese bookseller. The Japanese are astute, but I could not imagine who in Seoul would be found to buy a work in three volumes on the Epistle to the Corinthians. But as I was turning away, between volume two and volume three of this treatise I noticed a little book bound in paper. I do not know what induced me to take it out. It was called *The Complete Poker Player* and its cover was illustrated with a hand holding four aces. I looked at the title-page. The author was Mr John Blackbridge, actuary and counseller-at-law, and the preface was dated 1879. I wondered how this work happened to be among the books of a deceased missionary and I looked in one or two of them to see if I could find his name. Perhaps it was there only by accident. It may be that it was the entire library of a stranded gambler and had found its way to those shelves when his effects were sold to pay his hotel bill. But I preferred to think that it was indeed the property of the missionary and that when he was weary of reading divinity he rested his mind by the perusal of these lively pages. Perhaps somewhere in Korea, at night and alone in his mission-house, he dealt innumerable poker hands in order to see for himself whether you could really only get a straight flush once in sixty-five thousand hands. But the owner of the shop was looking at me with disfavour so I turned to him and asked the price of the book. He gave it a contemptuous glance and told me I could have it for twenty sen. I put it in my pocket.

I do not remember that for so small a sum I have ever purchased better entertainment. For Mr John Blackbridge in these pages of his did a thing no writer can do who deliberately tries to, but that, if done unconsciously, gives a book a rare and precious savour; he painted a complete portrait of himself. He stands before the reader so vividly that I was convinced that a wood-cut of him figured as a frontispiece and I was surprised to discover, on looking at the book again the other day, that there was nothing of the kind. I see him very distinctly as a man of middle-age, in a black frockcoat and a chimney-pot hat, wearing a black satin stock; he is clean-shaven and his jaw is square; his lips are thin and his eyes wary; his face is sallow and somewhat wrinkled. It is a countenance not without severity, but when he tells a story or makes one of his dry jokes his eyes light up and his smile is winning. He enjoyed his bottle of Burgundy, but I cannot believe that he ever drank enough to confuse his excellent faculties. He was just rather than merciful at the card-table and he was prepared to punish presumption with rigour. He had few illusions, for here are some of the things that life had taught him: 'Men hate those whom they have injured; men love those whom they have benefited; men naturally avoid their benefactors; men are universally actuated by self-interest; gratitude is a lively sense of expected benefits; promises are never forgotten by those to whom they are made, usually by those who make them.'

It may be presumed that he was a Southerner, for while speaking of Jack Pots, which he describes as a frivolous attempt to make the game more interesting, he remarks that they are not popular in the South. 'This last fact,' he says, 'contains much promise, because the South is the conservative portion of the country, and may be relied on as the last resort of good sense in social matters. The revolutionary Kossuth made no progress below Richmond; neither Spiritualism, nor Free Love, nor Communism, has ever been received with the least favour by the Southern mind; and it is for this reason that we greatly respect the Southern verdict upon the Jack Pot.' It was in his day an innovation and he condemned it. 'The time has arrived when all additions to the present standard combinations in Draw Poker must be worthless; the game being complete. The Jack Pot,' he says, 'was invented (in Toledo, Ohio) by reckless players to compensate losses incurred by playing against cautious players; and the principle is the same as if a party should play whist for stakes, and all be obliged every few minutes to stop, and purchase tickets in a lottery; or raffle for a turkey; or share a deal in Keno.'

Poker is a game for gentlemen (he does not hesitate to make frequent use of this abused word; he lived in a day when to be a gentleman had its obligations but also its privileges) and a straight flush is to be respected, not because you make money on it ('I have never seen anyone make much money upon a straight flush,' he says) but 'because it prevents any hand from being *absolutely* the winning hand, and thus relieves gentlemen from the necessity of betting on a certainty. Without the use of straights, and hence without the use of a straight flush, four aces would be a certainty and no gentleman could do more than *call* on them.' This, I confess, catches me on the raw, for once in my life I had a straight flush, and bet on it till I was called.

Mr John Blackbridge had personal dignity, rectitude, humour, and common sense. 'The amusements of mankind,' he says, 'have not as yet received proper recognition at the hands of the makers of the civil law, and of the unwritten social law,' and he had no patience with the persons who condemn the most agreeable pastime that has been invented, namely gambling, because risk is attached to it. Every transaction in life is a risk, he truly observes, and involves the question of loss and gain. 'To retire to rest at night is a practice that is fortified by countless precedents, and it is generally regarded as prudent and necessary. Yet it is surrounded by risks of every kind.' He enumerates them and finally sums up his argument with these reasonable words: 'If social circles welcome the banker and merchant who live by taking fair risks for the sake of profit, there is no apparent reason why they should not at least tolerate the man who at times employs himself in giving and taking fair risks for the sake of amusement.' But here his good sense is obvious. 'Twenty years of experience in the city of New York, both professionally (you must not forget that he is an actuary and counsellor-at-law) and as a student of social life, satisfy me that the average American gentleman in a large city has not over three thousand dollars a year to spend upon amusements. Will it be fair to devote more than one-third of this fund to cards? I do not think that anyone will say that one-third is not ample allowance for a single amusement. Given, therefore, a thousand dollars a year for the purpose of playing Draw Poker, what should be the limit of the stakes, in order that the average American gentleman may play the game with a contented mind, and with the certainty not only that he can pay his losses, but that his winnings will be paid to him?' Mr Blackbridge has no doubt that the answer is two dollars and a half. 'The game of Poker should be intellectual and not emotional; and it is impossible to exclude the emotions from it, if the stakes are so high that the question of loss and gain penetrates to the feelings.' From this quotation it may be seen that Mr Blackbridge looked upon poker as only on the side a game of chance. He considered that it needed as much force of character, mental ability, power of decision, and insight into motive to play poker as to govern a country or to lead an army, and I have an idea that on the whole he would have thought it a more sensible use of a man's faculties.

I am tempted to quote interminably, for Mr Blackbridge seldom writes a sentence that is other than characteristic, and his language is excellent; it is dignified as befits his subject and his condition (he does not forget that he is a gentleman), measured, clear, and pointed. His phrase takes an ample sweep when he treats of mankind and its foibles, but he can be as direct and simple as you please. Could anything be better than this terse but adequate description of a card-sharper? 'He was a very good-looking man of about forty years of age, having the appearance of one who had been leading a temperate and thoughtful life.' But I will content myself with giving a few of his aphorisms and wise saws chosen almost at random from the wealth of his book.

'Let your chips talk for you. A silent player is so far forth, a mystery; and a mystery is always feared.'

'In this game never do anything that you are not compelled to; while cheerfully responding to your obligations.'

'At Draw Poker all statements not called for by the laws of the game, or supported by ocular demonstration, may be set down as fictitious; designed to enliven the path of truth throughout the game, as flowers in summer enliven the margins of the highway.'

'Lost money is never recovered. After losing you may win, but the losing does not bring the winning.'

'No gentleman will ever play any game of cards with the design of habitually winning and never losing.'

'A gentleman is always willing to pay a fair price for recreation and amusement.'

'. . . that habit of mind which continually leads us to undervalue the mental force of other men, while we continually overvalue their good luck.'

'The injury done to your capital by a loss is never compensated by the benefit done to your capital by a gain of the same amount.'

'Players usually straddle when they are in bad luck, upon the principle that bad play and bad luck united will win. A slight degree of intoxication aids to perfect this intellectual deduction.'

'Euchre is a contemptible game.'

'The lower cards as well as the lower classes are only useful in combination or in excess, and cannot be depended upon under any other circumstances.'

'It is a hard matter to hold four Aces as steadily as a pair, but the table will bear their weight with as much equanimity as a pair of deuces.'

Of good luck and bad luck: 'To feel emotions over such incidents is unworthy of a man; and it is much more unworthy to express them. But no words need be wasted over practices which all men despise in others; and, in their reflecting moments, lament in themselves.'

'Endorsing for your friends is a bad habit, but it is nothing to playing Poker on credit. ... Debit and credit ought never to interfere with the fine intellectual calculations of this game.'

There is a grand ring in his remarks on the player who has trained his intellect to bring logic to bear upon the principles and phenomena of the game. 'He will thus feel a constant sense of security amid all possible fluctuations that occur, and he will also abstain from pressing an ignorant or an intellectually weak opponent, beyond what may be necessary either for the purpose of playing the game correctly, or of punishing presumption.'

I leave Mr John Blackbridge with this last word and I can hear him saying it gently, but with a tolerant smile:

'For we must take human nature as it is.'

RAW MATERIAL

I HAVE long had in mind a novel in which a card-sharper was the principal character; and, going up and down the world, I have kept my eyes open for members of this profession. Because the idea is prevalent that it is a slightly dishonourable one the persons who follow it do not openly acknowledge the fact. Their reticence is such that it is often not till you have become quite closely acquainted with them, or even have played cards with them two or three times, that you discover in what fashion they earn their living. But even then they have a disinclination to enlarge upon the mysteries of their craft. They have a weakness for passing themselves off for cavalrymen, commercial agents, or landed proprietors. This snobbish attitude makes them the most difficult class in the world for the novelist to study. It has been my good fortune to meet a number of these gentlemen, and though I have found them affable, obliging, and debonair, I have no sooner hinted, however discreetly, at my curiosity (after all purely professional) in the technique of their calling than they have grown shy and uncommunicative. An airy reference on my part to stacking the cards has made them assume immediately the appearance of a clam. I am not easily discouraged, and learning by experience that I could hope for no good results from a direct method, I have adopted the oblique. I have been childlike with them and bland. I have found that they gave me their attention and even their sympathy. Though they confessed honestly that they had never read a word I had written they were interested by the fact that I was a writer. I suppose they felt obscurely that I too followed a calling that the Philistine regarded without indulgence. But I have been forced to gather my facts by a bold surmise. It has needed patience and industry.

It may be imagined with what enthusiasm I made the acquaintance a little while ago of two gentlemen who seemed likely to add appreciably to my small store of information. I was travelling from Haiphong on a French liner going East, and they joined the ship at Hong-Kong. They had gone there for the races and were now on their way back to Shanghai. I was going there too, and thence to Peking. I soon learned that they had come from New York for a trip, were bound for Peking also, and by a happy coincidence meant to return to America in the ship in which I had myself booked a passage. I was naturally attracted to them, for they were pleasant fellows, but it was not till a fellow-passenger warned me that they were professional gamblers that I settled down to complete enjoyment of their acquaintance. I had no hope that they would ever discuss with frankness their interesting occupation, but I expected from a hint here, from a casual remark there, to learn some very useful things.

One – Campbell was his name – was a man in the late thirties, small, but so well built as not to look short, slender, with large, melancholy eyes and beautiful hands. But for a premature baldness he would have been more than commonly good-looking. He was neatly dressed. He spoke slowly, in a low voice, and his movements were deliberate. The other was made on another pattern. He was a big, burly man with a red face and crisp black hair, of powerful appearance, strong in the arm and pugnacious. His name was Peterson.

The merits of the combination were obvious. The elegant, exquisite Campbell had the subtle brain, the knowledge of character, and the deft hands; but the hazards of the card-sharper's life are many, and when it came to a scrap Peterson's ready fist must often have proved invaluable. I do not know how it spread through the ship so quickly that a blow of Peterson's would stretch any man out. But during the short voyage from Hong-Kong to Shanghai they never even suggested a game of cards. Perhaps they had done well during the race-week and felt entitled to a holiday. They were certainly enjoying the advantages of not living for the time in a dry country and I do not think I do them an injustice if I say that for the most part they were far from sober. Each one talked little of himself but willingly of the other. Campbell informed me that Peterson was one of the most distinguished mining engineers in New York and Peterson assured me that Campbell was an eminent banker. He said that his wealth was fabulous. And who was I not to accept ingenuously all that was told me? But I thought it negligent of Campbell not to wear jewellery of a more expensive character. It seemed to me that to use a silver cigarette case was rather careless.

I stayed but a day in Shanghai, and though I met the pair again in Peking I was then so much engaged that I saw little of them. I thought it a little odd that Campbell should spend his entire time in the Hotel. I do not think he even went to see the Temple of Heaven. But I could quite understand that from his point of view Peking was unsatisfactory and I was not surprised when the pair returned to Shanghai, where, I knew the wealthy merchants played for big money. I met them again in the ship that was to take us across the Pacific and I could not but sympathize with my friends when I saw that the passengers were little inclined to gamble. There were no rich people among them. It was a dull crowd. Campbell indeed suggested a game of poker, but no one would play more than twenty-dollar table stakes, and Peterson, evidently not thinking it worth while, would not join. Although we played afternoon and evening through the journey he sat down with us only on the last day. I suppose he thought he might just as well make his bar chits, and this he did very satisfactorily in a single sitting. But Campbell evidently loved the game for itself. Of course it is only if you have a passion for the business by which you earn your living that you can make a success of it. The stakes were nothing to him and he played all day and every day. It fascinated me to see the way in which he dealt the cards, very slowly, with his delicate hands. His eyes seemed to bore through the back of each one. He drank heavily, but remained quiet and self-controlled. His face was expressionless. I judged him to be a perfect card-player and I wished that I could see him at work. It increased my esteem for him to see that he could take what was only a relaxation so seriously.

I parted with the pair at Victoria and concluded that I should never see them again. I set about sorting my impressions and made notes of the various points that I thought would prove useful.

When I arrived in New York I found an invitation to luncheon at the Ritz with an old friend of mine. When I went she said to me:

'It's quite a small party. A man is coming whom I think you'll like. He's a prominent banker; he's bringing a friend with him.'

The words were hardly out of her mouth when I saw coming up to us Campbell and Peterson. The truth flashed across me: Campbell really was an opulent banker; Peterson really was a distinguished engineer; they were not card-sharpers at all. I flatter myself I kept my face, but as I blandly shook hands with them I muttered under my breath furiously:

'Impostors!'

STRAIGHT FLUSH

I AM not a bad sailor and when under stress of weather the game broke up I did not go below. We were in the habit of playing poker into the small hours, a mild game that could hurt nobody, but it had been blowing all day and with nightfall the wind strengthened to half a gale. One or two of our bunch admitted that they felt none too comfortable and one or two others played with unwonted detachment. But even if you are not sick dirty weather at sea is an unpleasant thing. I hate the fool who tells you he loves a storm and tramping the deck lustily vows that it can never be too rough for him. When the woodwork groans and creaks, glasses crash to the floor and you lurch in your chair as the ship heels over, when the wind howls and the waves thunder against the side, I very much prefer dry land. I think no one was sorry when one of the players said he had had enough, and the last round of jack pots was agreed to without demur. I remained alone in the smoking-room, for I knew I should not easily get to sleep in that racket and I could not read in bed with any comfort when the North Pacific kept dashing itself against my port-holes. I shuffled together the two packs we had been playing with and set out a complicated patience.

I had been playing about ten minutes when the door was opened with a blast of wind that sent my cards flying, and two passengers, rather breathless, slipped into the smoking-room. We were not a full ship and we were ten days out from Hong-Kong, so that I had had time to become acquainted with pretty well everyone on board. I had spoken on several occasions to the pair who now entered, and seeing me by myself they came over to my table.

They were very old men, both of them. That perhaps was what had brought them together, for they had first met when they got on board at Hong-Kong, and now you saw them sitting together in the smoking-room most of the day, not talking very much, but just comfortable to be side by side, with a bottle of Vichy water between them. They were very rich old men too and that was a bond between them. The rich feel at ease in one another's company. They know that money means merit. Their experience of the poor is that they always want something. It is true that the poor admire the rich and it is pleasant to be admired, but they envy them as well and this prevents their admiration from being quite candid. Mr Rosenbaum was a little hunched-up Jew, very frail in clothes that looked too big for him, and he gave you the impression of hanging on to mortality only by a hair. His ancient, emaciated body looked as though it were already attacked by the corruption of the grave. The only expression his face ever bore was one of cunning, but it was purely habitual, the result of ever so many years astuteness; he was a kindly, friendly person, very free with his drinks and cigars, and his charity was world-famous. The other was called Donaldson. He was a Scot, but had gone to California as a little boy and made a great deal of money mining. He was short and stout, with a red, clean-shaven, shiny face and no hair but a sickle of silver above his neck, and very gentle eyes. Whatever force he had had to make his way in the world had been worn away by the years and he was now a picture of mild beneficence.

'I thought you'd turned in long ago,' I remarked.

'I should have,' returned the Scot, 'only Mr Rosenbaum kept me up talking of old times.'

'What's the good of going to bed when you can't sleep?' said Mr Rosenbaum.

'Walk ten times round the deck with me tomorrow morning and you'll sleep all right.'

'I've never taken any exercise in my life and I'm not going to begin now.'

'That's foolishness. You'd be twice the man you are now if you'd taken exercise. Look at me. You'd never think I was seventy-nine, would you.'

Mr Rosenbaum looked critically at Mr Donaldson.

'No, I wouldn't. You're very well preserved. You look younger than me and I'm only seventy-six. But then I never had a chance to take care of myself.'

At that moment the steward came up.

'The bar's just going to close, gentlemen. Is there anything I can get you?'

'It's a stormy night,' said Mr Rosenbaum. 'Let's have a bottle of champagne.'

'Small Vichy for me,' said Mr Donaldson.

'Oh, very well, small Vichy for me too.'

The steward went away.

'But mind you,' continued Mr Rosenbaum testily, 'I wouldn't have done without the things you've done without, not for all the money in the world.'

Mr Donaldson gave me his gentle smile.

'Mr Rosenbaum can't get over it because I've never touched a card nor a drop of alcohol for fifty-seven years.'

'Now I ask you, what sort of a life is that?'

'I was a very heavy drinker when I was a young fellow and a desperate gambler, but I had a very terrible experience. It was a lesson to me and I took it.'

'Tell him about it,' said Mr Rosenbaum. 'He's an author. He'll write it up and perhaps he'll be able to make his passage money.'

'It's not a story I like telling very much even now. I'll make it as short as I can. Me and three others had staked out a claim, friends all of us, and the oldest wasn't twenty-five; there was me and my partner and a couple of brothers, McDermott their name was, but they were more like friends than brothers. What was one's was the other's, and one wouldn't go into town without the other went too, and they were always laughing and joking together. A fine clean pair of boys, over six feet high both of them, and handsome. We were a wild bunch and we had pretty good luck on the whole and when we made money we didn't hesitate to spend it. Well, one night we'd all been drinking very heavily and we started a poker game. I guess we were a good deal drunker than we realized. Anyhow suddenly a row started between the McDermotts. One of them accused the other of cheating. "You take that back," cried Jamie. "I'll see you in hell first," says Eddie. And before me and my partner could do anything Jamie had pulled out his gun and shot his brother dead.'

The ship gave a huge roll and we all clung to our seats. In the steward's pantry there was a great clatter as bottles and glasses slid along a shelf. It was strange to hear that grim little story told by that mild old man. It was a story of another age and you could hardly believe that this fat, red-faced little fellow, with his silver fringe of hair, in a dinner jacket, two large pearls in his shirt-front, had really taken part in it.

'What happened then?' I asked.

'We sobered up pretty quick. At first Jamie couldn't believe Eddie was dead. He took him in his arms and kept calling him. "Eddie," he says, "wake up, old boy, wake up." He cried all night and next day we rode in with him to town, forty miles it was, me on one side of him and my partner on the other, and handed him over to the sheriff. I was crying too when we shook hands with him and said good-bye. I told my partner I'd never touch a card again or drink as long as I lived, and I never have, and I never will.'

Mr Donaldson looked down, and his lips were trembling. He seemed to see again that scene of long ago. There was one thing I should have liked to ask him about, but he was evidently so much moved I did not like to. They seem not to have hesitated, his partner and himself, but delivered up this wretched boy to justice as though it were the most natural thing in the world. It suggested that even in those rough, wild men the respect for the law had somehow the force of an instinct. A little shiver ran through me. Mr Donaldson emptied his glass of Vichy and with a curt good night left us.

'The old fellow's getting a bit childish,' said Mr Rosenbaum. 'I don't believe he was ever very bright.'

'Well, apparently he was bright enough to make an awful lot of money.'

'But how? In those days in California you didn't want brains to make money, you only wanted luck. I know what I'm talking about. Johannesburg was the place where you had to have your wits about you. Joburg in the eighties. It was grand. We were a tough lot of guys, I can tell you. It was each for himself and the devil take the hindmost.'

He took a meditative sip of his Vichy.

'You talk of your cricket and baseball, your golf and tennis and football, you can have them, they're all very well for boys; is it a reasonable thing, I ask you, for a grown man to run about and hit a ball? Poker's the only game fit for a grown man. Then your hand is against every man and every man's hand is against yours. Team-work? Who ever made a fortune by team-work? There's only one way to make a fortune and that's to down the fellow who's up against you.'

'I didn't know you were a poker player,' I interrupted. 'Why don't you take a hand one evening?'

'I don't play any more. I've given it up too, but for the only reason a man should. I can't see myself giving it up because a friend of mine was unlucky enough to get killed. Anyway a man who's damn fool enough to get killed isn't worth having as a friend. But in the old days! If you wanted to know what poker was you ought to have been in South Africa then. It was the biggest game I've ever seen. And they were fine players; there wasn't a crooked dodge they weren't up to. It was grand. Just to give you an example, one night I was playing with some of the biggest men in Johannesburg and I was called away. There was a couple of thousand pounds in the pot! "Deal me a hand, I won't keep you waiting," I said. "All right," they said, "don't hurry." Well, I wasn't gone more than a minute. When I came back I picked up my cards and saw I'd got a straight flush to the queen. I didn't say a word, I just threw in my hand. I knew my company. And do you know, I was wrong.'

'What do you mean? I don't understand.'

'It was a perfectly straight deal and the pot was won on three sevens. But how could I tell that? Naturally I thought someone else had a straight flush to the king. It looked to me just the sort of hand I might lose a hundred thousand pounds on.'

'Too bad,' I said.

'I very nearly had a stroke. And it was on account of another pat straight flush that I gave up playing poker. I've only had about five in my life.'

'I believe the chances are nearly sixty-six thousand to one against.'

'In San Francisco it was, the year before last. I'd been playing in poor luck all the evening. I hadn't lost much money because I never had a chance to play. I'd hardly had a pair and if I got a pair I couldn't improve. Then I got a hand just as bad as the others and I didn't come in. The man next to me wasn't playing either and I showed him my hand. "That's the kind of thing I've been getting all the evening." I said. "How can anyone be expected to play with cards like that?" "Well, I don't know what more you want," he said, as he looked at them. "Most of us would be prepared to come in on a straight flush." "What's that," I cried. I was trembling like a leaf. I looked at the cards again. I thought I had two or three little hearts and two or three little diamonds. It was a straight flush in hearts all right and I hadn't seen it. My eyes, it was. I knew what it meant. Old age. I don't cry much. I'm not that sort of man. But I couldn't help it then. I tried to control myself, but the tears just rolled down my cheeks. Then I got up. "I'm through, gentlemen," I said. "When a man's eyes are so dim that he can't see a straight flush when it's dealt him he has no business to play poker. Nature's given me a hint and I'm taking it. I'll never play poker again as long as I live." I cashed in my chips, all but one, and I left the house. I've never played since.'

Mr Rosenbaum took a chip out of his waistcoat pocket and showed it to me.

'I kept this as a souvenir. I always carry it about with me. I'm a sentimental old fool, I know that, but, you see, poker was the only thing I cared for. Now I've only got one thing left.'

'What is that?' I asked.

A smile flickered across his cunning little face and behind his thick glasses his rheumy eyes twinkled with ironic glee. He looked incredibly astute and malicious. He gave the thin, high-pitched cackle of an old man amused and answered with a single word 'Philanthropy'.

THE END OF THE FLIGHT

I SHOOK hands with the skipper and he wished me luck. Then I went down to the lower deck crowded with passengers, Malays, Chinese, and Dyaks, and made my way to the ladder. Looking over the ship's side I saw that my luggage was already in the boat. It was a large, clumsy-looking craft, with a great square sail of bamboo matting, and it was crammed full of gesticulating natives. I scrambled in and a place was made for me. We were about three miles from the shore and a stiff breeze was blowing. As we drew near I saw that the coconut trees in a green abundance grew to the water's edge, and among them I saw the brown roofs of the village. A Chinese who spoke English pointed out to me a white bungalow as the residence of the District Officer. Though he did not know it, it was with him that I was going to stay. I had a letter of introduction to him in my pocket.

I felt somewhat forlorn when I landed and my bags were set down beside me on the glistening beach. This was a remote spot to find myself in, this little town on the north coast of Borneo, and I felt a trifle shy at the thought of presenting myself to a total stranger with the announcement that I was going to sleep under his roof, eat his food, and drink his whisky, till another boat came in to take me to the port for which I was bound.

But I might have spared myself these misgivings, for the moment I reached the bungalow and sent in my letter he came out, a sturdy, ruddy, jovial man, of thirty-five perhaps, and greeted me with heartiness. While he held my hand he shouted to a boy to bring drinks and to another to look after my luggage. He cut short my apologies.

'Good God, man, you have no idea how glad I am to see you. Don't think I'm doing anything for you in putting you up. The boot's on the other leg. And stay as long as you damned well like. Stay a year.'

I laughed. He put away his day's work, assuring me that he had nothing to do that could not wait till the morrow, and threw himself into a long chair. We talked and drank and talked. When the heat of the day wore off we went for a long tramp in the jungle and came back wet to the skin. A bath and a change were very grateful, and then we dined. I was tired out and though my host was plainly willing to go on talking straight through the night I was obliged to beg him to allow me to go to bed.

'All right, I'll just come along to your room and see everything's all right.'

It was a large room with verandas on two sides of it, sparsely furnished, but with a huge bed protected by mosquito netting.

'The bed is rather hard. Do you mind?'

'Not a bit. I shall sleep without rocking tonight.'

My host looked at the bed reflectively.

'It was a Dutchman who slept in it last. Do you want to hear a funny story?'

I wanted chiefly to go to bed, but he *was* my host, and being at times somewhat of a humorist myself I know that it is hard to have an amusing story to tell and find no listener.

'He came on the boat that brought you, on its last journey along the coast, he came into my office and asked where the dak bungalow was. I told him there wasn't one, but if he hadn't anywhere to go I didn't mind putting him up. He jumped at the invitation. I told him to have his kit sent along.

'"This is all I've got," he said.

'He held out a little shiny black grip. It seemed a bit scanty, but it was no business of mine, so I told him to go along to the bungalow and I'd come as soon as I was through with my work. While I was speaking the door of my office was opened and my clerk came in. The Dutchman had his back to the door and it may be that my clerk opened it a bit suddenly. Anyhow, the Dutchman gave a shout, he jumped about two feet into the air and whipped out a revolver.

'"What the hell are you doing?" I said.

'When he saw it was the clerk he collapsed. He leaned against the desk, panting, and upon my word he was shaking as though he'd got fever.

'"I beg your pardon," he said. "It's my nerves. My nerves are terrible."

'"It looks like it," I said.

'I was rather short with him. To tell you the truth I wished I hadn't asked him to stop with me. He didn't look as though he'd been drinking a lot and I wondered if he was some fellow the police were after. If he were, I said to myself, he could hardly be such a fool as to walk into the lion's den.

'"You'd better go and lie down," I said.

'He took himself off, and when I got back to my bungalow I

found him sitting quite quietly, but bolt upright, on the veranda. He'd had a bath and shaved and put on clean things and he looked fairly presentable.

'"Why are you sitting in the middle of the place like that?" I asked him. "You'll be much more comfortable in one of the long chairs."

'"I prefer to sit up," he said.

'Queer, I thought. But if a man in this heat would rather sit up than lie down it's his own lookout. He wasn't much to look at, tallish and heavily built, with a square head and close-cropped bristly hair. I should think he was about forty. The thing that chiefly struck me about him was his expression. There was a look in his eyes, blue eyes they were and rather small, that beat me altogether; and his face sagged as it were; it gave you the feeling he was going to cry. He had a way of looking quickly over his left shoulder as though he thought he heard something. By God, he was nervous. But we had a couple of drinks and he began to talk. He spoke English very well; except for a slight accent you'd never have known that he was a foreigner, and I'm bound to admit he was a good talker. He'd been everywhere and he'd read any amount. It was a treat to listen to him.

'We had three or four whiskies in the afternoon and a lot of gin pahits later on, so that when dinner came along we were by way of being rather hilarious and I'd come to the conclusion that he was a damned good fellow. Of course we had a lot of whisky at dinner and I happened to have a bottle of Benedictine, so we had some liqueurs afterwards. I can't help thinking we both got very tight.

'And at last he told me why he'd come. It was a rum story.'

My host stopped and looked at me with his mouth slightly open as though, remembering it now, he was struck again with its rumness.

'He came from Sumatra, the Dutchman, and he'd done something to an Achinese and the Achinese had sworn to kill him. At first he made light of it, but the fellow tried two or three times and it began to be rather a nuisance, so he thought he'd better go away for a bit. He went over to Batavia and made up his mind to have a good time. But when he'd been there a week he saw the fellow slinking along a wall. By God, he'd followed him. It looked as though he meant business. The Dutchman began to think it was getting beyond a joke and he thought the best thing he could do would be to skip off to Soerabaya. Well, he was strolling about there one day, you know how crowded the streets are, when he happened to turn round and saw the Achinese walking quite quietly just behind him. It gave him a turn. It would give anyone a turn.

'The Dutchman went straight back to his hotel, packed his things, and took the next boat to Singapore. Of course he put up at the Van Wyck, all the Dutch stay there, and one day when he was having a drink in the courtyard in front of the hotel, the Achinese walked in as bold as brass, looked at him for a minute, and walked out again. The Dutchman told me he was just paralysed. The fellow could have stuck his kris into him there and then and he wouldn't have been able to move a hand to defend himself. The Dutchman knew he was just biding his time, that damned native was going to kill him, he saw it in his eyes; and he went all to pieces.'

'But why didn't he go to the police?' I asked.

'I don't know. I expect it wasn't a thing he wanted the police to be mixed up in.'

'But what had he done to the man?'

'I don't know that either. He wouldn't tell me. But by the look he gave when I asked him, I expect it was something pretty rotten. I have an idea he knew he deserved whatever the Achinese could do.'

My host lit a cigarette.

'Go on,' I said.

'The skipper of the boat that runs between Singapore and Kuching lives at the Van Wyck between trips and the boat was starting at dawn. The Dutchman thought it a grand chance to give the fellow the slip; he left his luggage at the hotel and walked down to the ship with the skipper, as if he were just going to see him off, and stayed on her when she sailed. His nerves were all anyhow by then. He didn't care about anything but getting rid of the Achinese. He felt pretty safe at Kuching. He got a room at the rest-house and bought himself a couple of suits and some shirts in the Chinese shops. But he told me he couldn't sleep. He dreamt of that man and half a dozen times he awakened just as he thought a kris was being drawn across his throat. By God, I felt quite sorry for him. He just shook as he talked to me and his voice was hoarse with terror. That was the meaning of the look I had noticed. You remember, I told you he had a funny look on his face and I couldn't tell what it meant. Well, it was fear.

'And one day when he was in the club at Kuching he looked out of the window and saw the Achinese sitting there. Their eyes met. The Dutchman just crumpled up and fainted. When he came to, his first idea was to get out. Well, you know, there's not a hell of a lot of traffic at Kuching and this boat that brought you was the only one that gave him a chance to get away quickly. He got on her. He was positive the man was not on board.'

'But what made him come here?'

'Well, the old tramp stops at a dozen places on the coast and the Achinese couldn't possible guess he'd chosen this one because he only made up his mind to get off when he saw there was only one boat to take the passengers ashore, and there weren't more than a dozen people in it.

'"I'm safe here for a bit at all events," he said, "and if I can only be quiet for a while I shall get my nerve back."

'"Stay as long as you like," I said. "You're all right here, at all events till the boat comes along next month, and if you like we'll watch the people who come off."

'He was all over me. I could see what a relief it was to him.

'It was pretty late and I suggested to him that we should turn in. I took him to his room to see that it was all right. He locked the door of the bath-house and bolted the shutters, though I told him there was no risk, and when I left him I heard him lock the door I had just gone out of.

'Next morning when the boy brought me my tea I asked him if he'd called the Dutchman. He said he was just going to. I heard him knock and knock again. Funny, I thought. The boy hammered on the door, but there was no answer. I felt a little nervous, so I got up. I knocked too. We made enough noise to rouse the dead, but the Dutchman slept on. Then I broke down the door. The mosquito curtains were neatly tucked in round the bed. I pulled them apart. He was lying there on his back with his eyes wide open. He was as dead as mutton. A kris lay across his throat, and say I'm a liar if you like, but I swear to God it's true, there wasn't a wound about him anywhere. The room was empty.

'Funny, wasn't it?'

'Well, that all depends on your idea of humour,' I replied.

My host looked at me quickly.

'You don't mind sleeping in that bed, do you?'

'N-no. But I'd just as soon you'd told me the story tomorrow morning.'

A CASUAL AFFAIR

I AM telling this story in the first person, though I am in no way connected with it, because I do not want to pretend to the reader that I know more about it than I really do. The facts are as I state them, but the reasons for them I can only guess, and it may be that when the reader has read them he will think me wrong. No one can know for certain. But if you are interested in human nature there are few things more diverting than to consider the motives that have resulted in certain actions. It was only by chance that I heard anything of the unhappy circumstances at all. I was spending two or three days on an island on the north coast of Borneo, and the District Officer had very kindly offered to put me up. I had been roughing it for some time and I was glad enough to have a rest. The island had been at one time a place of some consequence, with a Governor of its own, but was so no longer; and now there was nothing much to be seen of its former importance except the imposing stone house in which the Governor had once lived and which now the District Officer, grumblingly because of its unnecessary size, inhabited. But it was a comfortable house to stay in, with an immense drawing-room, a dining-room large enough to seat forty people, and lofty, spacious bedrooms. It was shabby, because the government at Singapore very wisely spent as little money on it as possible; but I rather liked this, and the heavy official furniture gave it a sort of dull stateliness that was amusing. The garden was too large for the District Officer to keep up and it was a wild tangle of tropical vegetation. His name was Arthur Low; he was a quiet, smallish man in the later thirties, married, with two young children. The Lows had not tried to make themselves at home in this great place, but camped there, like refugees from a stricken area, and looked forward to the time when they would be moved to some other post where they could settle down in surroundings more familiar to them.

I took a fancy to them at once. The D.O. had an easy manner and a humorous way with him. I am sure he performed his various duties admirably, but he did everything he could to avoid the official demeanour. He was slangy of speech and pleasantly caustic. It was charming to see him play with the two children. It was quite obvious that he had found marriage a very satisfactory state. Mrs Low was an extremely nice little woman, plump, with

385

dark eyes under fine eyebrows, not very pretty, but certainly attractive. She looked healthy and she had high spirits. They chaffed one another continually and each one seemed to look upon the other as immensely comic. Their jokes were neither very good nor very new, but they thought them so killing that you were obliged to laugh with them.

I think they were glad to see me, especially Mrs Low, for with nothing much to do but keep an eye on the house and the children, she was thrown very much on her own resources. There were so few white people on the island that the social life was soon exhausted; and before I had been there twenty-four hours she pressed me to stay a week, a month, or a year. On the evening of my arrival they gave a dinner-party to which the official population, the government surveyor, the doctor, the schoolmaster, the chief of constabulary, were invited, but on the following evening the three of us dined by ourselves. At the dinner-party the guests had brought their house-boys to help, but that night we were waited on by the Lows' one boy and my travelling servant. They brought in the coffee and left us to ourselves. Low and I lit cheroots.

'You know that I've seen you before,' said Mrs Low.

'Where?' I asked.

'In London. At a party. I heard someone point you out to somebody else. In Carlton House Terrace at Lady Kastellan's.'

'Oh? When was that?'

'Last time we were home on leave. There were Russian dancers.'

'I remember. About two or three years ago. Fancy you being there!'

'That's exactly what we said to one another at the time,' said Low, with a slow, engaging smile. 'We'd never been at such a party in our lives.'

'It made a great splash, you know,' I said. 'It was *the* party of the season. Did you enjoy it?'

'I hated every minute of it,' said Mrs Low.

'Don't let's overlook the fact that you insisted on going, Bee.' said Low. 'I knew we'd be out of it among all those swells. My dress clothes were the same I'd had at Cambridge and they'd never been much of a fit.'

'I bought a frock specially at Peter Robinson's. It looked lovely in the shop. I wished I hadn't wasted so much money when I got there; I never felt so dowdy in my life.'

'Well it didn't much matter. We weren't introduced to anybody.'

I remembered the party quite well. The magnificent rooms in Carlton House Terrace had been decorated with great festoons of yellow roses and at one end of the vast drawing-room a stage had been erected. Special costumes of the Regency period had been designed for the dancers and a modern composer had written the music for the two charming ballets they danced. It was hard to look at it all and not allow the vulgar thought to cross one's mind that the affair must have cost an enormous amount of money. Lady Kastellan was a beautiful woman and a great hostess, but I do not think anyone would have ascribed to her any vast amount of kindliness, she knew too many people to care much for any one in particular, and I couldn't help wondering why she had asked to such a grand party two obscure and quite unimportant little persons from a distant colony.

'Had you known Lady Kastellan long?' I asked.

'We didn't know her at all. She sent us a card and we went because I wanted to see what she was like,' said Mrs Low.

'She's a very able woman,' I said.

'I dare say she is. She hadn't an idea who we were when the butler man announced us, but she remembered at once. "Oh, yes," she said, "you're poor Jack's friends. Do go and find yourselves seats where you can see. You'll adore Lifar, he's too marvellous." And then she turned to say how d'you do to the next people. But she gave me a look. She wondered how much I knew and she saw at once that I knew everything.'

'Don't talk such nonsense, darling,' said Low. 'How could she know all you think she did by just looking at you, and how could you tell what she was thinking?'

'It's true, I tell you. We said everything in that one look, and unless I'm very much mistaken I spoilt her party for her.'

Low laughed and I smiled, for Mrs Low spoke in a tone of triumphant vindictiveness.

'You are terribly indiscreet, Bee.'

'Is she a great friend of yours?' Mrs Low asked me.

'Hardly. I've met her here and there for fifteen years. I've been to a good many parties at her house. She gives very good parties and she always asks you to meet the people you want to see.'

'What d'you think of her?'

'She's by way of being a considerable figure in London. She's amusing to talk to and she's nice to look at. She does a lot for art and music. What do *you* think of her?'

'I think she's a bitch,' said Mrs Low, with cheerful but decided frankness.

'That settles her,' I said.

'Tell him, Arthur.'

Low hesitated for a moment.

'I don't know that I ought to.'

'If you don't, I shall.'

'Bee's got her knife into her all right,' he smiled. 'It was rather a bad business really.'

He made a perfect smoke-ring and watched it with absorption.

'Go on, Arthur,' said Mrs Low.

'Oh, well. It was before we went home last time. I was D.O. in Selangor and one day they came and told me that a white man was dead in a small town a couple of hours up the river. I didn't know there was a white man living there. I thought I'd better go and see about it, so I got in the launch and went up. I made inquiries when I got there. The police didn't know anything about him except that he'd been living there for a couple of years with a Chinese woman in the bazaar. It was rather a picturesque bazaar, tall houses on each side, with a board walk in between, built on piles on the river-bank, and there were awnings above to keep out the sun. I took a couple of policemen with me and they led me to the house. They sold brass-ware in the shop below and the rooms above were let out. The master of the shop took me up two flights of dark, rickety stairs, foul with every kind of Chinese stench, and called out when we got to the top. The door was opened by a middle-aged Chinese woman and I saw that her face was all bloated with weeping. She didn't say anything, but made way for us to pass. It wasn't much more than a cubby-hole under the roof; there was a small window that looked on the street, but the awning that stretched across it dimmed the light. There wasn't any furniture except a deal table and a kitchen chair with a broken back. On a mat against the wall a dead man was lying. The first thing I did was to have the window opened. The room was so frowsty that I retched, and the strongest smell was the smell of opium. There was a small oil-lamp on the table and a long needle, and of course I knew what they were there for. The pipe had been hidden. The dead man lay on his back with nothing on but a sarong and a dirty singlet. He had long brown hair, going grey, and a short beard. He was a white man all right. I examined him as best I could. I had to judge whether death was due to natural causes. There were no signs of violence. He was nothing but skin and bone. It looked to me as though he might very likely have died of starvation. I asked the man of the shop and the woman a number of questions. The policeman corroborated their statements. It appeared that the man coughed a great deal and brought up blood now and then, and his appearance suggested that he might very well have had T.B. The Chinaman said he'd been a confirmed opium smoker. It all seemed pretty obvious. Fortunately cases of that sort are rare, but they're not unheard of – the white man who goes under and gradually sinks to the last stage of degradation. It appeared that the Chinese woman had been fond of him. She'd kept him on her own miserable earnings for the last two years. I gave the necessary instructions. Of course I wanted to know who he was. I supposed he'd been a clerk in some English firm or an assistant in an English store at Singapore or Kuala Lumpur. I asked the Chinese woman if he'd left any effects. Considering the destitution in which they'd lived it seemed a rather absurd question, but she went to a shabby suit-case that lay in a corner, opened it, and showed me a square parcel about the size of two novels put together wrapped in an old newspaper. I had a look at the suit-case. It contained nothing of any value. I took the parcel.'

Low's cheroot had gone out and he leaned over to relight it from one of the candles on the table.

'I opened it. Inside was another wrapping, and on this, in a neat, well-educated writing: To the District Officer, me as it happened, and then the words: please deliver personally to the Viscountess Kastellan, 53 Carlton House Terrace, London, s w. That was a bit of a surprise. Of course I had to examine the contents. I cut the string and the first thing I found was a gold and platinum cigarette case. As you can imagine I was mystified. From all I'd heard the pair of them, the dead man and the Chinese woman, had scarcely enough to eat, and the cigarette-case looked as if it had cost a packet. Besides the cigarette-case there was nothing but a bundle of letters. There were no envelopes. They were in the same neat writing as the directions and they were signed with the initial J. There were forty or fifty of them. I couldn't read them all there, but a rapid glance showed me that they were a man's love letters to a woman. I sent for the Chinese woman to ask her the name of the dead man. Either she didn't know or wouldn't tell me. I gave orders that he should be buried and got back into the launch to go home. I told Bee.'

He gave her his sweet little smile.

'I had to be rather firm with Arthur,' she said. 'At first he wouldn't let me read the letters, but of course I wasn't going to put up with any nonsense like that.'

'It was none of our business.'

'You had to find out the name if you could.'

'And where exactly did you come in?'

'Oh, don't be so silly,' she laughed. 'I should have gone mad if you hadn't let me read them.'

'And did you find out his name?' I asked.

'No.'

'Was there no address?'

'Yes, there was, and a very unexpected one. Most of the letters were written on Foreign Office paper.'

'That was funny.'

'I didn't quite know what to do. I had half a mind to write to the Viscountess Kastellan and explain the circumstances, but I didn't know what trouble I might be starting; the directions were to deliver the parcel to her personally, so I wrapped everything up again and put it in the safe. We were going home on leave in the spring and I thought the best thing was to leave everything over till then. The letters were by way of being rather compromising.'

'To put it mildly,' giggled Mrs Low. 'The truth is they gave the whole show away.'

'I don't think we need go into that,' said Low.

A slight altercation ensued; but I think on his part it was more for form's sake, since he must have known that his desire to preserve an official discretion stood small chance against his wife's determination to tell me everything. She had a down on Lady Kastellan and didn't care what she said about her. Her sympathies were with the man. Low did his best to tone down her rash assertions. He corrected her exaggerations. He told her that she'd let her imagination run away with her and had read into the letters more than was there. She would have done it. They'd evidently made a deep impression on her, and from her vivid account and Low's interruptions I gained a fairly coherent impression of them. It was plain for one thing that they were very moving.

'I can't tell you how it revolted me, the way Bee gloated over them,' said Low.

'They were the most wonderful letters I've ever read. You never wrote letters like that to me.'

'What a damned fool you would have thought me if I had,' he grinned.

She gave him a charming, affectionate smile.

'I suppose I should, and yet, God knows I was crazy about you, and I'm damned if I know why.'

The story emerged clearly enough. The writer, the mysterious J, presumably a clerk in the Foreign Office, had fallen in love with Lady Kastellan and she with him. They had become lovers and the early letters were passionately lyrical. They were happy. They expected their love to last for ever. He wrote to her immediately after he had left her and told her how much he adored her and how much she meant to him. She was never for a moment absent from his thoughts. It looked as though her infatuation was equal to his, for in one letter he justified himself because she had reproached him for not coming to some place where he knew she would be. He told her what agony it had been to him that a sudden job had prevented him from being with her when he'd so eagerly looked forward to it.

Then came the catastrophe. How it came or why one could only guess. Lord Kastellan learnt the truth. He not merely suspected his wife's infidelity, he had proofs of it. There was a fearful scene between them, she left him and went to her father's. Lord Kastellan announced his intention of divorcing her. The letters changed in character. J. wrote at once asking to see Lady Kastellan, but she begged him not to come. Her father insisted that they shouldn't meet. J. was distressed at her unhappiness and dismayed by the trouble he had brought upon her, and he was deeply sympathetic because of what she was enduring at home, for her father and mother were furious; but at the same time it was plain that he was relieved that the crisis had come. Nothing mattered except that they loved one another. He said he hated Kastellan. Let him bring his action. The sooner they could get married the better. The correspondence was one-sided, there were no letters from her, and one had to guess from his replies what she said in them. She was obviously frightened out of her wits and nothing that he could say helped. Of course he would have to leave the Foreign Office. He assured her that this meant nothing to him. He could get a job somewhere, in the colonies, where he would earn much more money. He was sure he could make her happy. Naturally there would be a scandal, but it would be forgotten, and away from England people would not bother. He besought her to have courage. Then it looked as though she had written somewhat peevishly. She hated being divorced, Kastellan refused to take the blame on himself and be made respondent, she did not want to leave London, it was her whole life, and bury herself in some God-forsaken place on the other side of nowhere. He answered unhappily. He said he would do anything she wanted. He implored her not to love him less and he was tortured by the thought that this disaster had changed her feelings for him. She reproached him for the mess they had got into; he did not try to defend himself; he was prepared to admit that he alone was to blame. Then it appeared that pressure was being brought to bear on Kastellan from some high quarter and there was even yet a chance that something might be arranged. Whatever she wrote made J., the unknown J., desperate. His letter was almost incoherent. He begged her again to see him, he implored her to have strength, he repeated that she meant everything in the world to him, he was frightened that she would let people influence her, he asked her to burn her boats behind her and bolt with him to Paris. He was frantic. Then it seemed that for some days she did not write to him. He could not understand. He did not know if she was receiving his letters. He was in an agony. The blow fell. She must have written to say that if he would resign from the Foreign Office and leave England her husband was prepared to take her back. His answer was broken-hearted.

'He never saw through her for a moment,' said Mrs Low.

'What was there to see through?' I asked.

'Don't you know what she wrote to him? I do.'

'Don't be such an ass, Bee. You can't possibly know.'

'Ass yourself. Of course I do. She put it up to him. She threw herself on his mercy. She dragged in her father and mother. She brought in her children; I bet that was the first thought she'd given them since they were born. She knew that he loved her so much that he was willing to do everything in the world for her, even lose her. She knew that he was prepared to accept the sacrifice of his love, his life, his career, everything for her sake, and she let him make it. She let the offer come from him. She let him persuade her to accept it.'

I listened to Mrs Low with a smile, but with attention. She was a woman and she felt instinctively how a woman in those circumstances would act. She thought it hateful, but she felt in her bones that in just that way would she herself have acted. Of course it was pure invention, with nothing by J.'s letter as a foundation, but I had an impression that it was very likely.

That was the last letter in the bundle.

I was astonished. I had known Lady Kastellan for a good many years, but only casually; and I knew her husband even less. He was immersed in politics, he was Under-Secretary at the Home Office at the time of the great do to which the Lows and I had been invited; and I never saw him but in his own house. Lady Kastellan had the reputation of being a beauty; she was tall and her figure was good in a massive way. She had a lovely skin. Her blue eyes were large, set rather wide apart and her face was broad. It gave her a slightly cow-like look. She had pretty pale brown hair and she held herself superbly. She was a woman of great self-possession, and it amazed me to learn that she had ever surrendered to such passion as the letters suggested. She was ambitious and there was no doubt that she was very useful to Kastellan in his political life. I should have thought her incapable of indiscretion. Searching my memory I seemed to remember hearing years before that the Kastellans were not getting on very well, but I had never heard any details, and whenever I saw them it looked as though they were on very good terms with one another. Kastellan was a big, red-faced fellow with sleek black hair, jovial and loud-voiced, but with little shrewd eyes that watched and noted. He was industrious, an effective speaker, but a trifle pompous. He was a little too conscious of his own importance. He did not let you forget that he had rank and wealth. He was inclined to be patronizing with people of less consequence than himself.

I could well believe that when he discovered that his wife was having an affair with a junior clerk in the Foreign Office there was a devil of a row. Lady Kastellan's father had been for many years permanent Under-Secretary for Foreign Affairs and it would have been more than usually embarrassing for his daughter to be divorced on account of one of his subordinates. For all I knew Kastellan was in love with his wife and he may have been teased by a very natural jealousy. But he was a proud man, deficient in humour. He feared ridicule. The role of the deceived husband is difficult to play with dignity. I do not suppose he wanted a scandal that might well jeopardize his political future. It may be that Lady Kastellan's advisers threatened to defend the case and the prospect of washing dirty linen in public horrified him. It is likely enough that pressure was brought to bear on him and the solution to forgive and take his wife back if her lover were definitely eliminated may have seemed the best to adopt. I have no doubt Lady Kastellan promised everything she was asked.

She must have had a bad fright. I didn't take such a severe view of her conduct as Mrs Low. She was very young; she was not more than thirty-five now. Who could tell by what accident she had become J.'s mistress? I suspect that love had caught her unawares and that she was in the middle of an affair almost before she knew what she was about. She must always have been a cold, self-possessed woman, but it is just with people like that that nature at times plays strange tricks. I am prepared to believe that she lost her head completely. There is no means of knowing how Kastellan discovered what was going on, but the fact that she kept her lover's letters shows that she was too much in love to be prudent. Arthur Low had mentioned that it was strange to find in the dead man's possession his letters and not hers; but that seemed to me easily explainable. At the time of the catastrophe they were doubtless given back to him in exchange for hers. He very naturally kept them. Reading them again he could relive the love that meant everything in the world to him.

I didn't suppose that Lady Kastellan, devoured by passion, could ever have considered what would happen if she were found out. When the blow fell it is not strange that she was scared out of her wits. She may not have had more to do with her children than most women who live the sort of life she lived, but she may for all that not have wanted to lose them. I did not even know whether she had ever cared for her husband, but from what I knew of her I guessed that she was not indifferent to his name and wealth. The future must have looked pretty grim. She was losing everything, the grand house in Carlton House Terrace, the position, the security; her father could give her no money and her lover had still to find a job. It may not have been heroic that she should yield to the entreaties of her family, but it was comprehensible.

While I was thinking all this Arthur Low went on with his story.

'I didn't quite know how to set about getting in touch with Lady Kastellan,' he said. 'It was awkward not knowing the chap's name. However, when we got home I wrote to her. I explained who I was and said that I'd been asked to give her some letters and a gold and platinum cigarette-case by a man who'd recently died in my district. I said I'd been asked to deliver them to her in person. I thought perhaps she wouldn't answer at all or else communicate with me through a solicitor. But she answered all right. She made an appointment for me to come to Carlton House Terrace at twelve one morning. Of course it was stupid of me, but when finally I stood on the doorstep and rang the bell I was quite nervous. The door was opened by a butler. I said I had an appointment with Lady Kastellan. A footman took my hat and coat. I was led upstairs to an enormous drawing-room.

'"I'll tell her ladyship you're here, sir," the butler said.

'He left me and I sat on the edge of a chair and looked round. There were huge pictures on the walls, portraits you know, I don't know who they were by, Reynolds I should think and Romney, and there was a lot of Oriental china, and gilded consoles and mirrors. It was all terribly grand and it made me feel very shabby and insignificant. My suit smelt of camphor and it was baggy at the knees. My tie felt a bit loud. The butler came in again and asked me to go with him. He opened another door from the one I'd come in by and I found myself in a further room, not so large as the drawing-room, but large all the same and very grand too. A lady was standing by the fireplace. She looked at me as I came in and bowed slightly. I felt frightfully awkward as I walked along the whole length of the room and I was afraid of stumbling over the furniture. I can only hope I didn't look such a fool as I felt. She didn't ask me to sit down.

'"I understand you have some things that you wish to deliver to me personally," she said. "It's very good of you to bother."

'She didn't smile. She seemed perfectly self-possessed, but I had a notion that she was sizing me up. To tell you the truth it put my back up. I didn't much fancy being treated as if I were a chauffeur applying for a situation.

'"Please don't mention it," I said, rather stiffly. "It's all in the day's work."

'"Have you got the things with you?" she asked.

'I didn't answer, but I opened the dispatch-case I'd brought with me and took out the letters. I handed them to her. She accepted them without a word. She gave them a glance. She was very much made up, but I swear she went white underneath. The expression of her face didn't change. I looked at her hands. They were trembling a little. Then she seemed to pull herself together.

'"Oh, I'm so sorry," she said. "Won't you sit down?"

'I took a chair. For a moment she didn't seem to know quite what to do. She held the letters in her hand. I, knowing what they were, wondered what she felt. She didn't give much away.

There was a desk beside the chimney-piece and she opened a drawer and put them in. Then she sat down opposite me and asked me to have a cigarette. I handed her the cigarette-case. I'd had it in my breast pocket.

'"I was asked to give you this too," I said.

'She took it and looked at it. For a moment she didn't speak and I waited. I didn't quite know if I ought to get up and go.

'"Did you know Jack well?" she asked suddenly.

'"I didn't know him at all," I answered. "I never saw him until after his death."

'"I had no idea he was dead till I got your note," she said. "I'd lost sight of him for a long time. Of course he was a very old friend of mine."

'I wondered if she thought I hadn't read the letters or if she'd forgotten what sort of letters they were. If the sight of them had given her a shock she had quite got over it by then. She spoke almost casually.

'"What did he die of in point of fact?" she asked.

'"Tuberculosis, opium, and starvation," I answered.

'"How dreadful," she said.

'But she said it quite conventionally. Whatever she felt she wasn't going to let me see. She was as cool as a cucumber, but I fancied, though it may have been only my fancy, that she was watching me, with all her wits about her, and wondering how much I knew. I think she'd have given a good deal to be certain of that.

'"How did you happen to get hold of these things?" she asked me.

'"I took possession of his effects after his death," I explained. "They were done up in a parcel and I was directed to give them to you."

'"Was there any need to undo the parcel?"

'I wish I could tell you what frigid insolence she managed to get into the question. It made me go white and I hadn't any make-up on to hide it. I answered that I thought it my duty to find out if I could who the dead man was. I should have liked to be able to communicate with his relations.

'"I see," she said.

'She looked at me as though that were the end of the interview and she expected me to get up and take myself off. But I didn't. I thought I'd like to get a bit of my own back. I told her how I'd been sent for and how I'd found him. I described the whole thing and I told her how, as far as I knew, there'd been no one at the end to take pity on him but a Chinese woman. Suddenly the door was opened and we both looked round. A big, middle-aged man came in and stopped when he saw me.

'"I beg your pardon," he said, "I didn't know you were busy."

'"Come in," she said, and when he had approached, "This is Mr Low. My husband."

'Lord Kastellan gave me a nod.

'"I just wanted to ask you," he began, and then he stopped.

'His eyes had caught the cigarette-case that was still resting on Lady Kastellan's open hand. I don't know if she saw the look of inquiry in his eyes. She gave him a friendly little smile. She was quite amazingly mistress of herself.

'"Mr Low comes from the Federated Malay States. Poor Jack Almond's dead and he's left me his cigarette-case."

'"Really?" said Lord Kastellan. "When did he die?"

'"About six months ago," I said.

'Lady Kastellan got up.

'"Well, I won't keep you any longer. I dare say you're busy. Thank you so much for carrying out Jack's request."

'"Things are pretty bad just now in the F.M.S. if all I hear is true," said Lord Kastellan.

'I shook hands with them both and Lady Kastellan rang a bell.

'"Are you staying in London?" she asked, as I was going. "I wonder if you'd like to come to a little party I'm giving next week."

'"I have my wife with me," I said.

'"Oh, how very nice. I'll send you a card."

'A couple of minutes later I found myself in the street. I was glad to be alone. I'd had a bad shock. As soon as Lady Kastellan mentioned the name I remembered. It was Jack Almond, the wretched bum I'd found dead in the Chinese house, dead of starvation. I'd known him quite well. It never struck me for a moment that it was he. Why, I'd dined and played cards with him, and we'd played tennis together. It was awful to think of him dying quite near me and me never knowing. He must have known he only had to send me a message and I'd have done something. I made my way into St James's Park and sat down. I wanted to have a good think.'

I could understand that it was a shock to Arthur Low to discover who the dead wastrel had been, for it was a shock to me too. Oddly enough I also had known him. Not intimately, but as a man I met at parties and now and then at a house in the country where we were both passing the week-end. Except that it was years since I had even thought of him it would have been stupid of me not to put two and two together. With his name there flashed back into my memory all my recollections of him. So that was why he had suddenly thrown up a career he liked so much! At that time, it was just after the war, I happened to know several people in the Foreign Office; Jack Almond was thought the cleverest of all the young men attached to it, and the highest posts the Diplomatic Service had to offer were within his reach. Of course it meant waiting. But it did seem absurd for him to fling away his chances in order to go into business in the Far East. His friends did all they could to dissuade him. He said he had had losses and found it impossible to live on his salary. One would have thought he could scrape along till things grew better. I remembered very well what he looked like. He was tall and well-made, a trifle dressy, but he was young enough to carry off his faultless clothes with a dash, with dark brown hair, very neat and sleek, blue eyes with very long lashes, and a fresh brilliant colour. He looked the picture of health. He was amusing, gay, and quick-witted. I never knew anyone who had more charm. It is a dangerous quality and those who have it trade on it. Often they think it enough to get them through life without any further effort. It is well to be on one's guard against it. But with Jack Almond it was the expression of a sweet and generous nature. He delighted because he was delightful. He was entirely without conceit. He had a gift for languages, he spoke French and German without a trace of accent, and his manners were admirable. You felt that when the time came he would play the part of an ambassador to a foreign power in the grand style. No one could fail to like him. It was not strange that Lady Kastellan should have fallen madly in love with him. My fancy ran away with me. What is there more moving than young love? The walks together of that handsome pair in one of the parks in the warm evenings of early summer, the dances they went to where he held her in his arms, the enchantment of the secret they shared when they exchanged glances across a dinner-table, and the passionate encounters, hurried and dangerous, but worth a thousand risks, when at some clandestine meeting-place they could give themselves to the fulfilment of their desire. They drank the milk of Paradise.

How frightful that the end of it all should have been so tragic!

'How did you know him?' I now asked Low.

'He was with Dexter and Farmilow. You know, the shipping people. He had quite a good job. He'd brought letters to the Governor and people like that. I was in Singapore at the time. I think I met him first at the club. He was damned good at games and all that sort of thing. Played polo. He was a fine tennis-player. You couldn't help liking him.'

'Did he drink, or what?'

'No.' Arthur Low was quite emphatic. 'He was one of the best. The women were crazy about him, and you couldn't blame them. He was one of the most decent fellows I've ever met.'

I turned to Mrs Low.

'Did you know him?'

'Only just. When Arthur and I were married we went to Perak. He was sweet, I remember that. He had the longest eyelashes I've ever seen on a man.'

'He was out quite a long time without going home. Five years, I think. I don't want to use hackneyed phrases, but the fact is I can't say it in any other way, he'd won golden opinions. There were a certain number of fellows who'd been rather sick at his being shoved into a damned good job by influence, but they couldn't deny that he'd made good. We knew about his having been in the F.O. and all that, but he never put on any frills.'

'I think what took me,' Mrs Low interrupted, 'was that he was so tremendously alive. It bucked you up just to talk to him.'

'He had a wonderful send-off when he sailed. I happened to have run up to Singapore for a couple of days and I went to the dinner at the Europe the night before. We all got rather tight. It was a grand lark. There was quite a crowd to see him off. He was only going for six months. I think everybody looked forward to his coming back. It would have been better for him if he never had.'

'Why, what happened then?'

'I don't know exactly. I'd been moved again, and I was right away north.'

How exasperating! It is really much easier to invent a story out of your own head than to tell one about real people, of whom you not only must guess the motives, but whose behaviour even at crucial moments you are ignorant of.

'He was a very good chap, but he was never an intimate friend of ours, you know how cliquey Singapore is, and he moved in rather more exalted circles than we did; when we went north I forgot about him. But one day at the club I heard a couple of fellows talking. Walton and Kenning. Walton had just come up from Singapore. There'd been a big polo match.

'"Did Almond play?" asked Kenning.

'"You bet your life he didn't," said Walton. "They kicked him out of the team last season."

'I interrupted.

'"What *are* you talking about?" I said.

'"Don't you know?" said Walton. "He's gone all to pot, poor devil."

'"How?" I asked.

'"Drink."

'"They say he dopes too," said Kenning.

'"Yes, I've heard that," said Walton. "He won't last long at that rate. Opium, isn't it?"

'"If he doesn't look out he'll lose his job," said Kenning.

'I couldn't make it out,' Low went on. 'He was the last man I should ever have expected to go that way. He was so typically English and he was a gentleman and all that. It appeared that Walton had travelled out with him on the same ship when Jack came back from leave. He joined the ship at Marseilles. He was rather low, but there was nothing funny about that; a lot of people don't feel any too good when they're leaving home and have to get back to the mill. He drank a good deal. Fellows do that sometimes too. But Walton said rather a curious thing about him. He said it looked as if the life had gone out of him. You couldn't help noticing it because he'd always had such high spirits. There'd been a general sort of idea that he was engaged to some girl in England and on the ship they jumped to the conclusion that she'd thrown him over.'

'That's what I said when Arthur told me,' said Mrs Low. 'After all, five years is a long time to leave a girl.'

'Anyhow they thought he'd get over it when he got back to work. But he didn't, unfortunately. He went from bad to worse. A lot of people liked him and they did all they could to persuade him to pull himself together. But there was nothing doing. He just told them to mind their own business. He was snappy and rude, which was funny because he'd always been so nice to everybody. Walton said you could hardly believe it was the same man. Government House dropped him and a lot of others followed suit. Lady Ormonde, the Governor's wife, was a snob, she knew he was well-connected and all that, and she wouldn't have given him the cold shoulder unless things had got pretty bad. He was a nice chap, Jack Almond, it seemed a pity that he should make such a mess of things. I was sorry, you know, but of course it didn't impair my appetite or disturb my night's sleep. A few months later I happened to be in Singapore myself, and when I went to the club I asked about him. He'd lost his job all right, it appeared that he often didn't go to the office for two or three days at a time; and I was told that someone had made him manager of a rubber estate in Sumatra in the hope that away from the temptations of Singapore he might pull himself together. You see, everyone had liked him so much, they couldn't bear the thought of his going under without some sort of a struggle. But it was no good. The opium had got him. He didn't keep the job in Sumatra long and he was back again in Singapore. I heard afterwards that you would hardly have recognized him. He'd always been so spruce and smart; he was shabby and unwashed and wild-eyed. A number of fellows at the club got together and arranged something. They felt they had to give him one more chance and they sent him out to Sarawak. But it wasn't any use. The fact is, I think, he didn't want to be helped. I think he just wanted to go to hell in his own way and be as quick as he could about it. Then he disappeared; someone said he'd gone home; anyhow he was forgotten. You know how people drop out in the F.M.S. I suppose that's why when I found a dead man in a sarong, with a beard, lying in a little smelly room in a Chinese house thirty miles from anywhere, it never occurred to me for a moment that it might be Jack Almond. I hadn't heard his name for years.'

'Just think what he must have gone through in that time,' said Mrs Low, and her eyes were bright with tears, for she had a good and tender heart.

'The whole thing's inexplicable,' said Low.

'Why?' I asked.

'Well, if he was going to pieces, why didn't he do it when he first came out? His first five years he was all right. One of the best. If this affair of his had broken him you'd have expected him to break when it was all fresh. All that time he was as gay as a bird. You'd have said he hadn't a care in the world. From all I heard it was a different man who came back from leave.'

'Something happened during those six months in London,' said Mrs Low. 'That's obvious.'

'We shall never know,' sighed Low.

'But we can guess,' I smiled. 'That's where the novelist comes in. Shall I tell you what I think happened?'

'Fire away.'

'Well, I think that during those first five years he was buoyed up by the sacrifice he'd made. He had a chivalrous soul. He had given up everything that made life worth living to him to save the woman he loved better than anything in the world. I think he had an exaltation of spirit that never left him. He loved her still, with all his heart; most of us fall in and out of love; some men can only love once, and I think he was one of them. And in a strange way he was happy because he'd been able to sacrifice his happiness for the sake of someone who was worthy of the sacrifice. I think she was always in his thoughts. Then he went home. I think he loved her as much as ever and I don't suppose he ever doubted that her love was as strong and enduring as his. I don't know what he expected. He may have thought she'd see it was no good fighting her inclination any more and would run away with him. It may have been that he'd have been satisfied to realize that she loved him still. It was inevitable that they should meet; they lived in the same world. He saw that she didn't care a row of pins for him any longer. He saw that the passionate girl had become a prudent, experienced woman of the world, he saw that she'd never loved him as he thought she loved him, and he may have suspected that she'd lured him coldly into making the sacrifice that was to save her. He saw her at parties, self-possessed and triumphant. He knew that the lovely qualities he'd ascribed to her were of his own imagining and she was just an ordinary woman who had been carried away by a momentary infatuation and having got over it had returned to her true life. A great name, wealth, social distinction, worldly success: those were the things that mattered to her. He'd sacrificed everything, his friends, his familiar surroundings, his profession, his usefulness in the world, all that gives value to existence – for nothing. He'd been cheated, and it broke him. Your friend Walton said the true thing, you noticed it yourself, he said it looked as if the life had gone out of him. It had. After that he didn't care any more, and perhaps the worst thing was that even with it all, though he knew Lady Kastellan for what she was, he loved her still. I know nothing more shattering than to love with all your heart, than not to be able however hard you try to break yourself of it, someone who you know is worthless. Perhaps that is why he took to opium. To forget and to remember.'

It was a long speech I had made, and now-I stopped.

'All that's only fancy,' said Low.

'I know it is,' I answered, 'but it seems to fit the circumstances.'

'There must have been a weak strain in him. Otherwise he could have fought and conquered.'

'Perhaps. Perhaps there is always a certain weakness attached to such great charm as he possessed. Perhaps few people love as wholeheartedly and as devotedly as he loved. Perhaps he didn't want to fight and conquer. I can't bring myself to blame him.'

I didn't add, because I was afraid they would think it cynical, that maybe if only Jack Almond hadn't had those wonderfully long eyelashes he might now have been alive and well, minister to some foreign power and on the high road to the Embassy in Paris.

'Let's go into the drawing-room,' said Mrs Low. 'The boy wants to clear the table.'

And that was the end of Jack Almond.

RED

THE skipper thrust his hand into one of his trouser pockets and with difficulty, for they were not at the sides but in front and he was a portly man, pulled out a large silver watch. He looked at it and then looked again at the declining sun. The Kanaka at the wheel gave him a glance, but did not speak. The skipper's eyes rested on the island they were approaching. A white line of foam marked the reef. He knew there was an opening large enough to get his ship through, and when they came a little nearer he counted on seeing it. They had nearly an hour of daylight still before them. In the lagoon the water was deep and they could anchor comfortably. The chief of the village which he could already see among the coconut trees was a friend of the mate's, and it would be pleasant to go ashore for the night. The mate came forward at that minute and the skipper turned to him.

'We'll take a bottle of booze along with us and get some girls in to dance,' he said.

'I don't see the opening,' said the mate.

He was a Kanaka, a handsome, swarthy fellow, with somewhat the look of a later Roman emperor, inclined to stoutness; but his face was fine and clean-cut.

'I'm dead sure there's one right here,' said the captain, looking through his glasses. 'I can't understand why I can't pick it up. Send one of the boys up the mast to have a look.'

The mate called one of the crew and gave him the order. The captain watched the Kanaka climb and waited for him to speak. But the Kanaka shouted down that he could see nothing but the unbroken line of foam. The captain spoke Samoan like a native, and he cursed him freely.

'Shall he stay up there?' asked the mate.

'What the hell good does that do?' answered the captain. 'The blame fool can't see worth a cent. You bet your sweet life I'd find the opening if I was up there.'

He looked at the slender mast with anger. It was all very well for a native who had been used to climbing up coconut trees all his life. He was fat and heavy.

'Come down,' he shouted. 'You're no more use than a dead dog. We'll just have to go along the reef till we find the opening.'

It was a seventy-ton schooner with paraffin auxiliary, and it ran, when there was no head wind, between four and five knots an hour. It was a bedraggled object; it had been painted white a very long time ago, but it was now dirty, dingy, and mottled. It smelt strongly of paraffin, and of the copra which was its usual cargo. They were within a hundred feet of the reef now and the captain told the steersman to run along it till they came to the opening. But when they had gone a couple of miles he realized that they had missed it. He went about and slowly worked back again. The white foam of the reef continued without interruption and now the sun was setting. With a curse at the stupidity of the crew the skipper resigned himself to waiting till next morning.

'Put her about,' he said. 'I can't anchor here.'

They went out to sea a little and presently it was quite dark. They anchored. When the sail was furled the ship began to roll a good deal. They said in Apia that one day she would roll right over; and the owner, a German-American who managed one of the largest stores, said that no money was big enough to induce him to go out in her. The cook, a Chinese in white trousers, very dirty and ragged, and a thin white tunic, came to say that supper was ready, and when the skipper went into the cabin he found the engineer already seated at table. The engineer was a long, lean man with a scraggy neck. He was dressed in blue overalls and a sleeveless jersey which showed his thin arms tattooed from elbow to wrist.

'Hell, having to spend the night outside,' said the skipper.

The engineer did not answer, and they ate their supper in silence. The cabin was lit by a dim oil-lamp. When they had eaten the canned apricots with which the meal finished the Chink brought them a cup of tea. The skipper lit a cigar and went on the upper deck. The island now was only a darker mass against the night. The stars were very bright. The only sound was the ceaseless breaking of the surf. The skipper sank into a deck-chair and smoked idly. Presently three or four members of the crew came up and sat down. One of them had a banjo and another a concertina. They began to play, and one of them sang. The native song sounded strange on these instruments. Then to the singing a couple began to dance. It was a barbaric dance, savage and primeval, rapid, with quick movements of the hands and feet and contortions of the body; it was sensual, sexual even, but sexual without passion. It was very animal, direct, weird without mystery, natural in short, and one might almost say childlike. At last they grew tired. They stretched themselves on the deck and slept, and all was silent. The skipper lifted himself heavily out of his chair and clambered down the companion. He went into his cabin and got out of his clothes. He climbed into his bunk and lay there. He panted a little in the heat of the night.

But next morning, when the dawn crept over the tranquil sea, the opening in the reef which had eluded them the night before was seen a little to the east of where they lay. The schooner entered the lagoon. There was not a ripple on the surface of the water. Deep down among the coral rocks you saw little coloured fish swim. When he had anchored his ship the skipper ate his breakfast and went on deck. The sun shone from an unclouded sky, but in the early morning the air was grateful and cool. It was Sunday, and there was a feeling of quietness, a silence as though nature were at rest, which gave him a peculiar sense of comfort. He sat, looking at the wooded coast, and felt lazy and well at ease. Presently a slow smile moved his lips and he threw the stump of his cigar into the water.

'I guess I'll go ashore,' he said. 'Get the boat out.'

He climbed stiffly down the ladder and was rowed to a little cove. The coconut trees came down to the water's edge, not in rows, but spaced out with an ordered formality. They were like a ballet of spinsters, elderly but flippant, standing in affected attitudes with the simpering graces of a bygone age. He sauntered idly through them, along a path that could be just seen winding its tortuous way, and it led him presently to a broad creek. There was a bridge across it, but a bridge constructed of single trunks of coconut trees, a dozen of them, placed end to end and supported where they met by a forked branch driven into the bed of the creek. You walked on a smooth, round surface, narrow and slippery, and there was no support for the hand. To cross such a bridge required sure feet and a stout heart. The skipper hesitated. But he saw on the other side, nestling among the trees, a white man's house; he made up his mind and, rather gingerly, began to walk. He watched his feet carefully, and where one trunk joined on to the next and there was a difference of level, he tottered a little. It was with a gasp of relief that he reached the last tree and finally set his feet on the firm ground of the other side. He had been so intent on the difficult crossing that he never noticed anyone was watching him, and it was with surprise that he heard himself spoken to.

'It takes a bit of nerve to cross these bridges when you're not used to them.'

He looked up and saw a man standing in front of him. He had evidently come out of the house which he had seen.

'I saw you hesitate,' the man continued, with a smile on his lips, 'and I was watching to see you fall in.'

'Not on your life,' said the captain, who had now recovered his confidence.

'I've fallen in myself before now. I remember, one evening I came back from shooting, and I fell in, gun and all. Now I get a boy to carry my gun for me.'

He was a man no longer young, with a small beard, now somewhat grey, and a thin face. He was dressed in a singlet, without arms, and a pair of duck trousers. He wore neither shoes nor socks. He spoke English with a slight accent.

'Are you Neilson?' asked the skipper.

'I am.'

'I've heard about you. I thought you lived somewheres round here.'

The skipper followed his host into the little bungalow and sat down heavily in the chair which the other motioned him to take. While Neilson went out to fetch whisky and glasses he took a look round the room. It filled him with amazement. He had never seen so many books. The shelves reached from floor to ceiling on all four walls, and they were closely packed. There was a grand piano littered with music, and a large table on which books and magazines lay in disorder. The room made him feel embarrassed. He remembered that Neilson was a queer fellow. No one knew very much about him, although he had been in the islands for so many years, but those who knew him agreed that he was queer. He was a Swede.

'You've got one big heap of books here,' he said, when Neilson returned.

'They do no harm,' answered Neilson with a smile.

'Have you read them all?' asked the skipper.

'Most of them.'

'I'm a bit of a reader myself. I have the *Saturday Evening Post* sent me regler.'

Neilson poured his visitor a good stiff glass of whisky and gave him a cigar. The skipper volunteered a little information.

'I got in last night, but I couldn't find the opening, so I had to anchor outside. I never been this run before, but my people had some stuff they wanted to bring over here. Gray, d'you know him?'

'Yes, he's got a store a little way along.'

'Well, there was a lot of canned stuff that he wanted over, an' he's got some copra. They thought I might just as well come over as lie idle at Apia. I run between Apia and Pago-Pago mostly, but they've got smallpox there just now, and there's nothing stirring.'

He took a drink of his whisky and lit a cigar. He was a taciturn man, but there was something in Neilson that made him nervous, and his nervousness made him talk. The Swede was looking at him with large dark eyes in which there was an expression of faint amusement.

'This is a tidy little place you've got here.'

'I've done my best with it.'

'You must do pretty well with your trees. They look fine. With copra at the price it is now. I had a bit of a plantation myself once, in Upolu it was, but I had to sell it.'

He looked round the room again, where all those books gave him a feeling of something incomprehensible and hostile.

'I guess you must find it a bit lonesome here though,' he said.

'I've got used to it. I've been here for twenty-five years.'

Now the captain could think of nothing more to say, and he smoked in silence. Neilson had apparently no wish to break it. He looked at his guest with a meditative eye. He was a tall man, more than six feet high, and very stout. His face was red and blotchy, with a network of little purple veins on the cheeks, and his features were sunk into its fatness. His eyes were bloodshot. His neck was buried in rolls of fat. But for a fringe of long curly hair, nearly white, at the back of his head, he was quite bald; and that immense, shiny surface of forehead, which might have given him a false look of intelligence, on the contrary gave him one of peculiar imbecility. He wore a blue flannel shirt, open at the neck and showing his fat chest covered with a mat of reddish hair, and a very old pair of blue serge trousers. He sat in his chair in a heavy ungainly attitude, his great belly thrust forward and his fat legs uncrossed. All elasticity had gone from his limbs. Neilson wondered idly what sort of man he had been in his youth. It was almost impossible to imagine that this creature of vast bulk had ever been a boy who ran about. The skipper finished his whisky, and Neilson pushed the bottle towards him.

'Help yourself.'

The skipper leaned forward and with his great hand seized it.

'And how come you in these parts anyways?' he said.

'Oh, I came out to the islands for my health. My lungs were bad and they said I hadn't a year to live. You see they were wrong.'

'I meant, how come you to settle down right here?'

'I am a sentimentalist.'

'Oh!'

Neilson knew that the skipper had not an idea what he meant, and he looked at him with an ironical twinkle in his dark eyes. Perhaps just because the skipper was so gross and dull a man the whim seized him to talk further.

'You were too busy keeping your balance to notice, when you crossed the bridge, but this spot is generally considered rather pretty.'

'It's a cute little house you've got here.'

'Ah, that wasn't here when I first came. There was a native hut, with its beehive roof and its pillars, overshadowed by a great tree with red flowers; and the croton bushes, their leaves yellow and red and golden, made a pied fence around it. And then all about were the coconut trees, as fanciful as women, and as vain. They stood at the water's edge and spent all day looking at their reflections. I was a young man then – good heavens, it's a quarter of a century ago – and I wanted to enjoy all the loveliness of the world in the short time allotted to me before I passed into the darkness. I thought it was the most beautiful spot I had ever seen. The first time I saw it I had a catch at my heart, and I was afraid I was going to cry. I wasn't more than twenty-five, and though I put the best face I could on it, I didn't want to die. And somehow it seemed to me that the very beauty of this place made it easier for me to accept my fate. I felt when I came here that all my past life had fallen away, Stockholm and its University, and then Bonn: it all seemed the life of somebody else, as though now at last I had achieved the reality which our doctors of philosophy – I am one myself, you know – had discussed so much. "A year," I cried to myself. "I have a year. I will spend it here and then I am content to die."

'We are foolish and sentimental and melodramatic at twenty-five, but if we weren't perhaps we should be less wise at fifty.

'Now drink, my friend. Don't let the nonsense I talk interfere with you.'

He waved his thin hand towards the bottle, and the skipper finished what remained in his glass.

'You ain't drinking nothin',' he said, reaching for the whisky.

'I am of sober habit,' smiled the Swede. 'I intoxicate myself in ways which I fancy are more subtle. But perhaps that is only vanity. Anyhow, the effects are more lasting and the results less deleterious.'

'They say there's a deal of cocaine taken in the States now,' said the captain.

Neilson chuckled.

'But I do not see a white man often,' he continued, 'and for once I don't think a drop of whisky can do me any harm.'

He poured himself out a little, added some soda, and took a sip.

'And presently I found out why the spot had such an unearthly loveliness. Here love had tarried for a moment like a migrant bird that happens on a ship in mid-ocean and for a little while folds its tired wings. The fragrance of a beautiful passion hovered over it like the fragrance of hawthorn in May in the meadows of my home. It seems to me that the places where men have loved or suffered keep about them always some faint aroma of something that has not wholly died. It is as though they had acquired a spiritual significance which mysteriously affects those who pass. I wish I could make myself clear.' He smiled a little. 'Though I cannot imagine that if I did you would understand.'

He paused.

'I think this place was beautiful because here for a period the ecstasy of love had invested it with beauty.' And now he shrugged his shoulders. 'But perhaps it is only that my aesthetic sense is gratified by the happy conjunction of young love and a suitable setting.'

Even a man less thick-witted than the skipper might have been forgiven if he were bewildered by Neilson's words. For he seemed faintly to laugh at what he said. It was as though he spoke from emotion which his intellect found ridiculous. He had said himself that he was a sentimentalist, and when sentimentality is joined with scepticism there is often the devil to pay.

He was silent for an instant and looked at the captain with eyes in which there was a sudden perplexity.

'You know, I can't help thinking that I've seen you before somewhere or other,' he said.

'I couldn't say as I remember you,' returned the skipper.

'I have a curious feeling as though your face were familiar to me. It's been puzzling me for some time. But I can't situate my recollection in any place or at any time.'

The skipper massively shrugged his heavy shoulders.

'It's thirty years since I first come to the islands. A man can't figure on remembering all the folk he meets in a while like that.'

The Swede shook his head.

'You know how one sometimes has the feeling that a place one has never been to before is strangely familiar. That's how I seem

410

to see you.' He gave a whimsical smile. 'Perhaps I knew you in some past existence. Perhaps, perhaps you were the master of a galley in ancient Rome and I was a slave at the oar. Thirty years have you been here?'

'Every bit of thirty years.'

'I wonder if you knew a man called Red?'

'Red?'

'That is the only name I've ever known him by. I never knew him personally. I never even set eyes on him. And yet I seem to see him more clearly than many men, my brothers, for instance, with whom I passed my daily life for many years. He lives in my imagination with the distinctness of a Paolo Malatesta or a Romeo. But I dare say you have never read Dante or Shakespeare?'

'I can't say as I have,' said the captain.

Neilson, smoking a cigar, leaned back in his chair and looked vacantly at the ring of smoke which floated in the still air. A smile played on his lips, but his eyes were grave. Then he looked at the captain. There was in his gross obesity something extraordinarily repellent. He had the plethoric self-satisfaction of the very fat. It was an outrage. It set Neilson's nerves on edge. But the contrast between the man before him and the man he had in mind was pleasant.

'It appears that Red was the most comely thing you ever saw. I've talked to quite a number of people who knew him in those days, white men, and they all agree that the first time you saw him his beauty just took your breath away. They called him Red on account of his flaming hair. It had a natural wave and he wore it long. It must have been of that wonderful colour that the pre-Raphaelites raved over. I don't think he was vain of it, he was much too ingenuous for that, but no one could have blamed him if he had been. He was tall, six feet and an inch or two – in the native house that used to stand here was the mark of his height cut with a knife on the central trunk that supported the roof – and he was made like a Greek god, broad in the shoulders and thin in the flanks; he was like Apollo, with just that soft roundness which Praxiteles gave him, and that suave, feminine grace which has in it something troubling and mysterious. His skin was dazzling white, milky, like satin; his skin was like a woman's.'

'I had kind of a white skin myself when I was a kiddie,' said the skipper, with a twinkle in his bloodshot eyes.

But Neilson paid no attention to him. He was telling his story now and interruption made him impatient.

'And his face was just as beautiful as his body. He had large blue eyes, very dark, so that some say they were black, and unlike most red-faired people he had dark eyebrows and long dark lashes. His features were perfectly regular and his mouth was like a scarlet wound. He was twenty.'

On these words the Swede stopped with a certain sense of the dramatic. He took a sip of whisky.

'He was unique. There never was anyone more beautiful. There was no more reason for him than for a wonderful blossom to flower on a wild plant. He was a happy accident of nature.

'One day he landed at that cove into which you must have put this morning. He was an American sailor, and he had deserted from a man-of-war in Apia. He had induced some good-humoured native to give him a passage on a cutter that happened to be sailing from Apia to Safoto, and he had been put ashore here in a dug-out. I do not know why he deserted. Perhaps life on a man-of-war with its restrictions irked him, perhaps he was in trouble, and perhaps it was the South Seas and these romantic islands that got into his bones. Every now and then they take a man strangely, and he finds himself like a fly in a spider's web. It may be that there was a softness of fibre in him, and these green hills with their soft airs, this blue sea, took the northern strength from him as Delilah took the Nazarite's. Anyhow, he wanted to hide himself, and he thought he would be safe in this secluded nook till his ship had sailed from Samoa.

'There was a native hut at the cove and as he stood there, wondering where exactly he should turn his steps, a young girl came out and invited him to enter. He knew scarcely two words of the native tongue and she as little English. But he understood well enough what her smiles meant, and her pretty gestures, and he followed her. He sat down on a mat and she gave him slices of pineapple to eat. I can speak of Red only from hearsay, but I saw the girl three years after he first met her, and she was scarcely nineteen then. You cannot imagine how exquisite she was. She had the passionate grace of the hibiscus and the rich colour. She was rather tall, slim, with the delicate features of her race, and large eyes like pools of still water under the palm trees; her hair, black and curling, fell down her back, and she wore a wreath of scented flowers. Her hands were lovely. They were so small, so exquisitely formed, they gave your heart-strings a wrench. And in those days she laughed easily. Her smile was so delightful that it made your knees shake. Her skin was like a field of ripe corn on a summer day. Good heavens, how can I describe her? She was too beautiful to be real.

'And these two young things, she was sixteen and he was twenty, fell in love with one another at first sight. That is the real love, not the love that comes from sympathy, common interests, of intellectual community, but love pure and simple. That is the love that Adam felt for Eve when he awoke and found her in the garden gazing at him with dewy eyes. That is the love that draws the beasts to one another, and the Gods. That is the love that makes the world a miracle. That is the love which gives life its pregnant meaning. You have never heard of the wise, cynical French duke who said that with two lovers there is always one who loves and one who lets himself be loved; it is bitter truth to which most of us have to resign ourselves; but now and then there are two who love and two who let themselves be loved. Then one might fancy that the sun stands still as it stood when Joshua prayed to the God of Israel.

'And even now after all these years, when I think of these two, so young, so fair, so simple, and of their love, I feel a pang. It tears my heart just as my heart is torn when on certain nights I watch the full moon shining on the lagoon from an unclouded sky. There is always pain in the contemplation of perfect beauty.

'They were children. She was good and sweet and kind. I know nothing of him, and I like to think that then at all events he was ingenuous and frank. I like to think that his soul was as comely as his body. But I dare say he had no more soul than the creatures of the woods and forests who made pipes from reeds and bathed in the mountain streams when the world was young, and you might catch sight of little fawns galloping through the glade on the back of a bearded centaur. A soul is a troublesome possession and when man developed it he lost the Garden of Eden.

'Well, when Red came to the island it had recently been visited by one of those epidemics which the white man brought to the South Seas, and one third of the inhabitants had died. It seems that the girl had lost all her near kin and she lived now in the house of distant cousins. The household consisted of two ancient crones, bowed and wrinkled, two younger women, and a man and a boy. For a few days he stayed there. But perhaps he felt himself too near the shore, with the possibility that he might fall in with white men who would reveal his hiding-place; perhaps the lovers could not bear that the company of others should rob them for an instant of the delight of being together. One morning they set out, the

413

pair of them, with the few things that belonged to the girl, and walked along a grassy path under the coconuts, till they came to the creek you see. They had to cross the bridge you crossed, and the girl laughed gleefully because he was afraid. She held his hand till they came to the end of the first tree, and then his courage failed him and he had to go back. He was obliged to take off all his clothes before he could risk it, and she carried them over for him on her head. They settled down in the empty hut that stood there. Whether she had any rights over it (land tenure is a complicated business in the islands), or whether the owner had died during the epidemic, I do not know, but anyhow no one questioned them, and they took possession. Their furniture consisted of a couple of grass mats on which they slept, a fragment of looking-glass, and a bowl or two. In this pleasant land that is enough to start housekeeping on.

'They say that happy people have no history, and certainly a happy love had none. They did nothing all day long and yet the days seemed all too short. The girl had a native name, but Red called her Sally. He picked up the easy language very quickly, and he used to lie on the mat for hours while she chattered gaily to him. He was a silent fellow, and perhaps his mind was lethargic. He smoked incessantly the cigarettes which she made him out of the native tobacco and pandanus leaf, and he watched her while with deft fingers she made grass mats. Often natives would come in and tell long stories of the old days when the island was disturbed by tribal wars. Sometimes he would go fishing on the reef, and bring home a basket full of coloured fish. Sometimes at night he would go out with a lantern to catch lobster. There were plantains round the hut and Sally would roast them for their frugal meal. She knew how to make delicious messes from coconuts, and the breadfruit tree by the side of the creek gave them its fruit. On feast-days they killed a little pig and cooked it on hot stones. They bathed together in the creek; and in the evening they went down to the lagoon and paddled about in a dug-out, with its great outrigger. The sea was deep blue, wine-coloured at sundown, like the sea of Homeric Greece; but in the lagoon the colour had an infinite variety, aquamarine and amethyst and emerald; and the setting sun turned it for a short moment to liquid gold. Then there was the colour of the coral, brown, white, pink, red, purple; and the shapes it took were marvellous. It was like a magic garden, and the hurrying fish were like butterflies. It strangely lacked reality. Among the coral were pools with a floor of white sand and here, where the water was dazzling clear, it was very good to bathe. Then, cool and happy, they wandered back in the gloaming over the soft grass road to the creek, walking hand in hand, and now the mynah birds filled the coconut trees with their clamour. And then the night, with that great sky shining with gold, that seemed to stretch more widely than the skies of Europe, and the soft airs that blew gently through the open hut, the long night again was all too short. She was sixteen and he was barely twenty. The dawn crept in among the wooden pillars of the hut and looked at those lovely children sleeping in one another's arms. The sun hid behind the great tattered leaves of the plantains so that it might not disturb them, and then, with playful malice, shot a golden ray, like the outstretched paw of a Persian cat, on their faces. They opened their sleepy eyes and they smiled to welcome another day. The weeks lengthened into months, and a year passed. They seemed to love one another as – I hesitate to say passionately, for passion has in it always a shade of sadness, a touch of bitterness or anguish, but as wholeheartedly, as simply and naturally as on that first day on which, meeting, they had recognized that a god was in them.

'If you had asked them I have no doubt that they would have thought it impossible to suppose their love could ever cease. Do we not know that the essential element of love is a belief in its own eternity? And yet perhaps in Red there was already a very little seed, unknown to himself and unsuspected by the girl, which would in time have grown to weariness. For one day one of the natives for the cove told them that some way down the coast at the anchorage was a British whaling-ship.

'"Gee," he said, "I wonder if I could make a trade of some nuts and plantains for a pound or two of tobacco."

'The pandanus cigarettes that Sally made him with untiring hands were strong and pleasant enough to smoke, but they left him unsatisfied; and he yearned on a sudden for real tobacco, hard, rank, and pungent. He had not smoked a pipe for many months. His mouth watered at the thought of it. One would have thought some premonition of harm would have made Sally seek to dissuade him, but love possessed her so completely that it never occurred to her any power on earth could take him from her. They went up into the hills together and gathered a great basket of wild oranges, green, but sweet and juicy; and they picked plantains from around the hut, and coconuts from their trees, and breadfruit and mangoes; and they carried them down to the cove. They loaded the unstable canoe with them, and Red and the native boy who had brought them the news of the ship paddled along outside the reef.

'It was the last time she ever saw him.

'Next day the boy came back alone. He was all in tears. This is the story he told. When after their long paddle they reached the ship and Red hailed it, a white man looked over the side and told them to come on board. They took the fruit they had brought with them and Red piled it up on the deck. The white man and he began to talk, and they seemed to come to some agreement. One of them went below and brought up tobacco. Red took some at once and lit a pipe. The boy imitated the zest with which he blew a great cloud of smoke from his mouth. Then they said something to him and he went into the cabin. Through the open door the boy, watching curiously, saw a bottle brought out and glasses. Red drank and smoked. They seemed to ask him something, for he shook his head and laughed. The man, the first man who had spoken to them, laughed too, and he filled Red's glass once more. They went on talking and drinking, and presently, growing tired of watching a sight that meant nothing to him, the boy curled himself up on the deck and slept. He was awakened by a kick; and jumping to his feet, he saw that the ship was slowly sailing out of the lagoon. He caught sight of Red seated at the table, with his head resting heavily on his arms, fast asleep. He made a movement towards him, intending to wake him, but a rough hand seized his arm, and a man, with a scowl and words which he did not understand, pointed to the side. He shouted to Red, but in a moment he was seized and flung overboard. Helpless, he swam round to his canoe, which was drifting a little way off, and pushed it on to the reef. He climbed in and, sobbing all the way, paddled back to shore.

'What had happened was obvious enough. The whaler, by desertion or sickness, was short of hands, and the captain when Red came aboard had asked him to sign on; on his refusal he had made him drunk and kidnapped him.

'Sally was beside herself with grief. For three days she screamed and cried. The natives did what they could to comfort her, but she would not be comforted. She would not eat. And then, exhausted, she sank into a sullen apathy. She spent long days at the cove, watching the lagoon, in the vain hope that Red somehow or other would manage to escape. She sat on the white sand, hour after hour, with the tears running down her cheeks, and at night dragged herself wearily back across the creek to the little hut where she had been happy. The people with whom she had lived

before Red came to the island wished her to return to them, but
she would not; she was convinced that Red would come back,
and she wanted him to find her where he had left her. Four
months later she was delivered of a still-born child, and the old
woman who had come to help her through her confinement
remained with her in the hut. All joy was taken from her life. If
her anguish with time became less intolerable it was replaced by a
settled melancholy. You would not have thought that among
these people, whose emotions, though so violent, are very tran-
sient, a woman could be found capable of so enduring a passion.
She never lost the profound conviction that sooner or later Red
would come back. She watched for him, and every time someone
crossed this slender little bridge of coconut trees she looked. It
might at last be he.'

Neilson stopped talking and gave a faint sigh.

'And what happened to her in the end?' asked the skipper.

Neilson smiled bitterly.

'Oh, three years afterwards she took up with another white
man.'

The skipper gave a fat, cynical chuckle.

'That's generally what happens to them,' he said.

The Swede shot him a look of hatred. He did not know why
that gross, obese man excited in him so violent a repulsion. But
his thoughts wandered and he found his mind filled with memories
of the past. He went back five-and-twenty years. It was when he
first came to the island, weary of Apia, with its heavy drinking, its
gambling and coarse sensuality a sick man, trying to resign himself to the loss of the career which had fired his imagination with
ambitious thought. He set behind him resolutely all his hopes of
making a great name for himself and strove to content himself
with the few poor months of careful life which was all that he
could count on. He was boarding with a half-caste trader who had
a store a couple of miles along the coast at the edge of a native
village; and one day, wandering aimlessly along the grassy paths
of the coconut groves, he had come upon the hut in which Sally
lived. The beauty of the spot had filled him with a rapture so
great that it was almost painful, and then he had seen Sally. She
was the loveliest creature he had ever seen, and the sadness in
those dark, magnificent eyes of hers affected him strangely. The
Kanakas were a handsome race, and beauty was not rare among
them, but it was the beauty of shapely animals. It was empty.
But those tragic eyes were dark with mystery, and you felt in them

the bitter complexity of the groping, human soul. The trader told him the story and it moved him.

'Do you think he'll ever come back?' asked Neilson.

'No fear. Why, it'll be a couple of years before the ship is paid off, and by then he'll have forgotten all about her. I bet he was pretty mad when he woke up and found he'd been shanghaied, and I shouldn't wonder but he wanted to fight somebody. But he'd got to grin and bear it, and I guess in a month he was thinking it the best thing that had ever happened to him that he got away from the island.'

But Neilson could not get the story out of his head. Perhaps because he was sick and weakly, the radiant health of Red appealed to his imagination. Himself an ugly man, insignificant of appearance, he prized very highly comeliness in others. He had never been passionately in love, and certainly he had never been passionately loved. The mutual attraction of those two young things gave him a singular delight. It had the ineffable beauty of the Absolute. He went again to the little hut by the creek. He had a gift for languages and an energetic mind, accustomed to work, and he had already given much time to the study of the local tongue. Old habit was strong in him and he was gathering together material for a paper on the Samoan speech. The old crone who shared the hut with Sally invited him to come in and sit down. She gave him *kava* to drink and cigarettes to smoke. She was glad to have someone to chat with and while she talked he looked at Sally. She reminded him of the Psyche in the museum at Naples. Her features had the same clear purity of line, and though she had borne a child she had still a virginal aspect.

It was not till he had seen her two or three times that he induced her to speak. Then it was only to ask him if he had seen in Apia a man called Red. Two years had passed since his disappearance, but it was plain that she still thought of him incessantly.

It did not take Neilson long to discover that he was in love with her. It was only by an effort of will now that he prevented himself from going every day to the creek, and when he was not with Sally his thoughts were. At first, looking upon himself as a dying man, he asked only to look at her, and occasionally hear her speak, and his love gave him a wonderful happiness. He exulted in its purity. He wanted nothing from her but the opportunity to weave around her graceful person a web of beautiful fancies. But the open air, the equable temperature, the rest, the simple fare, began to have an unexpected effect on his health. His temperature did not soar at night to such alarming heights, he coughed less and began to put on weight; six months passed without his having a haemorrhage; and on a sudden he saw the possibility that he might live. He had studied his disease carefully, and the hope dawned upon him that with great care he might arrest its course. It exhilarated him to look forward once more to the future. He made plans. It was evident that any active life was out of the question, but he could live on the islands, and the small income he had, insufficient elsewhere, would be ample to keep him. He could grow coconuts; that would give him an occupation; and he would send for his books and a piano; but his quick mind saw that in all this he was merely trying to conceal from himself the desire which obsessed him.

He wanted Sally. He loved not only her beauty, but that dim soul which he divined behind her suffering eyes. He would intoxicate her with his passion. In the end he would make her forget. And in an ecstasy of surrender he fancied himself giving her too the happiness which he had thought never to know again, but had now so miraculously achieved.

He asked her to live with him. She refused. He had expected that and did not let it depress him, for he was sure that sooner or later she would yield. His love was irresistible. He told the old woman of his wishes, and found somewhat to his surprise that she and the neighbours, long aware of them, were strongly urging Sally to accept his offer. After all, every native was glad to keep house for a white man, and Neilson according to the standards of the island was a rich one. The trader with whom he boarded went to her and told her not to be a fool; such an opportunity would not come again, and after so long she could not still believe that Red would ever return. The girl's resistance only increased Neilson's desire, and what had been a very pure love now became an agonizing passion. He was determined that nothing should stand in his way. He gave Sally no peace. At last, worn out by his persistence and the persuasions, by turns pleading and angry, of everyone around her, she consented. But the day after, when exultant he went to see her he found that in the night she had burnt down the hut in which she and Red had lived together. The old crone ran towards him full of angry abuse of Sally, but he waved her aside; it did not matter; they would build a bungalow on the place where the hut had stood. A European house would really be more convenient if he wanted to bring out a piano and a vast number of books.

And so the little wooden house was built in which he had now lived for many years, and Sally became his wife. But after the first few weeks of rapture, during which he was satisfied with what she gave him, he had known little happiness. She had yielded to him, through weariness, but she had only yielded what she set no store on. The soul which he had dimly glimpsed escaped him. He knew that she cared nothing for him. She still loved Red, and all the time she was waiting for his return. At a sign from him, Neilson knew that, notwithstanding his love, his tenderness, his sympathy, his generosity, she would leave him without a moment's hesitation. She would never give a thought to his distress. Anguish seized him and he battered at that impenetrable self of hers which sullenly resisted him. His love became bitter. He tried to melt her heart with kindness, but it remained as hard as before; he feigned indifference, but she did not notice it. Sometimes he lost his temper and abused her, and then she wept silently. Sometimes he thought she was nothing but a fraud, and that soul simply an invention of his own, and that he could not get into the sanctuary of her heart because there was no sanctuary there. His love became a prison from which he longed to escape, but he had not the strength merely to open the door – that was all it needed – and walk out into the open air. It was torture and at last he became numb and hopeless. In the end the fire burnt itself out and, when he saw her eyes rest for an instant on the slender bridge, it was no longer rage that filled his heart but impatience. For many years now they had lived together bound by the ties of habit and convenience, and it was with a smile that he looked back on his old passion. She was an old woman, for the women on the islands age quickly, and if he had no love for her any more he had tolerance. She left him alone. He was contented with his piano and his books.

His thoughts led him to a desire for words.

'When I look back now and reflect on that brief passionate love of Red and Sally, I think that perhaps they should thank the ruthless fate that separated them when their love seemed still to be at its height. They suffered, but they suffered in beauty. They were spared the real tragedy of love.'

'I don't know exactly as I get you,' said the skipper.

'The tragedy of love is not death or separation. How long do you think it would have been before one or other of them ceased to care? Oh, it is dreadfully bitter to look at a woman whom you have loved with all your heart and soul, so that you felt you could not bear to let her out of your sight, and realize that you would not mind if you never saw her again. The tragedy of love is indifference.'

But while he was speaking a very extraordinary thing happened. Though he had been addressing the skipper he had not been talking to him, he had been putting his thoughts into words for himself, and with his eyes fixed on the man in front of him he had not seen him. But now an image presented itself to them, an image not of the man he saw, but of another man. It was as though he were looking into one of those distorting mirrors that make you extraordinarily squat or outrageously elongate, but here exactly the opposite took place, and in the obese, ugly old man he caught the shadowy glimpse of a stripling. He gave him now a quick, searching scrutiny. Why had a haphazard stroll brought him just to this place? A sudden tremor of his heart made him slightly breathless. An absurd suspicion seized him. What had occurred to him was impossible, and yet it might be a fact.

'What is your name?' he asked abruptly.

The skipper's face puckered and he gave a cunning chuckle. He looked then malicious and horribly vulgar.

'It's such a damned long time since I heard it that I almost forget it myself. But for thirty years now in the islands they've always called me Red.'

His huge form shook as he gave a low, almost silent laugh. It was obscene. Neilson shuddered. Red was hugely amused, and from his bloodshot eyes tears ran down his cheeks.

Neilson gave a gasp, for at that moment a woman came in. She was a native, a woman of somewhat commanding presence, stout without being corpulent, dark, for the natives grow darker with age, with very grey hair. She wore a black Mother Hubbard, and its thinness showed her heavy breasts. The moment had come.

She made an observation to Neilson about some household matter and he answered. He wondered if his voice sounded as unnatural to her as it did to himself. She gave the man who was sitting in the chair by the window an indifferent glance, and went out of the room. The moment had come and gone.

Neilson for a moment could not speak. He was strangely shaken. Then he said:

'I'd be very glad if you'd stay and have a bit of dinner with me. Pot luck.'

'I don't think I will,' said Red. 'I must go after this fellow Gray. I'll give him his stuff and then I'll get away. I want to be back in Apia tomorrow.'

'I'll send a boy along with you to show you the way.'

'That'll be fine.'

Red heaved himself out of his chair, while the Swede called one of the boys who worked on the plantation. He told him where the skipper wanted to go, and the boy stepped along the bridge. Red prepared to follow him.

'Don't fall in,' said Neilson.

'Not on your life.'

Neilson watched him make his way across and when he had disappeared among the coconuts he looked still. Then he sank heavily in his chair. Was that the man who had prevented him from being happy? Was that the man whom Sally had loved all these years and for whom she had waited so desperately? It was grotesque. A sudden fury seized him so that he had an instinct to spring up and smash everything around him. He had been cheated. They had seen each other at last and had not known it. He began to laugh, mirthlessly, and his laughter grew till it became hysterical. The Gods had played him a cruel trick. And he was old now.

At last Sally came in to tell him dinner was ready. He sat down in front of her and tried to eat. He wondered what she would say if he told her now that the fat old man sitting in the chair was the lover whom she remembered still with the passionate abandonment of her youth. Years ago, when he hated her because she made him so unhappy, he would have been glad to tell her. He wanted to hurt her then as she hurt him, because his hatred was only love. But now he did not care. He shrugged his shoulders listlessly.

'What did that man want?' she asked presently.

He did not answer at once. She was too old, a fat old native woman. He wondered why he had ever loved her so madly. He had laid at her feet all the treasures of his soul, and she had cared nothing for them. Waste, what waste! And now, when he looked at her, he felt only contempt. His patience was at last exhausted. He answered her question.

'He's the captain of a schooner. He's come from Apia.'

'Yes.'

'He brought me news from home. My eldest brother is very ill and I must go back.'

'Will you be gone long?'

He shrugged his shoulders.

NEIL MACADAM

CAPTAIN BREDON was good-natured. When Angus Munro, the Curator of the museum at Kuala Solor, told him that he had advised Neil MacAdam, his new assistant, on his arrival at Singapore to put up at the Van Dyke Hotel, and asked him to see that the lad got into no mischief during the few days he must spend there, he said he would do his best. Captain Bredon commanded the *Sultan Ahmed*, and when he was at Singapore always stayed at the Van Dyke. He had a Japanese wife and kept a room there. It was his home. When he got back after his fortnight's trip along the coast of Borneo the Dutch manager told him that Neil had been there for two days. The boy was sitting in the little dusty garden of the hotel reading old numbers of *The Straits Times*. Captain Bredon took a look at him first and then went up.

'You're MacAdam, aren't you?'

Neil rose to his feet, flushed to the roots of his hair, and answered shyly: 'I am.'

'My name's Bredon. I'm skipper of the *Sultan Ahmed*. You're sailing with me next Tuesday. Munro asked me to look after you. What about a stengah? I suppose you've learned what that means by now.'

'Thank you very much, but I don't drink.'

He spoke with a broad Scots accent.

'I don't blame you. Drink's been the ruin of many a good man in this country.'

He called the Chinese boy and ordered himself a double whisky and a small soda.

'What have you been doing with yourself since you got in?'

'Walking about.'

'There's nothing much to see in Singapore.'

'I've found plenty.'

Of course the first thing he had done was to go to the museum. There was little that he had not seen at home, but the fact that those beasts and birds, those reptiles, moths, butterflies, and insects were native to the country excited him. There was one section devoted to that part of Borneo of which Kuala Solor was the capital, and since these were the creatures that for the next three years would chiefly concern him, he examined them with attention. But it was outside, in the streets, that it was most thrilling, and except that he was a grave and sober young man he would have laughed aloud with joy. Everything was new to him. He walked till he was footsore. He stood at the corner of a busy street and wondered at the long line of rickshaws and the little men between the shafts running with dogged steps. He stood on a bridge over a canal and looked at the sampans wedged up against one another like sardines in a tin. He peered into the Chinese shops in Victoria Road where so many strange things were sold. Bombay merchants, fat and exuberant, stood at their shop doors and sought to sell him silks and tinsel jewellery. He watched the Tamils, pensive and forlorn, who walked with a sinister grace, and the bearded Arabs, in white skull-caps, who bore themselves with scornful dignity. The sun shone upon the varied scene with a hard, acrid brilliance. He was confused. He thought it would take him years to find his bearings in this multi-coloured and excessive world.

After dinner that night Captain Bredon asked him if he would like to go round the town.

'You ought to see a bit of life while you're here,' he said.

They stepped into rickshaws and drove to the Chinese quarter. The Captain, who never drank at sea, had been making up for his abstinence during the day. He was feeling good. The rickshaws stopped at a house in a side street and they knocked at the door. It was opened and they passed through a narrow passage into a large room with benches all round it covered with red plush. A number of women were sitting about – French, Italian, and American. A mechanical piano was grinding out harsh music and a few couples were dancing. Captain Bredon ordered drinks. Two or three women, waiting for an invitation, gave them inviting glances.

'Well, young feller, is there anyone you fancy here?' the Captain asked facetiously.

'To sleep with, d'you mean? No.'

'No white girls where you're going, you know.'

'Oh, well.'

'Like to go an' see some natives?'

'I don't mind.'

The Captain paid for the drinks and they strolled on. They went to another house. Here the girls were Chinese, small and dainty, with tiny feet and hands like flowers, and they wore suits of flowered silk. But their painted faces were like masks. They looked at the strangers with black derisive eyes. They were strangely inhuman.

'I brought you here because I thought you ought to see the place,' said Captain Bredon, with the air of a man doing his bounden duty, 'but just look-see is all. They don't like us for some reason. In some of these Chinese joints they won't even let a white man in. Fact is, they say we stink. Funny, ain't it? They say we smell of corpses.'

'We?'

'Give me Japs,' said the Captain. 'They're fine. My wife's a Jap, you know. You come along with me and I'll take you to a place where they have Japanese girls, and if you don't see something you like there I'm a Dutchman.'

Their rickshaws were waiting and they stepped into them. Captain Bredon gave a direction and the boys started off. They were let into the house by a stout middle-aged Japanese woman, who bowed low as they entered. She took them into a neat, clean room furnished only with mats on the floor; they sat down and presently a little girl came in with a tray on which were two bowls of pale tea. With a shy bow she handed one to each of them. The Captain spoke to the middle-aged woman and she looked at Neil and giggled. She said something to the child, who went out, and presently four girls tripped in. They were sweet in their kimonos, with their shining black hair artfully dressed; they were small and plump, with round faces and laughing eyes. They bowed low as they came in and with good manners murmured polite greetings. Their speech sounded like the twittering of birds. Then they knelt, one on each side of the two men, and charmingly flirted with them. Captain Bredon soon had his arms round two slim waists. They all talked nineteen to the dozen. They were very gay. It seemed to Neil that the Captain's girls were mocking him, for their gleaming eyes were mischievously turned towards him, and he blushed. But the other two cuddled up to him, smiling, and spoke in Japanese as though he understood every word they said. They seemed so happy and guileless that he laughed. They were very attentive. They handed him the bowl so that he should drink his tea, and then took it from him so that he should not have the trouble of holding it. They lit his cigarette for him and one put out a small, delicate hand to take the ash so that it should not fall on his clothes. They stroked his smooth face and looked with curiosity at his large young hands. They were as playful as kittens.

'Well, which is it to be?' said the Captain after a while. 'Made your choice yet?'

'What d'you mean?'

'I'll just wait and see you settled and then I'll fix myself up.'

'Oh, I don't want either of them. I'm going home to bed.'

'Why, what's the matter? You're not scared, are you?'

'No, I just don't fancy it. But don't let me stand in your way. I'll get back to the hotel all right.'

'Oh, if you're not going to do anything I won't either. I only wanted to be matey.'

He spoke to the middle-aged woman and what he said caused the girls to look at Neil with sudden surprise. She answered and the Captain shrugged his shoulders. Then one of the girls made a remark that set them all laughing.

'What does she say?' asked Neil.

'She's pulling your leg,' replied the Captain, smiling.

But he gave Neil a curious look. The girl, having made them laugh once, now said something directly to Neil. He could not understand, but the mockery of her eyes made him blush and frown. He did not like to be made fun of. Then she laughed outright and throwing her arm round his neck lightly kissed him.

'Come on, let's be going,' said the Captain.

When they dismissed their rickshaws and walked into the hotel Neil asked him:

'What was it that girl said that made them all laugh?'

'She said you were a virgin.'

'I don't see anything to laugh at in that,' said Neil, with his slow Scots accent.

'Is it true?'

'I suppose it is.'

'How old are you?'

'Twenty-two.'

'What are you waiting for?'

'Till I marry.'

The Captain was silent. At the top of the stairs he held out his hand. There was a twinkle in his eyes when he bade the lad good night, but Neil met it with a level, candid, and untroubled gaze.

Three days later they sailed. Neil was the only white passenger. When the Captain was busy he read. He was reading again Wallace's *Malay Archipelago*. He had read it as a boy, but now it had a new and absorbing interest for him. When the Captain was at leisure they played cribbage or sat in long chairs on the deck, smoking, and talked. Neil was the son of a country doctor, and he could not remember when he had not been interested in natural history. When he had done with school he went to the University of Edinburgh and there took a B.Sc. with Honours. He was looking out for a job as demonstrator in biology when he chanced to see in *Nature* an advertisement for an assistant curator of the museum at Kuala Solor. The Curator, Angus Munro, had been at Edinburgh with his uncle, a Glasgow merchant, and his uncle wrote to ask him if he would give the boy a trial. Though Neil was especially interested in entomology he was a trained taxidermist, which the advertisement said was essential; he enclosed certificates from Neil's old teachers; he added that Neil had played football for his university. In a few weeks a cable arrived engaging him and a fortnight later he sailed.

'What's Mr Munro like?' asked Neil.

'Good fellow. Everybody likes him.'

'I looked out his papers in the scientific journals. He had one in the last number of *The Ibis* on the Gymnathidaw.'

'I don't know anything about that. I know he's got a Russian wife. They don't like her much.'

'I got a letter from him at Singapore saying they'd put me up for a bit till I could look round and see what I wanted to do.'

Now they were steaming up the river. At the mouth was a straggling fishermen's village standing on piles in the water; on the bank grew thickly nipah palm and the tortured mangrove; beyond stretched the dense green of the virgin forest. In the distance, darkly silhouetted against the blue sky, was the rugged outline of a mountain. Neil, his heart beating with the excitement that possessed him, devoured the scene with eager eyes. He was surprised. He knew his Conrad almost by heart and he was expecting a land of brooding mystery. He was not prepared for the blue milky sky. Little white clouds on the horizon, like sailing boats becalmed, shone in the sun. The green trees of the forest glittered in the brilliant light. Here and there, on the banks, were Malay houses with thatched roofs, and they nestled cosily among fruit trees. Natives in dug-outs rowed, standing, up the river. Neil had no feeling of being shut in, nor, in that radiant morning, of gloom, but of space and freedom. The country offered him a gracious welcome. He knew he was going to be happy in it. Captain Bredon from the bridge threw a friendly glance at the lad standing below him. He had taken quite a fancy to him during the four days the journey had lasted. It was true he did not drink, and when you made a joke he was as likely as not to take you seriously, but there was something very taking in his seriousness; everything was interesting and important to him – that, of course, was why he did not find your jokes amusing; but even though he didn't see them he laughed, because he felt you expected it. He laughed because life was grand. He was grateful for every little thing you told him. He was very polite. He never asked you to pass him anything without saying "please" and always said "thank you" when you gave it. And he was a good-looking fellow, no one could deny that. Neil was standing with his hands on the rail, bare-headed, looking at the passing bank. He was tall, six foot two, with long, loose limbs, broad shoulders, and narrow hips; there was something charmingly coltish about him, so that you expected him at any moment to break into a caper. He had brown curly hair with a peculiar shine in it; sometimes when the light caught it, it glittered like gold. His eyes, large and very blue, shone with good-humour. They reflected his happy disposition. His nose was short and blunt and his mouth big, his chin determined; his face was rather broad. But his most striking feature was his skin; it was very white and smooth, with a lovely patch of red on either cheek. It would have been a beautiful skin even for a woman. Captain Bredon made the same joke to him every morning.

'Well, my lad, have you shaved today?'

Neil passed his hand over his chin.

'No, d'you think I need it?'

The Captain always laughed at this.

'Need it? Why, you've got a face like a baby's bottom.'

And invariably Neil reddened to the roots of his hair.

'I shave once a week,' he retorted.

But it wasn't only his looks that made you like him. It was his ingenuousness, his candour, and the freshness with which he confronted the world. For all his intentness and the solemn way in which he took everything, and his inclination to argue upon every point that came up, there was something strangely simple in him that gave you quite an odd feeling. The Captain couldn't make it out.

'I wonder if it's because he's never had a woman,' he said to himself. 'Funny. I should have thought the girls never left him alone. With a complexion like that.'

But the *Sultan Ahmed* was nearing the bend after rounding which Kuala Solor would be in sight and the Captain's reflections were interrupted by the necessities of his work. He rang down to the engine room. The ship slackened to half speed. Kuala Solor straggled along the left bank of the river, a white, neat, and trim little town, and on the right on a hill were the fort and the Sultan's palace. There was a breeze and the Sultan's flag, at the top of a tall staff, waved bravely against the sky. They anchored in midstream. The doctor and a police officer came on board in the government launch. They were accompanied by a tall thin man in white ducks. The Captain stood at the head of the gangway and shook hands with them. Then he turned to the last comer.

'Well, I've brought you your young hopeful safe and sound.' And a glance at Neil: 'This is Munro.'

The tall thin man held out his hand and gave Neil an appraising look. Neil flushed a little and smiled. He had beautiful teeth.

'How do you do, sir?'

Munro did not smile with his lips, but faintly with his grey eyes. His cheeks were hollow and he had a thin aquiline nose and pale lips. He was deeply sunburned. His face looked tired, but his expression was very gentle, and Neil immediately felt confidence in him. The Captain introduced him to the doctor and the policeman and suggested that they should have a drink. When they sat down and the boy brought bottles of beer Munro took off his topee. Neil saw that he had close-cropped brown hair turning grey. He was a man of forty, quiet, self-possessed in manner, with an intellectual air that distinguished him from the brisk little doctor and the heavy swaggering police officer.

'MacAdam doesn't drink,' said the Captain when the boy poured out four glasses of beer.

'All the better,' said Munro. 'I hope you haven't been trying to lure him into evil ways.'

'I tried to in Singapore,' returned the Captain, with a twinkle in his eyes, 'but there was nothing doing.'

When he had finished his beer Munro turned to Neil.

'Well, we'll be getting ashore, shall we?'

Neil's baggage was put in charge of Munro's boy and the two men got into a sampan. They landed.

'Do you want to go straight up to the bungalow or would you like to have a look round first? We've got a couple of hours before tiffin.'

'Couldn't we go to the museum?' said Neil.

Munro's eyes smiled gently. He was pleased. Neil was shy and Munro not by nature talkative, so they walked in silence. By the river were the native huts, and here, living their immemorial lives, dwelt the Malays. They were busy, but without haste, and you were conscious of a happy, normal activity. There was a sense of the rhythm of life of which the pattern was birth and death, love, and the affairs common to mankind. They came to the bazaars, narrow streets with arcades, where the teeming Chinese, working and eating, noisily talking, as is their way, indefatigably strove with eternity.

'It's not much after Singapore,' said Munro, 'but I always think it's rather picturesque.'

He spoke with an accent less broad than Neil's but the Scots burr was there and it put Neil at his ease. He could never quite get it out of his head that the English of English people was affected.

The museum was a handsome stone building and as they entered its portals Munro instinctively straightened himself. The attendant at the door saluted and Munro spoke to him in Malay, evidently explaining who Neil was, for the attendant gave him a smile and saluted again. It was cool in there in comparison with the heat without and the light was pleasant after the glare of the street.

'I'm afraid you'll be disappointed,' said Munro. 'We haven't got half the things we ought to have, but up to now we've been handicapped by lack of money. We've had to do the best we could. So you must make allowances.'

Neil stepped in like a swimmer diving confidently into a summer sea. The specimens were admirably arranged. Munro had sought to please as well as to instruct, and birds and beasts and reptiles were presented, as far as possible in their natural surroundings, in such a way as to give a vivid impression of life. Neil lost his shyness and began with boyish enthusiasm to talk of this and that. He asked an infinity of questions. He was excited. Neither of them was conscious of the passage of time, and when Munro glanced at his watch he was surprised to see what the hour was. They got into rickshaws and drove to the bungalow.

Munro led the young man into a drawing-room. A woman was lying on a sofa reading a book and as they came in she slowly rose.

'This is my wife. I'm afraid we're dreadfully late, Darya.'

'What does it matter?' she smiled. 'What is more unimportant than time?'

She held out her hand, a rather large hand, to Neil and gave him a long, reflective, but friendly look.

'I suppose you've been showing him the museum.'

She was a woman of five-and-thirty, of medium height, with a pale brown face of a uniform colour and pale blue eyes. Her hair, parted in the middle and wound into a knot on the nape of her neck, was untidy; it had a moth-like quality and was of a curious pale brown. Her face was broad, with high cheek-bones, and she had a rather fleshy nose. She was not a pretty woman, but there was in her slow movements a sensual grace and in her manner as it were a physical casualness that only very dull people could have failed to find interesting. She wore a frock of green cotton. She spoke English perfectly, but with a slight accent.

They sat down to tiffin. Neil was overcome once more with shyness, but Darya did not seem to notice it. She talked freely and easily. She asked him about his journey and what he had thought of Singapore. She told him about the people he would have to meet. That afternoon Munro was to take him to call on the Resident, the Sultan being away, and later they would go to the club. There he would see everybody.

'You will be popular,' she said, her pale blue eyes resting on him with attention. A man less ingenuous than Neil might have noticed that she took stock of his size and youthful virility, his shiny curling hair and his lovely skin. 'They don't think much of us.'

'Oh, nonsense, Darya. You're too sensitive. They're English, that's all.'

'They think it's rather funny of Angus to be a scientist and they think it's rather vulgar of me to be a Russian. I don't care. They're fools. They're the most commonplace, the most narrow-minded, the most conventional people it has ever been my misfortune to live amongst.'

'Don't put MacAdam off the moment he arrives. He'll find them kind and hospitable.'

'What is your first name?' she asked the boy.

'Neil.'

'I shall call you by it. And you must call me Darya. I hate being called Mrs Munro. It makes me feel like a minister's wife.'

Neil blushed. He was embarrassed that she should ask him so soon to be so familiar. She went on.

'Some of the men are not bad.'

'They do their job competently and that's what they're here for,' said Munro.

'They shoot. They play football and tennis and cricket. I get

431

on with them quite well. The women are intolerable. They are jealous and spiteful and lazy. They can talk of nothing. If you introduce an intellectual subject they look down their noses as though you were indecent. What can they talk about? They're interested in nothing. If you speak of the body they think you improper, and if you speak of the soul they think you priggish.'

'You mustn't take what my wife says too literally,' smiled Munro, in his gentle, tolerant way. 'The community here is just like any other in the East, neither very clever, nor very stupid, but amiable and kindly. And that's a good deal.'

'I don't want people to be amiable and kindly. I want them to be vital and passionate. I want them to be interested in mankind. I want them to attach more importance to the things of the spirit than to a gin pahit or a curry tiffin. I want art to matter to them, and literature.' She addressed herself abruptly to Neil: 'Have you got a soul?'

'Oh, I don't know. I don't know exactly what you mean.'

'Why do you blush when I ask you? Why should you be ashamed of your soul? It is what is important in you. Tell me about it. I am interested in you and I want to know.'

It seemed very awkward to Neil to be tackled in this way by a perfect stranger. He had never met anyone like this. But he was a serious young man and when he was asked a question straight out he did his best to answer it. It was Munro's presence that embarrassed him.

'I don't know what you mean by the soul. If you mean an immaterial or spiritual entity, separately produced by the creator, in temporary conjunction with the material body, then my answer is in the negative. It seems to me that such a radically dualistic view of human personality cannot be defended by anyone who is able to take a calm view of the evidence. If, on the other hand, you mean by soul the aggregate of psychic elements which form what we know as the personality of the individual, then, of course, I have.'

'You're very sweet and you're wonderfully handsome,' she said, smiling. 'No, I mean the heart with its longings and the body with its desires and the infinite in us. Tell me, what did you read on the journey, or did you only play deck tennis?'

Neil was taken aback at the inconsequence of her reply. He would have been a little affronted except for the good-humour in her eyes and the naturalness in her manner. Munro smiled quietly at the young man's bewilderment. When he smiled the lines that ran from the wings of his nostrils to the corners of his mouth became deep furrows.

'I read a lot of Conrad.'

'For pleasure or to improve your mind?'

'Both. I admire him awfully.'

Darya threw up her arms in an extravagant gesture of protest.

'That Pole,' she cried. 'How can you English ever have let yourselves be taken in by that wordy mountebank? He has all the superficiality of his countrymen. That stream of words, those involved sentences, the showy rhetoric, that affectation of profundity: when you get through all that to the thought at the bottom, what do you find but a trivial commonplace? He was like a second-rate actor who put on a romantic dress and declaims a play by Victor Hugo. For five minutes you say this is heroic, and then your whole soul revolts and you cry, no, this is false, false, false.'

She spoke with a passion that Neil had never know anyone show when speaking of art or literature. Her cheeks, usually colourless, flushed and her pale eyes glowed.

'There's no one who got atmosphere like Conrad,' said Neil. 'I can smell and see and feel the East when I read him.'

'Nonsense. What do you know about the East? Everyone will tell you that he made the grossest blunders. Ask Angus.'

'Of course he was not always accurate,' said Munro, in his measured, reflective way. 'The Borneo he described is not the Borneo we know. He saw it from the deck of a merchant-vessel and he was not an acute observer even of what he saw. But does it matter? I don't know why fiction should be hampered by fact. I don't think it's a mean achievement to have created a country, a dark, sinister, romantic, and heroic country of the soul.'

'You're a sentimentalist, my poor Angus.' And then again to Neil: 'You must read Turgenev, you must read Tolstoy, you must read Dostoyevsky.'

Neil did not in the least know what to make of Darya Munro. She skipped over the first stages of acquaintance and treated him at once like someone she had known intimately all her life. It puzzled him. It seemed so reckless. When he met anyone his own instinct was to go cautiously. He was amiable, but he did not like to step too far before he saw his way before him. He did not want to give anyone his confidence before he thought himself justified. But with Darya you could not help yourself; she forced your confidence. She poured out the feelings and thoughts that most people keep to themselves like a prodigal flinging gold pieces to a scrambling crowd. She did not talk, she did not act, like anyone he had ever known. She did not mind what she said. She would speak of the natural functions of the human animal in a way that brought the blushes coursing to his cheeks. They excited her ridicule.

'Oh, what a prig you are! What is there indecent in it? When I'm going to take a purge, why shouldn't I say so, and when I think you want one, why shouldn't I tell you?'

'Theoretically I dare say you're right,' said Neil, always judicious and reasonable.

She made him tell her of his father and mother, his brothers, his life at school and at the university. She told him about herself. Her father was a general killed in the war and her mother a Princess Lutchkov. They were in Eastern Russia when the Bolsheviks seized power, and fled to Yokohama. Here they had subsisted miserably on the sale of their jewels and such objects of art as they had been able to save, and here she married a fellow-exile. She was unhappy with him and in two years divorced him. Her mother died and, penniless, she was driven to earn her living as best she could. She was employed by an American relief organization. She taught in a mission school. She worked in a hospital. She made Neil's blood boil, and at the same time embarrassed him very much, when she spoke of the men who tried to take advantage of her defencelessness and her poverty. She spared him no details.

'Brutes,' he said.

'Oh, all men are like that,' she replied, with a shrug of her shoulders.

She told him how once she protected her virtue at the point of her revolver.

'I swore I'd kill him if he took another step, and if he had I'd have shot him like a dog.'

'Gosh!' said Neil.

It was at Yokohama that she met Angus. He was spending his leave in Japan. She was captivated by his straightforwardness, the decency which was so obvious in him, his tenderness and his consideration. He was not a business man; he was a scientist, and science is milk-brother to art. He offered her peace. He offered her security. And she was tired of Japan. Borneo was a land of mystery. They had been married for five years.

She gave Neil the Russian novelists to read. She gave him

Fathers and Sons, Anna Karenina, and *The Brothers Karamazov.*
'Those are the three peaks of our literature. Read them. They
are the greatest novels the world has ever seen.'

Like many of her countrymen she talked as though no other
literature counted, and as though a few novels and stories, some
indifferent poetry, and half a dozen good plays had made whatever else the world has produced negligible. Neil was fascinated
and overwhelmed.

'You're rather like Alyosha yourself, Neil,' she said, looking
at him with eyes that were now so soft and tender, 'an Alyosha
with a Scotch dourness, suspicious and prudent, that will not let
the soul in you, the spiritual beauty, come out.'

'I'm not a bit like Alyosha,' he answered self-consciously.

'You don't know what you're like. You don't know anything
about yourself. Why are you a naturalist? Is it for money? You
could have made much more money by going into your uncle's
office in Glasgow. I feel in you something strange and unearthly.
I could bow down at your feet as Father Zossima did to Dimitri.'

'Please don't,' he said, smiling, but flushing a little too.

But the novels he read made her seem a little less strange to
him. They gave her an environment and he recognized in her traits
which, however unusual in the women he knew in Scotland, his
mother and the daughters of his uncle in Glasgow, were common
to many of the characters in Russian fiction. He no longer wondered that she should like to sit up so late, drinking innumerable
cups of tea, and lie on the sofa nearly all day long reading and
incessantly smoking cigarettes. She could do nothing at all for
days on end without being bored. She had a curious mixture of
languor and zest. She often said, with a shrug of her shoulders,
that she was an Oriental, and a European only by chance. She had
a feline grace that indeed suggested the Oriental. She was immensely untidy and it did not seem to affect her that cigarette-
ends, old papers, and empty tins should lie about their living-
room. But he thought she had something of Anna Karenina in her
and he transferred to her the sympathy he felt for that pathetic
creature. He understood her arrogance. It was not unnatural that
she despised the women of the community, whose acquaintance
little by little he made; they *were* commonplace; her mind was
quicker than theirs, she had a wider culture, and she had above all
a sort of tremulous sensitiveness that made *them* extraordinarily
colourless. She certainly took no pains to conciliate them. Though
at home she slopped about in a sarong and baju, when she and

Angus went out to dinner she dressed with a splendour that was somewhat out of place. She liked to display her ample bosom and her shapely back. She painted her cheeks and made up her eyes like an actress for the footlights. Though it made Neil angry to see the amused or outraged glances that her appearance provoked, he could not in his heart but think it a pity that she should make such an object of herself. She looked grand, of course, but if you hadn't known who she was you would have thought she wasn't respectable. There were things about her that he could never get over. She had an enormous appetite and it fashed him that she ate more than he and Angus together. He could never quite get used to the bluntness with which she discussed sexual matters. She took it for granted that at home and in Edinburgh he had had affairs with a host of women. She pressed him for details of his adventures. His Scotch pawkiness helped him to parry her thrusts and he evaded her questions with native caution. She laughed at his reticence.

Sometimes she shocked him. He grew accustomed to the frankness with which she admired his looks, and when she told him that he was as beautiful as a young Norse god he did not turn a hair. Flattery fell off him like water from a duck's back. But he did not like it when she ran her hand, though large, very soft, with caressing fingers, through his curly hair or, a smile on her lips, stroked his smooth face. He couldn't bear being mussed about. One day she wanted a drink of tonic water and began pouring some out in a glass that stood on the table.

'That's my glass,' he said quickly. 'I've just been drinking out of it.'

'Well, what of it? You haven't got syphilis, have you?'

'I hate drinking out of other people's glasses myself.'

She was funny about cigarettes too. Once, when he hadn't been there very long, he had just lit one, when she passed and said:

'I want that.'

She took it out of his mouth and began to smoke it. After two or three puffs, she said she did not want any more and handed it back to him. The end she had had in her mouth was red from the rouge on her lips, and he didn't want to go on smoking it at all. But he was afraid she would think it rude if he threw it away. It somewhat disgusted him. Often she would ask him for a cigarette and when he handed it to her, say:

'Oh, light it for me, will you?'

When he did so, and held it out to her, she opened her mouth so that he should put it in. He hadn't been able to help wetting the end a little. He wondered she could bear to put it in her mouth after it had been in his. The whole thing seemed to him awfully familiar. He was sure Munro wouldn't like it. She had even done this once or twice at the club. Neil had felt himself go purple. He wished she hadn't got these rather unpleasant habits, but he supposed that they were Russian, and one couldn't deny that she was wonderfully good company. Her conversation was very stimulating. It was like champagne (which Neil had tasted once and thought wretched stuff), 'metaphorically speaking'. There was nothing she couldn't talk about. She didn't talk like a man; with a man you generally knew what he would say next, but with her you never did; her intuition was quite remarkable. She gave you ideas. She enlarged your mind and excited your imagination. Neil felt alive as he had never felt alive before. He seemed to walk on mountain peaks, and the horizons of the spirit were unbounded. Neil felt a certain complacency when he stopped to reflect on what an exalted plane his mind communed with hers. Such conversations made very small beer of the vaunted pleasure of sense. She was in many ways (he was of a cautious nature and seldom made a statement even to himself that he did not qualify) the most intelligent woman he had ever met. And besides, she was Angus Munro's wife.

For, whatever Neil's reservations were about Darya, he had none about Munro, and she would have had to be a much less remarkable woman not to profit by the enormous admiration he conceived for her husband. With him Neil let himself go. He felt for him what he had never felt for anyone before. He was so sane, so balanced, so tolerant. This was the sort of man he would himself like to be when he was older. He talked little, but when he did, with good sense. He was wise. He had a dry humour that Neil understood. It made the hearty English fun of the men at the club seem inane. He was kind and patient. He had a dignity that made it impossible to conceive of anyone taking a liberty with him, but he was neither pompous nor solemn. He was honest and absolutely truthful. But Neil admired him no less as a scientist than as a man. He had imagination. He was careful and painstaking. Though his interest was in research he did the routine work of the museum conscientiously. He was just then much interested in stick-insects and intended to write a paper on their powers of parthenogenetic reproduction. An incident occurred in connexion with the experiments he was making that made a great impression on Neil. One day, a little captive gibbon escaped from its chain and ate up all the larvae and so destroyed the whole of Munro's evidence. Neil nearly cried. Angus Munro took the gibbon in his arms and, smiling, stroked it.

'Diamond, Diamond,' he said, quoting Sir Isaac Newton, 'you little know the damage you have done.'

He was also studying mimicry and instilled into Neil his absorbed interest in this controversial subject. They had interminable talks about it. Neil was astonished at the Curator's wonderful knowledge. It was encylopedic, and he was abashed at his own ignorance. But it was when Munro spoke of the trips into the country to collect specimens that his enthusiasm was most contagious. That was the perfect life, a life of hardship, difficulty, often of privation and sometimes of danger, but rewarded by the thrill of finding a rare, or even a new, species, by the beauty of the scenery, and the intimate observation of nature, and above all the sense of freedom from every tie. It was for this part of the work that Neil had been chiefly engaged. Munro was occupied in research work that made it difficult for him to be away from home for several weeks at a time, and Darya had always refused to accompany him. She had an unreasoning fear of the jungle. She was terrified of wild beasts, snakes, and venomous insects. Though Munro had told her over and over again that no animal hurt you unless you molested or frightened it, she could not get over her instinctive horror. He did not like leaving her. She cared little for the local society and with him away he realized that life for her must be intolerably dull. But the Sultan was keenly interested in natural history and was anxious that the museum should be completely representative of the country's fauna. One expedition Munro and Neil were to make together, so that Neil should learn how to go to work, and the plans for this were discussed by them for months. Neil looked forward to it as he had never looked forward to anything in his life.

Meanwhile he learned Malay and acquired a smattering of the dialects that would be useful to him on future journeys. He played tennis and football. He soon knew everyone in the community. On the football field he threw off his absorption in science and his interest in Russian fiction and gave himself up to the pleasure of the game. He was strong, quick, and active. After it was all over it was grand to have a sluice down and a long tonic with a slice of lemon and go over it all with the other fellows. It had never been intended that Neil should live permanently with the Munros.

There was a roomy rest-house at Kuala Solor, but the rule was that no one should stay in it for more than a fortnight and such of the bachelors as had no official quarters clubbed together and took a house between them. When Neil arrived it so happened that there was no vacancy in any of these messes. One evening, however, when he had been about four months in the colony, two men, Waring and Jonson, when they were sitting together after a game of tennis, told him that one member of their mess was going home and if he would like to join them they would be glad to have him. They were young fellows of his own age, in the football team, and Neil liked them both. Waring was in the Customs and Jonson in the police. He jumped at the suggestion. They told him how much it would cost and fixed a day, a fortnight later, when it would be convenient for him to move in.

At dinner he told the Munros.

'It's been awfully good of you to let me stay so long. It's made me very uncomfortable planting myself on you like this, I've been quite ashamed, but now there's no excuse for me.'

'But we like having you here,' said Darya. 'You don't need an excuse.'

'I can hardly go on staying here indefinitely.'

'Why not? Your salary's miserable, what's the use of wasting it on board and lodging? You'd be bored stiff with Jonson and Waring. Stupids. They haven't an idea in their heads outside playing the gramophone and knocking balls about.'

It was true that it had been very convenient to live free of cost. He had saved the greater part of his salary. He had a thrifty soul and had never been used to spending money when it wasn't necessary, but he was proud. He could not go on living at other people's expense. Darya looked at him with her quiet, observant eyes.

'Angus and I have got used to you now. I think we'd miss you. If you like, you can pay us for your board. You don't cost anything, but if it'll make you easier I'll find out exactly what difference you make in cookie's book and you can pay that.'

'It must be an awful nuisance having a stranger in the house,' he answered uncertainly.

'It'll be miserable for you there. Good heavens, the filth they eat.'

It was true also that at the Munros you ate better than anywhere else at Kuala Solor. He had dined out now and then, and even at the Resident's you didn't get a very good dinner. Darya liked her food and kept the cook up to the mark. He made Russian dishes which were a fair treat. That cabbage soup of Darya's was worth walking five miles for. But Munro hadn't said anything.

'I'd be glad if you'd stay here,' he said now. 'It's very convenient to have you on the spot. If anything comes up we can talk it over there and then. Waring and Jonson are very good fellows, but I dare say you'd find them rather limited after a bit.'

'Oh, well, then I'll be very pleased. Heaven knows, I couldn't want anything better than this. I was only afraid I was in the way.'

Next day it was raining cats and dogs and it was impossible to play tennis or football, but towards six Neil put on a mackintosh and went to the club. It was empty but for the Resident, who was sitting in an arm-chair reading *The Fortnightly*. His name was Trevelyan, and he claimed to be related to the friend of Byron. He was a tall fat man, with close-cropped white hair and the large red face of a comic actor. He was fond of amateur theatricals and specialized in cynical dukes and facetious butlers. He was a bachelor, but generally supposed to be fond of the girls, and he like his gin pahit before dinner. He owed his position to the Sultan's friendship. He was a slack, complacent man, a great talker, not very fond of work, who wanted everything to go smoothly and no one to give trouble. Though not considered especially competent he was popular in the community because he was easy-going and hospitable, and he certainly made life more comfortable than if he had been energetic and efficient. He nodded to Neil.

'Well, young fellow, how are bugs today?'

'Feeling the weather, sir,' said Neil gravely.

'Hi-hi.'

In a few minutes Waring, Jonson, and another man, called Bishop, came in. He was in the Civil Service. Neil did not play bridge, so Bishop went up to the Resident.

'Would you care to make a fourth, sir?' he asked him. 'There's nobody much in the club today.'

The Resident gave the others a glance.

'All right. I'll just finish this article and join you. Cut for me and deal. I shall only be five minutes.'

Neil went up to the three men.

'Oh, I say, Waring, thanks awfully, but I can't move over to you after all. The Munros have asked me to stay on with them for good.'

A broad smile broke on Waring's face.

'Fancy that.'

'It's awfully nice of them, isn't it? They made rather a point of it. I couldn't very well refuse.'

'What did I tell you?' said Bishop.

'I don't blame the boy,' said Waring.

There was something in their manner that Neil did not like. They seemed to be amused. He flushed.

'What the hell are you talking about?' he cried.

'Oh, come off it,' said Bishop. 'We know our Darya. You're not the first good-looking young fellow she's had a romp with, and you won't be the last.'

The words were hardly out of his mouth before Neil's clenched fist shot out like a flash. He hit Bishop on the face and he fell heavily to the floor. Jonson sprang at Neil and seized him round the middle, for he was beside himself.

'Let me go,' he shouted. 'If he doesn't withdraw that I'll kill him.'

The Resident, startled by the commotion, looked up and rose to his feet. He walked heavily towards them.

'What's this? What's this? What the hell are you boys playing at?'

They were taken aback. They had forgotten him. He was their master. Jonson let go of Neil and Bishop picked himself up. The Resident, a frown on his face, spoke to Neil sharply.

'What's the meaning of this? Did you hit Bishop?'

'Yes, sir.'

'Why?'

'He made a foul suggestion reflecting on a woman's honour,' said Neil, very haughtily, and still white with rage.

The Resident's eyes twinkled, but he kept a grave face.

'What woman?'

'I refuse to answer,' said Neil, throwing back his head and drawing himself up to his full imposing height.

It would have been more effective if the Resident hadn't been a good two inches taller, and very much stouter.

'Don't be a damned young fool.'

'Darya Munro,' said Jonson.

'What did you say, Bishop?'

'I forget the exact words I used. I said she'd hopped into bed with a good many young chaps here, and I supposed she hadn't missed the chance of doing the same with MacAdam.'

'It was a most offensive suggestion. Will you be so good as to apologize and shake hands. Both of you.'

'I've had a hell of a biff, sir. My eye's going to look like the devil. I'm damned if I apologize for telling the truth.'

'You're old enough to know that the fact that your statement is true only makes it more offensive, and as far as your eye is concerned I'm told that a raw beef-steak is very efficacious in these circumstances. Though I put my desire that you should apologize in the form of a request out of politeness, it is in point of fact an order.'

There was a moment's silence. The Resident looked bland.

'I apologize for what I said, sir,' Bishop said sulkily.

'Now then, MacAdam.'

'I'm sorry I hit him, sir. I apologize, too.'

'Shake hands.' .

The two young men solemnly did so.

'I shouldn't like this to go any further. It wouldn't be very nice for Munro, whom I think we all like. Can I count on you all holding your tongues?'

They nodded.

'Now be off with you. You stay, MacAdam, I want to have a few words with you.'

When the two of them were left alone, the Resident sat down and lit himself a cheroot. He offered one to Neil, but he only smoked cigarettes.

'You're a very violent young man,' said the Resident, with a smile. 'I don't like my officers to make scenes in a public place like this.'

'Mrs Munro is a great friend of mine. She's been kindness itself to me. I won't hear a word said against her.'

'Then I'm afraid you'll have your job cut out for you if you stay here much longer.'

Neil was silent for a moment. He stood, tall and slim, before the Resident, and his grave young face was guileless. He flung back his head defiantly. His emotion made him speak in broader Scots even than usual.

'I've lived with the Munros for four months, and I give you my word of honour that so far as I am concerned there is not an iota of truth in what that beast said. Mrs Munro has never treated me with anything that you could call undue familiarity. She's never by word or deed given me the smallest hint that she had an improper idea in her head. She's been like a mother to me or an elder sister.'

The Resident watched him with ironical eyes.

'I'm very glad to hear it. That's the best thing I've heard about her for a long time.'

'You believe me, sir, don't you?'

'Of course. Perhaps you've reformed her.' He called out, 'Boy. Bring me a gin pahit.' And then to Neil. 'That'll do. You can go now if you want to. But no more fighting, mind you, or you'll get the order of the boot.'

When Neil walked back to the Munros' bungalow the rain had stopped and the velvet sky was bright with stars. In the garden the fire-flies were flitting here and there. From the earth rose a scented warmth and you felt that if you stopped you would hear the growth of that luxuriant vegetation. A white flower of the night gave forth an overwhelming perfume. In the veranda Munro was typing some notes, and Darya, lying at full length on a long chair, was reading. The lamp behind her lit her smoky hair so that it shone like an aureole. She looked up at Neil and, putting down her book, smiled. Her smile was very friendly.

'Where have you been, Neil?'

'At the club.'

'Anybody there?'

The scene was so cosy and domestic, Darya's manner so peaceful and quietly assured, that it was impossible not to be touched. The two of them there, each occupied with his own concerns, seemed so united, their intimacy so natural, that no one could have conceived that they were not perfectly happy in one another. Neil did not believe a single word of what Bishop had said and the Resident had hinted. It was incredible. After all, he knew that what they had suspected of *him* was untrue, so what reason was there to think that the rest was any truer? They had dirty minds, all those people; because they were a lot of swine they thought everyone else as bad as they were. His knuckle hurt him a little. He was glad he had hit Bishop. He wished he knew who had started that filthy story. He'd wring his neck.

But now Munro fixed a date for the expedition that they had so much discussed, and in his careful way began to make preparations so that at the last moment nothing should be forgotten. The plan was to go as far up the river as possible and then make their way through the jungle and hunt for specimens on the little-known Mount Hitam. They expected to be away two months. As the day on which they were to start grew nearer Munro's spirits rose, and though he did not say very much, though he remained quiet and self-controlled, you could tell by the light in his eyes and the jauntiness of his step how much he looked forward to it. One morning, at the museum, he was almost sprightly.

'I've got some good news for you,' he said suddenly to Neil, after they had been looking at some experiments they were making, 'Darya's coming with us.'

'Is she? That's grand.'

Neil was delighted. That made it perfect.

'It's the first time I've ever been able to induce her to accompany me. I told her she'd enjoy it, but she would never listen to me. Queer cattle, women. I'd given it up and never thought of asking her to come this time, and suddenly, last night, out of a blue sky she said she'd like to.'

'I'm awfully glad,' said Neil.

'I didn't much like the idea of leaving her by herself so long; now we can stay just as long as we want to.'

They started early one morning in four prahus, manned by Malays, and besides themselves the party consisted of their servants and four Dyak hunters. The three of them lay on cushions side by side, under an awning; in the other boats were the Chinese servants and the Dyaks. They carried bags of rice for the whole party, provisions for themselves, clothes, books, and all that was necessary for their work. It was heavenly to leave civilization behind them and they were all excited. They talked. They smoked. They read. The motion of the river was exquisitely soothing. They lunched on a grassy bank. Dusk fell and they moored for the night. They slept at a long house and their Dyak hosts celebrated their visit with arrak, eloquence, and a fantastic dance. Next day the river, narrowing, gave them more definitely the feeling that they were adventuring into the unknown, and the exotic vegetation that crowded the banks to the water's edge, like an excited mob pushed from behind by a multitude, caused Neil a breathless ravishment. O wonder and delight! On the third day, because the water was shallower and the stream more rapid, they changed into lighter boats, and soon it grew so strong that the boatmen could paddle no longer, and they poled against the current with powerful and magnificent gestures. Now and then they came to rapids and had to disembark, unload, and haul the boats through a rock-strewn passage. After five days they reached a point beyond which they could go no further. There was a government bungalow there, and they settled in for a couple of nights while Munro made arrangements for their excursion into the interior. He wanted bearers for their baggage, and men to build a house for them when they reached Mount Hitam. It was necessary for Munro to see the headman of a village in the vicinity, and thinking it would save time if he went himself rather than let the headman come to him, the day after they arrived he set out at dawn with a guide and a couple of Dyaks. He expected to be back in a few hours. When he had seen him off Neil thought he would have a bathe. There was a pool a little way from the bungalow, and the water was so clear that you saw every grain of the sandy bottom. The river was so narrow there that the trees over-arched it. It was a lovely spot. It reminded Neil of the pools in Scotch streams he had bathed in as a boy, and yet it was strangely different. It had an air of romance, a feeling of virgin nature, that filled him with sensations that he found hard to analyse. He tried, of course, but older heads than his have found it difficult to anatomize happiness. A kingfisher was sitting on an overhanging branch and its vivid blue was reflected as bluely in the crystal stream. It flew away with a flashing glitter of jewelled wings when Neil, slipping off his sarong and baju, scrambled down into the water. It was fresh without being cold. He splashed and tumbled about. He enjoyed the movement of his strong limbs. He floated and looked at the blue sky peeping through the leaves and the sun that here and there gilded the water. Suddenly he heard a voice.

'How white your body is, Neil.'

With a gasp he let himself sink and turning round saw Darya standing on the bank.

'I say, I haven't got any clothes on.'

'So I saw. It's much nicer bathing without. Wait a minute, I'll come in, it looks lovely.'

She also was wearing a sarong and a baju. He turned away his head quickly, for he saw that she was taking them off. He heard her splash into the water. He gave two or three strokes in order that she should have room to swim about at a good distance from him, but she swam up to him.

'Isn't the feel of the water on one's body lovely?' she said.

She laughed and opening her hand splashed water in his face. He was so embarrassed he did not know which way to look. In that limpid water it was impossible not to see that she was stark naked. It was not so bad now, but he could not help thinking how difficult it would be to get out. She seemed to be having a grand time.

'I don't care if I do get my hair wet,' she said.

She turned over on her back and with strong strokes swam round the pool. When she wanted to get out, he thought, the best thing would be if he turned his back and when she was dressed she could go and he would get out later. She seemed quite unconscious of the awkwardness of the situation. He was vexed with her. It really was rather tactless to behave like that. She kept on talking to him just as if they were on dry land and properly dressed. She even called his attention to herself.

'Does my hair look awful? It's so fine it gets like rat tails when it's wet. Hold me under the shoulders a moment while I try to screw it up.'

'Oh, it's all right,' he said. 'You'd better leave it now.'

'I'm getting frightfully hungry,' she said presently. 'What about breakfast?'

'If you'll get out first and put on your things, I'll follow you in a minute.'

'All right.'

She swam the two strokes needed to bring her to the side, and he modestly looked away so that he should not see her get out nude from the water.

'I can't get up,' she cried. 'You'll have to help me.'

It had been easy enough to get in, but the bank overhung the water and one had to lift oneself up by the branch of a tree.

'I can't. I haven't got a stitch of clothing on.'

'I know that. Don't be so Scotch. Get up on the bank and give me a hand.'

There was no help for it. Neil swung himself up and pulled her after him. She had left her sarong beside his. She took it up unconcernedly and began to dry herself with it. There was nothing for him but to do the same, but for decency's sake he turned his back on her.

'You really have a most lovely skin,' she said. 'It's as smooth and white as a woman's. It's funny on such a manly virile figure. And you haven't got a hair on your chest.'

Neil wrapped the sarong round him and slipped his arms into the baju.

'Are you ready?'

She had porridge for breakfast, and eggs and bacon, cold meat, and marmalade. Neil was a trifle sulky. She was really almost too Russian. It was stupid of her to behave like that; of course there was no harm in it, but it was just the sort of thing that made people think the things they did about her. The worst of it was that you couldn't give her a hint. She'd only laugh at you. But the fact was that if any of those men at Kuala Solor had seen them bathing like that together, stark naked, nothing would have persuaded them that something improper hadn't happened. In his judicious way Neil admitted to himself that you could hardly blame them. It was too bad of her. She had no right to put a fellow in such a position. He had felt such a fool. And say what you liked, it was indecent.

Next morning, having seen their carriers on the way, a long procession in single file, each man carrying his load in a creel on his back, with their servants, guides, and hunters, they started to walk. The path ran over the foothills of the mountain, through scrub and tall grass, and now and then they came to narrow streams which they crossed by rickety bridges of bamboo. The sun beat on them fiercely. In the afternoon they reached the shade of a bamboo forest, grateful after the glare, and the bamboos in their slender elegance rose to incredible heights, and the green light was like the light under the sea. At last they reached the primeval forest, huge trees swathed in luxuriant creepers, an inextricable tangle, and awe descended upon them. They cut their way through the undergrowth. They walked in twilight and only now and then caught through the dense foliage above them a glimpse of sunshine. They saw neither man nor beast, for the denizens of the jungle are shy and at the first sound of footsteps vanish from sight. They heard birds up high in the tall trees, but saw none save the twittering sunbirds that flew in the underwoods and delicately coquetted with the wild flowers. They halted for the night. The carriers made a floor of branches and on this spread waterproof sheets. The Chinese cook made them their dinner and then they turned in.

It was the first night Neil had ever spent in the jungle and he could not sleep. The darkness was profound. The noise was deafening of innumerable insects, but like the roar of traffic in a great city it was so constant that in a little while it was like an impenetrable silence, and when on a sudden he heard the shriek of a monkey seized by a snake or the scream of a night-bird he nearly jumped out of his skin. He had a mysterious sensation that all around creatures were watching them. Over there, beyond the camp-fires, savage warfare was waged and they three on their bed of branches were defenceless and alone in face of the horror of nature. By his side Munro was breathing quietly in his deep sleep.

'Are you awake, Neil?' Darya whispered.

'Yes. Is anything the matter?'

'I'm terrified.'

'It's all right. There's nothing to be afraid of.'

'The silence is so awful. I wish I hadn't come.'

She lit a cigarette.

Neil, having at last dozed off, was awakened by the hammering of a woodpecker, and its complacent laugh as it flew from one tree to another seemed to mock the sluggards. A hurried breakfast, and the caravan started. The gibbons swung from branch to branch, gathering in the dawn dew from the leaves, and their strange cry was like the call of a bird. The light had driven away Darya's fears, and notwithstanding a sleepless night she was alert and gay. They continued to climb. In the afternoon they reached the spot that the guides had told them would be a good camping place, and here Munro decided to build a house. The men set to work. With their long knives they cut palm leaves and saplings and soon had erected a two-roomed hut raised on piles from the ground. It was neat and fresh and green. It smelt good.

The Munros, he from old habit, she because she had for years wandered about the world and had a catlike knack of making herself comfortable wherever she went, were at home anywhere. In a day they had arranged everything and settled down. Their routine was invariable. Every morning Neil and Munro started out separately, collecting. The afternoon was devoted to pinning insects in boxes, placing butterflies between sheets of paper and skinning birds. When dusk came they caught moths. Darya busied herself with the hut and the servants, sewed and read and smoked innumerable cigarettes. The days passed very pleasantly, monotonous but eventful. Neil was enraptured. He explored the mountain in all directions. One day, to his pride, he found a new species of stick-insect. Munro named it Cuniculina MacAdami. This was fame. Neil (at twenty-two) realized that he had not lived in vain. But another day he only just escaped being bitten by a viper. Owing to its green colour he had not seen it and was only saved from lurching against it by the Dyak hunter who was with him. They killed it and brought it back to camp. Darya shuddered at the sight of it. She had a terror of the wild creatures of the jungle and was almost hysterical. She would never go more than a few yards from the camp for fear of being lost.

'Has Angus ever told you how he was lost?' she asked Neil one evening when they were sitting quietly together after dinner.

'It wasn't a very pleasant experience,' he smiled.

'Tell him, Angus.'

He hesitated a little. It was not a thing he liked to recall.

'It was some years ago, I'd gone out with my butterfly net and I'd been very lucky, I'd got several rare specimens that I'd been looking for a long time. After a while I thought I was getting hungry so I turned back. I walked for some time and it struck me I'd come a good deal farther than I knew. Suddenly I caught sight of an empty match-box. I'd thrown it away when I started to come back; I'd been walking in a circle and was exactly where I was an hour before. I was not pleased. But I had a look round and set off again. It was fearfully hot and I was simply dripping with sweat. I knew more or less the direction the camp was in and I looked about for traces of my passage to see if I had come that way. I thought I found one or two and went on hopefully. I was frightfully thirsty. I walked on and on, picking my way over snags and trailing plants, and suddenly I knew I was lost. I couldn't have gone so far in the right direction without hitting the camp. I can tell you I was startled. I knew I must keep my head, so I sat down and thought the situation over. I was tortured by thirst. It was long past midday and in three or four hours it would be dark. I didn't like the idea of spending a night in the jungle at all. The only thing I could think of was to try and find a stream; if I followed its course, it would eventually bring me to a larger stream and sooner or later to the river. But of course it might take a couple of days. I cursed myself for being such a fool, but there was nothing better to do and I began walking. At all events if I found a stream I should be able to get a drink. I couldn't find a trickle of water anywhere, not the smallest brook that might lead to something like a stream. I began to be alarmed. I saw myself wandering on till at last I fell exhausted. I knew there was a lot of game in the forest and if I came upon a rhino I was done for. The maddening thing was I knew I couldn't be more than ten miles from my camp. I forced myself to keep my head. The day was waning and in the depths of the jungle it was growing dark already. If I'd brought a gun I could have fired it. In the camp they must have realized I was lost and would be looking for me. The undergrowth was so thick that I couldn't see six feet into it and presently, I don't know if it was nerves or not, I had the sensation that some animal was walking stealthily beside me. I stopped and it stopped too. I went on and it went on. I couldn't see it. I could see no movement in the undergrowth. I didn't even hear the breaking of a twig or the brushing of a body through leaves, but I knew how silently those beasts could move, and I was positive something was stalking me. My heart beat so violently against my ribs that I thought it would break. I was scared out of my wits. It was only by the exercise of all the self-control I had that I prevented myself from breaking into a run. I knew if I did that I was lost. I should be tripped up before I had gone twenty yards by a tangled root and when I was down it would spring on me. And if I started to run God knew where I should get to. And I had to husband my strength. I felt very like crying. And that intolerable thirst. I've never been so frightened in my life. Believe me, if I'd had a revolver I think I'd have blown my brains out. It was so awful I just wanted to finish with it. I was so exhausted I could hardly stagger. If I had an enemy who'd done me a deadly injury I wouldn't wish him the agony I endured then. Suddenly I heard two shots. My heart stood still. They were looking for me. Then I did lose my head. I ran in the direction of the sound, screaming at the top of my voice, I fell, I picked myself up again, I ran on, I shouted till I thought my lungs would burst, there was another shot, nearer, I shouted again, I heard answering shouts; there was a scramble of men in the undergrowth. In a minute I was surrounded by Dyak hunters. They wrung and kissed my hands. They laughed and cried. I very nearly cried too. I was down and out, but they gave me a drink. We were only three miles from the camp. It was pitch dark when we got back. By God, it was a near thing.'

A convulsive shudder passed through Darya.

'Believe me, I don't want to be lost in the jungle again.'

'What would have happened if you hadn't been found?'

'I can tell you. I should have gone mad. If I hadn't been stung by a snake or attacked by a rhino I should have gone on blindly till I fell exhausted. I should have starved to death. I should have died of thirst. Wild beasts would have eaten my body and ants cleaned my bones.'

Silence fell upon them.

Then it happened, when they had spent nearly a month on Mount Hitam, that Neil, notwithstanding the quinine Munro had made him take regularly, was stricken with fever. It was not a bad attack, but he felt very sorry for himself and was obliged to stay in bed. Darya nursed him. He was ashamed to give her so much trouble, but she would not listen to his protests. She was certainly very capable. He resigned himself to letting her do things for him that one of the Chinese boys could have done just as well. He was touched. She waited on him hand and foot. But when the fever was at its height and she sponged him all over with cold water, though the comfort was indescribable, he was excessively embarrassed. She insisted on washing him night and morning.

'I wasn't in the British hospital at Yokohama for six months without learning at least the routine of nursing,' she said, smiling.

She kissed him on the lips each time after she had finished. It was friendly and sweet of her. He rather liked it, but attached no importance to it; he even went so far, a rare thing for him, as to be facetious on the subject.

'Did you always kiss your patients at the hospital?' he asked her.

'Don't you like me to kiss you?' she smiled.

'It doesn't do me any harm.'

'It may even hasten your recovery,' she mocked.

One night he dreamt of her. He awoke with a start. He was sweating profusely. The relief was wonderful, and he knew that his temperature had fallen; he was well. He did not care. For what he had dreamt filled him with shame. He was horrified. That he should have such thoughts, even in his sleep, made him feel awful. He must be a monster of depravity. Day was breaking, and he heard Munro getting up in the room next door that he occupied with Darya. She slept late, and he took care not to disturb her. When he passed through Neil's room, Neil in a low voice called him.

'Hullo, are you awake?'

'Yes, I've had the crisis. I'm all right now.'

'Good. You'd better stay in bed today. Tomorrow you'll be as fit as a fiddle.'

'Send Ah Tan to me when you've had your breakfast, will you?'

'Right-ho.'

He heard Munro start out. The Chinese boy came and asked him what he wanted. An hour later Darya awoke. She came in to bid him good morning. He could hardly look at her.

'I'll just have my breakfast and then I'll come in and wash you,' she said.

'I'm washed. I got Ah Tan to do it.'

'Why?'

'I wanted to spare you the trouble.'

'It isn't a trouble. I like doing it.'

451

She came over to the bed and bent down to kiss him, but he turned away his head.

'Oh, don't.'

'Why not?'

'It's silly.'

She looked at him for a moment, surprised, and then with a slight shrug of the shoulders left him. A little later she came back to see if there was anything he wanted. He pretended to be asleep. She very gently stroked his cheek.

'For God's sake don't do that,' he cried.

'I thought you were sleeping. What's the matter with you today?'

'Nothing.'

'Why are you being horrid to me? Have I done anything to offend you?'

'No.'

'Tell me what it is.'

She sat down on the bed and took his hand. He turned his face to the wall. He was so ashamed he could hardly speak.

'You seem to forget I'm a man. You treat me as if I was a boy of twelve.'

'Oh?'

He was blushing furiously. He was angry with himself and vexed with her. She really should be more tactful. He plucked nervously at the sheet.

'I know it means nothing to you and it ought not to mean anything to me. It doesn't when I'm well and up and about. One can't help one's dreams, but they are an indication of what is going on in the subconscious.'

'Have you been dreaming about me? Well, I don't think there's any harm in that.'

He turned his head and looked at her. Her eyes were gleaming, but his were sombre with remorse.

'You don't know men,' he said.

She gave a little burble of laughter. She bent down and threw her arms round his neck. She had nothing on but her sarong and baju.

'You darling,' she cried. 'Tell me, what did you dream?'

He was startled out of his wits. He pushed her violently aside.

'What are you doing? You're crazy.'

He jumped half out of bed.

'Don't you know that I'm madly in love with you?' she said.

'What *are* you talking about?'

He sat down on the side of the bed. He was frankly bewildered. She chuckled.

'Why do you suppose I came up to this horrible place? To be with you, ducky. Don't you know I'm scared stiff of the jungle? Even in here I'm frightened there'll be snakes or scorpions or something. I adore you.'

'You have no right to speak to me like that,' he said sternly.

'Oh, don't be so prim,' she smiled.

'Let's get out of here.'

He walked out on to the veranda and she followed him. He threw himself into a chair. She knelt by his side and tried to take his hands, but he withdrew them.

'I think you must be mad. I hope to God you don't mean what you say.'

'I do. Every word of it,' she smiled.

It exasperated him that she seemed unconscious of the frightfulness of her confession.

'Have you forgotten your husband?'

'Oh, what does he matter?'

'Darya.'

'I can't be bothered about Angus now.'

'I'm afraid you're a very wicked woman,' he said slowly, a frown darkening his smooth brow.

She giggled.

'Because I've fallen in love with you? Darling, you shouldn't be so absurdly good-looking.'

'For God's sake don't laugh.'

'I can't help it; you're comic – but still adorable. I love your white skin and your shining curly hair. I love you because you're so prim and Scotch and humourless. I love your strength. I love your youth.'

Her eyes glowed and her breath came quickly. She stooped and kissed his naked feet. He drew them away quickly, with a cry of protest, and in the agitation of his gesture nearly overthrew the rickety chair.

'Woman, you're insane. Have you no shame?'

'No.'

'What do you want of me?' he asked fiercely.

'Love.'

'What sort of a man do you take me for?'

'A man like any other,' she replied calmly.

'Do you think after all that Angus Munro has done for me I could be such a damned beast as to play about with his wife? I admire him more than any man I've ever known. He's grand. He's worth a dozen of me and you put together. I'd sooner kill myself than betray him. I don't know how you can think me capable of such a dastardly act.'

'Oh, my dear, don't talk such bilge. What harm is it going to do him? You mustn't take that sort of thing so tragically. After all, life is very short; we're fools if we don't take what pleasure we can out of it.'

'You can't make wrong right by talking about it.'

'I don't know about that. I think that's a very controvertible statement.'

He looked at her with amazement. She was sitting at his feet, cool to all appearance and collected, and she seemed to be enjoying the situation. She seemed quite unconscious of its seriousness.

'Do you know that I knocked a fellow down at the club because he made an insulting remark about you?'

'Who?'

'Bishop.'

'Dirty dog. What did he say?'

'He said you'd had affairs with men.'

'I don't know why people won't mind their own business. Anyhow, who cares what they say? I love you. I've never loved anyone like you. I'm absolutely sick with love for you.'

'Be quiet. Be quiet.'

'Listen, tonight when Angus is asleep I'll slip into your room. He sleeps like a rock. There's no risk.'

'You mustn't do that.'

'Why not?'

'No, no, no.'

He was frightened out of his wits. Suddenly she sprang to her feet and went into the house.

Munro came back at noon, and in the afternoon they busied themselves as usual. Darya, as she sometimes did, worked with them. She was in high spirits. She was so gay that Munro suggested that she was beginning to enjoy the life.

'It's not so bad,' she admitted. 'I'm feeling happy today.'

She teased Neil. She seemed not to notice that he was silent and kept his eyes averted from her.

'Neil's very quiet,' said Munro. 'I suppose you're feeling a bit weak still.'

454

'No, I just don't feel very talkative.'

He was harassed. He was convinced that Darya was capable of anything. He remembered the hysterical frenzy of Nastasya Filipovna in *The Idiot*, and felt that she too could behave with that unfortunate lack of balance. He had seen her more than once fly into a temper with one of the Chinese servants and he knew how completely she could lose her self-control. Resistance only exasperated her. If she did not immediately get what she wanted she would go almost insane with rage. Fortunately she lost interest in a thing with the same suddenness with which she hankered for it, and if you could distract her attention for a minute she forgot all about it. It was in such situations that Neil had most admired Munro's tact. He had often been slyly amused to see with what a pawky and yet tender cunning he appeased her feminine tantrums. It was on Munro's account that Neil's indignation was so great. Munro was a saint, and from what a state of humiliation and penury and random shifts had he not taken her to make her his wife! She owed everything to him. His name protected her. She had respectability. The commonest gratitude should have made it impossible for her to harbour such thoughts as she had that morning expressed. It was all very well for men to make advances, that was what men did, but for women to do so was disgusting. His modesty was outraged. The passion he had seen in her face, and the indelicacy of her gestures, scandalized him.

He wondered whether she would really carry out her threat to come to his room. He didn't think she would dare. But when night came and they all went to bed, he was so terrified that he could not sleep. He lay there listening anxiously. The silence was broken only by the repeated and monotonous cry of an owl. Through the thin wall of woven palm leaves he heard Munro's steady breathing. Suddenly he was conscious that someone was stealthily creeping into his room. He had already made up his mind what to do.

'Is that you, Mr Munro?' he called in a loud voice.

Darya stopped suddenly. Munro awoke.

'There's someone in my room. I thought it was you.'

'It's all right,' said Darya. 'It's only me. I couldn't sleep, so I thought I'd go and smoke a cigarette on the veranda.'

'Oh, is that all?' said Munro. 'Don't catch cold.'

She walked through Neil's room and out. He saw her light a cigarette. Presently she went back and he heard her get into bed.

He did not see her next morning, for he started out collecting before she was up, and he took care not to get in till he was pretty sure Munro also would be back. He avoided being alone with her till it was dark and Munro went down for a few minutes to arrange the moth-traps.

'Why did you wake Angus last night?' she said in a low angry whisper.

He shrugged his shoulders and going on with his work did not answer.

'Were you frightened?'

'I have a certain sense of decency.'

'Oh, don't be such a prig.'

'I'd rather be a prig than a dirty swine.'

'I hate you.'

'Then leave me alone.'

She did not answer, but with her open hand smartly slapped his face. He flushed, but did not speak. Munro returned and they pretended to be intent on whatever they were doing.

For the next few days Darya, except at meal-times and in the evenings, never spoke to Neil. Without prearrangement they exerted themselves to conceal from Munro that their relations were strained. But the effort with which Darya roused herself from a brooding silence would have been obvious to anyone more suspicious than Angus, and sometimes she could not help herself from being a trifle sharp with Neil. She chaffed him, but in her chaff was a sting. She knew how to wound and caught him on the raw, but he took care not to let her see it. He had an inkling that the good-humour he affected infuriated her.

Then one day when Neil came back from collecting, though he had delayed till the last possible minute before tiffin, he was surprised to find that Munro had not yet returned. Darya was lying on a mattress on the veranda, sipping a gin pahit and smoking. She did not speak to him when he passed through to wash. In a minute the Chinese boy came into his room and told him that tiffin was ready. He walked out.

'Where's Mr Munro?' he asked.

'He's not coming,' said Darya. 'He sent a message to say that the place he's at is so good he won't come down till night.'

Munro had set out that morning for the summit of the mountain. The lower levels had yielded poor results in the way of mammals, and Munro's idea was, if he could find a good place higher up, with a supply of water, to transfer the camp. Neil and

Darya ate their meal in silence. After they had finished he went into the house and came out again with his topee and his collecting gear. It was unusual for him to go out in the afternoon.

'Where are you going?' she asked abruptly.

'Out.'

'Why?'

'I don't feel tired. I've got nothing much else to do this afternoon.'

Suddenly she burst into tears.

'How can you be so unkind to me?' she sobbed. 'Oh, it is cruel to treat me like this.'

He looked down at her from his great height, his handsome, somewhat stolid face bearing a harassed look.

'What have *I* done?'

'You've been beastly to me. Bad as I am I haven't deserved to suffer like this. I've done everything in the world for you. Tell me one single little thing I could do that I haven't done gladly. I'm so terribly unhappy.'

He moved on his feet uneasily. It was horrible to hear her say that. He loathed and feared her, but he had still the respect for her that he had always felt, not only because she was a woman, but because she was Angus Munro's wife. She wept uncontrollably. Fortunately the Dyak hunters had gone that morning with Munro. There was no one about the camp but the three Chinese servants and they, after tiffin, were asleep in their own quarters fifty yards away. They were alone.

'I don't want to make you unhappy. It's all so silly. It's absurd of a woman like you to fall in love with a fellow like me. It makes me look such a fool. Haven't you got any self-control?'

'Oh, God. Self-control!'

'I mean, if you really cared for me you couldn't want me to be such a cad. Doesn't it mean anything to you that your husband trusts us implicity? The mere fact of his leaving us alone like this puts us on our honour. He's a man who would never hurt a fly. I should never respect myself again if I betrayed his confidence.'

She looked up suddenly.

'What makes you think he would never hurt a fly? Why, all those bottles and cases are full of the harmless animals he's killed.'

'In the interests of science. That's quite another thing.'

'Oh, you fool, you fool.'

'Well, if I am a fool I can't help it. Why do you bother about me?'

'Do you think I wanted to fall in love with you?'

'You ought to be ashamed of yourself.'

'Ashamed? How stupid! My God, what have I done that I should eat my heart out for such a pretentious ass?'

'You talk about what you've done for me. What has Munro done for you?'

'Munro bores me to death. I'm sick of him. Sick to death of him.'

'Then I'm not the first?'

Ever since her amazing avowal he had been tortured by the suspicion that what those men at Kuala Solor had said of her was true. He had refused to believe a word of it, and even now he could not bring himself to think that she could be such a monster of depravity. It was frightful to think that Angus Munro, so trusting and tender, should have lived in a fool's paradise. She could not be as bad as that. But she misunderstood him. She smiled through her tears.

'Of course not. How can you be so silly? Oh, darling, don't be so desperately serious. I love you.'

Then it was true. He had sought to persuade himself that what she felt for him was exceptional, a madness that together they could contend with and vanquish. But she was simply promiscuous.

'Aren't you afraid Munro will find out?'

She was not crying any more. She adored talking about herself, and she had a feeling that she was inveigling Neil into a new interest in her.

'I sometimes wonder if he doesn't know, if not with his mind, then with his heart. He's got the intuition of a woman and a woman's sensitiveness. Sometimes I've been certain he suspected and in his anguish I've sensed a strange, spiritual exaltation. I've wondered if in his pain he didn't find an infinitely subtle pleasure. There are souls, you know, that feel a voluptuous joy in laceration.'

'How horrible!' Neil had no patience with these conceits. 'The only excuse for you is that you're insane.'

She was now much more sure of herself. She gave him a bold look.

'Don't you think I'm attractive? A good many men have. You must have had dozens of women in Scotland who weren't so well made as I am.'

She looked down at her shapely, sensual figure with calm pride.

'I've never had a woman,' he said gravely.

'Why not?'

She was so surprised that she sprang to her feet. He shrugged his shoulders. He could not bring himself to tell her how disgusting the idea of such a thing was to him, and how vile he had thought the haphazard amours of his fellow-students at Edinburgh. He took a mystical joy in his purity. Love was sacred. The sexual act horrified him. Its excuse was the procreation of children and its sanctification marriage. But Darya, her whole body rigid, stared at him, panting; and suddenly, with a sobbing cry in which there was exultation and at the same time wild desire, she flung herself on her knees and seizing his hand passionately kissed it.

'Alyosha,' she gasped. 'Alyosha.'

And then, crying and laughing, she crumpled up in a heap at his feet. Strange, hardly human sounds issued from her throat and convulsive tremors passed through her body so that you would have thought she was receiving one electric shock after another. Neil did not know if it was an attack of hysteria or an epileptic fit.

'Stop it,' he cried. 'Stop it.'

He took her up in his strong arms and laid her in the chair. But when he tried to leave her she would not let him. She flung her arms round his neck and held him. She covered his face with kisses. He struggled. He turned his face away. He put his hand between her face and his to protect himself. Suddenly she dug her teeth into it. The pain was so great that, without thinking, he gave her a great swinging blow.

'You devil,' he cried.

His violent gesture had forced her to release him. He held his hand and looked at it. She had caught him by the fleshy part on the side and it was bleeding. Her eyes blazed. She was feeling alert and active.

'I've had enough of this. I'm going out,' he said.

She sprang to her feet.

'I'll come with you.'

He put on his topee and, snatching up his collecting gear without a word, turned on his heel. With one stride he leaped down the three steps that led from the floor of the house to the ground. She followed him.

'I'm going into the jungle,' he said.

'I don't care.'

In the ravening desire that possessed her she forgot her morbid fear of the jungle. She recked nothing of snakes and wild beasts. She did not mind the branches that hit her face or the creepers that entangled her feet. For a month Neil had explored all that part of the forest and he knew every yard of it. He told himself grimly that he'd teach her to come with him. He forced his way through the undergrowth with rapid strides; she followed him, stumbling but determined; he crashed on, blind with rage, and she crashed after him. She talked; he did not listen to what she said. She besought him to have pity on her. She bemoaned her fate. She made herself humble. She wept and wrung her hands. She tried to cajole him. The words poured from her lips in an unceasing stream. She was like a mad woman. At last in a little clearing he stopped suddenly and turning round faced her.

'This is impossible,' he cried. 'I'm fed up. When Angus comes back I must tell him I've got to go. I shall go back to Kuala Solor tomorrow morning and go home.'

'He won't let you go, he wants you. He finds you invaluable.'

'I don't care. I'll fake up something.'

'What?'

He mistook her.

'Oh, you needn't be frightened, I shan't tell him the truth. You can break his heart if you want to; I'm not going to.'

'You worship him, don't you? That dull, phlegmatic man.'

'He's worth a hundred of you.'

'It would be rather funny if I told him you'd gone because I wouldn't yield to your advances.'

He gave a slight start and looked at her to see if she was serious.

'Don't be such a fool. You don't think he'd believe that, do you? He knows it would never occur to me.'

'Don't be too sure.'

She had spoken carelessly, with no particular intention other than to continue the argument, but she saw that he was frightened and some instinct of cruelty made her press the advantage.

'Do you expect mercy from me? You've humiliated me beyond endurance. You've treated me like dirt. I swear that if you make any suggestion of going I shall go straight to Angus and say that you took advantage of his absence to try and assault me.'

'I can deny it. After all it's only your word against mine.'

'Yes, but my word'll count. I can prove what I say.'

'What do you mean?'

'I bruise easily. I can show him the bruise where you struck me. And look at your hand.' He turned and gave it a sudden glance. 'How did those teeth marks get there?'

He stared at her stupidly. He had gone quite pale. How could he explain that bruise and that scar? If he was forced to in self-defence he could tell the truth, but was it likely that Angus would believe it? He worshipped Darya. He would take her word against anyone's. What monstrous ingratitude it would seem for all Munro's kindness and what treachery in return for so much confidence! He would think him a filthy skunk and from his standpoint with justice. That was what shattered him, the thought that Munro, for whom he would willingly have laid down his life, should think ill of him. He was so unhappy that tears, unmanly tears that he hated, came to his eyes. Darya saw that he was broken. She exulted. She was paying him back for the misery he had made her suffer. She held him now. He was in her power. She savoured her triumph, and in the midst of her anguish laughed in her heart because he was such a fool. At that moment she did not know whether she loved or despised him.

'Now will you be good?' she said.

He gave a sob and blindly, with a sudden instinct of escape from that abominable woman, took to his heels and ran as hard as he could. He plunged through the jungle, like a wounded animal, not looking where he was going, till he was out of breath. Then, panting, he stopped. He took out his handkerchief and wiped away the sweat that was pouring into his eyes and blinding him. He was exhausted and he sat down to rest.

'I must take care I don't get lost,' he said to himself.

That was the least of his troubles, but all the same he was glad that he had a pocket compass, and he knew in which direction he must go. He heaved a deep sigh and rose wearily to his feet. He started walking. He watched his way and with another part of his mind miserably asked himself what he should do. He was convinced that Darya would do what she had threatened. They were to be another three weeks in that accursed place. He dared not go; he dared not stay. His mind was in a whirl. The only thing was to get back to camp and think it out quietly. In about a quarter of an hour he came to a spot that he recognized. In an hour he was back. He flung himself miserably into a chair. And it was Angus who filled his thoughts. His heart bled for him. Neil saw now all sorts of things that before had been dark to him. They were revealed to him in a flash of bitter insight. He knew why the women at Kuala Solor were so hostile to Darya and why they looked at Angus so strangely. They treated him with a sort of affectionate levity. Neil thought it was because Angus was a man of science and so in their foolish eyes somewhat absurd. He knew now it was because they were sorry for him and at the same time found him ridiculous. Darya had made him the laughing-stock of the community. If ever there was a man who hadn't deserved ill usage at a woman's hands it was he. Suddenly Neil gasped and began to tremble all over. It had suddenly occurred to him that Darya did not know her way through the jungle; in his anguish he had hardly been conscious of where they went. Supposing she could not find her way home? She would be terrified. He remembered the ghastly story Angus had told them of being lost in the forest. His first instinct was to go back and find her, and he sprang to his feet. Then a fierce anger seized him. No, let her shift for herself. She had gone of her own free will. Let her find her own way back. She was an abominable woman and deserved all that might come to her. Neil threw back his head defiantly, a frown of indignation on his smooth young brow, and clenched his hands. Courage. He made up his mind. It would be better for Angus if she never returned. He sat down and began trying to make a skin of a Mountain Trogon. But the Trogon has a skin like wet tissue-paper and his hands trembled. He tried to apply his mind to the work he was doing, but his thoughts fluttered desperately, like moths in a trap, and he could not control them. What was happening over there in the jungle? What had she done when he suddenly bolted? Every now and then, against his will, he looked up. At any moment she might appear in the clearing and walk calmly up to the house. He was not to blame. It was the hand of God. He shuddered. Storm clouds were gathering in the sky and night fell quickly.

Just after dusk Munro arrived.

'Just in time,' he said. 'There's going to be a hell of a storm.'

He was in great spirits. He had come upon a fine plateau, with lots of water, from which there was a magnificent view to the sea. He had found two or three rare butterflies and a flying squirrel. He was full of plans to move the camp to this new place. All about it he had seen abundant evidence of animal life. Presently he went into the house to take off his heavy walking boots. He came out at once.

'Where's Darya?'

Neil stiffened himself to behave with naturalness.

'Isn't she in her room?'

'No. Perhaps she's gone down to the servants' quarters for something.'

He walked down the steps and strolled a few yards.

'Darya,' he called. 'Darya.' There was no answer. 'Boy.'

A Chinese servant came running up and Angus asked him where his mistress was. He did not know. He had not seen her since tiffin.

'Where can she be?' asked Munro, coming back, puzzled.

He went to the back of the house and shouted.

'She can't have gone out. There's nowhere to go. When did you see her last, Neil?'

'I went out collecting after tiffin. I'd had a rather unsatisfactory morning and I thought I'd try my luck again.'

'Strange.'

They hunted everywhere round the camp. Munro thought she might have made herself comfortable somewhere and gone to sleep.

'It's too bad of her to frighten one like this.'

The whole party joined in the search. Munro began to grow alarmed.

'It's not possible that she should have gone for a stroll in the jungle and lost her way. She's never moved more than a hundred yards from the house to the best of my knowledge since we've been here.'

Neil saw the fear in Munro's eyes and looked down.

'We'd better get everyone along and start hunting. There's one thing, she can't be far. She knows that if you get lost the best thing is to stay where you are and wait for people to come and find you. She'll be scared out of her wits, poor thing.'

He called out the Dyak hunters and told the Chinese servants to bring lanterns. He fired his gun as a signal. They separated into two parties, one under Munro, the other under Neil, and went down the two rough paths that in the course of the month they had made in their comings and goings. It was arranged that whoever found Darya should fire three shots in quick succession. Neil walked with his face stern and set. His conscience was clear. He seemed to bear in his hands the decree of immanent justice. He knew that Darya would never be found. The two parties met. It was not necessary to look at Munro's face. He was distracted. Neil felt like a surgeon who is forced to perform a dangerous operation without assistance or appliances to save the life of someone he loves. It behoved him to be firm.

'She could never have got so far as this,' said Munro. 'We must go back and beat the jungle within the radius of a mile from the house inch by inch. The only explanation is that she was frightened by something or fainted or was stung by a snake.'

Neil did not answer. They started out again and, making lines, combed the undergrowth. They shouted. Every now and then they fired a gun and listened for a faint call in answer. Birds of the night flew with a whirring of wings, frightened, as they advanced with their lanterns; and now and then they half saw, half guessed at an animal, deer, boar, or rhino, that fled at their approach. The storm broke suddenly. A great wind blew and then the lightning rent the darkness, like a scream of a woman in pain, and the tortured flashes, quick, quick, one on the heels of the other, like demon dancers in a frantic reel, wriggled down the night. The horror of the forest was revealed in an unearthly day. The thunder crashed down the sky in huge rollers, peal upon peal, like vast, primeval waves dashing against the shores of eternity. That fearful din hurtled through space as though sound had size and weight. The rain pelted in fierce torrents. Rocks and gigantic trees came tumbling down the mountain. The tumult was awful. The Dyak hunters cowered, gibbering in terror of the angry spirits who spoke in the storm, but Munro urged them on. The rain fell all night, with lightning and thunder, and did not cease till dawn. Wet through and shivering they returned to the camp. They were exhausted. When they had eaten Munro meant to resume the desperate search. But he knew that it was hopeless. They would never see her alive again. He flung himself down wearily. His face was tired and white and anguished.

'Poor child. Poor child.'